CW01213531

By S.M. WARLOW

Tales of The Phoenix Titan
Volume I - Heritage
Volume II - Invidious

TALES OF THE PHOENIX TITAN

VOLUME II

INVIDIOUS

S.M. WARLOW

COPYRIGHT

Copyright © 2023 S.M. Warlow

All rights reserved. This book or any portion thereof may not be reproduced or used in any manner without express written permission of the author.

This is a work of fiction. Names, characters, places, and incidents either are the product of the author's imagination or are used fictitiously. Any resemblance to actual persons, living or dead, events, or locales is entirely coincidental.

ISBN: 9798378869367

For Pamela Collinson.

"In politics the choice is constantly between two evils".

—John Morley

PROLOGUE: THE FALL
10 HOURS

The elevator doors opened with a creak, and Jack dragged his unconscious sixteen-year-old son, James, through the reception area and into the office belonging to Theodore Jareth. The Society's chairman was long gone, likely aboard one of his top secret escape shuttles, fleeing the attack before the Revenant destroyed what remained of Earth.

James was out cold, but that was the intended effect of the drugs that the Society's goons had injected into the boy. Jack figured that at least his son wouldn't remember the ordeal they'd put him through in the last forty-eight hours: *silver lining.*

Theodore Jareth's office was on the thirty-fourth floor of Jareth Banking's corporate headquarters in London: the kind of place Jack avoided by design. The office was functional, with a desk, a computer, an ergonomic chair and access to a private helipad.

The chopper was still there. *Good.*

For the first time since the Revenant attack began, Jack looked to the sky he'd lived beneath his entire life. Black smoke replaced the white clouds, and deep crimson painted the once blue celestial sphere like an omen of things to come. Logic dictated that the only remaining course of survival was to flee. There was no point in fighting. There had never been any point in fighting: the Society had seen to that.

The war between the Revenant and what remained of

Earth's various militaries had raged for ten hours, and most of the world had fallen. There were pockets of resistance out there fighting the good fight, but without central coordination, they would fail.

With James over his shoulder, Jack pushed through the office doors and out toward the helipad. The air was thick and humid, and the smell of fresh fires permeated the air. He moved quickly, rushing toward the helicopter in the hopes of escaping the corporate headquarters.

Then he stopped as the six-two hulking mass of Eric Garland stepped out from the chopper. Like Jack, Garland was an Earth Defense Alliance agent, trained to be a blunt instrument for the governments of Earth. Say what you will about the EDA, but they produced the deadliest soldiers known to man, and they happened to be Earth's second best-kept secret.

Garland was a tall, broad-shouldered American: a former US marine with extensive experience in combat ops. Moreover, he was a man who'd lost his wife and child in the last twenty-four hours. All thanks to the Society.

"You son of a bitch," Garland pointed his pistol at Jack.

"They didn't give me a choice, Eric," Jack said, trying his best to plead with the man. "They went after my father; they took my son: what else was I supposed to do?"

Garland's jaw twitched, agony hidden behind his dark green eyes. "The Society killed my family, Jack".

"I know…"

Garland glowered. "Did you do it?"

"No," Jack answered. "It was the same guys that kidnapped my son… they're down in the basement, but I doubt you'll get much conversation out of them".

Garland said nothing; rage and grief and misery filled his visage. It didn't matter what Jack said; the man was blinded by despair. And now he was standing in Jack's way: slowing him from saving his family and getting the hell off Earth.

Jack lowered James to the floor, aware that he'd need both hands for what was next.

"Listen to me, Eric; we can still get out of here," Jack

said, pleading with the man he considered a friend. "I know where one of those Society shuttles is. We can still escape before this planet goes to hell".

Garland's eyes narrowed, and he shook his head.

"I don't want to hurt you, Eric," Jack warned.

Garland said nothing, his finger poised on the trigger. It was at that moment that Jack knew there was no reasoning with him. On the one hand, Garland was a good man, and Jack didn't like to kill good men. In addition, he'd also killed a dozen people in the last ten minutes, including the Society's principal enforcer, Götz Richtofen. He'd grown tired of killing and wanted the day to end, but alas, the need to survive was greater.

Garland squeezed the trigger. Jack darted right, barely avoiding the bullet as it flew past him. Without hesitation, Jack pulled his sidearm and returned fire, but Garland was as well trained in combat as any EDA agent. The American dropped to the floor and fired a precise round into Jack's handgun, sending the weapon flying from his hand and over the edge of the helipad.

Jack stopped, raised his hands, and Garland adjusted his razor-sharp aim to target Jack's heart.

"You're fuckin' criminal, Jack," Garland yelled, bitterness and anger swelling in his voice. "You should die for what you did!"

He wasn't wrong. Jack would question the decisions he'd made that day until the end of his life.

"This doesn't have to be the way, Eric," Jack said. "The Society is still out there. If we get off Earth, we can stop them once and for all. We can make them pay".

With a clear head, Eric Garland might've considered it, but emotions were high, and the man was bereft of everything he once held dear. The anger in his eyes suggested he'd pull the trigger, ending Jack's life then and there. But something in Eric Garland's expression seemed tentative, as though logic was waging war against the emotional epicentre of his being.

Then a single, horrible gunshot rang out.

Garland gripped a gaping wound on his chest. Blood

poured from between his fingers. A look of primal fear and hostility and a hint of regret came across Garland's face. It was awful watching the death of a friend: something Jack had seen too much of in the last twenty-four hours.

In the moment, Jack's intuition told him that the worst possible thing had happened: he'd failed to shield his son from the horror of being a killer. He glanced back for a split second to confirm his suspicion, and there several metres behind was James, clutching Richtofen's smoking revolver.

Jack turned to Garland, who stumbled and staggered, and finally crumbled to the floor in a heap. The impact was awful; a ferocious, unforgiving thump as the two-hundred-thirty pound mass collided with steel.

A huge part of Jack wanted nothing more than to grab his friend and do whatever he could to revive him. Immediate surgery could —potentially— save his life: the wound was below the heart, and the exit wound on Garland's back meant it had passed straight through him.

But there were no hospitals left, and even if there were, the Revenant would wipe them out in the next few hours.

Time was of the essence, and Jack had to think of those he loved.

He looked at James, still sitting on the floor with the smoking pistol, looking so shocked he might hurl. Jack moved to his son and gently pulled the gun from his grasp.

"You okay?" he asked.

James stared at Garland with no expression for a moment. Garland coughed and spluttered on the floor, unable to move.

"Better than that guy," James answered.

"Where'd you get this?" Jack asked, holding out the pistol.

"I snatched it of Richtofen," James paused and looked at his father, "What happened down there?"

Jack's eyes hardened. "I took care of Richtofen".

James didn't say anything. There was a good chance the trauma and shock of the last day were finally starting to hit him. Jack hadn't even asked what the Society subjected him to during his time as their prisoner. He'd not had the chance.

"What now?" James asked, staring at the bleeding horizon with dismay.

Jack gestured to the chopper. "We're getting out of here, using one of their shuttles, but first we're going back for our family".

"We don't have time to save them," James insisted, with defeat and dread in his voice. "We shouldn't go back."

Jack pulled his son to his feet, refusing to listen to the cowardice. Yes, James was young, and he'd been through an ordeal, but that was no excuse to abandon those who mattered most.

Jack grabbed Garland's pistol, knowing it would come in handy. Garland stared at him with judgement and rage as he lay dying on the floor. Jack refused to look him in the eyes.

He handed James the pistol; "We leave no one behind. We're going back for them, and that is final".

11 HOURS

The flight across war-torn London was unpleasant. The streets were filled with Revenant troops and ground vehicles, making light work of whatever resistance was out there. The funny thing was that the enemy didn't seem to have an air force, which made the flight surprisingly easy.

It was a strange concept, but Jack figured these creatures were space-faring aliens that could charter the cosmos. And besides, the RAF and Nato's Allied Air force were probably toast by this stage. All the resistance on the streets was civilian, and it didn't look like it was going well.

After an hour's flight, Jack set the chopper down in a big field close to his parent's home on Macon Close. He climbed from the helicopter, noting that several houses in the surrounding area were already on fire.

The weird zipping chorale of alien gunfire could be heard coming up the street: that meant Revenant were nearby. Father and son versus the alien threat, Jack didn't like those odds one bit.

He peered at James, still clutching Garland's pistol. He looked more alive now, as though the shock of it all had melted away: albeit momentarily. Jack knew that everything going on would take its toll on James and that he'd need to deal with that one day.

But not today.

As Jack and James made their way toward the Stephens family home, the sound of gunfire seemed to dissipate. To Jack's well-trained ear, he estimated that the weapons fire was coming from a house further up the street. That meant he still had time: he could still save them.

His father, Bill, had bought the family home over thirty years ago: a magnificent yet understated detached house complete with a big garden for the dogs and grandchildren to roam. It was the house where Jack had grown from a boy to a man, and it was mostly the same for James.

As Jack made his way up the long gravel driveway, he noticed the front door had been smashed off its hinges. Without hesitation, he signalled to James to hurry, and moments later, they entered the house.

Together, father and son pushed through the entrance hall, carefully checking every corner as they moved: both armed with nothing more than pistols. Jack could only hope that the Revenant had moved off and left the Stephens family intact.

Logic dictated that James was correct earlier. Perhaps running the hell away was the right thing to do, but Jack couldn't do that. The last day had taught him that family mattered more than anything else. He was pretty sure his father was dead, thanks to the Society, and he didn't want any more deaths on his hands. If he could save them —any of them— he would.

That would begin to make up for everything.

As soon as Jack entered the kitchen, he knew something wasn't right. Blood was splattered against the white cupboards, and there was a smell of burning in the air. He didn't see it at first, then as he turned the corner, passed the trendy kitchen island fitted last autumn, he saw it: *his mother's body.*

She'd been shot. Recently. Minutes if not seconds, ago. The semi-cauterised wound on her heart had come from one of the Revenant's energy weapons. He felt sick to his stomach and didn't know how to process it. Then he looked at James, who seemed completely and utterly bewildered by the grizzly sight.

Under normal circumstances, he'd hug his son and tell him everything would be alright, but fate had other plans. The sound of yelling —of human yelling— came from the rear of the property.

Someone was out there.

Together, they dashed through the house, checking the corners for anything hostile. They passed through the library, which had seen better days, and entered the lounge: or at least what was left of it.

The coffee table was split in half and upturned. Bill Stephens' prize armchair had been torn to shreds. A long family portrait taken a year prior was covered in a grey liquid that looked like oil. Jack was then confronted by the sight of a body on the floor. It wasn't human. In fact, it was so far from human that it frightened him a little. The thing had a huge, bulbous head filled with jagged teeth and weird unmoving eyes. Its skin was torn and scarred in over a dozen places, and its claws looked sharp enough to break steel. Whatever the atrocity was, it had died from a fire iron to the skull. The same metal implement Jack's father had used to stir fires on cold wintery nights was buried in the monster's cranium.

When Jack turned toward the wall, he was met by a far grizzlier sight.

His brother-in-law, Dylan Carter, had been run through by something that looked like a spear, impaling his bloodied carcass to the wall, three feet off the ground. Jack figured the big, dead monster thing had killed him, but Dylan had taken the ugly fucker down with him.

Fearless. Typical Dylan.

The sound of yelling was still there, somewhere toward the gardens. As much as Jack wanted to pull Dylan's body from the wall, he couldn't ignore the cries for help. He spared a thought for his mother and Dylan, then proceeded toward the garden, not knowing that what lay ahead would change everything.

There was a raised voice which Jack recognised immediately: his sister, Liza. Dylan must've bought her some time by fighting off the creature in the lounge. Jack rushed forward, following the sound of Liza's voice, until he reached his mother's prize garden.

He saw Liza, two hundred yards ahead, placing herself directly between her son, Nathan, and the Revenant soldiers. There were two of them, both in the same greyish black armour, looking entirely out of place against the flowers and plants that had once served as the backdrop for family barbeques.

Liza had been shot; there was a wound on her torso from one of their energy weapons. Despite her injury, Liza Carter —nee Stephens— bravely stood her ground, refusing to let the aliens near her child. One of the Revenant was talking, and it sounded like English, but Jack didn't have the capacity to process it. All he saw were two armed hostiles, cornering what remained of the family.

Jack sprung forward, willing to save his sister and nephew, but before he could take aim, one of the Revenant fired the killing shot. Liza Carter collapsed to the floor as the single round from the hostile's energy weapon tore through her chest.

In that single moment of awful horror, Jack's eyes pivoted from Liza to her young son. The boy, no older than five, watched as his mother fell to the floor in a heap.

Something akin to an animal shriek of primal rage emerged from Jack's mouth. He wasn't even aware of it, but the Revenant were. They took their eyes off the boy and focussed on Jack and James, running toward them with guns raised.

The first went down with ease. It didn't matter if you were some ugly fucked up, ghoulish soldier wearing armour over your torso; a bullet to the brain still killed. The creature's head snapped to one side, and a cloud of grey fluid splattered against the geraniums.

By the time the second realised what was going on, it was too late. James shot him twice in the shoulder, forcing the Revenant to drop its gun. Once Jack was within a metre, he readied himself to execute it with a single shot to the head, but something stopped him.

He saw human eyes beneath the helmet. This person was not like the others at all. He wasn't alien. He was human. That raised a shit ton of questions for Jack, but all he saw at the moment was the guy who'd murdered his sister.

Jack fired a round into the man's knee, blowing out blood, muscle, and viscera. The Revenant man screamed in agony: that was different from the others. Real. Human.

As the man writhed on the floor, Jack drew his eyes to Liza. She was gone: likely dead before she'd hit the ground. Nathan was there, curled up in a ball against the fence — terrified. Jack knew what had happened in the last few minutes would stay with the boy forever. *How could anyone let go of trauma like that?*

The simple answer was that they didn't recover; they just learned to live with it. Nathan was now an orphan. That moment of horrific violence would impact him forever, and it was all thanks to a conscious, sentient Revenant—a human man, currently squirming and twitching on the floor.

"James," Jack called out to his son. "Get Nate out of here. He doesn't need to see what happens next".

James looked at him, then at the wounded man on the floor. He didn't question his father's authority. He scooped Nathan from the ground and returned to the house with the child in his arms.

Jack looked at the man on the ground, his hand trembling. *The sentient Revenant was an officer of some sort, maybe a CO? Jack wondered if perhaps that was how they worked. Maybe a conscious commanding officer gave the orders, and the weird zombie-like footsoldiers followed them without question?*

He considered shooting the man in the head, but that was too good a death. Jack wouldn't afford such luxuries for the man who'd killed his sister and orphaned his nephew. He holstered his pistol and kicked the Revenant's energy weapon aside. Then, as he stared down at the officer, Jack's hands balled into fists.

After that, there was a gap in his cognition: a blinding, uncontrollable flash of savagery from a place of bloodthirsty madness. The human mind was fragile, and Jack had been subjected to the worst twenty-four hours imaginable. Everything had taken its toll, and now he allowed himself to lose his mind in the haze.

When his awareness returned, he was looking at what had once been a face, now resembling a crushed bloom of blood and gore. Jack had shown him no mercy. No remorse —just like the Revenant man had shown Liza. He should've been horrified by the state of the soldier's body, but Jack felt nothing, only an ache in his arms and hands. He stared at his knuckles, wondering if the blood upon them was his, the officer's or both?

Liza was on the floor, her cold, dead eyes looking at Jack as though passing judgment. He shut the thought of guilt down: *there'd be plenty of time for that later.* He crawled to her body and cradled her for a moment.

"I swear I'll make it right," Jack sniffed as he gently closed her eyelids. "I'll take care of the boy: treat him like my own. I promise".

He laid a farewell kiss upon her forehead and gently lowered her down. A huge part of him wanted to bury her and the others: to mourn each of them.

But that wasn't an option.

Jack returned to the house, finding James holding Nathan, who'd seemingly passed out from the shock. A harrowing expression was painted across James' boyish teenage features as he stared aimlessly at one of the flowerbeds.

"We've gotta go," Jack said, trying to keep his voice free of emotion. "There ain't much time left".

James' eyes flicked upward, numb and indifferent. "You killed that guy…"

"He had it coming," Jack growled. Then nodding to Nathan, "Did he say anything?"

James shook his head as he held the small boy close.

Jack sighed, trying to bite back the pain. “We’ve gotta head east”.

James’ eyes hardened as he processed the words. “What’s east?”

“The last Society escape shuttle,” Jack answered. “The three of us are getting the hell out of here”.

12 HOURS

Before Jack killed him, Götz Richtofen was showboating about his supposedly *grand* escape plan: arrogantly assuming that he stood a chance in combat against an EDA field agent. Sure, Richtofen had put up a fight, but his undoing had been in that showboating. He’d shown his hand and unintentionally screwed over one of his Society overlords in the process: *his beloved brother-in-law Sir Alastair Roth.*

“Roth will be waiting for me at his estate with a comfortable shuttle,” he’d said boastfully. “Then I can watch this rock burn in comfort during the thirteenth hour”.

Of course, that hadn’t happened, and Richtofen had met a grizzly demise and the end of a sharp axe back at Jareth banking headquarters. Unwittingly and unknowingly, he’d given Jack a chance at survival. *It was the least he could do.*

Before leaving the family home for the last time, Jack hurriedly grabbed a bunch of family photos and stuffed them into a leather duffle. He raided his father’s office, taking two of the old man’s hunting rifles and a box of ammo. *He knew he’d need them: Roth wouldn’t be happy to see him again, that was for sure.*

Alastair Albon de-Freiherr Roth was Theodore Jareth’s right-hand man: a modest captain of industry who preferred to stay out of the limelight. That fact made much sense in hindsight, but it didn’t matter in the grand scheme of getting the hell off Earth.

Roth had a shuttle, and in Jack’s eyes, that was enough

to make him the enemy.

With James and Nathan in tow, Jack doubled back to the helicopter, and seconds later, they were back in the air, soaring above the burning English countryside. For thirty minutes, they flew east, low enough to make out landmarks and roads. While Jack piloted, James clutched Nathan in one arm while navigating using an old map.

A half-mile from Roth's estate, Jack put the chopper down to avoid detection. Then he, James and Nathan travelled on foot to the property. It was a huge stately home: grand and opulent *—the sort of thing that likely once belonged to a Duke or Lord.* The grounds were extensive, around forty acres, complete with orchards, fields, water parterres and even a foot maze. Roth had done very well for himself, or the Society had made things happen for him.

Jack didn't see anyone as he surveyed the north face of the house and surrounding gardens. There was no sign of Roth or any henchmen, which left him to wonder if Roth was spineless enough to flee earlier than agreed with Richtofen.

There came a sudden loud hiss from the rear of the building, and something in Jack's gut told him it was the noise of a Society escape shuttle. The commotion sounded slightly like a jet prepping its engines before take-off, but a roar to the cacophony felt different to Jack's well-trained ears.

He peered at James, still carrying Nathan over his shoulder. The boy was conscious now but hadn't said a word. It was a real example of childhood trauma playing out before Jack's eyes, and as much as he wanted to comfort the boy, he knew he couldn't. Not yet: not until they were all safe.

"Listen to me," Jack said to James. "Whatever happens next, I need to know you've got my back".

James swallowed a lump in his throat. "Always".

Jack acknowledged it. Then, with the efficiency of a fully-fledged EDA operative, he pushed up toward his target with James and Nathan not far behind. They rushed through the beautifully kept grounds, heading east while using a set of high bushes for cover; *just in case Roth had people watching*. Jack turned a corner; his gun pointed toward any potential threat lurking against the side of the building.

He waited: breathed. Then pushed up, following the hissing sound emanating from the rear of the house. He stopped at the corner and checked for anyone behind James.

There was nobody.

Jack turned his attention to the shuttle in the back garden. The hissing noise was still there, as was the sound of footsteps and voices. He peeked around the corner, spotting two mercenary types armed with assault rifles patrolling the area. A third was waiting on a docking ramp, closely watching everything to the south.

Then Jack laid eyes on Alastair Roth, busy ushering his wife and two small children to the shuttle. Roth was a rotund bastard with a chinless facial structure that somehow made him look pompous regardless of the situation. He was older than Jack by a good decade, if not more.

Jack looked at the shuttle. It was enormous: far bigger than Roth or anyone needed. By Jack's guess, you could comfortably stuff at least thirty people into the damn thing and still have room for a dozen more.

This was how the Society was riding out the apocalypse: in luxurious greed. *What better way to ring out the end of the world than by not aiding your fellow man?* Jack's blood boiled at the thought, but he wouldn't lose control.

He switched out his pistol for one of the hunting rifles he'd picked up earlier. He checked the magazine and the sights and considered any changes to the wind. The patrolling guys were farther out, maybe two hundred yards from Jack's current position. The third was stationary, but he had the high ground and what looked like a sniper rifle.

Jack took aim, lined up the lookout's head in his sights, and considered the wind again. He breathed. He squeezed the trigger: and waited for the red bloom of blood to appear. Then upon confirming the kill, Jack switched targets to the patrolling guys. The first went down in a cloud of blood, and his buddy quickly followed.

Jack waited a heartbeat, checking for any other Society goons in the area. There were none. Then Jack spotted Roth dip his head out of the shuttle door to look at the sudden commotion. He disappeared into the shuttle and began screaming at what Jack assumed was a pilot.

"Take off, take off now!"

Jack didn't wait. He slung the hunting rifle back over his shoulder and switched back to his pistol: much better for close quarters. He dashed to the shuttle, ensuring that James was at his back: wary that this new-fangled spaceship could lift off without warning.

But it didn't. The Society shuttle, like its NASA cousins —for lack of a better word— needed time to warm up. That gave Jack the time he needed to board.

Roth was there, hands raised, shielding his wife and children. He looked like a man terrified, and yet also like a man ready to make a deal. Jack kept his gun trained on Roth as he entered the shuttle.

The interior was incredibly spacious, with white leather seats and a storage area containing crates of wine, painted canvases and clothes—capacity for a hell of a lot more people.

"You son of a bitch," Jack spat, resisting the urge to put a bullet in Roth's head. "You did this.. you and Jareth."

Roth cowered slightly, his eyes wide and fearful. "Mr Stephens, you must know that—"

Jack screamed, "Is Theodore Jareth aboard this shuttle?"

Roth shook his head and stammered. "N- No. He was in Paris. He's dead.. we think".

That was some good news, at least, but Jack wasn't done. He pressed the barrel of his gun against Roth's skull, and the children and wife began panicking and crying and all the other natural responses to imminent danger. A part of Jack was happy that they could experience a slither of the terror that James and Nathan had been subjected to.

"What about my father?" Jack hissed.

Roth looked at him, cowardice in his eyes. "I don't know".

"What do you mean you don't know?"

"The Ural mountains are gone, Mr Stephens," Roth insisted, panic to his tone. "There's nothing left".

Jack pulled his gun away and felt something wash over his being —*grief perhaps?* His mother and sister were gone, and by the sound of things, so was his father. But at least he had James and Nathan: that was something.

He turned to James, standing at the shuttle entrance watching the whole thing play out like some surreal performance. James set Nathan down on one of the chairs before moving up the shuttle. Jack handed his son the hunting rifle. What he said next was the hardest thing he'd said in his entire lifetime. But it was necessary if they hoped to survive.

"Watch them," Jack said, gesturing to Roth and his family. "If any of them move, you shoot them. Got it?"

James looked at the floor, bewildered. "Got it".

Jack nodded at his son and began a slow walk to the next compartment —the cockpit. Along the way, he passed Nathan, who simply stared into space without expression. The boy's eyes were glazed over like the lights were on, but no one was home.

12 HOURS 30 MINUTES

The pilot didn't put up any fight at all. As soon as he saw Jack's gun, the man threw up his hands in surrender and insisted he wasn't military. That was bullshit, of course, but Jack figured he needed the guy to fly the shuttle, so better to keep him alive.

After a few threats of violence, Jack convinced him it was best to depart now rather than later. Naturally, the pilot obliged, and after a few pre-flight checks and ensuring everyone —including the Roths— were strapped into their chairs, the shuttle lifted off. It wasn't a straight-shot vertical take-off like the traditional space shuttle. The vessel seemed to move more like a plane, moving upward but charting a horizontal course at around a thousand feet.

It was a wonder how the Society had kept technology

like it a secret for so long. On the face of things, humanity had barely scratched the surface of space travel, yet that wasn't the case. The shuttle was a feat of engineering prowess, and the Society had thousands of the things ferrying the chosen few to safety while leaving the rest to die.

While Jack supervised the pilot, he took a moment to look at what remained of the dead landscape. Thick columns of smoke rolled upward from a town on the horizon. Where once a peaceful residential estate had been situated near a lake, now all that remained was a crater. Revenant ground forces were there, gathering the dead.

"Okay," the pilot exhaled. "Going for ascent in five.. four.."

Something below caught Jack's eye: *a tiny beacon of hope? Redemption?* The bus was moving along a baron road heading south: toward the city —toward the Revenant. From the sky, Jack couldn't tell how many people were on board, but he knew they wouldn't survive long.

Jack made a choice. Too much life had been lost, and it was about time he started keeping that promise to Liza. At that moment, Jack could do the one thing the Society refused to do: save people.

"Take us down and intercept that bus," Jack ordered the pilot. "Now".

12 HOURS 40 MINUTES

The shuttle touched down a hundred yards ahead of the bus, and the vehicle growled to a halt. Jack passed through the passenger compartment, where James was still watching the Roths like a hawk; his hunting rifle pointed squarely at them.

"What is this meaning of this?" Roth yelled at Jack. "Why are we landing?"

Jack said nothing.

He pushed up to the rear airlock and opened it up. He paced the landing ramp and spotted a big man climbing from the bus with a nervous expression. That was when Jack saw the number of passengers inside. The bus was well over capacity: full of men, women and children who just wanted to escape the apocalypse.

Jack returned his gaze to the nervous driver, who was entirely unsure what to make of the Society shuttle.

"You folks need a ride?" Jack asked.

The driver nodded hurriedly.

Over five minutes, Jack, the bus driver, and some passengers emptied the shuttle of Roth's possessions, much to the Society man's chagrin. Before long, Jack was staring at a pile of exquisite wine, beautiful art pieces and designer clothes all dumped on the road. It had to be the most valuable pile of fly-tipping known to man.

By Jack's estimate, there were forty additional people aboard. He should've felt better knowing that forty souls would continue, thanks to his choice, but it didn't.

How could it ever begin to make up for what he'd done?

With everyone aboard and accounted for, Jack sealed the airlock, ready to give the pilot the order to take off, when Roth stood from his seat. He moved a pace toward Jack, but James pressed the barrel of his rifle against Roth's pudgy chest.

"How dare you," Roth yelled at the top of his lungs. "These people are not entitled to this".

Jack didn't react immediately. On some conscious level, he was aware they didn't have much time, that Earth would soon die, but Roth struck a nerve that had been plucked too many times that day.

He grabbed Roth by the windpipe, forcing the obese rat to the airlock: intending to kill the man one way or the other. Everything around Jack muted and a kind of tunnel vision set in. All he saw was Roth choking, spluttering, begging for his life. He didn't notice James tugging at the back of his shirt, or the bus driver yelling at him to take it easy.

What pulled him back to reality was Roth's children sobbing in the corner. The daughter curled up in a ball, shielding her eyes from the sight, while the son —no older than Nathan— looked on, screaming and protesting.

Jack stopped and considered. He couldn't do it: much

as he wanted to. If he were to kill Roth in front of his children, he'd be doing what the Revenant did to Nathan.

It wasn't right.

He released his grip, and Roth slipped down the bulkhead, gasping for air: the colour purple filling his usually pasty complexion.

Jack straightened up, looking at James. "Shoot him if he starts fucking around again".

James didn't question it.

Jack glanced at Nathan, still sitting on his chair. The boy stared back at him with some clarity. Neither of them said a word.

12 HOURS 50 MINUTES

The pilot took off soon after, and the shuttle lifted toward the sky. What followed was a vertical climb to the clouds — steeper than anything Jack had ever experienced. It wasn't like flying in a jet or the tasks the EDA made him face in basic. No, this was the kind of thing astronauts trained their whole lives for.

When they reached space, Jack laid eyes on the Revenant fleet and forced himself to stay in the moment. It was unlike anything he'd ever seen. The dark grey machines spanned miles in length, obscuring everything around them. The ships were firing on Earth's surface, levelling what Jack knew as Copenhagen. Entire continents were gone. The oceans had turned to a strange grey colour and nothing about the Earth looked like it was supposed to.

"Wow," the pilot gasped.

"So, how the fuck do we get past them?" Jack said, pointing at the Revenant ships.

The pilot shrugged; "I was told they'd let us pass".

Sure enough, he was right. Less than five minutes later, a squad of smaller Revenant ships flew by as if the shuttle never existed. Jack breathed a sigh of relief, as did the pilot. All the anxiety in the cockpit melted away for a heartbeat.

"What now?" Jack asked.

The pilot exhaled. "My orders were to take Mr Roth to the moon".

Everything suddenly clicked in Jack's mind. The Society was heading to the EDA's lunar facility, where they could reboot humanity and start anew: all while watching the Earth burn.

13 HOURS

The pilot spotted it first, and Jack had to force his brain to process it. Somewhere between the moon and Earth, a strange blue light formed in space. It looked like an electrical storm crossed with a giant rip to the naked eye. Then spaceships began to emerge from within, but they weren't like the Revenant. The new vessels were similar in scale but seemed somehow more civilised. There was no vicious angular design: no ominous dark grey colouring.

These ships were different.

To Jack's surprise, the new vessels began to fire on the Revenant, and all hell broke loose. Waves of laser fire filled space. Small fighter-like ships appeared in the same flashes of brilliant blue light, engaging the Revenant's fighters.

"What the hell is going on?" the pilot said.

Jack was lost for words.

He watched the battle unfold, willing his primitive human mind to process it. Before he could begin to put together the pieces, an alarm emerged from the pilot's console.

"It's a transmission," the pilot said. "What the hell do we say?"

Jack didn't know how to answer the question. First — technically second— contact: it should've felt monumental, but given the circumstances he didn't know how to feel. Jack noticed his hand shake as he tapped the communications console and listened.

A woman's voice filled the tiny cockpit, and Jack felt the hairs on his arms stand to attention.

"People of Earth, this is Admiral T'dalam of the

Commonwealth of planets. We are here to evacuate you to safety," the voice said over the communicator. "Any vessels in the area, please proceed to the nearest Commonwealth ship. Lifeboats will be deployed for anyone on the surface".

Jack moved to the window. He saw hundreds —maybe thousands— of rectangular spacecraft breaking away from the larger frigates and heading toward what was left of Earth. Smaller fighters flanked the cubic lifeboats, cutting through Revenant fighters as they passed by.

A minute later, one of the lifeboats stopped before the shuttle and deployed a pair of metal arms that locked around Jack's escape craft. The proximity gave Jack a chance to look at the pilot.

She was human.

Not Revenant.

Human.

In what should've felt like a historical moment, the only thing Jack could do was raise a hand in greeting. The pilot returned the gesture.

CHAPTER ONE
ROUSSEAU

On most Commonwealth planets, the architecture was uniform and egalitarian, rarely breaking away from the prescribed design that the communist regime deemed the moral choice. For Titus Rousseau, many 'wealther worlds reminded him of the brutalist Soviet-era buildings he'd seen across Europe before the Fall. Everything from the dull colour pallet to the regimentation of civilian dwellings was an eery reminder of the past. Seeing a typical 'wealther planet, with all its identical cookie-cutter buildings, didn't inspire Titus in any way —in fact, it served as another reason to hate the Commonwealth.

In their fleeting moment of existence, the people of Earth had built colosseums, cathedrals, and grand palaces fit for kings and queens. It was all meant to inspire greatness for the generations to come: to show them that progress was possible.

Fortunately, Rousseau wasn't on a typical Commonwealth planet. He was on the Capital World of Valour: the central nexus for the communist aristocracy. Unlike their secondary systems, the Capital Worlds were luxurious and exorbitant: everything that went against the supposedly socialist values of the Commonwealth's Founders. Of course, that was why Communism failed —a central power always held the cards. In a way, Titus found the whole thing to be genius. The Commonwealth's leadership and *star citizens* would convince the rest of the population to be grateful for the scraps they were given. Meanwhile, those who lived on the Capital Worlds would live a life of decadence.

As the sun rose over Valour, orange rays of light peaked through the skyscrapers peppering the horizon. In his sixty-seven years of life, Titus Rousseau would've never taken notice of such an ordinary sight, but today felt different: like the start of something new: something monumental. Today was the day of the Earther Withdrawal Ballot, otherwise known as the EWB.

Despite months of kicking and screaming like a scolded child, the Commonwealth Council eventually agreed to the terms of a public ballot. The population of Paradisium would go to the polling stations, and today, they would vote on one of two options: remain in the Commonwealth or leave to become an independent world.

Rousseau suspected that the only reason why the 'wealth had agreed to the terms was that Grand Master of the House, Inon Waife, was up for re-election.

On the surface, it seemed odd that a dictatorial regime went through the theatre of elections and debates as if they were a representative democracy. At first, Titus assumed that it was just smoke and mirrors to create the illusion of freedom, but when he thought about it more, the answer was right in front of him. He wanted Paradisium to fail. That way, he'd have a shining example for other planets considering separatism and thus ensure Commonwealth control.

As Titus Rousseau left the confines of his hotel room, an aide handed him a datapad preloaded with the latest polling projections. Titus waited until he was sitting comfortably in his inner-planet transport before reading the reports. Whilst his entourage of analysts and aides loaded onto the limousine-type craft, Titus reviewed and scrutinised the projections. The graphs and spreadsheets reminded him of his business days before Paradisium: back when he and his husband ran a small empire of hedge funds and investment groups. As usual, the numbers were looking strong. Early forecasts out of Paradisium suggested that over sixty percent were in favour of separatism.

One of Titus' analysts handed him a cup of coffee before remarking on the visualisations on his datapad;

"It looks like we are well on track, sir," the eager young man said. "Today should be a very good day for us!"

Titus shrugged as he returned the datapad. "Just because we are predicting a victory in the polls doesn't mean we've secured it yet".

The analyst looked stunned —almost fearful— at what he'd said. It suddenly occurred to Titus that the young man was a recent hire; he was a former number cruncher for Roth Industries. The terrified young analyst was likely accustomed to abuse and who-knows-what-else for being wrong. Fortunately, that wasn't the way Titus operated. People were people: they made mistakes, and he'd seen his fair share of Alastair Roth's management style in the Society.

"Can I give you a word of advice?" Titus said to the young man.

"Of course, Mr Rousseau".

"They say with age comes perspective," Titus gestured to the datapad with all the numbers. "Don't ever, ever assume that anything is as it appears".

▲

When Titus arrived at the Commonwealth Assembly, he was surprised by the number of protestors outside. If there was one thing the 'wealthers were good at, it was being outraged by something their government told them to be outraged by. There was a rabble of soft socialists armed with placards outside the perimeter fences, shouting abuse at anyone walking past. Titus knew they wouldn't dare aggravate the Commonwealth soldiers guarding the main gate, but he still felt on edge.

Knowing that people viewed him as a bigot for his part in the EWB felt so out of place. He'd been a victim of bigotry for most of his life, called every homophobic slur under the sun, simply because of who he loved, and yet now, the 'wealthers saw him as the bigot for simply supporting freedom.

Entry into the Assembly hall was easy, and once Titus had cleared security, he felt any hint of his anxiety melt away. Knowing that any violent protestors would have to get past soldiers and corporate mercenaries before they could even get inside made Titus feel better.

The Assembly Hall was a large open room, laid out with chairs and tables for the guests. A stage was erected against the back wall, with lighting and a giant screen above. All the theatrics of it reminded Titus of the award ceremony's he'd attended back on Earth: like someone had plucked out a memory of a red-carpet Hollywood event and rebuilt it in the strange post-Fall world that he now lived in.

The voting wasn't starting for another ten minutes, so the hall was only at seventy-five percent capacity. Titus knew that the others would be running late or showboating with the press, neither of which was his style. Instead, Titus preferred efficiency and a degree of personal moderation.

What surprised him was that only a handful of the Society's members were amongst the rabble of so-called celebrities and career politicians. He saw people such as Ethan Hancock, Alan Washington and Xu Lei amongst the crowd. They mingled and pretended to look interested in everything going on, but they were all there for the same reason as Titus: Alastair Roth —the chairman of the Society — was especially interested in the EWB.

Titus picked an empty table on the far side of the room, away from the riff-raff, the press and his brothers and sisters from the Society. There was no need to celebrate just yet. Yes, the forecasts indicated a landslide victory, but Titus didn't want to put all his eggs in one basket. If the vote swung the other way by some miracle, there was no doubt in his mind that the Commonwealth would seek to break apart Paradisium's culture and push their political message, as they had with so many other worlds before.

The chair beside Titus was suddenly pulled out from

under the table, and someone in a blue velvet jacket sat down next to him. When Titus turned to look, he saw the snake-like eyes of David Jareth: the man who'd enabled the EWB to happen.

Jareth wasn't a member of the Society. He ran in similar circles, but he didn't engage with any of it. His father, the late-great Theodore Jareth, was the previous chairman of the Society: a man that Titus both respected and feared. The same could not be said of David Jareth. Yes, he was enigmatic and charming and brilliant, but he wasn't dangerous —not in the grand scheme of things anyway.

"Titus..." Jareth said with a nod.

"Hello, David," Titus replied. "I am so glad you could make it for such a monumental day".

"The separatist dream has been alive on Paradisium for over a quarter of a century. I wouldn't miss this for the world". Jareth's lips pressed thin, and he offered an entirely unreadable smile. "You decided to attend alone?"

Titus couldn't be sure if the question was intended as some sort of insult. Jareth knew he'd remained unmarried since the Fall: he knew what Titus lost on that fateful day. But of course, Titus Rousseau remained calm and polite: as was good etiquette.

"This is hardly a social affair".

Jareth's expression shifted to something far less friendly than it had been before. There was a hardness to his eyes that suggested what Titus could only assume was offence, but Jareth's rat-like smile remained nonetheless.

Jareth chuckled to himself, "You and I both know that *if* the result swings in favour of separatism, this *gathering* will soon devolve into a social affair. I hear that the champagne is already on ice".

He stared at Titus until he eventually broke eye contact. That was the way David Jareth operated: he liked to believe he was in control.

"If some people choose to celebrate, who am I to judge," Titus shrugged. "This is a monumental occasion after all".

“Oh, but of course it is. After all, it’s been twenty-six years since *our people* gave up control”.

“Our people?”

Jareth’s smirk hinted at something insidious

“*Our* people,” he repeated.

For a moment, Titus wondered if Jareth was referring to the Society. But, as always, when it came to David Jareth, it was impossible to tell. That was one of his many flaws; Jareth was mysterious for the sake of it. It was the very reason why he’d never cut it in the Society, regardless of whether he’d chosen to be a part of the group or not. Yes, the suppression and control of the masses required you to maintain the lie that you were an ordinary man, but being a member of the Society required transparency with your fellow brothers and sisters. After all, *if they couldn’t trust you, why would they maintain the greatest lie in Earth’s history with you?*

Jareth opened something on his datapad, checked it, then stood as if to excuse himself. He glanced at Titus with a smile that was friendly but entirely false.

“I’m sorry, I must attend to some important business,” he said, patting Titus on the shoulder. “Make sure you enjoy the celebrations, old boy. A victory such as this only comes around once in a lifetime”.

Titus nodded the strange comment away, assuming it was simply Jareth being his usual cryptic self. There was no reason to call him out on his use of the term *old boy* despite the fact there were only a few years between them. Titus reminded himself that today a victory would be announced, and *if* it went the way he was expecting, then the political future of Paradisium would be his for the taking.

▲

As the results began to pour in, so to did the attendees at the Commonwealth Assembly. All of the Society’s members were there, blending in amongst the crowds of would-be politicians and hopeful fools trying to network for business.

Even Alastair Roth and his son Christian appeared: though the former disappeared into one of the side rooms for a meeting. Titus looked on eagerly as the ballots grew and took shape. For about ten hours, the number in favour of separatism grew to over fifty percent, then it seemed to fluctuate between fifty-five and sixty for what felt like a lifetime. Then, the northern hemisphere results came in, and the number spiked to over seventy percent.

The separatist dream was finally realised. Paradisium was free. Markus Holland made a speech to the crowd about liberty and daring to dream. Then the champagne flowed, just as David Jareth predicted. And so, Titus Rousseau celebrated the victory, raising a glass with his fellow Society brother, Alan Washington.

"Novus Ordo Seclorum".

▲

By the early hours of the morning, Titus had consumed more champagne than ever before in sixty-seven years of life. He'd never been one for drinking excessively, even during his early years as a stockbroker on Wall Street. But tonight had been different. For the first time in what felt like forever, the Society had a meaningful victory.

Separatism meant the corporations could operate without the heavy taxation imposed by the 'wealth. The hard-working men and women of Paradisium would finally see the fruits of their labour. The younger, lazy generations would no longer have the luxury of free housing, medical or food. They'd have to stand on their own two feet. At last, the people would be forced to become self-reliant and, in doing so, become more industrious —just as it had been before the Fall.

Of course, one of the Society's goals was implementing a capitalist system, at least on the surface. They'd never really allow a two-bit bottom feeder to ascend beyond reasonable means —that was how you lost control of the system. The key to maintaining control was illusion: the Society would make the everyman believe in whatever they wanted them to believe. In Titus' mind, there was a beauty to be found there, as though they were machiavellian puppet masters, pulling the strings and watching the game unfold over generations. That was how the Society operated: in the shadows.

After drinking one too many glasses of champagne, Rousseau decided to call it a night. He exchanged gentlemanly handshakes and hugs with his colleagues, as was the appropriate custom for a man of his position, and left the celebration before the sunrise. Titus was escorted to his inner-planet transport, flanked by four bodyguards and the trip back to his hotel was pleasant.

His hotel was situated in the diplomatic quarter of the central city. Like all of the Commonwealth Capital Worlds, a strange luxuriousness seemed to radiate from the area that was entirely out of place for a supposedly socialist culture. Of course, Rousseau ignored the hypocrisy. He'd rather sleep in a place of extravagance than a communist slum.

When Titus reached his room, he dismissed his bodyguards and wished them a good night's sleep. Sure, they were the gruff military types with shitty conversational skills, but Titus hoped that he could inspire them to improve by setting a good example.

Once inside his dimly lit room, Titus threw his suit jacket over the back of a chair, then placed his folded tie and cufflinks on the marble dressing table opposite. He let out a tired sigh as he moved into the room to activate the shades. Almost tripping over in his semi-drunken state, Titus used the back of a long leather chair to steady himself.

Then he realised, something was wrong.

Titus felt the cold barrel of a gun press against his skull. There was weight to the weapon, meaning it was made from metal and not carbon composites. That told him, whoever his attacker was, they had money to afford a decent firearm.

"What do you want?" Titus said, his voice cracking under the pressure of the situation. He quickly raised his hands in surrender. "There's a gold watch on the dressing table. It's yours if you walk away right now".

Silence lingered in the air for a moment.

"Sit down, Mr Rousseau. I've got some questions, and you are going to answer them".

The voice was undeniably male, though distorted by a vocal scrambler that sounded aggressive and robotic. That meant whoever was holding the gun was also wearing a mask.

"What do you want to know?" Titus asked. "I've got money... I've got resources—"

The gunman grabbed him by the shoulder and pulled him away from the windows with considerable strength. After Titus was shoved into a chair, he got a good look at his attacker. The masked man wore a long black combat jacket atop modified armour that hugged his stocky frame like a glove. The mask he wore was made from dark cloth and gave no hint of the face beneath.

Titus forced himself not to scowl. "Who are you? What do you want?"

Without saying a word, the gunman's hand moved to the inner pocket of his jacket, and he produced an envelope.

At least it wasn't another gun.

Titus was shocked when the six-foot-two shadow gently handed him the envelope.

"Open it".

Reluctantly, Titus unpeeled the envelope and glanced at its contents. He couldn't help gulping when he saw his signature on the almost-thirty-year-old documents. The paperwork was tied back to a research facility deep in the Ural mountains, long before the Fall. It was a venture that Titus had overseen on behalf of the Society, under the orders of Theodore Jareth.

"Where did you get all of this?" Titus said, his mouth growing dry. "Whatever you think I did—"

"I have questions about the Russian facility, Mr Rousseau". The shadow's voice was calmer than it had been earlier. "I'd like you to answer my questions honestly; otherwise, this exchange becomes far more violent. I can already tell that you are a civilised man, so let's not go down that path".

Titus didn't appreciate the threat, but at the same time,

he recognised it was very real. He nodded to the shadow, and the masked man stepped back and holstered his firearm.

"What do you want to know?"

"You hired a team, led by Doctor Bill Stephens, to research something your people found in that mountain.." The shadow paused for breath, and the list of names of those who'd be interested in such information began to fill Titus' head. "Why did you hire Bill Stephens?"

That wasn't a question Titus expected at all.

Involuntarily, his brows knotted, and his neck twitched.

"Doctor Stephens had an... interesting track record with unusual phenomena," Titus answered with a shrug. "He found something similar in the Artic, but the EDA destroyed it. In Russia, I presented a different opportunity for Stephens and his team: a meaningful opportunity".

Silence lingered again, but this time the masked man moved to the bottle of whiskey on Titus' stand and handed it to him. It was a strange gesture: almost gentlemanly.

"Did Doctor Stephens get the anomaly working?"

That was an incredibly specific question. Only a tiny portion of people knew about the artefact buried under the Ural mountains from all those years ago, and all of them were in the Society. *It prompted Titus to think, who would want him dead, and why?*

"Yes," Titus answered. He took a long sip of the whiskey, hoping the strong booze would calm his nerves. Then after swallowing, he added, "They got it working for the most part".

The masked man nodded. "Is that why you ordered the hit on Doctor Stephens and his team? Did they find out too much?"

"So that's what this is all about?" Titus mused as he stared into the soulless mask of his attacker. "Who are you under there? Some vengeful relative of the research team? Because I've got news for you, that was over a quarter of a century—"

The shadow grabbed Titus by the throat and squeezed on his windpipe. The robotic voice of the attacker turned hostile. "Who ordered the hit?"

Titus choked under the pressure of the big man's chokehold for several seconds before being released from the grip.

"The orders came from over my head; Theodore Jareth via Roth," Titus coughed. "I had no say in the matter at all. You have to believe me..."

The masked man backed away, and suddenly all of the professionalism returned to their exchange. Titus tried to analyse the situation as he would anything else, but his nerves were starting to overpower the senses. The gunman was male, likely human, professionally trained and seemingly had a personal tie to the slaughtered research team. To find relatives of that group wouldn't be difficult at all.

The shadow considered Titus for a moment before asking "What happened to the anomaly?"

Titus forced himself not to sound sarcastic. "It went up in flames with the research team and the rest of Earth..."

Something shifted inside the gunman; a tiny jolt of human emotion he carried in his shoulders and neck. Maybe it was rage or grief, but it was there nonetheless.

"I want you to think very carefully about your answer to this next question, Mr Rousseau". The shadow leaned forward in anticipation, his finger around the trigger of his gun. "Since the Fall, has anyone in the Society found an anomaly like the one in Russia?"

The question gave it all away. Suddenly it all became clear to Titus. The masked man wasn't under the employ of a Society member, and he wasn't some whack-job seeking revenge for a bunch of nobody researchers.

This man was working for someone with an agenda. He was working for David Jareth —a man obsessed with Enkaye technology. He'd invested countless resources into finding out everything he possibly could about the galaxy's forerunners. Plus, he was the only person outside the Society who could get ahold of old documents like the ones in Titus' hand.

Titus stared at the shadow, knowing that the masked

man had been sent there for a reason: to extract information by any means necessary. He was David Jareth's loyal attack dog: a monster who wouldn't think twice to kill a man in cold blood.

The gunman raised his voice, "Has anyone found another anomaly?"

For Titus, answering the question was impossible. Say nothing or betray the Society: either way, he was a dead man. Knowing that his life was coming to an abrupt end, felt terrible, but he wouldn't betray his brothers and sisters.

There was honour in that.

Titus slowly climbed to his feet to match his killer's stance; refusing to die on his knees while begging for his life. Instead, he would die an honourable death: protecting the Society from those who would seek to harm it.

Titus straightened up and regarded his murderer with a look of anger and acceptance.

"The next time you see Mr Jareth, tell him that his father would be disgusted by what he has become," Titus replied, keeping his voice free of emotion.

The shadow nodded as though he saw some courage in it as well.

"The Society's days are numbered," he said, stating it as fact. "All of you are going to pay for what you did to Earth".

Titus nodded quietly in acceptance. Then, he took one final swig from the bottle of whiskey, placed it down and said his last words.

"Novus ordo seclorum".

A gunshot followed, and the last thing Titus Rousseau thought about was his late husband, Eli. He hoped that through death, they'd be reunited again.

CHIMERA

Chimera fired his silenced pistol. The bullet seared into Rousseau's skull with a thud, spilling blood and brain against the neutral coloured walls and carpet. The lifeless body fell backwards, crashing to the ground. It was the kind of death that was too good for a Society member, but that was the way Jareth wanted it: *as clean as humanly possible.*

As Chimera holstered his gun, he looked into Rousseau's dead eyes. He should have felt bad for killing someone in cold blood, but he didn't feel anything at all. Instead, Chimera took comfort in the fact that what he was doing was for justice.

It was for all those who'd died in the Fall.

CHAPTER TWO
ASTRILLA

At over ten thousand metres in height, Takara was the second-largest mountain on Pelos Three: rising from the forest and disappearing into the clouds. When she was thirteen, Astrilla and her peers climbed to the highest peak as part of a training exercise. At the time, Elder Xanathur had called it a lesson in perseverance, which Astrilla and her classmates had casually dismissed. The funny thing was that with age came perspective, and now eighteen years later, Astrilla saw just how right Xanathur had been. She and her classmates had spent days hiking and climbing the harsh terrain to reach the top. Astrilla hadn't appreciated the struggle or the cold temperatures, but looking back, she realised that Xanathur had instilled a sense of unbridled perseverance in her. *Perhaps it was that same determination that kept her alive on the Messorem.*

Takara was nothing less than a giant stone wall, and from where Astrilla and Nathan stood, it looked to offer little to no purchase. Fortunately, they had no plans to scale the mountain, which came as a relief to Nathan. Instead, they were there to investigate an Enkaye temple not far from the base.

"Remind me again," Nathan said as he looked at the giant mountain ahead. "Why did you insist that we hike?"

"It's not healthy to spend every waking moment aboard your ship, especially when you are planetside," Astrilla shook her head and pointed to the trees surrounding them.

"Fresh air and the sounds of nature cleanse the soul".

Nathan's brow arched, and Astrilla half-expected him to respond with something sarcastic, but to her surprise, he did no such thing. Instead, Nathan looked at the slowly setting sun, considered something then dropped his backpack.

"I think we should make camp here," he said with a tired sigh. "Besides, poking around an old temple after dark feels like a bad move".

As always, some part of Astrilla wanted to push ahead, but it was hard to argue with Nathan's point. All safety issues aside, Astrilla was exhausted, not to mention hungry.

▲

By the time they had made a campfire and deployed a sleeping pod, night had set in. Dinner simmered in a covered pan atop a pile of neatly raked coals. While Nathan reviewed the notes that Elder Xanathur supplied, Astrilla sipped tea and quietly looked at the night sky in contemplation. She took a great deal of comfort, knowing that she'd be sleeping under the same stars that she had growing up.

"Looks like Xanathur's records on the temple are pretty vague," Nathan said as he deactivated his datapad. As he checked on the food, Nathan continued to talk, "I really hope we get a win this time. It'd be good to find something half-interesting".

"I hope so," Astrilla nodded. "It doesn't feel like we've made a notable discovery for a while".

The crew of the Phoenix Titan had spent the last eleven months investigating Enkaye ruins in Commonwealth space and to some success. Their discoveries had varied from old Enkaye texts to elaborate murals, but the most significant breakthrough —at least for Astrilla— was a single word: *Ganmaru*.

It was a name referenced in all the Enkaye's latter records over several dozen times, but most importantly of all, *Ganmaru*, was considered to be a significant threat to the Enkaye. The initial assumption was that the Ganmaru were a race of hostiles that wiped out the Enkaye. However, further discoveries seemed to indicate that it was, in actuality, a plague that swept across the galaxy, wiping out a large proportion of the Enkaye race. Then all of the records ceased, and presumably, so did the galaxy's forerunners.

The crew of the Phoenix had been unable to unearth any documents or records since, but it was still a monumental breakthrough. Regardless of whatever *Ganmaru* was, Astrilla felt as though she was closer to understanding her ancient predecessor's downfall. It was something: a hint or possible explanation for what happened all those thousands of years ago.

"So," Nathan said as he checked on the food bubbling away on the fire. "Are you gonna tell me why you *really* forced me to hike all this way out here?"

He banged a wooden spoon against the rim of the pot and looked at Astrilla sceptically.

"I told you already," she replied casually. "You need time away from the ship".

It was the very question Astrilla had been hoping to avoid all day. But, the truth was that she needed Nathan away from the newscasts and all the coverage circulating Paradisium and the EWB. She'd hoped that the prospect of exploring a new temple, plus the long hike, would take his mind off everything. But, alas, her paramour had grown to know her almost as well as she knew herself.

Nathan spooned two portions of the hot soup into bowls and handed one of them to Astrilla.

"C'mon, let's be honest here," he said. "It's the EWB, isn't it?"

Astrilla sighed in what she could only describe as mild frustration. The Earther Withdrawal Ballot was a highly controversial topic that the entire galaxy was watching closely, including the three Earthers aboard the Phoenix.

The political movement had been spearheaded by what Gordon called, Paradisium's elite. They were high-rolling businessmen, celebrities and politicians: the people that would benefit most from separatism.

"With the ballots and the debates all over the newscast, I thought you could use a break from it all," Astrilla said. She paused to take a spoonful of soup. "I don't see why you, Gordon and Russell are so transfixed by the whole thing. You don't see the Paradisians as your people; Gordon can barely stand the company of anyone outside of the ship, and Russell practically chewed your arm off at the prospect of leaving Paradisium".

"I care because of Jareth," Nathan answered. "He's got invested interest in this thing. That's bad news for all of us; I know it".

Astrilla knew he would say it before he said it, and she understood why he was so concerned. Jareth had tried to manipulate Nathan into giving him the Messorem, which Nathan had correctly refused. There was no denying that giving a weapon of that magnitude to a sociopath like Jareth would've been disastrous.

"David Jareth will do what David Jareth has always done; he will make money however possible," Astrilla shuffled beside Nathan while balancing her bowl of soup in one hand. "Personally, I think you need to take your mind off of things and focus on the good. We aren't on the run from the Revenant anymore; we have a wonderful crew, and we are making groundbreaking discoveries with the work we are doing—"

"Plus, we've got each other," Nathan cut her off mid-sentence.

His words carried with them a warmth that still felt bizarre to Astrilla: certainly not bad, but odd nonetheless. After ten months of being lovers or paramours —whatever they were calling their relationship— Astrilla still had to remind herself now and then that she wasn't alone anymore. Of course, it wasn't in Nathan's nature to get overly sentimental, and to Astrilla, that was just fine: that was who he was. But she couldn't deny that it felt refreshing on those occasions when Nathan said something corny or romantic. It was the kind of thing that made her feel alive.

Nathan wrapped an arm around her shoulder and continued, “It’s not that I’m ungrateful for all the good stuff: I’ve never been happier. What keeps me up at night is the thought that Jareth could quickly become another Seig if he’s left unchecked. That bastard was desperate to get his hands on the Messorem—”

“And you made the right call,” Astrilla interrupted. “All you can do is act in the here and now, and that’s what you did with Jareth in the first place: that’s why he doesn’t have the Messorem. That’s why you and I, and our crew, are still alive”.

Yes, her words were harsh, but they came from a place of affection, which Astrilla reinforced by squeezing Nathan’s hand. Astrilla knew she was right, and she suspected that Nathan knew it too. His need to carry the weight of the galaxy’s problems wasn’t new, but it had undoubtedly evolved and grown. After Nathan found out that he was an Enkaye half-breed, things changed. Rather than shouldering his own burdens and perhaps those of his crew, he’d begun to worry more about the galaxy at large, which was a weight that no one deserved to carry: not even a descendant of the Enkaye.

▲

Astrilla woke several hours later to the sound of rainfall and thunder. Having spent most of her life on Pelos Three, she’d grown accustomed to the frequent stormy showers that would occur almost every other day. The sound was a pleasant reminder that she was home or at least her home away from home. Astrilla knew that the Phoenix Titan was starting to fill that role now, and she willingly embraced that fact.

Nathan stirred beside her. Then in a gruff and groggy voice, he asked, “Is that thunder?”

“It wouldn’t be Pelos without a storm,” Astrilla answered.

Nathan mumbled something incoherent in his state of

semi-slumber and then went quiet. Astrilla hoped that he would go back to sleep and get some meaningful rest. In recent weeks, especially with all the talk of Paradisium and the EWB, Nathan struggled to sleep, and when he did, violent nightmares plagued his mind.

Astrilla lay between the covers for several minutes, listening to the storm, hoping that it would send her to sleep. There was something meditative about the white noise that muted her thoughts and enabled her to doze off. She drifted toward slumber, but Nathan's voice pulled her back to consciousness.

"I was dreaming," he said flatly. "I saw a forest on a planet somewhere... very far away".

"Well, that makes a pleasant change," Astrilla said, turning over to face him. "Was it like the forests here on Pelos?"

Nathan paused for a short moment, leaving Astrilla to wonder if he was talking in his sleep.

"No," he shook his head. "Something terrible was on that planet. I can't explain it, but it felt as though something under the trees wanted to..." Nathan paused and looked upward in a thoughtful manner. "It's like this thing was desperate to be whole again. I don't know how to explain it..."

Astrilla placed a hand on his arm and moved in closer. At least his dream —or vision— wasn't bloody and violent: there had been more than enough of those in the past. Nathan focussed his gaze on Astrilla, and he said in a low voice;

"You still believe we are part of this whole Enkaye plan, right?"

Astrilla nodded, "Of course. Why do you ask?"

"I'm struggling to get my head around what it all means," Nathan sat up in the bed. "Are we just supposed to wait for something to happen, or do we need to be the ones to seek out the next part of the plan?"

"What do you think we're doing right now?" Astrilla replied as if stating the obvious. "Since the Messorem, we have been working tirelessly to understand our forerunners.

We've learned more about them in a year than entire generations have in hundreds of years".

"I know, but I can't explain the thought that the Enkaye intended for us to do more than just investigate ruins," Nathan said. "With all the bad stuff in the galaxy, surely we are supposed to do something".

Astrilla smiled and placed her hand on his cheek, feeling the coarse hairs of his beard against her palm.

"I love you," she said tenderly before hardening her voice slightly. "But we can't just go out into the galaxy and find King Baylum or David Jareth or root out all the corruption in the Commonwealth. You and I are just two people. We may be part-Enkaye, and we may well have a part in some elaborate plan, but we must allow destiny to present itself to us; not go in gung-ho".

Nathan chewed the inside of his cheek reflectively. Then with an almost smirk, he said, "When did you get so good at talking me out of going into shitty situations with guns-blazing?"

"For the record, I don't think I could ever talk you out of that," Astrilla replied. "All I know is that when destiny, or fate, or the Enkaye plan, presents itself, we will face it together".

Nathan seemed to accept her answer, and he was drifting to sleep once again within a few minutes. It was funny to think that when Astrilla first met Nathan Carter aboard the Vertex, he'd been a capable but uncaring vagabond with little thought for the galaxy at large. But, since then, he'd grown into a compassionate and protective leader who saw the bigger picture.

NATHAN

Considering that strange dreams had broken most of Nathan's sleep, he was surprised at how well-rested he felt by morning. Less than thirty minutes after waking, he'd washed, changed into fresh clothes and boiled a canteen of water. Once Astrilla was ready to leave, they packed down the sleeping pod and began the short hike to the temple.

As Nathan sipped on a flask of coffee, he took the time to reflect on his dreams. Something innate told him that it wasn't the same as the visions he'd experienced during the search for the Omega, but at the same time, they weren't normal either. He'd seen something lurking under a vast forest that simply didn't belong there. In a way, it felt broken —no, not broken— just not whole. Whatever the thing was that Nathan felt in that dream, it was desperate to escape.

By the end of his coffee, Nathan concluded that it didn't matter. If it were an Enkaye vision, Astrilla would've seen it too, which she hadn't. *So maybe his brain was simply doing what was normal.* Perhaps the combination of REM sleep and the right conditions had allowed his mind to produce something coherent from his subconscious. *Maybe dreams were just dreams? That was entirely human. And perhaps it was entirely Enkaye as well? Who said that they didn't dream too?*

The entrance to the temple was situated on the east side of Takara, buried under a few hundred years of moss and rumble. Astrilla made light work of the debris with the help of an elemental summon, and before long, the shape of what had once been became clear. A white stone archway was set into the mountain and led into a dark tunnel. As Nathan led the way, he activated a flashlight hooked to his backpack. The additional light allowed him to make out old Enkaye hieroglyphs and markings carved into the walls. They were similar to those Nathan had seen back on the Messorem but seemed somehow older.

They followed the long tunnel for over half a kilometre, by which point Nathan was sure they were walking beneath the mountain. The further he walked into the perfectly symmetrical passage, the more Nathan felt he was walking across an airlock. The whole thing was all too perfect —as though the Enkaye had meticulously carved every inch of the tunnel using a precise tool.

"It's remarkable, isn't it?" Astrilla said as if she could tell what he was thinking.

"It sure is," Nathan answered as he examined the walls. "I'm no architect, but this tunnel should've collapsed years ago. How the hell did they cut such a perfect path?"

Astrilla looked at Nathan the way she did whenever he asked an impossible question. "Maybe they used some sort of mining laser," she shrugged. "Something that would generate the kind of heat that could fuse all the rock and minerals. Either that or they built some supporting structures around the tunnel that we simply cannot see".

"Well, whatever they did, it certainly stood the test of time," Nathan said.

Less than a minute later, the tunnel opened out onto a small cylindrical room, no larger than the galley aboard the Phoenix. When none of the dormant technology reacted to his presence, something in Nathan's gut told him that this temple —like the last few— was a total bust. If the Enkaye technology were in working order, it would've detected his or Astrilla's presence immediately. Things would inevitably start moving or changing when that happened, but unfortunately, that wasn't the case on this occasion.

"Shit..." Nathan said with a disappointed sigh.

CHAPTER THREE
RUSSELL

A year after leaving Paradisium and joining the crew of the Phoenix Titan, Russell Johnson felt like a new man. His life had changed beyond all recognition, and more importantly, *he* had changed for the better.

Gone was the day-in-day-out grind of serving cocktails to entitled Paradisians, replaced by a yearning for adventure. The whole experience had made Russell realise that he was, in actuality, a young man with his entire life ahead of him, where before he felt defeated and condemned to a life of boredom and menial labour.

There was no argument that the sudden overnight change to his life was overwhelming, but he wouldn't change it for all the money in the world. Russell had gone from tending a bar on Paradisium to fighting in one of history's greatest battles. Now he was part of the very crew that were leading the charge when it came to Enkaye research. As a result, he'd learnt more in a year than at any point in his entire life.

Russell awoke to the smell of fresh coffee and the sound of banging on the hull. In his half-awake state, the noise sounded like gunfire, which forced him to sit up in bed, ready to take on whatever it was shooting at the ship. Two seconds later, he realised that the mechanics were starting early to get a good look at the Phoenix's engine.

The ship was by no means in a bad state. In fact, it was in the best condition Russell had ever seen, but Vol had insisted that the Phoenix undergo an extensive maintenance check while they were planetside.

It had been two days since they'd landed at Pelos Three, and Russell was surprised to find that he hadn't grown impatient. For over six months, the Phoenix had travelled between Enkaye ruins across the galaxy: bouncing from one planet to the next. As a result, Russell had grown accustomed to life on the go, which was a welcome change from his days on Paradisium. The problem now was that the prospect of staying still for too long terrified him. *Maybe that's what twenty-two years on the same god-forsaken rock would do to someone? Perhaps it was the reason why he'd grown to resent Paradisium so much.*

Despite yearning to stay between the confines of his comfortable bedsheets, Russell knew that sleep at this stage was a waste of time. At best, the mechs would be working for the next ten hours, and he found it difficult to drown out external noises. Russell dragged himself out of bed pulled on a pair of dark jeans and an old sports jersey that had once belonged to his father.

When he entered the living area, Russell found Gordon Taggart staring pensively at the newly installed monitor at the bar. The screen was divided into two windows, one displaying the Commonwealth newscast and the other, live news from Paradisium. The fact that Gordon was watching both in tandem should have said something profound about his political affiliation, but Russell had learned that the doctor was far more complicated than he appeared.

There was no doubt that Gordon was detail-orientated, but his need to analyse every possible eventuality bordered on obsessive. Of course, Russell didn't judge the old man for his quirks. In fact, he enjoyed Gordon's company immensely. And besides, they mostly agreed that the EWB was a farce, designed to make the rich richer and the poor poorer: something that most Paradisians were either too stupid or too proud to understand.

"Morning, Doc," Russell said as he grabbed a clean cup from the bar.

Gordon was too transfixed by the opposing newscasts

playing out before him to reply. Rather than peel the old man away from his thoughts, Russell instead decided to focus on a more pressing matter, namely a fresh cup of coffee. He paced across the bar and tapped in his order for an espresso with a single scoop of Corianth sweetener: just the way he liked it in the morning. As the coffee machine gurgled to life, Gordon turned his attention away from the screen.

"Sorry," Gordon said.

"No problem," Russell shrugged. Then, he pointed at the screen, "What's happened with the EWB?"

Gordon looked at him as though he'd said something stupid. It took Russell a moment longer than it should have to realise that something was up. What he saw on the screen —on the Commonwealth side anyway— was a scrolling ticker tape under the news reporter that read;

BREAKING NEWS: PARADISIAN BALLOT RESULTS. SEPARATISM: 75.1%. REMAIN: 25.9%. TURNOUT: 68.3%.

"Damn," Russell said, drawing the word out to two syllables. "When did the results come out?"

"About a half-hour after you went to bed..." Gordon answered, without peeling his gaze from the screen.

Russell shook his head as he took in the result. "I ain't surprised they voted that way, but shit... three quarters voted for separatism. That's way higher than I expected".

Gordon's eyes didn't hint at complete agreement. Trying to understand the odd mannerisms of the doctor was difficult, but over the last few months, Russell believed he had a good grasp on when the old man was irritable: this was not it.

Gordon tapped his knuckle against the bar, "There was only a sixty-eight percent turnout. That's more of a concern than the result itself".

The coffee machine chimed behind Russell in a cheery tone that meant his drink was ready.

"Why?" Russell shrugged as he moved to grab his

drink. "Sixty-eight percent is better than nothing. Besides, I'm pretty sure that even if you got all the non-voters together and they voted to stay, none of it would make a difference".

"That is beside the point," Gordon said, his voice growing severe yet teacherly. "Almost a thirty percent of the adult population abstained from voting. Just think about those numbers for a moment..."

It was hard for Russell to imagine a third of Paradisium's adult population. A slither of them would be like him: born after the Fall, with little-to-no understanding of what life on Earth was really like. He wondered if any of them would really care about the things the Commonwealth had done for their people. Russell presumed not, but then again, he did, so surely that meant someone else would too.

Then again, there were the people a decade older than him —the same generation of Earthers as Nathan. They were often referred to as the *scarred generation* on Paradisium. Many had witnessed the horrors of planetary slaughter first hand as children and a result many suffered severe psychological trauma. As a generation they had the highest suicide rate on Paradisium, though it wasn't reported much in the media. Russell could understand why that group would levy some blame toward the 'wealth.

The problem in Russell's mind was that the scarred generation could have only made up a quarter of Paradisium's population, whilst his own —at least of voting age— would've been barely ten percent. That meant the rest of the vote came from the older residents: people who'd been adults at the time of the Fall. Arguably, those people had lost the most, and in a way, Russell could understand why they'd side with separatism.

It was easy to argue that maybe he'd have felt the same way had he been born twenty or thirty years earlier, but in his heart, Russell knew that wasn't the case. Yes, the Commonwealth had made mistakes. Yes, it was a very flawed government, but it was a damn sight better than the alternative: better than the Revenant. *Maybe the people of Paradisium had lost sight of that?*

Russell forced himself to remember that none of it mattered now. The voting had finished, and Paradisium had made up its mind.

Russell and Gordon watched the coverage of the EWB results for another hour. It was strange watching both news outlets in parallel, but Russell finally understood why Gordon did it. There was some validity in both arguments, but what was more interesting was the way both news reports used almost war-time language throughout. The 'wealthers referred to the ordeal as a betrayal, while the Paradisian media hailed the victory as a great day for freedom. Despite being completely different messages, both intended to do the same thing —create division.

NATHAN

At the end of a very long hike, the last thing on Nathan's mind was a meeting with the Evoker Elders. He wanted nothing more than a hot shower followed by an hour or two of sleep. Unfortunately, that wasn't the way things went when the expensive maintenance of your ship was at the behest of the Elders. It also didn't help that one of those Elders was his lover's disapproving surrogate mother-figure. Every time he saw Yuta, he felt obliged to filter himself, as though saying the word *fuck* was a sure-fire way to give the old woman a heart attack.

Elder Xanathur was slightly different. He was a friendly old coot who'd seen more of the galaxy than his peers, resulting in a practical, no-nonsense mindset, which Nathan could appreciate. Where the others saw Nathan and his crew as a thorn in the side, Xanathur seemed to gravitate toward them.

As for the rest of the Elders, they didn't understand Nathan: *how could they?* He was many things, and a clean-cut Evoker scholar wasn't one of them. At his core, Nathan Carter was a son of Earth, the Captain of the Phoenix Titan, the man who'd faced King Seig in combat and won. Yet, despite knowing all of those things, the Evoker Elders looked at him as though he didn't belong: as though they were disappointed in Astrilla for choosing such an uncouth paramour.

The tricky thing was that the Elders didn't know the whole truth about Nathan Carter. They didn't know that he was an Enkaye half-breed, like Astrilla. They weren't even aware that he could occasionally summon elemental energy like an Evoker. The fact that his surrogate-mother-in-law —or whatever the hell Yuta was— didn't know those facts often left Nathan to wonder if keeping his heritage a secret was the right call.

Before leaving the Phoenix, Harrt was adamant that a mole was working for the Revenant. That didn't mean to say that the traitor was inside the Evokers, but Nathan knew that people talked. If the Elders knew what he *really* was, word would travel and eventually, it would paint a target on the Phoenix and his crew. That was something he wouldn't allow to happen again.

Elder Yuta's *room of learning* had all the earmarks of an office. There was a small desk with an upturned display at the back of the room. Glass windows built between the ornate stone pillars boasted an impressive view of the forest below. Yuta was already standing when Nathan and Astrilla arrived, and when Nathan examined the room, he noticed a distinct lack of chairs.

Guess I'll stand, he thought.

A strong aroma of incense filled Nathan's nostrils as he waited for Astrilla and Yuta to finish their initial exchange. The strange not-quite-cinnamon scent reminded Nathan of Earth for one reason or another, evoking memories of cookies and the autumnal seasons when the leaves would turn red, and the weather would change. Those times seemed so distant now: like the memories belonged to some carefree stranger and not himself.

Something Yuta said dragged Nathan away from the nostalgia that filled his mind. For a split second, he wasn't sure how long his attention had drifted, but neither Astrilla or Yuta had noticed, so it couldn't have been long.

"Do you agree with Xanathur's reports?" Yuta asked.

Nathan stared blankly at her for a moment, then shook away the daze. "The temple was a complete bust, just like Xanathur said. Even with Astrilla's presence, nothing switched on. So I guess we write this one off".

Yuta nodded. "I recommend you speak with Xanathur when he returns: we'll need to update our records".

Nathan nodded, and the conversation shifted from temples to the news of the day.

"The reports on the EWB keep coming in," Yuta said, moving around her desk and tapping her screen. "I've not seen the Commonwealth politicians and Admiralty so active on a subject that doesn't relate to the Revenant".

"In the grand scheme of things, Paradisium is one of thousands of member worlds," Astrilla said. "Does it matter if one planet leaves? It's not like the Commonwealth are losing military assets or a meaningful contribution to the war effort".

"You tell me, child," Yuta lifted her open palms as if to shrug. "Paradisium is the first world to leave since the Commonwealth's formation. I hear that the Master of the House grows wary".

Nathan started to speak, then stopped. He noticed Yuta was staring at him. She raised her thin grey eyebrows, hinting as though she were welcoming his comments. *That was a first.*

"You think the Commonwealth are afraid of losing control," Nathan surmised. "You think there will be some kinda domino effect?"

He was surprised that Yuta nodded in response.

"If Paradisium strikes out on its own and proves successful, many others could follow," Yuta tapped on the screen again, and a holo-projector spun up in the middle of the room. She glanced at Nathan again, "Master of the House, Inon Waife, is not a fool, but he is a true believer in the state. If someone were to provoke him —for example, David Jareth— we could have a very unpleasant situation on our hands".

"You mean war?" Nathan said bluntly.

The room went quiet, leaving only the sound of the holo-projector to fill the void.

Yuta cleared her throat; "What I mean to say is that the Commonwealth will take their eyes off of the Revenant. That is something *we* cannot allow to happen".

Nathan's first impulse was to wonder if Yuta had meant to include him and the crew in her generalisation. He most certainly was not an Evoker; neither was Russell, Vol or Gordon. It didn't matter, but he had to wonder what she meant by saying that.

The second impulse was to admit that Yuta was entirely right. The Commonwealth were like a starving bear in the wild, angry and easy to provoke, while Paradisium was the idiot with a stick ready to poke the bear and hope not to get mauled in the process.

Nathan wondered what a Commonwealth versus Paradisium war would look like. In his head, he pictured Jareth Corps' advanced ivory white ships and drones. Sure, they make a dent, but the truth was that the 'wealthers had the numbers. Even with all the other corporate militaries out of Paradisium, the outcome was the same: the 'wealth would undoubtedly win.

So that begged the question; *why was David Jareth doing all of this? What could he possibly have to gain?*

It was at that moment that Nathan realised that Yuta had summoned him there for a reason. Astrilla could've easily told the old woman that their excursion to the mountainside temple was a complete bust, but she'd specifically requested his attendance.

A hologram finally emerged from the projector, displaying a planet not far from the Pelos System, not far from corporate space. At most, the journey would be four hours in the slipstream, with a short burn toward the planet.

"I asked you both here because I've got something that will be of interest to you," Yuta said, looking at Nathan.

In response, Nathan shrugged as if to say, *I'm all ears*. Yuta's frown lingered for all but a heartbeat. Then she gestured at the holographic planet in the middle of the room.

"This is Levave, a former terraforming project that belonged to the Illuminators up until fifteen years ago". Yuta stopped and shifted her gaze to Nathan. "I assume you are familiar with the Illuminators, Captain Carter?"

"Not personally, but I know enough," Nathan answered. "They're a group of monks that allied with the 'wealth a few centuries back. Back in the days when I shipped aboard the Loyalty, there were these rumours about them..."

"*Rumours?*" Yuta's brow raised. She exchanged a brief look with Astrilla before turning back. "Please tell me about these *rumours...*"

Nathan couldn't be sure if her eyes were judgemental or surprised.

"Well," he said, stretching the word out. "I heard the Illuminators swore off combat, even against the Revenant. Rather than fighting in the war, they spend their days farming and terraforming new worlds. Problem is that the 'wealthers don't like people who don't do as they say".

Yuta's expression showed that she was impressed by his knowledge.

"That is partially correct," Yuta replied. "I'm sure the Commonwealth would be happier with the Illuminators if they used their power and resources for war, but the fact is that they need the Illuminators as much as the Illuminators need them".

"And why's that?"

"Terraforming is an art form," Yuta replied. "In over three hundred years, the Illuminators have turned hundreds of dead worlds into completely habitable ecosystems. In the last three centuries, only one of those worlds has been considered a failure..." Yuta gestured to the holographic planet above her desk. "The weather systems on Levave were considered to be overly reactive, and the project was abandoned several years ago".

"So, what's so important about this planet now?" Nathan said, trying his best to remove all the scepticism from his voice.

Yuta tapped something on her screen, and a smaller hologram in red was overlayed on top of Levave. When

Nathan looked closer, he saw it was of a satellite in orbit of the planet.

"The Evokers have a monitoring beacon in orbit," Yuta said. "We use it to monitor the storms for research. Usually, the readings are interesting, but nothing out of the ordinary. That is until today. Eight hours ago, our beacon detected a spike of energy inside one of the Illuminator temples, and we'd like you to go and investigate".

Nathan fought the urge to be blunt, but he was pretty sure it sounded downright rude when he spoke:

"Why us? Why can't you send one of your students or study crews?"

To his surprise, Yuta's expression didn't change. She must've anticipated his reaction.

"I'm asking you because the spike in the energy almost matches that of your Enkaye droid," she said.

The prospect of what Yuta said sent a chill down Nathan's spine. If the spike was Enkaye, like the droid, then something must've switched it on. Nathan's mind raced at the thought of another Messorem buried deep beneath Levave's surface. *Maybe that was what his dream had hinted at?* Of course, if it weren't Enkaye, that would be the kind of fluke that erred on the ridiculous. In Nathan's experience, there was no room in the galaxy for coincidences: not after everything that had happened to him.

"Do any of the Illuminator surveys mention any Enkaye structures on the surface?" Astrilla asked.

"No," Yuta shook her head. "Levave would've been nothing more than a barren wasteland in the days of the Enkaye Dynasty. According to Xanathur's records, all that's down there is the abandoned Terraforming station".

"The spike in energy readings seems to say otherwise," Nathan said. "If it is Enkaye, then that means something awoke that tech..."

Yuta lifted her brows expectantly.

"Fine," Nathan nodded. "We'll head to Levave and investigate once the Phoenix is good to go".

Yuta offered up a smile to Nathan that was entirely false. She was doing her best to hide her sense of victory from her weathered old face. It was pretty infuriating, but Nathan did his best to swallow his annoyance.

▲

After finishing the meeting, Nathan and Astrilla took a slow walk back to the docking pad. The gentle afternoon drizzle that came over Pelos Three served as decent background noise for Nathan as he tried to organise his thoughts.

The spike that the Evoker beacon had detected was strange, but it was a single thread among a billion others: like pointing out a single star in the night's sky. Remarkable and unique, but also one of many distinctive spikes. When Nathan split the image of the readouts against those of the Enkaye droid, he could see some similarities. Some peaks and lows twinned at similar intervals, but at the same time, the curves of those lines separated, almost resembling two waves in the ocean.

Usually, Nathan would be the first to admit that he wasn't the expert on such things, but there was no denying that there was something to it.

CHAPTER FOUR
VOL

Vol Volloh prepped the engines as the sun began its leisurely stroll below the horizon. Beside her in the copilot's chair, Nathan checked the Phoenix's internal systems. She knew everything was running as intended; the Evoker mechs had done their job to the highest standard possible. Of course, Vol had already checked long before Nathan had gazed at his screen, but a second set of eyes never hurt —at least that was what Harrt used to say.

Nathan nodded, confirming that all systems were green across the board. Without ceremony, Vol flipped the switches on her controls, and the Phoenix roared to life. Within seconds, the ship soared beyond the clouds and thereafter, it entered the cold embrace of space.

The jump into the FTL slipstream was perfect —no, it was better than perfect. Before Vol had even braced herself for the jolt that usually followed the sudden acceleration, the ship's onboard systems anticipated it and adjusted the gravity to compensate.

The Phoenix Titan was a masterclass in ship engineering long before the battle of the Messorem, but now after months of upgrades and the time for maintenance, it had become something more.

There were times that Vol had to remind herself that she wasn't travelling aboard an old hauler or a rickety Linkrider. In her head, the Phoenix existed somewhere between military gunship, yacht and racer, yet somehow it was none of those things. Instead, it felt like home. That's what mattered most.

Once the ship stabilised inside the slipstream, Nathan unbuckled himself from the chair and cleared his throat. Vol didn't need her sixth sense to tell that the Earther was stressed and slightly overwhelmed by his own thoughts. She knew the way he subtly communicated his frustrations. He tapped his foot on the ground, tensed his jaw and would breathe out for longer. The signals weren't obvious, and Nathan probably didn't realise he was doing any of them, but Vol had shipped with him since Yenex. She'd grown to know those around her. That was, in some way, the advantage of shipping with the same people for the long haul. The flights between systems, while confined to the Phoenix, felt like stepping into a tiny, private universe that only those who filled the space could understand.

Again, Vol noticed Nathan exhale for longer than he usually would. She turned to face him. "So, what are we gonna do if we find another Enkaye droid on this planet?"

Nathan looked at her and considered the question. "Well," he scratched his beard. "If it's a droid, something must've powered it up. If that's the case, we may be looking for one of my long lost relatives..."

Despite his comment sounding sarcastic, there was more than a hint of hope behind it. Before Vol could probe any further, Nathan climbed from his chair with a resigned huff that meant he needed a drink.

"You want one?" he asked, gesturing with an invisible glass in his hand.

Vol politely declined, and once Nathan left the room, she checked a couple of the Phoenix's systems to ensure that everything was ship-shape, which of course, it was. After a few seconds, Vol's datapad let off a joyful beep that meant she'd received a new message.

When she read the text that said, *from Commander Harrt Oxarri*, Vol forced herself to take a deep, sobering breath.

At that moment, she immediately found herself regretting saying no to a drink.

As far as Vol was aware, there were no hard feelings between her and Harrt. There had never been anything between them, besides friendship. Vol had missed that companionship every single day since he'd left, but it wasn't the primary source of her not-quite-heartache —if that's whatever it was that she felt. Instead, the thing that stung the most was the what-ifs, and the could've beens if Harrt chose to stay, which he hadn't.

Instead of staying, Harrt accepted his promotion in the Commonwealth military as part of an elaborate plan that he and Leviticus Dines had made together. Harrt's mission aimed to root out the corruption inside the Commonwealth's highest echelons, which hopefully included the person —or people— that sold out the Phoenix and her crew during the hunt for the Omega.

The whole thing was honourable and brave and all the other reasons why Vol had a soft spot for Harrt. But it was still foolish and reckless. There were times when Vol wished she'd asked Harrt to reconsider what he was doing, but of course, he'd have done it anyway. Harrt Oxarri wasn't the kind of man that could turn a blind eye to injustice.

He'd lost family, friends, his previous crew, and most importantly of all, he'd lost the one thing he'd believed. While most would consider Harrt's change of view toward the Commonwealth as a moment of eye-opening clarity, Vol saw it as something far less victorious. It was like Harrt had lost faith in a deity that never existed, and now he was trying to rebuild that same entity.

It was only when Nathan sat down beside her that Vol realised that she'd been staring at the screen for several minutes. She promptly shut down the datapad and stuffed it in her pocket, hoping that the Earther hadn't noticed.

"I take it that's Oxarri again?" Nathan said as he sank back into his chair. Vol frowned but didn't reply, which only prompted Nathan to ask, "When's the last time you and he spoke?"

Vol could tell that he already knew the answer, which meant that Nathan didn't intend it as a question. Instead, he was allowing Vol the opportunity to open up to someone —or vent. Of course, that wasn't how she operated. Whatever she and Harrt had shared wasn't romance or anything close to that. They'd been good friends and nothing more.

Vol understood Harrt's reasons for leaving, and part of her admired him for it. The problem was that another part of Vol selfishly wished that he'd stayed: that he'd given whatever they could've been a chance. Harrt would have probably been happier with that alternative too, but as always, he'd done what he'd always done and put everyone else above himself.

That was why Vol hadn't spoken to him for over six months. Every time she saw his dark eyes and regimented 'wealther haircut, she saw the man who'd chosen duty over the could've been.

It sucked, but that's the way it was, and nothing was going to change it. A big part of Vol wanted to share some of that conflict with Nathan and the others, but the problem was none of them would really get it. Vol had been widowed at a very young age, only to find something resembling a relationship that was then ripped away. *How could any of the crew understand that?*

Vol pushed her seat back and reclined, placing her boots on the Phoenix's dashboard. She looked at Nathan, wary that she'd not answered his question promptly.

"It's complicated..." she said, keeping her tone as light and chipper as possible. "Harrt's gotta do what Harrt's gotta do..."

Nathan seemed to soften his eyes in an accepting manner. It was almost as though his features said, *I know what you're saying is bullshit, but I understand.* He promptly changed the subject of their discussion, shifting topics to the maintenance of the Phoenix. It made his earlier question seem casual and not intrusive, which they both knew was bullshit, but Vol appreciated it.

She felt grateful that the Earther was looking out for her as a good captain should.

JARETH

Years ago, somebody told David Jareth that a wise man could learn a great deal from his enemies. He couldn't remember who that person was or if they'd said it to him before or after the Fall, but it was something he'd applied to all aspects of his life.

Forty years ago, Jareth started his career at the family business, Jareth Banking and Investments, as a lowly admin assistant. Despite being the son of the mighty Theodore Jareth, banking tycoon and legend of the sector, he'd never been given an easy break, and he'd never asked for one. In those early days, he'd looked at his peers to understand how he could rise above the pack. He had to understand who was the best at presenting; who had the soft skills to navigate complex tasks; who could integrate with the people that made the big decisions. Knowing all of those things meant that he could identify the threats to his progress. It meant that David Jareth could learn and adapt and, most importantly of all, evolve from those around him. Like a sponge, Jareth soaked up the skills of those around him, and when the opportune moment came, he put them to good use. *He identified his enemy and learnt what he needed in order to surpass them.*

That was how everything in his life had worked. He'd married the woman that everyone else desired because he outsmarted the competition. He'd formed Jareth Corps because everyone else was too scared about the 'wealth and the Revenant to develop a private military. Where there was an opportunity, David Jareth would find it, use it or destroy it. That was his way. That was the way it had to be.

Whoever told him those words was correct; there was much to learn about the enemy. The only problem with that statement was that it often left Jareth wondering *who his true enemy really was.*

He understood the nature of the Commonwealth, and to an extent, he understood the Revenant. They were no different from the kind of people Jareth had learnt about in his school days. Earth's history was littered with influential people who believed their ideology was the only course for humanity. Wars, crusades and other acts of genocide had taken place under the guise of forging a better world. The 'wealth and the Revenant were no different and were both guilty of the same crimes.

Maybe that spoke volumes about the nature of intelligent life?

Regardless of when or where they were, the weak-willed consequential types would rise and cause hard times. That was just nature.

There was no denying that the Revenant and the 'wealth were enemies to what remained of Earth. It was a cold, hard fact, and Jareth knew it would be a problem long after his time. So, rather than focus on what he couldn't solve, David Jareth turned his attention to his immediate enemy —the Society.

It was a choice he'd made on the day of the Fall. It would have been an impossible choice for most men, but for Jareth, it was something he had to do because nobody else could. Thanks to his privileged position, he'd seen first-hand what the likes of Alastair Roth, Titus Rousseau and even his own father were willing to do in the name of forging a better world. It was something Jareth couldn't allow to continue, but it wasn't as simple as pulling a trigger.

The Society's influence had spanned centuries, and since its formation, had controlled the masses through the power of manipulation. During the days of Earth, they'd held the cards to almost everything. Media, stock markets, wars, terrorists, all of it was the Society. To them, the world was a stage, and they were the puppet masters. The Society didn't care about politics or religion or anything like it. All they were concerned with was the continuation and growth of their power.

That was why they'd allowed the Fall to happen. That was why they'd helped Baylum in the destruction of Earth and the murder of billions. The —then— Revenant Prince offered them something that they could never achieve alone —a cultural cleansing of the highest magnitude. That was why Jareth chose the Society as his enemy. He knew it would take time and patience, but at least he'd be able to take action. Once the right pieces were in play, he would act, and avenge all those who'd died in the Fall.

He'd waited many years for the opportunity to present itself, and eventually, it came in the form of Leviticus Dines at the Battle of the Messorem. The data that Dines was forced to hand over became the seed that sprouted into the EWB and eventually into the glorious tree that would be vengeance and justice.

Jareth stared at his datapad: at the image of Titus Rousseau's cold, dead face. He felt nothing. Rousseau was nothing more than a pawn in the grand scheme of things: a name in a long line of people due a comeuppance. There was a gunshot wound in Rousseau's forehead and a long trail of blood that stained his once-proud face.

Jareth closed the image, and in its place, formed the open communication with the assassin, Chimera. The call was audio-only: no visual or holographic imagery at all. That was the way Chimera worked. He didn't like the world to see his face beneath the mask, even though Jareth had seen it a few hundred times before. Theatre was everything to the efficient gunman.

"Well done, old boy," Jareth said into his datapad. "I trust Rousseau's staff have found the body?"

"They found him in the early hours," Chimera answered, his voice carrying the type of distortion that meant he was wearing his mask. "They didn't raise the flag until a few hours afterwards, which means someone senior on his staff is working for the Society too".

Jareth nodded in agreement, even though the hitman couldn't see him on his datapad.

"How would you like me to proceed?" Chimera asked. "Fawas Hussein's ship is still docked on Valour. I can go and—"

"No," Jareth interrupted.

He brought up an image of the confirmed Society members on his datapad and sent it to a large screen ahead of him. There were more blank entries than Jareth preferred, but it was all he had to work with. By nature, the Society worked in the shadows and rarely came out into the light. Still, Jareth had amassed enough data to know who most key players were. He considered the screen for a moment, then sent a picture of the next target to Chimera.

"I think we need someone with a looser tongue," Jareth said. "We need to find out if Roth really has access to another Project Erebus, and if he does, we need to know how he intends to power it".

At the other end of the communication, Chimera was silent. Jareth imagined the seasoned gunman, staring at the picture of his next target with significant consideration.

"Martin Cleave?" Chimera said, his voice flat and cold. "What are your orders?"

A wise man can learn a great deal from his enemies.

The words rang out in Jareth's skull as he thought about it. Chimera could extract information with brute force, but David Jareth would be the mastermind behind the Society's downfall. He had to play his part in the violence that was to come.

His answer to Chimera was simple. "Find Martin Cleave and bring him to me alive".

ASTRILLA

The FTL slipstream was silent. Other than the slight hum of the Phoenix's engines, there was nothing but peace. With a couple of hours of travel remaining, Astrilla elected to meditate in one of the unused cabins toward the back of the ship. Initially, she found the room was colder than expected but quickly acclimatised once she settled into a meditative state. For a while, the passage of time seemed to slow, and Astrilla's awareness transcended the chilly cabin and entered a state of peace and reflection.

Inside the deep recesses of her mind —and, perhaps soul— Astrilla saw a long and winding path before her. She saw great pain and agony behind her and in its place was a renewed sense of purpose. She was sure that everything she'd suffered aboard the Messorem had somehow been intended, and as a result, now seemed redundant. She was no longer scared of what had passed, and she embraced the feeling with the strength of a thousand suns.

There was peace in that thought, and for a time, it distracted her from the long path ahead. When she finally shifted her focus to the future, all she saw was a jumble of near-absolute disorientation. There was no peace there, and Astrilla forced herself to embrace that as well. It was better to accept that life would have its hurdles rather than expecting a smooth ride.

After what felt like an eternity, her consciousness began its slow return to the moment. She noticed the calming thump of her heartbeat amidst the white noise of the Phoenix. The gentle chill of recycled air caused goosebumps to form on her skin, and for a second, Astrilla let her thoughts linger there in the empty space. Serenity washed across her very being. Body and mind, and maybe even spirit, became aligned once again.

It took Astrilla longer than usual to realise that her eyes were already open. She became aware that she was staring at the cabin wall for no particular reason. As she climbed to her feet, she noticed that her mouth was dry and that the skin on one of her knuckles felt coarse.

She'd learned long ago that returning from a deep meditation wasn't always pleasant at first. The mind had a profound ability to block out and ignore certain subtle sensations, and mild discomfort was one of them. Often Astrilla would return from meditation and notice a few dozen things felt different. Fingernails would feel harsher; individual hairs would seem heavier; skin felt tighter or drier than it had been before. But, in a way, that was the purpose of the art form. The mind would leave, reflect, return and notice.

"Go now and face whatever the universe has in store for you with vigour," Elder Xanathur said inside Astrilla's head.

Astrilla took a deep breath and considered the mantra.

Then when she was ready, she shuffled across the floor and grabbed her all-terrain boots. As she pulled on the heavy footwear, Vol's voice came through the ship-wide comms:

"This is your ten-minute warning, folks," Vol said, her voice chirpy as usual. "I don't wanna scrape anyone off the bulkhead today, so get yourselves prepped for the FTL drop".

Astrilla smiled at her friend's camaraderie, threw a jacket over her shoulders and made for the cockpit. As she walked through the Phoenix's living space, the smell of fresh coffee hit her nostrils. Russell and Gordon were sitting at the bar, watching a politically-charged Paradisian newscast and commenting on the presenter's angry viewpoints.

"What a fascist pig," Russell said, shaking his head at the screen in outrage. He turned to Gordon and gestured at the screen, "Who the hell hires someone like this?"

"Someone with some very worrying political views," Gordon grimaced. "He's almost as awful as Markus Holland".

Out of nothing but sheer curiosity, Astrilla glanced at the source of the Earther's indignation. On the screen was a stocky man in his late forties, who seemed to be shouting into the camera as though it were his worst enemy. There was a certain rage about it all that seemed inflammatory — as though it was intended to make its viewer as angry as the presenter.

"We have only just begun to resist our oppressors, and I'm sure that we will continue to fight against their tyranny. They are the ones that could have saved our people, and they didn't. Instead, they forced us to live under their boot for the last quarter of a century. I don't know how this is all going to end, but I'll tell y'all this, if they want war, they better believe they'll get one".

Astrilla watched the impassioned rant for over thirty seconds. It was hard to tell if the presenter's anger was real or simply an act for the cameras. The frenzied rampage seemed like fuel to a fire. After a few more sentences, the man practically frothed at the mouth and had to stop to drink while on air.

"Who is that man?" Astrilla said.

"That is the shill media," Russell replied, pointing at the screen.

"His name is Dallas Emerick," Gordon cut in. "He's a whack-job from Earth who did the rounds on a few shitty local newscasts on Paradisium".

"I've never heard of him," Astrilla shook her head.

"I doubt you would have," Gordon interjected. "Emerick was a real pariah on Paradisium up until a few years ago. For a long time, nobody would hire him, thanks to his big mouth and extreme views. For years, he did the rounds on pirate newscasts, and now here he is —on primetime news".

"It's fuckin' worrying," Russell added, his voice grave. "There are more and more people like Emerick popping up on the major Paradisian newscasts. Even Markus Holland is getting his five minutes of fame which is deeply concerning. It's like someone's trying to whip up a storm".

Astrilla wasn't sure what to make of it all. She understood that Earther —or rather Paradisian— culture was very complicated. On the surface, a Paradisian's societal value was measured by the impact they made through influence, which for the most part, was a status awarded to celebrities and public figures.

For Astrilla, this was an alien concept. The Evokers didn't operate that way at all. Instead, people were celebrated for their contribution to the study of the universe or something truly extraordinary: *such as defeating King Seig and saving all life in the known galaxy.*

Astrilla had visited Paradisium in the past. She'd seen first hand the reality of their pampered culture and understood it well enough to see it for what it was. The majority of people she'd seen appeared to spend their days lounging around in the sun. The worst part was that they did all of that while documenting every second of their humdrum lives for the social feeds: as though they were performers for a captive audience.

As Astrilla watched Dallas Emerick screaming into the camera, she felt the weight of the tragedy that had befallen Earth, and it wasn't the Fall. She realised at that moment that the Enkaye had intended for the people of Earth to do great things —to lead the universe through evolution. But sadly, that wasn't the case.

Paradisium had become a culture of ego-centric narcissists in the space of a single generation. Of course, that thought didn't apply to all people on the planet, but it was still enough for Astrilla to feel a level of strange heartbreak on the matter. The people who lived on Paradisium were so obsessed with celebrity culture that they failed to see their true potential.

That was the tragedy she felt as Dallas Emerick roared at the camera.

CHAPTER FIVE
NATHAN

From space, Levave looked like nothing more than a dull, lifeless rock. The once-proud Illuminator terraforming project was not pleasing to the eyes in any way, shape or form. Beneath coils of green cloud was an expansive auburn desert that made up over ninety percent of the planet's surface. The rest was a small patch of what was technically water, albeit with a hint of something corrosive that told Nathan not to drink it. Yet, as unappealing as Levave looked from orbit, Nathan still felt the drive to go and uncover all the Enkaye secrets left behind.

If Yuta was correct, something must've activated on the surface, and if that were the case, something must've switched it on. In his imagination, Nathan pictured another living Enkaye wandering the barren surface. The thought wasn't implausible either. Moshia, the Enkaye that Nathan and the crew encountered at the Lunar Facility, had been very much alive when they'd met. If the same happened on Levave, Nathan could get some questions answered. Maybe he could finally understand his purpose in the grand Enkaye plan. Of course, that was a daydream, and Nathan knew there was little room in the universe for such niceties.

Vol took the ship down through the thick green clouds and landed the Phoenix less than a kilometre from the point of interest. As Nathan unstrapped himself from the chair, he noticed Vol was eyeballing the environmental read-outs with the kind of scepticism he'd grown to expect of her.

"So, does it look like the air outside is going to kill us?" he asked.

Vol made a clicking noise with her tongue and shook her head. "No, but the sand is gonna be a bitch to scrape out of the air filters". She pointed at something on her monitor and added, "I'm a little concerned about this electrical storm to the east. It might be good for me to hang back here and keep the engine warm just in case it starts changing course".

Nathan glanced at her screen. "Sure, there's more than enough of us heading out anyway".

Vol smiled, but there was a hint of ambiguity behind it. Nathan wasn't sure if she was simply tired or if the message from Harrt had brought up some unresolved feelings. Either way, he recognised that Vol needed some time to herself. She returned to the pilot's seat, and Nathan swung around to look at the others.

Astrilla was standing at the holotable, looking thoughtfully at a projection of the nearby area, overlaid with Yuta's data and the Phoenix's scans. The ship was picking up signs of a crater at the point of interest. In contrast, the Evoker data didn't highlight anything at all, suggesting that something must've changed in the last few hours. According to the scans, the crater was only a few metres wide. As Nathan looked closer, he noticed that it looked more like something had exploded out of the ground.

"It doesn't look right at all, does it," Astrilla said thoughtfully.

"No," Nathan shook his head.

He swiped on the holotable and queried the Phoenix's systems to scan the area for life signs. The job ran in a few seconds and returned the information that nobody, besides basic wildlife, was on the continent.

"Guess we should go take a look," Nathan said.

Over his shoulder, Gordon was configuring a device that he'd hooked up to his datapad. It looked like a small microphone, but the tiny spinning receiver hooked up beside it suggested that it was a proximity sensor.

"You know the Phoenix can run scans on the area, right?" Nathan said.

Gordon snorted knowingly to himself. "One thing I've learnt about Enkaye technology over the years is that it does a very, very good job of deceiving us lesser beings".

Nathan accepted the cryptic response for what it was and instead proceeded to sling a jacket over his torso. When he was done, Nathan made his way over to Russell, who was checking a pair of rifles for ammo. For a moment, Nathan considered telling the former barkeep that the weapons were unnecessary for the job. They were on a virtually uninhabited planet, deep in 'wealther space. It was highly unlikely they'd encounter anything hostile, besides the wildlife, of course. But even then, the likelihood of encountering anything that vaguely resembled a threat was slim. Despite that logical thought, Nathan couldn't shut out the voice of Jack nagging at the back of his mind.

Better to be safe than dead, Jack said with a cocksure grin. *Of course, you could go out there unarmed like some fuckin' peace-loving hippy, but I sure as hell ain't savin' you if it goes sideways.*

It was hard for Nathan to tell if it was something that Jack had said back in the day or if he imagined it.

Eleven years had passed since the Mirotose Station incident: the day Jack and most of the Loyalty's crew were slaughtered by a heavily armed militia. Nathan was no closer to understanding who had murdered his uncle and former crewmates on that fateful day.

In the year since the Messorem, Nathan had grown to suspect that David Jareth had some involvement in the matter. After all, Jareth owned a private security company that undoubtedly had the resources to pull it off. He had the influence and power to cover his tracks as well. The only problem was that Jareth didn't have a clear motivation for doing it. The one thing Nathan knew about the man was that he didn't act out of emotion. Everything was part of his plan, and Jareth didn't have an apparent reason to murder Jack. He'd completely denied it when he and Nathan met on Paradisium and instead alleged that Jack had, in fact, been working for him.

Naturally, Nathan didn't believe Jareth, but he had nothing else to go on. All he could do was trust his gut, and it said that Jareth wasn't to be trusted. It didn't say *this is categorically the man who murdered Jack.*

Russell handed him a loaded rifle and a few spare clips. "Just in case, right?"

Nathan considered the gun, and Jack's voice scratched at his skull again; *better to be safe than dead.*

RUSSELL

A few days after the Battle of the Messorem, the crew spent an evening debating the right name to give the Enkaye droid. In Russell's opinion, simply calling it *droid* felt insensitive. It wasn't like the toaster or his datapad; the thing clearly had some understanding of what was going on around it. When the crew was hunting the Omega, the droid had the makings of a personality, plus it had aided them in more ways than one. It had resurrected Nathan; led them to Lunar and Moshia, then during the fight aboard the Messorem, it carried the nuke. The way Russell figured, they all owed the droid for what it had done and giving it a cool name felt like a good start.

Russell pushed for the name *Limbs* as both a nod to an old baseball player and as a reference to the droids, spider-like appendages. Of course, his was one of many that the crew threw around. Eventually, the name Kyp was selected from the pile. Astrilla suggested it because a character in one of the many religions formed from the Enkaye mythos shared that name. Gordon had backed her up on the choice as well. The doctor said that although the spelling wasn't the same, the name had been of significance to his days of study.

As Russell looked at the floating droid, he wondered what exactly was going through its mind. Kyp would spend its days keeping the Phoenix Titan meticulously clean, all while observing the crew and their behaviour. At first, it was like having a notetaker in the room, but over time the feeling faded as the droid seemed to learn from its observations.

The thing floated beside Astrilla as they were preparing to disembark. The Evoker was reviewing the local area on her datapad while Kyp supervised. It wasn't clear whether the droid was watching her or the hologram, but either way, it seemed awkward.

"Did you wanna come and take a look at this planet with us?" Russell said as he stepped beside the droid.

Kyp's ocular sensor focussed on him without any expression. An internal component inside the droid whirred as it seemed to consider his question.

"I should stay," Kyp replied. The droid didn't explain why. Instead, it shifted its gaze to the hologram, then to Astrilla. "There are no others like you here. I am sure of it".

As the Evoker was about to say something, the droid turned and floated out of the room as though it had somewhere else to be. Astrilla raised her brows in surprise, and Russell simply shrugged.

"That's one hell of a personality it's developing," Russell remarked.

Thirty seconds later, the airlock opened onto the planet of Levave, and Russell was the first to walk down the boarding ramp. As he disembarked, the first thing he noticed was the strange acrid smell of the air. The scent was powerful and somehow reminded him of a solvent he used during his time as a barman to clean beer taps.

Gordon told him that the smell resulted from an overabundance of zinc in the strange copper-coloured sand that made up the rolling deserts of Levave.

As Russell took his first step, he noticed that the crunch of the sand beneath his boot felt entirely different from the golden beaches on Paradisium. It was like walking through sweaty flour, despite no visible moisture on the ground.

Over his shoulder, Russell could hear Gordon fumble

with his datapad and the odd-looking attachment that the old man had retrofitted to the device. First, there came a series of beeps and boops, then a hum.

Gordon pointed to a nearby dune, "About a kilometre north".

"Then what the hell are we waiting for?" Russell said, excitement and impatience lifting his voice an octave. "Let's get going!"

"Hold up, kid," Nathan said as he walked down the docking ramp. The curly-haired captain of the Phoenix Titan disembarked the ship, and the moment his boots touched the sand, his brows knotted in the same way Russell's had seconds earlier. Nathan looked at his feet, then at Russell and Gordon. "That is some really weird sand..." He remarked before shrugging it off. "Anyway," Nathan said before handing Russell a comms device. "You left this back on the ship".

Russell took the device from him and synced it up with the Phoenix's comms array. A small beep followed, indicating that the ship was monitoring his location in real-time. In Russell's short experience, it was good to have someone keeping an eye on all of them, especially on unfamiliar worlds. Within a minute or two, the group proceeded to hike toward the point of interest —or, as Nathan called it, the weird *reverse-crater-thing.*

Along the way, Russell listened to Astrilla and Gordon's conversation about the planet and the mysterious group that had failed to terraform it. Initially, Russell struggled to understand why the Illuminators had aborted the operation. Sure, the deserts smelled weird, and virtually no plant could sustain life in the sand, but that was entirely solvable through the 'wealth's technology. The main thing was that the air was safe to breathe, which was considered the primary benchmark for a habitable world. As he listened to Gordon and Astrilla's conversation, Russell decided to speak up:

"So, why exactly couldn't someone settle here?" he asked. "I mean, I get it... the place isn't exactly the Capital

Worlds, but y'know.." Russell shrugged. "There is oxygen here...right?"

"True," Astrilla said thoughtfully. "Besides the lack of water on the planet, the Illuminators abandoned this project because of the violent weather systems".

"Weather systems that they changed by accident," Gordon cut in. "I read some of the public reports; the storms are not pleasant..."

"What do you mean?" Russell asked.

"Typhoons average at about four hundred miles per hour here," Gordon replied with a shrug. "That'd be about twice the size of the largest one ever recorded on Earth".

"Not to mention the incredibly violent electrical storms," Astrilla added. The Evoker seemed to force herself to reign herself in. "Good thing we aren't forecast for anything like that for the next few hours".

JARETH

David Jareth stared at the loaded revolver upon his desk. It was an old weapon from the days of Earth —an unmodified trinket from a long-forgotten era. The chamber was designed to hold up to six bullets that the gunman would manually load one by one. The grip was worn but functional, and the barrel was as intact as the day it was forged.

In many ways, Jareth could appreciate that it probably belonged in the museum of Earth, and maybe one day it would end up there, but not yet. The gun still had a part to play in Jareth's grand plan of vengeance.

He did not consider himself a man of violence, even though he'd taken lives, both first hand and as the man to give the order. Yes, there was blood on his hands, but it was the blood of evil people: Revenant and criminals and kingpins and all the other boogeymen who'd seek only to harm others. That was the difference between David Jareth and the Society. He killed because it was the right thing to do, whereas the Society did it because they could.

It may not be a righteous path, but it's the right one.

Notifications had been flooding his private feed since the EWB's victory a few days prior. Every message imaginable had come across his desk in the last forty-eight hours, everything from angry 'wealthers accusing him of being a bigot, brown-nosing business associates offering their congratulations, and even a few hopeful fools hoping to capitalise on the EWB's success. To Jareth, none of them mattered, so none of them got his attention.

The outraged 'wealthers would eventually find something else to focus all of their hate on. The brown-nosers would simply assume that his lack of response was due to the glamourous yet busy lifestyle. Then there were the hopeful fools, vying for his investment; Jareth wouldn't even dignify them with a split-second of his attention.

Only one notification mattered, and it came to him in the form of a message from his ship's captain: *Chimera is requesting to dock. He says he has a prisoner.*

Titus Rousseau was one of many in a long list of people that Jareth had sworn revenge: not for himself, but for the people of Earth. Martin Cleave would be the next name he'd scratch from his list, but only after answering Jareth's every question.

Weak men have loose tongues.

Jareth rose from his seat, adjusted his collar and jacket, then grabbed the antique revolver from his desk. He walked through his flagship's long and illustrious corridors toward the brig, and as he arrived, the unpleasant sound of screaming became apparent.

Two armed men flanked the doors to the brig and stood to attention as Jareth approached. One of them flinched as Martin Cleave's deafening howl was replaced by the sound of fist meeting flesh. Chimera was doing what he did best, and there was no doubt that it could frighten even the most hardened of soldiers. Even during his days of employment at Jareth Corps, Ralph Hayward found Chimera and his methods to be alarming —that spoke volumes for the anger Chimera held toward the Society. Yes, Chimera was a man, but he had the soul of someone who'd lost absolutely everything. That was what made him the perfect blunt instrument for the undertaking that he and Jareth shared.

Another loud strike came from behind the doors and was followed by a shriek from Martin Cleave. Jareth nodded politely to the guards as though what was going on in the next room was simply business as usual. He thought about making a witty remark but decided against it and instead passed by them and entered the brig.

In the dim light of the cell, two indistinct outlines caught Jareth's eye. The first was the immoveable six foot two frame of Chimera, still in his mask. Even in the presence of a man about to be put to death, Chimera refused to show his face. The second was Martin Cleave —former politician and a middle-ranking Society member. More importantly, he was very good friends with Alastair Roth, which meant he likely knew of Roth's plans. Cleave was chained to the ceiling by his wrists and bore the look of a beaten and bloodied ragdoll.

As Chimera stepped aside, Jareth stepped into the light to face Cleave directly. Somewhere within Cleave's delirious, post-beaten brain, the wheels began to turn as he looked at Jareth. His almost lifeless eyes flickered, and with what Jareth assumed was a broken jaw, he made a hateful scowl.

"Traitor..." Cleave spat a mouth of blood onto the floor. He nodded at Chimera, then turned his eyes to Jareth. "This thug is one of yours, isn't he?"

Jareth felt the cold grip of the revolver in his left hand. He wanted nothing more than to shoot Cleave between the eyes. *It was the least he deserved for the part he'd played in the Fall.* When Jareth spoke, his voice was calm and collected, free of the hatred he felt inside.

"I'm afraid you are right, old boy," Jareth said, nodding his head in Chimera's direction. "*He* is my most trusted collaborator".

"What the fuck do you think you are doing, David?" Cleave spat. "You don't realise what'll happen if—"

"If what?" Jareth interrupted him. "The Society will come and find me because I've kidnapped one of Alastair

Roth's most trusted lieutenants?" Jareth stepped an inch closer to Cleave. He felt powerful at that moment: not in an influential and meaningful way, but in a physically intimidating way. It wasn't a feeling that Jareth was used to. He looked at Cleave, trying his best to remain calm as always. "Listen here, Martin, and listen well. I've been waiting a very long time to right some wrongs that my father made before the Fall, and you are one of his many, many wrongs".

Cleave rolled his eyes and let out a sigh that implied impatience. "Does your sense of entitlement know no bounds?" Cleave said, lurching against his restraints.

Jareth could already sense Chimera reach for his sidearm, but he signalled the mercenary to hold. Cleave snarled as he leaned forward, "It's pathetic that you are still jealous that Alastair became the chairman of the Society and not you. The fact that your father was able to put aside his paternal duty in selecting his heir speaks volumes".

Jareth felt the weight of his revolver. Killing Martin Cleave was within his power now.

"Alas, old boy, you couldn't be further from the truth," Jareth said with a cool smirk that implied he was still in control. He waited and glared into the eyes of the man he intended to murder. Then without taking his eyes off of Cleave, Jareth issued an order to Chimera, "Wound him, but don't kill him".

The speed with which Chimera drew his pistol and fired at Cleave's torso was impressive. A cloud of blood sprayed against the wall, and for a while, the only sound that Jareth heard was the primal shriek that came from his prisoner. Cleave's body writhed against the restraints that held him, and for some reason, Jareth found himself sickened by what he was watching.

It may not be a righteous path, but it's the right one.

"Shut him up," Jareth said to Chimera. "He needs to answer my questions".

Chimera grabbed Cleave by the back of the head and forced him to look Jareth in the eyes. The screams slowly reduced to whimpers, and Jareth was able to ask the question he'd been waiting years to ask:

"Does Alastair Roth or anyone in the Society have access to another Project Erebus?"

Cleave's eyes darted from one direction to the other, and he tried to form the words "Fuck you". There it was — the makings of the lie. That was the bare minimum that Jareth needed to know, but he knew there was plenty more to extract. Chimera yanked on Cleave's hair, and the Society member groaned in pain.

"So, Alastair does control another Project Erebus," Jareth concluded with a smug look on his snake-like face. "Where is it, Martin? Where did he find it?"

Martin Cleave failed to resist. Chimera beat the man for what felt like minutes, but Jareth was sure was only seconds.

It may not be a righteous path, but it's the right one.

Jareth pulled his datapad as he repeated the question to Cleave. "Where is Roth hiding Project Erebus?"

This time Cleave's voice filled with defeat, and he pointed to a planet on Jareth's datapad. It was a world located deep within the Breach, far beyond the Corporate systems and far from the Commonwealth's reach.

"Helia," Cleave coughed. "The planet is called Helia".

Jareth nodded in consideration, then shut down the datapad. "So, this is what Baylum gave Roth in return for finding the Messorem?"

Cleave didn't say a word, but Jareth knew he was right.

The last of Jareth's questions was arguably the most important of all. He imagined pointing the gun at Cleave's head and pulling the trigger. He wanted to do it, but not yet.

"How does Roth intend to power his new Project Erebus?" Jareth asked.

Cleave's lips curled upward knowingly. "He's got himself a nice little Enkaye battery to open it," Cleave hissed. "All he's waiting for is delivery from the new King of Darkness".

"When?" Jareth demanded.

Cleave tried to shrug in his restraints, but Jareth could see as clear as day through the diversion, as could Chimera. The mercenary grabbed a knife from his jacket and twisted it into Cleave's ribcage: deep enough to cause agony but not enough to kill.

David Jareth raised his voice above Martin Cleave's screams and repeated the question: "When and where is he making the trade with Baylum?"

"Christian Roth's Estate on Haydrium!" Cleave yelped. "The night of the EWB celebration... Please... just stop".

Jareth nodded to Chimera, and the mercenary pulled the knife away from Cleave's torso and stepped back. A moment followed, wherein Jareth could see opportunity in what Cleave was saying. Baylum and Roth were to be in the same place at the same time. That was a once in a lifetime shot to take out the two men who'd wronged Earth the most.

Then, something else crossed Jareth's mind. Project Erebus required a living Enkaye to power it, just like the Messorem. All of Jareth's latest intel hinted that Nathan Carter and Astrilla were in the Pelos System, lightyears from the Society or the Revenant, who likely did not know the pair were of Enkaye descent.

So that begged the question: "Who is the Enkaye battery that Roth intends to use?"

Jareth waited, and Cleave smiled his bloody, almost toothless smile. It was the first time since he'd entered the room that it felt like Martin Cleave was in control.

"Come closer," Cleave lowered his voice.

The name whispered into Jareth's ear was unexpected, but he hid his surprise well from the prisoner. In Jareth's mind, he'd often picture his scheme as a giant game of chess that had more than four teams and many different pieces —each moving toward alternating objectives. The name that Martin Cleave had spoken was of a rook — maybe even a knight— who'd been taken off the board so long ago that Jareth hadn't even considered it a possibility.

He looked at Cleave, who was about ready to enter the begging phase of their exchange. David Jareth could already picture the former politician pleading for his life in a manner that would be embarrassing for all parties. A part of Jareth wanted to watch the bastard squirm; after all, it was the least he deserved. But Jareth reminded himself, *it may not be a righteous path, but it's the right one.* Cleave was a criminal with the blood of billions on his hands. He'd helped Roth and Baylum in their grand conspiracy: the Fall.

Cleave did not beg or plead. He looked at Jareth with a smug and knowing expression. Raising the antique revolver, David Jareth took aim at Cleave's head. Animal fear, rage, and the desire to live filled the eyes of the former politician, but Jareth shut out the very human impulse to spare. People like Cleave, like Roth, like Rousseau and Baylum, deserved nothing less than death.

"You will not succeed, David," Cleave said as he licked his lips. Then in his final breath he said the words of the Society, "Novus Ordo Seclorum".

Martin Cleave's head exploded in a haze of blood and brain. His almost headless carcass flailed back but remained upright thanks to the chains that had held him in a standing position. The once off-white cell walls now looked like something that Pollock would've painted if crimson had been on his pallet.

It may not be a righteous path, but it's the right one.

Jareth handed the gun to Chimera, and for a long while, they were silent together. A small trail of smoke bloomed from where Cleave's head had been split in half. It reminded Jareth of a cigarette moments after being stubbed out.

Yes, it was violent, but it was for the greater good.

Jareth turned to Chimera, "I think you and I need to RSVP to the EWB celebration on Haydrium, my old friend. It looks like we've finally got our shot at taking out Baylum and Roth at the same time".

"Two birds, one stone," Chimera summarised. "Who's the battery?"

"Nobody of significance," Jareth lied..

CHAPTER SIX
NATHAN

Nathan stopped at the edge of the *not-quite-crater-thing's* mouth and stared down into darkness. Just as the Phoenix's scans indicated, the hole wasn't a bowl-shaped depression made from something striking the surface. It was, in fact, more like a sandy blister created by something bursting from within. As Nathan peered down into the no man's land of the opening, Russell deployed a small drone to scan the area.

"We gotta find out how far down this goes," Nathan said to the former barkeep. "Can you try and get a good view of the nearest opening?"

"Sure thing," Russell replied as he launched the spherical drone into the crater.

As Russell piloted the device using his datapad, Nathan walked to Astrilla, who was staring into the distance. He didn't need to ask if the Evoker was picking up on something; he could already tell from how she looked subtly removed from everything going on around her.

"What is it?" Nathan asked.

Astrilla blinked, and clarity returned to her expression. She shook her head as though clearing the fog from her mind. Finally, after a deep, sobering breath, she answered

"There was great suffering here". Astrilla paused as if to consider her thoughts.

Nathan nodded at the ambiguous statement and made sure to recheck his holstered gun. He didn't know the specifics of how the Evoker abilities worked; all he knew was that they were rarely wrong. So if Astrilla said there was violence, that meant there was violence.

Better to be safe than dead, Jack said inside Nathan's head.

"Nathan, come take a look at this," Gordon called out.

The doctor stood about a hundred yards north of the crater's mouth. He was scanning something in the ground that seemed out of place, and as Nathan headed toward him, he saw what had attracted Gordon's attention. Imprinted on the weird coppery sand were a dozen faded footprints: each leading from the area where Gordon stood. As Nathan drew closer, he began to make out four deep recesses in the sand, each measuring about two metres in width and depth, spread out across an area roughly the same size as a gunship.

"Looks like whoever was here is long gone," Gordon pointed at the deep marks in the sand.

"I see tracks leading to the crater," Nathan said, thinking of the gun holstered to his hip.

The voice of Jack filled his mind once again, but this time his uncle simply said, *hate to say I told you so.*

RUSSELL

Russell's drone returned its scans to his datapad a few minutes later. The crater wasn't as deep as Nathan initially thought, and after some time to safely rig up a ladder and harness system, Russell found himself volunteering to go down first.

The climb was easy. After months of ascending and descending the Phoenix's gunnery chambers in simulated gravity, Russell had developed quite the knack for ladders. Before taking his final step, Russell pulled his gun and prepared himself to land on the same mushy sand as above. As his boot touched the floor, Russell was surprised to find that it was as hard as steel. The shine of his flashlight confirmed that the ground was made from a dark metal-like substance. A chill ran down Russell's spine as he examined the material. It was the same greyish-green material that made up the Messorem, not to mention the various Enkaye sites that he'd visited in the months since. The metal was a highly sought after commodity, known on the black markets as Arcane.

"Russell?" Gordon's worried voice came from above. "Are you okay down there?"

"Yeah!" Russell yelled. "Think we've got ourselves an Enkaye temple down here".

It took less than two minutes for Nathan, Astrilla and Gordon to descend into the pit and join Russell at the bottom. Once they were together, the group seemed to default into their roles when exploring a new site. Russell checked for anything out of the ordinary. Gordon would begin collecting samples and talking to himself in hushed, thoughtful tones. Russell guessed that the Enkaye temples served as a stark reminder to the couple that they were the last descendants of a race of figurative gods. He could imagine it was likely an easy thing to forget when you weren't thinking about it 24/7.

Russell noticed something out of place in the dark cavern walls that he simply couldn't ignore. Against the greyish-green of Arcane, he spotted a patch of the hieroglyph covered slabs that seemed slightly discoloured from the rest. When he pushed against it, Russell felt some give in the wall along with a tiny rush of air from the cracks. He shoved it again for good measure and confirmed his suspicions.

"Over here," Russell called to the others.

"What have you got?" Nathan said.

Russell gestured to the off-colour patch of wall, "Looks like a door of some sort, but it's real heavy!"

Nathan nodded thoughtfully, and Russell was pretty sure he knew what his captain was thinking. *Can we push that thing, or should I just get Astrilla to blow a giant hole through the wall?* Russell hoped for the latter, as did his spine. For a moment, he thought Nathan would actually roll with it, but he found himself quickly disappointed. Nathan handed his gear to Astrilla and Gordon, then rolled up his sleeves.

Guess we're pushing this thing, Russell thought.

NATHAN

For the better part of five minutes, Nathan and Russell pushed the stone tablet forwards. Nathan couldn't help but wonder if all the effort was to no avail, but he dared not stop just in case he lost all momentum.

"C'mon, we've got this," Nathan said behind gritted teeth. He dug the heels of his boots into the ground to gain some extra leverage.

Suddenly, the stone shifted back an inch. Then a meter. Before long, Nathan and Russell had pushed the slab aside and created a clearing into a deep tunnel set against the Arcane walls. Nathan shared a breathless, brotherly chuckle with Russell, then gestured to Astrilla to hand him the canteen.

As the Evoker handed him the water, she smirked and gestured at the now-moved slab. "You know, I could've moved that for you". A slight, incandescent flare of elemental energy flickered in her palm as she spoke, but Nathan was too busy chugging water to answer.

"Didn't see you volunteering," Russell panted as he pressed back against the wall.

"Well, you never asked," Astrilla shrugged. "Besides, now I know a few new Earther swear words to add to the list".

It was the kind of levity that the crew had developed in the months since the Messorem. It made Nathan think of the Loyalty and the family he and Jack and James had made there, but at the same time, it reminded him of the slaughter at Mirotose Station.

He recalled the deaths of Myles Taylor, Cobie Boud, Lish Ataga and imagined the others that he'd either scrubbed from his mind or that he'd not witnessed. For a long time, the butchery that took place on Mirotose Station all those years ago had served as a trauma for Nathan.

Now, it was a chilling reminder that he was the one responsible for a crew of his own. Nathan had no intention of allowing history to repeat itself. The crew —his crew— were family, and nobody was going to take that away.

Nathan tossed his canteen to Russell, and the former barkeep wasted no time knocking back the contents. As Nathan caught his breath, he looked at Gordon:

"So, what are we looking at down here?" Nathan asked.

Gordon looked up, then back down to this datapad, then back to Nathan. "These readings are off the charts," he said nervously. "If I didn't know any better, I'd say we were standing inside the Messorem again".

Nathan circled Gordon to look at the screen. The readings showed a giant pocket of what looked like electrical energy coming from the tunnel Nathan had just opened.

"What do you think we're dealing with here?" Nathan asked, looking the doctor in the eye.

Gordon's expression seemed to harden. "If I were a betting man, which, as you know, I'm not. I'd say at minimum we're looking at a piece of working technology".

▲

The tunnel went on for the better part of three hundred metres and eventually opened out onto a vast, dome-shaped chamber. Lights tried and failed to activate as whatever Enkaye tech remained recognised Nathan and Astrilla's presence. Without proper illumination, a shroud of darkness lingered on the walls, leaving Nathan with a slightly nervous feeling in his chest. Something about the place put him on edge, but he couldn't quite put his finger on why. The structure was no different from any other Enkaye temple he'd visited, but he got the impression that death was waiting there in the darkness.

"You feel it too?" Astrilla said as she stepped ahead of him, a white ball of light in her palm. "The violence I spoke of earlier…."

Nathan nodded but didn't say anything. Instead, he drew his gun, almost sure that someone —or something— was in the shadows. He signalled to Russell and Gordon to do the same.

"Fan out and proceed with caution," Nathan said in a low voice.

They split up, though still in visual range of one another. Astrilla went left, moving with the confidence of a seasoned warrior —her hands ready to burn anything that dared to challenge. Russell and Gordon went right but far more sheepish than the Evoker. That left Nathan to explore the middle-ground.

As he wandered the strange structure, Nathan couldn't help wonder what its purpose had been during the Enkaye's reign. It was a room buried beneath a vast desert with no discernable landmarks surrounding it. Of course, the thought crossed his mind that maybe Levave had been different back then, but still, he couldn't ignore the *very human* way he was experiencing it now.

Darkness shrouded the place like it was a curtain, and the smell of burning began to fill Nathan's nostrils. It was a scent that evoked violent memories at the back of Nathan's skull. Among a few dozen, the one that stuck out the most was the death of King Seig aboard the Messorem —when Astrilla had hurled a burning elemental summon through the Revenant King's heart.

Nathan wasn't sure why his psyche had conjured up such a bizarre memory, but it was there, and he forced himself to accept its presence. As soon as he did, Nathan realised that the strange aroma was of death and chaos: it was the smell of burnt flesh and armour.

"Guys!" Russell's voice came from the end of the tunnel. "Come check this out!"

Nathan pushed his thoughts aside and moved toward the source of Russell's call. On the right side of the room, Nathan found Russell and Gordon standing at what appeared to be the edge of a seemingly bottomless pit.

"Watch your step," Gordon advised.

Nathan carefully peered over the edge of the endless void. The strange sense of violence and death was strong there. Once Astrilla joined them, she looked into the pit as well before quickly turning to Nathan:

"This isn't right..." she shook her head.

Nathan wasn't sure why, but he knew that he agreed. He knelt at the mouth of the pit and held his hand over the edge. Something electrical fizzed in the open space, causing the hairs on his forearm to stand to attention.

"What the hell?" Nathan said to himself. He became aware that Russell was mimicking his movement, also reaching his hand across the pit. "Do you feel that as well?" Nathan asked him.

Russell shook his head. "No, nothing... just air..."

What Nathan felt pass over his skin was not a gentle breeze. He was sure that whatever it was, it was intended to deceive. Nathan carefully withdrew his hand, feeling the strange static fade as he did so. Without warning the others, Nathan drew his pistol and fired it into the place where his hand had been. The gunshot rang out around the hall, which was entirely normal.

What followed was not.

The sound was like glass shattering, contrasted by a bassy distorted scream. Though the sound faded after a split second, Nathan could feel the impact in his gut. He shifted his gaze to the space where he'd fired the single round and was stunned by what he saw. Above the supposedly endless pit was a large crack of green light hanging in mid-air.

It looked like a fracture in a pane of glass made from nothingness. The emerald light that peaked through the hairline break expanded and grew like a flower to the sun.

"What the hell?" Russell exclaimed.

"It's a projection... that'd explain the energy readings," Gordon concluded. The old man stepped to Nathan's side and asked, "How did you know?"

Nathan shrugged in response, "I just... knew".

The group was silent for a few seconds as they watched the illusion break down. The crack spread, creating a thousand splinters of green light, spanning the entirety of the false pit. Finally, the bogus image shattered into pieces so small that they could've been grains of sand.

Once the projection cleared, it became very apparent to Nathan that whoever had set the thing intended it as a means to conceal what lay beneath. At the bottom of a far more shallow pit were the bodies of over a dozen heavily armoured mercenaries. All had been human, and all had been corporate enforcers.

"These bodies are not long cold," Astrilla said as she peered down. "At most a day".

Nathan climbed into the pit, which was, in fact, less than a metre deep, and rolled one of the dead men onto his back. The first thing Nathan noticed was a deep and seared depression in the man's chest. It was a wound created by a powerful elemental summon intended only to kill. The armour the dead man wore was white and unmarked, without visible logos or hints at who his employer had been.

Nathan hadn't realised that Gordon had also climbed into the pit until the doctor called out to him, "Nathan, you might want to take a look at this one".

The headless corpse that Gordon was pointing at was still holding a weapon. Nathan took a close look at the gun and immediately recognised it as a modified pre-fall assault rifle. It was the shell of an M4 carbine, retrofitted with top of line components, some of which were Jareth Corps produced.

"What the fuck is this?" Nathan said, swinging his head to look at Gordon. "Is this all Jareth Corps technology?"

"Not all of it," Gordon replied. "I see Jareth Corps combat suits, but the guns are all wrong".

Gordon was right. Everything the small army carried was a strange mish-mash of items, which wasn't how corporate enforcers typically rolled. If you worked for Jareth Corps, you were kitted out with the top-of-the-line Jareth Corps gear, not a mixture of everything on the market.

"Do you think these people were working for Jareth Corps?" Gordon asked nobody in particular.

"They've gotta be Jareth Corps mercs," Russell concluded from above.

Nathan was instantly taken back to his exchange with David Jareth aboard the Messorem, moments after he and Astrilla defeated King Seig. Jareth had shown just how desperate he was to get his hands on working Enkaye tech.

He'd practically begged Nathan not to destroy the Messorem, even going so far as to say that Nathan *should let the people of Earth thrive again.* It stood to reason that the mercenaries were Jareth Corps employees, and they'd likely been trying to plunder the temple for artefacts.

"It doesn't matter who these people were," Astrilla said apologetically as she looked down at Nathan and Gordon. "The question is who —or what— killed them". Astrilla pointed at the bodies, "Whoever attacked these people could cast elemental summons, far greater than anything I ever could".

Nathan had barely considered it up until that point. He'd been too preoccupied with *who* the dead had been that he'd glossed over the grizzly wounds that peppered them. Someone with the ability to summon elemental energy — like an Evoker— had done this, *but why?*

To Nathan, the wounds looked as vicious as anything Astrilla could throw, but he was hardly the expert. Yes, Nathan had summoned elemental energy in the past — thanks to his Enkaye heritage— but that was once. If Astrilla said the killer was powerful, then she was right.

"Check this out," Gordon said, pointing at one of the bodies.

The doctor knelt beside a corpse of a dark-skinned human. Whoever they'd been had died from a sustained blast of elemental energy to the torso: making light work of their unmarked armour.

"Look," Gordon said, pointing at something inside the ruptured chest plate. Without any hesitation, Gordon yanked a small, dark component from the innards of the combat gear and held it up for Nathan to see.

"What is it?" Nathan asked.

"It's a combat recorder," Gordon handed him the device. "Granted, it's a very damaged combat recorder, but I may be able to access the contents back at the ship".

Nathan looked at the marble-sized thing in his hand and tried his best to ignore the dried blood that covered the lens. As he held it up to the light, Nathan saw the corporate logo of Jareth Corps embossed on the surface.

"Get it back to the ship and crack it open," Nathan said. "We need to find out what the hell happened here and who these people were".

HARRT

Harrt Oxarri, Commander of the Commonwealth Warship, Artemis, stared at the Capital World of Valour from orbit. He and his crew of three-hundred loyal 'wealthers had been directed to oversee traffic control in the system for the last week. It was a mind-numbingly dull assignment, and Harrt could see it on the faces of his crew.

Officially, the Admiralty had expressed nervousness that the Revenant may use the EWB as an opportunity to strike at the Capital worlds, which as a good citizen, Harrt agreed with. The eyes of the galaxy were firmly set on the Commonwealth and Paradisium now. It stood to reason that King Baylum could act at that moment, though it was unlikely. The Revenant hadn't been seen since the Battle of the Messorem. Of course, nothing had happened within Capital space beside a couple of shipping violations.

Where an average CO would be frustrated by the assignment, Harrt saw it as a different opportunity entirely. His executive order came from Admiral Dolian Wexell, and he was one of a few dozen that Harrt and Leviticus Dines had in their list of potential traitors. Getting close to Wexell was a crucial part of their shared investigation: either to rule him out entirely, find out he was the mole or to discover some other sordid skeleton that was hiding in the closet.

Logic dictated that the mole was a high ranking Commonwealth official: someone with access to military intel and political sway to keep things hidden.

Dines suspected it was a politician, but Harrt was almost positive that it was someone inside the Admiralty. It had happened before with Densius Olbori, so it could easily happen again. The traitor had sabotaged the Vertex, tried to capture Astrilla on more than one occasion and leaked the Phoenix's location to Seig during the hunt for the Omega.

Whoever the traitor was, Harrt was not willing to let them get away with it. He wanted to find them and make them pay, but not just for vengeance sake. The sooner Harrt unearthed the corruption inside the Commonwealth, the sooner he could get back to the Phoenix: back to Vol and his friends.

In his new role as Commander, Harrt found the whole thing surprisingly straightforward. He was serving in a time of relative peace, which the Commonwealth hadn't known since its formation. Rather than fighting in battles or policing challenging trade routes, the Artemis had spent most of its time escorting aid ships or ferrying politicians back and forth.

The one thing Harrt enjoyed about command was getting to know his new crew. He had some genuinely remarkable comrades onboard. Some were fresh-faced recruits from the academy, eager to learn from the Hero of Maru Seven, while others were the kind of seasoned veterans that Harrt could share a drink with while sharing war stories. One of those veteran officers included Harrt's first-mate, Lieutenant Jaudi Meera.

They'd served on the same ship, many years ago, when Harrt had been little more than a greenhorn. He'd served under Jaudi's command for a few years and respected her for how she led by example. Jaudi was strong-willed and understood that the 'wealth was flawed in more ways than one. Most importantly, Jaudi Meera was trustworthy, which for Harrt, counted for a lot these days, though he hadn't told her about his investigation into the mole, nor did he intend to.

Once the bulk of his shift had ended, Harrt retreated to his quarters, intending to rest. He spent a good thirty minutes reviewing his messages, hoping that Vol had responded to his latest attempts to strike up a dialogue. Of course, she hadn't replied. *Maybe she'd been busy with life aboard the Phoenix and simply hadn't seen his messages? Or perhaps, she was still annoyed.* Harrt knew it was the latter, but he didn't want to face that reality.

Fighting his impulse to review any more messages, Harrt climbed from his desk and took a look out of the giant window that spanned an entire wall of his room. From the Artemis' current position, the extensive traffic flowing in and out of the system looked like ants flooding to a nest.

As Harrt was about to pour himself a glass of Kor, he was interrupted by a communication chime. Reluctantly, he placed his bottle down and answered the request. The image loaded up before him, and a small projection of Jaudi appeared. She wore her curly grey hair tied back, which somehow made her dark eyes seem slightly more intense.

"Apologies for disturbing your bunk time," Jaudi said unapologetically.

Harrt could tell she wasn't sorry in the slightest. As a former Commander, Jaudi was no stranger to the long hours associated with a ship's command.

"Everything alright?" Harrt asked as he climbed from the chair.

"There's an incoming communication for you from outside the system, some guy calling himself an old friend".

"An old friend?" Harrt raised his brows involuntarily. "Did they give you a name?"

"Nope," Jaudi said with a shrug. "We tried to tell him you weren't available, but he's refusing to take no for an answer. Usually, I wouldn't interrupt my CO's beauty sleep, but pretty sure you did this to me back in the day when you broke that drive core..."

Harrt sighed, sensing the camaraderie in her voice.

"You make one mistake, and twenty-five years later, it comes up in these situations," he said with a smile. Then in a more serious manner, "Patch whoever it is through. I'll take care of it".

Jaudi nodded, and within seconds the hologram shifted. The face that formed in her place was not what Harrt had expected at all.

Ralph Hayward, head of security for Jareth Corps, stood with his broad arms folded one atop another. Hayward wore what looked like a combat vest atop a dark t-shirt that strained to contain his broad shoulders. He regarded Harrt with a stoic nod of greeting that said, *hello, and, yes, I'm still in control of the situation.*

"Commander Oxarri..." Hayward said, keeping his tone light and professional.

"This is certainly unexpected," Harrt said, peering into

the projection. "I'm not gonna lie, Mr Hayward, there's not many 'wealthers that would entertain a conversation with a Jareth Corps employee".

For one reason or another, a hint of smugness filled Hayward's expression.

"Well," Hayward began. "Guess it's a good thing I don't work for Jareth Corps anymore".

Harrt leaned forward on his desk. "Change of contracts?" he asked. "Perhaps a change of heart?"

To Harrt's surprise, Hayward chuckled to himself at his attempt at verbal sparring.

"What do you want, Hayward?" Harrt said, cutting to the chase.

"Long story short, I need people I can trust. I need the crew of the Phoenix Titan".

"Why?"

"Because, Commander Oxarri, you and I both know a thing about working for corrupt leaders..." Hayward let his words hang in the air for a moment. Then with a raised brow, "I notice the device you are transmitting from is heavily encrypted. Most Commonwealth CO's don't hide their comms log.."

"What's your point?"

"There are people inside the Commonwealth whose interests align with King Baylum: you know it, and I know it. I can't say too much over this transmission, but I'm working with someone who needs your help, and I think it'd be in both our interests to work together".

CHAPTER SEVEN
VOL

For over ten minutes, Vol sat in quiet contemplation as she stared at the unread message from Harrt Oxarri. The gentle blue of the text lingered on the screen as though it were gently nudging her to open it. Vol reclined in her chair and took a deep breath. Then as if trying to summon up courage, she sipped from the bottle of Kor that she often kept stashed in the pilot's armrest. Once again, she looked at the flashing text:

Unread message from Harrt Oxarri.

She took another swig from the bottle. "Screw it," Vol said, shaking her head at nobody in particular. She extended her index finger and was about ready to open the message when something caught her attention.

The mechanical beep and whir of the Enkaye droid — now known as Kyp— grew louder as it entered the cockpit. The strange spider-like ganglia that spilt from its spherical body were hard at work, cleaning the walls and ceiling as it floated by.

Vol glanced at the droid, and it looked back without emotion. The single ocular sensor in the middle of its body blinked once and shifted subtly from turquoise to cyan.

"You okay there, Kyp?" Vol asked, stashing her datapad in the armrest.

The droid remained in place and stopped its obsessive cleaning routine. The thin, wiry arms went slack and drifted down, implying that Kyp was about to engage in conversation.

"Something has been puzzling me," it said, sounding almost thoughtful.

The droid's speech function had only evolved over time. Before, it had barely been able to formulate single words, now like a child, it was soaking up the necessary language to communicate with those around it. That was the strange thing about Enkaye tech; it grew and developed.

"And what exactly is puzzling you?" Vol asked.

The droid was still for a moment, then it drifted closer to her as it spoke. "Why is it that you, the better pilot aboard this ship, take on the co-pilots function?"

Vol wrinkled her nose involuntarily. "Why would something like that be puzzling you?"

"I understand that the Captain is still learning, but, in the event of an emergency, wouldn't it be logical to have the most skilled person aboard piloting?"

"There won't be any emergencies, Kyp," Vol said, trying her best to reassure the droid. "Besides, if anything does go wrong, I'm still here".

"But for how long?"

"What do you mean?"

Kyp buzzed and whirred for a couple of seconds as if it were trying to pick its words carefully. "Commander Oxarri left this ship, as did Chief Koble".

The droid's matter-of-fact statement hurt more than Vol cared to admit. Kyp was utterly unaware of it, of course, but it still stung like hell. Harrt was gone, and Vol felt his absence every single day.

'wealther bastard, Vol thought, but she didn't mean it.

When it came to Vol's friendship with Koble, that was very different. The Sphinax had been her partner-in-crime since Yenex —since they'd been plotting against Viktor Venin— long before Nathan or Harrt or the Phoenix itself. Koble had been a reliable and loyal friend. In many ways, that companionship was something that had pulled Vol out of a stupor of mourning, depression and suicidal thoughts. Koble had made a significant impact on her life, and Vol realised that she'd barely acknowledged his absence in recent months. *Maybe because her potential romance with*

Harrt had been all-consuming? Had she been a lousy friend to Koble?

That crescendo of negative thoughts stung even more now.

Despite the salt in an open wound feeling that washed over her, Vol bit back her not-quite-tears. She reinforced her resolve by taking a large mouthful from her bottle, even though she was pretty sure Kyp couldn't understand what crying was.

"Doctor Taggart says that attrition is completely natural," Kyp continued to speak, oblivious to the thoughts in Vol's head. "It concerns me that without you, this ship won't have a competent pilot".

Vol cleared her throat and looked at the droid. The ocular sensor shifted again, and this time it looked directly into her eyes. She wondered if Kyp was picking up on the anxieties of the crew, and herself.

"I ain't going anywhere, Kyp," Vol said, trying her best to sound reassuring.

"While I appreciate your attempts at comfort, you can't guarantee that," the droid said, its voice very matter-of-fact. "Despite the advanced gravity compensators installed on this ship, there is still a 0.01% chance of stroke in a Uvan female of your age. Plus, I ran calculations for sudden decompression and for FTL failures and—"

Vol interrupted, "You learn by observation, right?"

Kyp blinked but didn't say anything.

"How about you stick by me when I'm showing Nathan how to fly this thing, so you learn as well".

The droid hummed thoughtfully, then it almost rocked its spherical torso like a nod. It was a strangely human gesture that made Vol realise that Kyp was remarkable. A machine, yes, but remarkable nonetheless.

As the droid floated away, Vol grabbed her datapad from the armrest and looked at the unread message from Harrt Oxarri. Before she allowed herself to think about opening it, she deleted it.

▲

Fifteen minutes later, Nathan and the others returned to the Phoenix. Before any of them had stepped into the cockpit, Vol felt the wariness that shrouded the group. It was a rare emotional cocktail that Vol had sensed from others before but never from the crew. It was a twist of disgust, a dash of confusion and just a hint of intrigue, which resulted in something far more ambiguous than it should have been.

Astrilla was the first into the cockpit, and when Vol turned to look at the Evoker, she saw an expression that looked like caution. Although she couldn't read Evokers, Vol didn't need her sixth sense to know that something had rattled her friend.

"You found something". Vol said it as a statement rather than a question.

Astrilla nodded, but a commotion came from the living area before she could speak. Russell's deep voice filled the room as he entered.

"I mean... what the hell was that back there?" he said to Nathan and Gordon, who followed him inside. "Who piles up a bunch of bodies like that?"

"We will soon find out," Gordon answered as he held up a small black

device in his hand. "We'll just need a bit of time..."

As Nathan circled the holotable, Vol cleared her throat, getting the attention of the others. There was silence for an awkward moment, then Vol spoke up:

"What exactly did you find?"

From Russell, she sensed an aversion to what he'd seen. When it came to Gordon, there was a more methodical and factual way of processing everything.

Nathan was the odd one out. He'd always been the odd one out. Reading Nathan was almost as difficult as reading Astrilla. Vol likened it to breathing underwater or opening a book with no pages or cover.

"The place was stripped bare," Nathan said. "All we found was a bunch of dead mercs".

Nathan unbuckled his holster and placed it down on the holotable. He then pulled his datapad from his pocket and loaded a series of scans onto the projector. Every picture was violent, but Vol didn't shy away from the gore. Death was death, and she'd seen her fair share back on Yenex before joining the crew.

The dozen dead mercs were all human, and every single one of them had died from elemental summons, but that wasn't what interested Vol. She cast her eyes over projections and schematics of the modified armour and weapons that the group were carrying. It was all non-standard gear for corporate enforcers but too high-end for simple mercenaries.

"This isn't all you found, is it?" Vol said, looking at Gordon. She pointed at the black sphere in his hand. "Is that a combat recorder?"

"It sure is," Gordon answered as he handed her the small device.

Vol looked at the thing as Gordon grabbed his toolkit from one of the lockers. She noticed the Jareth Corps logo on the back and looked straight at Nathan.

"Jareth Corps..." she said.

Nathan nodded. "We just need to crack that combat recorder, and then we'll have some answers".

"I can't crack this thing," Vol replied. "The encryption will be too—"

Gordon snatched the device from her hands and proceeded to carry it to a nearby console. He plugged a green cable into the recorder then beckoned Kyp toward him. As Vol looked at the old man, she realised exactly what he had in mind.

"We use Kyp," Gordon said. "The processing power from the droid should —after some time at least— break through military encryption. Plus, it'll be a good learning curve for our little mechanical friend".

Within seconds, the droid, the recorder and the console were linked up with several cables. Kyp remained in place, and its ocular sensor flashed between green, blue and an odd shade of purple that Vol had never seen from the droid.

"Well?" Nathan said as he looked at the droid. "How does it look in there?"

Kyp whirred a few times.

"Messy," the droid answered flatly.

"Can you break it open?" Gordon asked.

Kyp's eye shifted colours a couple of times, then clarity returned to its not-quite expression.

"I'll need time," Kyp said. Then as though considering something, it said, "Give me forty-eight uninterrupted hours".

Nathan nodded in agreement. The clarity and focus left Kyp's eye, and the droid went static and lifeless as it hovered in the air. Vol found the sight of the floating and empty vessel kind of creepy. The droid looked like a dead spider that had become tangled inside its own web. Rather than acknowledge it, Vol looked at the rest of the crew.

"So," she said. "What now?"

NATHAN

Taking the Phoenix up to orbit was —relatively speaking— an easy manoeuvre. It was something Nathan learned back in the days when he'd served aboard the Loyalty. The difference was that the Phoenix was an advanced titan-class frigate that pretty much doubled as a military gunship, whereas the Loyalty had been a bucket of bolts.

When behind the controls of the Phoenix, taking off felt smooth, and the power behind its glorious engines was apparent. When executing a take off in the Loyalty, it felt like dragging a dozen dead whales to the surface of an ocean made entirely of syrup. So when Nathan found himself at the Phoenix's helm, he'd have an almost involuntary desire to push the ship as hard as humanly possible. It was a habit that Vol was slowly coaching out of him, but every now and then, he felt old habits creeping back.

Once the ship was safely travelling in the void of space, Nathan released helm control to Vol. He spent all of five minutes sending Elder Yuta his less-than-detailed report of what they'd found, attached all the images and necessary data, then hit send. A small part of him hoped that the lack of orderliness to his report would piss the old woman off, but the rest of him was too tired to care.

For what felt like years, but was months, Nathan had carried the weight of so much upon his shoulders. There was the lives of his crew, the truth of his Enkaye heritage, the supposed destiny that came with it, the Revenant, David Jareth and whatever game he was playing. Every ounce of every burden took its toll, and Nathan finally realised that he needed some time to stop.

Once his report had gone into the network and was en-route to Yuta, Nathan made his way to the living area. He stopped at the recently updated bar and reached for a clear bottle. Gordon pulled up a seat beside him and leaned on the bar.

"Can you pour one for me?" the doctor said.

"Sure". Nathan grabbed another glass and served a double for each of them. Neither of the men toasted before drinking, and instead, they sat in companionable silence.

"Do you think those mercenaries were Jareth Corps?" Gordon said, looking into nothing but thin air.

"What do you think?" Nathan asked.

"I think if they were, then David Jareth has many irons in the fire," Gordon replied. "Shouldn't be a surprise, really. He is a captain of industry with a penchant for all things Enkaye related. I suspect he's trying to find a way to leverage the EWB into something that pays dividends".

Nathan considered the doctor's rationale and found himself conflicted.

"Don't get me wrong, Jareth is an opportunist, and he sure as hell loves a bit of Enkaye tech, but I don't think the EWB and all the other bullshit has anything to do with money". Nathan filled their glasses as he spoke. "The thing is, Jareth showed his hand aboard the Messorem. He showed me that he's motivated by power; that's what gets him up in the morning".

Gordon watched Nathan with a sceptical expression. The brown eyes behind his glasses looked thoughtful, as though the years had given him extra insight into the world around him.

"Money is power," Gordon said.

Nathan picked up his drink and knocked back a mouthful. "Jareth said to me that that the people of Earth deserve to be at the top of the food chain. It's like he's got some sort of superiority complex".

Gordon sighed. "Some people just have trouble letting go".

"It's more than that," Nathan shook his head. "After we took down Seig, Jareth begged me to hand the Messorem over to him. What if he's looking for another weapon? What if he knows what I really am? What if he knows that I am Enkaye?"

Gordon removed his glasses and placed his hand on Nathan's shoulder. "How could he possibly know something like that? The only people who know are the people you trust most".

"What about Jack?" Nathan said. "He was working for Jareth for years; he could've—"

"Jack wouldn't do that to you," Gordon cut him off. "He wouldn't".

It was an odd statement to make. Considering that Gordon had never rushed to Jack's defence in the past, it seemed wildly out of place now. Nathan sat up in his chair and eyed Gordon thoughtfully as the old man sipped from his glass in a slightly sheepish manner.

"You know there was no love lost between your uncle and I," Gordon said. "Before the Fall, I only met him a handful of times, and he struck me as an arrogant bastard back then. On the last occasion I saw him… well, lets just say it didn't go well".

"That's another tale for you to tell me about," Nathan said. It was a story Nathan had heard only minor details about, mainly from Koble. Legend had it that Gordon Taggart had struck Jack and got away unscathed, which was a rarity in Nathan's experience.

As always, Gordon barely acknowledged the comment. "Despite the history, I share with Jack, I do not believe he would tell a man like David Jareth that you, and he and his son, were —or in your case are— children of gods... effectively speaking of course".

"If that's the case, what the fuck was Jack doing working for Jareth?" Nathan shook his head. "It's like he was trying to paint a fuckin' target on my back... working for the one guy in the universe who's got a crazy obsession with the Enkaye..."

Gordon looked at him with sympathy. "Knowing Jack, he probably saw a means to an end. That's why we are all sitting aboard this ship, right?"

The doctor had an excellent point. Somehow Jack knew everything that was going to happen, and he'd made plans to help Nathan through his journey. The Phoenix had been stashed on Paradisium by Jareth: simply waiting for Nathan to reemerge. Jareth Corps knew to utter the words, *never let them see you bleed* at the opportune moment. He'd left Nathan messages that had led to Gordon joining the crew. Jack had known all of it, ten years before it had happened.

As Nathan was about to take another swig, Vol's voice came over the internal communicator.

"Nathan, we've got an incoming message". Her voice was filled with apprehension. "You ain't gonna believe this..."

▲

As Nathan neared the cockpit, he heard the sound of Russell's voice raised in an almost combative state. He was arguing with someone whose husky voice sounded oddly familiar to Nathan, but he couldn't quite place it.

"If you wanna talk to the cap, you go through me first," Russell said, his voice booming up the hall. Nathan could imagine the young man puffing out his chest to look like a tough guy.

"You listen here, *cosmo*, if you don't put your Captain on right now, I'll bust your ass back to that crap-shack on Paradisium!"

"I'd like to see you try *roid-rage*," Russell taunted.

As Nathan rounded the corner and entered the cockpit, he saw Vol sitting in the co-pilot's seat, watching Russell's exchange with whoever was on the other end of the hologram. The Uvan nodded in the direction of the holotable as if saying, *you should probably step in now*.

Nathan nodded and walked by her to get a look at the communication. Ahead of Russell was the holographic projection of Ralph Hayward, former head of security for Jareth Corps. Nathan had heard on the grapevine that the American had broken away from his corporate master months ago, but the reason for it was unknown.

Before Hayward could utter a word of retaliation to Russell, Nathan stepped into his line of view. Hayward's dark eyes shifted onto Nathan, and a look of practised restraint filled the man's razor-sharp expression.

"Captain Carter," Hayward nodded in greeting. "It's been a long time".

"Not long enough, I'd say," Nathan replied. "I heard you left Jareth Corps?"

Hayward's brow lowered a degree. "That'd be about right".

"What do you want?" Nathan asked.

"I need your help".

Nathan stepped back, "You need *my* help?"

"Believe me, this isn't exactly ideal for me either," Hayward folded his arms. "Obviously, I can't say too much—there are bugs everywhere".

"Try..." Nathan said, feeling his jaw ache where he'd been clenching out of frustration.

Hayward exhaled; "I need you to meet with someone with vital interests that align with your own. Just in case I need to spell it out to you...never let *them* see you bleed," Hayward said, shifting his weight from one foot to the other. "*If* you did bleed... who knows what *they* might find..."

Something in Nathan's gut shifted as he realised what Hayward was implying. He wondered if the big man was referring to his Enkaye heritage. It seemed more than likely, which begged a few dozen questions that Hayward seemed reluctant to answer over comms.

"Do you get what I'm saying?" Hayward asked.

Nathan stared at the hologram and nodded. "Yeah, I get you," Nathan said. "Transmit the rendezvous coordinates; we'll see you soon".

▲

Ralph Hayward's coordinates were less than three hours from Levave, so Nathan wasted no time plotting the FTL jump. Once the Phoenix was safely travelling through the slipstream, he relinquished control of the ship to Vol, intending to catch an hour to rest. He didn't leave the semi-comfort of the pilot's seat, just in case Vol needed to get a break and someone needed to take over. Nathan was finally starting to realise that having only two pilots aboard —one of which was capable— wasn't going to be enough if the day-to-day continued to be as demanding as it had been in recent days.

That meant hiring a new crewmate, which was far from ideal. Nathan liked to keep his circle of trust small, so bringing somebody new was a contradiction to the rule. He tried his best to shut out the thought as he threw his jacket over his body and settled into the soft leather of his pilot's chair. It took a while to fall asleep, even with the white noise of the FTL and the droning hum of Kyp's processors over his shoulder, but eventually, he fell into slumber.

He dreamt briefly of the desert where he'd met Bill Stephens during the Battle of the Messorem. It was almost the same as Nathan remembered; the brown park bench, the golden sand, and the gentle breeze were all present, but the apparition of his grandfather was not.

The word *elsewhere* lingered in the empty space, and Nathan felt drawn away.

He saw the entity buried near the molten core of an entirely forested planet. The thing craved to be whole again. Its anger and rage were so wild that they were practically palpable. Whatever it was, called to Nathan in a haze of whispers that made no sense.

Before Nathan could say a word, he was suddenly thrown from the dream and back to where he laid: back to the Phoenix's cockpit. The FTL drop warning buzzed its earache-inducing melody, and Nathan's eyes opened wide. It took him a moment to shake off the sleepy haze, but once he did, he wasted no time in shutting the alarm down. Beside him, Vol was checking something on her monitor, either unaware of his dreams or too polite to comment. After putting out a ship-wide communication to the rest of the crew, instructing them to buckle up for the FTL drop, Vol turned to him:

"So," she said musically. "Ralph Hayward..."

The name sat in the air for a moment.

"Yeah..." Nathan growled. "Didn't see that one coming".

"Sounded like he knew a thing or two about you that he probably shouldn't". Vol tapped the console beside her. "So, how do you suppose that happens?"

▲

The idea of meeting with Ralph Hayward didn't feel right. Yes, Hayward had helped Nathan and Astrilla back when they'd searched for the third piece of the Omega on Paradisium, but he'd done so because those were his orders from the boss. Hayward had been a corporate man back then: eager to please management to grow his capital. Nathan had seen enough of the corporate shills to know precisely how they operated, and he didn't imagine Hayward as any different.

The drop from the slipstream was smooth, and the Phoenix Titan barely rocked as it floated into the empty void. Nathan had executed several FTL drops since acquiring the Phoenix, but this drop, in particular, felt damn near natural.

"Very good," Vol complimented him from the co-pilot's seat. "Looks like you're getting the hang of this!"

Nathan nodded in acknowledgement as he unhooked himself from his seat.

He joined Russell, Gordon and Astrilla around the holotable as the Phoenix scanned the area. The rendezvous location was between 'wealther and corporate space, a few thousand miles shy of a massive gas giant.

Initial scans threw up readings from the hydrogen-heavy planet, and Gordon narrowed the search parameters. The Phoenix's systems searched for ships nearby: Jareth Corps first, Revenant second, civilian freighters last.

Better to be safe than dead, Jack's voice itched at the back of Nathan's head.

The search task took the Phoenix a matter of seconds, and what it returned was magnificent. The lone ship orbiting the gas giant was unlike anything Nathan had ever seen. The long thin vessel, bore a grey hull on the top half while the bottom was a deep crimson red. The shield generators were on the top side of the vessel outstretched, almost resembling the sails of a boat. A series of high powered, military-grade laser cannons spanned both the port and starboard sides, effectively creating a kill zone on either side of the ship. The bow and stern were covered by gunnery chambers similar to the Phoenix Titan's.

"She's magnificent," Gordon exclaimed as he looked at the holographic projection. The doctor adjusted the image to zoom in. He then moved his glasses to the bridge of his nose and leaned on the holotable. "It looks like this ship has been modelled after the old man-o'-war boats... must have cost a bloody fortune".

Nathan returned to the pilot's station to see the approaching vessel with his own eyes. He saw gold letters painted across the starboard bow that read, *Sadalmelik.*

"Hmm," Gordon mused. "Sadalmelik: that's an old Arabic word. I think it means *luck of the king...* or something like that".

To Nathan, it was a prehistoric language he'd only ever heard about from older Earthers. He'd never encountered a single person who spoke Arabic. Chances were that only a tiny percentage of people on Paradisium still used it as a first language. It left Nathan wondering, *who the hell Hayward was working with.*

His thought dissolved as the proximity alarm began to scream. Suddenly, the blue and white flashes of an FTL drop materialised a couple thousand kilometres ahead of the Phoenix. Nathan was about ready to spin the ship around and get the hell out of there, but something made him stop. A small Commonwealth shuttle emerged from the slipstream: big enough for a crew no greater than four.

"This situation keeps getting weirder," Russell said from the holotable.

Nathan ignored the comment as preliminary details of the 'wealther shuttle populated his screen. He scanned the info then dismissed it almost as quickly as it appeared. Nathan pulled up a new window to the comms system and opened a channel to the small 'wealther transport and the strange, Galleon-styled vessel. Both ships accepted the transmission, and Nathan's monitor split into two panes. Ralph Hayward's square-jawed visage filled one while the calm and collected face of Commander Harrt Oxarri filled the other.

The look of surprise on Harrt's face mirrored Nathan's as they looked at one another through the open channel. Rather than show his hand to a potential threat, Nathan chose to downplay his astonishment in front of Hayward. To his relief, Harrt did the exact same thing. It was funny how after a year apart, both of them fell into the same rhythm and pattern.

"Glad to see y'all made it," Hayward said, lifting his palms in what Nathan assumed was a faux shrug. What sounded a lot like sincerity filled the American's deep voice: "In all seriousness, thank you for coming and keeping this on the down-low".

"I guess we can all appreciate that subtlety is required at times like these," Harrt said diplomatically.

"That it is," Hayward nodded and pressed something on his console. A set of docking instructions appeared on Nathan's display as Hayward continued to talk. "I'll meet you at the airlocks".

Hayward waited for all but a second before killing his comm. Nathan assumed he'd done it to avoid entertaining any standoffs about the meeting location. Yes, it was rude, but there was no denying Hayward's ruthless efficiency: no doubt a skill he'd gained through years of corporate servitude.

The window where Hayward was, vanished from the screen, leaving just the feed of Harrt. Nathan looked at his friend through the comms channel and offered a friendly smile.

"You think this is a trap?" Nathan asked.

Harrt exhaled in what Nathan assumed was sarcasm. "Guess there's only one way to find out."

CHAPTER EIGHT
NATHAN

Hayward was at the airlock to meet the crew as promised. Somehow the American seemed bulkier than the last time Nathan saw him, and yet despite that, Nathan wasn't the slightest bit intimidated. Sure, all two-hundred and fifty meaty plus pounds of Ralph Hayward was standing directly in Nathan's path, but he was no different from any other big, dumb gun-for-hire.

All the crew, besides Kyp, accompanied Nathan into the intersected airlocks between the three ships. Astrilla was at his side, looking deceptively calm, though she was ready to strike anything that posed a threat. A strange sensation in Nathan's gut told him that Hayward had no intention of harming the crew: after all, he had no reason to do so. Plus, he'd seen Astrilla's combat abilities first hand. *As good a shot Hayward might've been, it'd never be enough to take down an Evoker*, but regardless Nathan chose to take a pistol: as did Vol and Russell.

Gordon was the only one to —technically— go in unarmed. When Russell asked him why, the old man simply replied, "If Hayward wanted us dead, there would be a dozen Jareth Corps drones here".

At the mid-point of the airlock, Hayward stood with his arms folded, trying to look professional and formidable at the same time.

Harrt was already at the intersection between the three ships, keeping his distance from Hayward. Nathan could see the sceptical look on the 'wealther's face from a mile away.

"Welcome to the Sadalmelik," Hayward said. Then with a smile that didn't suit him, he added, "This is like some good ol' family reunion".

Nobody acknowledged it. Nathan was sure that it was a poor attempt to lighten the mood, but another part of him took the comment as antagonistic. The last time he and much of the crew encountered Hayward, he'd been nothing more than a callous and uncaring corporate man.

For a long awkward moment, nobody said a word until finally, Hayward conceded and broke the silence. "Glad to see most of you made it.."

"*Most* of us?" Astrilla said, her brows knotting.

"He means, Koble," Russell interrupted, attitude oozing from his voice.

"That I do, *Cosmo*," Hayward said, his voice lifting a degree. The American elevated his hands into little gun shapes and mockingly fired at Russell. It was intended to look like jest but simply looked aggressive.

When Hayward's gaze wandered back to Nathan, his expression fell back to the same professionalism as before.

"Your Sphinax friend told me in no uncertain terms to go screw myself. It would appear that people have a bit of distaste for those who previously worked for Jareth Corps".

"Can you blame them?" Russell said. "All I see is a corporate lapdog in some fancy-ass ship. So, how about you tell us what the fuck we are doing here?"

"How about you shut your damn mouth," Hayward raised his voice and took a stride closer to the former barkeep.

Russell threw out several obscenities and insults as he approached Hayward. Nathan promptly stepped between them, placing his hand on Russell's chest and halting the young man before the situation escalated. Nathan turned to Hayward and looked the American dead in the eyes.

"My hot-headed crewmate has a very good point," Nathan began. "It's about time you told us why we are here".

Hayward offered up an expression that looked a mix of hyper-focused and stoic: like he was tracking prey on a hunting trip.

"Follow me," he said. "There is someone you need to meet".

▲

The Sadalmelik's internal walls were made from a white ceramic material designed to look like marble. Paintings and canvases were hung at precise intervals, giving the ship an almost museum-like quality. Whoever Hayward was working with, Nathan could only imagine the kind of wealth they commanded. Even from space, it was easy to tell that the Sadalmelik was a finely constructed custom-made ship, and that kind of thing wasn't cheap. Nathan's attention was drawn to Gordon, who gestured at one of the paintings.

"Is that what I think it is?" Gordon whispered.

The framed image was a landscape painting of what looked like a small village. Giant swirls of blue and white had been painted in the sky while contrasting yellow and white circles had been layered on top. Each brushstroke on the canvas was deliberate and looked sloppy to the naked eye, with copious amounts of paint on every marking. Despite the messy nature of the painter's technique, there was a strange beauty to the thing that Nathan couldn't deny.

"I don't know..." Nathan said, looking at Gordon then at the painting. "What the hell is it?"

"That painting is a Van Gogh," Gordon said, his voice low and thoughtful. The old man adjusted his spectacles and considered the painting as he looked at it. "How the hell did this survive the Fall?"

Nathan became aware that they were falling behind the others, so he promptly moved Gordon along. In a hushed tone of voice, Nathan said, "Is Van Gogh supposed to mean something to me?"

"You'd have been too young," Gordon nodded to himself, then after a moment of quiet contemplation, he shook his head, "It can't be the real thing..."

Suddenly, Hayward spoke from the front of the pack, "Oh, it's the real deal alright, so hands off the goods".

The expression that filled Gordon's face was a mix of scepticism and wonder. Nathan wasn't sure what the big deal about the painting was, but he could see the awe that filled Gordon's eyes.

"Who exactly is this ally of yours?" Gordon asked. "That painting should've burned with the rest of Earth decades ago; who the hell owns something like that?"

"Let me introduce you to him". Hayward stopped at a pair of white double doors, which he promptly pushed open.

The room looked like a viewing observatory with several chairs and couches arranged in neat rows. A single long window covered the entirety of the wall and provided a glorious view of the gas giant they were orbiting. Nathan's eyes were drawn to a man, leaning against the window and staring at space.

Hayward cleared his throat, and the stranger turned to face the crew of the Phoenix Titan. He was a human male —likely an Earther— mid-to-late-forties, with dark skin and long black hair that flowed down to his shoulders. He boasted a perfectly maintained beard, which complemented his jawline well, and he wore a purple suit with a black undershirt that seemed to be more of a statement than anything else.

"Thank you all for coming," he said, with an accent that Nathan couldn't place. "I apologise for the secrecy in bringing us all together, but as we all know, these are difficult times and it's very hard to trust others".

Nathan noted how the purple-suited man took the time to look each of them in the eye. It was a conscious and intended action designed to build trust and rapport. He'd seen the very same qualities in David Jareth, Guttasnype and all the other people who'd tried to influence him in the past. *He hadn't fallen for their bullshit, and he wasn't about to start now.*

"So, who are you?" Nathan asked.

The man stepped forward, and to Nathan's surprise, didn't offer up a rehearsed answer. Instead, he extended his hand to shake.

"My apologies, Captain Carter. I know who all of you

are; therefore, it is only right that you know who I am. My name is Tariq Mahmoot, and I am a survivor of the Fall — just like you".

There was a moment of awkward silence as Tariq's hand lingered in the air. Nathan considered the handshake, then cautiously, he obliged.

"So," Nathan began. "Mind telling us what this is all about?"

Tariq's expression softened, and he smiled. Again, it didn't seem rehearsed, which meant he was either an excellent liar or genuine about whatever his intentions were.

"As I said before, we live in difficult times," Tariq said, turning to the window. "The Commonwealth is in disarray, led by corrupt bureaucrats and politicians who are too blind to see that they are on the verge of total societal collapse. The Criminal Syndicate and the corporates seek out joint ventures that position them to gain more power. Meanwhile, the Paradisians have finally realised the separatist dream, and now the destiny of what remains of Earth's people is being led by an incredibly dangerous group of elites. And while all of this is going on, nobody notices King Baylum rebuilding his forces in the Juno galaxy, just waiting for the opportune moment to strike everyone".

Tariq turned to face Nathan again, his hair sweeping in the air. It looked dramatic, and Nathan was sure it was intended to look that way.

"To answer your question, Captain Carter, I brought you all here because I need trustworthy allies, and I need those allies for a very important mission".

The silence felt ominous. Everything Tariq said about the 'wealth, the Revenant and the Syndicate was right, but that didn't mean he could be trusted.

"Why us?" Harrt asked.

Tariq's focus shifted from Harrt to Nathan, and his eyes sharpened. "Mr Hayward tells me that you refused to give David Jareth the Messorem. Is that true?"

"Yes," Nathan nodded.

"That fact alone tells me that you are the kind of people that will stand against evil. I brought you all here because, once again, the galaxy at large faces a threat that has hidden in the shadows for decades".

Again, there was silence. Nathan waited, and he hoped the others would follow his lead. He wanted the awkwardness to stretch: to understand how Tariq would react. If the man chose to fill that void of conversation with something akin to a sales pitch, then it was easy to conclude that he was full of shit. The same would apply if Tariq said nothing as well, only he'd look like a moron as well as being full of shit. There was, however, a chance that Tariq was genuine. If that was the case, the next words that came out of his mouth would be meaningful.

Tariq scratched his beard and nodded sympathetically at Nathan, then to Astrilla. "Very well," he mused. "I will make this as straight to the point as possible. I know what both of you are. I know that you are of Enkaye descent".

Nathan felt his heart skip. Adrenaline coursed through his veins like fuel to an engine. He felt an instinct that urged him to reach for his gun. His mind played out different scenarios wherein he'd shoot Hayward first, then Tariq. The moment passed as neither Tariq nor Hayward moved. It became crushingly apparent that neither man had hostile intentions.

Nathan tried his best to ignore the dryness that crept into his mouth and instead glanced at Astrilla. She looked just as surprised as he did. Nathan turned to Tariq, keeping his voice low and threatening.

"How the fuck do you know about that?" It made him sound more like Jack than he cared to admit.

Tariq cleared his throat and gestured in Astrilla's direction. "Less than a year ago, Prince Baylum —as he was then— had over two dozen capture contracts on her head. Seig had over a hundred. Almost every bounty hunter and corporate hit-person in the Outer worlds was searching for an Evoker who could power an Enkaye ship. It doesn't take a genius to figure it out".

Nathan stepped closer to Tariq. "And what about me? How do you know?"

Nobody outside of the Phoenix's crew knew about his

heritage. *Nobody*. It was a need-to-know fact reserved for only those Nathan trusted the most.

"Your cousin, James, has been a part of my operation for almost a decade," Tariq said, trying to look sympathetic. "I know that you and he haven't spoken in a long time, but I need you to put that aside. He's in grave danger, and I need your help to save him".

Nathan didn't hear the second part of what Tariq said. All he heard was the name James.

James Stephens, son of Jack. Cousin to Nathan. A man Nathan would've once called brother. James Stephens, one of only three confirmed survivors of the Mirotose Station incident. James Stephens, the addict who'd destroyed the Loyalty and killed over a hundred civilians in the process.

James —fucking— Stephens.

Just thinking the name made Nathan's teeth ache. He couldn't help but wonder how his cousin survived the harshness of the galaxy. The last time Nathan saw him was over a decade ago, and he'd been a pathetic mess: an addict, hooked on the outer-worlds narcotic, Ice.

Even before discovering the electric highs of the drug, James had what many described as a *problematic* attitude. He'd been arrogant and cocky, and most of the Loyalty's crew tolerated it, but only because Jack was his father. Hitting the captain's kid wouldn't be well received. It stayed that way for many years, but once James discovered Ice, his behaviours changed: exacerbating his already reckless nature beyond all recognition.

Sure, he had problems before, but the Ice made him something worse: callous and violent. Koble and many others didn't appreciate the sudden change, but they stayed mostly silent. It was only when James botched his part of a job that Nathan and the crew called him on the bullshit.

Things almost got violent, but Jack, along with James' girlfriend, Merri, had stepped in and stopped it. Jack committed to getting his son clean, as did Merri. Of course, both failed to meet that promise, but it wasn't their fault.

By the time anyone noticed James' problem, it was too late. In many ways, Nathan blamed Merri or at least levied some blame with her. She'd been sleeping with James for years. They were close: very close.

Did she honestly expect Nathan and the rest of the Loyalty's crew to believe that she didn't know about his drug habit?

To look back on the situation now, Nathan realised that Merri had simply been a hopeless fool. A loving, caring woman, yes, but a loyal and gullible moron nonetheless. Sure, some blame sat with her, but James was his own man, and he was the one with the problem.

James —the addict— Stephens.

Nathan tried not to think about it too much, but the memory of his last encounter with James was forever etched into his brain. He still remembered the expression of rage on James' face after the Mirotose Station Incident. It was like looking at the makings of a monster, but at the time, Nathan hadn't paid attention to it. Among other things, Nathan had been overwhelmed and injured, and James' ranting was the last thing he needed to worry about. He'd watched most of his friends from the Loyalty die in what could only be described as a slaughter. All the others, including Jack, were missing and presumed dead. *How was Nathan supposed to know what James had been planning behind his seething, rage-filled eyes?*

James Stephens: the man who couldn't control his rage.

They'd waited at the rendezvous location for hours, hoping that someone —anyone— from the crew would arrive. Unfortunately, James had other plans, and after waiting for Nathan to go into the town to gather info, he highjacked the Loyalty.

Nathan could still remember the gut-churning moment when he saw the Loyalty crash into the Xung-Sin hideout. In a rampage of drug-fuelled insanity, James murdered over a hundred people, the majority of which were civilians.

James Stephens, the junkie murderer.

After the crash, the next few hours were an emotional whirlwind that now seemed blurry in Nathan's mind. He'd helped the emergency services put out fires and pulled people from the wreckage. Some were still alive; others were less lucky. One of them had been a child, no older than eight. It was horrible. Then something happened, and Nathan was never too sure why, but he chose to check for James' location —just in case.

His datapad returned a ping on the other side of town: a seedy nightclub with an equally sleazy name. So Nathan walked there, unsure what he'd find when he arrived. He found James hunched over a bar with a drink —alive and well. High as a fucking kite, yes, but a hell of a lot more alive than the people he'd killed.

Nathan didn't recall much of his final conversation with James, but he knew that he'd brought up the civilian casualties. He knew that the number of dead was already in excess of forty and still climbing. James simply didn't care that he'd killed innocents. He'd looked at Nathan with a foggy yet angry stare as though Nathan's protests about right and wrong were insignificant.

"Their lives mean nothing," James spat before turning back to his drink and dismissing everything Nathan said. That was the moment everything changed.

James Stephens: dead to me.

In Nathan's memory, he'd started the fight: he could remember that much. All the anger and outrage at James: all the sadness for his dead crew: all the adrenaline from the escape from Mirotose Station boiled over. He remembered grabbing a glass bottle and smashing it over the back of James' skull. Everything else after that was a blur of red-hot violence.

The next thing that registered inside Nathan's head was a confused memory of having sore fists. He'd beaten James to a bloody pulp in that nightclub. He'd broken his cousin's arm in several places, and he was pretty sure that James was on death's door. Blood was all over the illuminated glass dance floor, and the fifty-or-so patrons were stood in stunned, terrified silence.

Nathan became aware that he was pointing a pistol at his cousin: the same weapon James had attempted to use during the fight. The fact that James had pulled a gun confirmed just how far gone he was. James Stephens was no longer family. He was a worthless junkie bastard who'd die in a ditch with a needle in his arm.

That night, Nathan walked away and never looked back. The funny thing was that even now —more than ten years later— he didn't regret his actions. He stood by his decision to beat the living crap out of James, and he'd do it again.

James Stephens: not even worth the bullet.

Nathan realised that he'd been quiet for too long: lost in the trauma that had been his final moments with his cousin. Tariq and Hayward studied his reaction, *meaning they knew Nathan and James' history.*

James Stephens: the ultimate litmus test.

Nathan tried his best to hide his disgust, but it was difficult. He noticed an ache in his jaw, where he unconsciously tensed and took a deep breath, exhaling through his nostrils and willing for some form of semblance to wash over him.

A million different things to say ran through Nathan's mind, but when he finally spoke, it felt like someone else's words: "James... is alive?"

It was a fair and reasonable question, but speaking it aloud didn't feel natural. Tariq must've expected something else because once Nathan asked the question, he shared an almost stunned look with Hayward. It was as though they were exchanging a tiny conversation that only they were privy to. It was the first time Nathan saw the calm facade drop between the pair. There was real, human emotion there. *But for James? Really?*

Tariq cleared his throat. "There is much I need to explain. Myself, James, Mr Hayward and our small crew have been a part of an undercover operation for the last decade".

For the first time since entering the room, Vol spoke up, "Investigating what?"

Nathan could see her colourful brows lower, and her eyes widened as she asked the question. The Uvan was doing her utmost to ensure the situation was above board. Of course, she could read the minds of others, or at least their intentions, so she must've sensed some apprehension.

"We have been investigating an elite group based out of Paradisium known as the Society," Tariq said, picking his words carefully. "This may come as a shock to you, but we believe that they have been collaborating with Baylum long before the Fall".

"Earthers helping the Revenant?" Nathan raised his brows. "Why would anyone do that?"

"Why, indeed?" Tariq said. "As much as I'd like to speculate on the subject, we —"

Nathan cut him off. "Give me one good reason I should put my crew in danger to save him?"

"Besides, the obvious Enkaye heritage?" Tariq asked.

Nathan nodded.

Tariq spoke for over a minute, providing a testimony that painted James as a completely changed man. The words *honourable* and *trustworthy* were thrown in for good measure too. When Hayward's turn came, the American spoke plainly, which Nathan appreciated.

"Your cousin has got some cahoonas," Hayward said, his voice gruff and serious. "Roth Industries was among the hardest to infiltrate. I was sure James would turn up in a body bag, but I was wrong. He's been tracking Alastair Roth for a very long time. Thanks to your cousin, we have amassed a shit-ton of data on the Society".

It sounded beyond unbelievable: James Stephens: a changed man?

Nathan realised something as he stared at Hayward. It shouldn't have surprised him, given everything they'd discussed, but for some reason, it did. Hayward looked at him as if to say, *go ahead and ask your question.*

"When you and I first met, were you undercover in Jareth Corps?" Nathan said.

Hayward nodded, "Ten years of my life that I'm never getting back".

There was a dedication to his voice, and it made Nathan realise that he and Tariq were men who believed in their cause. *Maybe James was like them now?*

Tariq took a step closer to Nathan, "The truth of the matter is that the Society has James prisoner. They, like I, know what he is, and more importantly, we suspect that the Society is planning on giving him to Baylum".

James Stephens: Enkaye halfbreed and battery for dangerous advanced technology.

"So," Tariq began. "Will you help us?"

James Stephens: family?

"I want every ounce of intel you have on the Society, and the Revenant shared with my crew, so we can validate your story," Nathan said, counting out demands on his fingers. "I want a full briefing on everything you know about the trade".

"Of course," Tariq nodded.

"I want a full manifest of your crew and any other operatives you're working with".

Tariq nodded: "Done".

As accommodating as Tariq appeared, Nathan still wasn't buying it entirely. The whole thing still felt a little sketchy, and Nathan felt he needed some additional guarantees. He gestured to the crew to head back to the Phoenix, but he remained in place, keeping his eyes fixed on Tariq.

"One more thing," Nathan said with severity. "We run this operation together. If me and my guys are on the ground, so are you".

Tariq nodded. "I wouldn't have it any other way".

CHAPTER NINE
HARRT

When Harrt stepped aboard the Phoenix Titan, he immediately felt at home. Despite the minor changes to the bar and living area, it was like he'd never left. For a fleeting moment, Harrt had forgotten that a year had passed since the battle of the Messorem: since he and Leviticus Dines had agreed to their unauthorised covert operation. Nearly a year on, they'd made very little progress, and stepping back into the Phoenix —the home he'd left behind— made him feel regretful. Harrt hadn't wanted to go. He'd gone to the Admiralty intending to resign, but Dines had talked him out of it: appealing to the idealist 'wealther within him.

Yes, it was a patriotic path, but it was also a lonely one.

Seeing Vol again brought that thought home. She'd changed but only a little from the mental image that had formed in Harrt's mind. Her pink skin was a little darker than he remembered, and her hair carried more purple tones than it had before. Selfishly, the first thought that crossed his mind was to try to repair the damage to their not-quite friendship, but of course, duty called.

Tariq and Hayward had brought them there for a valid reason, and now specific steps had to be followed. The data they'd provided Nathan with had to be verified, then a joint plan would be built. The rescue of an Enkaye half-breed had to come before everything else. Lives were at stake, and if Baylum got his hands on another half-breed, he could power any Enkaye artefact he wanted.

For an hour, the crew sifted through the multitude of files that Tariq provided. Nathan's cousin, James Stephens, appeared to be an efficient operative, which seemed odd given what Harrt had heard about the man. James had been undercover within Roth Industries for several years, working under the guise of an administrative assistant. Day to day, he processed sensitive paperwork and monitored stacks of business data. In reality, James had spent his time keeping a close eye on Alastair Roth's movements.

There were pages and pages of entries, each one detailing top executive meetings: who'd attended, agenda points, financial transactions and agreements. At first, the data was all very vanilla. Shady, yes, but nothing that none of the other corporations were doing. Then, as time went on, James' entries changed as he progressed through the ranks of Roth Industries. They began to paint a more seedy picture: a business controlled by a man whose ego outweighed his blind ambition.

It was only when James was promoted to an executive role that his entries became far more detailed: implying that he had greater access to the inner workings of Roth industries. Mentions of corporate espionage and collaborations with the Criminal Syndicate began to fill the pages. There was talk of complex transactions with some fishy-looking Outer-worlds businesses. But none of them were Revenant. Then a list of associates to Roth followed.

This was the Society, or at least a few of its members. Four names kept cropping up in James' reports; David Jareth, Markus Holland, Martin Cleave and Alan Washington. James had noted in his entries that he couldn't verify the extent of the Society's numbers, but he speculated that it was likely in the hundreds: with Cleave and Holland identified as crucial, senior members. Names, locations, a speculative hierarchy and hints of Society involvement with the Messorem began to crop up.

It painted a picture of a vast network of former and current Paradisians who had some involvement with Roth industries, but James had failed to pick out its leader.

By all accounts, not just James', but Tariq's other operatives, the Society and its members were highly elusive. They met in private; their communications were encrypted, and there was no actual proof of their existence: nothing tangible anyway.

They were —in essence— the boogeymen of Paradisium.

Eventually, James' communications changed tone. He began to sound worried, then fearful, then paranoid. For a while, he suspected that his cover was blown but couldn't confirm it. Then in his final message, James had broken all protocols and contacted Tariq directly via a scrambled comms channel.

"They know I'm an Enkaye, not sure how but I'm totally fucked. Datapad and all devices purged. Corporate enforcers are on me, gonna try and hijack a shuttle and get the fuck out. I will attempt to make contact in twenty-four hours".

Then there was nothing for four days. Slowly Tariq's network of four spies went silent, with the last reporting that Christian Roth —son of Alastair— was holding James prisoner at his private estate on the planet Haydrium. In addition, an EWB celebration was to be the backdrop for a secret meeting with Baylum.

"I'm no expert, but all this data seems real," Harrt said, looking at the rest of the crew. "I'd like to share it all with Dines to verify, but I think Tariq and Hayward are telling the truth".

Nobody said a word for a long time. The whirring sound of the Enkaye droid —now called Kyp— filled the cockpit. To Harrt's surprise, Vol was the one to break the silence: not because she hadn't said a word to him up until that point, but because none of the others had beaten her to the punch.

"I agree," Vol said, tossing her datapad onto the holotable with resignation. "When we were on the Sadalmelik, I could read everything in the room: Tariq and Hayward are telling the truth. This data backs everything up".

"I'm inclined to agree," Astrilla said. "Tariq invited us into his home, fully armed, knowing what we as a group are capable of. He would be a fool to try and deceive us."

Harrt noted the sceptical frown on Nathan's face. The Earther was leaning with his elbows on the holotable, his jaw clenched tight, and his eyes sharp and penetrating.

"I hate to admit it, but I think you guys are right," Nathan concluded. "I grew up with James: I'd like to think that I know how he operates. He wouldn't do something like this unless he truly believed it".

"Meaning what exactly?" Astrilla asked as she tugged her dark hair into a ponytail.

Nathan sighed and closed his eyes. He proceeded to lower his head to rest against the holotable, suggesting discomfort with what he was about to say next.

"When we escaped the Fall, we did it aboard Alastair Roth's private shuttle," Nathan said, not lifting his head. "I don't remember that much about it, but what I do was pretty bad. Jack threatened Roth: threatened to murder his wife and kids if he didn't comply".

The crew looked stunned. Even the look in Astrilla's eyes suggested she had no idea of that detail in Nathan's life. Harrt noticed Gordon's hardened yet outraged expression: no doubt something to do with the secretive yet tumultuous relationship he'd shared with the fabled Jack Stephens.

"One thing that really sticks out is the way Roth protested when Jack took the shuttle down and saved a bunch of people," Nathan continued. "Roth was outraged — more than outraged— by the fact that Jack was actually saving people. It was like Roth wanted them to die. If you ask me, everything Tariq and Hayward, and well... fuck, even what James has said in his reports all sound just like the man I saw the day of the Fall".

They were silent for a long moment.

Russell stretched until the joints in his arms gave a pop, then casually sat back in one of the comfortable cockpit chairs and thoughtfully pressed all of his fingers together.

"So, what happens now?" Russell said. "What do we do?"

"We've gotta do it," Gordon said, his voice sounding more reluctant than usual. "We all know what happens when an Enkaye device has the appropriate battery".

He was right.

The Capital World of Unity was a testament to that fact. Trillions died from a single blast of the Messorem's firing array, and all it had taken was an individual with Enkaye heritage to make that happen.

Nathan stood and adjusted a stray chunk of his long hair. He looked at all of them and sighed with what looked like hesitance.

"All those in favour of busting my dumbass, junkie cousin out of a shitty situation, raise your hands".

Unanimously, the entire crew, including Harrt, put their hands up. Nathan eyeballed the others, and reluctantly raised his own. Evidently, the Earther wasn't rushing for a family reunion anytime soon.

▲

"We've got a problem".

It was a sentence that nobody wanted to hear the moment Tariq and Hayward stepped into the Phoenix, and yet, there it was. Four simple words that didn't fill newly made allies with confidence.

"We've got a big fuckin' problem," Hayward added, changing up the formula slightly by including an Earther expletive. It made no difference from how Tariq had said it seconds earlier, only far less polite. Harrt could already picture the frown on Nathan's face before he'd even looked. Not because of the cursing, Nathan used that word a lot, but because of the statement.

On the Phoenix's holotable, Hayward loaded up a complex projection of a local star map. A single point appeared, deep in the Outer Worlds, where the corporations operated.

"So," Hayward said, putting his meaty hands behind his back in a military-like fashion. "As I said before, *we* have ourselves a problem".

Despite the bulky Earther's calm outward appearance, his voice hinted the opposite. Hayward sounded seriously concerned, which seemed odd given what Harrt had seen of the man in the past.

"What is it?" Harrt asked.

Hayward zoomed in on the star map, where the marker had been placed. The image shifted to a grey, industrial-looking world that reminded Harrt of Yenex.

"This sorry rock is the planet, Haydrium," Hayward said, gesturing to the floating hologram. "Roth Industries runs a great deal of its mining operation through here, but that's beside the point. Haydrium is the home of Christian Roth: son of Alastair Roth".

Hayward pulled in a new window to overlay the projection of the planet. A small three-dimensional schematic formed inside the new pane of what looked like a giant floating palace. It was as though someone had lifted a small country from the planet's surface and given it the ability to defy gravity.

"This is Hawtrey house, otherwise known as the third Roth estate". The inflexion in Hayward's voice implied a distaste for the decadence. "As you've seen from our intel, the Society is going to use the cover of a private EWB celebration to hand James over to Baylum".

"And what better time and place to do it," Tariq added. "A five-hundred-acre maze filled with hundreds, if not thousands of guests. It'll be easy for the Society to slip away in all the chaos. This is smoke and mirrors at its finest".

Nathan stepped closer to the holotable, and Harrt watched as the Earther expanded the image of Hawtrey house to the largest it could possibly go. He leaned on the holotable, closely examining the structural diagram with meticulous attention.

Seeing Nathan Carter, Captain of the Phoenix Titan, with that look in his eyes, reminded Harrt of the moments before the Messorem: when he and Nathan and the others had planned the operation that saved the Commonwealth.

Nathan said, "Okay, so it's their home turf, lots of aerial defence systems and likely a few hostiles. We can work with this".

"There's more," Hayward said, his voice growing severe. "You know how I said we've got a big problem?"

Hayward collapsed the image of Hawtrey House and returned the hologram to the star map, where a new point appeared. It was in the opposite direction of Haydrium: a pulsing green marker just outside the Candela System, bordering on the verge of Syndicate territory.

Hayward brought up a new window; this time, it was a photograph of a blonde human woman in business-like attire, no older than her mid-thirties. Harrt recognised her from the data records. She was Claire Lawrence, one of Tariq's missing operatives.

"I presume you've familiarised yourselves with our data?" Hayward said. "Claire was one of our best, our engineer who doubled as a secretary for her cover story. She had access to a bunch of potential Society members, including Alastair Roth, Gary Jordan, Titus Rousseau, Alan Washington, Fawas Hussien—"

"You mean men?" Vol interrupted him. "Was she—"

"No," Hayward cut the Uvan off before she could finish. "Sure, a pretty young thing like her could charm the hell out of any dirty old man, but she had a classy way of doing things".

"There is no doubt that weak men have weak resolve," Tariq added. "But Claire was exceptional; she was the finest engineer either of us has ever known. She amassed a wealth of intel, but all of it was stored in an encrypted data vault aboard her shuttle".

"Let me guess," Vol said. "She tuned the data vault to transmit once every thirty days to avoid detection?"

"Thirty-seven," Hayward nodded. "She said the number seemed random enough to not draw attention".

"Damn, that's smart..." Vol replied.

"Unfortunately, we lost all line of communication with Claire two weeks before James," Tariq said, trying to move the conversation along. "The last time she made contact, Claire mentioned suspicious communications between Alastair Roth and a Commonwealth Councilman".

Harrt felt a cold chill run down his spine, and he involuntarily shivered. He wondered if Tariq's operative had stumbled onto the same mole he and Dines had been searching for all those months.

"What happened to her?" Harrt asked, his voice lifting with interest.

Hayward looked downward, evidently not wanting to provide the answer he had to give.

"We presumed she was dead, as did James in all of his communications around the time," Hayward sighed. "James tried to check out the shuttle, but it was gone. So this leads us to our big problem. Thirty minutes ago, Claire's transponder went live. Her shuttle is broadcasting an emergency signal out of the Candela System".

"You really think it's her?" Gordon spoke up, his voice sounding a little sarcastic. "She disappears, then on the eve of a Society and Revenant powwow, it just happens to start up like magic".

"No," Tariq replied. "It's more than likely that she's dead, but the databanks are what's important here. They were designed to emit this particular signal if someone was trying to tamper with them... if that's the case—"

"Then your operative has intel that the Society doesn't want anyone seeing," Harrt concluded. "Intel that potentially implicates a Commonwealth official incahoots with Roth and Baylum. So, they take the shuttle to the edge of space where the signal will take longer to transmit, then destroy it all before anyone notices".

Russell raised his hand: "Couldn't they just like... I dunno.. blow it up? Shoot the shit out of the databanks?"

"Fortunately, Claire was a very thorough engineer," Tariq answered. "In the event of absolute, systemic failure, Claire rigged those data-drives to transmit on a wide-band frequency. Every man, woman and child within two systems would receive that data. So the Society will need to tread very carefully and bypass all of the security and failsafes in order to remove those files".

Vol whistled. "This lady sounds like my kinda engineer". She paced for a moment, squinting as though she were deep in thought. After a matter of seconds, she turned to Hayward with action in her voice: "How many layers of firewalls and protection did your engineer put in place? I need to know how many hours we have on the clock..."

"Around twenty-four, maybe thirty hours," Tariq replied with a shrug.

"Then we ain't got any time to waste," Vol said, looking at Nathan then the rest. "Clock's ticking".

▲

The plan was simple enough, though Harrt wasn't entirely comfortable with it. Two objectives, with two rapidly decreasing timeframes, separated by several star systems. To Harrt, that meant only one thing; divide and conquer, which immediately set off alarm bells inside his head.

Sure, Tariq and Hayward were backed up by years and years of data. They'd seemingly been honest with the crew from the get-go. Even Vol, with her sixth sense, trusted what they were saying. And yet, despite all of those things, Harrt didn't feel comfortable with the setup.

During their discussions, he'd half-expected Hayward and Tariq to choose one objective for their crew and the Sadalmelik, which implied something foul was at play. To his surprise, however, Tariq suggested the opposite.

"As a token of goodwill, I am happy to split my crew to make this work," he said. "I can see that this needs to be a collaborative and trustworthy alliance. Therefore, I will accompany the team that goes after James while Hayward and our small crew help with the data vault".

"You really wanna put yourself in the line of fire?" Nathan folded his arms, his brows lifted in surprise.

"I don't expect you to undertake this alone," Tariq said. "I'm coming with you. James is my friend, and I will not see him used to fuel the Revenant's next genocide".

Harrt could see the scepticism he'd come to expect of Nathan as the Earther eyeballed Tariq to the nth degree. It was something Harrt could see in himself. Now that he was —like Nathan— responsible for the lives of a crew, Harrt could relate. He could almost picture the inner workings in Nathan's head as though they were his own.

With every choice Nathan now made, he had to consider the risk to his crew.

"Fine," Nathan said to Tariq. "Given the time restraints, we'll plan the operation en-route".

There was a hint of warning to Nathan's voice. The kind of tone that said *screw with me or mine, and I'll kill you:* Harrt recognised that one immediately.

"We still need to discuss saving, Claire," Hayward said, either oblivious to the tension or bulldozing through it. "If we are splitting this thing for the sake of... *unity,* then who is coming with?"

Harrt felt his gut clench the moment Vol answered him.

"By the sound of things, you guys are gonna need a decent engineer to crack open those databanks," she said. Vol looked at the others and shrugged: "Guess I'm the only person for the job".

At that very moment, Harrt made a choice. It was impulsive, formed out of the attachment he felt for Vol and the desire to keep her safe. He also reminded himself that any intel that hinted at the Commonwealth mole had to be protected. If he could finally crack the case, he wouldn't need to wear the uniform or pretend to be something he wasn't.

"I think it's only wise that I go as well," Harrt said to the group. "I'll bring Dines into the fold too. If those databanks contain any info about a Commonwealth mole, then I need to make sure that it's kept safe and handled properly".

He only got a moment to glance at Vol. Her expression was half-angry, half-unsurprised. She'd likely read his mind and knew that what he'd said was only half the story, but Harrt didn't care. He wasn't exactly going to try and have an awkward conversation in such an open setting.

"Dines.." Hayward sighed knowingly. "Not looking forward to meeting the guy I kinda screwed over".

"It'll be fine," Harrt lied. "Dines will understand... I think".

NATHAN

Nathan watched from the Phoenix's cockpit as the Sadalmelik, along with Harrt's shuttle, jumped into the FTL slipstream. It felt strange watching his friends fly off into the unknown with Ralph Hayward, of all people. Yet, he knew this was the way it had to be done.

The horrible truth of the matter was that the mole had to be shut down, and James had to be saved. Yes, allying with Tariq and Hayward was risky, but Nathan knew he needed the allies.

As he stared at the holographic projection of Hawtrey house, Nathan thought about the strategy he'd use to rescue James. Guns blazing simply didn't feel right: especially with a mix of Paradisium's elite and members of the Criminal Syndicate present. There would be hired guns and corporate enforcers, plus Revenant in attendance, and he knew that he needed to be smart when planning the operation.

What I need is a man on the ground.

That thought evolved, and Nathan saw a method to the madness. He needed someone who could talk-the-talk, walk-the-walk and looked an awful lot like a member of the Criminal Syndicate. He needed someone who could be a wolf—or in this case, a Sphinax— in sheep's clothing.

There was only one man for the job: Koble.

CHAPTER TEN
KOBLE

"Wake up..."

Koble didn't dream often, but it was usually pleasant if he did. Normally, he dreamt of something relaxing, such as fishing, but it hadn't been that way since returning to Pluvium. Now, it was of the Phoenix Titan, or sometimes even the Loyalty: a less-than subtle subconscious craving to return to his life of adventure.

"Wake up".

This time he dreamt that he and Merri Tautana were trying to catch fish using huge nets that were the size of the universe. The only problem was that the ocean was empty, and the fish could fly.

Dream-Koble didn't understand what was going on, and *Dream-Merri* found the whole thing hilarious. *Semi-conscious-Koble* understood that his old friend wasn't there. She was dead, and more importantly, she'd never been that happy in life. Ergo, he was dreaming.

As soon as he realised that fact, a star exploded in the distance, and all Koble saw was a raw white light that penetrated his corneas.

He was snapped from his gentle slumber by the bright rays of the sun burning into his furry eyelids. Instinctively, Koble rolled onto his side in an attempt to shield himself from the light, longing to return to the dream, but he failed once a voice filled the room.

"Wake up, Koble".

It took Koble a matter of seconds to put together the pieces in his mind; someone had opened the curtains, and now they were telling him what to do. He was in between the covers of his bed back on Pluvium. The place he'd been before was a dream, and Merri Tautana had died in the Mirotose Station incident.

"C'mon, wake up". It was the unmistakable voice of Koble's close advisor and mother, Krell. He tried to ignore her, willing himself to fall back into slumber and see Merri again, but he knew that his efforts would be futile. More sunlight poured into the room as Krell opened the other three pairs of shades, including one in the ceiling above his bed.

"Gah," Koble groaned, raising his paw to block out the light. "Close those damn curtains!" He grumbled before rolling back over and burying his face in a pillow.

"I can't believe I have to wake you up in the afternoon. You're Chief now," Krell asserted from the window. "You're forty-three cycles old, not a boy anymore. You can't keep spending every night partying; that's a young man's game."

"I am still young," Koble muttered from his pillow. "Besides, last night was an important business meeting..."

Technically, he wasn't lying. Koble had spent the previous night with several young and up and coming Sphinax entrepreneurs. It was his chiefly duty to host guests, and it was tradition to ensure that the patrons were blind stinking drunk before engaging in any *business talk*.

"You need to get your fur-trimmed," Krell continued, glancing down at his thick matted coat. "You should pay Nestor a visit; he'll get you looking like a sophisticated leader".

Koble lifted his head from his pillow and scowled at his mother. In the space of a few seconds, she'd rudely awoken him, called him lazy, reminded him that he wasn't as young as he pretended to be, and now was pulling him up on the state of his luscious fur-coat.

Despite his mother's comments, Koble knew that she wasn't wrong. Pluvium was still in the early days of recovering from twenty years of dictatorship and poverty.

Kornell had pretty much bankrupted the economy, and now Koble was responsible for fixing that.

That, unfortunately, meant spending hour after boring hour of meetings with dignitaries, councillors, business-types and of course the press. It wasn't the life he'd imagined for himself at his age, but then again, he'd spent over half his life living as a criminal.

A year after taking up the mantle, he'd achieved a lot. People were happy again; they were being fed again. Production of wheat-based foods and vegetables went up quickly as Pluvium's first eco-domes opened. Then Pluvium's economy began to recover.

Thousands of small businesses and ventures began to open. The shipping industry followed and now was almost back to its pre-civil war days. Real Sphinax alcohol was being made again for the first time in over a decade, and the experts were calling it the most exciting development for all Sphinax-kind.

The main problem was the fishing industry, which had been Pluvium's main export back in the day. Sadly, Kornell's administration had shown little respect for the ecosystem, allowing the corporations to dump waste into the vast, beautiful oceans. A large patch of the sea had been rendered non-viable, but there were options to reverse the damage, but they were expensive, which meant external investment.

Hence Koble's hangover.

"Meeting with Kibola, the brewery master, to discuss his new blend is not the same as attending a political summit," Krell replied. "You can't turn up to those things looking like a walking hairball".

"My coat is fine just the way it is, mother," Koble growled.

"I'm sure Rain and Nero will squeeze a trim into your busy schedule," she replied. "Your breakfast meeting with Rain is in twenty minutes down in the gardens. Maybe some meat will soak up the remaining booze".

▲

"Heavy night, boss?" Rain drawled.

The blue-furred Sphinax grinned from his chair as Koble made his way to their table. As always, Rain was there in his fedora, looking suave and charming and like a man half his age. Somehow Rain had shaken off his hangover well. He'd been at the event the previous night and drank his fair share, and yet he didn't look affected at all.

Koble took a seat opposite and immediately noticed the hot breakfast of various meats waiting for him on the table. He wasted no time in grabbing a piece of fish and devouring it.

"So," Koble said with his mouth full. "What's the latest?"

This was a daily tradition between the pair. Rain would update Koble on the latest news and developments on various subjects while they shared breakfast.

Rain was, in essence, his vice-chief—if there was such a thing. Having spent the last twenty years as a vital member of the Sphinax Resistance, Rain always had a good read on the people's opinion. Koble valued that input immensely as it helped him make the best decision for the people.

Like all mornings, Rain grabbed his datapad from the table and started with the most recent headlines.

"Hmmm," Rain mused. "Let's see... EWB, blah blah blah..."

"Pass," Koble chewed. He had no patience for the Paradisian's political movement or the people behind it.

Rain tapped his datapad, scrolling to the next story. "An EWB front runner has been found dead".

Koble immediately stopped eating and his ears pricked up. He stared up at Rain and then hurriedly chomped through the mouthful and gulped it down.

"Was it Jareth?" Koble asked, his voice filled with anticipation.

"Afraid not," Rain answered as he glossed through the article. "The dead guy was called Titus Rousseau. Ring any bells?"

"Nah," Koble shook his head and continued to eat.

Every headline was related to the EWB, and Koble didn't have the time or energy to focus on it. Of course, he knew he'd have to take stock of the Paradisium situation eventually. With the Earther-refugee world now independent, it could make a potential trading ally, but Koble was sceptical.

Rain ran through the rest of the headlines, then switched to the day's messages and appointments.

"Chieftess Alluci of the Parivia tribe has requested an audience," Rain said.

Koble stopped and raised his brow. "Another proposal?"

Yes, there had been multiple proposals in the last year, and no, Koble wasn't interested.

"Could well be..." Rain chuckled. "Shall I have the admins pencil in an appointment?"

"Is she hot?" Koble chewed.

"She's two-hundred cycles old," Rain replied. "Probably old enough to be my grandmother".

"A simple no would have sufficed. Anything else?"

Rain continued to scan the messages for several seconds, then lifted his eyes; "Did you know that the Phoenix Titan is on the way here?"

Koble sat up in his chair excitedly.

"Are you serious?" Koble clapped his paws together.

Rain shrugged, "It says they're only a few hours away".

When Koble finished chewing a piece of fish-rib, he placed the picked bone on his plate. "Break out a bottle of something suitable for a human palette, and tell the mechs to be on standby. I want those guys treated as best as possible".

Rain nodded, "You got it, Boss".

RUSSELL

For years, Russell had yearned for adventure. He'd spent all his life on Paradisium, and by age eleven, he realised he'd seen everything there was to see: the same beach, the same buildings, the same people. And so, the fantasy of joining a crew and getting the hell away from Paradisium was born.

It was to be a boundless journey to the stars, filled with the kind of experiences that would change him from a boy to a man. That was all well and good, but never in his years of daydreaming had Russell taken the time to consider the time-consuming exercise of FTL travel. It could be boring as hell, but Russell found ways to keep busy. He'd sleep; read; jog the ship's corridors, and —on occasion— cook for the others. Staying occupied was the key, but that was harder to do when you were heading toward a potentially dangerous mission.

It was too early to sleep, and Russell knew that jogging and cooking weren't appropriate, so he sought comfort in music. Once he had his trusty over-ear headphones, Russell poured himself a whiskey from the bar and settled in a comfortable armchair. From his datapad, he listened to a variety of old Earth music ranging from old blues tracks right through to urban hip-hop.

He must've drifted off at one point as when he opened his eyes, Gordon was sitting in the chair opposite, and the ice from his whiskey had melted inside the glass. An old gentle jazz number that Russell didn't recognise was playing, so he gave it a moment and waited to see if he enjoyed it. While he listened to the light baritone vocals, Russell glanced at Gordon then at the book in his hands. It was old, the spine was worn, and the corners of the hardcover were creased. The words *Macbeth by William Shakespeare* were embossed into the surface.

Russell reached for the bottle of whiskey on the coffee table and poured himself another glass as he studied Gordon's engrossed expression. Out of nothing but sheer curiosity, Russell pulled off his headphones and called out to the doctor.

"Looks like you're enjoying that one, Doc".

Gordon glanced up and nodded. He set a bookmark down on his page and placed the book on the table between them.

"You wanna know something funny? I hated this book when I was younger," Gordon remarked.

Russell took a sip of his whisky and gave a puzzled look at the doctor. It was such a strange comment as Gordon didn't tend to change his mind about things.

"So, what changed?" Russell asked.

"Maybe Macbeth is like blue cheese? Maybe it gets better as you age?" Gordon said. "I think it's this funny realisation that Earth is long gone. Our culture, our history and all that remains are battered, old relics like this book. Kinda like the music you're listening to".

"You may have a point there," Russell shrugged, then pointed at the book. "So what's this one about?"

Gordon climbed to his feet and slowly walked over to the bar to get himself a glass. "Macbeth is the story of a man who becomes consumed by his own ambition".

"Sounds kinda morbid."

"Oh, it is, but it's a part of our literary history," Gordon said as he returned to his chair. "When I'm done reading it, I'll lend it to you".

"Yeah, sure, why not," Russell said. He went to pull his headphones back over his head and settle back down into his chair, but Gordon halted him and pointed at his datapad.

"So, what are you listening to?" Gordon asked.

"This one is called…." Russell paused and then glanced at his datapad. "Fly me to the moon. Not a bad number; the guy has a smooth voice".

Gordon was seemingly taken aback by the mention of the song's title. It was an expression Russell had never seen on the man: a mix of nostalgia and sadness.

"You never mentioned you had that one in your collection..." Gordon said, his voice cracking as he spoke.

"You've never asked..." Russell shrugged. Then noticing the slight twinkle in the old man's eye, he asked, "You alright there, doc?"

Gordon beckoned him to hand over the datapad, and Russell obliged. The doctor disconnected Russell's headphones allowing the music to spill from the speakers and fill the room. Gordon smiled at the hopeful-sounding tune, but it wasn't an expression of happiness. It was more like sentimentality and a longing for something that had once been. Russell had seen the same look on other Paradisians, particularly those who'd survived the Fall as adults.

"That takes me back," Gordon muttered into his glass. "I've not heard that song since, well... Earth".

The doctor sank back into his chair and closed his eyes, uncharacteristically lost in the track. To see Gordon so consumed by something as simple as old Earth music was a strange sight to behold.

The song finished, and Russell shut off his datapad before the next track in his queue could begin. Gordon rubbed his eyes, then took a mouthful of his drink for good measure.

"Funny how music can evoke old memories..." he mused.

"You wanna talk about it?"

Russell could see the discomfort on Gordon's face from a mile away. The old man didn't open up often, especially about his life before the Fall, but after sinking another mouthful of alcohol, Gordon acquiesced.

"About... thirty years ago, I went to Seattle to visit my mother and step-father for Christmas. They used to host these parties every year and pretty much invited their entire apartment complex," Gordon paused and finished off the rest of his drink. "There would be music, egg-nog, dancing; y'know people having a merry time".

"Sounds nice".

Gordon began to refill his glass. "I was probably a few years older than you are now, and I'd been working as part of a research project for a while, so I didn't visit home too often. Anyway, I met this girl at the party —Helena— a new neighbour of my mother's." Gordon's eyes softened at the mention of the name. "We were in conversation for a while, and I remember that song playing, and she asked me to dance. That's right, me... dancing".

Russell breathed laughter at the thought.

"So, this Helena was pretty special to you?" he said.

Gordon nodded. "She was a wonderful person with a truly remarkable mind: insightful, funny, witty..."

"Was she a scientist?

"A researcher," Gordon said with a smile. "But well on her way to getting her doctorate".

"Sounds like the perfect woman for you".

Russell paused, noticing that Gordon's smile had fallen.

"She was..." Gordon sighed into his glass, then climbed to his feet. "Think I'll hit the hay for a while. The last thing I need is a hangover with Koble potentially coming aboard." As Gordon passed by, he patted Russell on the shoulder. "I appreciate the drink and the company".

"Anytime".

VOL

For the better part of two hours, Vol tried to keep herself busy. Avoiding a super-personal conversation with Harrt was her primary objective, so she wandered the vast halls of the Sadalmelik. She spent an hour examining Tariq's collection of Earther-art, which was mainly comprised of paintings that seemed beautiful but entirely pointless. When Vol found herself growing bored, she opted to explore the guts of the ship.

What she found was impressive. The engineering deck, while small, was utterly immaculate: almost as good as the Phoenix. The armoury was stocked with enough guns and ammo to fight a small war.

It was only when Vol stumbled into the galley that she came face to face with Harrt. The 'wealther sat at the table, with a datapad and a glass of something that looked like kor but smelled entirely different.

She could read him at that moment —*a mix of delight, regret and nerves.*

Harrt had removed his military uniform and instead opted for something more casual: a jacket of black fibre-cotton atop a white shirt and dark trousers. His hair was tidier and far more in line with the prescriptive 'wealther look that many males the same age preferred, but Vol could see beyond it. The clothing suited him and seemed reminiscent of the time they'd spent aboard the Phoenix — back when things had somehow been more chaotic and more simple.

For a long moment, they were silent together.

"I—" Harrt started, then stopped himself. He peered at her as if looking for the right words, then, after a deep breath, continued. "It's good to see you again".

Vol nodded in response, though it was hard to simply smile his words away. Seeing him in the flesh for the first time in ages was strange, and Vol wasn't quite sure how to process it. She could, of course, return the sentiment. That would be the civil thing to do, and it really was, in a way, good to see him, but it wasn't natural —like a half-lie. Of course, at the other end of the spectrum, Vol could give him a piece of her mind and really let the 'wealther know how much he'd hurt her, but that wouldn't be right either. In the end, Vol decided to choose the middle ground:

"How's the life of command?"

Vol could feel Harrt's uncertainty at that moment, but it didn't stop him from answering.

"Boring," he said with a shrug.

"And the investigation?"

"We've had a couple of leads: nothing concrete, but hopefully Hayward's operative will be precisely what we need to find the traitor".

"Let's hope so".

There was silence once again, and this time Vol could sense his intentions. He wanted to rebuild: wanted to be whatever they'd been before, but the problem was that while he regretted his choice in leaving the Phoenix, he'd do it again.

Harrt sighed and invited her to take the seat opposite and slid the bottle of brown liquor across the table. She reluctantly took the chair and allowed the 'wealther to pour her a drink.

"The last few months have been tough," Harrt said into his glass.

"They sure have," Vol nodded.

Vol necked the sharp, bitter drink in her glass, and it gave her a little ounce of courage to speak her mind.

"I hate not having you aboard the Phoenix," she said into her glass.

Harrt's lip twitched, "I miss you too. Every single day. I wish things could be different".

"But they aren't," Vol said quietly, hoping that it would put a cap on their emotional exchange.

She was wrong.

"It's not that simple," Harrt replied, emotion in his voice. "I wish—"

"After you killed Olbori, you came back different," Vol cut him off with a slight hint of anger to her voice. "I thought you were going to retire from the 'wealth. When you told me that you were going to fight the injustice inside the Commonwealth from within... it—"

The words, *broke my heart* lingered on Vol's lips, but she daren't speak them aloud. Instead, she composed herself, took another sip of alcohol and breathed.

"It hurt," she said. "But I get it. I—"

Harrt cut her off. "For years, I wanted nothing but revenge. I always thought that killing Olbori was the answer to all my problems, but I was wrong. After the Messorem, I realised that Olbori was just a byproduct of the Commonwealth's corruption. He betrayed them because they'd betrayed him and so many others. It's a vicious cycle, and I don't think I can allow it to continue: not after the traitor killed my crew aboard the Vertex and tried to kill us".

"I get it," Vol nodded.

"Then how do I make this right?" Harrt asked. "I know we weren't exactly... *courting,* but that doesn't matter. I miss my friend, and I just—"

"I stopped replying to your messages because I can't cling on to this whole, what could've been shit. I know you chose duty over whatever the hell we were because that is the kind of man you are". Vol held his gaze from across the table, his dark eyes staring back at her. "You are a kind and honourable man, Harrt, and I miss having you aboard the Phoenix every single day. But I cannot be a reason for you to stop fighting for what you believe in. Yeah, the 'wealth kinda sucks, and it needs good people to make it right again: people like you".

"I—"

"*This* is your calling," Vol continued, with finality in her voice. "I realised a while ago that you need to do this. Otherwise, you'll never find peace. I had to do the same: I had to kill Grecko for what he took from me to find my version of peace".

Vol didn't know why she'd said it. Technically it was true, but emotionally it was a complete and utter lie, but Harrt couldn't read her like she could him.

Harrt looked down, "Vol... I—"

She shook her head, necked the rest of her drink, and placed the glass down on the table. "You and I are good, but there's just a lot to figure out, and right now isn't the best time. We've got a mission and a 'wealther traitor to find. Let's focus on that first".

Vol could feel her eyes strain against her brows as she realised that her expression had grown from emotional to down-right cautioning. She stepped away after that: *better to keep things transactional for the time being.*

INTERLUDE
ROTH

Alastair Albon de-Freiherr Roth raised his glass to toast. Through the airlock doors, Roth stared at the coffin containing the body of his late Society-brother, Titus Jean-Michel Rousseau. The morning after the EWB results, Rousseau's security detail found him, slumped on the floor with a bullet in his brain: executed like a feral dog.

Thankfully, Rousseau's staff were on Roth's payroll. Like good little worker bees, they didn't report the death to the 'wealth until Roth had the body in his possession. There were two very good reasons for that. The first was that Rousseau deserved the honour of a Society funeral. No post mortems. No organ harvesting, like the 'wealthers would prefer. Yes, Roth didn't like Rousseau, but he hated the Commonwealth more. Not letting them have their way felt entertaining. His second reason for getting the body away from the 'wealthers was simple: the murder of a well-known EWB supporter on the night of the EWB's victory on a 'wealther Capital World was stardust. It was the kind of thing that Roth, and the Society, could use to create drama, turmoil and distractions: fuel for a fire.

Standing beside him were a small cohort of Society brothers and sisters. They all tried to look sad and mournful, but Roth could see through the facade like glass.

You are all just a pack of wolves, Roth thought to himself.

The truth was that each and every one of them and their descendants had become a little more powerful. Rousseau had been a single, homosexual-widower without no offspring or successor to claim his role; ergo, his family's vote in Society decisions was gone forever.

Regardless of his brothers and sisters perceived gain in power, Alastair Roth was still the man in charge. He'd been the Chairman for over twenty-five years, and while it had been a *problematic* tenure, it had given Roth ample time to prepare.

It was the master plan that would place him in a position where he'd always deserved to be, all while dealing with those who'd opposed him or questioned him. Roth was a man who should've been an emperor or a monarch or Julius Caesar himself, but that wasn't reality. He was a man who intended to change the course of history: a man who could lead the universe toward a bright and prosperous future.

But before he could do that, Roth needed something that had been stolen from him a quarter of a century prior. He needed Project Erebus and all the power and glory that it contained.

It was time for his pièce de résistance: the ultimate gambit. The one chance he had to destroy those who stood in his way while obtaining the kind of power that only gods could dream of.

Roth looked at Rousseau's casket one last time. Then as he raised his glass, he spoke the words that had defined generations of Society members throughout the ages.

"Novus Ordo Seclorum".

The wolf-pack repeated his words and raised their glasses in false honour of their fallen brother. Roth hit the execute button on the airlock, and Titus Rousseau's casket floated into the nearby star.

▲

Within an hour of sending the wolves back to their respective ships, the Featon jumped to FTL en-route to Haydrium, where the EWB celebration would take place. Not on Paradisium —not with the riff-raff. This extraordinary private event was designed to be a soiree of the grandiose variety. That was why Roth chose his son's private estate on the corporate world to host the event. They needed to set the stage for everything that was to come: *an overture that would lead to the most glorious first act.*

Up until the EWB, Roth's first-born, Christian, had spent most of his days lounging within the confines of Hawtrey House: an estate paid for by his father. That all changed after the EWB. Christian recognised that the Society needed him to play his part, and he'd stepped up. *It was about bloody time.* Christian's home —if it could be called such a thing— was a five hundred acre monument to luxury: a floating island that soared high above the clouds and no doubt tickled Christian's many superiority complexes.

It was the perfect location for the celebration that would act as the backdrop for Roth's overture.

A few hours later, the Featon docked at Hawtrey House on the east wing. As Roth stepped into the house, he was greeted by the garish mix of not-quite-Elizabethian architecture mixed with Christian's preference for bold and colourful decoration.

It was no surprise that Christian wasn't there to meet his father. He'd spent the previous night partying at the EWB results ceremony; likely, chatting up some pretty young thing of any persuasion. Usually, Roth would turn a blind eye to his son's debauchery and indulgences, but things had now changed. Things would continue to change. Yes, Christian was a man who'd grown up in the wonderful extravagance of Paradisium, but he was also a Roth. He was the man who one day would inherit the mantle of Chairman. Christian would fill the shoes of men whose legacy could still be felt today: men like Theodore Jareth, like Truman Oswald.

He certainly wasn't there yet.

Alastair Roth was greeted on entry by three of his most trusted security experts. The most senior of the three men present, Bradley Austin, was an unassuming looking fellow. He was muscular and broad and tall, but he didn't look like a man capable of violent murder or vicious torture at all.

Austin looked like a man who frequented American football games and drank cheap beer straight out the can. And yet, despite that, Bradley Austin was among the most efficient killers that Roth had ever employed. He was a fierce attack dog who would only heel to a few select superiors, including Roth and his otherwise indisposed manager.

Austin had been leaning on a table when Roth stepped into the room, and he immediately jumped into military-like attention, an act that pleased Roth greatly.

That's right, dog, Roth thought. *Heel, speak, paw and roll over.*

Austin regarded his master with a nod. "Welcome, sir".

Roth waited: allowing silence to drag just a moment too long. "Are we all set for the theatrics?"

"Yes, sir. The cargo is stowed inside a containment chamber aboard a private shuttle, ready to go".

"And he's stable?" Roth asked.

"Yes, sir".

It was perfect. *Well, almost perfect.* In an ideal world, the likes of Alastair Roth wouldn't need to share the same air with someone like Bradley Austin, but sacrifices were necessary.

Roth offered the slightest hint of praise to the three security experts, and after a few other questions regarding the security detail for the party, he excused himself. He made his way through the vast mansion that doubled as Christian's summer home while two aides carried his bags and suit. At the centre of the west hall, Roth noticed a particularly vulgar pink statue placed in the middle of the room. It was a metallic eyesore that looked an awful lot like a Horrus holding an axe in battle. The sight of the thing left Roth to wonder how much his petulant son had spent on such a pointless monstrosity.

His thought was quickly interrupted when a member of Christian's staff approached him. The woman carried herself with sharp and efficient professionalism that told Roth that he must've hired her. He racked his brains for a moment, trying to recall the name. He knew that she was one of Mao Chen's children, the one who could play the violin at a grade eight standard.

"Mr Roth," she said, bowing politely —subserviently. "I hope your travels were comfortable".

"They were".

"I am delighted to hear that..."

Roth could tell from the mild flicker in her eyes that the next thing she would say was uncomfortable. He didn't make it easy for her by asking. Instead, he waited for her to speak.

"One of the guests has arrived earlier than expected," she said nervously. "The staff didn't have a room prepared, so we told Mr Jareth to wait in the Magdelena hall".

Roth felt his heart pulse with fire, but he did an excellent job of hiding his outrage. He regarded Rachel Chen —that was her name— with a friendly nod.

"Thank you, Ms Chen. I shall go and pay my dear old friend a visit".

▲

The Magdelena hall was a vast and expansive auditorium built on Hawtrey House's third and fourth basement levels. It was by far one of the most expensive rooms in the building. Boasting an architecture inspired by the Italianate style, the theatre-type room was designed as a place of culture.

Roth had hoped that his son would use the exorbitantly priced holographic entertainment suite to host cultured evenings of opera or maybe ballet, but that was not the case. Instead, Christian left the room dormant, and on the rare occasions he did use it, it'd be a party ground.

When Roth entered the hall, he was surprised to see that all overhead LEDs were off. The only source of illumination was from the stage, where a hologram of the Paradisian Philharmonic Orchestra was displayed. The projection was pristine and looked as though the orchestra was really there performing live.

The playback was around three-quarters of the way through Beethoven's 9th symphony. Roth could tell because he'd listened to classical music since he was a boy. When it came to the greats, he knew every note, every rise, and every fall as though it were the back of his hand.

As Roth walked the empty aisles, he took note of the hundreds of unoccupied, vacant seats. The desolation of the sight had a ghostly feel that should have made him feel nervous, but instead, it filled him with a sense of power. The Magdelena Hall —a monument to sophistication— was something that would stay in the Roth family for generations. His children, grandchildren and all the others that would follow would have exclusive access to only the most refined pieces of Earth's past. Not all the other —lesser— forms of media.

To Roth, *that was a true inheritance to leave behind.* But unfortunately, it wasn't enough: not while power sat with the 'wealth, Baylum and anyone else.

He'd been thinking a lot about that recently —what one left behind. Legacy was everything. Men could bury themselves in riches and trinkets, but death came for everyone in the end. All that mattered was the impact you made on the world. Yes, Roth had contributed to the Society, and made history with his part in the Fall, but it wasn't enough: *not yet.*

There was one more thing he needed to do, and even then, his work wouldn't stop there.

Roth had realised many years ago that power —true power— had to sit with those who deserved it: people with the balls to make hard choices but refined and educated enough to understand the bigger picture. The wise and mighty Theodore Jareth was undoubtedly one of those people, but he was long gone. It was tragic, yes, but his death meant new leadership, and with David Jareth uninterested in the Society, it created the role that Roth now inhabited.

Sometimes water was thicker than blood after all.

David Jareth was sat on the second row, with one knee folded over the other, watching the symphony play out in front of him with intrigue. Roth couldn't be sure if Jareth had any genuine appreciation for the art he was taking in, or if he were simply posturing. While Roth and Jareth shared an entirely false mutual respect for one another, there was no love lost between them. That was just fine. Jareth used Roth, and Roth used Jareth: a means to an end —at least on the surface.

In truth, Roth truly despised the man. He always had. In Roth's eyes, the just-about blonde swine that was David Jareth was nothing compared to his father. Theodore Jareth had been a man of vision.

Selfish, yes. Bigotted, yes, but a visionary nonetheless.

David Jareth, on the other hand, was a man who'd turned his back on the Society: a man who'd not only insulted his lineage but also broken a tradition that had lasted centuries. By refusing the privilege of membership, David Jareth had created chaos, and Roth had seen his opportunity: his route into the highest echelons of the Society.

In some way, Roth should have been grateful for Jareth's choice all those years ago, but he wasn't. Roth quietly hated the man. He hated him for breaking Theodore Jareth's heart; he hated the smug way he looked at everything. But most importantly, Roth hated Jareth because years ago, he'd aided the criminal, Jack Stephens: the man who'd threatened Roth and his family on the day of the Fall.

Your time is coming, Mr Jareth, Roth thought. *Soon.*

"You're incredibly early," Roth said as he approached.

"Apologies, old boy," Jareth said with a false smile. "I hate to impose but, my ship hit a snag on the way back from the Capital Worlds. I hope you don't mind".

Yes, it was suspicious, and no, Roth didn't fall for it.

"Of course not," Roth lied, taking the seat beside Jareth.

On the arm of his theatre chair, Jareth had stowed a bottle of chilled white wine, which he promptly presented like the trophy body of an elk after an excruciating hunt.

"Well, it'd be only right to share this bottle of Chateau Galton with my host," Jareth said, pouring them each a glass. "My staff tell me it's a bottle from the 1930s, but unfortunately, the label must've suffered some damage".

Jareth was posturing: Roth noted that. There was very little point in showboating over something as trivial as a —*at most*— two-thousand dollar wine to someone like Alastair Roth. Back on the Featon, he had a small collection of wines and ports, one of which was worth at least sixty-thousand. In the wine cellar of his private residence on

Paradisium, Roth had fine alcohols that would fetch triple or even quadruple the price of the thing Jareth was pouring.

In the end, it didn't matter. Jareth's wine was entirely trivial in the grand scheme of things. They were two men with an unspoken hatred for the other that had lasted for decades. It was a cold war of the cultivated variety that Roth would win.

After Jareth handed him the expressive smelling wine, they raised their glasses to toast: as was the custom for gentlemen of Paradisium.

Jareth said, "To the separatist dream."

There was a musical clink as the glasses touched. The wine was dry and bold. Delectable but lacking the kind of kick that Roth preferred. *Nothing beat a good, hearty red.*

"You didn't hear about Titus?" Roth asked, surprised that he'd not toasted to the dead.

Jareth sipped his drink thoughtfully, then after setting his glass down with care, he answered: "Yes —terrible business. Does anyone inside your... *circle...* have any idea what happened?"

It was funny that Jareth worded it that way: *your circle.* In other words, he was referring to the Society, but he refused to say it aloud.

"Not yet." Roth answered.

"Do you think it was suicide?"

Roth chuckled at the ridiculous notion.

"Your father once said to me that a life of buggery would rot a man's mind". Roth said, nostalgically reflecting on the words of his mentor. He said it because he knew that Jareth would feel uncomfortable with the bigotry. He let the discomfort hang long enough for Jareth to cringe. "Titus led a... *questionable lifestyle* for many years. He could've killed himself with drink and drugs when we were much younger men, but he didn't. So to answer your question: no, I don't think Rousseau killed himself. He didn't have the balls".

Jareth breathed laughter at the comment, but the tone of voice he used next conveyed something else —*deception, perhaps?*

"I will assign my best investigative unit to Titus' case," Jareth said. "We must bring whoever is responsible to justice".

Alea iacta est, old boy. The die has indeed been cast.

"I'll drink to that," Roth said, raising his glass again. As the victorious vocal chorale of *Ode to joy* filled the hall.

CHAPTER ELEVEN
GORDON

A very wise man once told Gordon, *When it comes to alarm clocks, buy the one with the most unpleasant sound. It'll motivate you to get up in the mornings and make you more productive.*

And so he did, and every day for the last twenty years, he'd awoken to the unbridled squawk of his datapad. The sound was close enough to the alarm-clock radio he'd owned back on Earth. On occasion, it could fool him into believing the last quarter of a century had been a bad dream.

This was not one of those times, and Gordon immediately shut off the squealing alarm with urgency. He climbed from his bed and dressed, taking a moment to glance around his tidy cabin. His room aboard the Phoenix was immaculate, with a few keepsakes from his house on Paradisium: a small stack of literature; framed photographs of days gone by; a potted succulent and a painted canvas: all of them were a piece of Earth, including the painting that was of the Paris skyline, though not entirely accurate.

He'd been thirty-two, the day of the Fall, so he remembered Earth and its many cultures in all its flawed glory. That was the difference between Gordon and all the hardcore Paradisian separatists. He saw Earth for what it really was: neither perfect nor imperfect, just something that was that now wasn't. Like all survivors of the Fall, Gordon had a story of tragedy —of people he'd loved and lost— but his perspective was entirely unique. Nobody else would understand what he went through in Russia, just like he wouldn't understand anyone else's experience. Still, he imagined most Paradisians had a far more straightforward escape than him, particularly those in the elite.

Gordon had fought to survive on the day of the Fall, whereas many —not all— had walked onto top-secret shuttles and left Earth to burn. For that very reason, he knew that he could never be a true Paradisian. He was nothing like the rest of Earth's survivors, or at least the ones who'd stayed on Paradisium. Of course, the Commonwealth had arrived at the thirteenth hour and saved millions, but Gordon's story of survival would always be different from those evacuated on lifeboats.

Before he'd come aboard the Phoenix, Gordon had suffered nightmares for many years. Most of the time, they were memories or at least emotions from the day of the Fall. It wasn't an everyday occurrence, but every time the nightmares reared their ugly head, Gordon felt the trauma all over again.

The previous night, Russell had played *that-damn-song,* and it had evoked a powerful memory of Helena: another tragic loss in his story. He'd not thought about their first meeting for at least a month, but the music had brought it all back —the good times and, of course, the bad.

It had been twenty-six years, and not a day had gone by that he hadn't thought of Helena. He still felt the weight of her death like it'd had happened yesterday. In many ways, it felt wrong to still cling to her after so long, but Gordon wanted to honour the woman he'd loved. He glanced at one of the framed photographs on his mantle —a picture of him and Helena in their younger days. He acknowledged the calamity of it all, how he wished things were different, then summoned the strength to start his day.

It was, in a way, a silent prayer. Gordon acknowledged the events that had led him to that very moment in time. He recognised those who'd made him who he was today: his mother, his stepfather, Helena, Bill, Donnie, and all the others that he'd lost. He allowed himself to feel the weight of their deaths, then closed out the thought and shelved it alongside the burden of Jack Stephens' greatest secret.

Fuck you, Jack, Gordon thought. *Fuck you for shouldering your crimes on Koble and I. Fuck you for what you did.*

Usually, saying the words aloud —even if it were a whisper— made him feel better. Gordon noticed the anger in his gut and the mild impulse to clench his fists as he recalled his final conversation with Jack over fifteen years ago.

I hate you for what you did, Gordon thought. *I hate you for encumbering me with your guilt.*

Then he released his anger onto the universe. It felt mildly better, but the sting remained.

It would always remain.

Gordon left his quarters and headed straight to the bar for a coffee: as was his morning routine. As he passed into the living area, Gordon stumbled across Tariq, who was on his knees in the middle of the room. At first, Gordon thought he'd fallen over but quickly realised that the middle-eastern man was in the middle of his prayers. While Gordon wasn't a religious man, he showed his respect to Tariq by not disturbing his ritual. When Tariq was finished, he climbed to his feet and carefully rolled up his red prayer mat.

Tariq nodded politely, "I hope my praying didn't make you uncomfortable?"

"Not at all" Gordon shook his head while pouring a coffee. "I just didn't have you down as a man of faith".

Tariq took a seat at the bar, and Gordon offered him a coffee which Tariq accepted.

"I only found faith after the Fall," Tariq said as Gordon fetched a second mug. "Once I made it off Earth, I looked out on the vastness of space and came to the realisation that all of this, the alien races, the thousands of planets that sustained life for millions of years is not an accident". Tariq spoke gently, his eyes locked on Gordon's. "In a way, I realised the scale of it all: that we are mere cells when compared to the grand scale of this universe".

Noticing a fingerprint on his thick glasses, Gordon removed

his specs and polished them with the end of his plaid shirt.

Tariq leaned on the bar; "Forgive me if this is forward, but are you a man of faith, Doctor Taggart?"

Gordon considered his response; placed his thick glasses back on his face.

"Not that kind of faith".

The coffee machine pinged, and Gordon handed Tariq a fresh cup

"Ah," Tariq mused. "But you have faith in something: that means a lot in this strange world. Your faith may not be in God or in spirits or karma, but it is undoubtedly in something".

Gordon kept his response brief, "Where does your faith lie, Tariq?"

Tariq smiled enigmatically. "I have faith that all of this is part of a higher purpose. That all of this is part of God's plan".

"God's plan? Or the Enkaye's?" Gordon questioned.

There it was: the awkward man of science versus man of faith moment that Gordon hoped to avoid. Rather than challenge Tariq's beliefs, Gordon kept talking, hoping to keep everything conversational;

"We know that the Enkaye were on Earth. It's been theorised that they had something to do with constructing the pyramids. We know first-hand that they were trying to create Earthling-Enkaye hybrids. Let me ask you this, what if your god is simply a little grey man?"

It was a poignant theory that Gordon had been working on for some time. *What if the Enkaye had created life in the galaxy?* Gordon had just seen a slither of what the Enkaye technology was capable of doing.

Was it really outside the realms of possibility that they could design intelligent species, planets or even the universe itself?

"If my god is a little grey man and life has been manipulated by a long-dead, technologically advanced race, I'd simply ask three questions." Tariq paused as he stared at Gordon. Then counting on his fingers, "Why would they manipulate these events in such a way? If they did, why create us? And most important of all, who created them?".

KOBLE

Koble couldn't help but grin as he watched the Phoenix Titan begin its slow descent. The ship he'd once called home emerged from the clouds, and it made Koble feel nostalgic. Seconds later, the unmistakable boom of the Phoenix's engines became apparent. The trees around Koble and his greeting party shook, sending red autumn leaves scattering around the landing pad like confetti at a party.

The welcoming committee accompanying Koble consisted of five bodyguards plus his mother and Rain. All wore grey-hoods over their heads with the exception of Rain, who, of course, donned his signature brown fedora. The grey hood was a popular symbol of the Sphinax Resistance: reserved for those who'd stood against Kornell's authoritarian regime during the Pluvium Civil War. Though Koble had fought and lost in that campaign, he refused to wear the hood. Not because his fur was wildly out of control —as his mother would tell people— but because he felt that Pluvium needed to move on. Clinging to the past didn't aid progress; in fact, it did the opposite.

It was Sphinax tradition for a chief to greet notable guests with their entire cabinet, but Koble didn't want to create a scene. Nathan was transmitting dark, meaning that he was trying to keep things subtle. And besides, Koble's cabinet consisted of stuffy and boring administrators who wouldn't appreciate the crew of the Phoenix Titan.

While the rest of the welcoming committee shielded their eyes from the breeze that the Phoenix kicked up, Koble kept his eyes locked on the ship. Small blue flames from the impulse balancers crackled to life on the hull, adjusting the ship's speed and angle. Koble savoured the familiar mechanical whir of the landing gears as the Phoenix touched down: albeit rather harshly. It wasn't the smoothest landing that Koble had seen, suggesting that Vol wasn't behind the stick.

Less than a minute later, the boarding ramp emerged from the Phoenix's port side, and the airlock door opened. Koble's smile grew more as Russell Johnson emerged from the ship. Somehow the former barkeep looked older than the mental image Koble had stored. Russell shot him a wave, then proceeded to disembark with Gordon following close behind.

"How you doing, kid?" Koble said as he pulled Russell into a friendly hug.

Russell groaned under the immense pressure of Koble's grip but still managed to fathom a response:

"I'm good, man. It's good to see you".

Koble released Russell and moved to Gordon. The Doctor stopped, examining Koble's thick-fur coat from a distance, then extended his hand to shake. There would never be a brotherly greeting between them, which was fine. Koble was and would always be loyal to Jack Stephens, whereas Gordon saw the man as the root of all evil, at least that was Koble's understanding of the matter.

It wasn't to say that Koble had a problem with the man. He found Gordon to be polite and pleasant, but there would always be tension between them. After all, they were the only two people in the galaxy who knew the horrible truth about Jack. At least they could both agree that Jack's secret stayed secret and that Nathan should never find out the truth.

"Good to see you, Doc!" Koble said. Rather than shake his hand, Koble pulled the Earther into a tight embrace, which he knew Gordon would hate but did it anyway.

"Good to see you too," Gordon said awkwardly as he patted Koble on the back.

It was hard to tell if he was being truthful.

Koble's eyes turned to the boarding ramp where Nathan and Astrilla had already disembarked. He embraced them both simultaneously: one giant arm per human.

"It's good to see you guys," Koble said as he released the pair from his hold. He gestured at Nathan's hair and beard, "Nate, you're looking more and more like a Sphinax every time I see you".

Before Nathan or Astrilla could say a word, Koble's attention was drawn back to the Phoenix. A human male with dark skin, long flowing hair and groomed facial hair stood at the airlock. He wore a black silk shirt tucked into suit trousers, with his sleeves rolled up to the elbows. As he walked down the ramp, the man threw on a jacket that matched his slacks: giving him the look of a corporate man.

Koble raised his brow to Nathan, "New crewmate?"

"Not exactly," Nathan replied.

"Chief Koble," the suited man said, bowing his head respectfully. "My name is Tariq Mahmoot. It is good to make your acquaintance."

Speaks like a corporate guy, Koble thought.

Koble was about ready to question the situation when Nathan shot him a severe expression. Koble knew the Earther's look all too well; he'd seen it many times before, usually when things were about to go sideways. It was Nathan Carter's way of saying; shit just got real.

"We need to talk," Nathan said, urgency in his voice.

▲

Koble chose a room at the town hall as a good place for them to gather. The room was just about big enough to host the crew of the Phoenix, as well as Koble, his mother and Rain. Once everyone was settled down, Koble looked at Nathan.

"So... we're all here..." he said. "Let's hear it".

The suited man, Tariq, spoke at Koble, Rain, and Krell for over twenty minutes. Everything he said from the elite Earther conspiracy to enact the Fall, right down to James — the junkie— Stephens operating as a spy sounded beyond the realms of possibility: especially the latter. Nathan, Gordon and Astrilla chipped in where appropriate, but Tariq did most of the talking.

"So let me get this straight..." Koble said, leaning back in his chair. He pointed across the room at Tariq, hoping to create a dramatic effect with what he said next. "You have been investigating David Jareth and all those other rich assholes for ten years.... and of all the people in the galaxy, you chose Ralph Hayward as you're second in command?"

Koble became aware of at least two members of the Phoenix's crew, sighing in frustration as he made the comment.

"Hayward is not my second in command," Tariq said, his voice only slightly defensive. "He is a trusted companion who has been dedicated to this cause since day one".

"Correct me if I'm wrong but wasn't that protein-riddled steroid the one who handed all the 'wealther data to Jareth?" Koble said, looking at Nathan then back to Tariq.

"He was deep undercover," Tariq replied, the inflexion in his voice growing irritable. "Mr Hayward did what he had to in order to maintain his cover".

"You wanna know something about your pal Hayward?" Koble said, his voice hostile with just a hint of sarcasm. "When my crewmates were being held captive aboard a Revenant warship, your pal refused to help us. Instead, he was too busy screwin' around watching the Jareth Corps warships fly around".

Tariq's eyes narrowed, "What do you not understand about the words *deep undercover*?"

"Guess that makes it alright then..." Koble folded his arms.

Tariq looked offended, but Koble didn't care. He'd seen enough of Hayward's actions to know what kind of man he was dealing with.

On the other side of the room, Nathan stood. "We can argue about this all day, but the reality of the situation is that time is working against us. We checked out Tariq's data — everything. It all checks out".

Koble sighed and reached a tankard of hearty Sphinax Grog. As he clasped the heavy cup between both paws, he shrugged in acceptance.

"Fine, whatever, Ralph Hayward's a dick; let's just move on," Koble said. He could tell that Tariq wanted to cut in there and reaffirm his stance that Hayward was a brave and honourable man, but Koble refused to give him a chance and instead continued speaking. "So, James is a secret agent now? That's a new one, even for him. So, how the hell did he get captured?"

"We don't know," Tariq said with regret in his voice. He checked his watch and continued, "The last message I received from James was four —no five— days ago. He said that they knew he was Enkaye. After that, James went completely dark, as did the rest of my network".

Koble assimilated all the information as he drank from his tankard. The thought of James Stephens being able to do anything, let alone espionage, sounded insane. The last time Koble had seen the man, he'd barely been able to stand up straight: so consumed by his addiction that he barely resembled a functional human being. Then it dawned on Koble that he'd been thinking about it all wrong. Nathan had come to him for a reason, and it wasn't for a Loyalty crew reunion.

"What do you need me for?" Koble asked.

Nathan pulled a datapad from his pocket and sent a burst of data to the holoprojector on the wall. A three-dimensional image formed in the centre of the room. It was a home fit for royalty: a giant estate built upon a gravity-defying floating island.

"Hmm," Koble mused as he climbed from his chair. He gestured to the holographic palace, "This is one of those Avix Platforms, right?"

"Correct," Nathan nodded. "The Roth party is an invites-only affair, and security will be tight".

"Not a problem Nate. We faced more firepower on the Messorem," Koble grinned. "Plus, we've got Astrilla this time. She'll tear through any of these Society mercs".

Silence filled the gap, suggesting to Koble that his plan wasn't appropriate.

"Going in guns blazing is not an option," Tariq shook his head. "If they get any hint that their handoff is in jeopardy, they will get James as far away from there as possible".

Koble sat forward, untucking his paws from behind his head. He looked at Nathan, "How do you wanna play this?"

Nathan plotted two markers on the hologram: the first at the entrance to the Roth estate and the second at the base.

"The way I see it, we divide and conquer," Nathan began. "One team will infiltrate the party and tracks Roth, to the trade. We gather evidence of this conspiracy so we can shut them down properly".

"Little bit subtle for my liking, but okay," Koble snorted.

Undeterred by the interruption, Nathan continued;

"Meanwhile, the second team will infiltrate the security hub, placing EMP charges here and here," Nathan highlighted two points on the lower levels of Roth's island. "Once the first team has confirmed the location of the trade, we blow the charges, knocking out all power to the house, but not the engines keeping the thing in the sky".

Koble considered the plan. He saw the rational reason for saving James, though he immaturely would've left the junkie to rot —at least on a personal level.

"Okay, Nate," Koble said. "I'll help you plant those EMP charges and save your douche-bag cousin. It's been a while since I've seen some—"

"We need you to be in the first team," Astrilla interrupted.

What she said made little sense. Koble was a firearms expert: arguably the best shot in the galaxy. *Why waste his skills on shadowing a bunch of rich assholes?*

"There will be a considerable number of guests; Society, Corporations, possibly Revenant and of course members of the Criminal Syndicate," Astrilla said. "We need you to go in and pose as someone".

It took Koble a moment to realise what she was implying. Then like a bucket of ice water to the face, the realisation hit him. She was asking him to assume his brother's identity. Kornell had been a former business partner of David Jareth, a Don in the Criminal Syndicate, and likely an associate to the Society.

Koble scoffed at Astrilla then broke into a sarcastic chuckle.

"I hate to break this to you guys, but Kornell and I don't look anything alike". Koble jovially nudged Rain, "Do these humans think we all look alike?"

To Koble's surprise, his mother spoke up. "You and Kornell are brothers, after all. When you were children, even I struggled to tell you apart".

Koble scoffed again. "Kornell barely has a summer coat of fur, and I have the fur of a true warrior, and—" he paused, uncomfortably looking back at Nathan, who made the gesture of scissors at him. "Ah crap," Koble muttered.

NATHAN

Nathan had never been to Pluvium before, but he'd heard enough that he'd formed a mental picture of it over the years. Koble and a handful of the Loyalty's crew had spoken of a lush green world, wherein its inhabitants had respected the natural beauty of its vast forests, even going so far as to build towns and entire cities among the gaps in the trees. Nathan had always imagined it as an almost idyllic fairy-tale world, with little cottages laced between the branches.

To say that actually seeing Pluvium had shattered the illusion was wrong. Sure, it wasn't a rustic village carved from some old fantasy tale, but it wasn't far from beautiful either. From the town square where Nathan stood, he could tell that the townspeople were thriving. Market traders were busy selling, a series of boats moved in and out of a modest harbour with the day's latest catch, and a group of builders were fabricating a new structure using nothing more than wood.

As Nathan stared at the evolving landscape of Pluvium, Rain joined him. The blue-furred Sphinax was smoking a pipe that had the distinct aroma of Pluvium Vine: a delicacy among the Sphinax.

"Amazing isn't it," Rain said as he gestured to the town square. "Our people suffered under Kornell's boot for two decades, and during that time, this place fell apart. After Kornell's loyalists surrendered, we landed here, and I'll tell you now it didn't look anything like this".

"I see that Koble is doing a great job as Chief," Nathan replied.

"The people of Pluvium are an industrious bunch," Rain smiled as he drew from his pipe slowly. "In a year, the people have been able to rebuild so much that was lost, and progress will only continue with stable leadership".

Nathan knew what Rain was implying.

"You know I'm coming with you, right?" Rain said bluntly.

Though Nathan didn't know the Sphinax well, he'd always liked Rain. Of course, he was as charming as hell, but the thing Nathan appreciated most was that he cut to the chase pretty damn quick. There was never any tiptoeing around potentially tricky subjects. If something needed to be said, Rain would say it.

"You must understand that I need to keep Koble safe," Rain said. "And you need a combat pilot behind the stick of the Phoenix. No offence intended, but you are not as skilled as your Uvan friend. I'd feel safer knowing—"

"You don't need to sell me on your piloting abilities," Nathan interrupted. "Facts are facts, and I need to be on the ground for this operation. It'd be good to have an experienced pilot on our side for this one".

CHAPTER TWELVE
HARRT

After four hours in the slipstream, Harrt found himself becoming restless. Wandering the sterile white halls of Sadalmelik reminded him too much of government buildings. Vol wasn't overly forthcoming with conversation either; *after all, who could blame her?* After their brief exchange, Vol had disappeared into one of the guest cabins and not come out since. That meant that Harrt could either continue exploring the Sadalmelik until the rendezvous with Dines, or he could make nice with Hayward and his crew.

Harrt tried the first option for a while, but there was only so many white corridors a man could stomach before getting bored. And so, he made his way to the Sadalmelik's command centre. Hayward greeted him with friendly open arms, then introduced him to the Sadalmelik's five-man crew. All of them were just like Hayward: stocky, Earther types with big personalities and strange humour. Harrt recognised the camaraderie immediately, but it was not his to share. He was an imposter amongst the Earthers, and Harrt doubted they'd ever accept him, so he kept his distance, acted politely, and didn't say anything stupid.

It was interesting to observe Ralph Hayward among his *true* crewmates. Harrt found it hard to separate the man he saw before him versus the man that had worked for Jareth Corps. Hayward shared smiles and laughs with his crew, and he appeared to command respect, but it wasn't respect bred out of fear —it was one of fealty. They were united in their mission to bring the corrupt to justice.

Harrt saw the middle ground as plain as day.

When Hayward was finished talking with his crew, he approached Harrt and placed his hand on his shoulder; "I think it's time you and I had a chat".

Hayward led him back to the room where he'd met Tariq earlier that day. The blue streams and ribbons of FTL bathed the room in flashing lights that reminded Harrt of swimming beneath the ocean. The moment ended as soon as Hayward hit the lights.

The big Earther retrieved a bottle and two glasses from a unit on the far side of the room. The alcohol was clear and odourless: Harrt didn't recognise it. They toasted before taking their seats. Hayward looked uncomfortable as he shifted his broad shoulders. The Earther stretched out, trying to look relaxed but failing to do so on every level. Eventually, he gave up and leaned forward to meet Harrt's gaze.

"I understand your apprehension, I really do, but I can assure you we are the good guys in this situation. What happened last time—"

"In my experience, the people who say they are the good guys are usually the bad ones," Harrt interrupted. Something was tickling at the back of his mind —a question he needed to ask. "All of your operatives were covering these Society members and turned up data on all of them. How come you didn't find anything on Jareth in eight years?"

Hayward knocked back his liquor and promptly refilled his glass. He didn't seem surprised by Harrt's question; in fact, he'd probably anticipated it.

"David Jareth is one of the most intelligent people I've ever met," Hayward said, scratching his greying beard. "The man certainly knows how to cover his tracks".

"So you never found a link between him and the Revenant?"

"Jareth? No. Never". Hayward's chuckle was sardonic in nature. "Don't get me wrong, Jareth Corps does some... questionable things, but David Jareth actively despises the Revenant".

"And he's still a member of the Society?"

Hayward made a musical sound that was somewhere between uncertain and thoughtful. "Maybe. Maybe not".

"That's kinda non-committal," Harrt said, raising his eyebrow in suspicion.

"Thing you've gotta understand is that Jareth is an enigma. He's interested in the Enkaye —borderline obsessed. He truly believes that the Enkaye wanted Earthers to inherit their place in the galaxy".

"So... what? He's not a member of the Society?"

"David Jareth's only goal is to put the people of Earth at the top of the food chain. Whereas the Society's interest is in putting themselves at the top". Hayward's voice was flat and matter of fact as he spoke. "See the difference there?"

Harrt nodded.

"I spent years working very closely with Jareth. He spent every waking moment trying to build his little empire: granted, Jareth Corps didn't always do the right thing, but..." Hayward paused for thought. "Jareth was always in pursuit of a bigger objective".

"Just because he thinks he's doing something good doesn't make him right," Harrt leaned forward in his chair.

"Spoken like a true 'wealther," Hayward raised his glass. "We could talk about Jareth all day, but that ain't gonna help anything".

Harrt blinked, unsure how to respond. "So, what did you wanna talk about?"

Hayward leaned in, "I need you to understand that I am not your enemy. Sure, shit was pretty rough when I was undercover, but I had to—"

"What's in this for you?" Harrt cut in, with almost severity in his voice. "Tell me why this mission is so damn important".

He figured there was no point in dancing around the topic, and Hayward seemed to appreciate it.

Hayward breathed. "Saw some pretty bad stuff during the Fall: it changed everything".

"What do you mean?

"When the Fall happened, I was twenty-one years old, just started as a beat cop in New York City".

Harrt understood maybe two-thirds of what Hayward said.

"What's a cop?" It was an Earther idiom he'd not heard before, and it didn't sound like cursing.

"Law enforcement," Hayward clarified. "I'd been on the job for about a year when the Fall happened. Don't get me wrong, I'd seen some bad shit before that day, but... they don't prepare you for the kinda things I saw during the Fall. To say I saw the worst of my people on that day would be an understatement". Hayward was quiet for a long moment. The bulky Earther sipped at his drink, then after a long sigh, he continued. "I was lucky. I got scooped up by a 'wealther lifeboat, but I saw things that made me question everything".

Harrt raised his brow.

"I saw soldiers turn their weapons on civilians trying to board a private shuttle," Hayward's voice became low. "Man, woman or child, it didn't matter. They were under orders from someone, to gun down anyone who tried to get aboard".

The image formed in Harrt's mind shook him to the core, and he could tell from the darkness in Hayward's voice that what he'd experienced was undoubtedly ten times worse.

"The shuttle belonged to this guy, Michael Goldman. Some slick banking type," Hayward waved his words away, likely realising that most of what he said meant nothing to Harrt. "Anyway, I get close enough to see these shuttles. These things were fuckin' huge: big enough for... I don't know... dozens? Maybe hundreds of passengers. So these soldiers formed a barricade around Goldman's place and opened fire the minute the civilians got close".

Hayward's voice cracked. He stopped, took a sip of his drink, and looked at Harrt with reservation.

"It was fuckin' merciless," Hayward said. "The funny thing is that Michael Goldman left those soldiers behind. They killed for a man who didn't give a shit about them. How fucked up is that, right?"

Harrt could hear the pain in his voice, despite the hardened look in Hayward's eyes.

"That's rough," Harrt nodded.

"I escaped Earth, thanks to one of your 'wealther lifeboats," Hayward tipped his glass at Harrt as though he were vicariously toasting the entire Commonwealth. "I was one of the lucky few, but there was still this issue of Michael Goldman. That asshole murdered a whole bunch of people right in front of me". Hayward shook his head in anger. "So when I got to Paradisium, I tracked that bastard down to his big new mansion, filled with art and statues and wine and all this other priceless bullshit from Earth. Then I realised that Michael Goldman had stuffed that shuttle full of *things:* not people. That asshole murdered people so that he could airlift some fucking wine off of Earth".

Harrt's gut turned at his statement. He'd never heard anything so awful. Sure, he'd heard Nathan's account of the Fall, but Hayward's was something else entirely.

"I killed Goldman," Hayward said without emotion. "I smashed his head against a priceless renaissance-era statue, and I didn't feel a thing. So when Tariq comes to me years later and tells me about the Society and all that other shit, it ain't too hard to convince me to join him".

"Goldman was a member of the Society..." Harrt said, saying it as a statement rather than a question.

Hayward nodded. "He was. Low ranking, but yeah, he was a Society guy. And guess what? All those Society pricks escaped aboard private shuttles, leaving billions to die".

"Is this whole thing about revenge for you?" Harrt asked. "Because I've been down that path before. It's not—"

"This is about justice," Hayward interrupted. "This is for all those people they conspired against. Tariq is more than right on this one. I don't know if it's the Society as a whole or a group of them, but they colluded with the Revenant, long before the Fall".

Harrt relived the moment he'd killed Densius Olbori aboard the Messorem. It made him realise that he and Hayward weren't that different after all. They were both men searching for justice.

"I've seen your data," Harrt nodded. "The problem I've got is that all your evidence about the Society is—"

"Ropey?"

Harrt's jaw twitched, and he nodded. "I didn't wanna say that, but sure".

"There's one fact I wanna throw at you," Hayward said, grabbing the bottle and refilling both their glasses. "This is a little tidbit that one of our operatives told me several years ago. If this doesn't convince you, I dunno what will".

"Let's hear it".

Hayward leaned in; "During the Fall, two thousand Commonwealth lifeboats travelled to the Earth's surface, collecting survivors, but only half made it back."

"Okay..." Harrt said, anticipating more from the Earther. "It was a battlefield... the Revenant had dug in on the planet. They'd probably set up anti-aircraft weapons and had fighters in orbit".

"Naturally," Hayward agreed. "But you wanna know the weird thing. The Revenant didn't shoot down any of the private shuttles".

He slid a datapad across the desk for Harrt to review. Harrt saw a list of Earther names and shuttles clashed against a publicly listed Commonwealth report on the skirmish. Hayward leaned over, then dragged his finger across the screen, overlaying the original diagram with all the known members of the Society. It was still guesswork, but the circumstances were downright remarkable. Hundreds of private shuttles without a single record in the 'wealther documents: *as though someone scrubbed all record of those ships from existence.*

ASTRILLA

"You look rather regal," Astrilla said.

Koble shuffled into the Phoenix's living area, looking like half the Sphinax he'd been just two hours prior. His previously thick and matted fur was cut from inches in length to mere millimetres. He no longer bore the look of a fluffy walking rug and appeared somehow far more refined. The haircut style reminded Astrilla of Kornell, which was exactly what Nathan intended. If Koble could fool Astrilla into believing that he was Kornell, he could hopefully do the same with the Society's party guests.

"Damn, Koble, you look like a real gentleman," Russell mocked from the bar.

Koble huffed in frustration as he placed his bags down. "Such a waste of good fur".

"It'll be worth it," Astrilla said, trying to reassure the Sphinax. "Besides, fur grows back".

Koble snatched the bottle of liquor that Russell offered him and scowled. "Yeah, but it's James Stephens," he shrugged with annoyance. Koble wrestled the cap from his bottle and tossed it into the disposal behind the bar. "Of all the people in all the galaxies, why the hell did it have to be James..."

"Whoa," Nathan said as he entered the room and saw Koble. "You had me fooled for a moment there. I honestly thought you were Kornell".

"That ain't a compliment, Nate," Koble said.

"Just think, it'll be just like that job back in the day. That one at the Amaluna Casino," Nathan patted Koble on the shoulder. "You remember that one, right?"

"Yeah," Koble scoffed. "If memory serves correctly, I was the one doing all the shooty-shooty-bang-bang, and you were the sucker with short hair in a dumbass suit. Oh, and might I add we had to save James' ass on that occasion too!"

The nostalgic conversation went back and forth for a few more minutes, and Astrilla found herself learning something new about Nathan's past. All his stories about the Loyalty and its crew were often vague, but the information seemed to flow freely when Koble was around: *after all, he'd lived that life beside Nathan.* Still, every time Astrilla heard about the Loyalty and its escapades, she found it harder and harder to reconcile the Nathan from those tales and the man she now called her lover. That wasn't to say that it changed how she felt about him, more like she was peeling back the curtain to a scene that she wasn't supposed to be a part of.

With that thought in mind, Astrilla proceeded to the cockpit, leaving Nathan and Koble to continue their conversation. It was good to see Nathan relax a little: albeit for a moment. The topic of James was a tricky one. Nathan had told her the story of his cousin once, and even then, Astrilla could tell that the whole thing was an emotive topic.

We must worry about getting James to safety first, Astrilla told herself. *Let's worry about the potential family drama after the fact.*

In the cockpit, Rain was at the helm, marvelling at all the consoles with a giddiness that made him seem decades younger. Though Astrilla had never seen his piloting first-hand, she'd heard enough from Vol and Koble to know they were in safe hands. Yes, Nathan could fly the ship from A to B, but he wasn't combat-ready. With Vol absent, that had left a considerable risk, and to now have an experienced pilot at the helm made Astrilla feel safe: *or at least safer.*

"I said it before, but damn, this is one hell of a ship," Rain said with an excited smile.

"I'm guessing the Phoenix is a little bigger than the fighters you are used to?"

Rain grinned, "Oh don't you worry, I'll make this baby move like a fighter".

"You sound awfully confident," Astrilla said, sitting in the co-pilot's seat.

Rain breathed laughter. "Confidence is the greatest weapon you can have in your arsenal". He paused and looked at her with a thoughtful expression. "After all, this is the ship of Jack Stephens".

Astrilla smiled, though it wasn't genuine, and she was pretty sure Rain knew it. Jack was yet another tricky subject: not as tricky as James, but rather an enigma that would never be solved.

Astrilla had watched Jack's final message to Nathan more than a hundred times. The video that he'd buried deep with the Phoenix's logs was a strange confession that raised more questions than answers. Jack Stephens had looked through his holo-recorder moments before death and recorded a message that seemed vague and, in a way, pointless.

"I'm hoping that by now you are starting to see that the Enkaye's plan is the real deal," Jack had said.

What plan?

How do you know they had a plan?

What is said plan, and what does it mean?

Astrilla couldn't understand the motivation behind it, and for hours she watched and watched. Nathan seemed to accept it with one viewing, but Astrilla couldn't let it go. There had to be an explanation.

Astrilla meditated on the subject an awful lot, and eventually, she concluded that she would never have an explanation. Despite that, the very notion of who Jack had been fascinated her. He was, after all, the man who'd raised her paramour: the man who'd sacrificed himself to protect the Loyalty's crew. And yet Jack hadn't been the one to meet Nathan in his vision aboard the Messorem. That duty had fallen on Nathan's long-dead grandfather, Bill.

Trying to make sense of it hurt Astrilla's jaw.

"You know that Jack Stephens is a name that my people will never forget," Rain mused as he tapped the nav terminal. Then with a chuckle, "What a crazy bastard".

"What do you mean?"

Rain looked back at her with surprise. "Well, Jack fought for our side in the Civil War. That guy stood his ground against an entire troupe of Jareth Corps mercs so that I could evac a bunch of civilians".

"He did?"

"Oh yeah," Rain said, as though stating something obvious. "Bravest man I ever knew. Well, maybe except for your... *boyfriend?* I mean, he did stand toe-to-toe with the Revenant king twice... that's gotta count for something, right?"

Astrilla nodded, feeling the need to meditate on Rain's testimony of Jack. It was another brushstroke on the canvas still forming in her mind. It would never be a finished picture, but that didn't mean it couldn't be understood.

▲

In her meditation, Astrilla saw something fall from the stars. It crashed into the ground, sending plumes of crimson into the air. For a time, she saw hatred manifest itself in the form of dark swirling shadows around the crater. A thirst for revenge ignited a fire that burned like a star. The thing twisted in the inferno, morphing into something new: something with purpose.

Then there was only a word: *Chimera.*

Astrilla didn't know what it meant, but she could tell it was important: that the universe needed her to know it. She accepted the message that fate bestowed upon her and allowed herself to wake.

Astrilla's head was on Nathan's chest, his heartbeat slow and his breathing deep. She was sure that the Earther was asleep, but the moment Astrilla pulled herself up, he shifted his arms.

Blue light from the slipstream spilt into the room from the window, allowing Astrilla to make out the silhouette of her lover's face, his eyes open and full of purpose.

"Did I wake you?" she said, laying her head on the pillow beside him.

"No," Nathan shook his head. "Too much to think about to sleep. I just wanna be here in this quiet moment with you before everything starts getting... less peaceful. Savour the good moments and all that stuff".

Astrilla reached out and took his hand. They lay together in companionable silence for a long while with only the faint sound of the engines bleeding into the room. In that moment of tranquillity, their bodies wrapped together comfortably, and Astrilla felt herself drifting off again.

As she began to fall back into slumber, she asked, "What is a Chimera?"

Nathan didn't reply and instead snored quietly.

JARETH

Christian Roth's estate was so large that it boasted its own private restaurant on the outskirts of the property. Back in the days of Earth, it would've been the kind of place where only the finest chefs would work. Jareth could almost imagine a soiree of upscale new york types sitting at the empty table opposite him. They'd be weekending from their jobs on wall street to enjoy an evening of fine dining that equated to a month's salary, and they'd describe the experience as *transcendent* or *luxurious*.

As it happened, the place was entirely empty when Jareth arrived: spare the chef and a crew of remarkably attentive waiters. Of course, it filled up as more of Roth's guests began to appear, ready for the night's festivities. Most of them were of the Paradisian Elite, not necessarily Society members, but the upper-crust has-beens of Earth: a celebrity chef, an actor with several awards to her name, a once notable stockbroker, a former American vice president, whose party allegiance Jareth couldn't recall. All of them were a by-product of something that probably should have changed the day of the Fall, but alas, celebrity culture ventured forward. Naturally, Jareth turned on the charm to make it look like he was one of them. He shook hands and gave hugs as though he were greeting old friends, all the while cursing them for clinging to the achievements of days gone by.

Jareth was not one for status or politics or fame. In his younger days, when he'd studied at Featon Academy, he may have desired those things, but he'd been a very different person. Back then, he'd been nothing more than a boy, raised in an influential and powerful family, but like the rest of the world, he'd been blissfully unaware that beyond the boundaries of Earth, there was a galaxy-spanning war that had raged for centuries.

In those formative years, and even as a young man, Jareth rubbed shoulders with the crème de la crème of Earth —people like those he was surrounded by now. He was raised into believing that one day he would control the Society just like his father and grandfather before him, but after the Fall, Jareth's eyes were opened. He saw the stars, the planets and all the possibilities that came with it. Yes,

Earth was gone, but something new had to be forged from the tragedy.

The people of Paradisium had to do better. They had to grow, evolve and change, but many of them refused to do so. Where Jareth embraced that change, they did not. Where he found purpose and a newly found sense of morality, the Paradisian elite clung to the old ways: to the red-carpet Hollywood bullshit, to the old political ideologies that no longer mattered.

And then there was the Society, still operating in the shadows, still conspiring with Baylum to ensure their continuation. It made him feel sick with anger.

When Christian Roth entered the restaurant, his magnetic presence drew the attention of all the has-been losers. There was no doubt that he was the dynamic type: the kind of man who back in the days of Earth would've been groomed for a high-flying career in modelling or acting or maybe even a world leader. Christian was nothing like his father in looks. He was a tall, square-jawed fellow with blondish hair and a swimmer's body. He mingled about the guests for a while, turning on the false charm in a way that made Jareth wonder *if he hated all the bullshit too.*

When Christian reached Jareth's table, he smiled his well-rehearsed smile and shook his hand vigorously.

"Mr Jareth, I'm very glad you could make it," he said, beaming from ear to ear.

The sincerity was false, just like his father's. Jareth noticed it immediately, but he also noted that where Alastair Roth used the facade in a cold-war manner, Christian used it in a blissfully unaware kind of way. In short, Christian was not as dialled into the situation as his father. *That was interesting.*

"I wouldn't miss it for the world," Jareth replied, his false cordiality perfect enough to fool the young idiot. "I'm very much looking forward to the night's celebrations. It's high time that Paradisium had something grand to celebrate. Thank you so much for hosting this historic event".

"Anytime, David".

"I'm very much looking forward to the show. Where exactly would be the best view?"

For a beat, the facade dropped, and Jareth could see uncertainty in the younger Roth. Something was there: *a hint of surprise? Perhaps shock?*

Naturally, Christian's charming yet planned smile returned within nano-seconds.

"Ah, I see someone let slip that we have fireworks planned for this evening." Christian's chuckle was bogus: a cover for the truth. "We've got a guy from Klemix who put on the fireworks display for Queen Krartie's coronation last year. I'm told he fills the rockets with diamonds and these little shards of gold that make the whole experience that little bit more magical".

"Ah, only the best".

"Naturally," Christian smirked. "I'm told that the view will be especially wonderful in the east gardens".

The east gardens: not the north or the south or the west. East: away from the guarded rooftop terraces that Chimera identified earlier. That was where the trade would occur; Jareth was sure of it.

"Very good," Jareth smiled falsehood. "Then I shall keep my lips sealed so that the rest of your guests enjoy the surprise".

Christian bid him farewell with another handshake and made his way to the next group of adoring party-goers. Once he was out of sight, Jareth pulled his datapad and sent an encrypted message to Chimera, who was tucked away somewhere hidden, keeping an eye on everything and everyone at Hawtrey House.

In your professional opinion, what does an ostentatious fireworks display imply?

They are covering for something in the sky, Chimera replied. *Maybe something on the roof.*

Jareth considered it, then replied to his associate. *I need you on the ground tonight. Something doesn't feel right.*

CHAPTER THIRTEEN
NATHAN

As the crew gathered in the cockpit for the mission briefing, Nathan stared out the window at the planet, Haydrium. He didn't need the ship's sensors to tell him what kind of world he was looking at. Like all mining planets, a large proportion of the land was awash with immense man-made structures that evoked memories of Yenex. It was an atypical corporate world, designed solely to generate profit from exploitation. According to public records, the bulk of the mining operation took place on the southern hemisphere, where Roth Industries and its subsidiaries would drill for anything they could sell.

"Doesn't look like much of a tourist destination," Rain said, twiddling his long whisker as he spoke.

"What a dump," Koble drawled from the co-pilot's chair. "Why the hell would one of Alastair Roth's kids choose a place like this to live?"

"Christian Roth selected this planet himself," Tariq answered. "I don't need to tell you that planets like this are a cesspit of sex, drugs and whatever else".

"Ah," Koble nodded. "So, the Roth kid fancies himself as a bit of a playboy".

At the holotable, Nathan brought up a recent image of Christian Roth. "He's hardly a kid," he said behind gritted teeth.

It was hard to reconcile the photograph of the smug-looking heir to the Roth fortune with the child that Jack had threatened on the day of the Fall. Christian Roth had been nothing more than a frightened little boy back then, but twenty-six years had passed since, and like Nathan, he'd grown into a man now in his early thirties. Nathan had researched Christian Roth and what he'd found was pretty much what he expected. The man was more or less a boy: a spoiled man-child that had secured a well-paying job doing fuck all at the family business. He'd been involved in bar brawls and even faced arrest on Paradisium for burning down a bar not that dissimilar from the one where Nathan met Russell. All of the Paradisian media, accompanied by Tariq's intel, painted a picture of the kind of man Christian Roth was: an entitled and overindulged frat-boy, who'd never grown out of his teenage years.

"Looks can be extremely deceiving," Tariq mused as the crew gathered around the holotable. "James never confirmed it, but one of my other operatives heard... well, let's just say... Christian Roth *could* be a particularly dangerous individual".

"Him? Dangerous?" Russell said with a flat voice bordering on sarcasm as he pointed at Christian Roth's photo. "I saw hundreds of idiots just like him on Paradisium. Sure, he's pretty ripped, but that's only because momma and papa paid for the good muscular enhancements. Trust me, this asshole won't have a clue if he goes toe-to-toe with someone".

Nathan noticed the way Tariq's brows knotted at Russell's statement. It was almost as though he were irritated with the former barkeep for suggesting that he was wrong.

"As I said, looks can be deceiving," Tariq said with finality to his voice. The middle-eastern man shifted his gaze to Nathan, "Shall we begin?"

As Nathan was about to start his briefing, Rain cut in. The giant blue Sphinax tossed his fedora onto the holotable, distorting Christian's image for a split second as the hat passed through. He shifted through the photos of the known Roth associates until it landed on David Jareth's picture.

"How exactly does Jareth fit into this whole situation?" Rain asked, looking first at Nathan then at Tariq.

"Jareth has been occasionally linked to the Roths through my investigation," Tariq answered. "We don't know to what degree, but there are records of private meetings —"

"I know, I know," Rain replied, waving both paws in the air. "But you have to ask yourself, why would someone as smart as David Jareth link himself to these people".

"Power and riches," Tariq shrugged. "Powerful men like Jareth, like Roth are easily enticed."

Rain shook his head in disagreement, "I fought against Kornell and Jareth Corps in the Pluviam Civil War. From the firepower they had, I'd say that Mr Jareth has more than enough money and power to be content. Something about his involvement feels off".

"I'm inclined to agree," Gordon said from the sidelines. "David Jareth is not a fool. If he's doing something, he's doing it for a reason."

Sensing an off-subject debate between Gordon, Rain and Tariq, Nathan decided to shut it down. There was no time to debate.

"If he's there and incriminates himself, then we capture him," Nathan said.

"Surely, you mean, take him out?" Koble said, making a gun gesture with his paw.

"I mean capture. Jareth has questions to answer: questions about Jack, about Mirotose Station, about the Society".

"Fine," Koble sighed, slowly lowering his finger guns in what looked like embarrassment. "Let's get this show on the road".

At the holotable, Nathan brought up the schematic of Hawtrey House, overlaid with his annotations and notes. He ran through the mission and the key objectives one more time, ensuring that everyone knew their part. Essentially, the mission hadn't changed at all. The first team comprising of Koble and Tariq would infiltrate the party and pose as guests, bugging the likes of Roth and Jareth.

"Evidence is essential," Tariq said.

The second team led by Nathan would enter via the lower levels. From there, they would commandeer the security control centre, and blow a series of electro-magnetic pulse bombs, knocking out all power to the house, gardens and most importantly, the aerial defence grid. With Roth's anti-aircraft guns out-of-action, the Phoenix, with Rain at the helm and Gordon at the guns, would keep the airspace clear, thus halting the trade. The ground teams would then reunite, get James to safety, and get the hell out of there.

It sounded simple enough on paper, but Nathan could see where things could go sideways. They still weren't entirely clear on how many men Roth had at his disposal. The schematics of the house were six months old, and Christian Roth could've made alterations in that time. In addition, there was the air-support situation. With the right pilot, the Phoenix could certainly hold her own in close-quarters combat, but the problem was that nobody could predict what Baylum would send to make the trade.

Nathan hoped that the Revenant king would play into the Society's desire to remain subtle. If that were the case, the newly-crowned King would send a Revenant Royale and maybe a few fighters as backup, which the Phoenix Titan could undoubtedly handle. The problem was that Baylum was an unknown entity, and he could very well send a full-blown warship —or even an armada— into the mix.

That would make things a lot more complicated.

No plan is set in stone, kid, Jack's voice played out in Nathan's mind. *If shit hits the fan, you adapt.*

When Nathan finished his briefing, nobody offered a protest or even a mild challenge. It made him feel like all those years of planning heists alongside the rest of the Loyalty's crew had been worthwhile. Nathan could see the plan —flaws included— and he knew it had a solid chance of working.

He glanced at the clock on the holographic projection, looked at his crew and nodded. "Gear up".

RUSSELL

Seeing Koble with short fur was weird, but Russell adjusted to his pal's new look after a few hours. Seeing the Sphinax in formal clothing seemed beyond the realms of possibility, and yet there he was, wearing a stylish maroon jacket and outlandish gold jewellery.

Tariq had also dressed for the occasion, looking like he'd been cut straight from an old-Earth spy movie. His blue three-piece suit, accompanying four-knot tie, and sleek silver watch made him appear cool and sophisticated.

"Y'all ready for this?" Russell asked as he offered Koble a loaded handgun.

"Me? I was born ready," the Sphinax laughed as he tucked the ceramic weapon into his breast pocket.

Russell nodded, knowing that Koble's bluster and bravado was likely a cover for some mild nerves. He offered a loaded pistol to Tariq, but the middle-eastern man politely declined.

Tariq gestured to the inside of his suit jacket, "I prefer my own weaponry. Besides, if all goes according to plan, we won't need to fire a single shot".

When has anything ever gone to plan? Russell thought but didn't say aloud.

Two minutes later, the Phoenix landed at a busy public spaceport to offload Koble and Tariq. From there, the pair would charter a high-end transport to Hawtrey House. Rather than arrive at the party in an advanced gunship, Koble and Tariq would turn up like all the other guests: *in a limo.* Subtlety was the key to their part of the operation. They needed to blend in and look like sharp, refined gentlemen: which they undoubtedly did.

As Russell was closing the airlock, Koble turned to him:

"Stay safe, kid".

Russell nodded, "Good hunting".

Within seconds, the Phoenix was back in the busy skylanes, camouflaged amongst the dense air traffic. Russell made his way back to the cockpit, where the rest of the crew gathered. Rain was busy at the helm, whistling a folksy tune that Russell hadn't heard before. Astrilla sat in one of the chairs, looking decidedly calm while Nathan quietly checked his pistols for ammunition.

"You good cap?" Russell asked.

"Yeah," Nathan nodded to a loaded assault rifle on the holotable. "All set for you".

Russell took up the gun, checked that the sights and barrel were set up to his liking, then placed it back down. He hoped he wouldn't need to kill anyone on this mission, but realised it was probably a foregone conclusion: the guns and weaponry told him that much. Russell had killed Revenant before, but that wasn't the same as killing a living, breathing —thinking— being. Killing a Revenant —convert or otherwise— wasn't the same: they were psychopaths. When it came to the Revenant, it was kill or be killed.

But then, the Society was working with the Revenant. They'd conspired to destroy Earth together. They were about to trade an Enkaye half-breed with Baylum. The last time that happened, trillions died in the Battle of the Messorem.

Ergo, the Society were kinda like Revenant.

It was a justification —albeit a shitty one— but it cleared some of the fog in Russell's mind. He would kill if he had to.

"If they aren't Revenant, we shoot to wound," Nathan said from over his shoulder. "We only kill as a last resort. Got it?"

"Yeah," Russell replied, feeling part of his anxiety melt away. "Got it".

KOBLE

Hawtrey House was everything Koble expected. It was an entirely lavish property, intended as a declaration of status rather than a home. The estate was built atop a giant floating sky-island, nestled comfortably amongst the clouds. It was a rarely seen type of construction that Koble had only ever seen on a few occasions, typically reserved for those with more money than taste. The sky-island itself was designed to look like a natural gravity-defying anomaly: like a mountain ripped from the ground, flipped upside down and left in the sky, never to come back down.

"How much money does Roth industries make?" Koble asked Tariq.

The dark-skinned human glanced out of the cab

window and clenched his jaw with a scowl. Tariq gestured to Roth's estate, "Enough to afford something like that".

The main house was a strange type of architecture that Koble didn't recognise, with several wings and outbuildings that spanned about two-thirds of the estate. In addition to the swanky buildings, there was a meticulously well-maintained garden, a swimming pool and a gold fountain at the entrance.

Koble couldn't help but gawk at the sheer scale of the grand, floating palace. The whole thing was a testament to sheer decadence: the kind of thing that would outrage the average 'wealther. In Koble's mind, he imagined that the Roths had built the small slice of paradise as a message to Haydrium's workers, toiling away on the surface.

It said, *We are superior to you in every possible way. We enjoy luxury while you labour away below.*

The thought made Koble's fur stand to attention.

The cab joined a small queue of a dozen others, each offloading its well-dressed passengers at the entrance of Roth's estate. The first thing Koble noticed was that it wasn't just humans in attendance: there were Uvans, Sphinax, Horrus, Troars, even a Florus, which was a rare sight in and of itself. The next thing he spotted was a surprisingly large security detail at the front gate, checking IDs and invites as though they were about to enter a government building.

"Don't worry," Tariq looked at him and handed over a forged invite and ID. "Getting past security such as this is my specialism".

Koble checked the documents, then peered at the guards.

"You better be right about this," Koble muttered.

"I give you my word".

▲

As it happened, Tariq's word was good, which came as a relief. When Koble handed his forged ID and invite to a meat-head looking guard, he was pretty sure that the jig was up. As it happened, the beefy-looking human simply nodded and allowed him to enter the grounds. This was his moment to blend in: to look and behave like his brother. As Koble stared around the hundreds of gala-dressed visitors, he realised just how challenging his objective was.

Back in the days aboard the Loyalty, Koble never objected to being *the recon-guy*. He'd once had a knack for blending in with a crowd and surveying what he and the crew would be up against. Unfortunately, it had been a long time since his days on the Loyalty, and on most of those occasions, Koble had been blending in with common criminals and outer world scumbags. The people he now found himself among were a more cultivated and pretentious form of scum.

I think I may be a little out of practice, Koble thought.

The same could not be said for Tariq. The Earther appeared to be in his element, moving through the crowd with a gentile yet slightly arrogant demeanour. His presence didn't draw attention —didn't make anyone question why he was there. Koble realised that he had to do the same.

Koble took his own advice and pushed his concerns to the back of his mind. He reminded himself that his dark fur coat had received a trim and that he was dressed and styled for the occasion in the finest clothing money could buy. All he had to do was act like Kornell.

Koble and Tariq made their way up a white stone path toward the main house. Guests mingled in small huddles while waiting staff drifted between the groups with trays of alcohol.

Koble turned to Tariq and whispered, "You know it's kinda weird how calm you are right now".

Tariq didn't reply, instead gazing quietly at the house ahead. There was a crowd of at least three dozen around the gold fountain. Most were partygoers, but Koble could see security guards in the mix too, which wasn't surprising in the slightest.

To the right side of the stately home, Koble saw the swimming pool where a group of scantily clad humans had made themselves at home. Loud music thumped from a bar beside the pool, and the smell of something akin to Pluvium Vine emanated from the area.

"This Christian Roth guy isn't subtle about spending the family money," Koble remarked with a lowered voice.

Tariq replied in a low whisper. "Since the Fall, Alastair Roth has amassed a fortune through mining, the Society and the Criminal Syndicate. It would appear that the apple doesn't fall far from the tree".

As they drew closer to the house, they passed a particularly loud group. Koble chose not to look, but Tariq nudged him to do so.

"We aren't in the best of company," Tariq said in a low voice. He subtly hinted at a group of older human men: all smoking cigars and trying to outdo one another in conversation while playing a game of *who's-got-the-most-douchebag-laugh.* One of the geriatrics, in particular, wore a red jacket made entirely of diamonds.

"That one with the shiny jacket is Adrian Walker," Tariq said, his eyes locked on the man. "He's not a Society member, though he is an investor in the Yong-Pung Initiative".

"Yeah, he's also against working with the Revenant," Koble said. Then with a shrug, "We kinda gate-crashed a Criminal Syndicate meeting when we captured my brother. Kornell was trying to encourage the rest of his pals to work for Baylum. Walker was pretty pissed off and he walked".

Tariq made it clear that he was not amused by Koble's loose tongue. He clenched his jaw and sighed through his nostrils as they continued toward the house. Koble made sure to grab a drink from one of the passing waiters —both to blend in and take the edge off.

When they finally got to the house, Tariq looked at him with a severe expression. "This is where we split up. I'll cover the upper floor; you blend in and do not attract attention to yourself".

"You do realise my brother isn't the blending-in type"

"Then do what he would do," Tariq growled. "Comm-check?"

Koble checked the tiny comm-link tucked inside his ear and nodded to confirm he had a good signal. Tariq did the same, then they split up.

Koble passed another armed guard, and as he entered Hawtrey House, his eyes widened. It was a vast hall, so large that Koble was sure he could land the Phoenix inside and still leave room for a hundred-or-so guests. As he tried his best to blend in, Koble wandered with an air of superiority —just like Kornell. The more and more he took in, the harder it became to hide his shock. The sheer excess of the house was beyond all comprehension.

The floor was made from a dark stone that Koble was sure was Arcane. The walls were decorated with a contrasting diamond-infused white paint intended to look self-indulgent. To top it all off, there was an impressive collection of art, which didn't seem so bad on the surface until, over the comm, Tariq identified them as historic relics from Earth.

"The elite packed their shuttles with riches and paintings and wine and left their fellow man to burn," Tariq said, with anger in his voice. "This is why I do this. This is why I want justice".

As Koble entered the next giant hall-sized room, he allowed his eyes to dart from patron to patron, checking every guest to see if they were on Tariq's shit-list. Koble couldn't escape the feeling in the pit of his stomach that told him he was exposed. Anyone at that party could have been an old acquaintance of Kornell's, and if they were close with him, it'd be game over.

Koble's attention was drawn to a suited man approaching him. For the shortest moment, Koble prepared himself to play the part of Kornell, but then he spotted the tray of champagne in the human's hand.

"Would you care for an aperitif, sir?" the waiter asked. "The champagne is a restored Hennessy from Mr Roth's private collection. Quite a treat for such an auspicious occasion". His voice carried a pretentiousness that could only be found on Paradisium. He wasn't a Society member or even an Elitist. He was simply a man trying to impress a bunch of rich assholes in the hope of becoming a rich asshole himself.

"Sure," Koble said, grabbing two glasses from the tray without any care for decorum.

The waiter moved off, and Koble necked the first glass.

"That's already your second drink," Tariq said over the comm in a low voice.

"Don't worry, you'll thank me later. Drinking helps my aim," Koble replied. He then took a more conservative sip from the second glass as a group of well dressed older women passed by.

"Focus," Tariq said. "We need to get eyes on Roth, Jareth, Washington —any of them".

"I got this," Koble whispered as he sipped the champagne. "Just let me do my—"

"Jareth on your ten o'clock," Tariq cut him off.

Koble looked, and on the left side of the room was David Jareth: the man who'd funded Kornell's side during the Pluvium Civil war. The man who was —in part— responsible for the deaths of thousands of Sphinax. Koble pushed aside the rage that bubbled up in his chest and watched the Earther from afar. Jareth was deep in conversation with an elderly looking human with a cane under one arm and a far younger woman on the other. The thing that caught Koble's eye was neither Jareth nor the old guy. A strange figure dressed in black combat gear and a matching mask flanked Jareth like a bodyguard. He —or she— stuck out like a sore thumb once spotted, but up until that point had blended in like a shadow.

"Who's the muscle with Jareth?" Koble said into the comm.

There was a long pause.

"Well, well, this must be the legendary Chimera..." Tariq replied, with a hint of worry to his voice. "I thought he was just a myth"

Koble sipped his champagne. "Who the hell is he?"

Tariq was quiet for a moment. "Mr Hayward was never able to confirm his existence. All we ever found was tales of a skilled assassin who solely worked for Jareth".

"Doesn't look that deadly," Koble remarked.

"Trust me, if the rumours are true, this operation just got a whole lot more complicated".

"So," Koble drawled. "I should avoid the walking spectre of death?"

"Yes".

Koble was about ready to turn and walk the other way when he heard a loud voice to his right that drew everyone's attention. Christian Roth entered the room as though he were a celebrity, and people flocked to him as such.

"Well, quite frankly, I think this is an opportunity to take back control from the 'wealth. We can finally be our own sovereign democracy once again." Christian spoke far louder than he needed to. Koble had seen the same move in dozens of rich kids in the past. *Speak louder than you needed to get the attention of everyone else around you.*

Douchebag, Koble thought.

"Taxation, defence, education, it's all within our control again." Christian continued to ramble, and the idiots around him lapped it up. "And the best part of it all, we are now free!"

"Quite right," an older Earther in the pack said. "In years to come, people will look at separatist men like yourself as heroes".

"Why, thank you, my friend!" Christian said, raising his glass to the gentleman. "But we did not do this because we wanted to be called heroes. We did this because we believe in democracy".

"Hear hear," a voice came from the crowd.

Everything about Christian, from his expensive suit, bleached teeth and bodily enhancements, screamed elitist. Koble watched the magnetic Earther as he worked the group of avid supporters with grace.

"To the future of Paradisium," Christian raised his glass to toast, and the others followed.

"Can I not just shoot this arrogant little bastard right now?" Koble spoke quietly into the communicator.

"I'd rather you didn't," Tariq said flatly. "I'm going to follow Jareth. You keep eyes on Christian".

"Copy that".

A small round of applause erupted from ahead, and Koble assumed he'd missed some witty remark from Christian

Roth. He was laughing and smiling as he joked with the group. Koble went to a nearby table and grabbed an item of food that was dressed up to look like a delicacy but more resembled something he'd smoke.

He kept his eyes on Christian for a while, watching the man charm everyone he came across. When it was finally Koble's turn to be welcomed by the host, Christian offered him a handshake.

"I don't believe we've had the pleasure," Christian said, setting his intense blue eyes on Koble as he squeezed his paw. "Christian Roth; director of marketing at Roth industries. But you already know that... right?"

Christian chuckled pretentiously and waited for Koble to do the same. The grip on Koble's paw tightened. The handshake was designed as a condescending move to assert status: *let the Sphinax know that the Paradisian was in charge*.

In reality, Koble could've crushed his soft human hand without any significant effort, but he pushed aside the impulse, knowing that he needed to blend in. Koble laughed as Kornell would: in a showy and pompous manner that made him seem like part of the furniture.

It was awkward as hell, but Christian seemingly fell for it and released his grip on Koble's paw.

"I am Kornell, former Chief of Pluviam," Koble lied. "Senior member of the Syndicate and now a simple investor, looking for the next big thing. I see a lot of potential with this separatist movement".

"You don't say?" Christian replied, his voice both thoughtful and sceptical. "I heard you got overthrown?"

Koble did his best Kornell-styled scoff, making sure to lace it with dismissiveness.

"A minor setback," Koble replied. "Those rebels will suffer when I return to power".

"And so they should," Christian replied, handing Koble a business card. "Drop me a message sometime; we should talk about some opportunities".

Koble took the card. "I'll take it under consideration".

Christian's smile was well-rehearsed. He patted Koble on the shoulder in an overly friendly manner. "Enjoy the party, *Chief*".

Koble exhaled in relief as he watched Christian sleuth his way across the room to another group of adoring guests. It was strange watching the man switch between intense intimidation to charming, laughing political-type.

"You handled that well," Tariq said through the comm.

"You were listening?"

"About twenty percent. I was a little busy keeping an eye on Mr Jareth".

Koble moved to a staircase at the back of the hall to get a better view of the party and to keep eyes on Christian from afar.

"What's Jareth doing?" Koble asked.

"Standing by the staging area, he's talking with Andrea Longcroft, daughter of a politician from Earth," Tariq replied. "Wait…"

Tariq's voice suddenly filled with urgency. For thirty seconds, all Koble could hear through his communicator was the sound of Tariq moving through a crowd. There was a short silence before Tariq replied;

"That is very interesting," Tariq mused.

"What is?"

"It would appear that Mr Jareth and his accomplice are heading away from all the celebration," Tariq said. "Where in the world are they going?"

CHAPTER FOURTEEN
VOL

Leviticus Dines was a strange-looking human. Vol was sure that he was decades younger than his silver hair and beard implied. Humans aged different from Uvan's, so it was sometimes difficult to pinpoint, but Vol knew by looking at Dines that he wasn't much older than Nathan or Astrilla. He was undoubtedly younger than Harrt by a good decade, and yet he seemed so much more burdened and weathered.

The Sadalmelik met Dines on the outskirts of the Candela System: not far from where Tariq's operative was broadcasting. The Commonwealth Agent had travelled aboard a small gunship with a crew of five marines that he described as *loyalists to the cause*.

When Dines came aboard the Sadalmelik, he looked visibly uncomfortable: as though everything and everyone around him was a threat. His thoughts were far more evolved than that, and Vol got an excellent read on the man. Leviticus Dines was a man who believed in the values of the Commonwealth, but he'd seen and done too much in the name of leaders who didn't share the same values. He politely shook hands with Harrt, and Vol, then when he got to Ralph Hayward, Dines stopped.

Vol could feel his resentment.

There was no denying that Hayward had screwed him over during the battle of the Messorem. Dines had been put in an impossible situation and handed over all the data that led to the EWB. Dines was branded a traitor by his own people, despite being the man who'd led the battle against Seig when nobody else would.

Hayward offered his hand to Dines, "No hard feelings, pal. I was undercover... you know how it is".

Dines' reply came in the form of a hard-right hook that snapped Hayward's head to one side. As Harrt and the Sadalmelik's crew were about to step in, Hayward halted them.

"It's okay," the big man said, rubbing his jaw. "I had that coming".

There was no humour in Dines' expression. His angular jaw twitched, and his fists were clenched so tight that there was practically no colour left in his knuckles.

"Let's get one thing straight," Dines growled. "When this is all said and done, I want a full debriefing with you, this Tariq Mahmoot guy and the rest of your crew. I want all of David Jareth's secrets. Every last one of them. You got me?"

Hayward nodded amicably. "Sure thing".

"Good," Dines nodded. Then turning to Harrt, "Let's see what you've got".

▲

Claire's shuttle —the Equus— was more like a luxury yacht than a transport: not what Vol had expected at all. It was a long, slim vessel that easily doubled the Phoenix in length. The ship was transmitting from what looked like a barren area of space, far from any known shipping routes or stations. Vol sensed that it was made to look like she'd broken down mid-flight or maybe even suffered a failed FTL drop. If Tariq's suspicions were correct, Claire was already dead, and the Society was simply trying to crack the codes to her data vault.

"So," Dines mused as he leaned on the Sadalmelik's holotable. "Tell me about the part where your operative stumbled on a communication between Alastair Roth and a Commonwealth Councillor".

"I wish there was more to it than that," Hayward said. "We lost contact with her after she reported it. Then all my other guys started falling off the map too".

Dines furrowed his brow. "Wait, you lost all of your guys in the field?"

"Most of them," Hayward admitted.

Dines straightened, and the frown that filled his expression was of irritation: as though Hayward were saying something amateurish. "Sounds like you've got a leak in your bucket".

"The hell I do!" Hayward raised his voice and puffed out his chest as though Dines had said something wholly insulting. "Who the fuck do you think you are coming aboard my ship and—"

"We don't have time for this," Harrt said, stepping between the pair before they could square off. "We need to get to that ship and stop them from purging all of that data. It might be the only shot we've got to prove that there's a conspiracy".

"He's right," Vol said with her best take-no-prisoners tone. "We've gotta act now. You guys can deal with macho bullshit when we've got the job done, but for now, you've gotta put it all aside and deal with this thing before we lose the chance".

After a few seconds of posturing and glaring intensely at one another, both men conceded. Vol could tell from their thoughts that Hayward and Dines agreed with her and saw the bigger picture, though neither wanted to back down or show weakness in front of the other.

Harrt gestured to the holographic representation of the nearby system. "Any thoughts on how we do this?"

"I don't like the look of this setup," Dines said, gesturing to the starmap. "One lone ship in the middle of nowhere like this... something feels off".

"What'cha thinking?" Hayward folded his arms. "We ain't got time to wait around".

"That, we can both agree on," Dines said, adjusting and rotating the hologram. He plotted a marker on Claire's shuttle, then brought up a sphere representing the ship's potential short-range communication capability. "We've got to disable that ship as quickly possible: take out the engines, the power, maybe even life support".

"So, we take out the FTL engine on Claire's shuttle with a well-placed missile," Vol surmised, leaning across the holotable and pinpointing three locations on the yacht-type shuttlecraft. "Once we are sure they can't get away, we board, take any prisoners and crack that data vault open".

"I couldn't agree more," Dines said with a nod. Then looking at Hayward, "You wanna be a part of the boarding party?"

Hayward's smile seemed more like a challenge to Dines than amusement. The big Earther shrugged with his giant, meaty hands and winked at Dines sarcastically. "I wouldn't have it any other way, cupcake".

▲

The Sadalmelik's pilot was an old Earther, referred to by his crewmates as *Scruffy*. He was a quiet man with a potbelly and a large white beard that came down to his chest, and for some reason, his aftershave reminded Vol of her father. His real name was, in fact, Malcolm, and he'd once served as part of something called the air force back on Earth. Vol had picked up on those little facts just by listening in to the thoughts of Hayward's crew.

"So he's a good pilot?" Vol said, looking at Hayward.

The big man checked a heavy-looking assault rifle and raised his brow to the question. "You mean old Scruffs? Yeah, he's the best pilot I've ever known".

"And you are confident he'll be able to handle a combat situation?"

"That'd be about right," Hayward said, handing the rifle to one of his men. He must've sensed that she was about to offer a protest, so he quickly cut her off. "The fact is that the Sadalmelik is not your ship. Scruffy is my pilot, and he's been flying this thing for years. You are a guest aboard this ship, and we need you to deal with the data vault".

Vol nodded reluctantly, and Hayward responded by handing her a combat vest.

"I know the score," he said, softening his voice. "It's hard to let go: especially when you're good at it, right?"

Vol pulled the combat vest over her head, refusing to answer. Hayward checked the straps on her torso and proceeded to check his gun rack for a suitable weapon. She could sense something at the back of Hayward's mind: *hope maybe?* His focus was on the mission, but a part of him held onto the idea that Claire was alive.

An announcement alarm followed, signalling the crew of the Sadalmelik it was go-time.

"C'mon," Hayward said, gesturing toward the airlock. "Let's do this".

HARRT

The surprise attack on the Equus was over almost before it even began. Dines' gunship approached from the bow, drawing the attention of whoever was onboard the shuttle and prompting them to open fire. Fortunately, the Sadalmelik was able to sneak in from the stern and launch a single missile, killing the engines and primary power aboard the Equus in a single blast.

Inside the airlock, Harrt checked his rifle and waited for the signal. A deep rumbling shook the Sadalmelik as it began docking procedures. Harrt knew that at that very moment, Dines and his team would be boarding from the starboard side —likely near engineering. That meant that whoever was aboard the Equus would need to divide their forces to face their boarders.

The Sadalmelik's boarding party consisting of Harrt, Vol, Hayward, and two crewmates who would take the port side. Dines and his guys would have the headstart, but that was fine, they had the numbers and the skillset to take the brunt of any resistance.

Fifteen seconds later, there was a rumble as the charges detonated. The Sadalmelik's airlock opened with a hiss, and

Hayward stepped forward to take point. Harrt followed Hayward and his men, who'd already fanned out into a military-like formation.

The room they entered was a long, thin corridor covered in a haze of white gas from the emergency systems: *no doubt the attack had caused a few fires.*

Decorative wooden panels covered the walls, giving the place a sleek, modern aesthetic. Hayward and his men activated targetting lasers on their guns, and precise green bars of light filled the space as they began to move deeper into the ship.

While Hayward and his guys led from the front, Harrt and Vol covered the rear. Harrt sealed the airlock, ensuring that nobody could board the Sadelmelik without raising a request for entry. It was an excellent way to ensure that nobody would try and make a quick getaway. Harrt joined Hayward and his team upfront as they pushed toward a wide living space.

All of a sudden, there was a burst of gunfire from ahead, and something soared past Harrt's ear. He didn't comprehend the fact that one of the Sadalmelik's crew had gone down in a haze of blood until he'd pulled Vol into cover, behind what he could only assume was a bar. He looked at the Uvan, and she nodded to signal that she was okay. Vol took up her gun and began firing blindly at the attackers.

Someone yelled, "Contact!"

Harrt was pretty sure that was Hayward, but his brain didn't comprehend it under the circumstances. To his right, a man in partial combat gear burst through a doorway with his gun raised, ready to leverage his advantage against Hayward and his team.

Harrt didn't allow that to happen. He fired twice, the first round missing entirely, but the second caught the man directly in the head. Harrt confirmed the kill, then shuffled back into cover. Bullets continued clanging off the faux wooden walls and glass bottles above the bar as gunfire rained throughout the space.

Hayward and his crewmate were to the left, further ahead than Harrt and Vol but very much exposed to the enemy. Ahead, there were at least four active shooters, two who'd positioned themselves behind an upturned table and another pair who were using a doorway for cover.

For a few seconds, Harrt was pretty sure they'd be fighting until the ammo ran dry, but then something changed. A blast of something elemental passed through one of the walls, carrying with it the mangled body of another armoured hostile.

It looked like an elemental summon.

"What the fuck?" one of the hostile's yelled but was drowned out by gunfire from Hayward's group.

Harrt looked where the elemental summon originated. A hazy cloud of debris and dust kicked up where the interior wall gave way under the attack. Harrt was sure that there was heat emanating from the area. He raised his gun as a figure stepped out from the smoke.

Whoever he was, he wasn't one of the hostiles. He was an Evoker: *Harrt was sure of it.* He was a young caucasian male bordering somewhere between his teenage years and adulthood with a head of blue hair that suggested some Uvan genetics in the mix. He looked unwell, thin, gaunt and bloodied: as though he'd been in a vicious fight seconds earlier.

What followed was chaos. The Evoker cast a summon directly into the men Hayward was fighting. All three hostiles exploded on impact, sending blood and entrails up the walls and ceiling. The fourth and final man ran at him with a knife, but despite the Evoker's apparent injuries, he caught the attackers arm, bending it back until bone and ligament shattered.

The gunman screamed. "You—"

He didn't finish his sentence.

The Evoker snatched the knife from the mercenary's limp hand and plunged it deep into the hostile's throat. Harrt looked on in a mix of horror and confusion as the Evoker hacked into the man without mercy. It was an unusual sight to behold after all; an Evoker looking worse for wear, killing someone without a shred of grace.

The Evoker tossed the dead man aside and looked at Harrt and the others with a wary expression. He was shaking, frightened, maybe even drugged with an inhibitor that made things seem out of alignment.

"Take it easy there, son," Hayward's loud commanding voice filled the room. "We ain't hostile. We're friendly".

The Evoker twitched as he looked at the gun in Hayward's hands. The way he breathed heavily implied to Harrt that he'd been drugged with something potent.

Harrt stepped out of cover, placing his gun on the bar and gently moved toward the Evoker. "I'm Commander Harrt Oxarri of the Commonwealth warship Artemis; we mean you no harm".

"Commonwealth?" the Evoker blinked at Harrt, then at Vol and Hayward and all the others. "The big one isn't Commonwealth. He's like the ones who've been holding me here".

"He's an Earther, but he doesn't mean you any harm," Harrt said, trying to sound reassuring. "What's your name?"

"I.." the Evoker stumbled. "I'm Cadu."

The Evoker breathed something that looked halfway to relieved, then he stumbled forward clumsily. Harrt moved to steady the kid but quickly found the young man collapsing into his arms. As the Evoker fell unconscious, Harrt gently lowered him to the ground.

"Well... shit," Hayward said as he leaned down to check the boy's pulse. He gestured at a series of wounds on the Evoker's arms and wrists. "Looks like he's been through hell". Then to one of his crewmates —a surly-looking Earther who went by the name Riggs: "Get this kid back to the Sadalmelik, and get some damn meds into him".

"You got it, boss," Riggs replied, reaching down to grab the Evoker. He hoisted the kid over his shoulder and carried him back to the airlock.

Harrt looked over at Vol, who was checking on the wounded crewmate from the Sadalmelik.

As their eyes met, Vol shook her head, an action that said everything it needed to:

"He's gone," Vol said, directing her gaze to Hayward.

The big man stiffened.

"Goddamnit," Hayward growled.

▲

Harrt, Vol and Hayward moved through the upmarket vessel with military-like precision. They cleared rooms, checked corners and remained silent throughout using hand signals as their primary form of communication. At first, Harrt hoped that no more hostiles were remaining, but the sound of gunfire suddenly erupted from up ahead. It was coming from the front of the ship: no doubt the cockpit, where the hostiles were likely making a final stand. Hayward directed them toward the commotion, but as the group drew closer, the gunfire seemed to fade.

As Harrt turned a corner, he saw Dines and his marine unit standing in the cockpit with an instrument that looked out of place. The thing looked like metre-tall metallic barrel, with several dents in the side where the hostiles had made a last-ditch effort to destroy it. It was the data vault: Harrt was sure of it. Without asking, Vol rushed over and began plugging her datapad into one of the access ports.

"How long do you think it'll take?" Harrt asked.

"Depends on how good Hayward's engineer is," Vol replied.

Harrt nodded and proceeded to leave the Uvan to her own devices. *Better to let her focus on the task at hand than be a distraction.* At the other end of the room, Dines was leaning over one of the control panels, trying to pull any valuable data that he could.

"Did you meet much resistance?" Dines asked, not taking his eyes off the screen.

"We lost one of the Sadalmelik's guys in the gunfight," Harrt replied. "Then we were saved by an Evoker".

That caught Dines' attention. The silver-haired Agent turned with a quizzical expression on his face. "Say that again?"

Harrt explained how the Evoker —Cadu— had bested the hostiles, then collapsed in a heap. He also pointed out that the kid had clearly been injured —perhaps tortured. As always, Leviticus Dines carried a sceptical look on his chiselled face.

"I need to debrief that Evoker as soon as possible," Dines said. "Something doesn't feel right about this setup; I get the feeling that—"

The panel beside Dines began to alarm. It wasn't a standard alert. Harrt could tell from the loud audio chime that it was intended to catch the attention of everyone in a fifteen-metre radius of the cockpit.

Harrt turned, but his eyes were drawn to the window ahead of him. Outside, something that looked like an energy storm flared to life. Blue strands of lightning formed against the backdrop of the starfield. Harrt recognised it as an incoming FTL drop: but it wasn't a small ship at all.

The shape that emerged from the slipstream was a looming grey mass the size of a warship. Harrt knew its angular, violent design as soon as he laid eyes on it.

"Revenant..." Dines said, his breath quickening.

"We gotta get the fuck outta here," Hayward yelled.

Everything in Harrt's mind slowed.

Harrt couldn't disagree with the Earther's curse-filled statement, but there was a big problem: They'd knocked out the Equus' drive and onboard systems before boarding. That meant the only way to escape was via the Sadalmelik or Dines' gunship, and Harrt was pretty sure the Revenant would open fire before that was even possible.

He became aware of Dines yelling into his comms device: "Get the gunship in a defensive position, hold off any missiles!"

Harrt turned to look at Vol. She was still thumping her datapad, trying to extract the intel from the data vault. There was no time for that now.

In the space of a heartbeat, Vol yanked the cable from her datapad and called to Hayward. The Earther rushed over and ripped the vault from its housing. Harrt was pretty sure it would wipe all the data inside, but it was necessary. If there was a tiny slither of hope that the intel was there, they had to take the chance. Harrt joined Hayward, helping the big man to pull the cylindrical device from the wall. It gave way a second later, and Hayward hoisted it onto his shoulder.

"Go!" Hayward yelled.

Vol grabbed Harrt by the forearm, and they rushed to catch up with Dines, his men, and the last remaining crewman from the Sadalmelik. As they retraced the route back through the Equus' sleek, modern corridors, the ship rocked.

It felt like something had exploded off the starboard bow.

Harrt was pretty sure that they had all but a minute left to live. Experience told him that the Revenant ship would be launching alert fighters and targetting the Equus with its own primary cannons. Sure, Dines' gunship could cause a mild distraction —maybe buy them a few seconds— but it was a much smaller craft with far less weapons capability.

Regardless of the facts, Harrt felt the very primal instinct to live. He didn't want to die. He didn't want Vol to die there. And so he ran as fast as his legs would allow.

The Equus shifted as something breached the port bow. Oxygen flooded toward the breach, and Harrt felt the unmistakable pull of depressurisation.

He kept hold of Vol, practically dragging her toward the Sadalmelik. Ahead, he saw the airlock but didn't allow hope to fill his mind. At the door, Hayward's man was fumbling with the override controls: likely waiting for the Sadalmelik's pilot to open the doors.

Behind, Harrt heard Hayward barking into the comm: "Scruffy! Open the fucking doors!"

The airlock opened and cold air whipped by Harrt as it was dragged toward the front of the Equus. There was a mad dash into the bridge between the two ships: Hayward's man, then the marines, then Dines.

"Go!" Harrt yelled, pushing Vol through the door first.

Another explosion shook the Equus, and Harrt felt the vibration in his gut. *Something had collided with the front of the ship.* The flow of oxygen grew stronger, and Harrt found himself becoming light-headed. He followed Vol into the boarding passage and tapped the door controls, sealing the airlock behind them.

The rush of air toward the Equus ceased. The ground beneath Harrt's feet vibrated as the passage linking the Sadalmelik, and the Equus began to retract. He didn't bother looking back and instead rushed up the tunnel.

Something changed.

There was a bright flash in Harrt's peripheral vision as the Equus exploded. He realised too late that something broke the sealed passage where he was standing. Behind, the tunnel lurched violently, and Harrt felt himself being dragged away from the Sadalmelik.

All his training at the Commonwealth academy kicked in. Harrt ignored the fact that there was no air to breathe and instead concentrated on the fact that his lungs were empty.

That was a good thing. If he held his breath —like his subconscious told him— he'd burst a lung.

He pushed aside the reality that he was freezing cold.

As he felt himself pulled toward space, Harrt fought against the current. He dug his hands into the floor of the boarding tunnel and crawled toward the Sadalmelik.

In his oxygen-starved brain, he saw blinking lights. The world around him began to dim. Then there was a semi-darkness: that felt cold. Part of him wanted to drift toward it, but the other part wanted to live. He listened to that instinct, burrowing his hands into the ground and clinging on for dear life.

He became aware of something —no, someone— grabbing ahold of him. Harrt could barely open his eyes, but when he did, he saw Vol. She was crudely tethered by a chain from inside the Sadalmelik. Harrt wanted to say something, but his lungs and body and brain simply couldn't process it.

Something inside the Sadalmelik retracted the cord around Vol. Then like a particularly stubborn fish swimming upstream, the pair of them moved against the current.

Seconds later, Harrt's awareness shifted, and he was inside the Sadalmelik. The air that filled his lungs was heavy and warm. Vol was knelt beside him, with her hands on his chest. Hayward was sitting against a wall yelling into his communicator, and Dines looked like a man who'd seen one too many events like the one they'd just been through.

Hayward's voice shifted to something akin to surprise. Harrt didn't hear the words at first, but as the air flowed into his lungs, it caught up to him.

"Scruffy, say that again?" Hayward barked.

The voice on the other side of the communication was emotional and overwhelmed, but Harrt was pretty sure he made out the reply.

"You heard me; a 'wealther warship just took that big-ass motherfucker out. Dropped into the area and blew that big Revenant bastard to kingdom come".

"What ship?" Dines demanded.

Scruffy's reply sent a chill down Harrt's spine: "It's called the Artemis. Oxarri, that's your ship, right?"

CHAPTER FIFTEEN
ASTRILLA

The last time Astrilla performed a dropship manoeuvre, it had been at Mirotose Station alongside the Sphinax Resistance when they'd captured Kornell. There was something profoundly worrying about throwing oneself out of a moving ship and into a hostile environment. Granted, it had worked at Mirotose Station, but there was no reason to assume the same would apply here and now. The forthcoming release from the airlock would be at several hundred thousand feet.

Turning to her, Russell raised his brow. Despite his justifiably anxious expression, the former barkeep looked the part of a professional dropship artist.

"So, you've done this a few times, right?" Russell asked.

Astrilla nodded, "I have".

"Huh," Russell mused, then looked to Nathan, "And you've done this as well, cap?"

Nathan pulled the harness around his chest tight, securing a rifle to his back. "It's been a few years, and it wasn't exactly the same scenario, but sure, I've done this...*kinda*". Nathan's voice trailed off, and he unholstered his pistol to recheck the ammo for the ninth time that hour.

Russell looked at them both, then with a shrug, "So... any pointers?"

"Yeah," Nathan said, pushing the magazine into his gun with a snap. "Breathe slow. Focus on where you are heading and whatever you do, don't look down".

Russell nodded and secured a breathing mask over his face.

"You guys ready back there?" Rain's voice came over the comm.

Once she'd secured her mask, Astrilla replied, "We're ready".

The three of them moved to the airlock, waiting for Rain's signal. Astrilla could hear her heart beating as the Phoenix banked downward. If everything went according to plan, she and the others would drop from the Phoenix, and after a few thousand feet, they would land safely.

"Coming up on the target launch site," Rain said. "Launching in three.... two... one".

The airlock in front of Astrilla opened, and a rush of cold air flooded the room. For a heartbeat, her mind told her to retreat: *to run back to safety*. Astrilla refused to give in to that impulse, thinking instead that she wouldn't allow the Revenant to take another Enkaye half-breed like they'd done with her.

Astrilla threw herself out of the Phoenix, aware that Nathan was behind her, and Russell was slightly further ahead. For a split second, she felt weightless: as though she were floating. Then gravity took hold. She plunged down through dark clouds as though fired from the Phoenix's cannons. Astrilla ignored the cold, pushing aside the part of her *—mostly—* human brain that screamed, *this isn't natural.* Instead, she concentrated on the landing location.

Hawtrey House was ahead, and Astrilla allowed herself to look out at the sheer magnitude of everything around her. By comparison to the rolling metropolis of Haydrium's cities, Roth's floating island was nothing more than an anthill. Then again, *scale was everything, especially when looking at the world from a hundred thousand feet.*

The HUD inside Astrilla's helmet highlighted the destination and predicted trajectory of her fall. At first, the landing site was wildly small: a yellow box highlighting the lower levels of Roth's floating island. But as gravity did its job, the destination grew rapidly.

As Astrilla stared at the target below, her consciousness wandered to a place that felt oddly distant. She saw an old bench in the middle of a barren desert where someone *—or something—* was supposed to meet her, but they were absent.

"I cannot do this alone," a voice said across the dunes.

Astrilla barely had time to react as her heads-up-display began to alarm wildly. She was heading toward the target at a dangerous speed and was much farther ahead than Russell: who'd dropped five seconds earlier. Without any second thought, she punched on the dropship gear, and the backpack fired the deceleration mechanism. The short-term thruster on Astrilla's back yanked her away from gravity's whim, slowing her descent to a controllable level. She breathed easy as her momentum slowed and navigated so that she was ten-or-so feet above an industrial-looking walkway. Astrilla landed gracefully, as she'd been taught in her years of study at the Evoker Enclave. Seconds later, Nathan and Russell landed safely. Astrilla discarded her burnt-out backpack, tossing it over the edge of the railing to the city below.

As Nathan and Russell drew their guns, Astrilla spoke into the comms:

"We've landed".

GORDON

Gordon looked over a live holographic projection of Hawtrey House. The strategic plan was overlaid with markers that pinpointed the precise locations of the crew. Koble and Tariq were at the party: split apart but close enough to not cause concern. The audio from their comms channel came through speakers inside the cockpit. Gordon listened to their exchange intently, hearing familiar Paradisian celebrity names that he'd rather forget, as well as something that piqued his interest.

"Who's the muscle with Jareth?" Koble's voice boomed over the speakers.

Gordon could hear fear in Tariq's voice: "This must be the legendary Chimera. I thought he was just a rumour".

Gordon wasn't sure what to make of it, but logic told him that if Tariq was worried, something wasn't right about the situation. He pulled up a heat scan of the Roth Estate, hoping that somehow he could pinpoint the precise location of David Jareth and the man accompanying him, but it was impossible. The bulk of Roth's house lit up like a Christmas tree from the scan. There were hundreds —if not thousands — of partygoers inside the house alone.

"Tell me, my friend," Rain said from the pilot's seat. "What exactly is a Chimera?"

Gordon didn't want to get into a discussion about mythology with the Sphinax, so he kept his answer brief:

"Nothing good".

With Nathan, Astrilla and Russell on the ground, the Phoenix's role in the operation was to withdraw to a safe distance and wait for the EMP. Once detonated, all non-essential power in and around Hawtrey House would fall, thus allowing the Phoenix to return and provide aerial cover for the ground teams.

Now comes the waiting game, Gordon thought as he sat down.

Once again, he had the familiar view of the packed skylanes. Visibility was relatively good despite dark clouds forming in the night's sky. From the co-pilot's seat, he could see the Roth manor and the industrialised city several thousand feet below.

"I don't like this," Gordon remarked. "If the Revenant show up, this whole situation could go sideways very quickly".

"Fear not, my friend. Your ship is currently under the control of one of the finest pilots in the galaxy," Rain offered a confident smile. "I've fought against Jareth warships, Revenant and an entire Horrus militia. None of them have stopped me so far".

Gordon dismissed the comment, assuming it was nothing more than typical Sphinax bravado. Sure, Rain was an excellent pilot: he'd more than proved that during the Battle of the Messorem, but Gordon was a glass-half-empty kinda guy and for good reason. Experience had taught Gordon that death was around every corner. It didn't matter if you were the best or worst pilot; if the numbers were stacked against you, that was it —s*imple mathematics.*

"Mind if I ask you something?" Gordon turned to Rain.

"Sure?" the Sphinax shrugged.

"Wasn't it Jareth Corps that played a significant part in Kornell's rise to power?"

Rain shifted uncomfortably in his chair. "Jareth Corps is the only reason why Kornell and his band of thugs won".

"So, why'd Jareth do it?"

"They say that in return for his services, Kornell gave David Jareth access to all the Enkaye temples on Pluvium".

"All of the temples?" Gordon raised his brow. "You mean all three of them?"

Rain nodded. Then, "David Jareth started a war, so he could get his hands on the trinkets of a long-dead race. I just don't get how anyone can turn their sense of morality off like that".

"Jareth believes that the Earthers were destined to inherit the Enkaye's power and technology. The man is obsessed with putting the people of Earth back on the map. He thinks that Enkaye tech is the only way to do so."

Kyp buzzed momentarily in the corner, still processing the data from the recovered combat recorder. As Rain continued to talk, Gordon checked his watch. It was just over twelve hours until Kyp completed the hack. With everything that had gone on since finding the dead mercenaries on Levave, Gordon had almost forgotten about the droid. Given the current circumstances, the murdered cohort of mercenaries seemed trivial, but still, Gordon couldn't help but wonder what killed all those people in such brutal fashion. It was fascinating, in a morbid way, but it wasn't as pertinent as the matter at hand. The rescue of James Stephens had to take precedent, so Gordon pushed his wonder aside *—for now.*

He wondered what kind of man James had become. Yes, he was the son of Jack, but he was also the grandson of Bill: Gordon's mentor and friend from long ago. The last time Gordon saw him, James had been a young, grumpy teenager, and they'd barely interacted. At the time —and still, maybe today— Gordon had a mild aversion to children, teenagers and pets, so he'd likely avoided conversation with James back then.

Just don't be like Jack, Gordon hoped. *Be better. Please.*

Gordon was suddenly dragged away from his thoughts as Rain continued to waffle about the war. The Sphinax seemed blissfully unaware that he'd drifted away from their conversation, so Gordon didn't acknowledge it out of sheer social anxiety.

"I was lucky..." Rain furrowed his dark brow: clearly uncomfortable with whatever he was recounting. "In the war, we made our final stand at Triumph Place; hauled up in the old city hall," Rain said, his voice low and thoughtful. "We were outmanned and outgunned fifty-to-one. Kornell and Jareth's combined forces were on us, and I was pretty sure I was about to die".

"How did you get out?"

Rain smiled as he answered; "Jack Stephens".

Gordon felt his heart sink and his gut tighten at the mere mention of the man, who he loathed more than anyone —or anything— in the universe.

"Jack volunteered to *parle*. That crazy son-of-a-bitch went out there alone and faced Kornell and Jareth's main commando guy armed with only a pistol and machete".

"Did he now?" Gordon tried his best to sound impressed, but it was difficult. He didn't like talking about Jack. In fact, he'd made it his mission to forget the man. The memory and legacy of the former EDA agent hung onto Gordon like an enormous weight on his shoulders.

Rain talked for a while about *the legendary Jack*, and Gordon did his best to ignore it. After all, Gordon was one of the few people who knew *the real* Jack: not the heroic man that Rain —and many others— described. Finally, when Rain was done regaling Gordon with the tale, he capped it off with a statement that made Gordon feel sick.

"Jack was a true hero".

Gordon fought the urge to reply. He wanted to tell the Sphinax that *Jack Stephens was not a hero. That he was a crook and a liar and a killer.*

But of course, he said nothing. Much to Gordon's chagrin, preserving the lie —no, the myth— of Jack was all that mattered now.

NATHAN

The lower floor of Hawtrey House was a total contrast to the grounds above. Where Koble and Tariq were exploring an exquisite, stately home, Nathan, Astrilla, and Russell found themselves sleuthed through an almost military-like facility.

Upon entering the building, they encountered a trio of unsuspecting guards, who were taken out quickly and quietly. In Nathan's view, avoiding detection was the key to the entire operation. He hoped they could maintain that status-quo throughout, but experience told him that probably wouldn't be the case. So he settled for the idea that avoiding detection was vital until fate said otherwise. Everything else after that was good fortune.

After a few more minutes of stealthily navigating the facility, the group stumbled upon a dark warehouse filled with giant floor-to-ceiling racks. When Nathan activated his flashlight, he saw what was stored there and found himself open-mouthed in shock. He saw thousands upon thousands of valuables: everything from paintings and sculptures to a collection of classic sports cars.

The sheer decadence of Roth's collection was stupefying but not surprising in any way, shape or form. Jack had always maintained that Paradisians were greedy and only interested in material items. And it appeared that the Roth family fit that statement like a glove.

As much as Nathan wanted to comment on everything he was seeing, he forced himself back into the moment: back into the operation. He raised his rifle and continued through the warehouse until they were back on track.

▲

The large doors to the security centre were unguarded: *that was the good news*. The bad news was that they were sealed from the inside, meaning that the only way to get in was to force them open. Practically speaking, that wasn't a hindrance: Astrilla could break the doors down in a matter of seconds using elemental summons. The problem was that once the doors were busted open, everyone inside would be aware of it and would raise the alarm: drawing the unwanted attention they were trying to avoid.

There was no other option, but that didn't mean Nathan couldn't deploy a little pragmatism. He shouldered his backpack and pulled the additional EMP charge that he'd packed earlier.

When it comes to weaponry or ammo, bring spares, Jack's voice spoke inside his head.

Nathan was quick to rig the charge to detonate upon impact. Basically, it was now a grenade that wouldn't create an explosion but would temporarily take out most —if not all— the security centre's electrical devices. It wasn't ideal, but it would buy enough time to deal with whoever was staffing the security centre. Tariq's intel had loosely estimated a team of five, but that meant very little in reality. For all Nathan knew, there could be two dozen, or there could be one.

He gave Astrilla the signal and watched as she raised her palms upward. The air around her whipped up as though she were standing in the eye of a hurricane. A bolt of cyan energy formed at her fingertips: corkscrewing around her hands, wrists and forearms until all Nathan could see was an iridescent glow. As Astrilla unleashed the elemental summon, the reinforced bunker-style door exploded inward. The smell of melting steel filled the corridor, and thick acrid steam plumed outward. Before anything or anyone could react, Nathan tossed the rigged EMP charge into the security centre.

The electromagnetic pulse that followed was a contained blast that only affected equipment within a ten-to-fifteen foot radius. First, there was a crackle from inside the security centre, then a panicked yelp. Then all the lights around the former door flickered and died in quick succession.

"Move," Nathan ordered.

Gunfire erupted around the room. By Nathan's best guess, there were three —maybe four— active shooters. Two at the front were armed with nothing more than a pistol; they were also the ones who'd taken the brunt of Astrilla's initial attack. One at the rear had dug in behind cover and used what sounded like a modified Earth MP5.

The first two were unconscious within seconds, as Russell fired a stun round into each of them. The guy armed with the MP5 angled his weapon over the edge of the now-defunct holotable and sprayed burst after burst of weapons fire toward them.

Nathan quickly darted into cover, placing himself ahead of Astrilla and Russell by several metres. Bullets whipped across the room, suggesting that the gunman knew he was outnumbered. When the hostile stopped to reload, Nathan rushed from cover and placed himself in a flanking position. The mercenary-turned-security guard didn't spot him in time. Nathan fired a shot that sent the man flying to the ground in a heap.

"Is it me, or is this way too easy?" Nathan said, peering at Russell and Astrilla.

"Who knows... maybe the universe is actually on our side, for once," Russell shrugged. The former barkeep swung his backpack over one shoulder and began to rustle inside for items. He produced the EMP charges that Nathan gave him earlier. "Just show me where and I'll get to work on planting these things," Russell said.

Nathan gestured to the next room, where the critical systems to the manor were housed behind another sealed door. Once Astrilla had blown the door down with a summon, Russell rushed inside and began planting the charges. The Roths had clearly designed the place with a view of making interference as tricky as possible: keeping the basic electrical systems behind a security centre and two gunfire-proof doors pretty much proved that point.

Nathan glanced around the security centre, checking if any systems had come back online or even survived the small EMP blast. Most hadn't, but a few overhead monitors provided live footage from a security feed in the garden. It wasn't a bad thing *—it at least confirmed that a rigged EMP could work temporarily—* but Nathan had hoped they could use all of the security systems to keep an eye on things in the house. Sadly, that wasn't the case, but he still had Tariq and Koble as his eyes and ears above.

Nathan tapped on his communicator: "Koble, Tariq, what's your status?"

There was a long pause, then Tariq replied, "There is a crowd forming around a stage in the gardens. Looks like someone is going to make a speech."

Nathan checked his datapad, seeing Tariq and Koble's positions plotted on the schematic of the house. Koble was near the staging area in the west garden, while Tariq was several floors above, watching from what Nathan assumed was a balcony.

"Do you still have eyes on Jareth?" Nathan asked.

"Partially," Tariq answered behind a pant. It sounded like he was darting from room to room, trying to avoid detection. "Jareth and Chimera moved away from the crowd a few minutes ago. They've been heading to the upper floors for a while now. I'm trying to stick to his tail and find out where he's going".

"Copy that; keep us updated," Nathan said. "Koble? What's going on? Are you still tracking Christian Roth?"

"Yup," the Sphinax chewed. Nathan imagined him gnawing on a snack as he spoke. "Little Roth's been busy; lots of hugs, handshakes and crappy jokes. Looks like he's heading for the stage to make the big speech".

"Surely the Roths are drawing more attention to themselves?" Astrilla said from the back of the room. "I thought the Society were supposed to be more subtle than this?"

Koble's witty reply came back over the communicator; "These assholes are just trying to impress their pals".

JARETH

When it was announced that Christian Roth was set to make

a speech, a strange air of excitement came over the guests: like an old rock band were about to make a comeback after decades of hiatus. Jareth never appreciated Earth's celebrity culture, but he understood enough not to question why someone like Christian could amass such a following. He was, after all, a handsome young man in the prime of his life: witty and charismatic and oozing with charm.

But that was only on the surface.

A crowd migrated toward a staging area at pace: desperate to get a good view of Christian as he delivered what would be a historic speech. With most partygoers distracted by the glitz and glamour, Jareth had the opening he and Chimera needed to navigate Hawtrey House.

According to the intel that Chimera amassed, there were three methods to get to the roof. The first —and most direct— was a service elevator that ran from the lower levels to the top floor. Sure, it was a time-saver, but the problem was that Roth had two guards posted at every entrance. Chimera was an outstanding combatant and no doubt could best a pair of guards in seconds, but it would mean leaving bodies hanging around, and there were too many people and too many alarms.

The second route was a long, fire safety approved staircase that practically ran beside the elevator shaft. It was a direct route, but there was a high chance that Roth's administrative staff would use it to pass between the offices below and the house above. That left the third option, sneaking through the manor, into the library on the top floor, then into Christian's rooftop garden. From there, it would be easy: get to James Stephens, inject him with a lethal arterial bomb, wait for Baylum and Roth to show, then flip the switch.

It was terrible to know that James Stephens, son of Jack, would be caught up in the mix, but Jareth knew this was the only way. *The lives of the many outweigh the lives of the few.* Project Erebus, the Society and the Revenant King could be stopped in one fell swoop. That was worth more than the life of one man. The problem was that Chimera couldn't know it was James Stephens being traded. If he did, drama could ensue, and Jareth couldn't afford that: *the galaxy couldn't afford that.*

As he and Chimera sleuthed through Roth's giant manor, Jareth was sure to keep an eye on the path ahead. There was a feeling in the pit of his stomach that suggested they were being watched, but Jareth put it down to nerves. He wasn't a man of combat like Chimera, so being on the frontlines felt entirely alien, but Jareth had to be there: *he had to be the one to put an end to Roth and Baylum.*

He had to make right the wrongs of his father.

Chimera moved with a quiet confidence that suggested they were relatively safe. When they came upon a pair of Society henchmen, Chimera dispatched them with the kind of brutal yet silent efficiency that was expected.

The man, now known as Chimera, was once a field agent for the Earth Defense Alliance. He'd been trained in all manners of combat and, despite his age, showed no sign of slowing down.

Most people would feel intimidated by Chimera, but it wasn't the case for Jareth. He recognised that he and the hitman were no different, despite a number of differences that back in the days of Earth would've seen them in entirely different circles. Jareth and Chimera served a common cause, and that made them allies.

As they came upon the library, Jareth stared at the massive floor-to-ceiling bookcases that filled the room. There were glass display cases at regular intervals that contained priceless items from Roth's collection.

"Their greed knows no bounds," Jareth said as he looked upon a handwritten version of something victorian and no doubt valuable.

Chimera didn't acknowledge the comment immediately. Instead, he checked the corners of the room with his gun raised, making sure that nobody was waiting for them.

"Coast is clear," Chimera said, pointing to a staircase at the back of the room. "Let's get this over and done with".

▲

Despite having minimal combat training, Jareth knew to examine his surroundings when entering a hostile environment. He noted the exits, places to take cover, and hiding spots. As it happened, the rooftop was quieter than he'd expected. Two armed guards were the only thing guarding Christian Roth's rooftop garden, and they were silently subdued by Chimera in the space of a heartbeat.

The east wing of the house was covered in a sloping roof, whereas the western side was entirely flat, with a landing pad at the centre. Jareth counted four doorways on each corner of the west roof where a civilian shuttle was being unloaded by three unarmed warehousemen.

Chimera lifted his pistol, but Jareth stopped him.

"No need to kill postmen, old boy, just deal with them in a non-lethal manner".

Chimera nodded, and seconds later, the three civilians were down. *Unconscious but not dead.* Jareth stepped over one of them and looked to the shuttle where a containment chamber containing James Stephens was ready to be offloaded.

This was the critical moment. *Chimera couldn't know the truth.*

"Stand watch, old boy," Jareth said casually. "I'll deal with this".

Thankfully, Chimera nodded in agreement.

Jareth proceeded toward the containment chamber and stopped at the casket shaped device.

He waited until Chimera turned his back, then brushed aside thick condensation from the glass viewing pane.

Despite his medically induced unconscious state, James Stephens was almost the spitting image of his father, Jack. His blondish hair was beginning to show early signs of grey, and his wide jaw reminded Jareth of the first time he and Jack met all those years ago. Then subtle differences told him that he was looking at a very different man.

Where Jack had been clean-shaven, James maintained a full beard. Where Jack's eyes had been prominent, James had a more sunken look to them. In a way, Jareth felt sorry to use the son of Jack in such a way, but he had no other choice. This was the one and only shot to take out Roth and Baylum once and for all. *Jack would understand.*

Realising he had little time to waste, Jareth subtly removed a syringe from his jacket pocket. He found the input valve for the intravenous system, and without hesitation, he stabbed the needle into it. Jareth pushed down the plunger, injecting James Stephens with the arterial bomb that would kill the galaxy's greatest criminals.

"Please forgive me," Jareth whispered to the unconscious man inside. "This is the only way. I hope you understand".

The device would be embedded within thirty seconds. After that, Jareth would have to wait for the right moment and transmit the detonate code. After he'd said his part, David Jareth returned to Chimera.

"Let's go," Jareth said. "We need to—"

Jareth was too slow to notice the sighting laser on his chest, but Chimera wasn't. The big man shoved Jareth to the ground as a high calibre laser flew past them. It was a sniper round from what Jareth assumed was the southern roof. Chimera whipped around, placing himself between Jareth and the shooter, and opened fire.

"Move," Chimera yelled. "Get to the stairwell".

Jareth wasted no time in following the command. He darted across the roof, narrowly avoiding a second round from the sniper. Gunfire from Chimera continued to ring out as Jareth ran, and for a moment, he was sure that Chimera confirmed the kill. As he neared the door to the stairwell, it burst open, and Jareth came face to face with a group of mercenaries, led by the notorious serial killer, Bradley Austin.

As Jareth backed up, Alastair Roth stepped out from the mercenaries with a victorious smile on his rotund face.

"Well, well," Roth said triumphantly. "Looks like someone strayed away from the celebration".

CHAPTER SIXTEEN
NATHAN

With the charges planted, Nathan, Astrilla and Russell headed toward a service lift, which would take them as far as the top floor. Once there, they could then detonate the EMP and take a single flight of stairs to the roof and free James. On paper, it sounded simple, but Nathan had learnt to expect the worst in pretty much all situations.

As the elevator began its ascent, Nathan checked that his handgun was loaded before opening a comms channel to the crew.

"Charges are planted; we're en route to the roof. Expect the EMP to go off in two minutes," he said. "Rain, Gordon, keep the Phoenix out of the area for another two minutes after the blast. We can't risk the ship going down".

"But of course, my friend. Don't worry, your ship is in safe hands". Rain's voice was buttery smooth.

Nathan nodded, even though the blue-haired Sphinax couldn't see him. "Just be ready".

Nathan turned his attention to Koble and Tariq, who were still inside the house, keeping an eye on the party. "Koble, Tariq, what's the latest?"

"Looks like Roth Junior is taking the stage any minute," Koble replied. "Can't wait to see the look on this douchebag's face when all the lights go down, and we ruin his five minutes of fame".

Nathan could almost picture Koble's smug, satisfied smirk but quickly addressed Tariq, aware that he'd not replied throughout the exchange.

"Tariq?" Nathan said.

There was no reply.

"Tariq?"

Static filled the channel.

As Nathan shut down the comms, Astrilla said, "That can't be good".

He didn't reply.

A minute later, the service lift stopped on the top floor. The doors opened up onto a totally different environment from the lower levels. Where before, the group had been exploring a sterile metal environment, they now found themselves in something akin to a high-end hotel lobby. The plush cream carpet was soft underfoot, and walls had been papered to precision. The primary source of light came from a series of crystal chandeliers, which were hung from the art-deco style ceiling.

As Nathan stepped out of the elevator, the sound of thunderous applause came from the gardens. It sounded like a concert, or maybe even a protest march: the kind of thing Nathan had only ever heard through recordings or news broadcasts.

A thousand voices cheered in adulation for well over a minute.

Nathan looked at Russell, "Prep the charges".

CHRISTIAN

Christian was the heir to the Roth fortune, the future chairman of the Society and —soon— the first president of Paradisium. At thirty-two years of age, Christian was considered one of the galaxy's hottest up-and-comers.

His public persona —up until that point— was that of *the philanthropist-bad-boy:* at least that's what his public relations agent had told him.

The *real* Christian was, in many ways, the antithesis of

what the press made of him. Sure he liked to party, drink and enjoy the delicacies of the good life, but he was also highly intelligent —groomed to be the next great man of the Roth family.

The audience *—no, Christian's audience—* cheered and applauded him as he took to the stage accompanied by a musical track that sounded both victorious and powerful. He soaked in the adoration like it was a fresh hit of Ice, and it felt fucking amazing.

When the cheering died down, Christian stood in silence, looking at the faces of those who would one day be his subjects. This was his moment to shine: to re-invent himself. No longer would Christian Roth be the *petulant, spoiled whorehound.* After this momentous moment, he would be *Christian Roth: visionary.*

He took a deep breath, cleared his throat and began.

"Revenge for the fallen..."

A gentle murmur rippled amongst the crowd.

Christian pulled the microphone from its stand and glared out at his adoring followers. He let his words linger before continuing:

"Revenge for the fallen!" Christian repeated, this time with more aggression.

He knew at that moment that every eye in the audience was on him, and he liked the way it felt.

"Revenge. For. The. Fallen".

When the audience repeated his words, Christian consciously hid his pleasure.

"My friends, I was just a boy when I survived the Fall. I remember the day our world —our Earth— was ripped away from us. I remember the smell of burning bodies. I remember".

Christian paused for effect, pretending to bite back of tears of patriotism.

"I remember the bloodshed and the violence inflicted on our people on that terrible day. I remember the injustice. I remember the fear".

NATHAN

Thanks to Koble's close proximity to the stage, Nathan could hear Christian Roth's voice through the comm feed. He couldn't help but clench his fist at the man's blatant lies. Nathan knew all too well where the Roth family had been on the day of the Fall: hiding on a private shuttle, unwilling to save anyone but themselves.

Astrilla must've sensed his anger as she turned and glanced at him. Nathan's gaze met hers, and he sighed.

"The Roths were hiding," Nathan muttered as Christian's speech continued to play. "It's all bullshit —all of it."

CHRISTIAN

"Ever since the Fall, the 'wealth has forced their rules and laws upon our people," Christian yelled. "Well, I've got some news for Inon Waife and his precious council: that is not a democracy. *That* is a dictatorship. We have proven that we —the free people of Paradisium— disagree with that way of life".

There came a roar of applause in response. It lasted far longer than Christian expected, but he wasn't complaining. The almost devout way in which his adoring fans responded made him feel unstoppable.

"Yesterday, we proved that the people of Paradisium will not be bullied. The people of Earth —of Paradisium— voted in favour of the EWB. Nobody will stop us from carving out our own destiny. Nobody!"

As Christian took a deep breath, yells of agreement came from the audience. He heard everything from *aye* to *bloody right* to *fuck the 'wealth* in the space of seconds.

They were eating out of the palm of his hand: s*heep to the slaughter.*

"This gathering is to honour the brave men and women who fought for our independence: who fought for our EWB. The people who pulled us from the yoke of an unelected communist regime and restored democracy and freedom to our lands".

Christian allowed himself to smile as the crowd cheered for him. This was *his* moment, and nothing would stop him from going down in history.

"Tonight, my friends, we honour those who fought for our future".

NATHAN

Nathan stopped at the metal fire door for the stairwell. He pulled his handgun from its holster, knowing that once they got to the southern roof, there would likely be a battle. Christian Roth's arrogant voice continued through the communication, spouting lies and deceit to the crowd of gullible morons below. Nathan checked his datapad, confirming that the Phoenix was outside the blast radius, then turned to Russell.

"Can I shut this asshole up now?" Russell said, holding the detonator in anticipation.

"Do it," Nathan said.

CHRISTIAN

Christian wondered how the history books would record that very moment. He imagined that the scholars would liken it to Demosthenes, who rallied the Athenians to take up arms against the forces of Phillip of Macedo. The everyman of Earth —or Paradisium— would draw a comparison to Churchill or maybe even Abraham Lincoln: *one for those with a basic knowledge of history*. His brothers and sisters of the Society would see a great deal of Alastair Roth in Christian, likely seeing him as more youthful and dynamic and —perhaps— more prosperous than the current chairman. Regardless, the Society would look at Christian and realise that when he took power, he was not to be challenged: that his rule was sacred.

Most importantly of all, Christian kept the eyes of a thousand fools locked on him whilst his father initiated the greatest —if not craziest— plan in recent history. Maybe it would work, and Alastair Roth would reap the power of Project Erebus. The Roth family would become unstoppable, and there would be no 'wealth, no Revenant and no Society.

True power, at the hands of the pure.

As he gave his closing remarks, Christian gestured to one of the stagehands to pass him a fresh glass of champagne to toast. It felt right to cap off such a legendary moment with a tribute to distract the gullable masses.

When he finally had his drink, Christian thrust it into the air, and many of his adoring supporters began to follow.

"Tonight, my friends, let us raise our glasses in honour of the heroes who not only secured our future but also the future of our children and grandchildren".

Dozens, then hundreds, then maybe even thousands of glasses were raised at his command. Again, Christian felt the pulse of adrenaline, knowing that they worshipped him.

"To the bold and the brave. To a new dawn. To a—"

Suddenly all of the lights on the stage fell dark, and the microphone in Christian's hand fell silent. Something rocked the entirety of his floating palace that felt like a mild tremor. It wasn't an explosion, but Christian could've sworn he felt a change in the air. He swung his head around, noticing that the lighting around Hawtrey House had failed.

As his crowd began to stir in confusion, Christian's stage manager ran over to him with a dead datapad in her hand.

"Don't worry, probably just a power cut. We'll get the guys in engineering to reboot the system".

Christian's heart sank into his stomach. This was supposed to be his time to shine —his monumental entry into the history books. It had gone so well until that point, but now it was marred by a power failure.

Christian's embarrassment turned to rage, and he grabbed the stage manager by the throat, pinning her to the wall —out of sight of the audience. The small woman gasped under his grip but didn't dare resist.

"Get me my fucking power back now!" Christian hissed. "Make it happen, or I will have your head".

JARETH

"Well, well, looks like someone has strayed away from the celebrations…" Roth's voice oozed with condescension.

Jareth hadn't heard him use that particular tone for many years: likely in the pre-Fall era, when Jareth's father had been the Society chairman and Roth his protege. Somehow Roth figured out what he'd been planning for the last few months, and now David Jareth was staring at a small army of Society mercenaries: *all with their weapons trained on him*.

Over his shoulder, he became innately aware that Chimera hadn't dropped his gun and was now pointing it at the men flanking Roth. The situation was terrible, but if Jareth could lure Roth into the open, then perhaps there was still a chance.

"Did you really think you could pull one over on me, David?" Roth said as he stepped out of the stairwell. "I've known for decades that you have been plotting revenge against me..."

Jareth didn't say anything, and the hum of James Stephens' containment chamber filled the silence.

"When they told me that Titus Rousseau was dead, I suspected it was you," Roth continued. "When they told me that Martin Cleave had vanished, I knew. I know you've been out of the loop with the Society and our ways for decades, so let me refresh your memory on how things work. We control; we manipulate; we exploit and influence the course of history to meet our wants and desires. We know all, see all and control all. Did you really think that you could stop us from achieving our goals, David?"

Again, Jareth said nothing. He could almost imagine Chimera's thought process for getting them out of the situation. The masked man would be pulling on every ounce of his EDA training, assessing Roth's men to the last detail and lining up the optimum escape route.

For a heartbeat, something about the air changed. At first, it was subtle: a pulse or a hum that seemed to bypass natural sensation. Then Jareth felt the hairs on his body stand to attention as though he'd suffered a static shock from a balloon. What followed was something akin to a vibration: that would just about move dust from shelves.

Then all the lights died. The hum of James Stephens' containment chamber ceased, and Jareth knew three facts about the situation.

One: something that felt like an EMP blast had detonated inside Hawtrey, killing the power to most —if not all— electrical devices. That raised a slew of questions by its own merit, but he didn't have the time to think about it.

Two: the arterial bomb inside Stephens' veins was now inert. Sure it was still a floating piece of nanotech that the body would naturally consume in the next few days, but it was no longer the lethal explosive Jareth needed.

The third and most pressing fact was that Chimera now had his opening, and Jareth had to get away from the fighting that was about to commence.

Darkness settled, and without thinking, Jareth darted to the floor as bullets and laser fire began to fly. By design, Chimera used the dark to his advantage, camouflaged within it like a shadow against the black of space. The only hint of the masked man's ever-changing position was the odd burst of gunfire that lit up the area around him.

Jareth didn't worry about his associate: he didn't need to. Chimera was experienced enough to get out of situations just like this with minimal effort. He'd done so a hundred times before: just as the EDA trained him. Jareth bellycrawled until he was far enough away from the carnage that he could blend in with the shadows. He took cover behind a steel heating vent not far from where Jareth believed Chimera had last been.

A red, fiery light suddenly illuminated the roof as Roth's men began popping flares about the place. Jareth lifted his head from cover, spotting Chimera toward the west, fighting off two gunmen with unsurprising ease. Alastair Roth was still at the entrance to the stairwell, flanked by a half dozen guards, barking orders to the rest of his men to shoot Chimera.

Suddenly, one of the men beside Roth keeled over, and a spray of blood flew up against the wall. Jareth was certain that the silenced gunshot hadn't come from Chimera. When he turned his head to look at his masked accomplice, the big man was still in the process of pummelling one of the Society goons.

The fighting ceased as a suited man of middle eastern descent stepped out from the stairwell behind Roth, his dual pistols trained on both the Society chairman and Jareth at the same time.

"Tariq Mahmoot..." Roth smirked knowingly. "We meet at last".

The name rang bells inside Jareth's head, but he couldn't place it: not there, not in a stressful combat situation. Jareth was about ready to reach for the gun concealed behind his suit jacket when Tariq's gaze snapped to him.

"I wouldn't do that if I were you, Mr Jareth," he warned.

Whoever Tariq Mahmoot was, he was either brave or stupid. He stood amongst a crowd of heavily armed Society mercenaries —plus Chimera— armed with two pistols, which meant he was either a brilliant shot or had some sort of plan. Still, Jareth was pretty sure that Tariq had perfect aim on both him and Roth at the same time.

"Mr Chimera," Tariq said while keeping his gaze locked on Jareth. "Drop that pistol, or I will be forced to shoot your employer".

Jareth turned his head slightly to look at the masked mercenary and gave a slow nod of approval. Chimera tossed his pistol to the ground, but Jareth knew the mercenary would be concealing a second weapon on his person.

Tariq's gaze didn't waver as he stared at Jareth, though something wasn't right about his expression. Jareth had lived through enough board meetings and negotiations to know when someone was taken aback by a strange circumstance.

Regardless, Jareth raised his palms in a not-quite-surrendering fashion, hoping the middle-eastern man would assume he was complying. Tariq's jaw clenched as he glared at Jareth, but his head quickly snapped to Roth.

"Have your men open that containment chamber this instant," Tariq ordered.

Alastair Roth glanced around at his men before laughing. "I will do no such thing. Of course, you are welcome to try for yourself..."

That was the moment Tariq Mahmoot allowed emotion to break his cool demeanour: Jareth could see it from a mile away. The dark eyebrows on Tariq's face lowered, his nostrils flared, and his eyes grew wide with anger. Something learned over years of experience told Jareth that Tariq Mahmoot held a personal interest in that very situation. Perhaps Roth had wronged him in the past, or maybe he was a close friend or lover of James Stephens.

Either way, the man was reacting with emotion and not with logic. It would be easy to conclude that Tariq was a simple gun for hire if it were the latter, but it wasn't the case. Roth had pushed Tariq's buttons, knowing he'd get a reaction in response: *that was how Roth worked.*

The question was, *what kind of reaction?*

Then*, could Jareth use it to his advantage?*

Tariq edged closer to Roth with hatred in his voice, peeling his attention away from Jareth and Chimera. Tariq screamed at the top of his lungs, "Open the chamber now!"

That was the moment to react.

In a swift movement, Chimera pulled his second pistol and pointed it at Tariq, Roth and the dozen or so mercenaries. Jareth knew that this was to be the shit storm: *the moment to potentially fear for one's life.*

He knew Chimera's pistol likely held ten —*maybe twelve*— rounds. The masked man could do an awful lot of damage with that.

Chimera would kill Roth first —per the mission. Then he'd shoot Mahmoot and anyone else in Roth's band of thugs until he ran out of ammo.

Naturally, gunfire and violence were to be expected, but what Jareth heard next sounded more like a crack of lightning. A short, precise burst of Elemental Energy erupted from the south roof, colliding with Chimera's pistol and casting the weapon from the masked man's grip.

"Nobody moves a muscle," someone yelled from the shadows. "Hands up, or we start shooting".

Jareth hadn't heard the voice in a while, but he placed it immediately. It belonged to the man who sleighed King Seig at the battle of the Messorem. The same man who'd refused to give the Enkaye war machine to his own people. A man whose estranged cousin was lying in the containment chamber mere metres away.

The voice belonged to the Captain of the Phoenix Titan.

Nathan Carter.

Nathan moved from the shadows, armed with a heavy assault rifle. Despite the long dark hair and beard, Nathan reminded Jareth of Jack Stephens. There was something about how he moved: how he assessed the situation was eerily similar.

Seeing him there was entirely wrong. It was the kind of thing that Jareth hadn't anticipated: the kind of thing that would lay waste to months of scheming and plotting. Sure, Jareth had expected things to not go precisely to plan. He'd theorised a plethora of ways in which his entire operation to take down Roth and Baylum could go awry, but Nathan Carter was not one of them: *why would he be?*

Jareth realised that something was horribly wrong. *He wondered if Roth had outplayed him or if the universe simply saw the whole thing as a big joke.*

Regardless, only two things mattered now: *killing Roth and escaping.*

NATHAN

A light drizzle began to fall from the skies as Nathan pointed his gun at the group before him. David Jareth was to the left, taking cover behind a metal ventilation shaft, still in his dinner jacket and looking far more collected than he had any right to be.

Alastair Roth was almost unrecognisable from the picture in Nathan's head. Granted, when Nathan escaped the Fall aboard Roth's evac shuttle, the man had been far younger and thinner.

Now, Roth was decades older, much wider and somehow amused by the situation. He had jowls that sagged beyond his weak jawline. His white-circled sun-tan eyes and strange off-grey comb-over hair didn't lend to his overall appearance.

He looked like a caricature: what someone thought a victorian-era politician should look like.

Despite Jareth and Roth —two titans of Paradisium— being there, they weren't the thing that caught Nathan's attention.

Jareth's associate, the masked man in black, looked like something that didn't fit. Whoever he was, the mercenary clearly had a taste for the theatrical, but despite the get-up, Nathan knew his type all too well. He was a professional gun-for-hire. Not the kind of slop that would work for the Criminal Syndicate, nor a crazed lunatic with a gun. No, this mercenary was the kind that came with a hefty price tag or —perhaps worse— a cause to believe in.

This was the man Koble had spoken about over comms.

The walking spectre of death.

The one called, Chimera.

Nathan took point, moving to within metres of the standoff, with Astrilla and Russell at his side. He was aware that Russell had a gun directed at Jareth while Astrilla kept her eyes on Roth's militia. Tariq was in the mix as well, with his pistols aimed at Roth, and there humming away in the background was the containment chamber that held James.

"Carter?" Jareth said, his voice full of shock. "What in the world are you doing?"

"Shut your mouth!" Nathan barked as he moved in.

He trained his gun on Roth, who was now surrounded by his entourage of armed thugs: men creating a wall of human shields around the Society Chairman. *That was the kind of loyalty you couldn't buy.*

"Welcome to the party, Captain Carter," Alastair Roth smirked. "I've been waiting for this moment for a very long time".

On the surface, Roth's arrogance seemed dramatically misplaced, but Nathan had seen his type before: the kind of man who wouldn't admit defeat, even with a gun to his head. *Maybe he wasn't that different from the man Jack had threatened on the day of the Fall?*

"Open the containment chamber," Nathan ordered. "Now!"

Roth's smile was feral and triumphant as he glanced down at the gold watch on his wrist. The old man whistled something musical that seemed victorious and out of place under the circumstances. Nathan was about ready to issue a threat when Roth's eyes peeled upward and met his gaze once again.

"I'm sorry, Captain Carter, but I'm afraid that is no longer an option," Roth said. "You see, there's a hard lesson that people like you need to learn about the Society..."

A gust of wind passed across the space where they stood, and Nathan could tell in the pit of his stomach that something wasn't right. In the space of a heartbeat, Nathan sensed something in the atmosphere change. An inhuman and unnatural force bore down in the skies above, pushing the air outward like something exploding in the clouds.

"The Society always wins," Roth declared.

Blue lightning manifested as something huge poured out of an FTL slipstream, dangerously close to Hawtrey House. The ship was a jagged, vicious-looking beast, big enough for a crew of hundreds and a mutant horde of thousands.

It was a Revenant Behemoth: a warship designed only for the monarchy.

The only thing Nathan heard before the fighting commenced was the voice of David Jareth: "Oh, bugger," he said.

Gunfire erupted on the roof as a portion of Roth's men ushered the Society Chairman to safety. The remainder of Roth's thugs began to open fire on everyone else, including Chimera.

Nathan took up his gun and fired, aware that Astrilla and Russell were behind him, safely fighting from behind cover. Nathan moved left, hoping to get some momentum and place himself behind James' containment chamber, but he was forced to reroute toward Jareth's last position near the vents.

Nathan found Jareth cowering behind the metal chimney, attempting to wrestle a pistol from his dinner jacket. Before Jareth could pull the gun, Nathan punched the old man in the head, sending him to the floor in a heap.

As Nathan was about ready to make another dash toward the containment chamber, something heavy collided with him. The masked man —Chimera— charged at Nathan: pushing him back toward the edge of the roof.

Yes, the mercenary had caught him off guard, but Nathan knew how to handle brawlers like him. Yes, they'd take a nasty tumble, but he could prepare himself for that. Much to the masked man's surprise, Nathan grabbed ahold of the protective vest on Chimera's torso.

With the additional weight of Nathan combined with his own forward momentum, Chimera lost his footing, and the pair fell back down at least two storeys. They crashed through a canopy above one of the many concrete balconies of Hawtrey House.

Nathan landed hard, but he was able to put some distance between himself and the mercenary. Chimera's coat was caught in the mix of what had been the canopy and its frame. He was immobile for a moment but quickly ripped his arm from his sleeve and stood ready to face Nathan.

That was when Nathan saw it: *the tattoo on Chimera's forearm.*

It was a familiar design: an angry wolf barring its teeth, ready to strike. It was the same design Nathan had on his handgun —the gun he'd inherited from Jack. It was a tattoo that Nathan had seen before: inked onto his uncles forearm.

Suddenly the world closed in, and a million questions filled Nathan's head, but the only thing he could do was look at the masked combatant before him and say in disbelief:

"Jack?"

CHAPTER SEVENTEEN
HARRT

Despite feeling worse for wear, there was an urgency to the situation that helped clear the haze from Harrt's mind. Yes, he'd been partially exposed to the hard vacuum of space while escaping the Equus, but he didn't have the luxury to stop and undergo a medical examination. The Revenant Warship that had dropped in and destroyed the Equus and Dines' gunship had been one thing, but to see the Artemis —his ship— swoop in and save the day was something else. In his mind, Harrt could almost justify the Revenant's presence, but he couldn't do the same for the Artemis. The whole point of this operation with Hayward, Vol, Dines and the Sadalmelik was to keep the Commonwealth out of it: thus keeping the mole outside the loop.

And yet, his ship was there, and it had destroyed the Revenant aggressors.

Harrt limped through the Sadalmelik, despite Vol's advice to catch his breath, to see it with his own eyes. Over his shoulder, Hayward and Dines were arguing about the situation with raised voices, with Hayward accusing the Agent of *calling the 'wealth for backup.*

Harrt knew all too well that wasn't the case. If Dines had done as Hayward said, there would be more than a lone Warship out there. In his head, Harrt knew he needed to shut down Hayward's yelling, but something primal told him that he needed to get a look from the cockpit. *He needed to confirm if it really was the Artemis.*

As the cockpit doors opened, the Sadalmelik's pilot, Scruffy, gave Harrt an uneasy look. The big bearded man gawped at him for a few seconds, evidently noticing his pale complexion from hard vacuum exposure.

"You don't look so good, man," Scruffy said.

"It doesn't matter," Harrt shook his head, pushing past the pilot. "I've been through worse".

Then he saw her outside the window, the Artemis —his ship— and Harrt's worst fears were confirmed. Somebody —the mole— had gotten to his crew and put them there.

Maybe the mole was aboard his ship? What if they'd tracked him there? What if the mole wasn't working alone? Every possible scenario played out in Harrt's mind, but they all boiled down to the same question: *why was the Artemis there?*

Harrt whipped his head around to look at Scruffy, "Have they hailed us?"

"Twice in the last two minutes. What do we do?"

Hayward barged into the cockpit, barking orders into his communicator like it was going out of fashion: "Gimme a goddamn status update on that Evoker kid, Riggs. Tell me he isn't dead". Hayward stopped dead in his tracks as he gazed upon the Artemis. For what felt like a long moment, Hayward was silent: frozen in either fear or realisation that he was potentially staring down the guns of a fully-fledged 'wealther Warship. The status update on the Evoker snapped Hayward back to the moment, though he switched the thing off as soon as Riggs confirmed that the Evoker was stable.

"Well, shit," Hayward said, taking a long, sobering breath as he stepped closer to the cockpit window. "And there I was hoping to keep things simple".

"What the hell are they doing here?" Dines said to no one in particular.

There was no easy explanation to his question. Harrt had left his ship back in Capital World Space and hadn't told anyone of his whereabouts —with the exception of his XO, Lieutenant Jaudi Meera. Even then, he'd given false details of his destination and route. After all, anything concerning the 'wealther mole required a degree of subtlety.

So that left a few options in Harrt's mind to explain the presence of the Artemis. On the one —optimistic— hand, the Artemis could have a tracker planted on his shuttle, though Harrt had swept the ship pretty thoroughly before taking off. On the pessimistic hand, the 'wealther mole could've somehow gotten wise to Harrt and Dines' plan and taken control of the Artemis and brought it there to slaughter all of them.

But, if that were the case, we'd already be dead, Harrt thought.

The pilot's station yelped with an incoming comms request, and Scruffy called out to Hayward; "Boss, they are hailing us again... what do you wanna do?"

Hayward's expression implied tense internal calculation. He made a long sighing noise as he leaned on one of the consoles.

"Okay, Oxarri," Hayward licked his lips nervously. "Time to put the cards on the table: how much do you trust your XO?"

"With my life," Harrt answered.

"You sure about that? Because right now, we could be playing into the hands of your 'wealther mole". Hayward left enough room for a long uncomfortable pause. The sound of the comms request filled the silence like a countdown clock. Hayward folded his arms, "I don't need to tell you how screwed we are if you're wrong".

"I trust my crew with my life," Harrt reaffirmed. "That includes my XO".

Hayward's eyes darted to Dines as if asking the Agent if he agreed. As always, Dines offered a wary expression followed by a *semi-certain* nod.

"Lieutenant Jaudi Meera is one of the Commonwealth's most decorated officers. She has a military career spanning over forty years, and all of it has been in combat against the Revenant," Dines said. "If we can't trust her, we can't trust anybody".

"Let's hope she's the one in command on that ship," Hayward snarled. Then, looking to Scruffy, "If I give you the signal, jump this fuckin' ship into FTL and get us the hell outta here".

Scruffy nodded, though Harrt could tell from the look in his eyes that the pilot knew a move to FTL would be a death sentence. With such close proximity between the ships, the Sadalmelik wouldn't have ample time to spin up the engines, without getting blasted into a million tiny pieces.

Hayward looked at Harrt, "You better be right about this, Oxarri". Then, the muscular Earther signalled Scruffy to go ahead with the comm-link.

The window shifted to a visual comms display, and the image of Jaudi Meera formed. Most people would never guess Jaudi's age by her looks. For a woman pushing seventy, who'd hardly undergone any de-ageing treatments, she looked positively younger than her file implied. Sure, her thick, wiry hair was more grey than black these days, and the skin around her neck was a little looser, but Jaudi still looked formidable.

"Unidentified vessel, this is the Commonwealth Warship Artemis. Power down your FTL drive and—" Jaudi paused halfway through her well-rehearsed military address and squinted. Then her voice shifted an octave, "Commander? What the hell are you doing here?"

"I could ask you the same question," Harrt said, keeping the suspicion out of his voice. "Our last orders were to stay in Capital World space; what happened?"

Jaudi's eyes narrowed: "The Commonwealth received word of Revenant activity out here. We were redirected to investigate and confirm, and well, we confirmed it alright."

Dines stepped forward, placing himself in view of the broadcast: "Lieutenant Meera, who gave you the order?"

Jaudi's face was expressionless, but Harrt could almost see the wheels turning inside her head. He realised at the moment that the entire bridge crew would be watching the exchange, likely putting two and two together, just like Jaudi.

"Who gave you the order?" Dines repeated.

Jaudi shifted in her chair; then, in a low, serious tone, she answered: "They came from High Command: signed and sealed orders from the Master of the House: Inon Waife".

Her answer caused the hairs on Harrt's arms and neck to stand. Sealed orders from the four highest-ranking military officers in the 'wealth were one thing, but to have the signature of Inon Waife —the 'wealth's elected leader— was something else entirely.

The news left Harrt with more questions than he thought possible, and when he looked at Dines, the silver-haired Agent looked back with an equally overwhelmed expression.

"Lieutenant Meera, I think we are all being played for fools," Dines said. "I recommend we jump both of our ships to a safer location immediately. Have your most trusted people sweep the Artemis for any bugs or tracking devices. Shut down all outbound comms except for your own private channel."

Jaudi's brow raised at the request, and she looked at Harrt. "Do you agree with this, Commander?

"I do".

GORDON

Before the EMP blast, Gordon spent some time staring at Hawtrey House from the co-pilot's station, likening the floating monstrosity to the neon-soaked casinos of Las Vegas.

It was a symbol of decadence and greed: the kind of thing that spoke of the selfish nature of the Paradisium elite. But after Nathan's team detonated the EMP, the manor fell into complete darkness, and Gordon's comparisons to a long-dead city seemed entirely moot. Where before, the floating island looked like a dressed up spectacle, now it appeared as nothing more than a pitch-black shell of its former self.

"Two minutes to wait, then the fun begins," Rain said, rubbing his paws together in anticipation.

For sixty seconds, the pair were silent, simply watching the countdown on one of the displays between them. Suddenly the Phoenix's proximity sensors went haywire. Alarms began to scream throughout the cockpit, and Rain scrambled to the pilot's controls as fast as his body would allow. The blue-haired Sphinax jerked the ship backwards, and Gordon felt his guts jolt with the sharp movement.

Several miles ahead, a large Warship exited an FTL slipstream inside the atmosphere of the planet. It was an incredibly dangerous thing to do, especially considering the packed skylanes in and around Haydrium, but when Gordon looked closer, he realised that consideration for the traffic was the least of their problems.

"Is that a Revenant Warship?" Gordon said, pointing at the irresponsible vehicle.

"Uhhh," Rain said nervously. Then after swallowing a lump in his throat, "That's a Revenant Behemoth."

The humongous shard-shaped vessel stretched for miles, completely eclipsing Hawtrey House. Unlike the traditional Revenant warships, the Behemoth was decorated with black and gold decals all along the body: symbols from the Revenant holy texts.

"Last time we saw one of these, it was carrying King Seig," Gordon remarked.

"Well, at least he's dead," Rain replied, scratching his brow. "I guess we need to worry about getting the guys out and making a quick getaway. Maybe if we get them at—"

A new alarm began to blare out of one of the consoles, cutting the Sphinax off mid-sentence.

Rain tapped on the screen several times, then said behind gritted teeth: "Ah man... that's not so good..."

Gordon glanced out of the window ahead, spotting dozens of smaller fighters launching from the Behemoth. At first, it looked like the ships were heading to the city, but it quickly became apparent that they were heading for the Phoenix.

"Is it just me, or does it look like those fighters are heading straight for us?" Gordon asked, hoping that his eyes were deceiving him.

"I think it appears that way because that's what's happening..." Rain gulped.

The words, *how on Earth could they know,* formed on Gordon's lips, but when he turned to look at Rain, the Sphinax was yanking a safety harnesses over his upper body.

Rain said in a grave tone of voice, "Get in the gunnery chamber and shoot as many of them as possible".

The nav terminal was now awash with red blips heading straight toward them. Realising how incredibly outgunned they were, Gordon felt the anxiety wash over him.

As he hurried out of the cockpit, Gordon heard Rain talking to the ship as if it were a living being: "Okay, my giant metal darling, let's see what you are made of!"

▲

At some point in his childhood, Gordon's step-father took him to an amusement park. Gordon couldn't recall the theme park's name, but he remembered riding a particularly bumpy rollercoaster named the Red Gargantua.

He also remembered throwing up his lunch minutes after getting off the ride, but that was beside the point.

At the time, it had felt like the Red Gargantua was moving a million miles an hour, but that wasn't what upset Gordon's constitution. In his memory, he could picture being launched upward in the air at a seemingly unstoppable rate, then out of nowhere, feeling the drag back down to Earth —all whilst whipping around in a corkscrew-like fashion.

That experience turned Gordon off rollercoasters and carnival rides for life: vowing to never go near one again. Then the thought suddenly dawned on him, *what the hell am I doing aboard a bloody spaceship designed for high-speed aerial combat?*

As he darted out of the cockpit, Gordon felt the ship come alive under Rain's control. The engines rumbled, and thrust kicked in, creating the sense of not-quite motion-not-quite balance that made Gordon feel queasy. Before Gordon even made it through the Phoenix's living space, Rain forced the ship into what could only be described as an incredibly evasive manoeuver. The Sphinax must've dragged the ship into a tight barrel roll, but it was impossible to be sure, thanks to the onboard gravity simulators that strained to keep the Phoenix's interior on an even kilter.

By the time Gordon climbed the ladder to the top-side

gunnery chamber, near-miss weapons fire was rocking the Phoenix from side to side. Usually, the three-hundred-and-sixty degree view from the gunnery chambers was pleasant, especially while travelling through open space during non-combative moments.

This was not one of those times.

Instead of tranquillity, Gordon was greeted by carnage. Clouds and traffic and weapons fire whipped past as Gordon threw himself into the seat. He wasted no time strapping himself into the operating chair and activating the cannon control. As soon as he did so, the Phoenix highlighted the hostiles in the immediate vicinity. Gordon lined up the sights and began firing in a wide arc, hoping to shoot down the closest and most aggressive fighter first and then work back systemically.

There was a sudden crackle over the comm, and Russell's panicked voice emerged; "Rain, Doc, we could use some aerial support!"

Gordon noted the sound of gunfire behind the young man's transmission. *Evidently, things weren't going according to plan on the ground either.*

"We've got a bit of a problem of our own right now!" Rain said into the comm.

The Phoenix jolted as it entered one of the busy skylanes, going against the traffic. Gordon felt his gut rumble as Rain weaved the ship between the moving vehicles with absolute mastery. It was a brilliant manoeuvre —if a little showy— but Gordon saw the logic behind the tactic. Rain was using the oncoming traffic to deter the Revenant fighters from pursuing. Then it dawned on Gordon that they weren't up against traditional pilots with a sense of fear or morality; they were facing mutated Revenant soldiers.

Rather than fly between the approaching civilian frigates, the Revenant opened fire, mercilessly cutting a path toward the Phoenix. Gordon flung the cannons around, targetting one of the aggressors and firing until the thing exploded in a ball of fire.

"Get us out of this bloody skylane!" Gordon called out to Rain. "They are murdering civilians!"

Before Gordon finished his sentence, Rain snapped the Phoenix away and plunged the ship downward: toward the rolling metropolis below.

"What the hell are you doing?" Gordon yelped. "We can't take them on in open air!"

For a moment, Gordon thought he heard Rain chuckle.

"There's a hell of a lot of smog down there," Rain said in a slightly amused manner. "Wouldn't you agree?"

Gordon had to look out at the city below to confirm it, but Rain was entirely correct: thick green clouds of pollution filled the spaces between the giant towers and skyscrapers, masking the city beneath them.

"Hold on to your guts," Rain said. Then without waiting for Gordon's response, "Let's see how these bastards fly in low visibility!"

RUSSELL

The rooftop of Hawtrey House moved from standoff to warzone in what felt like a heartbeat. Nathan had pushed north-west toward Jareth and the containment chamber, while Russell stuck close to Astrilla on the westerly side. At the entrance to the northern stairwell, Alastair Roth was ushered away by a group of his bodyguards while more of his hired guns flooded into the battle.

Then, Russell saw the shadow —the man called Chimera— tackle Nathan. Russell pitched his rifle upward, hoping to shoot Jareth's henchmen before he could do any harm, but he was too slow to react, as Nathan and Chimera disappeared over the roof's edge.

"Quickly," Astrilla said, pointing at the containment chamber and Nathan's general direction. "We need to help Tariq and get James to safety!"

"What about Nate?"

"One thing at a time," the Evoker answered.

Through the darkness, Russell could barely see the

outline of Tariq, but as Roth's men deployed flares, red light filled the space around him. Tariq was taking cover behind the containment chamber, popping off gunshots at Roth's men that took out at least two of them in quick succession.

Russell followed Astrilla as she cast bolts of raw elemental energy at anyone close to Tariq. Despite feeling slightly ineffective in the battle — *at least, compared to the fully-fledged Evoke*r— Russell did what he could to support: taking down three Society goons as they darted away from Astrilla. Granted, Russell was using stun-rounds instead of anything lethal, but it did the job temporarily.

By the time they joined Tariq behind the Containment Chamber, Russell wished it was live ammo. More of Roth's army emerged from the northern stairwell, and the guys Russell had previously shot were brushing away the pain of his non-lethal rounds.

"Take 'em out now!" one of the mercenaries yelled.

An onslaught of gunfire followed, ricocheting against the Containment Chamber and sending sparks about the place. The chaos of the battle made it hard to tell how many soldiers Roth had at his disposal, but the number seemed to be growing by the second.

Russell quickly tapped on the comm-link in his ear, hoping that Rain and Gordon were coming to support. "Rain, Doc, we could use some aerial support!"

There was no reply. Or if there was, it was entirely drowned out by the sound of battle. It became quickly apparent that the Phoenix was —likely— occupied with the looming Revenant presence. That meant there wouldn't be any aerial support —for now anyway. Russell, Astrilla and Tariq were on their own, and they would have to fight their way out. *Using stun-rounds wasn't going to help the situation at all.*

It was kill or be killed.

Russell toggled the ammo control on his rifle, switching from non-lethal to lethal. He took a deep breath, willing that god, the universe, or even his own conscience could forgive him for what he was about to do.

He whipped out from behind the chamber, firing two shots into the opposing force. The first blast missed and ricocheted off one of the stairwell doors: careening into nothingness. The second, however, met its target and cut down one of Roth's men in a haze of blood. Russell scurried back into cover, trying to shut out the part of his brain that wanted to confirm whether the man was dead or injured.

When Russell was back in cover, Tariq grabbed him and gestured to the containment chamber with his thumb:

"I don't think this thing can take much more. If the internal systems fail—"

Russell cut him off, "We need to get it open. Fast". He turned to Astrilla, who was casting summons at the Society goons. "Can you give us some cover?"

The Evoker nodded and a heartbeat later, she leapt from cover, bolting toward the small army at pace. With an opening created, Russell and Tariq took ahold of a metal handle on the chamber's door and began to pull. They strained at the immense grip of the heavy metal seal, but it was no use; the door hadn't budged an inch.

"This ain't working," Russell yelled.

"No power means no oxygen," Tariq said with urgency. "James is running out of time".

ASTRILLA

When Astrilla moved from cover, she saw the collective mite of the Society's small army. For an average person, the thought of being confronted by a fourteen man team of moderately trained, well-armed soldiers would be hopeless, but for Astrilla, she simply saw fourteen hostile targets.

The Evoker training she had received as a child enabled Astrilla to harness the abilities gifted to her by the universe and the Enkaye. The likes of Elder Yuta and Xanathur taught her to effectively dispatch large groups of enemies when all other options had failed. Yes, killing wasn't ideal, but it served a purpose when your life was threatened.

The small army of Society thugs wasted no time in opening fire, sending a stream of bullets and laser-fire directly toward her. However, their efforts to gun her down were in vain. Astrilla cast a temporary wall of Evoker energy before herself, creating a shield that would protect her from the weapons fire for all but a heartbeat.

That was all the time she needed.

Once she was within three metres of the small army, Astrilla unleashed the full fury of her Evoker abilities. She rolled through the air in a single motion, like a feather caught in a tornado. In the time it took for Astrilla to close the gap, she'd already cast a series of summons that would meet their targets before her toes even touched the ground. She landed directly in front of an armoured mercenary, who was supposed to look all kinds of menacing. As it happened, Astrilla booted the man in the chest with such force that he physically lifted off of the ground.

The rest of the combat was a blur. Instinct took over, and for what felt like minutes, Astrilla's consciousness left her body: replaced by a combative being. It wasn't like fighting Revenant Soldiers: they were at least semi-predictable. No, combat against living, thinking beings was far more complex. Taking a Revenant life was —in a way— a service to the universe: not a good deed, but more like a preventative measure. Killing anything else was a far more visceral experience. Maybe that was why Astrilla's brain switched from normal to this strange out-of-body state? Perhaps it was to protect the compassionate part of her soul. Violence wasn't pretty; it certainly wasn't a good deed, but it was sometimes necessary, especially when other lives were hanging in the balance.

By the time Astrilla —the *real* Astrilla— was back in control, all she saw around her were bodies. Violence had resolved the situation —for now. Astrilla stopped, allowing herself to catch her breath. She knew that Roth's men were likely rallying, and it wouldn't be long before they or the Revenant retaliated in far greater numbers.

Suddenly, she felt the cold barrel of a gun pressed against the back of her head. The weapon had not been fired, which meant it wasn't one of Roth's men.

"Don't move," David Jareth said. "I don't want to hurt you".

Astrilla cursed at herself. She'd been so distracted by the attacking mercenaries that she'd taken her eye off Jareth. She raised both hands in surrender: not that she had any intention of giving up. This was simply a ploy to keep Jareth occupied.

"Your days of trading with the Revenant are over, Mr Jareth," Astrilla said. "Maybe it is you who should consider surrendering".

Jareth scoffed. "For an Evoker, you're not very smart, are you? Look around; before you lot showed up, Roth and his cronies had his guns on me. You have no idea what you've done".

"What's that supposed to mean?" Astrilla asked.

Sensing something akin to outrage in Jareth's voice, Astrilla turned her head to look at him out of the corner of her eye. There was something to what he was saying, but experience told Astrilla that the man couldn't be trusted.

Then again, Roth really had been pointing a gun at him.

Maybe there was some truth to what Jareth said?

Before Jareth could reply, he was struck over the head by Russell. The former barkeep slammed the butt of his rifle into Jareth's skull, sending the old man to the floor in a heap. Russell kicked Jareth's gun away and proceeded to turn the Paradisian elitist over using his boot.

Russell said, "He'll have one hell of a headache when he comes around, but he's alive."

"Good," Astrilla replied. "Restrain him. He has questions to answer".

Astrilla turned back to Tariq, who was still pulling at the containment chamber, attempting to open it by force. As Astrilla neared him, she realised something wasn't right: the chamber doors weren't shifting, and Tariq appeared panicked and flustered as he yanked on the handles.

"Stand aside," Astrilla ordered.

Tariq moved away as Astrilla placed her glowing hands on one of the four chunky metal hinges. She called upon the universe to grant her the power of fire: to summon an inferno hot enough to reforge steel. As her hands grew brighter, the metal began to sweat.

"I'll need covering fire," Astrilla said, turning her head to Tariq. "If any more of Roth's men show up, you need to keep them off my back".

"Understood," he nodded.

CHAPTER EIGHTEEN
NATHAN

When speaking about his one and only tattoo, Jack always presented the intricately designed piece as something that represented loyalty and brotherhood. Though in private, he always seemed to have a love-hate relationship with the ink. On the one hand, Jack got the same design minted onto his prized handgun —the same one Nathan held now. On the other hand, Jack would, on occasion, express a desire to remove the tattoo from his body.

Nathan could recall his uncle saying, *tattoos are for over-hyped liberals, weed-smoking hippies and prisoners that shiv each other in the back, and I ain't none of those.*

In all the years, Jack never mentioned where or why he'd got the thing —it just simply was. The black wolf design and Jack were one and the same. Where there was one, so too was the other.

Why the fuck am I staring at it now? Nathan questioned.

As Nathan stared across the three-metre gap between himself and the masked man known as Chimera, he saw the same tattoo —Jack's tattoo. Nathan felt his mouth become dry, and he was suddenly overcome by confusion.

It was impossible.

Jack had perished at Mirotose Station with the rest of the Loyalty's crew, and like any dead person, he'd been off the grid ever since. And yet there he was, dressed in dark attire with a black cloth mask covering his visage.

Nathan kept his gun —the one that previously belonged to Jack— trained on Chimera. The faceless mask gave away nothing. Despite the tattoo, Nathan noticed other things about the faceless spectre that drew his conclusions. Chimera was equipped with the same kind of weaponry; his build, stance, and how he carried himself was just like Jack. Even the risky attempt to tackle Nathan from the roof had Jack's name all over it.

"After all this time..." Nathan paused, unable to finish the sentence in a single breath. "How the fuck did you survive?"

Chimera tilted his head in a questioning manner but didn't say anything.

"It's been eleven years…." Nathan raised his voice. "All this time, you've been working for Jareth? Do you know what happened to us after you ran away? Do you know what I had to do to survive?"

From out of nowhere, Chimera reacted, flinging a combat knife at Nathan with ninja-like reflexes. Before Nathan could pull the trigger, the blade grazed his forearm. The feeling of sharp metal cutting into his flesh caused Nathan to take his eye off of Chimera for a split second. When his gaze returned a heartbeat later, Chimera was charging toward him.

This is gonna be one hell of a family reunion...

Chimera collided with Nathan with such force that it sent him crashing through one of the glass balcony doors and straight into Hawtrey House. Nathan had been so taken with the fact that he was staring at his *—supposedly—* dead uncle that he didn't even realise he'd put himself in a position of weakness. A million twinkling glass particles kicked up around him as he was forced through the door. Nathan landed hard but made sure to keep his eyes and face shielded from the shower of glass that followed.

The new room where he landed looked like a library, but it had a strange showroom-like quality like the rest of the house. As he shook off the daze, Nathan's brain kicked into combat mode, despite the fact that he was facing Jack. The first thing he realised was that his gun was no longer in his hand and was, in fact, several metres across the room.

As Nathan climbed to his feet, Chimera forced himself into the library, pushing aside a piece of stray doorframe that was precariously hanging from the wall.

"You have no idea what you've done, boy," Chimera said. The mask distorted the voice, making it completely unrecognisable. "You have ruined our one and only chance".

Nathan straightened up, feeling his knuckles click as he clenched his fists. He wasn't sure why Jack was doing what he was doing or why he was dressed like a phantom. He didn't know why the old man didn't recognise him. Regardless of Nathan's questions, all that mattered was the here and now. Jack posed a significant threat to the mission. He'd separated Nathan from the crew using violence, and now he stood in Nathan's way.

Chimera hurled a closed fist toward him, but it failed to meet its target. Nathan ducked underneath, spotting an opening in his aggressor's defences, which he exploited to maximum effect. Without pulling his punches, Nathan struck the mercenary twice in the chest, then followed up with a boot to the midsection.

As Chimera staggered back, Nathan went in for a follow-up attack, aiming to strike the masked man in the head and hopefully disable him. To Nathan's surprise, Chimera caught his fist before he could land the punch.

For a split second, the two men exchanged a stare. It was an odd moment that didn't feel right to the situation: as though Chimera recognised something he'd failed to see before.

Are you still in there, old man?

Suddenly, Chimera swept Nathan's feet from under him, and he crashed to the ground. As Nathan recoiled from the attack, the masked man began to circle him.

"Who taught you to fight?" Chimera said as he moved in.

Before Chimera could grab him, Nathan swung a fist, cracking the masked man in the jaw. Chimera staggered to the corner of the room, allowing Nathan ample time to climb to his feet and ready himself for more. His knuckles popped as his hands balled into fists. Nathan was worn and battered, but Chimera was close to exhaustion. *Maybe he was suffering from the tumble from the roof? Or perhaps Chimera was simply a much older man struggling to keep up with a far younger opponent.* Either way, the mercenary was on the defensive at last, and Nathan did not want to give him a chance to regroup.

As Chimera backed away, Nathan punched him across the face another two times, causing him to growl and desperately lash out. Nathan was able to avoid the wild swing and veered away, lunging towards his pistol.

He scooped up the weapon, but before taking aim, Chimera knocked the gun from his hands and struck Nathan across the head. The hard right hook forced Nathan to one side, leaving him staring up at the mercenary.

"You are quite the opponent," Chimera said, tipping his head slightly.

"Screw you," Nathan spat a mouthful of blood out on the floor.

Chimera grabbed Nathan by the collar of his shirt and pulled him to his feet. "You fight like an EDA Agent, but you are far too young to have learnt it on Earth... Who the fuck are you?"

Nathan didn't answer. He'd lost sight of his weapon but knew it was around two metres from his current position. He hoped that he wouldn't need to use it, but the mercenary —Jack— didn't seem to understand the situation.

In a move that Jack always referred to as *the last resort*, Nathan pushed off his back foot, whipping his head forward into Chimera's forehead. It was a brutal, unexpected headbutt that the mercenary didn't see coming. Nathan knew to expect it, so the impact was less of a shock but still hurt like hell. It was what many would call a dishonourable move, taught to him by Jack from way back in the day.

Why didn't he see it coming?

Chimera released his grip on Nathan and staggered back in a near drunken manner. That was when Nathan took the opportunity to strike, hoping that he wouldn't need to use the gun. He threw a punch to the ribs, then to the head, forcing Chimera back with every well-placed strike. Finally, Nathan went in for a kick that he hoped would subdue the man. His boot met the side of Chimera's head, and the masked man tumbled to the floor.

With Chimera down, trying to recover from the attack, Nathan scurried across the room, putting some distance between them. The gun was several metres away, and for a moment, Nathan hesitated to reach for it *—after all, it was Jack that he was fighting.*

Against better judgement, Nathan grabbed his pistol.

Chimera climbed to his feet and pulled a handgun from under his long black coat. Nathan could sense the big man setting his aim on his back. Using the very training that Jack bestowed upon him from an early age, Nathan rolled right and fired.

The gunshot didn't meet flesh, but it still met its target —Chimera's pistol. The gun flew from the masked man's hand, but only after discharging a stray round that flew wildly upward.

"Take off the mask," Nathan panted. "I said now, Jack".

Chimera tilted his head in what Nathan could only assume was curiosity: "What did you say?"

There came a sudden screech from above, so loud that both men stopped and looked up. The sound had originated from a chandelier, suspended at least twenty-five feet above Nathan's head. It was a majestic, beautiful piece of decor: surrounded by an impressive rose-style medallion. The problem was that it was now lurching away from where it was supposed to be.

A second creak followed, but this time the chandelier and its gaudy fixturing gave way. The shining, jewel-encrusted lamp plummeted to the ground, and Nathan's first reaction was to escape. He landed two metres away, slamming into the ground just in time to see the chandelier crash on top of Chimera, then through the floorboards and into the level below. Dust and debris and pieces of jewel kicked up into the air as the crown-shaped mass disappeared into the next floor. Usually, something like that would kill a man, but Nathan knew Chimera was reinforced to the eyeballs with top-spec Jareth corps armour. He'd likely have a few broken bones at worst and a splitting headache at best.

When the dust settled, Nathan spat out another mouthful of blood and climbed to his feet. He peered into the newly formed hole at the centre of the room. A few dozen metres below, Nathan saw a pile of debris but no sign of Chimera.

KOBLE

It was easy to pinpoint the moment before the EMP detonation. Koble had felt something in the air change: not like a shift in temperature or a breeze passing by, but more like vibration to whatever protons and neutrons and other *sciencey things* made up the space between spaces. Then as all the lights fell dark, Koble felt a surge of static electricity pass over his fur, causing the shorter-than-normal hairs on his body to rise.

After that, Koble watched Christian Roth's polished, statesmanly veneer peel away. Before, it seemed as though the Paradisian was in his element: delivering a speech for the ages during his one true moment in the sun. Of course, it had been dramatically ruined by the power outage, and Christian didn't take too well to the *interruption* at all.

In the space of ten —maybe fifteen— seconds, Christian Roth went from statesmen to spoilt-brat, and it was a curious sight to behold. Where earlier, he'd looked cultured and charming, now he was seething with uncontrollable rage.

For the better part of two minutes, Koble watched Christian berate his staff: even going so far as to grab one woman by the throat and scream at her. It was pretty clear that none of the employees would step in, either out of fear or blind loyalty, but Koble suspected it was the former.

There was something petulant about Christian that reminded Koble of his brother, Kornell. Sure, it was pretty easy to spot the similarities; the decadence of the house, the clothing, the food —hell, even the party itself— but there was something deeper. It was the arrogance, hubris and entitlement with which Christian armed himself. He truly believed that he was some kind of heroic champion, and that was precisely how Kornell worked: convinced that only his way, his thoughts, and his motives were righteous.

That thought alone told Koble all he needed to know.

After slapping the stage manager across the face, Christian looked ready to tear into another staff member, but he promptly stopped as the sound of gunfire drew his attention. The ruckus was undoubtedly coming from the roof. Koble's suspicion was confirmed seconds later when one of Roth's mercenaries plunged from the rooftop and into the swimming pool.

People in the audience screamed. In the hysteria of the moment, the crowd surged in two opposing directions. The majority rushed from the stage, heading away from the house, while a second and far smaller group moved into the house with gusto.

"Hmm," Koble mused to himself. "Patriots..."

He looked at the stage, noticing that Christian was heading back into Hawtrey House with a couple of his companions in tow. There was a militant way to the mob's movement that told Koble there was about to be a whole lot more trouble. From what he could ascertain, Christian was whipping his loyal followers into a frenzy: citing that terrorists were attacking and he needed help to defend his home.

It was just like Kornell.

Koble necked what was left of his champagne and followed Christian and his small mob into the east wing. Once there, Koble found a small security team handing out weapons to party-goers. It was strange to see a crowd of elitists brandishing military-grade assault rifles while wearing expensive dinner suits and party attire.

Koble watched from afar as Christian discarded his suit jacket and replaced it with a combat vest. Then one of his mercenaries handed him a custom pulse rifle decorated with tiny red crystals across the body and barrel: a cosmetic enhancement rather than functional. Once Christian was armed, he jumped atop a large wooden table to address his adoring congregation of locked-and-loaded socialites.

"Get to the roof and stop this carnage," Christian barked to his people. "There will be a sizeable reward for anyone who brings me one of the attackers alive".

Koble looked on as the mob headed to the stairwell with misplaced gusto. He counted at least two dozen in addition to a group of heavily armoured security personnel. They were all heading toward Nathan, Astrilla and Russell, and Koble knew he had to act.

"Kornell!" Christian yelled from across the almost empty room, beckoning Koble with a wave.

Koble politely obliged, though he became wary that his cover might have been blown when two big, burly-looking men flanked Christian on either side. They were the kind of guys Koble had seen a million times before; big dumb idiots that were good for one thing —smashing in skulls. Koble half-expected a three-on-one fight, but as he neared, Christian handed him a loaded gun.

"Looks like some degenerates are trying to interfere," Christian said. "Care to join me for a spot of hunting?"

Koble's smile was amiable.

Without a second thought, Koble slammed his rifle into Christian's face, forcing the elitist to the floor. Both of Christian's bodyguards were too slow —or too shocked— to react. Within a heartbeat, both men had joined their employer.

Once Koble confirmed there were no more threats in the area, he lowered his gun and moved to the big table where Christian stood earlier. He noticed several bottles of pricey champagne, there for the taking. It'd be a shame to let good booze go to waste.

"Don't mind if I do," Koble drawled as he shoved the bottles in his jacket pocket.

He moved back to Christian, realising that the man would no doubt whip up more trouble when he came around. Koble considered shooting him, then decided against it. Someone like Christian Roth would make a good prisoner: someone who would squeal under interrogation. Sure, he wasn't the mission, but there was no harm in being an overachiever.

Koble bound Christian's ankles and hands together using a tie from the curtains. Then he hoisted the unconscious Paradisian over his shoulder and made his way to the roof.

RAIN

Once the Phoenix plunged into the deep green fog covering the city, Rain felt slightly more control over the situation. He knew that using the smog would reduce visibility, but it was a risk he was willing to take. Flying on instinct rather than instruments was the cornerstone of his piloting experience, whereas the mutated Revenant pilots would undoubtedly find the situation far more challenging.

In a way, Rain couldn't have asked for a better distraction. The northern swamps of Pluvium had similar visibility during the winter seasons. Rain could fly circles around the wetlands when he was a boy, and Haydrium was *mostly* the same —minus the enormous skyscrapers and heavy traffic that filled the corporate world.

Glancing at his scanner screens with haste, Rain saw that the Revenant hadn't abandoned the chase. He pushed the Phoenix forward, carefully shifting between two neon-soaked towers. He could hear Gordon in the gunnery chamber above, firing at the pursuers. Seconds later, Rain felt a rumble of something exploding off the Phoenix's stern, followed by an almost celebratory sound from Gordon in the comms.

That was one of the hostile craft exploding. It was a start, but Rain knew there were many more in their vicinity. There was no doubt in his mind by this stage that the pilots chasing them were likely the best in Baylum's ranks: likely un-mutated sociopaths that genuinely believed in the Revenant creed. Regardless, Rain told himself that they weren't experienced enough *—or crazy enough—* to take him on in aerial combat. It was funny that he was the madman in the situation, considering he was fighting against genuine murderous psychopaths, but he figured there was a first —or second— time for everything.

He rolled the Phoenix between two buildings and darted beneath a crowded traffic lane. To his dismay, the Revenant fighters continued to chase him into the city. Lasers flew past the cockpit, and after a few seconds, one of the bolts glanced the Phoenix's bow, causing the ship to jolt violently.

Rain steadied the ship, then called out to Gordon, "Doctor Taggart, are you okay?"

"I'm fine, but I can't say the same about the top-side cannon".

Rain glanced at the monitor beside him, spotting quickly that the guns Gordon was operating had overheated. It wasn't ideal, but the Phoenix had a secondary gunnery chamber on the underside and weapons mounted at the front.

"Get on the other guns," Rain ordered.

"Working on it!"

The comm filled with sounds of hustling and heavy breathing as the Doctor moved between decks. Rain tried his best to shut out the noise and instead focussed on piloting through the maze of buildings, packed transit lanes and fog: all while dodging Revenant gunfire.

"C'mon, my metal darling," Rain said to the Phoenix. "We can do this!"

GORDON

Once he reached the belly-side gunnery chamber, Gordon strapped himself into the seat and switched on the cannon control. He glanced out of the window, spotting a dozen Revenant fighters in hot pursuit. It took three seconds for the weapons systems to come to life, but it felt like three hours. Impatiently Gordon tapped the console, willing the thing to boot up as fast as possible. Once the screen flickered to life and the system unlocked, Gordon took hold of the controls and began firing at the pursuing fighters. The cannons sent out a long string of green laser fire, cutting through three of the enemy crafts with ease.

"Nice shooting!" Rain said from the cockpit. Then after a pause, "Hold onto your fur; this one's gonna really hurt!"

All of a sudden, Gordon felt the Phoenix shift upward at an alarming rate. As the skyscrapers and fog disappeared from view, Gordon realised that they were climbing back up toward the clouds. The remaining fighters gave chase and continued to shoot at the Phoenix.

As Gordon returned fire, he yelled to Rain, "What are you doing? You are putting us out in the open".

Rain's response seemed to carry an almost cocky tone; "Like I said, Doctor Taggart; hold on to your fur..."

As the Phoenix rose, the night's sky filled Gordon's view. Then a heartbeat later, he felt the contents of his stomach turn as Rain drove the Phoenix back down in a corkscrew. Gravity mixed with thrust and inertia caused Gordon's ears to pop as the city closed in. His glasses fell from his face under the sheer velocity of Rain's aerial acrobatics.

"When I say, you spin the guns around and open fire on these bastards!" Rain said. Behind his voice, Gordon could hear the Sphinax flipping switches. "I'm gonna do something a little crazy..."

Resisting the pressure and weight of the rapid descent, Gordon returned his glasses to his face. He wrapped his hands around the cannon control and poised his thumbs over the firing mechanism.

He waited for what felt like an eternity.

Then, something about their plunge changed, and Gordon heard Rain through the comm.

"Now!"

Rain cut the Phoenix's main engine and, in its place, turned the impulse thrusters to maximum. The Phoenix Titan span one-hundred-and-eighty degrees on its nose, flipping like a coin.

The aerial move gave Gordon a perfect line of sight on the ten-or-so pursuers, and without hesitation, he pushed down on the firing control.

The cannons sent laser fire hurtling toward the Revenant ships. At the same time, Rain must've activated the forward weapons, as additional missiles and gunfire filled the sky, cutting into the fighters like a knife through butter.

The whole moment lasted a second, and when it passed, Gordon felt the Phoenix's engines kick in. The ship lurched back into the skies, passing the exploding fighters and flying shrapnel.

"That was one hell of a move," Gordon exclaimed.

"Ah, that was nothing," Rain replied cooly. "But I guess we shouldn't celebrate too soon; we need to get back to the others".

ASTRILLA

While Tariq and Russell held off the attacking mercenary force, Astrilla used an elemental summon to melt the hinges off of the containment chamber holding James. Time was working against them. James was no longer receiving a supply of oxygen to his blood. The number of hostiles seemed to be growing by the second, and Nathan had disappeared off the roof's edge while battling the masked mercenary.

Then there was the gigantic Revenant Behemoth to consider. The hulking mass of metal loomed in the skies, launching alert fighters that seemed to be heading away from Hawtrey House: as though they had a different objective: *likely the Phoenix.*

Which meant they were sitting ducks.

With that thought in mind, Astrilla pushed her elemental summon to burn as hard as the universe would allow. White-hot energy flew from her palms as she squeezed the containment chamber's hinges. Gunfire rang out around her as Russell and Tariq tried their best to hold off the enemy force. Sparks flew in every direction, and near-volcanic heat radiated around Astrilla.

She imagined fire and brimstone at her fingertips: tried to imagine the metal perspiring. A thought at the back of her mind edged its way forward: the campfire from days earlier.

Astrilla recalled the warmth from the coals and imagined what it would feel like to lift one with her bare hands.

The composite-steel hinges gave way, turning into a liquid paste that glowed a molten orange. Hot steam rose between Astrilla's fingers, and she pulled her hand away quickly out of nothing more than human instinct.

With nothing else to hinder her, Astrilla yanked the chamber open.

The man inside bore no resemblance to Nathan.

James had the thick-boned structure of a marine, not what Astrilla had expected at all. There was an unusual gauntness to his face, the kind that implied a history of drug abuse. His greying-blonde hair was short and tidy, but the beard on his neck was unkempt and wild.

Astrilla wasted no time checking for a pulse on his wrist, which, thankfully, she found. From a glance, James appeared mostly healthy, aside from an odd tightness in his breathing, which likely was the result of a nicotine habit.

Then Astrilla noticed something that made her stop.

On James' forearm were a collection of neatly arranged scars from his wrist to his elbow. As well as looking old, they also looked self-inflicted: *possibly something from his days as an addict.* They looked about the right size and shape for an Ice needle, and were pretty unsightly when you noticed them.

Without warning, James snapped up, grabbing Astrilla's wrist. His eyes were wild at that moment —all instinct with no logic. The panic on his face was primal, defensive, and confused by what was going on.

"Who are you?"

Thankfully, Tariq appeared at Astrilla's side, and James seemed to calm at the sight of a familiar face.

"Don't worry, my friend," Tariq said. "We're getting you out of here".

James released his grip on Astrilla and leaned back against the interior of his containment chamber. He breathed something that looked like relief, and relaxed as Tariq and Astrilla peeled the sedation needles from James' arms and torso. Once all the medical equipment and restraints were gone, Tariq helped James climb out of the chamber.

"I don't know how much longer we can keep this going," Russell yelled as he lunged into cover.

Astrilla nodded. While the former barkeep was entirely correct, Nathan and Koble were still unaccounted for, and the Phoenix was probably fighting off Revenant fighters. She spoke into the comms link hoping that someone would answer:

"Nathan, Koble?" Astrilla said. "Where are you?"

There was a long pause and then a crackle. Then there was a voice:

"I'm heading your way," Koble panted. "Just to warn you there's a shit-ton of Roth's men heading your way".

Astrilla turned to Russell, and the young man nodded to acknowledge the new information. Without hesitation, Astrilla continued into the comm-link: "Rain, please tell me you are heading this way?"

"Do not fear, my darling; we will be with you in due course," the cocky Sphinax replied. "We ran into a little... resistance up here".

Astrilla didn't bother pressing Rain for an ETA: she knew he'd make good on his word. Realising that Nathan was the only one not to respond, she spoke into the open channel:

"Nathan... where are you?""

CHAPTER NINETEEN
RUSSELL

Russell and Tariq assumed cover behind the containment chamber, exchanging gunfire with the Society mercenaries. All the while, James Stephens was coughing uncontrollably and looking worse for wear. Russell had been so engrossed in the gunfight that he'd been barely aware of the Phoenix Titan's approach. As the white and black ship swept in, a barrage of laser fire was unloaded into the hostile force. Most of Roth's men retreated into the stairwell, but those who decided to stay and fight were cut down by the Phoenix's superior firepower.

Within seconds, the rooftop was clear, and Rain's voice came through the comms; "Get aboard, my friends; the enemy will regroup. I can feel it".

As Tariq helped James to stagger toward the ship, Russell looked at Jareth. The old man was still unconscious with his wrists and ankles bound together by a piece of wire from the containment chamber. Without question, Russell slung Jareth over his shoulder and carried him to the Phoenix. Once aboard, Gordon helped Russell stow Jareth in one of the storage rooms, which had once —allegedly— been used as a brig.

"I'll keep an eye on him," Gordon said, with his trusty double-barrel shotgun to hand. "Go help the others aboard".

"Sure thing".

Russell rushed to the main cargo hold at the ship's stern, which Rain opened up to allow Tariq and James easy access. James was pale and gaunt in the face, with a lean body that seemed out of place for someone once hooked on outer-worlds narcotics. The greying-blonde man looked at Russell with a questioning expression as Tariq helped him sit.

"Who are you?" James asked with a weak voice.

"Name's Russell".

James' expression hung as though frozen inside the moment: likely an after-effect of the containment chamber. Then out of nowhere, his visage shifted to something more relaxed.

"Well, Russell, thanks for savin' my ass..." James replied breathlessly. "So, who the hell's in charge around here?"

ASTRILLA

Astrilla dashed to the roof's edge, where Nathan and the masked mercenary, Chimera, fell several minutes earlier. To her dismay, all she saw was a smashed canopy below that looked like it had sustained a heavy impact.

"Where are you, Nathan?"

All of a sudden, Astrilla's attention was drawn to the sound of heavy footsteps coming up the stairwell. Her first impulse was to prepare to attack, assuming that Roth's men had regrouped and were preparing for another assault. Astrilla ignited a blue elemental flame in her right hand, readying to strike. As the steps drew closer and closer, Astrilla raised her firey palm. The door burst open, and Koble stepped out with an unconscious human over one shoulder.

As soon he saw Astrilla, the Sphinax jumped in surprise; "Whoa," he yelped. "It's me."

Astrilla frowned but allowed herself to relax.

"Use your communicator," she said. Then as she extinguished the flame from her hand, she gestured to the man over Koble's shoulder. "Care to explain who that is?"

The Sphinax's smirk was wry and a little mischievous.

"So, I kinda went a bit off-plan," Koble said with a

shrug. "This guy is Christian Roth. I figured he'd be useful".

Astrilla rolled her eyes but didn't bother arguing. Yes, Koble had gone way off script, but there was a good chance that Christian was a part of his father's conspiracy.

"Get him aboard the Phoenix," she instructed.

Koble nodded, then stopped and looked around the area. "Where's Nate?"

Before Astrilla could reply, a series of gunshots flew past them. She turned her head and spotted a group of mercenaries heading straight toward them from the southern roof. Koble yanked her into cover inside the stairwell from where he'd come from. Then without hesitation, Koble booted the door shut to keep them both safe. Bullets and laser fire ricocheted off the door, which thankfully held under stress.

"I reckon that's about two dozen guys," Koble yelled.

Astrilla nodded. "There will be more of them soon if we don't hurry".

"Don't worry, I love a challenge". Koble took up his gun in one paw while balancing Christian with the other. As Koble moved toward the door, Astrilla grabbed him by the tail and pulled him away before he could do anything stupid.

"Don't be a fool," she said, yanking the Sphinax by his long tail. Astrilla gestured at the still unconscious Christian Roth, "Your aim will be impaired with that blithering idiot over your shoulder."

"Any other ideas?"

The sound of gunfire increased outside, no doubt where Russell, Tariq and maybe even the Phoenix were engaging in the fight. Then, Astrilla heard something in the comms. It was a faint crackle, but after a few seconds, the signal shifted, and Nathan's voice filled the channel:

"So, what did I miss?"

NATHAN

After his encounter with Chimera, Nathan skulked through the upper floors of the manor, trying to find his way back to the roof. It hadn't taken him long to find the southern stairwell, but the sound of an approaching crowd forced him to take cover in an office. Society mercenaries and armed party-goers rushed by without noticing his presence. The suited and booted types seemed oddly eager to get into the fight: as though the mere act of taking part somehow showed their commitment to Alastair Roth, or perhaps Paradisium as a whole.

It all seemed oddly out of place, but Nathan didn't have the time to think about it. He waited sixty seconds, then climbed the southern stairwell to the roof: following the crowd. At the top, Nathan found a lone gunman guarding the stairwell. He was one of the suited party-goers: likely someone who didn't know how to use the weapon he was carrying. Rather than shoot him dead, Nathan fired a round into the man's knee, sending him straight to the floor in a whimpering wreck.

Nathan moved up to the door and partially opened it to view the situation on the roof. He saw that the Society goons had split into two groups: one firing at the northern stairwell about eighty metres ahead and the second fighting with someone near the Phoenix. Distorted chatter came through the comms link, and Nathan could tell it was Astrilla and Koble. He quickly surmised that they were the ones pinned inside in the northern stairwell, so he pressed a finger to his ear and spoke:

"So, what did I miss?"

Astrilla was the first to reply. "Nathan, are you okay?

"Better than you guys right now," he answered. "I'm counting at least twenty out there. I might have to do something a little bold".

Astrilla's reply emphasised caution. "What are you proposing?" she said. "You can't take them all on by yourself. We should regroup on —"

Nathan cut her off as he moved from cover: "Wait for my signal".

At Koble and Astrilla's position, the combined force of armed party-goers and Society mercenaries were amassing outside the stairwell. Some were kitted out with riot shields and electric batons, while others carried more aggressive weaponry, including military-grade rifles.

A leading man from Roth's security force ordered his people to hold their fire. He raised a closed fist to his companions, signalling to move forward. Carefully the pack inched forward, and a lone mercenary grabbed the door handle.

That was the moment Nathan knew he had to act. Sure, Astrilla could fry all of them in a heartbeat, but she and Koble were pinned in an enclosed space. There was little to no chance of both of them surviving.

Before the merc's hand could touch the door, Nathan took aim and fired. The laser bolt caught the unsuspecting thug off guard and sent him toppling off the roof. As Nathan suspected, the combined force of Society mercenaries and armed merrymakers turned their attention on him.

I am part Enkaye, Nathan told himself.

In his mind, Nathan saw the place he'd gone during his final battle with Seig: the desert. He felt the warm sand between his toes, the cool breeze passing by, and the sun's warmth above. The vast dunes where he'd met Bill Stephens during the battle of the Messorem were precisely the same as before but with one significant difference. Bill was not there. Nobody was. And yet, despite the absence of a visible presence, someone spoke to Nathan across the sands.

"You have the power of a million generations within you. Make them proud son of Earth".

Nathan's mind returned to the darkened roof of Hawtrey House. He felt the cold air around him. There was sweat on his brow. His hair felt a little heavier than it had on the golden plains. His fists hurt from fighting. Then he saw the two dozen armed thugs pointing their weapons at him, ready to kill without mercy. Despite the threat of imminent death, Nathan did not embrace fear. Instead, he felt something entirely new: something powerful.

The small army was taken by surprise when Astrilla burst through the stairwell door, followed by Koble. The Evoker moved through the pack of mercs at speed, cutting down several of them in one manoeuvre.

"You have the power of a million generations within you..."

Nathan dashed into the fight, closing in on one of the thugs, who raised his riot shield in hopeful defence. Nathan slammed into the shield with his shoulder, pushing the man behind it off balance.

Another merc swept toward him with an electric baton. With a quick side-step, Nathan avoided the volatile fizz of the weapon and laid a hard punch into his attacker's head, forcing the mercenary to the floor. When Nathan turned his attention to the first hostile, he found the man reaching for a handgun, but before he could take aim, Nathan booted him.

With two attackers down and out, Nathan turned his attention to a suited man heading for Koble with his rifle raised. Nathan darted toward him and kicked the underside of his gun. The weapon discharged into thin air and distracted the armed-partygoer long enough for Nathan to nail him with a right hook. As two more thugs approached, Nathan swept up his pistol and opened fire, cutting both down in quick succession.

Then Nathan realised something. All of that violence had taken place in a matter of twenty-five seconds at most.

What the hell was that? he wondered.

A heartbeat passed.

All the hostiles were either dead or incapacitated. As he surveyed the area, it became apparent that between himself and Astrilla, they'd defeated an army of two dozen: with Astrilla doing most of the work.

"Clear," Nathan said, holstering his gun.

Upon hearing the word, Koble emerged from cover with Christian Roth slung over his shoulder in an unconscious state. The Sphinax was unharmed, and as he approached Nathan, he gestured to one of the dead mercs.

"That was... *new?*" Koble said, his voice lifting an octave. "I've never seen anyone move like that before".

"What do you mean?"

Koble raised his brow: "You were moving... *fast*".

Nathan didn't know how to respond, so instead, he said the first thing that came to mind. "Get to the ship".

Nathan watched the Sphinax run to the Phoenix while carrying Christian. When Nathan turned his attention to Astrilla, the Evoker gestured to his bleeding lip.

"Is that from the masked man that was with Jareth?" she asked.

A dark truth whirled there, that Nathan hadn't accepted.

"Probably," Nathan replied. Then, after pausing for thought, "I think the masked guy was Jack".

Astrilla blinked twice as though assimilating his words.

"Say that again?" she said.

"I think that Chimera guy is Jack," Nathan repeated. "He's got the same tattoo, he fights in the same way, all of it. It's Jack".

Astrilla seemed to mull it over for a few seconds, then, as though snapping back into the moment, she shook her head. "We've captured Jareth... James is safe. We're all here... that's all that matters".

She was right. With a Revenant Behemoth in the skies and all of the Society's goons in the house below, there was no point in sticking around. If Chimera was Jack, then Jareth could confirm it and then Nathan could take appropriate action.

Escaping was now the priority.

"Let's get out of here," Nathan nodded.

As Nathan and Astrilla drew closer to the Phoenix, a cold rain began to fall from the sky. Nathan's mind turned to James, who was now aboard his ship. They'd have to speak to one another for the first time in eleven years. They'd have to be civil. That was going to be a challenge.

Once Nathan was within a dozen metres of the ship, he could see Koble and Tariq lifting Christian into the cargo hold. Nathan wasn't sure exactly what to do with the elitist, but he figured he could deal with him once they were safely tucked in the slipstream.

Then Nathan felt a cold chill pass up threw his body like ice. It was an instinctive sensation designed to tell him that something wasn't right.

A gunshot fired into the air. Not at anyone in particular, but used as a way to draw attention. A distorted and angry voice came from the other side of the roof.

"Not one more step!"

Nathan and Astrilla stopped in their tracks and turned to face Chimera. From the targeting lasers mounted on Chimera's dual pistols, Nathan could tell that the masked man had a clean shot *—very Jack indeed.* It was more than likely that Chimera could gun down both of them with ease.

Chimera's yell was so loud that it could be heard on the Phoenix. Nathan became aware that Koble was reaching for his gun, but Chimera shifted his aim to the Sphinax:

"Don't try anything cute," Chimera said, focusing on Koble and Tariq inside the Phoenix. "Just give me Jareth, and I won't kill these two—".

Nathan interrupted him, "You really think you can move faster than an Evoker?"

Nathan shared a short glance with Astrilla, who was frozen in place. He knew that the Evoker was exhausted from combat, but he also knew that bluffing could buy Koble and the others some time *—maybe to activate the Phoenix's cannons.*

"I can shoot you both from here before you could even blink," Chimera said. "That'd be a hell of a gamble for anyone... including an Evoker". The mercenary called to Koble and the others, "You've got ten seconds".

As Chimera began a slow count down from ten, Nathan pondered how to get out of the situation. His gun was holstered, and Chimera was clearly at an advantage. Sure, Astrilla could cast a summon, *but was she quick enough to take him down at a distance?* Nathan didn't like those odds.

When Chimera got to three, Nathan interrupted him: "C'mon, Jack, you're not gonna shoot me. I know you, Jack Stephens. You are not a bad man".

Chimera stopped.

Although the black mask covered his face, it was easy to tell that he was taken aback by the mere mention of the name. To Nathan's surprise, Chimera slowly lowered his gun. Despite the mild rainfall and Nathan's distance from the mercenary, he could hear the man speak in a low voice to himself.

"Jack Stephens?" he said. "*Jack*—"

An explosion erupted within centimetres of Chimera's chest plate. A loud boom followed that made Nathan's ears pop. The force of the blow was so strong that it hurled Chimera back a good thirty feet. He flew threw the air, and collided with a chimney before veering back over the edge of Hawtrey House. The last thing Nathan saw of Chimera was the mask staring back at him.

Then Chimera disappeared.

Initially, Nathan assumed that the blast had come from the Phoenix, but to his surprise, the cannons hadn't spun up yet. It was only when Nathan got aboard the ship that he realised what had happened.

James Stephens leaned against the bulkhead, clutching a smoking grenade launcher that he'd grabbed from Koble's stash. He looked like hammered shit, but not in the way Nathan expected. Sure, he was pale as a ghost and seemed as breathless as an overweight Horrus, but there was a clarity to his eyes that told Nathan that his cousin was different.

James looked at Nathan, and lowered the grenade launcher with a laugh that suggested irony. As the cargo bay door sealed and the Phoenix lifted off, James nodded:

"Hello, Nate. It's been a long time".

VOL

The Evoker kid from the Equus looked terrible. By Vol's best estimate, the young man who'd identified himself as Cadu had been subjected to torture, starvation, and extreme dehydration. It was only when the Sadalmelik's crew got him to the medical bay that Vol understood the extent of his torment. Cadu's torso bore the marks of his suffering: everything from bruises to laser burns to nasty looking cuts around the ribs and even a bullet wound in the shoulder.

For the better part of an hour, Vol helped one of the Sadalmelik's crewmen with stabilising the Evoker. She wasn't a medical expert by any stretch of the imagination, but the same applied to Hayward's man, Langdon Riggs: he'd simply been the guy to carry Cadu from the Equus to the Sadalmelik. Despite the lack of medical training they shared, Vol and Riggs were able to get an intravenous into Cadu and treat the wounds on his torso. In addition, they'd completed those tasks during a short FTL transit, which Vol figured must be some kind of minor accomplishment.

Riggs had been trying to run a blood scan when the Sadalmelik's threat level dropped from one to two. It was a relief, but there was still anxiety in the room. Riggs was sure that the Society had injected something nasty in Cadu's blood flow and the Sadalmelik's equipment wasn't good enough to detect it.

Five minutes later, Hayward and Harrt arrived in the medical bay to check on the Evoker.

"Gimme the news," Hayward said. "Is he gonna live?"

"Hard to say, boss," Riggs shrugged. "I ain't no doctor, but I think they injected him with some nasty drugs to keep his elemental summons at bay".

Hayward folded his arms, "Meaning what exactly?"

"*Meaning* that we can only do so much with bandages and gauze," Riggs answered. "This kid needs a full brain scan, nerve detoxification, and maybe even blood therapy. If they got something into his blood, there's very little I can do with our gear".

"Let me get him aboard the Artemis," Harrt said, to Hayward. "My crew can treat him. We can save his life and get answers".

Hayward exhaled through his nostrils, and Vol could hear the what-if scenarios running through the big man's brain. Despite recovering part of Claire's data vault on the Equus, Cadu was the only real lead remaining, and if he died, then all of it would've been for nothing.

As Vol overheard Hayward's stray thoughts, she imagined the Earther making a pros-and-cons list inside his head. The problem was that there was a potential con for every pro and vice versa. If those potential cons became a reality, it would cost a lot more than the life of one Evoker.

Hayward had an emotional investment in the situation that reached far beyond his years undercover with Jareth Corps. He craved to know what happened to Claire on a base level, but also on a far higher plane of reasoning, Hayward didn't want the Society to get away scot-free. He wanted them to pay for their crimes, perhaps more than anything else.

After several tense seconds, Hayward replied to Harrt, "Do it. Get on the horn to your XO and get the kid the medical attention he needs, but as soon as he wakes up, I wanna question him".

▲

With Cadu in a stable condition, Vol excused herself from the medbay, leaving Riggs and Hayward to talk alone. There was an uneasy, mournful tension between the two men, rooted in the loss of their crewmate aboard the Equus. Vol didn't want to get in the middle of it, so she washed the blood from her hands and headed into the corridor. Harrt was leaning against the bulkhead, talking to someone on his datapad.

"I'll explain when I get aboard," he said with a sigh. "Just have the med techs prep for the patient".

A woman's voice came through the other side of the comm. "Understood. See you in a few minutes".

Harrt deactivated his datapad and stuffed it into his pocket. He pushed away from the bulkhead and offered up an exhausted smile as Vol approached. He looked a little worse for wear, still pale from the vacuum exposure, but better than he'd looked in the airlock.

"Thanks for saving me back there," he said. "What you did was—"

"Insane?" Vol raised her brows.

"Well, I was gonna go with brave, but sure, let's go with that..."

Vol nodded, "I just did what I know you would've done".

They shared a moment that was both companionable and awkward, and for that hair of a second, all the bullshit and drama melted away. It was like it had been before: two people from very different worlds, with different views, that simply cared for the other in a way that meant something more than it looked on the surface. It felt good to be in the space, and Vol allowed herself to embrace the feeling.

Harrt scratched his head; half-smiled and began, "I know things have been kinda difficult, but I —"

He was cut off by the sound of the Sadalmelik's internal comm-system, which seemed a lot louder to Vol than it had been earlier. Scruffy's voice filled the room through speakers in the ceiling, "All hands, prepare for docking: this ain't no drill, so let's try not to die".

When Scruffy's announcement ended, Vol looked at Harrt with a raised brow.

"Raincheck on this conversation?" he said.

"Yeah".

HARRT

When the Sadalmelik and Artemis docked, a musical ping came from one of the control panels, indicating that an air-tight vacuum was beginning to form between the two ships. Harrt knew that at that very moment, a squad of his marines would be prepping for a potential hostage situation: as was standard practice when the CO was aboard an unknown vessel for unknown reasons. When he shared his expectations with Hayward, the chunky Earther looked as though he wanted to protest but showed some restraint.

"Fine, but the rest of my crew and the data vault stay aboard the Sadalmelik," Hayward folded his big arms.

Harrt glanced at Dines, who —as always— wore a grim expression that made him look far older than his years. Harrt was expecting the Agent to argue, but to Harrt's surprise, Dines did the opposite.

"I think Mr Hayward makes an excellent point," Dines said as he straightened out his tattered, combat worn shirt. Then while motioning with a finger to Harrt, Hayward and Vol, Dines continued, "We don't mention the data vault to anyone outside this group, including Lieutenant Meera".

Nobody offered up a challenge.

"Oh, and one more thing," Hayward chipped in, his voice brash and unforgiving. "I don't want any members of your crew aboard this ship, or any 'wealther mandated inspections".

Harrt didn't argue: in fact, he agreed with him. The fact that the Artemis arrived when it did was beyond suspicious, but options were limited. The Evoker who'd been aboard the Equus could have information relating to the Society, the Revenant, and most importantly, the mole.

As the group waited for the airlock to finish its work, Vol handed Harrt a datapad with a bunch of complex coding schemes that looked almost alien to the untrained eye. Harrt looked at the blur of numbers and letters; unsure what to make of it all.

"What am I looking at?" he asked.

"This is the firewall that Claire put over the data vault," Vol answered. "It's gonna take me some time, but I think I can crack it".

"How long?"

"I mean, this would be a whole lot easier if we had Kyp, but he's still aboard the Phoenix trying to decode that combat recorder," Vol replied. She checked the time on her datapad, "All in all, I could crack this in a few hours".

Harrt was ready to say something profound when the airlock controls buzzed, and the lights around the hatch went green. A hiss of cold air arose from the ducts surrounding the still-sealed door.

"Contact me as soon as you crack it," Harrt said to Vol. "Nobody else".

She nodded before heading back into the bowels of the Sadalmelik. As Harrt watched Vol go, he felt the impulse to take her aside and straighten out all their problems: to repair that which was broken. It felt like things were getting back on track, but Harrt forced himself to remember that the mission came first.

"Never thought I'd be getting aboard a Commonwealth warship," Hayward grumbled, drawing Harrt's attention from his thoughts. "It's a fuckin weird feeling".

"First time for everything," Dines shrugged.

The hatch parted, and as Harrt suspected, four armed marines were there to greet them. Once Harrt stepped forward and made clear that he and the others were of no threat, the jugheads —his jugheads— lowered their weapons.

Lieutenant Jaudi Meera stepped through the pack of tough-looking soldiers —most of whom was twice her size — like the unstoppable force Harrt had always known her to be. Her bright eyes studied Hayward first, regarding him with an *almost* welcoming distrust. Jaudi's gaze flicked to Dines, and she nodded to him with the kind of politeness that was appropriate for the situation.

When Jaudi looked at Harrt, he felt as though he was back at the Commonwealth academy. Even though Harrt was now the CO and Jaudi the XO, their dynamic had never changed. She was and would forever always be *the* Jaudi Meera: the scourge of the skies.

"You're full of surprises, Commander," Jaudi said as she looked at Harrt. Then with a hint of sarcasm mixed with scepticism, she added, "Welcome back".

"Permission to come aboard?" Harrt asked, as was the custom.

"Granted," Jaudi nodded. Then when the Marines were out of earshot, she said, "Care to explain what's going on?"

INTERLUDE
ROTH

Hawtrey House —the third of the Roth family manors— was but a shell of its former self. Scorch marks covered the east wing, and a large proportion of the roof had been blown away in an explosion. The electrical systems were still going haywire. Worst of all, there was a gaping hole in the middle of the library that went down several storeys, and at the bottom was a smashed Brucbeck chandelier that had once belonged to Theodore Jareth.

Then there were the casualties. The death toll wasn't clear, but there had been several reports of injuries —some of which were life-threatening. In Alastair Roth's view, that part of it was far less important. People were expendable resources to exploit and use as he wished. All that mattered was the very real fact that Paradisian blood had been spilt on his land. *That, he could most certainly use.*

The trade for James Stephens had been interrupted. Tariq Mahmoot and the crew of the Phoenix Titan had played their role spectacularly and —mostly— according to plan. When he thought about it, Roth could already see the headlines:

"Commonwealth allies attack sovereign celebration".

"Evoker-funded mercenary gang kills x-number of innocent party goers".

"Political attack on Paradisium's freedom by radical fringe Commonwealth sympathisers".

That one was Roth's favourite.

It was almost perfect, but like all plans, there had to be a curveball. In Roth's experience, they were guaranteed. The key to dealing with them was to anticipate, to adapt and to react accordingly. Then if all went awry —which rarely happened in Roth's line of work— bursting the issue to minimise fallout was critical.

David Jareth was the curveball in this particular scheme, which seemed surprising given his early arrival at the party with his big, masked attack dog. For years, Roth had known that Jareth was a man consumed by jealousy and hatred, but he'd never expected the old fool to actually attempt a coup de grace against the Society. Hate them, yes. Sew seeds of discontent, perhaps, but to actually plot the assassination of Society members was a bold move indeed.

Maybe that was why Roth had been surprised to find Jareth on the roof in the first place? Sure, Roth had played the part of the all-seeing, all-knowing, machiavellian mastermind, but to be anything else would make him appear weak. That was something that Roth would not allow to happen. *After all, appearances were everything.*

Jareth was one of those people that had made Roth's kill list years ago, but to deal with him wasn't as simple as pulling the trigger. Jareth had supporters on Paradisium and in the Outer Worlds. Killing him could spark fallout, and that was something Roth couldn't afford. He imagined that Jareth's reasons for not attacking the Society over the decades were similar: everyone wanted to avoid repercussions. No, dealing with David Jareth was something that —had things gone to plan— could've waited until Project Erebus was fully realised.

Fate laughs at those who make plans, Roth thought.

Despite things not going entirely to plan, the overall objective had been achieved: Tariq Mahmoot played to his hand and involved the crew of the Phoenix Titan, and as a bonus, Jareth was taken out of the equation through sheer dumb luck. Now, Roth had the kindling to light a fire, the likes of which the galaxy had never seen before. The Society would do what it had always done and manipulate the masses to achieve its goals. This time, the only difference was that it would do so on a scale that hadn't been seen since the Fall.

No risk, no reward, as Theodore Jareth used to say.

For the hour that followed the attack, Alastair Roth felt rather pleased with himself, then Bradley Austin —one of his many henchmen— reported in:

"They took Christian, sir..."

Roth felt his gut cease and his heart thud.

"Pardon?" he said, desperately trying to remoisten his mouth as he spoke.

"The crew of the Phoenix Titan... they captured your son," Austin replied.

Roth considered Austin's statement, then instructed the mercenary to bring up the relevant security footage on his datapad. The video revealed that Christian had been attacked and subsequently carried off by a Sphinax masquerading as a party guest. According to the scans on the big creature's ID, he was Kornell, former Chief of the Pluvium System and a black-listed member of the Criminal Syndicate. Roth had met Kornell before, and the husky creature on-screen — while sharing some resemblance— was most certainly not Kornell.

Ergo, Roth could understand why his son would let down his guard, but at the same time, he felt a pang of disappointment with Christian. Over the years, Roth had spent a fortune ensuring his son was trained for such situations.

Before the Fall, successful businesspeople and their families were often targetted by lower-class miscreants: Jack Stephens had most certainly proven that on the day of the Fall when he barged onto Roth's private escaped shuttle and threatened his family with a gun. Even after the Fall, Roth had to ensure that his family line remained. Despite the safety of Paradisium, there were threats from all corners: Revenant, Commonwealth, the Criminal Syndicate and even those trying to usurp the Society's chain of command —all of them presented a danger to the Roth lineage.

And so, Christian and his sister were trained to fight and shoot. They were also taught what to do if they were taken hostage: in some way, that was a reassurance. Christian would know when to attempt an escape and when to keep his mouth shut. He'd know how to play mind games with his captors and could incapacitate them in close-quarters combat.

It's another curveball, Roth thought. *It can be course-corrected easily.*

He gestured to Austin, and the muscle-bound thug deactivated his datapad.

"See that, when the time comes, my son's liberation is at the top of your objectives," Roth ordered.

"Goes without saying, sir".

"Has there been any update on Jareth's man? The one they call Chimera?"

Austin cockily hoisted his gun over his shoulder; "I've got the guys searching the grounds, but the working theory is the Evoker got to him."

"So, in other words, he's been reduced to ash?"

"That's the theory, sir, but we'll keep searching".

It wasn't a satisfying answer for Roth at all. For years, the mercenary known as Chimera had served Jareth well. There were many rumours about his true identity: some of which had piqued Roth's interest, and then there were others that were entirely absurd. Still, Roth imagined there would be a certain satisfaction in unmasking Chimera before brutally killing him as he had countless others.

Roth looked at the giant Revenant Behemoth above, still floating against the red and orange morning sky. He knew who was up there.

"When is he coming down to see me?" Roth said, turning to Austin.

"Within the hour," Austin answered.

▲

Meeting with Baylum, the self-proclaimed King of reprisal, should've filled Roth with dread, but he wasn't scared at all. Yes, Baylum was dangerous, but his need for allies was far greater than his bloodlust. Where Seig had been a devout fool with near-infinite resources, Baylum was a pragmatist with significantly reduced numbers. The need to rebuild was top of his priorities, not praying to a river of broken Enkaye technology like his father before him.

Roth intended to exploit that weakness and use it for his gain. After all, *Baylum was but a pawn in his pièce de résistance.*

There was one thing to consider that made Roth slightly nervous when he thought about it. The brutal truth was that the Revenant had the numbers. Even after the defeat at the Battle of The Messorem, Baylum had a few billion soldiers at his disposal, whereas the Society had a few thousand. Despite that straightforward fact, it didn't matter unless things went very wrong, which Roth had no intention of allowing.

Taking on enemies in open combat wasn't the Society's style: the art of manipulation was, and Alastair Roth could have written a book on the subject. For now, he'd play the game. He'd smile and make nice, just as Theodore Jareth taught him all those years ago. Then when the opportune moment arose, Roth would deal with Baylum once and for all.

As he waited for Baylum in the atrium of Hawtrey House, Roth took out a cigar from his breast pocket and a monogrammed silver cutter. He sniffed the perfectly rolled stick and paused, examining the sophisticated scent of tobacco partnered with vodka. After taking a long pull on the cigar, Roth blew a large cloud of smoke as Baylum entered his domain.

The Revenant King was the walking embodiment of intimidation. He was larger than Roth recalled, both in muscle and in height. Unlike the previous times Roth had met with him, Baylum did not wear his crown or royal robes. Instead, he wore a long black coat that trailed down to his knees. His broad shoulders were covered by a pair of silver pauldrons, which added further to his impressive build.

Bradley Austin and another mercenary flanked Baylum as he silently walked across the room. Roth ordered his men to stand down with a wave of the hand, but the King still regarded him with an emotionless expression.

There was something horribly unnerving about pure-blooded Revenants that always sent a shiver of repulsion through Roth's skin. Unlike most species, purebloods had evolved in the cold vacuum of dark space —or as they called it, the Void. The impact of this evolutionary quirk was that Revenant eyes were entirely black. There was no way to discern where the iris began and the pupil ended.

There was only darkness.

As Baylum drew close, Roth made out the intricate details of the King's many tattoos, each representing a dominated world. His skin, though scarred and deformed, was covered in the sacred Revenant artwork. It was unnatural. It was inhuman. And yet, Roth shook the man's hand in what was intended to look like friendship.

"It is good to see you in the flesh, my old friend," Roth said, putting on his most charming tone of voice. "It's been far too long".

Baylum regarded him with a look of scrutiny, and when he noticed the cigar, he pointed at it. "I've never understood your species' obsession with self-destruction,"

"Maybe you should try one, " Roth took a pull and blew a ring of smoke into the air. "After all, cigars, fine cheeses and port were among the few things that deserved to be saved from Earth".

Baylum's expression hardened, though it wasn't a frown. *Chagrin, perhaps?* It was always hard to gauge the reactions of an inhuman creature that saw everything it did as holy or divine.

Still, there was no anger in Baylum's voice when he spoke. "I assume that everything is going according to plan?"

"For the most part," Roth nodded. "They interrupted the trade for the half-breed and killed a few dozen people in the process. Now my colleagues and I will rally the people of Paradisium against the Commonwealth. The masses will see this as an act of war, and the Society will use it. My brothers and sisters will direct our loyal subjects to amass around the Capital World of Valour".

"Good," Baylum said, his voice low and thoughtful. "I am pleased to share with you that Commander Oxarri boarded the Equus and took the bait as intended".

Roth leaned forward in anticipation, "And the Artemis? Did your spy—"

Baylum cut him off, "My *people* did precisely as intended. The Artemis intercepted the Sadalmelik, and soon it will receive new orders".

Roth puffed on his cigar, using the smoke to partially shield his smile. "That is excellent, your majesty. We are one step closer to Project Erebus".

"Let's hope you are right," Baylum said. "I want what lays inside Erebus".

Not as much as I do, Roth thought.

"Fear not, your majesty. The Society has been in control of the Earth's people for over two millennia. All it will take is a spark to light the fire we need".

Baylum nodded, "I'm leaving you with three of my Death Cruisers."

Roth almost choked on his cigar. "My dear friend, I will have the combined force of Paradisium's most patriotic fools at my disposal. Your support, while appreciated, is entirely unnecessary".

The last part was a lie, but Roth knew that he'd reinforce the notion that he was a loyal friend and ally by simply saying it.

"This is not a request," Baylum frowned. "Once you trigger the event, those ships will deploy into Commonwealth space to add to the theatre".

"If this is about the Phoenix Titan—"

"This is not about Nathan Carter or his crew," Baylum snapped. "This scheme we have devised is the most critical operation that either of us has ever attempted. The last time we undertook something like this was the Fall, and we both know how that turned out..."

The king's comment stung more than Roth cared to admit. The Fall was not considered a roaring success like many in the Society believed: in fact, Roth considered it a four-pronged failure. First, Bill Stephens destroyed the first Project Erebus, preventing Roth from becoming the most powerful being in the universe. *That one stung the most.* Second, the Commonwealth arrived, and millions who should've died on Earth survived and made it to the new world. Third, the wise and wonderful Theodore Jareth perished in his escape: likely mauled to death by an angry mob, but nobody could confirm the details.

Finally, there was Jack Stephens, the man who'd threatened Roth and his children, and who'd killed his beloved brother-in-law, Götz Richtofen. The man who'd dumped a few billion dollars worth of Roth's heirlooms and art pieces to save more gutter rats. It was a failure of the highest magnitude, and yet, Alastair Roth learned from his mistakes and the mistakes of others, such as Theodore Jareth.

"We cannot leave any room for failure. That is why *my ships* will support you". Baylum took a step closer to Roth, "If a time comes where the Phoenix Titan, its Captain or its crew are within our sights, remember this; I want Nathan Carter alive. Not dead. Do you understand me?"

Roth stared up into the dark, soulless eyes of the Revenant King. Despite Baylum's menacing stature looming over him, Roth stood his ground.

You will regret trying to intimidate me, Roth thought. *Project Erebus is mine.*

"Absolutely, your highness," Roth said, his voice polite and amicable. "The nephew of Jack Stephens will be yours".

CHIMERA

Despite his dislocated shoulder, many bruises and a headache that would last days, Chimera evaded Roth's security personnel with ease. Back in the days before the Fall, the man now known as Chimera operated as part of a top-secret government agency known as the EDA. It had been a hush-

hush, black-ops situation, where combat and stealth went hand in hand.

He'd been trained by the best to be the best.

Even now, twenty-six years on, he was pretty sure he could still sneak into the most secure buildings imaginable and evade detection. That was one of the many things that had been drilled into him. It was an ability that somehow became more than second nature: just like his capacity to fight and kill. Then again, the emotional curly-haired guy had proven to be quite challenging, but he'd also gotten lucky with the chandelier falling out of the ceiling.

While Roth's men scoured the house and grounds, Chimera took shelter in the hangar bay, which had been near the epicentre of the EMP blast. Under the cover of darkness, he waited.

Roth's men came to the hangars after about fifteen minutes. They entered in standard military formation, armed with stun weapons and lighting up the place with flashlights and flares.

Despite their presence, Chimera remained calm.

He waited.

He moved when he needed to do so.

He avoided detection.

Roth's men were none the wiser to his presence, and ten minutes later, they moved off. That was when Chimera took the opportunity to find the shuttle he and Jareth had arrived on. He spent the next hour laying low, as leaving too early could draw unwanted attention.

It gave him time.

First, Chimera popped his shoulder back into place while biting down on the inside of his mask. After that, he repaired his armour then set about getting the shuttle online.

An hour later, he carefully piloted the shuttle out of the hangars and to the city below, avoiding Roth's anti-aircraft guns on the top side. Chimera took the shuttle into one of the busy skylanes to obscure himself amongst the traffic. By this stage, there was little point in pursuing the Phoenix Titan. It'd be long gone by now, and Chimera's shuttle had limited FTL capabilities.

Besides, they wouldn't kill Jareth; he was far too valuable.

The mission had to continue, but objectives had to change. Chimera needed to understand Roth's movements in order to strike again. He waited another thirty minutes before running scans on Hawtrey House. The first thing that caught his eye was the sudden increase in Roth's security forces. Compared to the previous evening, Roth had seemingly quadrupled the number of armed mercenaries on the ground. Every ounce of Chimera's being could tell that something wasn't right.

He continued to investigate the incoming scans, checking for security alerts, incoming transmissions and the movement of ships from Hawtrey house. Then he saw it. A Revenant Royale landed at the manor, escorted by several fighters. Chimera's interest piqued, and he took the risk of activating an advanced surveillance drone from the confines of the shuttle. Not only was it undetectable to the naked eye, but it could also transmit video and audio to the shuttle. He watched intently as the drone flew threw the clouds to Hawtrey house. A figure stepped out from the shuttle that Chimera immediately recognised as King Baylum. He tracked the Revenant King through the manor until he reached the Atrium where Alastair Roth was waiting.

Chimera tuned the audio until he had an almost perfect signal. He watched intently as Roth and Baylum greeted one another. It was unusual to see it first-hand and not what Chimera expected at all. For years, he'd always assumed that Roth was subordinate to Baylum, but Roth's tone of voice implied that they were on even footing. Of course, both men believed that they were in control of the situation rather than the other, but that was simply the egos of weak-willed men: Chimera had known their type before.

"The nephew of Jack Stephens will be yours," Roth's voice reverberated around the shuttle.

Chimera stopped. It had been a lifetime since he'd heard that name spoken aloud, and yet this was the second —or third— time in twenty-four hours. That's what the curly-haired guy from the Phoenix Titan called him.

Jack Stephens...

Nathan Carter is Jack Stephens' nephew...

He was so lost in thought that he almost entirely took his eye off the mission. Chimera snapped himself back to the monitor and listened to Roth and Baylum's exchange three more times. It was clear that whatever the pair were planning, it was happening at the Capital World of Valour. A Commander Harrt Oxarri had taken the bait, and there, dead centre of it all, was the Phoenix Titan."

CHAPTER TWENTY
KOBLE

The escape from Haydrium was far easier than any of the crew anticipated. Despite being pursued by a couple dozen Revenant Fighters, Rain had easily out-manoeuvred them, and once they were clear of the planet's atmosphere, the jump to FTL was seamless. Koble breathed a sigh of relief when he saw the welcoming blue torrent of the slipstream. The Revenant would not be able to follow them, and by all accounts, the mission was a success.

"That was far too easy," Rain said as he unbuckled himself from the pilot's chair.

"Don't be paranoid," Koble replied, waving off his friend's comment. "Those bastards threw everything they had at us on the ground".

"They had a Death Cruiser, Chief. You don't just walk away from one of those things".

"Hey, we just did," Koble smiled.

Rain looked at him with a skeptical frown.

Koble placed a paw on his shoulder and presented Rain with one of the bottles of champagne he'd stolen earlier.

"Relax, old man," Koble said. "You did good".

Rain shot him a look that suggested disagreement, but Koble wrote it off as nothing more than nerves. He knew his blue-furred counterpart well. Despite Rain's suave nature, the old Sphinax always got overly edgy after a combat situation. It was just his way.

"C'mon," Koble said, gesturing to the champagne. "Let's crack one of these bad boys open".

▲

In the living area, Nathan was sitting on one of the barstools with his shirt off, allowing Astrilla to check the nasty bruises now forming on his ribcage. Koble looked at the injuries as he walked behind the bar to fetch a fresh glass.

"Looks rather painful, my friend," Rain said to Nathan as he leaned on the bar. "Did you get into some trouble down there?"

"You could say that," Nathan replied through his split lip.

Koble grabbed a medical kit from behind the bar and handed the Earther a repair pen. It wouldn't aid in the ribs, but it would certainly help the skin around his lip to heal.

"So, you fought that Chimera guy?" Koble said to Nathan as he handed Rain a tankard that probably wasn't champagne appropriate. "What the hell happened?"

Nathan's jaw tightened, and he looked at the ground for a long awkward moment.

"I think it was Jack," he said.

Koble took a step back. "What?"

Nathan dragged his gaze to Koble and looked the Sphinax in the eye. "Chimera fights like Jack. Got all the same moves; same gear; same build... same tattoo".

"Did you get the mask off him?" Koble asked.

Nathan was about to answer but stopped talking as Tariq and Gordon helped James past the living area and to one of the starboard cabins. Koble felt awkward sharing the same space as James, so he could barely imagine what it was like for Nathan. James was barely conscious and looked like he'd been through hell and back: which seemed ironic to Koble, given that the last time he'd seen James, he'd looked like a typical junkie.

Once Tariq and James were out of earshot, Nathan looked at Koble and answered his question. "I couldn't get the mask off of him".

Koble considered it for a moment, wondering if the legendary Jack Stephens could actually be Chimera. It was possible, but there were other circumstances that he couldn't ignore. For it to be Jack, it meant that he'd not only survived Mirotose Station, but he'd also laid low for the last decade: all while working for David Jareth.

It didn't make sense.

Astrilla frowned as she handed Nathan his shirt.

"Chimera's aim wavered when you said his name," she remarked. "Almost as though he were lowering his gun..."

"You mean right before James blew him off that roof with my grenade launcher?" Koble grimaced. Then after whistling through his teeth, "Ouch.."

"He was wearing enough armour to withstand much worse," Nathan asserted as he pulled his shirt over his head. "Fortunately, we have a prisoner aboard who knows the real identity of Chimera. I think it's time to get some answers".

"You want back-up?" Koble said, cracking his knuckles.

Nathan shook his head; "No. You guys contact Oxarri and Vol; find out where we rendezvous".

JARETH

When David Jareth opened his eyes, he felt an overwhelming ache inside his skull. It was the kind of pounding headache that he'd not experienced since his teenage years —the type of pain one would get from physical strain or combat. For several seconds, his eyes struggled to focus, and all Jareth could see was a single source of orange light in an otherwise darkened space.

Based on the lack of humidity and low hum coming from the back of the room, Jareth quickly deduced that he was aboard a ship. Out of nothing more than pure instinct, he attempted to move but quickly realised that he'd been unceremoniously bound to a chair.

As his vision began to clear, Jareth could just about make out the outline of another person at the other end of the room. The shadowy figure casually leaned against the wall while drinking from a shallow glass. The smell of Xandian mock-whiskey was there, but only ever so slightly. There was a certain devil-may-care attitude about the man opposite, and for a split-second, Jareth was sure he was looking at Jack Stephens.

All the telltale signs were there: everything from the dark and intimidating surroundings fit for interrogation to the custom pistol and even the cheap booze.

"It's been a long time, old boy," Jareth said into the cloudy haze.

The man in the shadows turned to look at him, and with a casual motion, he moved into the light. The outline of what Jareth assumed had been Jack shifted, and Captain Nathan Carter emerged from the darkness in its place. For the first time ever, Jareth saw the family resemblance, though it was only in demeanour and presence rather than appearance.

Nathan's dark hair had been tied back in a bun, showing his partially bruised face. He wore a holstered pistol atop a pair of dark denim jeans on his hip. It was the same gun that Jack carried back in the day: the same gun that Jareth sent to Nathan, as per his old acquaintance's instruction. Seeing the modified revolver in the hands of its intended owner filled Jareth with a strange sense of nostalgia.

"Welcome aboard the Phoenix Titan," Nathan said, sarcastically raising his glass. "I'm sorry to tell you that your trading days with the Revenant are over".

That was when all of it came rushing back to Jareth: the horrible realisation that his plan had failed. He recalled the rooftop gunbattle, Roth's smug look of victory, the EMP blast and injecting James Stephens with an arterial bomb.

All of his efforts and planning had gone to waste.

"You have no idea what you've done," Jareth spat angrily. "You bloody idiots haven't got the faintest idea of what you've done!"

There was silence. The sound of the Phoenix's engine filled the void. Nathan took a sip from his glass and savoured the taste as he glared back.

"Tell me something, David...you don't mind if I call you David, do you? I'm not really a titles guy".

Nathan knelt down to look him in the eye. The close proximity of the younger man allowed Jareth to make out his busted lip. The question that Nathan asked was the last one Jareth expected:

"Who is Chimera?"

"What?" Jareth scoffed. "Why in the world is he of concern to you?"

"Just answer the fucking question".

Jareth stared at Nathan as he attempted to put some rationale to it. There was something behind Nathan's dark brown eyes that Jareth had seen many times before. It was the innate yearning to find something lost. He thought long and hard about Chimera: about the man under the mask, and suddenly everything became clear.

"Let me ask you something, Captain Carter," Jareth leaned back. "Why did you capture me?"

Nathan stood up and frowned. "You and your pals are in bed with the Revenant. We caught you red-handed trying to trade an Enkaye half-breed with them".

"You think I am working with the Revenant?"

"Could have fooled me back there," Nathan shrugged.

Jareth replayed the whole rooftop shootout in his head, trying to imagine how it could've looked to the uninitiated. Admittedly, it didn't look great.

"I know how it looked," Jareth said, leaning against his binds. "But you must understand, I was trying to assassinate Baylum and Roth. I planted an arterial bomb on James, and it was my hope to detonate it once the Revenant King arrived".

"I don't believe a word you're saying," Nathan shook his head. "What was it you said to me before I destroyed the Messorem? Something about how I'd made an enemy out of you?"

Jareth scoffed. "Nothing more than impassioned words during a stressful moment. I assure you that my plan was to kill Baylum and Roth".

Nathan's brow lowered, and his lips pursed in thought. The Captain of the Phoenix Titan produced a datapad from his pocket and tapped the screen several times. Small holographic projections formed above the device; all were public domain press photos of Jareth and Roth at various EWB-related events.

"For someone who wants to kill Alastair Roth, you've sure had a big part in his political movement," Nathan mused. The look on his face was somewhere between sarcastic and irritated. "After all, you are the one that spearheaded the whole thing. You blackmailed the 'wealther data out of Leviticus Dines and handed it to Roth. You—"

"How dim are you, Carter?" Jareth cut in, elevating his voice to make him sound more in control of the situation than he was. "Nothing is ever as it appears on the surface. Yes, I spearheaded the movement. Yes, I met with Roth, and yes, I support the movement for Paradisian separatism".

"You aren't exactly making a great case for yourself," Nathan said, folding his arms.

Jareth frowned." Listen here, boy: the EWB serves two purposes. On the surface, the separatism of Paradisium from the Commonwealth, but it's what's under the surface that matters: what's always been under the surface."

"And what's that?"

"Those who control from the shadows: the Society," Jareth answered flatly. "Ever since the Fall, I've been trying to cast light on that which does not wish to be found. The EWB was the match to light the fires that I would use to find them and burn them".

Nathan Carter wore an expression of distrust that Jareth had seen before on the face of Jack. It was the same look Jack had given him when they'd first met all those years ago. Nathan strolled to the back of the room to refill his glass with a fresh dram.

"Why?" Nathan asked. "Why do you want the Society dead?"

Jareth smiled knowingly. "Because I know the truth..."

"What truth?" Nathan demanded.

The edginess on Nathan's face was apparent, and again it evoked memories of Jack. Jareth wondered if perhaps Nathan could be trusted with one of his closest kept secrets. After all, Jareth knew what Jack had done to get his son and nephew off Earth. Despite being a boy at the time, Nathan would have seen the kind of man Alastair Roth was. *Maybe he would understand?*

Jareth cleared his throat and opted for faith rather than logic for the first time in years.

"Before The Fall, a group of influential, powerful men, including Alastair Roth, betrayed our people".

"You mean the Society..."

Jareth nodded, "They made a pact with the —then— Prince Baylum. Not Seig. Baylum. That part is very important".

"Okay..."

"The Society gave Baylum access to all of Earth's defences, including those that weren't public knowledge. In return, the Society was granted safe passage for themselves and one-hundred thousand of Earth's *most refined citizens,* along with a host of terraforming gear and new sparkly technology to carve out their new —more sophisticated— Earth".

Nathan squinted: *half apprehension, half realisation.* Jareth could almost imagine the chill running down the young man's spine at that revelation.

"Of course, the Commonwealth arrived at the thirteenth hour and saved a lot more than the mere one-hundred thousand that the Society had cherrypicked to survive".

Nathan was quiet for a long time. The silence was awkward, but Jareth had anticipated it: after all, he was telling someone a cold, hard fact that had been buried for decades. What he said next would be uncomfortable, maybe even downright excruciating, but Jareth knew he had to say it: he had to test Nathan Carter to understand just how much the young man really knew about his uncle.

About the masterplan.

About the truth: the real truth.

"Do you now understand why Jack kept you away from Paradisium?"

Jareth could see the cogs turning inside Nathan's head. To Jareth's surprise, Nathan didn't answer the question. Instead, he took a long sip from his whiskey and then set it down on a crate at the back of the room.

"Who is Chimera?" Nathan said for the second time during their conversation.

The fact that he brought the conversation back around to Chimera told Jareth everything he needed to know. He saw the strings he could pull to get his way.

"Listen here," Jareth enunciated. "Let me go, and I'll tell you who Chimera is. You have my word".

Nathan's hand dropped to his holster. "Do you think I'm stupid?"

"Nathan, you must listen to me," Jareth said, staring back at the younger man. "Me being aboard the Phoenix Titan is part of Roth's plan. I don't know why, but this whole thing is wrong—"

"Who is Chimera?"

"I—"

Nathan pulled his gun from its holster.

"Answer the question!"

Jareth stared at Nathan, unphased by the gun pointed squarely at his skull. Much to Nathan's chagrin, Jareth shook his head. "I am a man of honour, Nathan. I swore to the man you know as Chimera long ago that I would keep his identity a secret. He is a man that does not wish to be unmasked".

"You are no man of honour," Nathan muttered. "You're just another bad person in a bad universe. I promise you, Mr Jareth, you will answer for your crimes: one way or the other".

Nathan holstered his gun and paced to the door. At that moment, Jareth realised he may have to break an old promise: that was the only way he was getting out of the situation.

"I suggest you take a hard look at those aboard your ship, Captain Carter," Jareth said, prompting Nathan to turn and look at him.

Nathan didn't dignify him with a response. The Captain of the Phoenix Titan turned and continued to leave. He slammed the light switch upon his exit, leaving Jareth in complete darkness. Out of nothing more than pure anger with Roth and the entire situation, Jareth screamed at the closed door.

NATHAN

Nathan strolled through the Phoenix's long corridor, past the galley and into the cockpit. He'd consciously gone the long way to avoid James. Nathan knew that eventually, he'd have to face his estranged cousin and have a very awkward conversation, but he wasn't ready for that.

Not now: not with everything that was going on.

He checked in with Rain, who'd spent the last fifteen minutes trying to make contact with Harrt and Vol. There was nothing, and the shared location data coming from the Sadalmelik was gone too. That didn't mean they were dead. It was more likely that the Sadalmelik was either laying low or had been forced to move from its previous location at pace.

"So..." Rain drawled. "Where do we go if we can't get in touch with your pals?"

"It's only been fifteen minutes," Nathan said.

"Still, I don't like flying without direction. So, what'll it be, Pluvium? The Evoker Enclave?"

"We'll figure it out," Nathan said. "In the meantime, get us into 'wealther space: as far from Paradisium and Jareth Corps as possible".

Rain made a noise that sounded agreeable, but Nathan was sure that the blue Sphinax wanted to get Jareth back to Pluvium for a speedy war crimes trial. Nathan couldn't allow that to happen: *not yet anyway*. He knew that a large portion of the Sphinax population wanted Jareth's head on a spike for his part in Kornell's rise to power, and a large part of Nathan was inclined to agree. The problem was that Jareth had a few dozen questions to answer, and Nathan had no intention of letting the Paradisian Elitist take a long walk to the gallows without first knowing every single detail.

After Nathan left the cockpit, he headed to his cabin and stowed his pistol and holster in his bedside cabinet. He figured that if he was going to talk to James, it'd be best to do so unarmed. It wasn't that Nathan couldn't trust his own sense of restraint; it was more the thought that rescuing James had taken a lot of effort and risk. Shooting James for one of his stupid, off-hand comments would erode all of it.

Nathan took a deep breath of courage and stepped out of his cabin. He made his way to the guest quarters he'd assigned for James and Tariq, but neither of them were there. Instead, Nathan found them in the living area, talking about Ralph Hayward and the Sadalmelik.

James was sitting in one of the Phoenix's leather armchairs, looking relaxed if slightly overwhelmed by his new surroundings. Nathan recognised the expression from years gone by: it was like the anxious look James would get after going a few days without a hit.

In the eleven years since they'd parted ways, he'd imagined confronting James a million times. He had a speech planned out in his head for years, but something felt different now. Being in the presence of his only living relative made Nathan feel conflicted. Maybe he'd grown wiser with age, or perhaps he'd let go of some of the anger he'd harboured for his junkie cousin.

Upon entry, Nathan exchanged a long stare with James before moving to the bar. Sensing the tension in the room, Tariq nodded to Nathan and took his leave. That was when a frosty silence fell over the living area. Nathan discarded his empty bottle and grabbed a fresh one from a shelf behind the bar. He then took two glasses and poured a portion into each.

Might as well get this over and done with, he thought.

Nathan moved to James.

He handed a glass to his estranged cousin and took the

seat opposite. The silence between them was broken only by the hum of the Phoenix's engine.

James looked just like his father in many ways: minus the eyes and brow, which seemed more concaved than Nathan recalled. At forty-two years of age, time had undoubtedly taken some effect on James' appearance. He was no longer the young, diminished-looking junkie that seemed to wear his skin rather than live in it. James' once blonde hair was starting to show the odd hint of grey. His beard was entirely unkempt, but Nathan suspected it wasn't intentional. Gone was the bloodshot, colourless expression: now replaced by clarity and something far more human. Gone was the gaunt, boney frame that shook with involuntary convulsions: replaced by a swimmer's body that looked —-mostly— healthy.

"Your hair is a lot longer than the last time I saw you," James said, finally breaking the silence. "I know this'll sound weird, but you look just like your father —like Uncle Dylan".

Nathan let the silence linger a moment longer and sipped from his drink. It was an odd comment, considering that the only real thing Nathan could remember about his father was his gruesome death at the hands of a Revenant Hunter.

Nathan cleared his throat and, when he spoke, kept his voice as low as possible.

"That's all you've got to say? Eleven years and the first thing you say is that? How about, thanks for putting your crew at risk to save my life? How about you're sorry you were such a fucking liability back in the day?"

He glared at James expectantly, hoping his cousin felt the weight of his words. James nodded, and his lips tightened. He hung his head and looked into his glass with a degree of something that looked like shame and guilt.

"I've been clean for years," James muttered. "Since I got off Ice, it's given me time to think".

"And what exactly have you been thinking about?"

James lifted his head.

"Everything with the Loyalty...it was all my fault. When you kicked the shit outta me in that bar, you were right to leave me there".

Nathan let out a bitter half-laugh that didn't even begin to summarise how he felt at that moment.

"I'm sorry, Nate," James murmured. "Really. I'm sorry for all of it".

Nathan had imagined James' half baked apologies a hundred times before. It didn't ease the pain of what had happened. *How could it?*

Nathan shook his head and straightened up in his seat. "That's it? You think saying *sorry* washes away all of the shit that happened?"

Nathan necked the rest of his whisky and decided to move back over to the bar, slamming his glass down in the process. He was well aware that years of pent up anger were starting to surface, and he was suddenly glad that he'd left his gun in his cabin.

"I—" James began to speak but was cut off immediately by Nathan.

"When you took the Loyalty —our home— and crashed it into the Xung-Sin hideout, you killed a lot of innocent people". Nathan paused for breath. "You had no proof that the Xung-Sin killed our crew at Mirotose Station: none whatsoever".

"You're right. I cost a lot of innocent people their lives," James admitted. "I did something entirely unforgivable. That's why I do what I do with Tariq and Hayward. I want to make amends for all the shitty things I did back in the day. Shitty things I did to you, to Merri and to all the others. I still have nightmares about Merri: about all the bad shit between us."

Nathan absorbed James' words for a moment, letting the inevitable pain wash over him. He longed for it to fade away, but it wasn't that simple. A decade's worth of pain and anger wasn't easy to drop. Nathan hesitated and forced himself to gather his emotions: to not react as he so desperately wanted.

"So, I heard about your escapades with the Revenant," James said, evidently trying to shift the subject. "Heard you and your crew were the ones that took out Seig?"

"Yeah," Nathan replied, still biting back his pent up anger. "We did".

James shifted awkwardly in his chair, then raised his glass. "Well then, here's to you, little cousin..."

The hard-edged way James said it was intended to sound clever —maybe even sardonic— but Nathan knew it was nothing more than a mask to hide how much the situation was weighing down on him. As James necked his drink, Nathan looked at his cousin with a darkened expression. They'd covered one awkward topic without resolution; it was only fitting that they addressed the other elephant in the room.

"We need to talk about Chimera," Nathan said in a slow and measured tone.

James stiffened and placed his empty glass down "What about him?"

"He fights just like Jack; he's got the same tattoo and even the same gear," Nathan said impatiently. "It's gotta be your father".

James shook his head, which surprised Nathan more than he cared to admit. *If there were any hope that Jack had survived after all this time, surely his son would care more than to shrug?*

"My father died at Mirotose Station," James said coldly. "You, me and Koble were the lucky ones".

"But the tattoos, James—"

"This is how *they* work, Nate," James interrupted. "They get inside your head and make you question everything so they can manipulate you further down the line. Trust me, it's how these Society fuckers work. Besides, Chimera —whoever he is— was stood in our way, and there was no way I was gonna let the Revenant strap me into some Enkaye death machine".

There it was: the moment of realisation.

Bill Stephens' only grandchildren stared at each other in quiet comprehension. They were both Enkaye: children of gods. It was the biggest elephant in the biggest room ever known to man, and neither had acknowledged the subject until that point.

"So I take it you've already heard?" James said.

"Yeah, I found out," Nathan answered. "How'd you figure it out?"

"When I was undercover at Roth Industries, I was cataloguing a bunch of old crap they'd been collecting; vases, wine, art. That was when I stumbled on an Enkaye relic," James sipped his drink. "So the thing switches on, and suddenly I'm looking at our grandfather. We sit and talk for hours, and he tells me everything. When it's all said and done, I'm back at Roth Industries looking at a painting, and only thirty seconds have passed. Crazy, right?"

Nathan considered what he'd said. James' experience sounded all too familiar. Sure, there were some differences, but Enkaye tech was still an unknown quantity, as was the bizarre, ghostly spectre of Bill Stephens that had appeared to both of them.

"I saw him too," Nathan said. "Aboard the Messorem: he told me what I am".

James leaned forward, his eyes narrow with frightened intrigue.

"No kidding…" he mused. "Man... did those little grey fuckers go outta their way to play some head games or what?"

Nathan said nothing.

"Nate, I know I can't erase what happened all those years ago," James said, climbing to his feet. "You have every right to hate me, but I want you to know that I ain't the addict I was before. I've changed, and I'm trying really hard to make things right again".

Nathan didn't reply to his cousin's attempt to make amends: too much damage had been done by his past mistakes. Even if James were a changed man, Nathan couldn't forgive him for what had happened: for all the innocent lives he'd taken.

Nathan squinted, unable to fathom a response because he simply didn't know what to say. He averted his gaze for a moment channelling his anger and discomfort into determination. He needed to get through the conversation, even if it was awkward as hell.

"We're trying to rendezvous with Hayward and a few of my guys," Nathan said with a razor-sharp focus. "They'll likely have a 'wealther agent in tow, and unfortunately, he'll probably want to debrief you".

James nodded longer than necessary.

"Yeah... okay," he sighed. "It was only a matter of time, right? Me and the guys on the Sadalmelik did everything we could; guess it's the 'wealther's turn now".

Out of nowhere, James placed his hand on Nathan's shoulder. It was a strange, almost brotherly gesture that felt incredibly out of place.

"Thanks for saving my ass. I owe you more than one," James said, sounding oddly sincere. "Dad would've been proud".

Nathan took a breath, refusing to allow himself an emotional response.

"Don't take this the wrong way, but I need to get some sleep," James said with a yawn. "I'm gonna hit the hay. What say you and I have a real talk once this is all sorted out?"

Nathan didn't answer. He pointed down the hall, "You and Tariq are in a room down there. Go get some rest".

"Thanks," James said before limping away.

CHAPTER TWENTY-ONE
VOL

Vol hunched over a terminal hooked up to the data vault recovered from the Equus. To say that the security safeguards that Claire had put in place were advanced was an understatement. In Vol's experience, she'd never seen anything quite so thorough. The first firewall was pretty complex, but Vol found a way to exploit a minor defect in the code: something only a master engineer of the black-market variety would understand. After she cracked the first layer of security, Vol discovered what lay beneath, and it made her throw a wrench across the room in frustration.

The Sadalmelik's pilot, Scruffy, looked at her blankly: "You alright there?"

Vol took a breath to quell her frustration: "Claire sure knew how to make life difficult".

Scruffy smiled in a sad, nostalgic fashion. It was pretty apparent that he believed that Claire was dead.

"So," Scruffy drawled. "What kinda puzzle has she left for us?"

Vol spun her terminal around for him to get a better look. The old Earther scratched his white beard as he eyeballed the visualisation. There were layers upon layers of code that would eventually break. The problem, however, was that Claire seemed to be the kind of engineer that preferred failsafes: *screw up the code enough times and the system could lock you out, erase everything or explode.*

Scruffy huffed at the screen. "I've got an idea," he said,

climbing to his feet. "Follow me".

The pair ventured toward the aft of the Sadalmelik, passing through the gallery-like corridors without even stopping to admire Tariq's art collection. They eventually came upon a storage room with crates and a few floor-to-ceiling lockers. After finding Claire's, Scruffy used a crowbar to jimmy open the door. Her personal effects were few and far between. There were some ragged leather-bound books, old makeup and beauty items and a few photographs pinned to the inner doors.

It was the first time that Vol got to see an image of the woman. She didn't look like the person Vol pictured in her mind. Claire was a blonde woman with sharp features and a seemingly friendly disposition: at least based on the photographs. One picture, in particular, caught Vol's eye: a shot of Claire and Hayward sitting on a beach with a couple of beers in hand, smiling at the camera.

"What's the story between those two?" Vol said, looking at Scruffy as he discarded the broken door mechanism.

"You mean Hayward and Claire?" He said, his bushy brows raising. "They are —were— tight".

"You mean lovers?"

"I wouldn't go that far," Scruffy shook his head. He grabbed one of the books from Claire's locker and started flicking through the pages. "In our line of work, especially the undercover guys, it's best that we don't form *attachments*. Claire and Hayward were just really good friends, I guess".

"It's a shame," Vol said, looking closer at the photo.

Scruffy continued flicking through pages, and his voice seemed to trail as he replied: "Yeah... well... if things were different... they—" Scruffy stopped and held out the open book. "Well, how about that".

Vol glanced at the pages, noticing that Claire had circled certain letters and phrases in different colours. It was a system; numbers to letters; letters to code.

"Is that a cypher?" Vol said.

Scruffy scratched his beard; "Let's go find out".

HARRT

As Harrt explained everything to Jaudi, she looked at him with the same pedantic scrutiny she'd used back when she'd been the CO and he the subordinate. It was like stepping back in time. Harrt told her every detail of what led him to that moment. He spoke of the Vertex and how the Revenant had shot it out of FTL over a year ago. He outlined his earliest suspicions of a mole inside the 'wealth, and talked about everything that happened at Paradisium during the search for the Omega: *how he suspected the mole had given away the Phoenix's location to the Revenant.*

The hardest part was explaining *why* he was doing what he was doing. Harrt told Jaudi about his final exchange with Densius Olbori, which was the whole truth: not what he'd falsified on his official report. He could almost see the anger in Jaudi's eyes as he outlined the final moments of the traitor responsible for Maru Seven.

As Harrt talked, Hayward leaned against the wall-long window at the back of the room, staring at the barren starscape. Leviticus Dines sat on a chair with his arms folded, looking like a man trying to mask his discomfort: *keeping secrets was, after all, his line of work: even if he trusted Jaudi, there was still risk there.*

Finally, Harrt spoke of the investigation that he and Dines had been working on for the last year, plus Hayward; the Sadalmelik; the Society; the Equus and everything else in between. When he finished talking, Jaudi took a deep, sobering breath and nodded slowly.

"That is quite the debrief," she remarked. Then turning to Dines, "Anything you'd like to add?"

Dines sighed through his nostrils and shook his head.

Jaudi's eyes returned to Harrt. "Who are your suspects?"

Harrt and Dines shared a look.

"We believe it's someone in the Admiralty or a councilperson," Dines said. "Whoever they are, they are damn good at covering their tracks".

"So that's it?" Jaudi replied flatly and shrugged in an

exaggerated fashion. "You two believe that corrupt people lead our precious 'wealth?"

An awkward —criminal— truth lived in the silence.

"Yes," Harrt said.

Jaudi breathed laughter.

"Well, it's about damn time," she said, her voice lifting an octave. "Always had my suspicions about a few of the Admirals, but working for the Revenant.. wow".

"We don't know for certain if it is an Admiral," Dines asserted. "The fact that you received signed and sealed orders from Inon Waife simply suggests we are dealing with someone within the highest echelons: that's all".

Jaudi looked at them both with scrutiny. "Do I need to remind you that executive orders on behalf of Inon Waife can come from the Council? What about the Evoker Elders or Commissioner Kamen? Hell, an Illuminator High Priest could be in on this".

"All highly unlikely, except the Councillors," Dines replied. "The way I see it, the head of the snake doesn't watch from afar. It's always attached to the body".

Hayward, who'd been silent until that point, turned to face the group. "The mole is a problem, but we can't act unless we know who they are." The Earther leaned on the table. "All that matters now is regrouping with the Phoenix; cracking that data vault, and getting answers out of that Evoker kid down in medical".

Harrt took a long breath and considered everything.

"I think we may need to get a little creative," he said. "The Phoenix and the data vault is one thing, but there is still the issue of this traitor looming over our heads. Regardless of who they are, we must create the illusion that everything is running smoothly: perhaps play to the mole's hand".

"So you want us to keep up appearances?" Jaudi said, leaning forward. "Make it look like the Artemis is obeying orders".

"We can't afford to raise any suspicion," Harrt nodded. "If we go dark, they'll know something is up, so we've got to try our best to look business-as-usual".

"Are you proposing we report in with High Command?" Dines lifted his brows.

"That's precisely what I'm proposing. It buys us a little more time and hopefully keeps the mole guessing".

Harrt was about to say something else when his internal communicator sounded. He answered it, and the medic's voice filled the room;

"Sir, it's the Evoker.... he's lucid".

▲

Harrt struggled to keep up with Hayward as the big man marched toward the medical bay. He'd left Dines with Jaudi while she contacted High Command to give them a false update. It wasn't ideal timing, but Harrt figured it'd be best if someone were in the room with Hayward whilst he questioned Cadu.

Harrt noticed stray glances from his crew as he wandered the wide and open corridors of the Artemis. He couldn't be entirely sure if they were simply acknowledging their CO or stopping to get a look at the hulking Earther moving through the ship like a man possessed. Rather than draw any additional attention to the matter, Harrt smiled and tried to look like everything was normal.

The Evoker kid —Cadu— was sat on a gurney, with various tubes and intravenous lines going in and out of his arms. He looked better than the last time Harrt had seen him, but that wasn't saying much.

Cadu was undoubtedly human with some Uvan mixed in the family gene pool. His dark blue hair was cut close to the scalp, while his brown eyes appeared entirely human. The early signs of patchy facial hair on his thin face told Harrt that Cadu was barely a man: perhaps nineteen years old.

"Commander Oxarri," Cadu said as he tried to stand. "I really must—"

"You really don't need to get up," Harrt said, halting the boy. "We just have a few questions—"

“Yeah,” Hayward cut in. “Like what the hell were you doing aboard the Equus, son?”

Harrt shot the Earther a disapproving scowl, but Hayward shrugged it off. When Harrt turned back to Cadu, the Evoker looked a little bewildered.

“Go ahead,” Harrt said reassuringly. “You’re safe now”.

Cadu jittered, then interlocked his fingers together in what Harrt could only assume was nerves.

“For the last week, I’ve been posted on the world of Inaxium Four as part of an architectural study. Four days ago, my group were attacked by a large Paradisian militia”. Cadu’s voice trailed off as he stifled a sob. “I tried my best, but there were just too many. They... killed everyone. I thought they’d kill me... but the commander ordered his men to take me alive”

Cadu sobbed into his hands, leaving Harrt to exchange an awkward look with Hayward.

“Why’d they want you alive?” Hayward asked.

When Cadu continued, his voice seemed distant: “They said something about taking me back for questioning. That I might be useful to someone called...” Cadu paused for thought. “I think the name was Holland”.

“Markus Holland?” Hayward barked.

Harrt recalled seeing the name in Tariq’s intel on the Society: a young man that James Stephens speculated was a member of the Society. Harrt turned his gaze to Hayward, and the big man nodded as if to say, *we need to talk about that later.*

Hayward looked at Cadu: “What happened next, kid?”

Cadu closed his eyes as if to compose himself. Harrt knew that at that moment, Cadu would be calling upon every ounce of his Evoker training to show strength and resolve.

“They had me aboard a transport skiff and were taking me to Paradisium —I think. For days, they beat me and drugged me with inhibitors... I thought I was going to die”. Cadu opened his eyes, and his eyes looked angry. “They must’ve received new orders because the skiff was redirected. The next thing I knew, I was being dragged onto that luxury shuttle”.

"You mean the Equus?" Hayward folded his arms.

Cadu nodded, and Harrt could see Hayward's jaw tighten in anticipation.

Hayward asked, "When they took you aboard, did you see a blonde woman?"

Cadu considered the question. "No, sorry, I didn't see anyone else... They moved me to a room while they took care of another task, and the next thing I knew, there was the sound of gunfire".

"You mean our incursion?" Harrt said.

Cadu nodded. "Yes. I awoke to find that the inhibitors were wearing off. I guess they must've been concentrating on whatever they were doing before".

The other task was Claire's data vault; Harrt was sure of it.

"Elder Xanathur always says to act when the time is right. I saw my opportunity to escape. So, I killed the guard stationed outside my cell. Then I stumbled upon your gunfight," Cadu stopped and looked thoughtful: as though he were trying desperately to recall something important. "The man whose throat I cut. He was the one in charge. I'm sorry I couldn't allow him to live... not after everything he did to me... he deserved a painful death".

The intimacy of the boy's confession and the fear and grief hit Harrt like a moving ship. The whole thing told him just how desperate to survive Cadu had been.

"It's okay," Harrt nodded, trying to show his sympathy for the boy.

"Is there anything else you can tell us?" Hayward asked, his voice far more severe than Harrt's. "Any detail, no matter how insignificant, could be useful".

Cadu drew his wounded arms away.

"There was one other thing..." Cadu said, staring at Harrt. The Evoker's gaze was on him like a weight. "I heard one of them saying something about the Capital World of Valour".

Harrt leaned forward at the mention of the world. A dark look passed over him as his mind raced through memories of the Messorem's strike on Unity.

"Do you remember what they said about Valour?" Hayward barked, his voice more urgent than angry. "Anything... anything at all!"

"It's all quite foggy," Cadu sighed. "I remember one of them saying that... *Holland* has big plans for Valour". Cadu leaned against his gurney, letting out an exhausted groan. "The bald man kept saying that he was looking forward to seeing the 'wealthers finally get some comeuppance".

A feeling of dread knotted in Harrt's gut. He didn't know precisely who *Holland* was, but it was pretty clear that he had hostile intentions.

Cadu looked at Harrt with a semi-urgent expression.

"I would appreciate it if we could contact Elder Xanathur and update him on my situation"

"We'll make contact as soon as possible," Harrt nodded. "In the meantime, you should rest up. The medics need to continue your blood therapy. You'll need your strength"

It was a reasonable request: after all, the Evokers were —in some part— considered allies, though they weren't aware of Harrt's investigation. Astrilla vouched for the four Elders stationed at Pelos Three, citing one of them as a mother figure, which had to count for something. Harrt trusted Astrilla, and Astrilla trusted the Elders. *Maybe it was time to bring them into the circle?*

"Thank you, Commander Oxarri," Cadu said, offering a weak hand. After shaking with Harrt, Cadu glanced at Hayward, "And you, Mr..."

"It's Hayward, son," the Earther said. "Ralph Hayward".

A friendly and appreciative smile flickered on Cadu's face as he offered his hand to Hayward. "Well, Mr Hayward, thank you for saving my life".

▲

After finishing the debriefing with Cadu, Harrt spoke with the Artemis' chief physicians. They gave him a quick rundown of the treatment Cadu would receive over the coming hours. It was pretty extensive therapy, but the kid needed everything he could. The fact that preliminary toxicology reports were unable to detect the inhibitors in Cadu's blood suggested the Society had only the finest resources at its disposal. In addition, the doctors suspected that he'd suffered a brain injury, likely affecting his short-term memory, which wasn't ideal considering Cadu could have more useful intel.

Once Harrt received the update, he told the doctors he wanted hourly updates. In addition, he also informed them that he would be posting two armed guards outside the med-bay, which, as expected, raised a few eyebrows.

Harrt found Hayward outside the med bay, leaning against a wall while checking his datapad. The Earther tried to look calm, but Harrt could tell he was stressed.

"Thoughts?" Hayward asked as he stood straight.

"The kid has been through hell; no doubt there," Harrt replied. "What I don't understand is why the Society would take him alive. It makes no sense".

Hayward shrugged his broad shoulders. "The only time I've known the Society to take live prisoners is when they need them for something: like James powering an Enkaye device. Roth and his cronies like to cover their tracks. If you leave too many people alive that know your secrets, the jig is up".

"So, why would they need an Evoker?"

"Beats me," Hayward said. "The interesting thing I got outta that convo was that the kid mentioned that the mercs were under the command of Markus Holland".

"Why is that significant?" Harrt asked. "Holland's name was all over James' intel".

"So that's the part that's never added up for me," Hayward said. "Markus Holland is a political mouthpiece for the EWB. He's a young and impressionable asshole who wants to be a big shot warrior for justice and change: a real influencer among certain groups on Paradisium".

"So?"

Hayward licked his lips thoughtfully; "The funny thing is that Markus Holland can barely tie his shoelaces, let alone engineer an attack on a Capital World. On paper, he's your guy. Think about it: an angry and very vocal Paradisian with some pretty strong anti-Commonwealth views".

"The Society is using Markus Holland..." Harrt concluded. "But why?"

"Now that is the golden question, " Hayward said.

VOL

Scruffy set up an algorithm on the Sadalmelik's computer that mapped out the cypher left by Claire. It clashed the words, numbers and letters across all the books Claire had on file, and after an hour of calculating, the system returned a few hundred passphrases.

While Scruffy was working, Vol created a program to calculate the probability of the potential passwords: cross-checking them against all the books and media from Claire's personal logs. It was important not to trigger any failsafe that could be on the data vault. From what Vol could tell, Claire was the meticulous type and had likely built-in countermeasures for anyone trying to tamper with her work.

For the better part of an hour, Scruffy and Vol worked through the potential passwords: validating each one to test its success rate. It took a while, but eventually, the system calculated the three most optimum results. Vol tentatively keyed the first password into the vault. She looked at Scruffy, and the old man nodded approvingly:

"Here goes nothing," she said, hitting the return key.

The firewall dropped, albeit partially. On-screen, three files were available, a holo-broadcast, a star chart and a third locked file that required a complex DNA scan.

"Where do you wanna start?" Vol asked Scruffy.

The bearded man swallowed a lump in his throat: "Start with the holo".

Vol tapped the file, and a three-dimensional projection of Claire formed above Vol's datapad, though she didn't look anything like the woman in the pictures. Gone were the glamourous clothes, the happy smile and the friendly eyes. Instead, Claire wore a combat vest over her torso and carried a heavy rifle, which she promptly stowed as she began to record. Her once magnificent blonde hair was covered in blood that was not her own. The audio was warped and distorted for the first ten seconds, then Claire's voice filled the room:

"I'm assuming my chances of evac are slim to none... guess I'm kinda screwed," she said with strange dark humour to her voice. "I dunno what happened, but Roth's mercs came after me. Bradley Austin is rounding up the staff to—"

Claire stopped to check her surroundings for something but quickly turned to the recorder.

"I dunno how much time I've got. They tracked the Equus and are breaching the hull as I'm recording. Tariq, Ralph, listen to me; Roth is planning something huge — something he calls his *pièce de résistance*. I was able to pull a file that I'm attaching to this holo".

Claire began to type into a terminal that was out of frame. She stared at the screen, undoubtedly anxious, watching her files uploading. Vol didn't need a sixth sense to know that the woman was desperate to get her intel to safety. Whatever she'd found had rattled her.

"The file is some sort of star map of the 'wealther Capital Worlds. It shows detailed routes in and out of the planet of Valour: military-level information that the 'wealthers don't just give away".

Something rocked behind Claire: as though her ship was struck by something. Electrical sparks flew from a bank of overhead LEDs, causing Claire to glance away for a beat.

"They've breached the airlock," she said. Claire looked at the camera with hardened eyes, "Tariq, I hope you know someone who can make sense of these fucking star maps. From my best guess, they are—"

Another impact struck the Equus, and Claire grabbed her gun.

"I think they will attempt some kind of attack on Valour. I don't know how or with what army, but all the intel I've found points to that outcome. There's also a name in that file… Beckett. Whoever that is, the Society wants them badly".

The orange flame of a blow-torch emerged from the blast door behind Claire. The metal began to melt away like butter, but Claire didn't allow her impending doom to hinder her. She continued typing as she uploaded a third file to the communication.

"So, here's the thing," Claire said breathlessly. "For the last few days, the Society has been tracking something called Subject C. They'd diverted a shit ton of security assets to finding this thing—"

Claire's voice trailed off as she watched the flames melt the door behind her. She hammered on a button below the camera in a hurried rush, and a cheery ping followed. Vol was sure that was the third file attaching to the communique.

"I don't know what to make of the last file," Claire said, shaking her head. "It's a video that Roth stored in his bedroom vault. I think the encryption is mapped to his DNA. Who knows maybe its a sex-tape, but it might be useful". She peered into the camera with a melancholy expression, "Ralph... I'm sorry things never worked out..." she paused as though biting something back. Once she'd composed herself, Claire gazed into the camera and smiled hopefully: "I'll be seeing you".

The door behind her gave way, and Society enforcers poured into the cabin. Claire turned her back on the holo-recorder and made her final stand. She fired into the pack of goons, taking two of them down, but it was to little avail. Gunfire filled the space around the holo recorder, and the footage ended as Claire was hit.

Vol felt daggers in her chest, as she looked at Scruffy. The old man looked positively bewildered by what he'd seen. She could feel a mix of pain and torment at the back of the Earther's head: he was genuinely hurt by what he'd seen, even though he already suspected that his shipmate was dead.

"Shit..." Scruffy managed.

▲

Vol went aboard the Artemis five minutes later, leaving Scruffy to grab a drink and toast his fallen comrade. Dines was waiting for her at the airlock. The silver-haired human escorted her through the utilitarian corridors of the 'wealther warship without saying a word. When they reached the doors to Harrt's cabin, Dines stopped outside.

"How bad is it?" he asked.

"Bad".

Dines led her inside the cabin, which was larger than Vol expected. Harrt's quarters were an immaculately clean, highly organised living space. The room was split into three separate areas, a bedroom, a lounge and an office though the whole thing was open-plan. Vol assumed it wasn't an aesthetic design choice. The standard-issue 'wealther furniture was prescriptive and lacked character or detail, all made from the same off brown carbon-metal composite.

Harrt and Hayward were at a holotable in the lounge, running searches on someone called Markus Holland. An unfamiliar woman in an officer's uniform was sitting behind Harrt's desk, checking her datapad for messages. Dines introduced the dark-skinned human as Lieutenant Jaudi Meera —Harrt's XO.

Vol got a good read of Jaudi immediately, which was rare. She was a tough old soldier who'd witnessed the worst of the worst and come out stronger. Vol sensed that Jaudi had known Harrt a very long time, but that wasn't the reason for her almost maternal loyalty. Something else was there: *friendship borne of shared pain.*

▲

Telling Hayward about Claire's death was one of the worst things Vol had ever done. Not because the big man was an emotional wreck but because Vol was drawing comparisons to her not-quite-relationship with Harrt. It was a stark realisation that people could be taken away in a single breath.

On the inside, Hayward was hurting; Vol could tell that much. There were the usual feelings of regret and sadness, but most of all, the big man was pissed off and craving revenge.

"I should review the footage," Hayward said as he stood up. "She might've—"

Vol halted him mid-sentence. "I've got an audio version and the attached documents for you on my datapad. You really don't need to see it, Ralph, trust me".

Hayward's jaw tightened, and for a moment, Vol wondered if the Earther was going to punch her for suggesting that he could be emotionally affected. The big man nodded with resignation, then turned to Harrt;

"You 'wealthers got any strong liquor on this ship? I need a fuckin' drink".

NATHAN

After finishing his conversation with James, Nathan decided it was time to get some rest. He climbed into bed beside Astrilla and tried to calm his racing mind, but it was to no avail. For over an hour, he debated if James had really changed in the last decade.

Years aboard the Loyalty had taught Nathan that James could lie his way out of anything: *especially if the situation concerned Ice*. But despite that early suspicion, Nathan couldn't deny that the man he'd spoken to in the living area seemed quite different— borderline sincere. The erratic behaviour was gone. James could hold a conversation without losing focus or his cool. He seemed to acknowledge the mistakes he'd made in the past and apologised: *that was a first.*

Recent events had been stressful. After saving James, capturing Jareth and confronting Chimera *—or Jack—* Nathan didn't feel any ease. Sure, the crew had completed a mission successfully, but he couldn't shake the feeling that he was in the middle of a potential shit-storm. The Phoenix was hauling two very prolific prisoners who could pose substantial political ramifications for both the 'wealth and Paradisium.

After an hour of staring at the ceiling, Nathan decided he'd give up his attempt to sleep and would instead check if comms had been reestablished with the Sadalmelik. He threw on some clothes and carefully tiptoed out of the room to avoid waking Astrilla.

Technically, the Phoenix was on the dusk-end of its day-to-night cycle, but every crewmember worked sleep into their schedules however they saw fit. As a result, the Phoenix's corridors, galley and living area were all dimly illuminated to simulate nighttime, and usually, it was pretty relaxing. As Nathan poured a coffee at the bar, he couldn't ignore the blue light spilling in from the cockpit and Koble's loud voice booming up the hall. He figured the Sphinax would be on the wrong end of the daily cycle, so he ventured into the room for some company.

Inside, Rain and Koble were at the pilot's station, playing a competitive card game. Gordon was on the right, working at a terminal where Kyp was still trying to access the combat recorder from days earlier. Judging from the frustrated look in Gordon's eyes, the droid was still working to break the complex encryption. It felt like weeks had passed since Nathan and the crew had discovered the dozen or so dead mercenaries on Levave. In reality, it had been two days. Granted, they'd been high pressured, stressful days, but in that whole time, the Enkaye droid had been working hard to crack the combat recorder they'd found on one of the bodies.

"Coffee ain't gonna help you sleep," Koble said, pointing at the mug in Nathan's hand.

"There's too much going on for me to rest," Nathan shook his head. "Any luck contacting the Sadalmelik?"

"We've got their location," Rain answered. "It's deeper into 'wealther territory than I was expecting, but it'll be about thirty minutes before we can transmit"

"Keep me updated," Nathan said.

It was good news at last, and Nathan felt an ounce of his anxiety melt away. If Harrt and Vol were in 'wealther space, that —likely— meant they'd achieved their objective and were now waiting somewhere safe.

Nathan moved to Gordon and Kyp in the corner of the cockpit. Gordon was standing beside the hovering Enkaye droid, checking on its status on a nearby monitor.

"What's the latest?" Nathan asked.

Gordon turned the monitor so that Nathan could take a look at the readouts. Everything on the screen indicated that the droid had broken the combat recorder's encryption, but was in some sort of rest mode.

"Kyp finished about an hour ago, but he says the file is for you," Gordon said. "I didn't wanna wake you".

Nathan turned his eyes to Kyp, and it buzzed to life, jerking toward Nathan almost drunkenly, which was strange considering it was a floating droid that didn't have legs or consume liquor.

"Kyp?" Nathan said. "What's up?"

"The footage was... difficult to process," Kyp replied, its voice distorting slightly. The ocular sensor on the droid's body shifted colours a few times. "I detect some errors in my code".

"Maybe you should go and run some maintenance tasks," Gordon suggested. "Just to be safe".

"I think that is wise," Kyp replied.

Gordon unplugged the half dozen cables from the droid's torso, and Kyp floated up and down the cockpit as though it were stretching its metaphorical legs. As it floated out of the room, Gordon got to work with uploading the cumbersome video to the Phoenix's holotable. Nathan wasn't a computer expert by any stretch of the imagination, but he could tell that the files extracted from the recorder were advanced: *the kind of combat encryption that only the big corporations could afford.*

"So," Gordon began. "How was the talk with James?"

"Awkward".

"Gotta start somewhere, right?" Gordon said, peering at the terminal. "Besides, I may have run a few tests on him while I was fixing him up. He's completely clean: no sign of drug abuse whatsoever. His tobacco habit isn't great, but it's far from Ice: at least as far as narcotics go".

Nathan didn't acknowledge Gordon's statement and instead gulped back a mouthful of coffee. Fortunately, the terminal between them chimed a few minutes later: indicating that the footage was available. As Koble and Rain joined them around the holotable to watch, Gordon tapped on the console:

"Let's see what we've got here," he said.

A holographic window formed, and a video began to play. For seconds there was only static. The footage settled on a first-person view of an industrial-looking cargo bay. Directly ahead, a group of mercenaries put on armour and checked their weapons. Nathan was certain that it was the same group the crew had found on Levave. The footage played out from the perspective of the commanding officer, an individual called Rhoades.

"Okay, y'all, the primary objective is simple: Capture Subject C," a gruff voice said. "Mr Roth wants him brought in alive". An uncertain murmur rippled across the mercenary pack as the commanding officer spoke. "You heard me: I said alive. Those are the orders"

Several minutes followed wherein the mercs landed on Levave and headed into the temple: the same temple where Nathan and the others found the dozen corpses two days prior. From what Nathan could ascertain from the shakey video, the mercenaries were tracking someone implanted with a locator tag. They followed a tight military formation, checking every corner and passage with meticulous care.

Suddenly the point-man signalled with a hand to halt. The CO, whose perspective Nathan and Gordon were following, moved to the front. The camera settled on a blood-soaked locator tag lying on the ground.

"Are you seriously telling me he pulled that thing out?" one of the mercs said. "How the fuck did he—"

"Shut your mouth, Hiller," the CO said, warily glancing over his shoulder. "Fan out... he's here".

Out of the darkness, something moved.

Nathan couldn't see it on the screen, but he could tell from how the footage jumped: likely the camera wearer's reaction.

"Contact! Contact!" One of the mercs yelled.

All of the soldiers —including the CO— began shooting toward something off-camera. The footage was jittery at best, and even with the Phoenix's systems trying to enhance the image, it was impossible to see who —or what— the soldiers were fighting.

Something that looked like an elemental summon flew from the shadows and smashed against one of the mercs. The armoured woman was flung out of sight in a cloud of blood and fire. As the brawling on-screen continued, more elemental energy could be seen whipping through the air, eliminating more and more of the armed goons until the CO was the last one standing.

All of the violence stopped, and the person wearing the combat recorder stood with a gun nervously pointed at the shadows.

"You know they'll never stop looking for you, Subject C".

A strange male voice came from the dark. "You should walk away while you still can".

"You know I can't do that," the CO replied. "You know what Mr Roth is looking for. It means too much to him".

"Alastair Roth has no idea what he's dealing with. Turn around and go back to Paradisium. This is your final warning".

A brief commotion followed, then a bolt of elemental energy struck the camera operator, and the footage turned static. Sound from the video continued to play, and the screams of the mercenary filled the Phoenix's cockpit until there was a violent, agonising crunch.

Static followed.

Gordon peered at Nathan, "That was unusual".

As Gordon moved to switch off the holotable, a new sound emerged from the footage. It sounded as though someone had deliberately yanked the combat recorder from the dead merc.

Subject C's voice came over the speakers: "Alastair Roth... as long as I draw breath, I will not allow you to open that which you call Project Erebus. Mark my words; I will stop you. I will find you, and I will end you for everything you and the Society did to me".

CHAPTER TWENTY-TWO
KOBLE

It took Koble a while to shake the weird feeling he got from watching the footage that Gordon played on the holotable. Initially, a haunting dread came over him, but he couldn't explain why: it was just a natural reaction to something pretty violent that had little explanation. After the third or fourth viewing, Koble realised that perhaps there was something constructive in the filmed violence: *somebody else had a problem with Roth and the Society.*

The enemy of my enemy is my friend, the imaginary Jack said inside Koble's mind.

Koble parked that thought as Rain pulled the Phoenix from FTL. The ship was now on the outskirts of 'wealther space, and Rain seemed confident that he could establish a comm-link with the Sadalmelik with the closer proximity. While Rain set up the communication, Koble leaned on the holotable beside Nathan and Gordon.

"You guys think Subject C is an Evoker?" Koble asked as he played with one of his whiskers.

Nathan shrugged, "You saw the same video I did".

Koble's eyes flicked to Gordon; "Can you —I dunno — clean up the footage or something?"

Gordon squinted through his glasses with a flat expression: "What you saw *is* the cleaned-up version. Even if we could improve the quality, I don't think that Subject C was in frame".

Nathan straightened up and stepped away from the holotable. "It certainly explains what happened to those mercs on Levave, but it also begs the question, *what did Roth do to piss this guy off?*"

Nathan was right, but there was no answering the question. The footage was days old, and Subject C was long gone. Something innate told Koble that there was more to it than the fifteen minutes of video, but there were more important things to focus on: *namely, Jareth and where they were taking him next.*

Koble's gut told him that the best place to go next was to the Evoker Enclave on Pelos Three, but nobody could make that call until they knew Harrt and Vol's situation. There was the option to take Jareth to the Pluvium system to stand trial for his crimes against the Sphinax, but that was tricky in and of itself.

The political landscape of Pluvium was delicate. It was a system of worlds that suffered for two decades under the boot of a fascist dictatorship: a regime that Jareth Corps aided during the Pluvium Civil War. Koble was the chief now, and his word was law, but in his experience, angry people could quickly evolve into angry mobs. He could easily imagine a horde of pissed off Sphinax tearing Jareth limb from limb —a fate Jareth deserved— but Koble wasn't willing to let the corporate man die until he'd spilt his secrets.

NATHAN

Fifteen minutes later, Astrilla, Russell and Tariq joined them in the cockpit as Rain established a clean connection to the Sadalmelik: though it was rerouted to a Commonwealth signature.

That raised some very uncomfortable questions.

As the others gathered around the holotable, Nathan checked the security feeds of the Phoenix's makeshift cells.

Jareth was sitting atop one of the empty shipping containers, looking decidedly relaxed about his situation. Christian Roth was the direct opposite, pacing back and forth in his cell, looking like a man offended by his surroundings.

The sound of Harrt's voice came from the holotable, drawing Nathan's attention away from his prisoners. He moved to the centre of the cockpit, where a projection of Harrt, Hayward, Vol and Dines formed. They looked like they'd been through hell and back, and what's more, Harrt was wearing his officer's uniform. That meant, they were no longer aboard the Sadalmelik: Nathan was sure of that much.

"We hit a snag," Harrt began. "Things got a little dicey. We lost people, and now we're aboard my ship — the Artemis".

The 'wealther's statement answered a handful of Nathan's questions but subsequently raised more. He felt the hairs on his arms stand to attention as he thought about the impact of Harrt and the others being aboard the Artemis. Subtlety was supposed to be critical to the operation, and a mile-long 'wealther warship was far from it.

"So, what happened?" Nathan asked. "I thought we were keeping the 'wealth out of this?"

For ten minutes, Harrt and Hayward gave a detailed account of their part in the mission. To Nathan's dismay, casualties were high. Not only had the Sadalmelik lost a crewman, but most of Dines' crew bore the brunt of the casualties fighting the Revenant Warship.

"I lost eight of the bravest marines I've ever known," Dines shook his head.

Nathan wanted to acknowledge the heroic sacrifice but he feared sounding disingenuous. The whole thing made him realise just how lucky he and those aboard the Phoenix had been at Hawtrey House.

Then there was the Evoker, Cadu. Astrilla recognised the name, identifying him as Elder Xanathur's understudy, though she couldn't admit to knowing him personally.

Nathan was pretty sure he'd seen the thin-looking guy around the Enclave in the past. Cadu was weird — that was the only word Nathan could use to describe him. He seemed like a loner that spent an unhealthy amount of time with Xanathur and didn't engage with anyone else —at least from what Nathan had observed.

Regardless of Cadu's social skills, he was still a fully-trained Evoker: lethal and dangerous if provoked. The fact that the Society kidnapped him told Nathan just how efficient their goons were. Evokers were notoriously hard to kill —or, in this case, disable. It meant that Roth and his organisation had the right arsenal at their disposal.

When Harrt explained the part about the Artemis dropping in and saving the day, Nathan felt his gut tighten. That part sounded suspicious as hell, and when Nathan glanced at Koble, the Sphinax shot him a look that said, *yeah, that ain't right.* The fact that the Artemis had shown up at that specific location at that precise time had the mole's fingerprints all over it, but the rationale didn't line up. After all, *why would the mole want to keep the Revenant and/or the Society from getting Claire's data?*

It didn't make any sense, and when Nathan questioned it, Dines was the first to answer:

"The Artemis received priority orders from Master of the House; Inon Waife. It could be pure coincidence, or it's proof that our mole has access to give supreme orders".

Russell made a clicking noise with his tongue.

"Why the fuck would the mole —who we know works in Baylum's interest— wanna destroy a Revenant Warship?"

There was an awkward silence.

"We ain't got the time to unpick that, Mojito," Hayward said, his voice severe. "The fact is we are where we are, and there's nothing we can do about that now".

The big man had a point, though the whole thing still didn't sit right with Nathan. The mole was clearly interested in the Equus; maybe they wanted Cadu and the data vaults destroyed, or perhaps there was something else aboard the ship that the others had overlooked. Either way,

Hayward was right in his assessment —there was no point in guessing; all they could do was react accordingly.

"What about the data vaults?" Astrilla asked Vol.

The Uvan looked awkwardly into the holo-recorder and nodded. Nathan could sense that something wasn't right when Hayward spoke instead.

"Hell of an engineer you've got here, Carter," Hayward said. "Yeah, she cracked the data vaults, alright. What we found.." the American paused for a beat, then directed his gaze at Tariq: "You should know, Claire's dead. She died getting us some pretty significant intel".

Tariq's head lowered, and his shoulders slumped. He pressed a thumb and finger to the corners of his eyes as though pre-empting tears of mourning. For that moment, Tariq had the look of a man who'd had the wind knocked out of him, but it was only for a heartbeat. His expression hardened, and his eyes formed a calm yet decisive expression.

"We shall avenge her, my friend," Tariq said. "Her death will not be in vain".

Hayward's jaw tightened, and he nodded.

Nathan asked, "So, what was the intel?"

Vol was the first to answer, "In short, the Society is planning an attack on Valour".

"That's a little vague, isn't it?"

Harrt cut in. "Cadu overheard his captors discussing something to do with an attack on Valour. The intel that Claire shared with us lines up with that. Roth has been looking at classified documents regarding military movements, flight plans: you name it. Everything points to some kind of assault".

For the first time since the conversation began, Gordon spoke up. "That'd be suicide. The Society may be powerful, but they aren't a galactic superpower. They certainly don't have a Messorem at their disposal".

"No, they don't," someone said. "They've got something worse".

James limped into the room with a lit cigarette in his mouth. With a quiet arrogance, he blew smoke from his nose as he stopped at the holotable. Nathan thought he'd forgotten the smell of burning tobacco, but as the distinct scent hit his nose, he was reminded of the Loyalty.

"Good to see you in one piece," Hayward said to James.

"Likewise, Ralph".

James looked around the Phoenix and its crew as he took a long drag on his cigarette. He looked nervous: as though what he was about to say next wasn't going to be easy.

"The Society calls it the *pièce de résistance,"* James said, looking around the room. "Long story short, Markus Holland kept cropping up, so I did a little digging. The day before I got captured, I broke into Holland's house and did a little snooping, and in doing so, I found something quite interesting".

"You mind elaborating?" Nathan said.

James nodded and blew a plume of smoke over the hologram, distorting the image for a beat. "Holland is plotting an assassination attempt on Inon Waife in an effort to destabilise the 'wealth. His main intention was to use some unhinged Evoker as the patsy".

"That'd explain Cadu," Vol interjected. "They captured him so that he would take the fall".

"Yeah, but that's not the point," James said. "The funny thing was that Roth had nothing to do with the planning of this assassination attempt. It was all Holland and his pals. I'm starting to think that maybe Roth isn't the man in charge. Maybe it's Markus Holland?"

Nathan noted the quizzical looks shared between Hayward and Tariq over the comm. They began to throw theories at one another, leaving Nathan to wonder if James' assumption had blown a giant hole in their years of careful espionage.

Astrilla waved away their speculations and spoke with gravity in her voice. "Regardless of who's leading the Society, this plot to assassinate Waife would disrupt the relationship between the Evokers and the Commonwealth. Why would they do such a thing?"

James took a final drag on his cigarette and stubbed it

out in an empty cup. "I guess they planned to have me hooked up to an Enkaye Warmachine by that point. The Revenant destroyed one Capital world when the 'wealth was united. Think about it, if you break down their leadership, cause political turmoil, and turn friends into foes, you've got a fuckin' opening right there".

"It's a do-over," Nathan surmised. "Baylum wants to finish his father's work, and the Society is helping him".

"Maybe," James shrugged as he put down his makeshift ashtray with exaggerated care. "All I know for sure is that the Society is planning something that'll lay the groundwork for Baylum".

The implication of that statement clung to the Phoenix's walls.

"There was one other thing," Vol said. "Claire mentioned that an arm of the Society was looking for someone. They've moved their forces around searching for some... well, I dunno, a prisoner? They call—"

"Subject C," Nathan interrupted her, and the Uvan looked surprised by his interjection. He quickly clarified: "Kyp was able to crack the combat recorder we recovered on Levave. It turns out that bunch of dead mercs were hunting Subject C".

Koble cut in boastfully, "It looks like Subject C handed them their asses".

Dines shook his head:

"We need to prioritise. This *Subject C* doesn't really matter in the grand scheme of things right now. Sure, it's great to know we aren't the only one fighting off Roth, but it's beside the point. The attack on Valour has to be a priority now. Lives are at stake. Plus, I didn't wanna say this, but you guys on the Phoenix are hauling two high value prisoners that could land you all sorts of problems".

"What are you suggesting?" Nathan narrowed his eyes.

"You get yourselves to Valour, then we put Jareth and Christian Roth into Commonwealth holding cells till we figure out the next move". The Agent looked at him apologetically. "It'd help take a few targets off your back and guarantee that all our work hasn't been for nothing".

Dines was right, though Nathan wasn't happy about it. He didn't care about Christian Roth: he was more a valuable asset with info on his father's operation. Jareth, on the other hand, was far more complicated. Sure, Nathan had questions regarding Jack and everything else, but on a personal level, he'd much rather see the elitist face justice on Pluvium. *That was a subject for another day.*

Nathan nodded at Dines. "We'll meet you at the Capital Worlds".

"Then I'll get a subtle communication to High Command to expect your arrival". Dines clenched his jaw. "I don't like this any more than you, but this situation has escalated beyond a simple rescue mission".

GORDON

Once Nathan and the others wrapped up their communiqué, the group dispersed. Astrilla set about contacting the Evoker Elders regarding the prisoner recovered aboard the Equus. Nathan, Koble and Rain stayed around the pilot's station to plot a clean route to Valour. This left Russell and Gordon to take watch of the prisoners: not that either man stood a chance of breaking free.

Russell led the way, and as the pair passed through the living area, Gordon saw James and Tariq raising a toast to their fallen crewmates from the Sadalmelik. While Russell grabbed a coffee from the machine, Gordon watched James from afar. It was strange to see him as a fully grown man rather than the vague memory Gordon had stored from aeons ago.

When Gordon first met Bill Stephens, James had been a small child —playing with a remote-controlled toy at the family home. He could still recall the blonde boy running about the place, happy and full of smiles. It was hard to reconcile that image with the man before him. James looked more like Jack now, except taller and somehow more approachable. The boy had grown into a man and then some. By Gordon's best estimate, James was now in his early forties, which felt far more ageing than he cared to admit. Granted, he'd been a young man when he'd first met Bill, but seeing James now made him realise just how many years had passed.

Russell nudged Gordon and gestured to the rear of the ship. "You coming?"

"You go ahead. I'll catch up".

"Alright, dude," Russell shrugged as he ventured toward the brig.

Gordon grabbed a snack from the bar while waiting for Tariq and James to finish their conversation. He didn't know why, but an odd itch at the back of his brain told him that he needed to speak to James: to talk to the man whose grandfather had changed his life forever. Tariq eventually excused himself from the lounge, leaving Gordon and James alone. It immediately gave Gordon a strange sense of deja-vu: reminding him of the first conversation he and Nathan shared.

"How are you feeling?" Gordon asked.

James shrugged with his eyebrows. "Well, the headache's a bitch, but at least this ship is quiet". He laughed at something that wasn't apparent to Gordon and climbed to his feet with a groan. "So, who are you?"

Gordon looked at him with surprise and relief;

"You don't recognise me?"

"Should I?"

Gordon shook James' hand. "I used to work with your grandfather. Granted, it was a very—"

"Listen, pal, I'm sure you're aware, but I'm a recovering Ice addict." James made a knocking motion against his skull, but his smile seemed affable. "Truth is that my memories pre-Fall are kinda foggy".

"Hell of a drug," Gordon replied.

"Well, that's kinda its intended use," James drawled. "Y'know, to make you forget the bad stuff. The dealers don't tell you that it can really screw with the human hippocampus. Uvan's can just about get away with it, but our kind.. not so much".

"I had no idea that it had that effect".

"Trust me, I was one of the lucky ones. Some of the other guys in my rehab group couldn't even remember their names".

Gordon took a step back, biting away a strange feeling that could only be described as a mix of sorrow and utter contempt: the former for James and the latter for Jack and his failure at parenting. Bill would've been horrified to learn that his grandchild suffered from such a terrible addiction. What made it worse was that Jack should've done something about it: *after all, that's what Gordon would've done if it were his child.*

"So, you knew my Grandpa Bill?" James said.

"I worked for him".

"Huh," James mused. "Interesting..."

Gordon was expecting him to pry deeper, just as Nathan had when they'd shared the same conversation.

He fully expected James to ask the tough questions.

Did my Grandfather make it off Earth? How did he die? When did he die?

All were things that Nathan asked, and Gordon had never fully answered. There was nothing to be gained by telling the whole truth and everything to lose by speaking it.

James smiled, "I'm sorry I need to rest for a while. This headache is pretty killer, but we should talk again soon. I'd love to hear more about Earth and the like".

"It'd be my pleasure".

James began to swagger in the direction of his cabin, but he turned back after a few paces. "What was your name again?" he asked in a friendly tone.

"Gordon. Gordon Taggart".

James nodded as though taking a mental note. The effects of Ice addiction were truly awful.

NATHAN

Rain estimated that a direct slipstream to Valour would take a little over three hours, so Nathan offered to take over the pilot's station so the Sphinax could have some much-needed sleep. He watched the slipstream for over thirty minutes, thinking about Chimera, Jareth, the Society, Subject C and all the other things racing through his tired mind.

It was all very complicated, and now, to add to that complexity, Nathan and the crew were heading to Valour —the heart of the Commonwealth. It was the last place anyone wanted to go, but it was the only option available that wouldn't cause political fallout for the Evokers or the Sphinax.

After some time, Nathan figured it was better to accept his decision rather than ponder it further. This was the situation, and there was nothing he or anyone else could do to change it. All that mattered now was what came next.

Nathan leaned into his chair and watched the blue ribbons of light pass over the Phoenix. It was an attempt to not think about anything, and for a brief moment, it worked, right up until the moment his mind wandered.

He saw the desert again, but it was different. There was no sunlight. The temperature was freezing, and the sand had turned to the colour of ash. Ahead, Nathan could feel a presence, desperate to be whole again. It writhed and screamed and fought, but the thing was unsuccessful in the end. His mind carved a shroud of pure darkness from the sand as if to represent the monster. It was like looking at smoke without a fire. The presence glared at him without expression. Nathan could only sense rage looming there:

It whispered a single word with a deep fractured voice that simultaneously sounded alien and human. "Erebus".

Nathan was snapped back to consciousness by the sound of his datapad chiming. He shook his head as if to clear the daze, realising that he'd fallen asleep at the stick.

His communicator chimed again.

It was fair to assume that Nathan's mind was now conjuring up strange dreams due to exhaustion and stress. He hadn't had a good night's sleep in what felt like a lifetime, and everything had been overwhelming recently, so Nathan brushed his concerns away and took up his datapad.

"What's up?"

"Nate," Russell's voice came over the channel. "You wanna get down to Cargo Two right now".

Nathan took a deep breath, knowing that Russell had a good reason to summon him. Nathan pressed his datapad to his forehead in an attempt to stay grounded.

"What's happened?" he said.

"Roth junior tried a lil' funny business when I took him some water," Russell answered. "I sorta... hit him. Now he's losing his shit: keeps punching the walls and demanding to speak with whoever is in charge".

After spending several seconds to regain some semblance of patience, Nathan replied, "Give me a moment".

▲

Cargo Two was the rarely used secondary storage space for the Phoenix. Often, the area was entirely dormant, but Vol had plans to convert the room into a third gunnery chamber —parts and expenses pending. In a way, Nathan was glad that the work hadn't started yet. Having prisoner cells had advantages, and he was reminded of that fact when he reached Cargo Two.

Russell stood in the hall, with his shotgun casually resting on his thigh. The former barkeep shot Nathan a raised brow: "Watch out, dude. That guy has got quite the mouth on him".

Nathan nodded and proceeded into the cell. Astrilla was in the corner of the room, watching Christian as he yelled profanities while slumped against the wall, resembling a petulant child. Blood was coming from Christian's nose, where Russell struck him earlier.

Christian regarded Nathan with a sour glare as he entered the room. His hubris and entitlement were as clear as day, and when he started speaking, there was genuine outrage in his voice.

"I presume that you are the one in charge?" Christian snarled.

"I am".

Christian looked him up and down and raised an eyebrow as though something about Nathan deeply offended him.

"When a man allows his prisoners to be beaten and threatened aboard his ship, I must truly question his honour," Christian snarled.

"You mean like you did to James?" Nathan folded his arms. "Beating and drugging him and then attempting to hand him over to the Revenant? Tell me something Christian, does that sound *honourable* to you?"

There was silence.

"Touché," Christian smirked pretentiously.

Nathan could tell that the man opposite was not expecting such a quick retort to his witty remarks. Nathan knew his kind: *people who enjoyed the art of verbal sparring because they believed they were superior.*

"Still," Christian drew the word out contemplatively. "One must question if you truly understand what an egregious error you've made in attacking Paradisium".

Nathan considered Christian for a moment, imagining what it'd be like to land a right hook into the overindulged playboy's head. Of course, he resisted the urge, knowing that a reaction was precisely what he wanted, but still it was nice to dream.

Nathan moved a pace closer, "When the people of Paradisium find out what the Society has been doing, they'll call for blood".

Christian stretched his neck and his vertebrae popped in bursts. He chuckled a mirthless laugh at Nathan. "You fools have no idea of what we are capable of doing. The people of Paradisium are nothing more than sheep who will blindly obey their shepherds." Christian stood as he'd delivered this speech, his face gleaming with the fervour of a prophet. Christian took a step closer to Nathan and stared at him with an imperious arrogance intended as threatening. "The Society has manipulated the masses since the dawn of the class system. What makes you think that *we* are not still in control?"

Christian wanted to elicit a reaction: that was something Nathan wouldn't allow. As Christian had said, *beating a prisoner wasn't the honourable thing*, even if it was incredibly tempting.

"When we land, the Commonwealth will take you into custody," Nathan growled. "Your criminal enterprise will go down in flames. When it does, the people of Paradisium will have their say about what to do with you and your father and all his pals".

Christian breathed laughter. He backed down, stepping away from Nathan and retreating to his slouched position beside the wall.

"You will regret crossing the Society," Christian sneered. "Mark my words: they will rain hell upon you and the ones you love until it makes the Fall look like child's play".

INTERLUDE
ROTH

Breakfast aboard Roth's flagship, the Featon, felt like a theatrical event. The eggs, bacon, and black pudding were from an exceptional replication firm specialising in premium taste experiences. The coffee was from a private plantation Roth acquired from the Criminal Syndicate five years prior. Even the fruit conserve spread across the crusty artisanal toast was made from genetically enhanced wild strawberries that fetched a surprisingly high price in the outer worlds.

It was the kind of luxury men like Alastair Albon de-Freiherr Roth deserved. Work hard, play hard: it was as simple as that. The riffraff would never understand that need for extravagance because they'd never really needed to graft for their success.

Award-winning chef Francios Beaulieu managed the Featon's kitchen. Before the Fall, he was famous for his various cooking shows. He owned restaurants in New York, Paris and Tokyo, all of which won many prestigious awards. He'd married a supermodel, invested millions into private equity, and became an incredibly wealthy man.

Not bad for someone who cooked eggs for a living.

All of it was thanks to the Society. They provided Francios with the means to build a small media empire, and in return, he would repay their *kindness*. Little did he know that the Fall would wipe out his award-winning restaurants, millions of dollars, supermodel wife, and his media empire, but that is precisely what happened. The Fall came. Francios survived —thanks to Roth— but his debt remained. Of course, he was incredibly grateful for the salaried position that Roth offered and took the job without question. In the blink of an eye, Francios Beaulieu went from being TV's favourite chef to Roth's private kitchen lackey.

It was one of many times where the Society —and Roth— had called on the debts of lesser, weaker people. Sometimes it resulted in violence or even murder. Other times it went smoothly —like in the case of Francios.

Markus Holland was the third kind of ambitious idiot: a man so consumed by his hubris that he didn't know he was being used. Holland always assumed that Roth was simply a smiling investor that shared his ideological beliefs and wanted nothing more than to mentor the next generation.

How wrong he was.

Like Francios, Holland craved fame and attention, but instead of award-winning restaurants and a media empire, he desired political influence: something Roth could undoubtedly exploit. At the time, Roth wasn't sure how he could use Markus Holland to his advantage, but he knew that one day he'd prove to have his uses. The Society invested into Holland and made him the public face of Paradisian separatism: *the warrior for justice, change and all the other political buzzwords that made activists froth at the mouth.*

For five years, the Paradisian press —which the Society controlled— gave Holland a platform to spew his ideology. It was just like it had been back in the days of Earth, but somehow easier and more targeted.

When Jareth provided the Commonwealth intel, the EWB was born. Roth's investment into Markus Holland began to pay dividends: creating a public face for the movement that wasn't associated with the Society. Throughout the campaign, Holland was the mouthpiece, inciting the morons of Paradisium into doing exactly as the Society —as Roth— wanted.

But now, the EWB was done. Roth's plan was in the early stages, and Holland's role needed to change. All it would take was some well-practised manipulation: something Roth was more than capable of doing.

Holland was a handsome fellow: six foot, medium build, dark skin, thirty-eight years of age with short hair and an impressive jaw-line. He looked every part the radical politician. Everything from the edgy expression in his hard eyes to the expensive grey suit fit for a US president screamed, *I am committed to my ideology.*

For thirty minutes, Roth fed Holland disinformation regarding the attack at Hawtrey House. It was the same story that would break in the Paradisian Press an hour later. Everything Roth said was either embellished or a complete lie: designed to trick the foolish into doing his bidding.

Throughout his story, Roth changed specific details to fit the narrative. The crew of the Phoenix Titan were referred to as a highly organised group of 'wealther supremacists—*perfect wording to rile up an easily outraged simpleton.* The number of casualties was multiplied to create a sense of atrocity. The capture of Jareth and Christian was played as a kidnapping *—a mild course correction where the plan had gone slightly awry.*

Naturally, the trade with Baylum was redacted. The odd witnesses that claimed a Revenant Warship was in the airspace were dealt with accordingly, and all wreckage was rapidly swept under the rug by Baylum's people.

In addition to his detailed account, Roth provided falsified reports and doctored footage that helped back up his false testimony: the same documents he'd already shared with the Paradisian media.

Fuel to the fire, as Theodore Jareth would say.

As Holland listened, Roth could almost see the cogs in his brain turning. He could see the sense of moral outrage boil on the man's chiselled features.

"Did they hurt you?" Holland leaned forward with an expression of genuine concern on his face.

Roth shook his head, "No. Fortunately, I have some courageous security experts under my employ".

He nodded to Bradley Austin, who'd been standing at the back of the room throughout the conversation. The attack dog acknowledged the recognition but didn't say a word.

Good dog, Roth thought.

Holland's expression darkened with fury.

"Have the kidnappers contacted you with their demands?" Holland asked.

"No".

As Roth hoped, Holland jumped to the conclusion: "This is a politically motivated attack".

"What do you mean?" Roth tried his best to sound like a worried geriatric.

"Think about it, the 'wealth captures two of our brightest citizens and throws them into a gulag. This is the Commonwealth's way of telling us that they are still in control, regardless of our separatism".

Roth peered at Austin with a rehearsed drama to his performance. "That explains the intel..."

As Roth hoped, Holland's ears pricked up at the lie: "What intel?"

There it was —opportunity.

The false narrative was almost too easy to spin: like giving poisoned candy to an egotistical baby. He told Holland that he'd received reliable intel from Jareth Corps, suggesting that the *Commonwealth Supremacists* were taking their *hostages* to the Capital Worlds.

"Inon Waife intends on making an example of my son," Roth said, trying and succeeding to sound like a worried parent. "We must do something about this, Markus".

Ever the warrior for justice and change, Markus Holland nodded in agreement. He lapped up the tall tale, the falsified documents, and even Roth's emotional, heart-wrenching performance, which could've won him a Hollywood award or two back in the day. Roth did what Roth did best. He manipulated. He lied. He used fraudulent evidence to substantiate every point. Roth's wit and cunning lured his prey into the web of deceit.

And so the fool believed whatever Roth wanted him to believe.

Holland said, "We will do something about this, my old friend. I promise we will get your son back from these fascists". He glanced at Roth tentatively, like a student awaiting a critical lesson from his teacher. "What would you advise?"

Alastair Roth hid his satisfied smirk all too well.

"We must rise above the 'wealth," Roth said. "We should meet this injustice with peaceful protest: show the galaxy that we are better than they are".

"How?" Holland asked.

"I have some thoughts," Roth answered, knowing that everything he'd say next would serve as the catalyst for things to come.

▲

Roth's plan of protest was simple, and Holland took it on board without question. *After all, why would he —a hopeful future president of Paradisium— take issue with the advice of his trusted mentor and confidant?*

The semi-fictitious scheme was the next phase of the pièce de résistance. Holland would address the people of Paradisium and appeal to the do-gooders, the patriotic and the downright ignorant, to take their ships and form a blockade of protest around the Capital World of Valour: blocking all transit from coming in or out of the planet.

For thirty minutes, Roth worked with Holland to write a compelling speech which would be broadcast on all Paradisian feeds within the hour. Through his words, Holland would evoke sentiments of empathy for the hostages, outrage for the Commonwealth's violent acts, and anger for the unjustified attack on their supposed liberty. If citizens didn't have a ship, Holland would encourage them through his sheer magnetism to do more; to do better for their fellow man. In Roth's experience, this simple term —to do better— would result in ten to twenty-five per cent of people acting out of guilt: clamouring to prove their virtue.

By the time the camera crews arrived at the Featon, Holland was ready to deliver his rousing speech to the masses. Roth watched the fool stand at a press podium like he were a president of times long past. On the backdrop behind him was the new Paradisian banner: a symbol of Earth accompanied by all the flags that once represented countries from around the world. It was to look like a historical moment to the everyman. The broadcast went live, and like the puppet he was, Markus Holland began his speech to the unwitting masses.

Brothers and sisters of Paradisium, it is with a heavy heart that I come to you on this day. Less than seventy-two hours ago, we voted in favour of a free and independent Paradisium. We secured the future of our children and our children's children, guaranteeing that they wouldn't have to live under a Commonwealth boot as we have for so very, very long.

There was no denying that Holland had a certain gravity to how he spoke. His voice carried a statesmanlike quality while sounding like a true man of the people. He was the perfect candidate for the role Roth had selected for him.

Our separatism was never intended to threaten the Commonwealth. We, the people of Paradisium, saw that our future was as an independent, sovereign world. Despite the many failings of the Commonwealth — particularly those concerning the Fall— we didn't harbour discontent. We looked to the 'wealth as a friend and ally during these uncertain times.

That part would appeal to the 'wealther sympathisers: the people who didn't want to rock the boat. Roth hoped that what followed would break their loyalty to the 'wealth and incite an emotional response.

That is why it pains me to tell you that they have torn away the olive branch we offered. Our former oppressors threw our kindness back at us. Last night a peaceful EWB celebration was attacked by a group of violent Commonwealth supremacists: brutally murdering several unarmed partygoers and injuring countless others.

Commonwealth supremacists: it was a perfect pair of words designed to make people feel threatened. After all, the Commonwealth was exclusionary, especially against those who fell outside their circle. The term *supremacist* spoke to the innate fear that Paradisium was a victim of bigotry, and the masses would believe every word of it.

After all, why would the everyman disagree with someone like Holland?

He was just like them: a man of the people.

In addition to the barbarianism, these radicals captured two of our citizens, David Jareth and Christian Roth: for unfounded crimes against the Commonwealth.

Holland's speech poured over the Featon's internal announcement system as it was broadcast to every news outlet on Paradisium. Roth felt jubilant as he listened to his mouthpiece say the words that would provoke the reactionists, the morons, the nationalists and the liberal sympathisers to do his bidding. It was the kind of genius that Roth could only associate with the wise and wonderful Theodore Jareth.

This is an attack against our freedom: against our liberty. We —the free people of Paradisium— can no longer remain silent. This senseless, unlawful attack on our democracy cannot be allowed. Mark my words, if we do not respond to this heinous, criminal act, then the Commonwealth will continue to assert its dominance over us until we are once again a part of their regime.

Roth imagined the faces of the few million Paradisians watching the newscasts: everyone from those intended to survive the Fall to those the Commonwealth saved. He pictured expressions of sombre agreement.

Like many of you, I was born and raised on Earth. I saw the Commonwealth's failure first-hand when the Revenant struck New York. They could've prevented the pain and suffering of our loved ones. They could've stopped the Revenant, but they didn't. They waited. They debated. They argued amongst themselves whether or not our species deserved to live. That is not a democracy founded on Unity. It is Evil. It is immoral.

The masses would be touched by Holland's words; *and who could blame them?* They —the ones born pre-Fall— had been through hell. Some felt guilty for the luxury bestowed upon them. Others were left with unimaginable trauma from what they'd experienced during the Fall. The generation that followed were raised by parents or grandparents who suffered one or more of those afflictions. Ancestral trauma coupled with survivor's guilt was a potent tool Roth could use to bring the darkest of feelings into the light.

I have lived under a Commonwealth sky long enough to recognise that their broken system is designed to oppress our kind. I've risked my life to bring justice to the many people impacted by Commonwealth supremacists by standing as a proud campaigner for the EWB. But today, I stand before you not as a campaigner but as a man of Paradisium —as a patriot of what was and can still be.

Holland paused for gravitas like the well trained, gullible mutt he was. As he stared into the cameras with his big brown eyes, Markus Holland looked like the saint and martyr for integrity and honesty. It was a powerful image that Roth knew would go down in the history books, not as a proud moment for freedom but as the precursor to a great tragedy.

And so, this is a call to justice. This is a call to dismantle a bigoted system that has oppressed us for decades. If we do not take a stand now, the 'wealthers will erode all we have worked for over the last year. Everyone has a role —no, a duty— not just to their fellow man but to those we lost in the Fall.

It was almost as though Project Erebus was calling out to Roth across the vastness of space. Helia was lightyears away, but still, Roth could feel it, just as he had before. He'd been so close to opening the singularity before, but it wasn't meant to be: *thanks to Bill Stephens and his team.* Finally, after twenty-six long years, Roth would be the one to harness the power of Project Erebus. He would unlock the Enkaye's greatest treasure. He would harness the power of gods and forge his perfect existence. Alastair Albon de-Freiherr Roth would do those things and more. Not Baylum or the Society or anyone else. It was to be *his* pièce de résistance and no one else's. Markus Holland and his ridiculous speech was simply the next phase.

We must not use this demonstration for selfish motives. We must not allow it to turn into a hostile situation. We are better than that because, unlike the 'wealthers, our resolve is steadfast and honourable. We are a united, proud people that will not lower ourselves to their level.

The pieces were moving on the galactic chessboard. All Roth needed to do now was wait. All of his investment into Markus Holland was about to pay off.

"Novus Ordo Seclorum," Roth whispered.

CHAPTER TWENTY-THREE
NATHAN

After hours of FTL travel, the Phoenix pierced through the slipstream and emerged into what Nathan could only describe as *natural space*. The ship's engine sent billows of lightning and cosmic energy tumbling forth, creating an effect that looked like a bullet emerging from an electrical storm. Punching the controls, Nathan watched the long silver torrents of the slipstream dissolve into space: replaced by a view of the stars and the Capital Worlds. It was the first time he'd returned to the system since the Battle of the Messorem. To say it was a completely different sight would be an understatement at best. Where before, scorched wreckages of warships from both sides floated in the endless void, there were now busy transit lanes packed with frigates.

A lump formed in Nathan's throat when he saw the thing that had once been known as the planet of Unity. It was undoubtedly the greatest casualty in the skirmish a year prior. Seig destroyed three planets with the Messorem. Two were farming colonies in the Ravow System, and the third was Unity: a Capital World with trillions of inhabitants. Thanks to the Messorem, Unity transformed from a utopian metropolis to fire and ash. Today, what had been the sixth Capital world was now a derelict and lifeless husk unable to sustain life: *much like Earth.*

"I hear the 'wealthers are discussing terraforming Unity," Koble said from the copilot's seat. The Sphinax shovelled a fork of fish stew into his mouth.

"Looks like it's gonna take some serious manpower," Rain said, leaning between Nathan and Koble and grabbing a piece of fish from Koble's cup.

"It's hard to believe that Seig did all that damage," Nathan shook his head in disbelief. "Just think if we hadn't stopped him—"

"But, we did". Koble cut him off.

The military presence around the Capital Worlds was apparent among the packed transport lanes. Two warships monitored the traffic while fighters patrolled the area.

A sudden inbound comms flagged on Nathan's display. When he opened the communique, a small hologram —no larger than a photograph— formed. The man in projection was a broad-shouldered Uvan male with blue skin and receding white hair, wearing the uniform of a senior officer.

"Captain Carter," the Uvan nodded in greeting. "I am Admiral Dolian Wexell of Commonwealth High Command. Agent Dines informed us of the situation. We understand that you and your crew apprehended some criminals attempting to conduct business with the Revenant?"

"That's right," Nathan nodded. "Dines seemed to think we'd get a target on our backs".

Wexell's eyes narrowed, and he transmitted a series of landing coordinates to the Phoenix; "I'm hereby ordering you to dock at this location. We'll provide the Phoenix Titan with fighter escort from here on out".

Nathan could almost feel Koble wince beside him, no doubt feeling the same reluctance that stemmed from years of Jack's warning regarding the 'wealth. Wexell oozed the kind of stereotypical patriotism that many associated with the Commonwealth. Even though Nathan had overcome certain aversions through his friendship with Harrt, it was still tricky to overcome his general sense of trepidation when confronted by a highly dutiful 'wealther.

"When you land, a group of marines will take your prisoners into custody," Wexell continued. "Do not get in their way".

"Understood," Nathan said, keeping it brief.

Wexell didn't say anything else, and his hologram dissolved into nothingness.

"Why is it that 'wealthers always come across so uptight?" Rain asked with a smirk. He gestured to Nathan to climb from the pilot's seat to take over. "They do realise that life is for living, right?"

"That's how they come off the assembly line," Koble said with his mouth full.

As Nathan unbuckled himself from his chair, six 'wealther fighters came into view. The small spacecraft flanked the Phoenix on every side, leaving Nathan to feel on edge, but he had no doubt that Rain would fly circles around them if things took an unlikely turn.

"I need to speak to Jareth one more time," Nathan said, looking at the two Sphinax. "I know this wasn't the plan. I still want him to stand trial on Pluvium".

Koble help up a paw. "Nate, we get it. Pluvium will have its justice one day, but that guy sitting in the brig knows a whole lotta stuff. First and foremost, we need to know if Chimera is Jack".

Nathan nodded, more to himself than Koble. "You wanna find out?"

KOBLE

Before meeting Jack and the Loyalty's crew, Koble had rarely ventured beyond the Pluvium System, but when Kornell rose to power, he was forced to flee the only home he'd known. Fortunately, Jack and the Loyalty's first captain, Theo Arturious, took him in and treated Koble like one of their own. In the first few months, Koble realised how narrow his view of the universe had been. He grew to understand the galaxy for what it was: not what his tutors and textbooks said. First-hand experience was one thing, but the life lessons and close mentorship of Jack cemented Koble's perception of morality and survival.

Among Jack's many lessons, one stood out more now than ever: *stay away from the Commonwealth*. The 'wealth at large would always put the needs of the state over the needs of the individual. That was fact, but Koble knew through his friendship with Harrt that it wasn't black and white. People could be shades of grey: just as Koble now thought of Jack —a kind and honourable man who'd made mistakes: the kind that should stay buried forever, just as Koble and Gordon agreed.

Koble wasn't sure why, but for one reason or another, he found himself recalling the day Jack confessed his sins.

The Loyalty had taken a job on Diem Nine, protecting a group of scientists during some violent labour strikes. It was supposed to be an easy job —*babysit a few dorks while they did scientific shit.* Of course, it hadn't been that easy.

When Jack and Gordon saw each other, things were frosty, and eventually it all spiralled into Gordon striking Jack while screaming bloody murder. Stranger still, Jack didn't fight back —not once.

That was entirely out of character for the Loyalty's captain. He wouldn't taken shit from anyone. Ever.

Six hours later, overcome with grief and shame, Jack attempted suicide, but fortunately, Koble had stopped him.

It was at that moment that Jack confessed to him the awful truth, and it shook Koble to the core. The memory of that would be forever etched into his brain. He'd tried to store it where it couldn't resurface, and most of the time, it worked, but there was the odd occasion where Jack's crime would hit Koble like a moving ship. He'd question the legitimacy of the man he'd called friend. He'd ask himself if covering up the truth was the right thing to do. Then, he'd think about the Jack he'd known: the principled man who'd saved his life and the lives of countless others. The man who'd raised his son and nephew single-handedly. The Jack who'd not only been a captain to the Loyalty's crew but also a friend, a confidant and a teacher. The man who sacrificed himself at Mirotose Station to save those he loved. Yes, Jack made mistakes in the past, but he'd spent a lifetime trying to atone. That was better than most.

That was the legacy of Jack Stephens.

When Koble and Nathan arrived at the brig, they found Gordon keeping watch. The doctor was sitting on one of the storage crates, reading an old book, with his shotgun casually resting over his lap.

"Any noise from them?" Nathan said, pointing to the pair of sealed cells.

"Not a thing," Gordon replied.

"Good," Nathan said.

The door to Jareth's cell opened with a hiss. Nathan was the first to enter the converted cargo bay, and Koble followed close behind. As he entered the room, Koble was overcome with a strange sensation that felt like it didn't belong. This was the first time he'd ever come face to face with Jareth: with the man who'd bank-rolled Kornell's rise to power. Koble should've felt angry and violent, but instead, he felt oddly placid about the whole thing. *Maybe it was because many other things were going on, or perhaps he'd outgrown the need for vengeance?*

Jareth sat in the middle of the room, his shirt from the previous night's soiree rolled at the sleeves and unbuttoned at the collar. He looked like a different man from what Koble pictured. Rather than appearing the part of the suave businessman, Jareth seemed defeated and exhausted. He still looked arrogant, but a certain glimmer had faded from his sharp human features.

Jareth lifted his head, and his eyes darted from Nathan to Koble and something akin to recognition filled the elitist's face.

"Chief Koble," Jareth exhaled. "We meet at long last".

Koble didn't say anything.

Jareth shifted his gaze to Nathan; "If I'm not mistaken, we've dropped out of the slipstream. Therefore, we must be close to wherever you are taking me. So,

Captain Carter, do me the courtesy of telling me where you are taking me?"

Nathan folded his arms. "Valour".

"*Valour?*" Jareth smiled ironically at the word and shook his head in disappointment. "It would appear that I overestimated you".

"What is that supposed to mean?" Nathan scowled.

Jareth glared at him with steely, unforgiving eyes: "It means you're making a grave lapse in judgement. Again. We are playing by the Society's rules now. If you are heading to Valour it's because Roth wants you to go to Valour".

"You seem mighty confident about that," Koble said, taking a step closer to the human.

"I expected more from you too, Chief Koble," Jareth hissed. "As Jack's right-hand man, I thought you'd be able to figure this out!"

Koble straightened, and the dark hairs on his torso stood upright. He felt his giant paws balling into fists.

"Funny, because Jack used to say you were a snake," Koble said. "I always figured you were the bastard that attacked us at Mirotose Station".

Jareth laughed to himself. "I'm one of the last people that wanted Jack dead". He paused as though considering his next words carefully. Jareth took on an apologetic expression as he said, "Much like yourself, Chief Koble, I am one of the few people who knew the truth about Jack Stephens: about Jack's involvement in the Fall".

Koble felt his heart sink into his stomach and his mouth turn dry. Everything seemed to slow down. Adrenaline flooded Koble's veins. Nathan's voice lifted in a tone of confusion, then in anger, but the words were jibberish in Koble's mind. Jareth's knowing eyes focussed on Koble's, and there in lay the truth.

Jareth knew. It wasn't a bluff. He knew. Koble wasn't sure how, but there it was. David Jareth knew the horrible truth about Jack, and saying that truth aloud was his attempt to sway the situation to his advantage.

Nathan's voice finally broke through the carnage in Koble's mind. "What is he talking about?"

Koble didn't say anything: his brain too busy processing everything. Time stood still until the second Koble realised that Gordon had entered the room: evidently noticing Nathan's yelling from the hall.

Jareth's eyes peeled away from Koble and settled on Gordon.

"I'm talking about the truth," Jareth said, almost apologetically. "The truth that all three of us have kept from Captain Carter".

With no other option left, Koble lunged forward, grabbing Jareth by the throat. He slammed the human against the bulkhead, hoping to crush his windpipe before he could utter another word.

"Put him down," Nathan ordered. "Now!"

Jareth offered no resistance, and his eyes were calm, as though he were challenging Koble to choke him out. The unmistakable bang of Nathan's gun, firing into the ceiling, erupted around the room. Koble knew it was a warning shot.

"I said put him down, Koble," Nathan yelled, his voice full of the rage and anger he'd hoped to avoid.

Koble loosened his grip on Jareth's neck but kept the elitist pinned against the wall. "Nate, trust me: you don't wanna hear what he's got to say".

"I'll be the judge of that," Nathan growled.

From the back of the room, Koble heard Gordon's mild-mannered voice fill the cell: "Koble's right, Nathan; this is something better left unspoken. Jack had his secrets for a reason".

"It's about time he knew," Jareth said, his expression a thin veil of empathy. "He deserves to know about the Fall and everything else that has been swept under the rug for all these years".

Gordon looked pale.

"How dare you!" He said, pushing forward with the kind of aggression that was more expected of Jack. "What good does the truth bring him? You have no clue—"

Nathan raised his voice so loud that it could've stripped paint from the hull.

"Shut up," Nathan screamed, moving in front of the doctor and blocking his path to Jareth. He waved a finger in Gordon's face, "Shut the fuck up!". Then turning to Koble, "Put him down. I ain't gonna ask again".

Koble debated snapping Jareth's neck right there. It'd be easy: a simple grab, squeeze and twist motion. The problem was the cat was already out of the bag. Nathan knew that he and Gordon had deceived him. With tremendous reluctance, Koble released Jareth, and Nathan pushed by him to get to the elitist.

"Talk," Nathan barked, grabbing Jareth by the collar. "What did Jack have to do with the Fall?"

Jareth held his gaze: "A time will come where you and I will sit and discuss everything. Personally, I think this conversation is better had with your..." Jareth paused to gesture at Koble and Gordon: "With your *crewmates*. My account of Jack's... *situation* is my own, and I suspect you would view it as one-sided".

Nathan's jaw clenched. The outrage and agitation on the Earther's face were more than apparent, making Koble all kinds of nervous.

Nathan bashed Jareth against the wall; "What did Jack do!"

Koble swallowed the lump in his throat as Jareth spoke the words that should've stayed buried until the end of time.

"Jack is one of the men responsible for the Fall".

Silence consumed the room, and Koble could hear his own heartbeat. Nathan appeared somewhere between confused and downright pissed off. Gordon looked like a man who wanted to give it all up.

Jareth continued, his voice surprisingly emotional. "The Society blackmailed him, and through his influence at the EDA, Jack unknowingly aided in the massacre of our people".

Nathan turned away from Jareth, looking at Koble and Gordon with an expression so raw it could break glass.

"Outside," he growled. "Now!"

As Koble and Gordon were led from the room, Jareth called out to Nathan: "When you realise that you have played into Roth's hand, come and visit me in the 'wealther gulag. We have much to discuss".

VOL

As the journey to Valour would take several hours, Jaudi organised guest quarters for Vol, Dines and what remained of his marines. Hayward returned to the Sadalmelik while Harrt went to the command deck. Vol's guest cabin was just down the hall from Dines. It was a standard-issue three-hundred square foot room with a tiny bathroom. There was a single bed, a desk and a window that looked out onto the slipstream. All of it lacked imagination and personality, just as she expected.

Vol made sure to lock the door behind her before rigging a simple override on the control panel that would cause it to alarm if anyone tried to bust in. She wasn't sure if the situation was improving, but figured it was better to be safe than sorry.

Despite the drab surroundings and partial sense of unease, Vol wanted nothing more than to rest. She undressed and placed her loaded gun under her pillow. She lay between the beige covers and thought of running water as a way to calm her mind, and eventually she drifted to sleep.

She awoke sometime later to the intrusive jangle of the door chime. At first, Vol didn't register it as something normal. A horrible tension crept up her spine, and instinctively she grabbed the pistol from under her covers and rolled out of bed with the gun trained on the hatch.

The door chimed again.

Vol cursed something in the old Uvan tongue and climbed from the bed. She hurriedly pulled on her clothes while keeping one eye on the sealed hatch.

"Who is it?" she said, keeping her pistol close.

A woman's voice came through from the other side.

"It's Lieutenant Meera: Oxarri's XO. The Commander asked me to come and get you".

"Why?"

Jaudi grunted in what sounded like irritation. "We're coming up on the Capital Worlds. He wanted to speak to you before we arrive".

Vol tried her best to read the woman's thoughts. Despite the four inches of steel dividing them, she could just about get a hint of something that felt *reasonably* genuine.

She holstered her gun and opened the door, allowing the Lieutenant inside. Jaudi was not what Vol expected of a 'wealther military officer. She seemed shorter than the average human female, perhaps fifteen pounds heavier too. Jaudi was definitely a decade beyond the average retirement age, yet Vol sensed she had the mind of someone twenty years younger.

Jaudi glanced at the gun on Vol's hip, but didn't acknowledge it. She was sharp enough to know not to do so.

"Okay," Vol said. "Take me to Oxarri".

▲

For several minutes, Vol and Jaudi walked in complete silence. It should've felt awkward, but Vol found herself lost in the sights and sounds of the Artemis. The corridors and junctions were alive: filled with bright, motivated officers productively going about their day-to-day routine. There was a certain pride in how the crewspeople carried out their duties that didn't surprise Vol in the slightest. She recalled once hearing that the 'wealth's most prized societal value was *efficiency,* which certainly explained why they showed such commitment to their craft. When Vol and Jaudi entered an ascending elevator, their silence dropped:

"So, I understand you're a pilot," Jaudi said, in an attempt to make idle chit-chat.

"I'm an engineer by trade, but you pick up certain skills along the way".

Jaudi chewed the inside of her cheek as she listened, and Vol sensed scepticism from the old woman.

"I read the reports on the battle for the Messorem. By all accounts, you and your crew are heroes," Jaudi said. "Plus, Harrt vouches for your skillset".

The elevator slowed and stopped at a floor that wasn't their destination. Two Horrus officers entered and offered casual salutes as they entered. Again, there was silence. Vol could feel an impulse at the tip of Jaudi's tongue: something she wanted to say that seemed controversial. She could tell how the Lieutenant rolled her jaw back and forth in contemplation. The Horrus officers disembarked three decks later. The doors closed with a whoosh, and Jaudi continued:

"By now, I'm sure you've read every one of my thoughts," she said stiffly. "So, how about we cut to the chase?"

Vol nodded.

Jaudi continued, "I've known Harrt Oxarri since he was a boy. I got him through the academy. Trained him. Took him under my wing. Attended his wedding—"

"I get it," Vol interrupted. "I don't question your loyalty at all. It's good that Harrt has such a supportive first-mate".

She'd hoped that by shutting down the conversation, Jaudi would drop the subject. Unfortunately, that wasn't the case. Jaudi hit the emergency brake on the control panel, causing the elevator to halt.

"Don't play dumb with me," Jaudi said. "I've seen how Oxarri looks at you, and there's no way you haven't noticed it either".

"Look, I know you are saying this because you care about him, but you gotta understand this is personal".

Jaudi exhaled, apparently attempting to maintain a level of cool-headedness. Vol could sense that the XO wasn't trying to pick a fight, but rather trying to protect Harrt.

"You gotta understand, Harrt and I go way back," Jaudi sighed, her eyes softening as she spoke. "I watched him grow from a spotty teenager into a man. I watched him marry the girl of his dreams". Jaudi took a long labouring breath. "I fought alongside him at Maru Seven... I stood beside him the day they buried his family".

Vol stepped back involuntarily: feeling the weight of Jaudi's thoughts and emotions from that potent memory. It was awful.

"I've not seen Oxarri look at someone like the way he looks at you in a really long time," Jaudi admitted, with a passion that spoke volumes. "Like you said, this is your personal business, but just do me one favour".

"What is it?"

"If you want to be with him, be with him. If you don't, let him move on," Jaudi said. "Since Maru Seven, Harrt's been a shell of the man I once knew. He seemed different after his *adventures* aboard the Phoenix. I just want the day to come where I can see my friend whole again."

Vol didn't need mind-reading abilities to sense the sincerity in Jaudi's voice. She genuinely cared for Harrt, more than most XOs would.

"You're a good friend, Jaudi," Vol said with a feint smile. "Here's the deal: when this is all said and done, I'll sit down with Harrt and figure this out".

Jaudi didn't return the smile. She simply stepped back, and nodded with a stiff upper lip.

Vol debated telling her that Harrt was lucky to have an XO who had his back as a method to kill the tension, but decided against it.

▲

Minutes later, Vol and Jaudi exited the elevator opened onto the hangar where the Sadalmelik was docked. The shuttle Harrt took days earlier to meet with Tariq, and the Phoenix's crew was stowed at the other end of the room, right next to the hangar doors, as if it was readying to leave. Harrt, Dines and Hayward were waiting at the centre of the room. The three men were in deep conversation, looking more agitated than Vol expected. From an initial read, she could tell something had come up. Hayward didn't like whatever it was, while Dines pictured worst-case scenarios in his head.

"What is it?" Vol said as she and Jaudi approached.

There was a rumble of uncertainty that shrouded the three men.

Dines was the first to answer: "It's the Paradisians. Markus Holland has instructed *all* of their ships, civilian, corporate or otherwise, to converge on Valour. Intel suggests they'll be in the system within the hour".

"This is the assault that Claire warned us about," Vol concluded. "But why send civilian ships? The Society isn't going to win a battle with a bunch of skiffs and yachts".

"She's right," Jaudi said. "Tactically speaking, it makes no sense. We usually have a few dozen warships in the system".

Harrt and Dines shared a sheepish glance.

"No, we don't," Dines sighed. "We've got three, including the Artemis. High command redistributed the fleet after we submitted our reports on the Revenant warship that attacked the Equus".

The mole had struck again, this time leaving the Capital Worlds open to assault. Despite the genius of whatever elaborate scheme the Society was pulling, something didn't quite add up. By all accounts, the Society didn't make mistakes. Surely they wouldn't be stupid enough to assume the 'wealther's defences rested in ships alone. Like the rest of the galaxy, Vol knew that every Capital World had ground-to-orbit defences capable of blowing warships to kingdom come. She suspected those weapons had undoubtedly received an upgrade since the Messorem. Even with every man, woman and child on Paradisium flying a spacecraft, they wouldn't make it as far as the ground.

But maybe that was exactly what the Society wanted. Vol thought about it more. Markus Holland was the one in the press, not Roth. *What if Roth wanted Holland to do something reactive and foolish?*

"What the hell happens now?" Vol asked, looking at the others.

Harrt exhaled, "Do you want the good news or the bad news?"

She folded her arms: "Bad news first, right?"

"Dines and I have been summoned by Inon Waife to an emergency summit on Valour," Harrt gestured to the shuttle behind them. "We are to answer the council's questions so they can make an *informed choice* about their next move".

Vol felt her hairs crawl. "What's the good news?"

"Elder Marx and Elder Repla are en route to debrief Cadu," Harrt said, trying to put a positive spin on the current situation. "Xanathur won't be far behind, but I'm told he's running a little late. The medical team informs me that Cadu's outlook is promising".

Hayward nodded in relief. "Might actually get some answers".

Jaudi made a clicking noise with her tongue. She looked at Dines and Harrt with a complex expression:

"During your investigation, did you ever rule out the possibility that your mole could be an Evoker Elder?"

That was a frightening prospect, that nobody had considered. Everyone with the exception of Dines seemed to flinch at Jaudi's proposal.

"It's implausible," Dines said.

Vol stared at him, brows raised. "You sure about that?"

Harrt's brow lowered and his head nodded back and forth as he processed the theory. "Some Elders have access to give executive orders. Plus, they all knew Astrilla's whereabouts when we were on the run from Seig. It's not impossible".

"And now three of the fuckers are heading for this ship," Hayward said. "Right as the Society is acting".

Hayward was right. The whole thing felt wrong.

"We contacted them," Dines said with finality. "I agree Elders have special access, but you'd be hard-pressed to find an Elder that wasn't completely committed to the creed".

Despite Dines' grim expression, Vol could read his every thought: he —mostly— believed in what he was saying. Not because he trusted the Evokers, but because he knew what the 'wealther aristocracy was like. He'd seen their cowardice, greed and malice first-hand, and it had cemented a strong gut feeling he couldn't ignore.

"This creates a difficult situation, doesn't it?" Vol summarised.

Hayward rubbed his giant hands together as he eyeballed her; "Could you mind-read an Evoker Elder?"

Her first impulse was to say *no* and join Harrt and rendezvous with the Phoenix on the surface. After all, she wanted to be in the middle of the action: doing whatever she could to save lives. Vol hadn't considered staying aboard the Artemis at all. Hayward's question prompted her to consider their predicament in a different light. Though she had difficulty reading Evokers, Vol recently had some luck with Astrilla. Sure, it had been a foggy, hazy mess, but she'd understood Astrilla's emotion at the time. Maybe staying aboard and attempting to read the Elders was the best course of action. It'd certainly help to clear some suspects off the board.

"If I'm around them a while, I *might* be able to do it," Vol said. "The problem is if they are hostile, how do we take them out?"

A smug grin formed on Hayward's face. "You let me and my boys worry about that. We've had our fair share of run-ins with Revenant Paladins before... same thing, right?"

"Not exactly," Dines frowned.

"When they arrive, divert them to a different hangar," Hayward said. "*If* they are planning something, we've got the element of surprise and a metric ton of inhibitor rounds aboard the Sadalmelik".

It was a clever play; send the Elders to an alternative hangar so they wouldn't see the Sadalmelik. Vol could get the read, then if things went sideways, the Artemis' security team and Hayward's guys could spring a trap.

With a rough plan formulated, the group went their separate ways. Hayward returned to his ship. Dines and Harrt climbed aboard the shuttle to head to Valour.

Before parting, Harrt and Vol shared a long look.

She softened her expression as she traced the shape of his dark eyes.

"Be careful down there," Vol said.

"You too".

CHAPTER TWENTY-FOUR
NATHAN

Jack Stephens: the man who screwed Earth. Nathan's mind whirled with that thought. Despite everything about his world crumbling inward, there was a strange reconciliation to his past, to the Fall —to Jack. Questions and memories coalesced in his brain like an unstoppable flood. A part of him hoped that Jareth was deceiving him, but the logical side of him knew that wasn't the case.

Nathan found himself consumed with a quiet rage that numbed everything around him. His mind didn't recognise the Phoenix touchdown on Valour. He didn't take note of the 'wealther marines boarding his ship and dragging Jareth and Christian Roth away: *the latter kicking and screaming like a petulant child.*

Instead, Nathan sat at the bar with a drink in hand: waiting for the two men he'd trusted to explain why they'd betrayed him. For a moment that seemed to last forever, Nathan wallowed in a state of defeat. Everything around him was muted. Astrilla was there using a stern tone with Koble and Gordon. Russell and Rain were snooping from the kitchen, refusing to get involved, while James and Tariq were nowhere to be seen.

When Nathan snapped back to reality, he heard Gordon arguing with Astrilla:

"That was never my intention," the doctor said. "We did what we had to".

Nathan slowly climbed to his feet, his hand tightening around his glass.

"You have exactly five seconds to tell me the truth," Nathan growled, his tone a warning. "What did Jack do?"

Gordon and Koble shared a not-so-subtle look. The lack of immediate answers made Nathan's blood boil, and he threw his glass against the bulkhead, sending shards of glass into the air.

"Tell me," he barked.

No doubt sensing that things could get messy, Astrilla stepped toward him. She likely knew better than anyone that the last few days were taking their toll. The lack of sleep, stress and, of course, the revelation that two friends had been lying to him was a recipe for disaster.

"Maybe we should take a walk..." Astrilla suggested.

The Evoker's attempt to diffuse the situation failed. Nathan moved around her and headed to Gordon and Koble with aggressive purpose. He didn't notice his hands forming into fists, nor did he recognise the rage filling his every motion. A sea of red craved to flood his senses, but the overwhelming desire to know the truth acted like a barrier.

Gordon's sigh implied failure.

"Jack was complicated," he said.

"That's not an answer!" Nathan snapped, fire flashing in his eyes.

Gordon must've recognised that anger and quietly moved to the bar for a seat. Following a long and laboured breath, he spoke;

"Before the Fall, there were theories about a group of politicians, celebrities, and business people asserting their control over the masses through media and government. This was the Society, and they induced countless atrocities throughout Earth's history: including the Fall".

Gordon swallowed a lump in his throat. He hesitated, shaking his head in what looked like disappointment.

"Jack was a senior EDA operative. He had access to many sensitive resources..." Gordon set his wide eyes on Nathan once again and they glimmered with sorrow. "Eight years before the Fall, the EDA launched an impenetrable satellite network over the Earth. It was secret, Enkaye-Earth hybrid tech: the ultimate defence against any potential alien attackers".

"And you just happen to know that for a fact?" Nathan folded his arms sceptically.

"Well, yes, I do," Gordon said. "Your Grandfather was one of the men to develop it".

Gordon paused, nervously trying to regain his breath. He peered at Koble, and the big Sphinax shrugged as if giving the doctor his blessing to say more.

"On the day of the Fall, someone within the EDA closed down that defence system. Earth would've lost the war regardless, but that satellite network would've bought us a great deal of time". Gordon stopped, his eyes conquered by fear, and apology. "That traitor was Jack".

Even though Jareth had said it earlier, the whole truth from Gordon hit him like a punch to the gut. It was agony. Worse than any gunshot or stab wound. The revelation of it all burrowed into Nathan's chest like an unwanted parasite.

Jack was many things, but he wasn't the kind of man that would stand by and allow the slaughter of his own people.

He was a man of Earth who held a seething hatred for the Revenant. A man haunted by the Fall: *that characteristic took on new meaning now.*

For the first time throughout the confrontation, Koble spoke up.

"It's not as black and white as Gordon is saying..." The Sphinax shuffled toward Nathan. "Jack was blackmailed by the Society. He had no idea what he was doing until it was too late".

Nathan failed to process all that part. He allowed himself to replay the Fall: to reconcile his experience with the accounts Gordon and Koble provided. Nathan remembered the grizzly deaths of his mother, father and grandmother in all their appalling detail. He embraced the disabling fear he'd felt on that day. Then a single memory plucked from the horror and tragedy came to the surface.

He saw Jack fighting off Revenant soldiers and rescuing him from certain death.

That was the brave man he'd always known.

Not a turncoat.

Not a coward.

Nathan felt Astrilla's soft hand against his shoulder. She shot steely glares at Koble and Gordon, evidently aware that Nathan was too overcome in the moment.

"What were they blackmailing Jack with?" she asked.

A pain-filled expression came across Gordon as he spoke; "As a backup, the Society sent hitmen after Nathan's Grandfather. I was with him when the Society attacked our research facility in Russia. They were under orders to capture Bill, but there were *other* forces at play and the whole thing turned into a bloodbath".

Silence whirled there for a beat.

"What do you mean *as a backup*?" Nathan said, noting the doctor's choice of words among all the other testimony. "If my grandfather was a backup hostage—"

"I was their leverage," James said from the corner of the room.

Nathan hadn't noticed his cousin, but he'd obviously been there long enough to hear what was happening. With all the raised voices, Nathan suspected half of Valour knew something was up.

James sleuthed into the living space with a cigarette between his lips. He sat down on the barstool beside Gordon and exhaled a thick cloud of smoke.

"Those Society fuckers kidnapped me," James admitted. "They told my dad they'd kill me if he didn't do as they said. They tried to kill me anyway, but Dad saved me. Then some EDA clown showed up, and things got dicey. Needless to say, I killed my first man that day".

Nathan shook his head. "I remember you and Jack arrived at the house. You guys saved me".

"Of course we did," James blew smoke. "Me and Dad escaped in a helicopter and went back to Grampa Bill's place. We wanted to get you all out... that's when we found you, Nate".

Nathan moved away from the pack, stomping from the bar to the mock fireplace at the opposite end of the room, analysing his memories in excruciating detail.

"How many—" Nathan's voice faltered as he tried to speak. With his voice failing to process the words he wanted, Nathan responded angrily. He slammed his fist on the mantel and glowered at Gordon and Koble. "Why the fuck didn't you tell me?"

The silence in the room was profound.

"Jack made me swear," Koble answered, his voice flat and surprisingly unapologetic. "He didn't want you, or James, carrying his mistakes".

Nathan's eyes snapped to Gordon, "And you?"

"Bad things happened in Russia, Nathan. The Society attacked us and—" Gordon stopped to bite back tears. "I lost everything and everyone that day, my fiancé, my friends and Bill. Your grandfather sacrificed himself to keep a weapon of sheer evil away from the Society's grasp: something so destructive it would've made the Fall look like nothing".

Gordon leaned back, his arms pressed tightly to his chest and his left leg shaking. Nathan had never seen the man so beset with emotion.

"I lost more than you could possibly imagine. Even after all of that, I continued to sacrifice. I gave up—"

Gordon forced himself to stop. It was a conscious effort: an attempt to prevent oneself from saying too much.

Seconds passed, and Gordon regained some of his usual stoic demeanour. He settled his hard eyes on Nathan:

"I'm sorry you had to find out this way, but this was the best thing for you".

In response, Nathan looked at Koble and Gordon with something akin to hatred, but he couldn't describe the feeling. It was a reaction to the moment: to the truth.

In the most civil tone possible, Nathan said, "Take all your shit and get the fuck off my ship. When I get back, I don't wanna see either of you".

Without anything else to say, Nathan headed for the airlock, ignoring the pleas and calls from the others as he departed.

ASTRILLA

Astrilla's immediate impulse was to follow Nathan, but unfortunately, that wasn't an option. Commonwealth marines tried and failed to stop him from leaving the hangar, evidently unprepared for someone to storm off as Nathan did. When Astrilla made it down the Phoenix's boarding ramp, the marines were up in arms, ordering her to return to the ship and await further instruction. She didn't really have a choice. Sure, she could ignore the guards and seek out Nathan, but it would create more tension with Commonwealth officials.

Astrilla's next instinct was to scold Koble and Gordon for their deception, but the pair avoided her like a Revenant Hunter.

She figured it was probably for the best. The crew had enough internal conflict, and Astrilla didn't want to add to the already heightened tension. She had to be the mediator, now more than ever.

Regardless of her feelings toward the matter, Astrilla needed to practice patience and resolve, so she tried to calm: positioning herself outside the Phoenix in the loading area. The marines steered clear of her, and for a while, there was something akin to tranquillity, but it wasn't meditative or reflective.

It felt like the eye of a storm.

Astrilla walked to the edge of the open hangar, which boasted an incredible view of Valour, though a series of large clouds loomed in the distance.

Despite being ninety percent covered in man-made cities, Valour was *mostly* magnificent. While Astrilla often took comfort in more natural environments, there was something unique about the central nexus of the 'wealth. There was a history of the Capital Worlds that couldn't be found elsewhere.

This was where the Commonwealth first came to fruition all those years ago. The founders met on Valour with a simple vision; to form a movement, to fight the Revenant. Those founders opposed the Revenant's tyranny and promoted a fair and equal civilisation. It was to be a culture in which no being would suffer discrimination or hate. Where there was no rich or poor. Where everyone worked together for a greater good. Unfortunately, the road to hell was paved with good intentions.

As Astrilla reflected on her thoughts of the Commonwealth and the sheer majesty of Valour's cityscape, she heard a pair of footsteps approaching. She turned, spotting James walking across the hangar toward her.

"Still no sign of him?" James asked.

"Nathan will return once he calms down," Astrilla answered confidently. "Trust me: he just needs a bit of time".

James stopped beside her and took a long look at the view. Astrilla could've sworn he was unimpressed by it, but he still faked an impressed look.

"Nate hasn't changed much," James remarked. He offered out his hand, "We've not been formally introduced".

"Astrilla," she shook the Earther's hand.

"So you're the girlfriend?" James remarked. "Guess that kinda makes us… *family*?"

Astrilla didn't quite know how to respond. The concept of *family* held an entirely different meaning to her. It wasn't about being blood relatives but about those you loved more than words could describe.

Once again, James pulled a cigarette and a lighter from his jacket pocket while waiting for a response. He placed the flame of his light against the rolled stick of tobacco, and the pungent aroma of nicotine filled the air around them. It was a continuous habit: likely a coping mechanism to deal with his former addictions.

"Welcome to the family," he said, making a toasting gesture with his cigarette.

"Why is it that every time I hear something new about *your* family, it's some grand, sweeping revelation?" Astrilla said, trying her best not to breathe in the smoke.

James laughed, almost choking in the process.

"Well, there's a straightforward explanation for that. My father was a liar, just like his father before him. So I'm gonna go out on a limb and assume it's probably genetic".

Astrilla had never met Jack, but somehow he felt like an instrumental part of the Phoenix's crew: *like a ghost haunting the ship*. Yes, Jack raised the man Astrilla loved, but his mistakes left behind wounds that weren't simple to repair.

James puffed smoke thoughtfully, "The sins of our ancestors stick with us for generations. Case in point, my father fucked up, and the consequence for that fuck-up is Paradisium and our current situation".

A murky truth lurked in his words.

"Still," James drawled. "I guess there's some good to be found in all this".

"How so?"

"Well, if you and my little cousin ever produce any offspring, he'll be a far better father than mine".

There was a heaviness to the Earther's voice that made Astrilla realise that he'd been holding onto a cluster of angry feelings for many years. Misery clung to him like a bad odour, and it seemed like Jack was the root cause of his pain.

James stubbed his cigarette on the floor.

"I'm gonna head back," he gestured to the Phoenix, then at the dark clouds looming over the city. "Storms coming in; you might wanna do the same".

Astrilla nodded, and as James began to stroll back to the Phoenix, she called out to him:

"James…" she said, halting the Earther mid-stride. "I disagree. The actions of our predecessors don't define who *we* are. History is littered with bad choices; it is up to us to learn from their mistakes".

James chuckled cynically. "You should get that printed on a fuckin' postcard or something".

▲

After Astrilla returned to the Phoenix, a chilly breeze quickened as the storm pushed southward. A slight drop in temperature followed, and a certain thickness of the air suggested that heavy rainfall would follow. When Astrilla reached the living area, she found Koble at the bar as though he'd been waiting for her. The Sphinax wore an unashamed expression to cover his remorse, looking like he had something to say, while also appearing incredibly sheepish.

"So, I tried to head out and find Nate," Koble drawled. "The marines sent me back. Apparently, we are to remain here until Inon Waife says otherwise".

"That can't be good," Astrilla frowned, feeling a shudder creep up her spine.

"Yeah, Russell overheard a couple of the marines talking. Apparently, we will be summoned to appear before the Commonwealth Council. I don't need to tell you that I can't afford to alienate Pluviam from the 'wealth".

"Are you worried about political ramifications?"

"The tribes have done just fine outside the 'wealth up until this point. If this jeopardises any potential allyship, we'll make do".

Astrilla didn't offer up a response. As an Evoker, she'd say to Koble that joining the Commonwealth was the best defence against the Revenant. To be united was the best way to survive: that was what the Commonwealth was designed to do. However, as the ipso facto first-mate of the Phoenix and someone who saw the 'wealth for all its flaws, Astrilla would say; being allies doesn't mean being the same.

She must've taken too long to reply, as Koble took her silence as disapproval for what happened earlier.

"Go ahead and say it," he said. "I'm surprised you've bit your tongue this long".

Astrilla took a deep breath and sat on the arm of one of the leather chairs at the centre of the room. She, like Koble, knew that an awkward conversation needed to occur.

"Why did you lie?" she said.

Koble spread his paws on the bar contemplatively. "I wanted to preserve the memory of my friend. Sure, Jack did something awful, but that doesn't change the fact that he was a good man".

Astrilla folded her arms.

"So you decided Nathan didn't need to know the truth?"

"Hey, it wasn't exactly my first choice, but you gotta understand I love Nate as a fleshy, meat-bag brother. Jack was important to me, and I loved him, but lying about his crimes wasn't for Jack; it was for Nate".

Astrilla looked at him quizzically.

"When I first met Nate, he was a young kid; still a little messed up from the Fall. You gotta understand Nate had no one besides Jack". Koble carefully considered his words. "What right did I have to ruin the memory of the man who was like a father to him?"

"You're suggesting that Nathan would be better off not knowing?"

Koble's voice lifted an octave: "I ain't suggesting nothing. I'm *telling* you he was better off not knowing. Now all he's gonna do when he thinks of Jack is think about the crime rather than the good man who raised him".

Astrilla was quiet for a moment. In many ways, she fundamentally disagreed with everything Koble said. The truth —no matter how difficult— had to be brought into the light, while deception, regardless of its intent, was wrong.

She experienced an odd sense of moral conflict when she applied that scenario to her own family: all massacred by the Revenant years ago. *Would she really want to know the truth? Maybe Koble had a point? Perhaps memory was better than reality?*

Astrilla looked at Koble: "Regardless of your rationale, you will fix this with Nathan". It wasn't a request or a question. It was instruction. It was an order.

Koble nodded; "Wouldn't have it any other way".

VOL

"Ten credits say our mole is an Evoker". Jaudi's voice was loaded with sarcasm.

Once Harrt and Dines departed, Vol was left with a nervous sensation that didn't sit right. The mole was real: she was more sure of that than ever. Only one question remained, and for one reason or another, Jaudi Meera was trying to place a bet on it as a way to break the tension.

"So," Jaudi quipped. "You gonna take the bet?"

"I hope you make shitty gambling choices," Vol replied.

The two women waited for the Evoker shuttle on the Artemis' starboard hangar: away from the Sadalmelik, where Hayward was prepping his men. It seemed crazy, and Vol wondered if maybe it was.

The Elders had been —mostly— kind to the crew of the Phoenix over the last year. To think one of them was aiding Roth and Baylum seemed insane, but everything else about the situation was equally nuts.

The shuttle docked with the Artemis no more than fifteen minutes after Harrt and Dines left. Vol and Jaudi watched the small grey craft touch down and waited for its occupants to disembark. Jaudi's plan was to meet the Elders upon arrival: making things seem business-as-usual.

Naturally, Vol agreed to join her, citing it as an opportunity to get close to the Elders and —hopefully— pick at their minds.

A boarding ramp emerged from the underbelly of the shuttle, creating a staircase for the Elders to disembark safely.

"This is where the fun begins," Jaudi sighed.

Vol appreciated the sardonic yet brutal honesty of the woman. Despite appearing outwardly confident, Vol could sense the fear concealed by Jaudi's candour.

"Let's just hope to the sun and stars that these guys aren't the mole," Vol replied.

"You and me both," Jaudi nodded as the Elders began to disembark.

The first was Elder Repla: a thin Sillix with green scales over skin that had darkened with age. Her yellow, reptilian eyes studied everything and everyone with scepticism.

Vol recognised her immediately from the Enclave on Pelos Three: though Repla rarely engaged with the Phoenix's crew. That was a role reserved for Yuta and on the rare occasion, Elder Xanathur, though his interactions with the crew were limited thanks to his busy schedule.

The second to step aboard the Artemis was a member of the Florus race —giant avian creatures whose existence teetered on the edge of extinction thanks to the Revenant. The Florus pulled back his hood, keenly examining his new surroundings with urgency. When his gaze settled on Vol, the Florus' expression turned to surprise.

"Welcome aboard," Jaudi said, addressing the Elders as they stopped at the end of the ramp. "I'm Lieutenant Jaudi Meera, acting CO of this vessel".

Jaudi did an excellent job of making things seem normal. Her formal greeting was well-rehearsed, and neither Evoker seemed phased by it.

Repla gazed at Vol, evidently recognising her, but refusing to acknowledge it immediately. Instead, the Sillix's intense golden eyes zipped back to Jaudi:

In a business-like tone, Repla said, "In addition to debriefing Cadu, we've been directed to support any negotiations that may arise. If the rumours of a Paradisian assault on Valour are to be believed, then the Artemis will be vital in keeping the peace.

"As always," Jaudi replied, stating it as though everything Repla said was no big deal.

"I'm sorry to say this, Lieutenant Meera, but your role in this situation could prove challenging over the next few hours," Repla said. "We are here to provide council".

"I welcome it," Jaudi said with a nod. "I'll have my people set up a station for you on the bridge, and we'll assign you a cabin each in due course".

The Florus raised a feathery arm and gestured to Vol: "You are the engineer from the Phoenix Titan, yes?"

Vol nodded, and the Florus' mouth amid his gold beak formed a gentle smile. He introduced himself as Agrion Marx and claimed to be an Evoker Elder once based on Pelos Three, though Vol didn't recognise him. Naturally, she'd recall seeing a Florus wandering the Enclave; they weren't exactly a credit-a-dozen.

Vol didn't need a mind-reading ability to know that Repla was growing impatient with Marx's polite small-talk. The Sillix audibly sighed, and her leg twitched nervously.

Vol took note of that.

She couldn't read either of them. Both Evokers' thought patterns seemed to emit the same vague blur that Astrilla did. There was simply nothing Vol could interpret: just blank static. The only thing she could feel was Jaudi's mild nerves.

The best course of action was to wait and see if one of the Evokers gave it all away. If one —or both— were the mole, they'd eventually slip up. Regardless of Evoker training, strong thoughts and emotions were hard to control: especially under stressful situations. Sure, it was said that the Sillix species didn't feel anything, but Vol knew first-hand that was an exaggeration. They felt fear, pain and love as much as any living creature. The difference was that the Sillix had evolved to not physically show emotion: so thoughts could certainly be plundered.

Jaudi led the Elders toward the elevator at the back of the hangar. Reluctantly, Vol followed, overly aware that she should appear nonchalant. She continued trying to delve into the thoughts of Marx and Repla, hoping that she could catch something —anything.

As the elevator began the long descent, Repla glanced at her: "Last I heard from Yuta, the Phoenix Titan was on Levave investigating that strange signal... did you turn up anything?"

The Sillix's glare was so incredibly stern that Vol stammered before she could formulate a decent response.

"Not much," Vol shrugged. "A bunch of sand and some dusty ruins. I'm sure Nathan submitted his report to Yuta a few days ago".

Marx turned his bird-like head toward them with an inquisitive look in his eyes.

"I really should make a request of Captain Carter or Astrilla to join you on your next Enkaye site investigation," Marx said, his voice friendly and cordial. "I've always found Enkaye ruins to be rather fascinating".

Vol couldn't tell if it was genuine, but her gut told her it was nothing more than idle chit-chat. She offered her best-forced smile and nodded:

"I'm sure we can accommodate you".

Repla made a clicking noise with her teeth; "That is assuming we can avoid the intergalactic incident that Captain Carter has caused..."

The atmosphere in the cramped elevator tightened. Vol wanted nothing more than to respond but decided against it.

This wasn't the time or place to get into an argument.

Thankfully, the elevator journey came to a swift end less than fifteen seconds later. Vol sighed with relief as Jaudi led the Elders into the Command Centre.

The Artemis' bridge was the nexus of flight and combat operations —a vast room on the forward bow, filled with consoles, work stations and about two dozen officers working hard to fulfil their duty. At the end of the room, there was a window spanning the entire length of the wall, boasting an impressive view of Valour from orbit. A staircase against the starboard wall led to a mezzanine floor with more consoles and crewspeople.

The officers stood to attention as Jaudi took to the bridge. The XO saluted and instructed her people to return to work. There was a formality to it that Vol expected but didn't quite know how to process. She'd never served in the military or worked in a formal environment. The whole thing seemed oddly official and sterile: just like the galaxy's perception of the 'wealth.

As the crew returned to duty, Jaudi faced the Evokers and gestured to a series of empty workstations:

"We'll set you up at these consoles. I'll have my senior Comms officer liaise with you to—"

"We must speak with Cadu," Repla cut in. "It is of the highest importance".

Jaudi nodded, though Vol could tell she didn't appreciate the interruption. The XO cleared her throat and rolled her head back as if to click something into place.

"As I was saying..." Jaudi began. "My senior Comms officer will liaise with you to provide clearance so that you can speak with Cadu in the med-bay".

"I don't understand," Repla frowned. "Why not now?"

Jaudi's eyes jumped to Vol and back again —as though trying to catch her attention. When Vol delved into Jaudi's thoughts, she overheard something intentional: *I'm trying to stall them. Get into their brains now!*

Jaudi smiled amicably at Repla: "I apologise, but this is standard procedure".

Despite the evolutionary Sillix quirk not to show emotion, Repla somehow looked positively irritated. Vol could've been sure the Evoker was ready to break something. That was the exact moment Vol heard a mild flicker from Repla's thoughts: two words *—typical 'wealthers...*

The Elders went about familiarising themselves with their workstations. It was obvious that Repla was frustrated by the delay to meet with Cadu, but Marx was entirely relaxed with the red-tape. *Maybe he'd been aboard a few too many 'wealther ships in the past?*

Jaudi passed Vol and walked to a Horrus officer a few metres away. The name tag on his jacket read: Ensign Imperi. Vol was close enough to overhear the conversation but not close enough to look a part of it. She didn't want to raise suspicions.

"Yes, Ma'am?" the Ensign looked up from his station.

In a low voice, she said, "I need you to subtly monitor the Evoker's workstations. Need-to-know basis. Can you do that for me?"

Imperi's jaw tightened, "Of course".

"Good," Jaudi nodded."Oh, and Ensign, take as much time as you need with their med-bay clearance".

CHAPTER TWENTY-FIVE
NATHAN

From space, Valour had been undeniably beautiful: a vast white city that spanned an entire planet while preserving healthy pockets of natural resources. From the ground, it was the opposite: at least in the district where Nathan found himself. In a strange and mundane way, Valour was nothing special. Ninety percent of the high-rise buildings were uninspired template-based towers, while the walkways and community spaces adhered to a strict, prescriptive design.

The citizens going about their daily lives were a completely different story. Most —if not all— had an outlandish sense of fashion, wearing bright-coloured outfits that looked overly expensive and bold eye makeup that seemed entirely unnecessary. Stranger still, it was impossible to pick out an elderly citizen, with most having undergone significant de-ageing therapies.

Harrt once mentioned that only prime citizens lived on the Capital Worlds: those who'd contributed the most to the 'wealth.

When Nathan asked how someone reached that status, Harrt's response was strange:

"All families are assessed based on their ability, needs and contribution to the 'wealth. The Capital Worlds are the most defended space in the universe; therefore, only the most valuable citizens should reside there".

On paper, there was a brutal rationale for that school of thought. Nathan disagreed with it and suspected that Harrt felt the same way. The Commonwealth was —supposedly— a communist regime: meaning the absence of social class, but that was not the case when it came to the Capital Worlds. The civilians seemed more privileged than other 'wealther planets: they were spoiled, just like the Paradisians.

The majestic yet bland architecture served as a mild diversion, but it wasn't long before thoughts of Jack, Gordon, and Koble were swimming around Nathan's head. He tried to shut them out, but it was to no avail. In the end, Nathan surrendered to the rush of thoughts and decided to mull them over. Naturally, the best place to do that was a watering hole, but the district Nathan found himself in had only bourgeois-looking restaurants and clothing houses.

Nathan picked one and pushed his way inside. The sign at the door read, *the Succession Social.* It was a high-end establishment with an immaculate interior. The bar and tables were made from black marble that reflected the low orange lighting. A couple of suited 'wealthers were drinking at the back, but otherwise, the place was empty.

Nathan pulled up a barstool, and the serving droid took his order: a glass of Kor. When the droid returned, Nathan found himself reaching for a credit chit to pay, but the droid ambled away: *everything was free to the prime citizens.*

As Nathan stared into his glass, he allowed the thoughts he'd been avoiding to swim to the surface. At first, he wasn't sure who to be angriest with. Koble had lied. Gordon had lied. But Jack had contributed to genocide.

Nathan took a swig from his glass, hoping to numb something internal. It failed, and a heartbeat later, that awful revelation crept into his mind like a spider. Jack was one reason for the Fall. He helped the Society and the Revenant to achieve their goals. Regardless of whether it was under duress or not, the fact remained: Jack betrayed his own kind. Nathan wasn't sure how to process that: he doubted he ever would.

Someone pulled the barstool beside him with a loud screech that distracted Nathan from his thoughts. At first, he assumed it was another entitled 'wealther, but when he turned to look, he saw the bespectacled face of Gordon

Taggart. There was a long silence, interrupted only by the serving droid taking Gordon's order.

"What the fuck are you doing here?" Nathan said.

"I managed to sneak past the marines," Gordon answered. Then with a slight sheepishness to his voice: "I followed you".

Nathan didn't look at him.

"I said, what are you doing here?"

"You deserve the whole story," Gordon said, turning on his seat. "You must understand that everything I did was in your best interest".

Nathan looked Gordon in the eye. The anger on his face must have been apparent as the doctor immediately straightened up. Nathan was pretty sure Gordon was expecting a swift uppercut for his deception.

With a low, controlled voice, Nathan said; "Say what you gotta say, then go". He shot the Doctor a *cut-to-the-chase* glare before taking a sip of his harsh liquor.

"I didn't come here to talk to you about Jack," Gordon began. "I came here to talk to you about your grandfather: about Russia".

Gordon drank from his cup as though willing some courage. When Nathan's eyes met his, there was a reluctant and unwilling honesty to them. Nathan huffed as he nodded to the doctor to continue.

Gordon set his glasses down on the bar; "Before the Fall, our team investigated paranormal and unnatural instances on Earth. Most were bullshit, but a handful shook me to my core, and every one of those had Enkaye fingerprints all over them". Gordon paused to sip his drink. "A few months before the Fall, our employers *—Sebastian Eli and Titus Rousseau—* found something in the Ural mountains".

Nathan recognised the name Titus Rousseau from Tariq's intel. He was an EWB campaigner with business interests in the Outer Worlds, suspected of being a mid-level player in the Society.

Gordon went on, "They called it Project Erebus".

Erebus —the word Nathan had heard in his dreams a dozen times.

Gordon shuddered at the mere mention of the word.

"Project Erebus was an Enkaye device that *reacted* with your grandfather. At first, we thought he had a stroke, but it turned out this machine was forcing images into his brain".

That piqued Nathan's interest.

"You mean visions?"

Gordon closed his eyes, and his brow deepened.

"Supposedly, Sebastian Eli was researching Project Erebus for many years. According to all sources, it was… Well, it wasn't what they said it was". Gordon shuddered at what he said next. "When the device spoke to your grandfather, it tried to warn him to stay away from it: to bury it and never speak of it again".

Nathan felt the tightness in his face loosen, and his expression turned to intrigue instead of anger.

Gordon lowered his voice and leaned in;

"Project Erebus was no vault. It was an Enkaye prison: designed to hold something evil. Bill's *visions* warned him about the thing inside, but Sebastian Eli and Titus Rousseau were under strict orders to extract whatever it was".

"Their orders came from the Society?"

Gordon nodded reluctantly. "With Titus Rousseau and Eli, we simply saw a very wealthy couple willing to fund our research, but of course, they were much more than that. They turned on us, and the Society struck our facility without remorse."

Nathan started to reply but stopped himself. A bitter taste crept up the back of his throat as his mind organised Gordon's account: imagining his grandfather and a group of scared scientists facing the worst humanity had to offer.

With a degree of urgency, Nathan lifted his gaze to meet Gordon's.

"Are you telling me that Alastair Roth killed my grandfather?"

"No," Gordon shook his head. "Bill died destroying Project Erebus. He knew the evil inside was dangerous, and wouldn't allow the Society to get their hands on it. Even then, I don't think anyone could control it; the prisoner was beyond human comprehension: a vile and twisted embodiment of hate".

Grave darkness whirled in Gordon's voice that was entirely new: *a genuine kind of terror.*

"What was it?" Nathan asked. "The prisoner?"

Gordon answered slowly; "It wasn't a thing you could see or touch. More like a presence. But you could feel the hatred and agony running throughout it".

"So, Project Erebus was destroyed in the Fall?"

"Thanks to Bill," Gordon nodded, and his lips lifted into a nostalgic smile. "He prevented Project Erebus from seeing the light of day, stopping the Society or anyone else from ever accessing the evil it contained".

The truth hurt, but the fact Nathan knew his grandfather died a hero took the edge off. And yet, despite that new knowledge, something dark tickled the back of Nathan's brain: his reoccurring dreams, wherein the word *Erebus* was uttered every night.

That had to mean something.

Nathan was about ready to make mention of that disturbing fact, but Gordon was already talking in a hushed but emotional tone.

"I'm not going to pretend that deceiving you was the right thing to do," he said, shaking his head. "I hated it, but Bill saved my life and was like a father to me. Repaying him meant more to me than you could possibly imagine".

Nathan nodded, and there was little else to say. They sat in silence for several minutes, and it was still very awkward, but it wasn't hostile like it'd been before. Nathan was still pissed that Gordon and Koble had lied about Jack, but Gordon's testimony was starting to make a little sense.

For a while, he wrestled with the idea of kicking Gordon and Koble off the Phoenix. He'd said it in the heat of the moment, but in truth, Nathan couldn't imagine being at odds with either man: they'd been through too much already, and family was important.

When Nathan was about ready to say more, something

interrupted him. The two suited guys at the back of the room called to the service droid in panicked, shrill voices:

"Get the newscast on right now!"

A giant screen on one of the walls flickered to life, displaying footage of thousands of ships amassing around Valour. Some were Roth Industries, a handful were Belfort Enterprises, but most were civilian transports. Many ships were decorated with a symbol that contained old flags and sigils from the days of Earth.

Nathan stood, his eyes transfixed on the screen.

There was no denying that some Paradisians would be pissed off with the unsanctioned capture of Jareth and Christian, but this was not the reaction Nathan expected. Paradisians struggled to move away from their sun-loungers and swimming pools, let alone go to war or protest. They certainly didn't decorate their ships with flags of long-forgotten countries either.

Nathan said to the service droid; "Can you turn the audio up?"

The droid followed his command and a reporter's voice filled the bar;

"That's right, Rami. We are getting reports of over five thousand Paradisian ships forming a blockade around Valour. The Commonwealth council hasn't issued a statement at this stage, but we will bring you the latest as this story develops. All hail our precious Commonwealth".

"This is the work of Alastair Roth," Gordon muttered. "We must—"

Before the doctor could finish his sentence, a group of four Commonwealth marines rushed into the bar. Once they spotted Nathan, they ran toward him.

"Captain Carter?" one of the marines said, not waiting for a reply. "Grand Master of the House Inon Waife requests your attendance at an urgent summit".

"Now?"

"Now".

▲

Nathan and Gordon were rushed to a military transport outside the Succession Social. They were packed into tight chairs between two big men in military uniforms. Within seconds, the inner-transport vessel was soaring high above the city with priority clearance over the rest of the traffic. Despite everything in the last hour, Nathan found it incredibly hard to ignore the dark, ominous clouds now filling the skies.

The military transport passed over several hundred miles of the cityscape, and eventually, there was a gradual change in the architecture of the buildings below. Slowly, the generic, white high-rises disappeared, and beautifully crafted skyscrapers, amphitheatres, and towers became the norm. There was a certain majesty to the space, implying that a great history began there: at the heart of Valour.

The inner-planet transport touched down in a square just outside the Council Chambers. There was a heightened sense of security around the site. Dozens of soldiers guarded the gates to the precinct, and beyond that, a tank patrolled the square.

With its pewter grey facade and impressive Corinthian-style columns surrounding the exterior, the building was a stunning nine-hundred meter tall example of majestic and patriotic romanticism. Crafted from an almost neoclassical design, it emanated a feeling of nobility and sophistication.

Above the main entrance stood a golden statue of the patron goddess of freedom, clasping a shovel in her right hand. Nathan didn't bother to ask what it symbolised.

Propaganda, he thought, while gazing into the lifeless eyes of the statue.

The marines escorted Nathan and Gordon through the main entrance, along a non-descript corridor into a vast, expansive room. The walkways were empty of almost everyone, save for a scattering of guards and a handful of exquisitely dressed officials. Nathan couldn't help but marvel at the sheer magnitude of the impressive government building.

He was directed through a security checkpoint, where he relinquished his gun while being scanned by an Icktus officer.

Upon clearing security, Nathan and Gordon were led up another long corridor to a reception area where Astrilla, Tariq and Koble were already waiting. Koble looked especially shamefaced when he and Nathan made eye contact, but neither acknowledged it.

Astrilla asked: "Did they tell you what's happening in orbit?"

"They didn't have to. It's all over the news feeds," Nathan answered. Then after looking at the others, "I presume Russell and Rain are back at the ship?"

"Correct," Astrilla nodded. "We've been summoned by name to this gathering".

"So, we're in trouble?" Nathan asked. "Or is this situation with Paradisians about to get much worse?"

He could recognise his paramour's habits from a mile away. Astrilla was the kind of silent that meant she knew the answer but didn't want to say it aloud. With the intensified military presence around the Council Chambers, it didn't take a genius to realise that the Commonwealth was readying itself for something violent.

Nathan looked at Tariq, who'd been listening to their conversation. Rather than scold the man for eavesdropping, Nathan invited his input:

"Thoughts?"

Tariq's jaw clenched. "It's the Society. For what purpose, I do not know, but I'll say this: we must act swiftly to avoid bloodshed".

"I'm with Mahmoot," Koble said, his voice more nervous than Nathan expected. "I say we take some affirmative action and deal with the Society the same way we dealt with Seig".

Nathan folded his arms: "Didn't I tell you I didn't wanna see you again?"

"You did," Koble said ruefully. "But I chose to ignore you. When all this drama is said and done, we can talk: let cooler heads prevail. I'll even let you hit me if it makes you feel better. I ain't walking away; not now. Not ever".

Before Nathan could respond, the door to the waiting

room hissed open, and Harrt was escorted inside by two marines. The 'wealther looked exhausted, as though he'd not rested for days. There was nervousness on Harrt's face, but something told Nathan it wasn't to do with the summit.

"Where are the others?" Astrilla said to Harrt.

"Dines is already with the politicians. Vol and Hayward are aboard the Artemis with my XO". Harrt ran his fingers through his greying black hair and sighed. He glanced at Nathan, then Astrilla, concern painting his face. "Two Evoker Elders boarded the Artemis to debrief Cadu, and a third is on the way".

Nathan shrugged. "So what's the problem?"

Harrt looked at his feet, his expression closing down. "We still don't know who the mole is".

"Are you proposing that our mole is an Evoker Elder?" Astrilla said, her voice lifting.

"I'm saying we can't rule anyone out," Harrt said. He checked his datapad, huffed at the screen then stuffed the device back in his pocket. "Worse still, since I landed, I've been unable to reach the Artemis via comms".

"The Paradisians must be blocking communications from the surface," Astrilla said.

"Let's hope you're right," Harrt replied.

▲

The Council Chamber was more like a courtroom than a house of congress. The room was hexagonal, with huge benches rising in levels along four of the five walls. Suited politicians of every species and gender were crammed into the seats and talking in hushed tones.

Dines stood in the middle of the room, looking like someone who'd undergone intense interrogation. As usual, he looked dour and stressed by everything around him.

As the massive doors to the Council Chamber closed, an ominous silence fell across the space. Against the fifth wall was a single raised platform, where Grand Master of the House: Inon Waife —leader of the Commonwealth— stood.

Nathan didn't know much about 'wealther politics, but he knew enough to know who the key players were. Waife was the —supposedly elected— leader of the Commonwealth, known for his egalitarian views and utter contempt for the Revenant. He'd faced re-election several times and won by a landslide on every occasion. Very few politicians had the balls to oppose him because the people loved him so much: *at least that's what the 'wealther media said.*

Waife was taller than Nathan expected, but he looked just like his picture in the press: a male Horrus with labrador-like facial features, wearing a long ceremonial gown and a surprising amount of jewellery for a communist leader. Waife's fur was white-blonde, while his eyes were a striking orange. He had a long snout that had seen some beautification therapy, and his dyed gold whiskers implied he was a man of refined taste.

Nathan couldn't help but notice the sound of his and the group's footsteps echoing as they walked across the stone floor to join Dines. With the absence of sound and all eyes in the room locked on him, Nathan felt a shudder. He glanced at the representatives seated on the benches. There were hundreds, many of whom regarded him with looks of either intrigue or indifference.

"Welcome," Waife said, with a deep voice that filled the room. "I must say, I was wondering how the crew of the Phoenix Titan would follow up the heroics aboard the Messorem. I suppose I finally have an answer".

There was a peal of awkward laughter from the stocks.

Heroics that saved your life, Nathan thought but didn't say aloud.

Waife continued; "A year ago, you saved the Commonwealth from annihilation, yet today you bring war to our doorstep?"

There was an unsettling hush as Waife fixed his eyes on Nathan.

"The principle of collective security is that all of us are accountable to one another. We must ensure that we don't put our fellow citizens into stressful situations they don't consent to. So, Captain Carter, please, explain to this mighty council why you have brought this situation upon us?"

It seemed weird, answering to a politician of all things. Nathan wasn't sure of the etiquette he had to use, but all eyes were on him, and he couldn't stay quiet for long.

"This was a—" Nathan began, but a Uvan delegate from the benches interrupted him.

"Point of personal privilege," the politician said, climbing to his feet. Waife nodded, and the Uvan continued. "For the sake of our comrades requiring translators, we'd like to remind Captain Carter that he isn't amongst his Paradisian brethren. He must speak clearly to the house".

Nathan craned his neck to look at the spindly-looking Uvan, who was climbing back into his chair with a self-righteous smirk.

"My thanks, Comrade," Waife said to the delegate. "Captain Carter, please enunciate your words".

Nathan took a breath and reminded himself that he wasn't there to punch anyone. Sure, kicking the crap out of the pompous asshole who'd talked over him would give him something to smile about, but there were bigger fish to fry.

"We undertook a dangerous mission to disrupt a trade with the Revenant," Nathan said, keeping his answer brief. He didn't want to give away the details of the mission —not yet anyway. He looked directly at the pompous Uvan delegate that interrupted him earlier. "Oh, and the Paradisians aren't *my* brethren".

As whining emerged from the stocks, Waife's stoic expression softened. The tall Horrus sat in his chair, allowing another representative to address the room.

She was a human female with green eye-makeup and matching hair; wearing a dress that looked more expensive than the Phoenix Titan.

"Point of personal privilege," the delegate said. "In respect of our comrades that are made anxious by the use of combative language or inflexion, I demand that Captain Carter remove any hostility from his tone".

Nathan failed to hide his scowl.

He realised —now surrounded by the 'wealth's decision

makers— that maybe there was a reason they looked to a strong dictator to call the shots. The delegation comprised of entitled, overly sensitive prime citizens who'd never made a tough decision. They were the privileged few who told themselves they served a tremendous socialist dream while selfishly expecting everyone to accommodate their needs and requirements. Inon Waife was simply the one with the most power, the loudest voice and the biggest cahoonas.

The people were nothing like Harrt, Dines, or any other 'wealther Nathan had ever met. Seeing the prime citizens made him realise that the 'wealth wasn't a communist regime at all. Sure, the systems outside Capital Space and the military adhered to a strict set of communist ideals, but the prime citizens were calling the shots while living a life of decadent luxury. It finally made sense why Dines was so confident that the mole was a 'wealther politician: they were the living embodiment of everything that went against their supposedly fair culture.

They preached fairness and equality while living the complete opposite.

A male Icktus from the front bench rose, and Waife welcomed his request to address the house. The politician stood and tossed his datapad down in front of him.

"I am Delegate Uom of the Saxion Cluster," he introduced himself. Then looking to Waife, "Point of inquiry: why, Captain Carter, did you not notify High Command of this mission?"

Dines stepped in front of Nathan and spoke for him;

"Delegate Uom, with all due respect, we did".

Uom scowled at Dines.

"The report *you* submitted, Agent Dines, was sent to High Command more than four hours after the mission and made minimal reference to the operation at Hawtrey House". Uom spread his arms wide as he gazed longingly at Waife. "It is said that when communication between us breaks down, our precious Commonwealth dies. With proper communication, a situation such as the one we now face could've been avoided".

Waife fixed his steely gaze on Dines.

"Our honourable comrade raises a good point," Waife said. Then to the broader group, "Your actions were reckless and impulsive".

Nathan stepped forward, and his tone grew gravelly:

"We were preventing a trade with the Revenant".

Uom lifted his palms into the air:

"Did you once consider the consequences?"

"I considered what the Revenant would do with another super weapon," Nathan scowled, but he pushed the anger aside and replied calmly. "Sadly, *Mr Uom*, none of us have the time to debate, whether my actions were right or wrong. Right now, a bunch of pissed-off Paradisians are in orbit, intending to trigger an attack".

The house erupted into laughter, followed by jeering and heckling, and Nathan didn't know how to react to the theatre of it all. Waife raised his paw, and his subjects slowly quietened.

Uom chuckled, dramatically wiping a tear from his eye.

"My boy, we have three Warships in the area. Not to mention our orbital canons that will reduce the Paradisians to ash if prompted to do so".

Dines looked at Waife, still standing on his raised platform, and offered his protest.

"Grand Master, we have proof of a conspiracy that includes members of the EWB movement and King Baylum. I believe this group are intentionally seeking an outcome of violence from this situation".

Waife made a tent with his fingers, and raised his brow thoughtfully; "To what end?"

Nobody could answer that question.

The Master of the House considered it for a moment. Then without ceremony, he took a small gavel from his desk and slammed it into the accompanying stone block. A sharp musical sound filled the chamber, and the delegation began to exit through doors in every corner of the room.

Waife had suspended the summit.

▲

The politicians took around two minutes to filter out of the room. Once they were gone, Inon Waife descended from a staircase to join Nathan and the others on the ground floor of the chamber.

"I sense there may be some substance to your argument," Waife said, rubbing his chin.

"So, you believe us?" Koble asked.

"Whether I believe you or not is of little consequence," Waife said. "I could give the order now and kill every Paradisian from here to Nebar Point with zero impact on my future as Grand Master". Waife pointed a finger to the ceiling; "Those fools up there could be dust in seconds. All I'd need to do is say the word".

"But you haven't," Nathan replied. "*Why not*?"

Waife's smile gave away nothing. He looked at Dines and Harrt, "For the same reason, I turned a blind eye to Commander Oxarri and Agent Dines investigating senior council members and military officials: I suspect that members of this council are conspiring against me".

Harrt and Dines looked at one another dumbfounded, and Waife shot the pair a knowing smile:

"Did you think I would not notice?" Waife shrugged. "I see all that goes on within my domain, gentlemen".

"But you allowed us to continue the investigation?" Dines said.

"Of course," Waife replied nonchalantly. "I wanted to see what you'd turn up and find out who in my council is reckless enough to betray our precious Commonwealth". Waife laced his fingers together as he turned to Nathan and the others; "You must understand that most of the delegation will not tolerate the aggressive stance that the Paradisium has taken; conspiracy or otherwise. The EWB was one thing, but this blockade is damning. I may be the Master of this house, but the democratic decision has the final say. Right now, it's impossible to ignore the six-thousand-plus ships blocking transmissions, traffic and essential goods from the citizens".

"Then give us time," Nathan argued. "Let me try and persuade Jareth to help".

Waife's brows knotted, "Jareth?"

Nathan's brow lowered; "He knows things about the group manipulating the Paradisians. If they are telling Paradisium that we killed or kidnapped Jareth, then let's prove them wrong. Let's get Jareth on camera, addressing those fuckin' idiots up there and expose the Society".

"You do realise we can't broadcast beyond the blockade..." Dines said.

"The blockade is our audience," Nathan said. "So long as we can transmit to the ships up there, that's all that matters".

Waife held up his paw in what Nathan assumed was realisation. The Horrus shifted his weight from one foot to the other and nodded to himself thoughtfully.

"This could be a viable option," he said. "Of course, all of it hinges on Jareth's compliance".

He was right: convincing Jareth to go along with the plan was the biggest challenge. Nathan could only hope the old man was enough of a patriot to prevent a war. After all, he'd made the EWB happen because he believed in Paradisian autonomy.

"Give me time," Nathan said, looking Waife hard in the eyes. "Let me to speak to Jareth..."

Waife scowled but didn't say anything. He paced slowly for an awkward amount of time. The sound of his heavy footsteps reverberated around the chamber.

Waife's eyes settled on Dines.

"Despite your... *mishandling* of the data pertaining to the Fall, I still believe that you are one of the bravest operatives in the 'wealth".

Dines didn't say anything.

Waife shifted to Harrt. "And you, Commander... your record speaks for itself: Hero of Maru Seven; slayer of Densius Olbori; a pilot with thousands of confirmed kills". Waife let the achievements hang in the air as he looked upon Harrt and Dines. "Do you gentleman agree with Captain Carter? Do you believe Mr Jareth is the key to solving this situation?"

"I do, Grand Master," Dines answered.

Waife glanced at Harrt, and the Commander nodded.

"Then get Captain Carter to the Containment Facility and secure Jareth's cooperation. You have two hours. After that, the fate of the Paradisians is out of my hands".

INTERLUDE
ROTH

As Alastair Roth gazed upon the magnificent blockade now spanning the entirety of Valour, one thought crossed his mind; *progress is not an illusion.*

In addition to the thousands of civilian ships now in orbit, several ivory-coloured Jareth Corps gunships had joined the protest, in solidarity with their kidnapped CEO. Thanks to a swift hostage-taking operation on Paradisium, Thomas Jareth and most of Jareth Corps' board were now in Roth's custody, which effectively rendered the business under *temporary* new management.

While standing at the communications centre of the Featon, Roth gazed through the window at the tens-of-thousands of stars that made up the galaxy and everything beyond. Roth knew that soon, he would rule every single planet, system and station out there; Project Erebus was all he needed to achieve that goal.

Everything was going according to plan, and there was no reason to assume that would change. The pieces were moving upon the galactic chessboard. Soon his rook *—or knight—* would make a bold move and take the enemy's queen out of the game. Patience was the key.

He looked upon the recently erected sound stage ahead, where a small film crew were preparing to broadcast Holland's address to the 'wealth. Roth's instructions to the filming crew had been clear: *make Holland look like a future leader of Paradisium.*

The soft lighting accompanied by in-camera smoothing effects would make Holland look pure and handsome and maybe a tad angelic, thus making fools believe, on a superficial level, that he was trustworthy. The backdrop containing the flags of Earth's fallen nations would appeal to the traditionalists: *people who'd survived the fall.* The speech was to be the crown jewel, invoking fear and outrage from the 'wealth while at the same time convincing the Paradisians that they were on the right side of history.

Like shooting fish in a barrel.

Roth could almost imagine Theodore Jareth smiling at him with approval. His old friend and mentor would call the pièce de résistance *an act of genius* or *a masterstroke in the art of political manipulation.*

When Markus Holland was ready to broadcast, he stepped out in front of the cameras, wearing combat armour as Roth instructed. Swapping his suit for military garb would only add to the illusion that Holland *—and by extension, Paradisium—* was fighting a war. Holland stood before the flags of nations long passed, and Roth smiled to himself. It was to be a broadcast that would go down in history, but not for the reasons Holland was hoping for. The film crew gave the signal, and Markus Holland looked into the camera with a steely yet well-rehearsed war-time determination:

This is a message to the Commonwealth from the free people of Paradisium. We demand the immediate release of our brothers, Christian Roth and David Jareth, who were unlawfully apprehended by a group of 'wealther supremacists acting under the direct orders of Inon Waife. As I broadcast this message, thousands of our ships have created a blockade around Valour, and many more will arrive in the hour. We will continue to block all transmissions to and from the surface until you meet our demands. The attack on the EWB celebration and subsequent kidnapping of two Paradisian citizens is illegal. It is an act of war. You have two hours to release our people. If you do not comply, we will retaliate. Justice for the fallen. Freedom for the living. Paradisium forever.

CHAPTER TWENTY-SIX
ASTRILLA

Once the discussion with Waife was over, guards escorted the group from the chamber. Astrilla was expecting another round of strict security screenings before being allowed to leave, but instead, the group were taken on an alternative route: circumventing the checkpoints and through a series of long, non-descript corridors to the main entrance.

To Astrilla's surprise, Elder Yuta was there, arguing with a senior marine. Her voice was urgent and nervous, but the soldier refused to allow her past.

"You don't understand; I must speak with them now," she said, raising her voice. "It is of the utmost urgency—"

Yuta's eyes shifted to Astrilla and the panic dropped from her features for a beat: as though the weight of the world was lifted from her shoulders.

"Sun and stars..." Yuta said when she reached Astrilla. "I've been trying to contact you for the last hour".

"Why?" Astrilla asked.

She glanced at her datapad. There were no unanswered messages, but the primary signal was intermittent, likely caused by the blockade.

Yuta seemed lost for words: downright bewildered. It was a look Astrilla had never seen the woman in the twenty-plus years she'd known her. Yuta's eyes filled with despair, and her hands twitched restlessly.

"We—" Yuta stammered, and she took a moment to regroup. "We've been betrayed". Yuta's gaze wavered, and she looked beyond Astrilla to Harrt: “Commander Oxarri, it brings me no pleasure to tell you this, but your crew aboard the Artemis are in grave danger”.

“What do you mean?” Harrt asked.

Yuta grimaced.

“We have reason to believe that Elder Marx is aligned with the Revenant”.

A brittle silence took ahold. Astrilla didn’t quite process it: nobody did. The implications of Yuta’s statement were far-reaching: far beyond anything Astrilla could conjure up in that heartbeat of time.

Marx was the traitor. It made so much sense, and yet it felt all wrong.

Koble asked, “What does this guy have to do with Oxarri’s ship?”

Harrt was quiet for a long moment; his eyes steely.

“Marx is aboard the Artemis debriefing Cadu”.

HARRT

As it happened, time could stand still. While Yuta gave her account of the situation, Harrt tried to ignore the sickening dread passing over his body. Thoughts of Vol, Jaudi, Hayward, and his three-hundred-man crew flooded Harrt’s mind. Every last one of them were in a closed environment with a dangerous Evoker turncoat.

Yuta explained that she and the three Elders from Pelos Three were notified of Cadu’s rescue less than a day prior. They’d all travelled separately, thanks to their assignments at the time. Yuta was the first to leave the Enclave, closely followed by Elder Xanathur, who’d been studying ruins on the Jurum plains.

At the time, Marx and Repla were at Pelos Seven meeting with an Illuminator Priest, and they’d left for Valour an hour after Yuta aboard the same ship. That all sounded good to Harrt, but when Yuta got to the part about Marx’s betrayal, he felt the panic creep up his spine.

“Xanathur contacted me during the slipstream leg of

the journey," Yuta began. "He said he had proof of Marx conspiring with the Revenant and a man called Roth..."

Harrt peered at Nathan, and the Earther looked back with a raised brow.

"Xanathur never made it to Valour," Yuta sniffled, looking like someone who didn't want to believe what she was about to say. She looked at Astrilla with sadness; "I'm so sorry, my dear, but all reports indicate that Xanathur's ship was destroyed".

There was a mix of emotions on Astrilla's face. Harrt had never seen her so taken aback.

That was the moment Leviticus Dines cut in; "Forgive me if this sounds insensitive, Elder Yuta, but do you have proof?"

Yuta scowled at the Agent. "I've known Elendrion Xanathur for the last fifty years. He is —was—- the most trustworthy man I've ever known. He would not have made such claims without reason".

Dines chewed the inside of his cheek, then pulled his datapad to scroll through the intelligence feed: no doubt in search of anything regarding Xanathur's murder.

Harrt didn't know Xanathur particularly well, but the old man had always been polite and friendly. Nathan even cited him as the best of the four on Pelos Three, which said a lot.

Still, as sad as it was that Xanathur was dead, there was still the issue of Marx aboard the Artemis: something had to be done. Mourning had to be put aside. Harrt pressed his hand to his forehead as Tariq began to speak:

"A mole within the Evoker ranks, with the inside track on all top-secret Commonwealth operations," Tariq surmised, peering at Harrt and Dines. "I think, gentleman, you've found your mole".

Harrt looked at Dines, and the silver-haired Agent sighed in defeat.

"We must take action," Harrt declared. "If Marx is aboard my ship, my crew and Vol and Hayward are at risk. We gotta do something. Right now".

Koble raised his paws as though shrugging.

"With that blockade in place, we won't be able to get a

message or even a ship up there to help them. How the hell can we act?"

A silence came over the group at the grim realisation.

Koble was entirely correct. Comms on and off of Valour were blocked, and getting a ship into orbit was suicide.

"There is one thing," Tariq said, stroking his tidy beard thoughtfully. "We may not be able to communicate with the Artemis, but we may be able to contact the Sadalmelik".

"How?" Nathan asked.

"The Sadalmelik has a working telegraph aboard," Tariq answered. "It's a little old-fashioned but—"

Koble cut in, "What the hell is a telegraph?"

"Old Earth tech," Gordon answered. "The transmission of text through radio waves, using on and off tones."

"We might be able to get a message up there and warn our people," Tariq said. Then looking at Gordon with urgency, "Could you help me rig up a makeshift transmitter?"

"I've got tools back at the Phoenix," Gordon nodded, then shifting his eyes to Harrt, "I could use your mechanical expertise on the Phoenix".

Harrt nodded, "Whatever I can do to help".

He noticed Gordon glance at Nathan as though asking permission. The exchange was odd, leaving Harrt to assume something dramatic happened between them earlier, but he didn't have time to pry.

"Do it," Nathan said. "In the meantime, me and Dines will pay Jareth a visit".

NATHAN

Nobody offered an argument: *not even Yuta*. That was saying something. They had a plan. It wasn't exactly foolproof, and it certainly wasn't even well put together, but it was something. The manual transmission to the Sadalmelik was a long shot, but it was the only viable option.

Part of Nathan wanted to risk it; grab the Phoenix and fly to orbit, kill Marx, grab Vol and save the day, but it wasn't that simple. Sure, the Phoenix was fast and had outrun a blockade in the past, but this was no ordinary protest. The latest numbers suggested that over six-thousand Paradisian craft were in orbit —not including the Jareth Corps warships. Nathan concluded that if he took the Phoenix into space, it'd be one versus thousands, and for the Paradisians, it'd be a piece of cake to shoot him down.

The group dispersed, heading out the main entrance. Heavy rain was falling from the sky, and there was the faint rumbling of thunder high above. Something alien amid the storm whispered to Nathan, but he couldn't be sure if it were real.

Erebus, the voice said, free of emotion or inflexion.

He glanced at the others, but nobody else noticed. The voice was a hallucination: Nathan was sure of it. Exhaustion was finally starting to get to him, but he didn't have time to rest.

His train of thought was broken as Koble approached. Naturally, Nathan was still angry with the Sphinax, but there were bigger fish to fry. Arguments and drama were officially paused.

Koble said, "If it's all the same to you, I wanna come with you to see Jareth". Before Nathan could respond, the Sphinax continued, "I know this whole Jack business is kinda... *unfinished*, but you ain't facing Jareth alone".

"He won't be alone," Dines interjected with a frown.

"Fine, let me rephrase that..." Koble licked his lips. "You ain't facing down Jareth… *without me*. If he wants to talk about Jack, I wanna be there. You ain't the only one that wants the truth".

Nathan looked at Dines for consent, and the Agent shrugged: "Fine".

Dines and Koble went ahead to get aboard Dines' inner-planet transport. Nathan was about to follow, but Astrilla halted him.

Considering that she'd learned of Xanathur's demise less than five minutes prior, she seemed unnaturally calm: *a mask for her grief perhaps?*

Nathan couldn't imagine what his paramour was going through. Xanathur was a man she'd known for more than two decades, as was Marx. To hear that one had died at the hands of the other must've been heartbreaking, and yet Astrilla was composed and ever tranquil.

She squeezed his hand: "are you okay?"

Nathan opted to put his own issues aside and instead focussed on his lover. He imagined the disbelief, disappointment and shock she was hiding behind her confident outlook.

"I'm fine," Nathan answered. "What about you?" He placed his hand against the back of her neck. "All this stuff about Marx is kinda unbelievable".

Astrilla looked at the floor:

"Honestly, I still can't believe it. Marx betraying the Evokers. It just seems so wrong".

He nodded in agreement. Nathan knew Marx professionally; the Florus always seemed objective and polite, but rumours circulated of emotional outbursts regarding the Revenant in lessons. Nathan never witnessed Marx lose his cool first-hand, but he'd heard enough stories to know there was substance to the chitchat. Before today Nathan would've said that Marx's impassioned flare-ups resulted from the near extinction of his race at the hands of King Seig.

The Florus were rarer than Earthers, so naturally, Marx had a reason to be angry. He'd lost family, friends and his home system as part of a Revenant attack.

Nathan could relate.

Now, Nathan's view on Marx had changed. Perhaps Marx would lose his cool over the Revenant because he overcompensated for his betrayal. By acting as the most enraged person in the room, he deflected the fact that he was in bed with the enemy.

Astrilla lifted her head, "I'll go back to the Phoenix and see what more I can do to help Gordon and Tariq with the transmitter. Are you going to be okay with Jareth".

"I'll do my best," Nathan nodded.

Astrilla and he embraced for a few seconds as the rain beat down. In the moment, Nathan felt safe, and he was pretty sure Astrilla felt the same.

There was no blockade, no Society, no Jareth, no Roth:

just peace in the arms of the woman he loved.

All good things had to come to an end. Letting his paramour go in a difficult moment felt wrong, but Nathan told himself that they both had important jobs to do. Vol's life, the lives of the Artemis' crew, and maybe millions more were hanging in the balance. He stepped away from Astrilla, then began the long walk to Dines' shuttle. Through the pouring rain, he heard the voice from earlier ring out around his tired mind:

Erebus, it whispered again.

VOL

The atmosphere aboard the Artemis was tense. With external comms jammed, there was an overwhelming sense of isolation aboard the ship. Scans of the immediate area showed two other 'wealther warships stuck amid the Paradisian blockade. The Athena and the Hermes were slightly smaller than the Artemis, with less firepower and crews of about two hundred, but still capable of wiping out a significant chunk of the blockade if prompted.

Thankfully, no such orders had been received, but that didn't mean anything in the grand scheme of things. The simple fact was that none of the warships could receive transmissions from the ground. The 'wealth and Paradisium could already be at war, and nobody would be any the wiser until somebody fired the first shot.

The observation deck looked out over the blockade surrounding Valour. The number of ships encompassing the planet had increased by twenty percent in the last half hour, and the number was growing. What surprised Vol the most was the aggressive positioning of the Paradisian ships around the Artemis: surrounding the warship and leaving little room for manoeuvre. Something about their strategy didn't feel right. Encircling a heavily armed warship seemed foolish, especially if things went south.

The situation escalated when a message was broadcast from within the blockade. The spokesperson that Paradisium selected was a young, reckless hothead called Markus Holland. He gave an impassioned speech demanding the immediate release of Jareth and Christian Roth while threatening the 'wealthers with affirmative action if they didn't comply.

It didn't take a genius to know that Holland wasn't the mastermind behind the blockade. Vol had seen a dozen just like him in the past: a boy in a man's body, working through the typical youthful drive to take risks, impress girls and cultivate wealth. Sure, he probably believed the bullshit he was spouting, but there was no doubt he could be dissuaded or manipulated easily: *all it took was a decent puppet master.*

Vol sat on the edge of her seat, her fingers laced over her knee, as she looked from the observation deck at the impressive yet threatening blockade. After a year aboard the Phoenix with its closed-in cockpit, the vast and incredible view before her seemed artificial: like watching a newscast on a big screen.

Maybe it isn't the view? Vol thought. *Perhaps it's just the context.*

The truth was that Paradisium could not survive against the 'wealth. They didn't have the numbers, resources or means to fight. The Commonwealth could lay waste to the Paradisians in a heartbeat, yet there they were, seven-thousand ships strong in protest of something they didn't truly understand. All the while, King Baylum —the real enemy— was out there in the great void rebuilding, regrouping and no doubt preparing to strike.

Vol's attention was drawn left, where Elder Marx was climbing the steps to join her. The expression on his face was unusual; somewhere between evaluating and critical. Despite being around both Evoker Elders for thirty minutes, Vol hadn't overheard any of their thoughts.

Marx strolled over and took the seat directly beside her. The Florus looked out on the blockade and disappointedly shook his giant bird-like head.

"Truly, this is a bizarre situation," Marx remarked, his eyes still glued to the scene outside. "The Commonwealth saves all of them from certain death during the Fall. Then twenty-six years later, here they are, ready to wage war".

It must have been apparent that Vol wasn't sure how to respond. The Florus craned his neck to regard her with a puzzled look before returning his gaze to the window.

"Humans are rather emotional creatures," Marx continued.

"That they are," Vol nodded. "Let's hope this situation will de-escalate".

Marx offered a cordial smile. "Let us hope so".

They sat in silence, the hum of a nearby air regulator and the murmuring of the bridge crew below as background noise. A moment later, Repla approached with a square-jawed marine in heavy combat gear.

"Come along, Marx," Repla ordered. "We've finally been given clearance to visit Cadu".

Vol could've sworn she heard irritation in her voice.

"Very well..." Marx climbed to his feet with a groan. He politely bowed his head to Vol, "May we hope that cooler heads prevail".

She nodded and watched the Evokers amble away with their marine escort. Once they were gone, Vol descended the staircase into the bulk of the command deck and found Jaudi at the centre.

"So much for stalling them.." she said, lifting her arms in semi-protest.

Jaudi shook her head.

"I could only hold out so long. The Sillix was looming over me the entire time, pushing to get some face-to-face time with Cadu... there is only so much bullshit I could spin. I was pretty sure she'd started to suspect something". Then, with tension in her voice, Jaudi asked, "Did you overhear anything?"

"Nothing," Vol sighed. "It's like trying to listen to music without ears or an audio implant: there's just nothing".

"So, we're no closer to knowing if they're hostile?"

"Pretty much".

Jaudi paced back and forth.

"We've got no comms, and we may have two Evoker

Elders that may or may not be working for the enemy". The Lieutenant's brow furrowed at her own grim assessment. "We gotta capture both of them".

Vol's head snapped to one side, and she locked eyes with Jaudi.

"What?" Vol said in stunned surprise.

"We've got no other options," Jaudi replied.

"A lone Evoker is one thing, but two—" Vol paused. "Taking on two would be suicide: taking on one is suicide. Besides, we don't know for sure if they are allied with the Revenant or not".

"But we can't rule it out either," Jaudi replied, her voice stern and decisive. "We don't have to take them out; just put them in a cell for a few hours..."

"I don't think that's wise..." Vol argued.

Jaudi frowned; "I've got a crew of three hundred aboard this tub, and I am responsible for every single one of them: not to mention the sheer firepower we're carrying". Jaudi pointed to the blockade out the window; "We are in a delicate situation here. We can't afford to let this ship come under enemy control, or a hell of a lot more lives will be at risk".

Jaudi was right, but Vol couldn't help but wonder how they could get an Evoker to stand down. She wished to the sun and stars that Astrilla were there; she'd know how to dismantle the tension and find a reasonable middle ground with the Elders. Alas, Astrilla wasn't there, and the situation required decisive action.

"Okay," Vol nodded tentatively. She drew a long breath, "Comms Hayward and the Marines... we gather a security detail and ask them to surrender".

"No comms," Jaudi shook her head. "If the mole is aboard, then they could be monitoring our internal channels. You head to the docks and summon Hayward and my security team. If we're quick, we may be able to corner them in the med-bay".

"This is crazy," Vol said.

"As crazy as it gets," Jaudi nodded.

GORDON

After leaving the Council Chamber, what remained of the Phoenix's crew —along with Tariq Mahmoot— returned to the ship via an inner-planet transport with a marine escort.

Harrt looked pensive and worried: understandable considering his crew and Vol were at significant risk. Astrilla seemed calm, but Gordon knew that the Evoker was likely screaming beneath her veneer of tranquillity and cool-headedness: *she was —mostly— human, after all.*

For one reason or another, Gordon found it impossible to interpret Tariq's mood. The middle-eastern man gripped what looked like rosary beads in his left hand. His eyes were closed, and his mouth twitched occasionally.

When Tariq's eyes opened, he eyeballed Gordon.

"It was a prayer," he said over the hum of the inner-planet transport.

Gordon pursed his lips together and nodded.

After that, nobody said a word throughout the ten-minute journey, and Gordon couldn't decide if it were simply nerves amongst the group or if his part in Nathan's deception had caused a frosty atmosphere. He decided on the former, not because he didn't feel guilty about his lies, but because he needed to focus on the task at hand.

Once they arrived at the Phoenix, it was straight down to business. Gordon gave an abridged version of the situation to Russell, Rain, James and Kyp. He explained that they were going to attempt to rig an old-style Earth telegraph via the Phoenix's Comms array —boosted by Kyp — to make contact with the Sadalmelik.

The group pulled together quickly, drawing up a plan and assigning roles. Gordon and Harrt ripped apart the innards under the Phoenix's comms panel to access the critical systems while Russell and Tariq rigged up a wiring post. Rain, James and Astrilla worked on the Phoenix's exterior, running a specific cable from the topside receiver and into the cockpit, which Gordon would hook into the wiring post, then Kyp and then the Comms console.

Devolving a highly advanced comms system, capable of sending and receiving messages across entire galaxies, back to a basic telegraph felt wrong. For hundreds of generations, Earth-kind could've only dreamed of communicating across the stars, yet Gordon was regressing an advanced piece of technology by a few centuries. He figured that one day he could put this story into his memoirs, right next to the chapter that outlined his part in the Battle of the Messorem.

The whole project took just under twenty-five minutes, and when it was near completion, Gordon called Kyp over. The droid obliged, and as Gordon crawled out from under the comms station, he yanked a length of wire from the desk.

"I don't think the captain will appreciate you making these *amendments*," Kyp remarked, its robotic voice sounding oddly human in the moment.

"I'll make it up to him," Gordon said, climbing to his feet and wiping the sweat from his brow. He held out the wire, allowing the droid to examine it. "I'm gonna have to plug you into the ship's communications system."

The droid studied the round piece of cable for less than a second.

"You wish to boost the signal?" Kyp asked.

"Boost is an understatement," Gordon replied. "I need you to push this message as much as your circuits will allow".

"Any signal we get out needs to be amplified enough to break through the blockade," Tariq added, grabbing a rag from the holotable to wipe his hands.

Kyp whirred at Tariq's statement, then allowed Gordon to plug the cable into its body. The droid seemed to process something for several seconds: it's ocular sensor flashing between green, orange and blue.

"Have you factored in the risk that one of the Paradisian ships may detect the signal?" Kyp asked. "Although this technology is rudimentary, data suggests that Paradisians collect old trinkets. What if one of their ships has one of these *telegraphs*?"

It was a valid point that Gordon hadn't considered: part

of him was impressed by the droid's quick thinking.

"Guess we've got no choice," Gordon said, peering at the others. "This whole thing is a roll of the dice, right?"

Nobody offered a challenge.

Tariq moved to the slapdash sounder, pressing it down. A continuous, droning hum followed: evoking memories in Gordon of old history lessons, war movies and museum visits as a child.

"Have faith, my friends," Tariq declared.

Gordon took a seat and watched Tariq transmit his message. The middle-eastern man tapped on the sounder, broadcasting a series of beeps and boops into the aether. At that moment, all Gordon could hope was that someone was listening to Tariq's prayer.

CHAPTER TWENTY-SEVEN
NATHAN

Dines' inner-planet transport shuttle was surprisingly spacious, with three separate spaces divided by faux-glass doors. There was a cockpit up front, with room for the pilot and perhaps one other person leaning against the rear wall. The passenger area at the centre was slightly larger, with three rows of bench-like leather seats. Nathan figured the ship could safely transport around nine passengers —eleven at a push. At the rear was a small cargo hold that wasn't in use.

As Dines steered the ship through the packed skylanes of Valour, Nathan took a seat in the central compartment, as far from Koble as possible. For the first five minutes, Nathan and Koble sat in complete silence. It was undeniable that neither man knew what to say to the other. To distract himself from the awkward muteness, Nathan pressed on the screen of his datapad, pretending to be busy.

Eventually, Koble climbed from his seat and moved across the cabin to the bench opposite Nathan. He shrugged as though his jacket was itchy, then took a deep breath.

"Listen.." the Sphinax paused, awkwardly craning his neck to look around. "About Jack—"

"Why did he tell you?" Nathan shot Koble a glare.

Koble leaned back.

"It's complicated".

"Then un-complicate it".

Koble's eyes narrowed, and his tail anxiously swayed.

"Contrary to all the shit Gordon may say, Jack wasn't evil. Yeah, he screwed up, but you gotta understand, he was haunted by the shit that went down during the Fall. He had no idea what the Society was doing. All he knew was that his son —and father— were in trouble, and he did everything he could to save them".

Nathan didn't say anything.

"You wanna know how bad it was for Jack?" Koble leaned forward and, with a low voice, continued, "He tried to kill himself: saw it with my own eyes. His guilt drove him to a place where he wanted to take his own life".

What Koble said came as a shock to Nathan. Jack had never been like the depressive type, more like the strong, stoic Captain that the Loyalty and her crew needed. Sure, he was dour and brooding, but Nathan never figured his uncle was the suicidal type. It left him wondering if perhaps he'd mistaken Jack's indifference for genuine despair.

Koble must have spotted the disbelief on Nathan's face. He continued talking, refusing Nathan the opportunity to speak.

"I found him one night with an empty bottle of something in one hand and a loaded pistol in the other". Koble's eyes turned down, and he hung his head in sadness. "I guess the drinking slowed Jack's reactions; I got the gun away from him".

In his head, Nathan tried to imagine a younger version of Koble wrestling a loaded weapon from the clutches of Jack, *the combat-trained government agent who could shoot a fly from fifty feet with both eyes closed.*

Koble lifted his head;

"That night, Jack told me everything that happened to him back on Earth. It was kinda… harrowing. Shook me inside and out. I dunno how he lived with a burden like that".

Nathan was silent.

"I told Jack that he had you and James and our crew to live for; that you were his responsibility," Koble continued. "I told him that he owed it to the people of Earth, including your parents, to make the universe a better place. I made him promise that he would live for you and James: to do the best he could".

Nathan gritted his teeth in an attempt to defeat the sense of overwhelming appreciation he felt for the Sphinax at that moment. Koble was loyal; Nathan could sense it. Everything that Koble had done was for Jack. It was the kind of loyalty that reminded Nathan of Jack's old adage; *blood might be thicker than water, but rivers and oceans run deeper.*

Nathan leaned forward, patting the Sphinax on the shoulder. He rushed to climb to his feet and took a few paces to the right, naturally refusing to appear vulnerable — even to Koble.

"Nate," Koble drawled. "There is one other thing..."

Nathan turned, "What is it?"

Koble's brow and whiskers lowered in unison. His expression turned from sentimental to cautious.

"When Jack told me about the Fall, he told me about the people that blackmailed him. Two names kept cropping up: one was Alastair Roth... the other was a guy called Theodore Jareth".

HARRT

The rudimentary device that Gordon called a *telegraph* was a bizarre sight to behold. The thing was made up of exposed wiring and components that looked like they'd give someone a nasty shock if they got too close. To Harrt, the machine looked like something from the dark ages: a pre-Commonwealth, pre-civilisation relic that simply didn't belong. The noise it projected when Tariq pushed down on the central mechanism was unpleasant to the ears, but Gordon assured everyone that it was normal.

Tariq must've been pressing the sounder for over two minutes, but to Harrt and the others, time seemed to drag. Eventually, Tariq stepped back, turned the audio dial to maximum, and static filled the cockpit.

"Moment of truth," Gordon said.

Tariq glanced at a gold watch on his wrist. "If the Sadalmelik can even get a transmission through, we may be waiting a while".

Russell gestured at the telegraph;

"So, What do we do now?"

"We wait," Gordon answered.

There was nothing else that could be done. Harrt sat in the cockpit with the others for a while, desperately awaiting a reply, but eventually, he felt the need to step away. The horrible buzz of the static was starting to drone on, and he figured it'd be best to grab a drink, clear his head and consider the next move.

A part of him wanted to take the Phoenix, fly into orbit and get his people —including Vol. Of course, it wasn't that simple. The Paradisians would shoot him on sight, and with tension on the ground, High Command would probably do the same. The Phoenix was fast, but Valour's orbital cannons combined with a few thousand Paradisian vessels —all with their weapons pointed in one place— reduced the probability of survival tenfold.

Harrt helped himself to a glass of liquor in the living area and slumped down in an armchair. He couldn't help but think of Vol and Jaudi. Knowing that they were in danger left him feeling sick to his stomach. Harrt owed his life to Jaudi several times over. She'd been a mentor to Harrt since he was a teenager; shown him how to be a leader; taught him what it meant to be a CO.

When it came to Vol, there were many things that Harrt wanted to say. Ever since leaving the Phoenix, he'd missed her more than words could describe. Sure, they had problems that needed working out, but now it seemed redundant.

Elder Marx was the traitor: the case was closed. The Commonwealth certainly didn't need him to command their ships on the battlefield; honestly, he wasn't sure if it was a government he wanted to serve any longer. Not because of the 'wealth's corruption but because Harrt wished to live his way: aboard the Phoenix with Vol and his friends.

Harrt imagined that Yuta's intel was wrong and that the

Artemis and her crew were safe. He pictured Vol returning safely to the surface. In his daydream, Harrt would embrace her and tell her that he wanted a life with her. After that, he'd march to High Command and resign from the service: *just as he should've done a year prior.*

Naturally, they'd try to convince him to stay, but Harrt would decline, stating that he'd completed two-and-a-half decades of service and that it was his time to go. Then he, Vol, and his friends would ride off into the sunset aboard the Phoenix Titan.

The fantasy made him feel better for a moment, but reality crashed upon him like the violent storm raging outside. The truth was that everyone aboard the Artemis was in grave danger, and there was nothing Harrt could do about it.

A sudden clang from the bar drew Harrt's attention. James Stephens was pouring himself a drink and looking at Harrt with an amiable smile. Harrt stared back, trying to pinpoint any familial similarities to Nathan, but there wasn't anything that stood out.

James didn't look like Nathan at all. He was mostly blonde with odd greys in the mix, with a thin face and prominent brow.

"So, you must be the cousin?" Harrt said speculatively.

James nodded from across the lounge. He tapped something on his datapad, then slowly swaggered from the bar with a tall bottle at hand. He set it down, then offered a hand to shake.

The first thing Harrt noticed was James' thick tattooed arms. The black designs were tribal, though Harrt couldn't pin them to a specific region. There was a harsh aroma of smoking herbs that clung to the Earther like an unwelcome shadow. It was pretty strange to be confronted by such a strong scent, but Harrt did his best to ignore it.

"You must be Harrt Oxarri: *the Hero of Maru Seven*?" James shook his hand. He tipped his glass to Harrt as he sat opposite; "Quite the prestigious title if you ask me".

"I wouldn't say my title is prestigious," Harrt replied.

"Hey, I've done my research," James shrugged. "Don't

take it as an insult. When I heard about my little cousin's heroics, I had to do my homework on all of you".

"And were you impressed with what you found?"

"Sure. At the time, I was deep undercover inside Roth's organisation, so I didn't exactly take it to the corporate book club".

Harrt nodded and sipped his drink: "I've never officially been undercover, but I know it's tough not knowing who you can trust".

James cracked a grin, which promptly disappeared behind his glass. When the Earther was done drinking, he leant forward and pressed the tips of his fingers together.

"You wanna know a secret, Oxarri?" James said, licking his lips. "I don't trust anyone. That is the one thing that's kept me alive all these years".

He sounded just like Nathan in the early days. The sentiment from James sent Harrt's mind back to the vagabond he'd survived with on Yenex, and it made him realise just how much Nathan had changed since.

Perhaps they are related, Harrt thought.

Harrt mimicked James' stance and leaned forward in his seat: "So, you don't trust anyone... does that include Tariq and Hayward?"

James laughed at the verbal challenge. "Don't get me wrong, those two are like brothers to me, but I'll never trust anyone fully".

There was an awkward silence as James stared at the two cubes of melting ice in his glass. The moment told Harrt more than any conversation could. James was a broken man, still suffering from the Fall and the life he'd led since: *just like Nathan had been.*

A notification from James' datapad broke the silence. He checked the screen but quickly disregarded it.

"Damn you 'wealthers have an efficient newscasts system," James said, stuffing the datapad into his pocket. He settled into his chair and asked, "Can I ask a personal question, Oxarri?"

"Sure".

"You lose anyone on Maru Seven?"

"I lost everyone".

"I'm sorry to hear that," James said, topping up Harrt's glass with more booze. "Nate doesn't remember much of the Fall, but I do. I remember everything: every single fuckin' detail. Is it the same for you with Maru Seven?"

Harrt nodded. "On Maru Seven, we were betrayed by one of our own; a man called Densius Olbori. Thanks to him, the Revenant had the advantage and were able to kill many people."

James frowned at that and shook his head. There was genuine anger and outrage in the Earther's face.

"It's Baylum's tactic in war," James replied stoically. "He gets a man on the inside, offers him power, riches, to do his bidding. If those don't work, blackmail, threats, and violence are just as effective".

"How do you know that?" Harrt asked.

James laughed bitterly: "Long story. You missed some drama with Nate, Koble and the Doc regarding my father".

Harrt wanted to pry into that statement. He'd noticed something wasn't quite right between Nathan and Koble earlier, but he'd figured it was nothing more than tension: *evidently that wasn't the case.*

James tipped his glass to Harrt; "Did anyone ever find the guy that screwed over your people?"

Harrt cursed the memory of Densius Olbori: the traitor.

He nodded to James' question;

"I found him and killed him".

James' arrogant smile seemed to grow out of nothing more than sheer delight, but his voice was stern and serious when he spoke.

"So, what did he say before you killed him? Did he apologise for all his wrongdoing? Did the bastard beg for his life?"

"No," Harrt shook his head. "I figure he knew one of us would catch up with him one day. I think Olbori saw some twisted irony that it was me to put him down".

James whistled in response. "Back on Earth, there was this saying: *what goes around comes around*".

"I took no pleasure in killing the man," Harrt clarified

swiftly. "It was just something that needed to be done".

There was another silence wherein the men stared back at one another. Harrt wasn't sure what to make of James Stephens. He was clearly still suffering from trauma. That, coupled with a form of anxiety that was undoubtedly an aftereffect of Ice addiction, made him seem slightly manic: at least socially.

James peered into his glass and began speaking in a slow, thoughtful tone, entirely different from seconds earlier.

"I was sixteen years old on the day of The Fall. My Dad wanted us to return to the family home and save my aunt, uncle, grandmother, and whoever else would be holed up there. Of course, none of them made it, except Nathan..."

The sudden shift in James' mood and subject matter made Harrt feel on edge. The behaviour seemed odd, but it was hard to tell if it was out of character. After all, Harrt had just met the man.

"I took my first life that day," James continued. "This guy. I shot him through the back and saved my father".

Harrt noticed a profound sadness in the man's eyes. His statement left a palpable weight in the air that seemed to linger long after the words left his mouth.

"Who was he?" Harrt asked.

James shook his head as though clearing a hazy fog from his mind. He hummed to himself as though desperately trying to recall details better left forgotten.

"He was just a guy". Clarity returned to James' expression, and he waved his hand as though dismissing his previous statement. "You know the thing that still gets me, Oxarri? The look in that guy's eyes the moment after I shot him. I shoot this prick in the back, and he looks me for —I dunno— a second... It was as if he was asking me… *why?*" James stopped, sipped his drink, then continued. "I shot him to save my father's life. Sixteen years old, and I got put in that situation".

With sympathy in his voice, Harrt said, "Sometimes we must do awful things to protect our loved ones".

James smiled, but this time it was more reflective than arrogant. He raised his glass to toast:

"To the people we lost and the fuckers in the ground for taking them. May the murderers burn for their crimes, and may our loved ones find peace".

It was a weird choice of wording, but rather than offend the Earther, Harrt reluctantly raised his glass.

NATHAN

On Nathan's thirteenth birthday, Myles, a member of the Loyalty's crew, gifted him a set of four books from Earth. They were tired, tattered old things that survived the Fall, with stained pages and broken spines, but Nathan appreciated the gesture nonetheless. Eighteen years later, he could barely remember the stories or the subject matter, but one memorable line would stay with him forever: *you can always judge a society by how they treat prisoners.*

Nathan was reminded of that quote when he laid eyes on the Commonwealth Containment Facility. The prison was an ugly metal sphere floating high above the surface, measuring five-to-six miles in diameter. There were no visible buildings below it, only a dark chasm that led down into infinite darkness. The sphere held its position via a series of mile-wide chains connected to towers at least five-to-ten miles away. Nathan could only assume that the prison —or gulag— was purposely designed to be secluded and difficult to access.

Dines docked at a landing pad reserved for military personnel. The blackened sky created an illusion of nighttime that was only broken by the occasional long torrent of lightning. Cold rain pummelled the landing pad as Nathan and Koble followed Dines into the facility.

They passed through a checkpoint where armed guards relieved Nathan, Koble and Dines of all weapons. It was the second time that day that Nathan had relinquished his gun; *it still felt just as uncomfortable as the first time.*

After, the trio were escorted through a series of dreary, grey corridors. Nathan noted cameras and automated turrets at regular intervals as he examined his surroundings. The place felt hostile, as intended by its designer. There was an unnatural stagnation to the air: *like it was supposed to make its occupants feel trapped.*

Eventually, they stopped at a pair of metal doors guarded by a mech-droid and a supervisor in full-combat gear. The officer peered at a datapad containing records of Dines, Nathan and Koble from the first checkpoint. He then reviewed Dines' ID and the order form direct from Inon Waife. The theatrical process lasted about five minutes, and eventually, the supervisor stepped aside.

"This is where we're keeping Jareth until he's processed," Dines said.

"Processed?" Nathan probed.

"We put em' in containment chambers," Dines shrugged as though it were no big deal.

It made sense. Living, eating, and breathing prisoners cost the 'wealth in resources. It was far easier to stash prisoners away in a comatose state where they couldn't hurt anyone or impact the 'wealth's precious bankroll.

Dines waved his finger at Nathan and Koble; "I'll be watching on the monitors in the next room. I don't want a hair of Jareth's head touched: do I make myself clear?"

Nathan nodded.

Koble shrugged.

The doors to the cell opened with a hiss. The room was square, with a bed in the right corner and a faux wall against the left, which Nathan figured was a bathroom. The whole thing was grey with no windows or personality.

In the middle of the cell, sitting on the floor in an orange prison jumpsuit, was David Jareth. Besides his blonde and grey hair being slightly out of place, he looked unaffected by his incarceration. The elitist regarded Nathan with a knowing smile as though he were still in control of the situation: *nothing had changed in the last few hours.*

Jareth smiled before speaking:

"The fact that you are here suggests that you now understand that something bigger is afoot". He licked his thin lips, lowered his brows and stared at Nathan for an awkward moment. "Would that be the case?"

Nathan sighed, but he didn't allow himself to look defeated. Strength in the face of adversity was a way to show men like Jareth —aka thinkers— that they were not the smartest in the room.

He faced Jareth's question decisively without hesitation or reluctance: "There's a blockade around Valour, led by a man called Markus Holland, but you and I both know that he isn't the one calling the shots".

Jareth chuckled ironically. "Let me guess, Mr Holland has demanded my immediate release?" Nathan didn't say anything, and Jareth continued, "This has nothing to do with me. It's all showmanship for something far greater".

"That's exactly why you are gonna help diffuse this situation," Nathan pointed at Jareth. "You are gonna go on a 'wealther newscast and tell them that you weren't kidnapped and that the Paradisians are idiots for following Holland into a war they can't win".

"Only half of that statement is true," Jareth laughed. "I didn't exactly board your ship of my own free will".

Nathan didn't rise to the argument.

"Will you help or not?"

Jareth's smile was enigmatic. "Before I answer that question, we must clear the air regarding several points... I need to know that you truly understand this situation".

Nathan resisted the urge to take a swing at the old man.

"What do you think people like Roth crave?" Jareth paused for dramatic effect but didn't allow enough time for anyone to respond."The answer is simple: power. Roth was a powerful man on Earth and became more powerful after the Fall. You must understand that it is a drug for these people. It'll never be enough, not for someone like Roth".

"Talk about stating the obvious," Koble mused. "I've known assholes like Roth since the Pluvium Civil War".

"Hah," Jareth snorted. "Please tell me you aren't comparing the likes of your brother to Alastair Roth?"

Koble folded his arms but stayed unusually quiet, looking angry enough to put his fist through Jareth's skull.

Jareth climbed to his feet, though the metal shackles around his wrists and ankles made it slightly harder for him to straighten to full height. He looked Koble hard in the eyes:

"Cards on the table; I aided your brother's rise to power. It was a mistake that I tried to rectify, but you must understand that there are greater threats to the galaxy than one power-hungry Sphinax with a daddy complex". Jareth shifted toward Koble and stopped about a foot away from him. "I helped Kornell because he gave me unlimited access to the Enkaye temples on Pluvium: something your father was unwilling to do: something I had to".

In a low and threatening voice, Koble said, "I hope all that blood on your hands was worth it".

Jareth slowly nodded.

The smugness was gone, and Nathan could've sworn he saw something akin to regret on the man's face.

Jareth moved away, and his gaze settled on Nathan:

"Let me ask, which side do you think I fight for?"

"Men like you don't fight for sides: you fight for yourselves," Nathan replied.

Jareth shook his head. "You don't have a bloody clue who I am. I have and always will fight for the people of Earth. I fight for democracy. I fight for the greater good".

"And what exactly is the greater good to you?" Nathan said, raising his voice. "You were involved in the Society: the same people who blackmailed Jack; who murdered billions in the Fall".

"I am no member of the Society!" Jareth stepped toward Nathan with a surprising amount of aggression. "I am the man who's been trying to dismantle them for the last two decades".

Silence answered for a beat.

"What are you talking about?" Nathan demanded.

Jareth raised his voice and puffed out his chest. "I told you back on the Phoenix... I was at Hawtrey House trying to kill Baylum and Roth—two birds one stone in one fell swoop".

"That sounds awfully convenient..." Nathan folded his arms. "You seriously expect me to—"

Jareth cut him off. "Martin Cleave; Titus Rousseau; Alexis Yeltsin; Zebadiah Moore; Johan Kraftczyk; Susan and Dennis Corey; Habib Marwan; Joseph Brandon; Boris Ingram; Theodore Jareth, and many more". He stopped to take a breath. His snake-like eyes darted from Nathan to Koble and back again. "All were members of the Society that I removed from the game".

"Is that bunch of random names supposed to mean something?" Koble said sceptically.

"Maybe not to you, but I'm sure Agent Dines is listening in," Jareth replied thoughtfully. "I'm sure he's well aware of Titus Rousseau's death a few days ago, and I have no doubt he's researching the others as we speak".

"Theodore Jareth?" Nathan said, dragging the name out for effect. "Relative of yours?"

Jareth clenched his jaw hard. "Theodore Jareth was the man who led the Society before Roth. During the Fall, he was the one who gave the order to blackmail Jack. He brokered the deal with Baylum and Seig". Jareth paused for a beat. Then, with a stiff upper lip, "He was my father, and I killed him".

There was a moment of silence as Nathan allowed the new information to sink in.

"You killed your own father?" Nathan said with a level of scrutiny to his voice. "Bullshit..."

Jareth's expression was stern, bordering on aggressive.

"I'll have you know that Jack wasn't the only one who saved a few civilians on the day of the Fall". Jareth cocked his head to one side and stared at Nathan knowingly; "That's right, Jack told me about your escape from Earth: about the bus load of people he saved".

Nathan said nothing.

Jareth continued, "Despite his crime, Jack wasn't a bad man. Much like your uncle, I too realised the danger of the Society when the Fall came. I *—like Jack—* came to understand that I was but a pawn in their game *—in my father's game*. That day I saw the truth. I saw dear old Theodore Jareth place the value of human life beneath that of a canvas painting: they all did".

Nathan was silent. Koble too. They watched Jareth slowly pace back and forth.

"That is why I have been picking off members of the Society," Jareth said. "The EWB served as the movement I needed to bring them out of the shadows and into the light". He stopped to breathe: "That is why I was on the roof of Hawtrey House with Chimera. I was going to end Baylum and Roth".

Nathan felt his fist clenching at the mention of the masked assassin. "Who the hell is Chimera?"

Jareth's expression was unreadable. "I don't think that's the question you need to ask right now".

Nathan edged closer, resisting the growing urge for violence. "Who is he?"

"Tell you what..." Jareth mused. "See that my terms are met, that I get through this alive, and not only will I assist in deescalating this situation, but I'll show you the man beneath Chimera's mask and answer every question you have".

Nathan didn't say anything.

"What are your *terms*?" Koble said.

Jareth kept his eyes on Nathan as he answered; "I want protection from your crew,"

"Why?" Nathan growled.

"I attempted to kill Alastair Roth. He will undoubtedly attempt to return the favour," Jareth said. "As it stands, I don't trust the 'wealthers, and if Jareth Corps ships are involved in this blockade, then it's likely that the Society has compromised my organisation: maybe my family".

Nathan glanced at Koble, and the Sphinax shrugged in resignation. They both knew that Jareth was calling the shots. If protecting him meant saving a few thousand lives on both sides, it was worth it.

Reluctantly, Nathan nodded. "We'll keep you safe: you have my word".

Jareth craned his neck to Koble. "And you?"

Koble looked pissed: more pissed than Nathan had ever seen him before. The Sphinax's brittle, dark fur stood to attention. His tail swayed from side to side.

"I won't kill you," Koble replied with a degree of restraint. "For now..."

There was a pause.

"Good enough," Jareth shrugged. Then almost resisting the urge to laugh, he said, "If I'm to appear on a newscast, it's probably best if I'm not in a prison jumpsuit and restraints".

CHAPTER TWENTY-EIGHT
VOL

As Vol rushed to the Sadalmelik, she could feel her heartbeat in her ears. Every fibre of her being willed her to sprint, but she couldn't do that. As Jaudi said, *everything needed to appear business-as-usual,* minimising the chance of the Evokers getting wind of the sabotage.

When Vol finally reached the docks, Hayward was waiting for her at the entrance with a heavy rifle to hand. He lowered the gun immediately and let out a sigh of relief. The big Earther looked positively rattled by something, and Vol could sense his anxiety drop for a moment, though it didn't last long.

Behind Hayward was a group of 'wealther marines, security officers and the Sadalmelik's small four-person crew. They were all gearing up, checking guns and armour as though they were about to go to war. Something had undoubtedly changed, and it filled Vol with dread. She hadn't even told Hayward the instructions from Jaudi, yet the combined forces of the Artemis' security teams and the Sadalmelik were preparing for something big.

"What the hell is going on?" Vol said.

Hayward's scowl could've meant anything.

"We got a communication from the surface," he said.

"How?"

"Old Earth-tech," Hayward waved his answer away as though it weren't relevant. "We're pretty sure it came from the Phoenix".

Vol folded her arms: "You're *pretty sure* it came from the Phoenix?"

"One-way comms: we couldn't reply," Hayward answered. "Besides the point: the method they used to get this message up here is old, but the signal was boosted by something fuckin' powerful. By the looks of things, they only had a small window to get their message out".

"What did it say?" Vol asked.

Hayward pulled a datapad from his combat vest and handed it over. A picture of Hayward and Claire was on the desktop background, smiling into the camera and looking like they didn't have a care in the world. Atop that picture was a blue dialogue window with a series of dashes on screen.

-- .- .-. -..- / .. ... / .- / - .-. .- .. - --- .-. .-.-.-

The code looked similar to the primitive comms devices that the Uvan Empire used in the dark ages: *starts and stops to transmit phrases*. Vol hit the audio button, and a series of ugly-sounding beeps played from the datapad. A translation replaced the code, and Vol felt her heart drop as she read the text:

MARX IS TRAITOR.

"Shit," Vol exhaled, handing the datapad to Hayward.

"Where is he?" he asked in a low voice.

"Med-bay: questioning Cadu".

Hayward didn't say anything. He instructed one of his guys to get Vol a rifle and a combat vest. Vol's first instinct was to decline, but given the situation, she had no choice. It would take a lot to bring down a hostile Evoker, and the security team would need all the help they could get.

Nervously she took the rifle and checked the stock, magazine and sights. It was a good gun: a modified Earth weapon that fired custom pulse rounds. Against a regular combatant, the rifle would kill very quickly, but its effectiveness against an Evoker was questionable at best.

"You said you've killed a Revenant Paladin in the past?" Vol looked at Hayward. "How'd you manage that exactly?"

Hayward gestured at the magazine on Vol's gun. "They're called Sanctum rounds. On impact, they exude a nasty airborne toxin that affects elemental summoners: like an inhibitor. We've also got grenades that do the same".

"Sounds too good to be true," Vol replied sceptically.

Hayward laughed. "Don't get me wrong; they ain't exactly silver bullets. You've got to put a shit-load of rounds into your target before noticing any significant effects. That's why we will keep our distance from Marx when we engage him in combat".

In theory, what he said made sense, but there was one problem: they weren't fighting in a big, open space. The Artemis was an enclosed environment, and Evokers had the ability to move incredibly fast. Given that fact alone, it meant that Marx had the advantage. Hayward must've seen the hopelessness in Vol's eyes. He placed a meaty hand on her shoulder:

"I know this ain't good, but we can't do nothing, right?" he said. "If Marx gets control of the Artemis, he'll have access to the ship's weapons systems. I'm pretty sure he could level two continents with that firepower".

At that moment, a chilling thought ran through Vol's head. She knew a standard warship would carry an array of projectiles, but this was —technically— a battlecrusier. It was the kind of vessel designed to be in the middle of a battlefield, engaging multiple large targets at once.

Hayward pulled his hand from her shoulder and nodded. Then to the group of marines, security officers and his crew, he called out;

"Move out, y'all, let's go hunt this traitor!"

JARETH

David Jareth had secured a deal. It was uneasy and slightly awkward, but it was there nonetheless. Nathan, Koble, Dines, and by extension Inon Waife had agreed to his terms. All he needed to do was appear on a 'wealther broadcast, and in return, he had the protection of the Phoenix's crew. It sounded easy at first. He'd appear on-screen wearing a clean suit and would calm the situation by informing the Paradisians that he was alive and well: not a prisoner. Of course, it was smoke and mirrors, but it would save lives and hopefully undo some of Roth's plan: though Jareth knew never to underestimate the man.

Once Jareth's terms were met, and he'd shaken hands to seal the deal, guards were sent in to remove his shackles. They provided him with his shoes and suit from the previous night —both cleaned to the point where they looked brand new. He was given privacy to shower, change and make himself look statesmanlike, which didn't take long. Despite Jareth's hatred of the theatrics and costuming of politics and celebrity culture, he knew how to look the part and make the pundits believe him.

Maybe it was an inherited skill from his father, or he'd been fighting a war of the cultivated variety for so long it had all become second nature.

Once Jareth was dressed and looking the part, Leviticus Dines entered the cell. Jareth had seen Dines' face in intel documents and the like, but the man seemed more surly in-person. Dines was at most forty years of age, but somehow, appeared a decade older. His hair was entirely silver, and his eyes looked tired: like they'd seen too much for one lifetime.

"I checked out those names you mentioned," Dines said. "You realise murder on a Capital World is a criminal offence, right? If you killed Titus Rousseau—"

Jareth cut him off.

"I did," he said shamelessly. "I suggest we put all that down to *diplomatic immunity*".

Dines scowled, avoiding eye contact for the first time since their exchange began. The Agent eyeballed a report on his datapad, then looked up:

"Zebadiah Moore killed himself whilst in Commonwealth custody".

"*Did he?*" Jareth smiled knowingly.

He sensed Dines becoming agitated, so he softened his approach as he adjusted the cuffs on his suit.

"Agent Dines, the people I have eliminated were vile individuals: people whose crimes extend beyond the Society. Every one of them was a threat, not just to Paradisium but also to the 'wealth. Of course, if you'd like to press charges against me—"

"I'm not talking about arresting you. I'm talking about finding out how far this conspiracy goes. I'd be interested in sharing a little intel when this is all said and done: *strictly off the record*".

Jareth exhaled laughter. There was a certain comedy to the situation that he found amusing: former prisoner now seen as a vital asset in more ways than one. They could carve those words into his gravestone.

"One thing at a time, Agent Dines".

▲

Ten minutes later, Jareth was escorted from his cell by two guards. Where before, he was dragged into the gulag without honour, now, he walked free of its monochrome confinement with dignity. He passed through a checkpoint without screening, then proceeded through the long, dull halls of the facility.

Nathan, Koble and Dines were waiting for him at a set of doors leading to the exterior: all of them looking impatient and irritated for one reason or another.

Outside, thick wind-driven blasts of rain lashed against the windows while dark clouds blocked out the sun.

When Jareth stopped beside his new *allies*, there was a moment of awkward silence. He could tell all three men were not happy with their uneasy alliance, but he refused to address the elephant in the room. Keeping them uncomfortable and unsure of his motivations was the only thing keeping him alive.

"So, gentlemen," Jareth said, clapping his hands together as though he were talking at a company retreat. "Shall we head to the nearest newscast station so I can save the day?"

"Slight change of plans," Dines said, waving his datapad. "High Command has locked down all the public newscast stations. Apparently, they could be targetted by the Paradisians".

There was some tactical validity to the Agent's statement.

If the blockade prevented transmissions beyond Valour's orbital range, it stood to reason that the military would identify newscast stations as high-risk targets. They were the only way to communicate with the planet's population. In the unlikely event of an all-out ground war, broadcast stations would be —tactically speaking— critical to the 'wealth.

"I presume you have an alternative?" Jareth asked.

Dines nodded, "My instructions are to bring you before the Commonwealth Council and Inon Waife. You —along with the Master of the House— will broadcast a joint address from the Council Chambers".

Jareth knew it was political theatre for Waife: he was likely the one to lock down the broadcast stations to ensure a joint address.

All at once, Waife, would embarrass the Paradisian protestors whilst sending a message that said, *I still own you.*

Waife knew he could break Paradisium's resolve with that single act. He'd get David Jareth, a proud citizen of Earth and Paradisium, the CEO of Jareth Corps, and ardent supporter of the EWB, to shake hands and smile and play the role of court jester.

It was political warfare, but there was no other option that Jareth could see that didn't result in bloodshed.

Refuse, and Roth would win. Comply and Paradisium would live to fight another day. It was as simple as that.

They proceeded into the freezing rain to the inner-planet transport. Dines headed into the cockpit while Nathan and Koble took seats at the centre of the small craft. Within seconds the shuttle was soaring away from the Containment Facility, and as Jareth peered at the floating sphere that served as a communist gulag, he swore he'd never enter a place like it again.

GORDON

Once Tariq transmitted his short message to the Sadalmelik,

things aboard the Phoenix slowed down. The crew milled about the ship's communal areas, looking almost as nervous as they had before the Battle of the Messorem.

For many reasons, Gordon found waiting around worse than anything, so he tried to stay busy. He monitored the Phoenix's comms array for a time, hoping to hear a response from the Sadalmelik, but eventually, that whittled down to waiting around as well. He retired to his cabin and tried to read, but again he found himself frustrated by the lack of doing. In the end, Gordon decided the best thing to do was tidy his belongings, empty the recycler and brew himself a fresh mug of coffee before heading out for some fresh air.

He strolled out of the Phoenix and into the open hangar where a couple of mechs were busy at work on what looked like a retired combat fighter. The dockmaster and an administrator stood outside the main office exchanging casual small talk while sharing a pipe.

The storm outside was still raging on, but the sound of heavy rain provided a white noise that Gordon embraced. He sipped the muddy contents of his mug for a few minutes, reflecting on the conversation he and Nathan shared earlier that day.

Jack's crime, the Society and Project Erebus were *mostly* out in the open, but Gordon had rightly kept certain details redacted. Even despite all the drama earlier, he was committed to keeping certain secrets.

All the pain and sacrifice and bloodshed had to be worth something.

The fact that Nathan heard the word *Erebus* in his dreams spoke to some primal instinct in Gordon's mind. Logically, Project Erebus was gone: sealed forever by Bill Stephens, then blown to hell by the Fall.

Still, human fear crafted from experience was a potent beast.

He'd seen what lay inside Project Erebus first-hand. Twenty-six years on, it still haunted him beyond all belief. There had been many sleepless nights where Gordon replayed his memory of what happened. Just thinking about it now made his gut knot, and the hairs on his arms stood to attention. In his nightmares, he saw it: violence and darkness and hatred and a desire to be whole again: evil incarnate.

But, thanks to Bill, it was gone.

The sudden sound of a gunship's engine caught Gordon's ear. He glanced up and spotted a white 'wealther troop transport docking at the other end of the hangar. A young bald man in full combat gear stepped out of the vessel to greet the dockmaster. They exchanged salutes and seemed friendly with one another: though Gordon could've sworn the bald man was irritated. More soldiers in the same heavy combat gear disembarked, and their numbers grew until Gordon gave up counting.

"That's a shit load of 'wealthers..."

Gordon didn't need to turn his head, to know that James Stephens was walking behind him. The awful smell of cigarettes that followed reminded Gordon of a long-dead friend.

It was odd to be around someone who chain-smoked like James. Gordon hadn't known anyone like it since before the Fall, and even then, he'd avoided smokers simply because he couldn't stand the smell.

Still, it reminded him of Earth: of who he once was.

James stopped beside Gordon and pocketed his datapad. He quietly looked across the hangar at the small militia, casually stretching their legs and sharing small talk.

Gesturing at the pack, James said, "If my father could see me now, on a 'wealther Capital World, this close to a bunch of commies, he'd be spinning in his grave".

Gordon considered his reply. He'd had enough conversation about Jack Stephens for one day, so he chose to speak of a far better man that they both knew well.

"Your grandfather used to have a few brilliant quotes for when he gave lectures," Gordon said wistfully. "Things of this world are in so constant a flux that nothing remains long in the same state".

"John Locke, right?" James tipped his cigarette and nodded. "I think I remember that one..."

Gordon couldn't help but smile.

“My Grampa was a good man, right?” James took a long drag from his cigarette and then blew the smoke up into the air.

“He was”.

James nodded; took another drag. “Ice kinda fucks with the brain. I’ve got some serious gaps in my memory, but I remember some good stuff. I remember barbecues and Christmas and... I dunno its blurry”.

Gordon felt his heart wrench. He'd attended the same events, but James clearly didn't remember him. Sure, it was a long time ago, but James deserved those good memories of his family: not the bad stuff that Jack shouldered on the boy post-fall.

“Can I ask a question about those times?” James asked. “There’s something that’s been bugging me”.

“Certainly”.

James stubbed his cigarette on the floor. “There’s a name that keeps cropping up in my head, and I just can’t place it”.

“What’s the name?”

James seemed to ramble for a moment. “I think it Barrett or Barber or Beckett or something like that”.

Beckett.

The world came to a standstill.

It was a name Gordon hadn’t heard since the Fall, and with good reason. Aubrey Beckett was dead and gone. Nobody living was supposed to know he even existed. Yet, somewhere in James’ fractured mind, he recalled the name of the man best left buried. Gordon felt himself grow nervous to the point of sickness. His mind raced with thoughts, and the palms of his hands started to sweat. He tried to say something, but something stopped the words from coming out right. Gordon paused and took a breath. He wasn’t doing a good job of keeping his composure.

James eyeballed him, “You alright there?”

Logic took over Gordon’s brain. He coughed, pretending that he’d choked on coffee and nodded.

“I’m fine,” he coughed again. Then holding up his mug, “Just went down the wrong way”.

James gently laughed.

"Barber, yes," Gordon nodded.

It was a lie: a vital lie.

A lie to preserve the truth.

"Barber was one of the lab assistants. Good guy. Died in Russia with the others".

"That's tragic," James shook his head.

Gordon felt the need to get away from the conversation. He quickly excused himself from James and headed in a direction that made it look like he was returning to the ship. He waited thirty seconds for James to move off and amble back to the Phoenix, then Gordon doubled back to rush out of the hangar and into the rain.

Hearing the name Beckett after so many years felt unnatural. It was a name that Gordon had practically forgotten, but it evoked an emotional reaction that he simply couldn't hide.

Gordon ventured through the downpour to an empty shelter. He didn't care that he wasn't wearing a jacket. The cold rain bombarded him, but Gordon took no notice. Decades of repressed panic set in at the mere mention of the name.

The shelter was three hundred yards from the hangar and devoid of life. Thunder crashed above, and the wind outside was blowing so hard the enclosure walls creaked under pressure.

Gordon slumped in the corner. He wiped a stray tear from his eye and took a moment to recover some semblance of composure. He climbed to his feet, readying himself to pace around until the cortisol raging through his body burned away.

Then something blunt struck him.

Before Gordon knew what was going on, the impact of whatever it was sent him slamming into the wall. He tried to call out for help but was unable to do so. The next thing Gordon felt was something slamming into the back of his skull.

Then darkness.

NATHAN

Agreeing to protect Jareth felt like the cherry on top of a dessert that was pretty much on fire, but as Jack used to say, *beggars couldn't be choosers*. As much as Nathan didn't like it, he and his crew were part of it now. Vol was in imminent danger, and the delicate situation that was the Paradisian blockade was a powder keg just waiting for a match. In addition, Nathan felt responsible for creating the problem. He'd gone to Hawtrey House to save James, thus providing Roth and the Society with the perfect conditions to rile up an already aggravated Paradisian populous.

The seating area of Dines' inner-planet shuttle was silent for most of the journey. Nathan checked his datapad for updates from the crew —of which there were none— then he swiped through the local newsfeed. There was a breaking news bulletin in bold red text on the front page.

Inon Waife, to make emergency address.

"Rather illuminating, isn't it?" Jareth said, leaning over to eyeball the headline. "The Commonwealth really is no different from any other government..."

Nathan didn't say anything. He tucked the datapad into his pocket and tried his best to ignore Jareth's smug, victorious expression.

"Tell me something, Nathan, how much do you remember of Earth?" Jareth asked. "Not what Jack or the others aboard The Loyalty told you as a child. I want to know what *you* remember".

Nathan was silent for two breaths. Most of his memories pre-Fall were foggy at best. There were a select few that Nathan cherished, but as soon as he allowed his mind to venture toward them, the Fall would overshadow everything. His distinction between good times and bad from back then was irrelevant because no matter what he tried, his mind would always veer toward the bad, so he shut the whole thing away.

He reminded himself of Jack's key lesson: *never let them see you bleed.*

When Nathan answered Jareth's question, he kept his answer brief to avoid recalling the Fall in all its gruesome detail.

"I remember enough".

"Let me tell you something about Earth," Jareth leaned in. "Our governments were run by men who didn't understand the people they ruled over. It was a world where those with riches prospered and those without failed. They'd label themselves with pretty political titles like conservative or liberal or freedom fighter, but they were all the same: corrupt, elitist pigs that didn't care about the people".

"And you do?" Nathan raised a brow.

Jareth smiled, dodging the question and continued his rambling.

"History has taught me one thing: power corrupts all people, regardless of idealogy". He gazed at Nathan as though waiting for him to acknowledge the statement. When Nathan did no such thing, Jareth continued, "I believe that the Enkaye saw past the immediate weaknesses of our people. They saw our true potential, and they intended for us to inherit their power".

"You wanna know what I think?" Nathan snapped. "I think the Enkaye didn't have a fucking clue what we'd become. The fact is that we didn't need the Revenant to wipe us out. We'd have taken care of that ourselves eventually".

Jareth lifted his brows.

"I disagree," he said. "You, my boy, are living proof that the Enkaye had a plan..."

The truth stood firm and unshakeable.

Jareth looked at Nathan with unwavering eyes, silently acknowledging the undeniable reality of his Enkaye heritage.

Nathan was taken aback.

Jareth knew. *But how?*

There was a very select group of people that knew the truth, and David Jareth was not one of them. Nathan kept it that way for good reason.

"Never let them see you bleed, Captain Carter," Jareth mused knowingly. "Never. Ever. Ever".

▲

Nathan didn't say another word to Jareth. Neither did Koble. Silence filled the shuttle for the better part of ten minutes, right up until the moment it neared the Council Chamber's air space.

To Nathan's confusion, he felt the shuttle turn off the designated path and head north, which was entirely wrong. He moved into the cockpit, where Dines was flying the ship with a particularly furious look in his eyes.

Dines was still on the communicator, frantically arguing with someone at the other end of the transmission. Nathan had never seen the man so enraged: he looked ready to put his fist through the comms panel.

"You don't understand; I have written orders from the Master of the House," Dines argued into the comms. He paused as the person on the other end said something, then continued, "I don't care what Admiral Deffu says. I am on direct orders from—"

The other person cut him off, and Nathan could hear the muffled shouting from Dines' earpiece.

The Agent's face grew red with anger, and out of nowhere, he yelled into the comms, "Then put Deffu on. Tell her Agent Leviticus Dines—"

Dines went silent. It was apparent that his comms weren't working. He pulled off the earpiece and launched it across the cockpit in frustration.

"What the fuck is going on?" Nathan asked.

Dines looked over his shoulder and huffed. "High Command has installed a no-fly zone. We're being ordered to land with the Phoenix and await further orders".

"You're joking, right?" Nathan said. "Just ignore them and land the fuckin' ship!"

Dines gestured to the window.

Nathan leaned in and got a look at an escorting fighter on the shuttle's starboard bow. Then he saw a second on the port side, further back than the first but close enough to make its intent clear.

"Shit," Nathan cursed. "What now?"

"Not much we can do," Dines said with resignation.

▲

Three minutes later, Dines landed his shuttle inside the same hangar as the Phoenix. The 'wealther fighters that had been escorting them from the Council Chambers veered away once the shuttle had touched down. Nathan wanted to question why they'd been so militant. Even by 'wealther standards, it seemed strange— but something stopped him when he looked out onto the hangar.

A platoon of around three dozen marines were waiting for them to disembark. Unlike typical 'wealther soldiers, the marines were clad from head to toe in thick green and black armour with helmets and dark visors. To Nathan, it looked like a faceless militia with no individuality. *Typical 'wealthers.*

"That's a lotta dudes," Koble remarked. "Friends of yours, Dines?"

Dines said nothing. He disembarked the shuttle and headed out into the hangar. He spoke with the Marine CO, checked something on a datapad, then walked back. The transactional conversation lasted less than thirty seconds.

"So?" Nathan said expectantly. "What's the word?"

"They were rerouted too," Dines answered. He pointed to the Marine CO; "The Corporal over there is awaiting orders from High Command. I'm gonna go out on a limb and assume that these guys are some sorta escort for us".

Nathan and Koble shared a look. It was odd how they still fell into the same intuitive methods of communication despite all the drama earlier.

Nathan eyeballed the Corporal. He was a human, about thirty years old, with a shaved head, dark eyebrows and a thin jaw. He was about five-nine, two-hundred pounds and looked pretty tough: like the scrappy cage fighters out of Peresopolis Station. For thirty seconds, the Corporal shared friendly banter with a couple of the guys from his unit; then, he took a communication on his datapad.

Despite feeling like something wasn't right, Nathan couldn't see anything out of place regarding the marines. They were typical 'wealther military types: proud, efficient and dangerous.

A moment later, the Corporal wandered to the shuttle. He offered respectful nods of greeting to Koble and Nathan, then directed his gaze to Dines.

"What's the update, Corporal?" Dines said, skipping any formalities.

"Markus Holland made some significant threats in the last half hour.

High Command is *concerned* that the Paradisians will commence an orbital bombardment," he said. "My orders have changed. My unit is to escort you and Mr Jareth to the Council Chambers on foot".

"Why on foot?" Nathan probed. "Surely we are safer in the skies?"

"I said the same thing, sir," the Corporal nodded. "It would appear that High Command has intel suggesting that Mr Jareth's life is at significant risk".

Just as Jareth said, Roth was keen to return the favour.

"How many in your platoon?" Dines asked.

"Thirty-five, including myself".

Dines looked at Jareth, then at Nathan and Koble. "You think Roth is bold enough to take on thirty-five marines?

"He sure as shit didn't have any issue forming the blockade," Nathan replied. He pointed at Jareth; "I'd sure as hell feel better keeping an eye on him with my people too: we did commit to protecting him after all".

The marine handed Dines a datapad. The Agent studied it for several seconds, then gave it to Nathan. On-screen were signed orders, direct from Inon Waife, co-signed by an Admiral Deffu of High Command.

"We'll move out once we get the ok," the Corporal said. Then with mixed emotion, he stared at Jareth, still sitting in a passenger chair.

Nathan noticed outrage in the man's eyes.

"Everything alright?" Dines barked.

"Yes, sir," the Corporal nodded. "Just thinkin' how crazy it is that one decadent capitalist could cause all this mayhem".

The Corporal straightened, realising he'd overstepped his mark. Dines was a superior officer, and Nathan guessed that free speech wasn't exactly a luxury among the ranks. The man was positively embarrassed beyond all words. Dines waved away the outburst and the man relaxed. He then committed to giving them the heads up once he received the all-clear and quietly took his leave.

With Dines keeping a close eye on Jareth, Nathan and Koble ventured back to the Phoenix, about a hundred yards from the shuttle. When they reached the ship, Nathan found James leaning against the hull. There was an edgy look in his eyes that Nathan recognised from years gone by. It was the same sneer his cousin would make before venturing to a scum-filled establishment to refill his stash.

Koble headed into the ship while Nathan stopped beside his cousin, suspecting that the stepped-up military presence was causing some unease. James watched the 'wealthers like a hawk while taking quick, anxious puffs on a cigarette.

"I don't like this," James whispered. He pointed at Dines' shuttle; "Is Jareth in there?"

"Sure is," Nathan nodded. "He's gonna address the Paradisians once we get the go-ahead".

"You guys need an extra gun out there?" James asked, gravity in his voice.

Nathan didn't want to say yes. James had been through hell, *but beggars couldn't be choosers*.

"Only if you're okay with that," Nathan nodded.

"Always," James puffed.

Nathan could see the panic on his cousin's face as he gazed at the platoon. Back in the day, James would've been climbing the walls at such a sight; either desperately seeking his next hit or waving a gun around like an idiot. He did neither of those things. Instead, James continued smoking, which Nathan realised was now a coping mechanism.

Ice for nicotine: there were far worse trade-offs.

"You ever wonder if things could be different?" James asked. "Y'know, like the Fall or Mirotose Station?"

"I realised a while back that there's no point in living in the past," Nathan placed a hand on James' shoulder. "I've accepted that, and I'm happier for it".

"I guess driving a sharp object through Seig's chest kinda helped," James muttered.

"Not that," Nathan shook his head and gestured to the Phoenix. "This crew made me a better person".

James nodded and breathed laughter; "When I got outta rehab, all I wanted to do was make amends for my fuck-ups. I didn't know what I'd do. Then I met Mahmoot, and he told me about the mission, and I knew that was how I could start to make things right".

Maybe it was old-times-sake or perhaps the brotherly bond they'd once shared, but Nathan found himself questioning all the hate he'd harboured for James over the years. Yes, he'd fucked up, but so had Jack. The fact was that James could've ended up dead in a ditch or plugged into some Enkaye death machine. But he wasn't. James was alive. More importantly, he was alive and trying to make the galaxy better. That was more than the junkie Nathan had once known.

What Nathan said next felt impulsive, but he knew in his heart it was only right.

"When this is all done, you and I should talk," Nathan suggested. "Y'know, work out all our bad blood and make things right again".

Nathan couldn't quite believe he'd said it. He'd clung to his resentment for James for over a decade, but seeing his cousin's vulnerabilities reminded Nathan of himself — before the Phoenix.

"What do you say?" Nathan said, trying to force an answer.

James' features softened, and the arrogant, sarcastic-looking smile Nathan had seen a million times before formed.

"You've gone soft!" James scoffed.

"I'm serious".

James rubbed a hand against his jaw as though he were mulling over a stray thought.

He chuckled, "I'll think it over".

INTERLUDE
ROTH

Two critical messages reached the Featon via scrambled channels. The first was from Baylum's spy —the Evoker. He confirmed that everything was in place aboard the Artemis —simply waiting for the order to execute. The communique, however, didn't come from the Artemis at all. Instead, it came from within the blockade, suggesting to Roth that Baylum's Evoker spy wasn't working alone and most certainly wasn't aboard the Artemis.

The second transmission originated from Valour's surface from Bradley Austin. It was text-based with no video or audio: scrambled, jumbled, and hard-coded so that none of the sheep in orbit could decode it. Thanks to the blockade scrambling all comms, Austin was required to broadcast to a vessel aligned relative to his position on the ground.

Line of sight was a beautiful thing.

Roth's Society brother, Alan Washington, had seen to that part of the plan: instructing his crew to hold the perfect geostationary orbit for when the key moment arose. In return, Washington would receive a place in Roth's new world: perhaps a star system of his own or a pretty title, like a knighthood.

Austin's message was simple: *Objective one complete. Awaiting your go on Objective two.*

Roth smiled his ruthless smile as he read the transcript. This was the critical hour of the pièce de résistance. Until then, all of Roth's scheming and manipulating had been relatively passive. No —important— blood had been spilled. Everything up to that point was about manoeuvring the pieces.

But now was the hour of violence.

Roth looked upon Valour from the comfort of the Featon. His zeus-class vessel was named after the school he'd attended as a boy. The Featon Academy of excellence was a highly exclusive educational institution: *reserved only for the best of the best of the best of the wealthiest of the most influential families on Earth.* The school held a special place in Roth's heart, not because he loved his time there, but for the profound impact it'd had on his life.

He'd been nothing more than a pound of wet clay the day he arrived; but upon departure, Alastair Roth was complete. Unlike most schools teaching Maths or English or Science, Roth learned what it was to be a man of the Society. He studied its history, legacy, and his family's part in the organisation. He came to understand what it meant to be better than the commoners. His efforts to learn even caught the eye of the Society's chairman, Theodore Jareth.

In those simpler pre-Fall days, the Society had a single objective: control of the masses. Back then, it was easy. the Society would nominate power-hungry morons to run Earth's many governments. Then, if they stepped out of line or went off-script, they were dealt with. If the population in a particular country was growing too fast, the Society would *handle* it. In the good old days, this meant releasing deadly contagions into the populous, or causing the odd natural disaster, or sometimes creating the perfect circumstances to trigger global conflicts.

Then there were the minor things; little ways to keep the masses pointing the finger at each other rather than those at the top. You could incite hatred between factions or races or sexualities or *anything, really.* People were easy to manipulate, especially when controlling politicians, celebrities and the media. One could fake a terrorist attack, crash the stock market, or simply elicit outrage as a means to an end.

Better days, Roth thought.

The Fall presented an opportunity: a chance to wipe the slate clean. With an ever-increasing population, the masses were getting wise. There had been a few cock-ups, and the Society was forced to take action in order to keep things unsullied. Theodore Jareth recognised that at the rate the populous was growing, it was only a matter of time before the gutter rats would learn to bite the hand feeding them.

If a shepherd has too many sheep, he loses control of the flock; Theodore Jareth's words were burnt into the back of Roth's mind: words spoken the day he brokered the deal with Baylum.

The Fall would've been a masterpiece had it gone according to plan, but three things prevented its perfection.

The first mistake came in the form of the first Project Erebus: a failed operation in Russia's Ural mountains that would've provided the Society with the means to kill Baylum when his back was turned.

The second botch was the untimely and mysterious death of Theodore Jareth, which plunged the Society into a leadership contest at the worst possible time.

The third and most fatal flaw came in the form of the Commonwealth: an unknown entity to the Society who arrived at Earth during the thirteenth hour of the Fall. The 'wealth saved far more civilian lives than anyone bargained for. The consensus was that Baylum lied about their existence for unknown reasons. Roth would never forget that betrayal.

Theodore Jareth's dream of a pure culture living on Lunar was left in shreds. What remained of Earth grew into Paradisium, and the rest was history.

Right up until the moment, another device identical to Project Erebus was discovered on the distant planet of Helia.

That was when Roth knew he had to trigger his *pièce de résistance.*

He needed to bide his time. To manipulate. To posture, to provoke. To invest in the right people. To wait until the right moment.

The Commonwealth would burn. Baylum would pay for his deceit, and Alastair Albon de-Freiherr Roth would rise to power.

As he looked at Valour, Roth realised that the critical moment had finally arrived. Roth took a glass from his cabinet and poured himself a brandy from a crystal decanter. He examined the dark liquid and swirled it with a flick of the wrist. He raised his glass as if toasting what was to come.

Roth pulled his datapad and established a private communique with the Featon's bridge commander.

"Cameron, it's time. Contact all our people, tell them —" Roth paused as if savouring the moment like his brandy. "Tell them it is time".

CHAPTER TWENTY-NINE
VOL

The Artemis' head of security was an orange-furred Horrus called Gane. He wasn't what Vol expected: a mild-mannered officer with a soft voice and a quiet disposition. Until Hayward shared his situational report, Gane remained in his formal military uniform instead of the combat gear. However, once Hayward got to the part about Marx and the main objective, Gane adopted a no-nonsense expression and pulled off his formal jacket, swapping it for a combat vest.

As one of Gane's men handed him a rifle, the Horrus sighed, "Take a job on a Warship. It'll be easy, they said..."

Gane's security team was around thirty-strong. That, combined with the Sadalmelik's crew and Vol, brought the grand total to thirty-five. It wasn't much against a fully-fledged Evoker, but Vol knew a small force could be highly effective: especially if the enemy wasn't expecting it.

Rather than use the primary elevator, Gane took the small army to a cargo lift: located in a part of the ship where they were less likely to cause disruption to the broader crew. For Vol, the journey to the med-bay deck felt as though it lasted a lifetime.

It was one of those times when she wished she didn't possess her sixth sense. Hearing the anxious thoughts of three dozen people simultaneously was enough to make anyone feel edgy.

Many believed *this was the day that they would die*. Others pondered the best way to kill an Evoker. A handful fantasised about not only killing Marx but being recognised as a hero of the 'wealth.

Then there was the Sadalmelik's crew.

Hayward kept his mind busy by recalling the words of an old Earth song with a funky beat and brass section. Scruffy was thinking about drinking rum from something called a coconut, and Riggs reflected on a former lover he'd known on Paradisium.

Staring death in the face brought up an array of emotions, but mostly it was fear.

Suddenly, the lift came to a screeching halt, and all the overhead lighting failed. Despite the nerves that Vol sensed among the small army, nobody flinched or reacted.

"What the hell happened, Gane?" Hayward said in a low voice. "Thought you said this was the best route?"

Flashlights illuminated the compact space.

"It is," Gane insisted. "You can only deactivate this lift from the main systems."

Vol felt Hayward's disposition change very quickly.

"Are you telling me Marx has access?" the Earther said.

"Could be a power failure," Gane replied. The Horrus looked around, shining his flashlight on the door, then to the ceiling. "The only way is up," Gane pointed at a hatch in the ceiling. He then looked expectantly at Hayward and the others, "Anyone gonna give me a boost?"

▲

It took eight minutes for the entire team to scale the maintenance ladder. As Hayward and Riggs pried the metal doors to access the main deck, dense, sticky air spilt into the elevator shaft from the gap. The main lighting was out too, replaced by emergency LED's on the floor and ceiling. It confirmed Hayward's earlier suspicion; *that Marx had access to the primary systems*.

The spooky part was that there were no signs of life: no 'wealther crew going about their work. *It was the definition of a ghost ship.*

"Where is everyone?" Gane whispered.

"We ain't got time to worry about that," Hayward replied. "Plan hasn't changed. We get to the medbay; find Marx and put him down".

As the group proceeded into the long, winding corridors of the Artemis, the clamminess in the air grew. Vol became aware of her boots sticking to the ground and the sweat coating her palms, making it challenging to hold her rifle.

They suddenly stopped at an intersection, where a scene of carnage and violence lay ahead. The walls were charred, smashed and covered in guts. Bodies of at least two dozen officers peppered the corridor: many killed by elemental energy. The acrid smell of burning flesh, blood and death lingered there like a shadow.

"Shit," Hayward gasped, looking at the destruction. He looked to Vol with urgency; "Fuck the no communications bullshit: get on the horn to Jaudi and tell her to lock down the bridge".

Vol didn't understand the Earther idiom, but she got the gist. She grabbed her datapad, attempting to establish a clear channel with Jaudi, but to her dismay, the signal refused to connect.

Vol tried again.

Still nothing: not even a dialtone.

Vol changed tactics, trying to contact the bridge directly.

Nothing.

No connection.

Worst case scenario, Jaudi was already dead, as were the bridge crew. Best case; interference from the blockade was obstructing comms.

Gane recommended they redirect to the bridge while a smaller party checked out the med bay. It was a logical suggestion. Hayward didn't look happy about it but ultimately agreed it was the best thing to do.

"I've gotta find Cadu," Hayward said. "We can't afford to lose him. Who knows what else he overheard on the Equus".

"Agreed," Vol said.

Gane nodded at them in understanding. As a gesture of

good faith, he selected five of his marines to accompany Vol and the Sadalmelik's crew to the med-bay. It wasn't the largest force, but Vol figured if they found Cadu or Repla alive, they could be a critical asset in the fight. They were Evokers, after all. Maybe —just maybe— there was a chance.

As Gane and his force of thirty were ready to move out, Hayward pulled the Horrus officer aside: "You get to the bridge, lock it down"

Gane nodded. "Good luck".

▲

The arena of in-person combat was not Vol's speciality. Sure, she could shoot a gun, and she'd killed before, but this situation did not play to her strengths. If she were behind the stick of the Phoenix, it'd be a different story. She'd have turrets, speed, sensors, agility, and everything that made aerial combat what it was. That was where she shone; not in infantry or hand-to-hand.

The Artemis was a scene of destruction. More bodies, blood, spent ammo, and death carpeted the corridors. It was vile: the worst thing she'd ever seen. In many places, the internal walls and ceiling were dented or burnt, where Marx had torn through wave after wave of enemy.

When they reached the med-bay, Hayward halted them at the entrance. The body of a med-tech was twisted and crushed into the bulkhead opposite the door: bones broken and contorted in all the wrong directions. Guts pooled beneath, prompting Vol to resist gagging at the gruesome sight.

Hayward made a gesture to move in. The Earther raised his gun into med-bay, and the group proceeded with him. Scruffy and Riggs moved with Hayward in an almost symbiotic fashion, checking corners with precision and ensuring nothing lurked in the darkness. The five 'wealther marines were pretty efficient too; clearing rooms systemically and methodically as 'wealthers would.

The med-bay looked like a place that had seen battle: as much as the corridors outside. There were giant, burning holes in the walls. The flooring was smashed and cracked. Storage cabinets at one end of the room were broken and shredded apart. Broken glass from the privacy shutters was everywhere. Medical gurneys were overturned or slewn against the far end of the long room. Scattered across the room were the bloody bodies of a dozen med-techs.

When the group reached the bed assigned to Cadu, Hayward stopped. The gurney was now a bent mass of steel mashed against the wall by something elemental. Green blood started there but dragged several metres across the room to a hole in the ground, where someone was pounded through the floor and down for several decks.

"That's Sillix blood," Vol whispered to Hayward. She shone her flashlight into the gaping chasm, not seeing an end to the darkness but knowing what likely lay at the end: the body of Repla.

As Vol brought her torch up, she noticed red blood beside Repla's. She moved her flashlight along the floor, tracking it across the walls, back to the ground and then to a body in the corner. Innards, blood, and feathers had exploded against the wall where he'd been pummelled by a powerful summon, but that killing blow wasn't enough for the murderer. No, they'd executed him even though he was a dead man. The severed head of Elder Agrion Marx lay metres from his body in a pool of crimson.

Vol's mind raced.

"What the fuck?" Hayward said in a low voice. "Is that—"

"Marx," Vol cut him off.

A grim darkness whirled there.

"If that's Marx…" Hayward stopped and considered it. "Shit".

That was when Vol realised the gravity of the situation. The mole had been aboard the Artemis long before Marx or Repla. In fact, he'd been brought to the Artemis by the Sadalmelik after he'd been *rescued.*

Vol felt a chill of realisation as she said the name aloud; "Cadu..."

Everything that happened aboard the Equus was intentional. Cadu was a plant, likely ordered to kill a few low-level Society thugs to look like a captive: to look like a man that needed saving. That explained why Cadu was so quick to execute the Society goon aboard the Equus —he couldn't afford to let the man speak. It explained why the med-techs couldn't detect an inhibitor in his blood— there never was one.

Cadu was an impostor.

"Son-of-a-bitch!" Hayward said.

NATHAN

The rainfall on Valour was torrential, plunging down in ferocious icy sheets in a way Nathan had never seen. He watched the storm from the dry comfort of the Phoenix, waiting for the marines to give the go-ahead. Having additional support to keep Jareth's head on his shoulders wasn't a bad thing, but Nathan wasn't entirely comfortable with it.

Many 'wealthers harboured ill-feeling toward Jareth, not just for his part in the EWB or the scandal surrounding his corporate tax-dodging, but because Jareth was the living embodiment of greedy capitalism: *the anthesis of the Commonwealth's socialist dream.* That was why Nathan elected to bring some of his own people: one, to keep watch of their allies, and two, ensure Jareth's survival.

He gathered the crew, plus Rain, James and Tariq, in the Phoenix's airlock to outline a plan. Nathan planned a big speech about how they all needed to put aside their differences with Jareth: *that this was for the greater good.*

The crew —plus guests— gathered, but Gordon was nowhere to be seen. It alarmed Nathan immediately. He questioned the others about Gordon's whereabouts. Russell said something about the Doctor going for a nap in his cabin, but the old man's quarters were vacant. Rain had passed Gordon in the kitchen an hour earlier, but again there was no sign of him there.

James spoke up, clicking his fingers as though recalling something: "We were talking outside about thirty mins ago. He excused himself, looking like he was heading back here".

"Clearly, he didn't..." Russell said.

Nathan could tell what Russell wanted to say: he'd thought the same thing ten seconds earlier: James clearly had an issue with parts of his short-term memory — *containment chambers could have that effect, as could Ice.*

Before Russell said something that could cause a tense situation, Nathan cut in to question James:

"You are absolutely sure Gordon was heading back into the ship?"

James nodded; "Positive".

Nathan was about ready to organise a search party, but as he was about to dish out commands, the airlock door opened with a hiss. Leviticus Dines stepped into the ship with Jareth at his side.

The Agent looked around the Phoenix's crew: "The marines have High Command's clearance. We're moving out in three minutes".

KOBLE

Koble didn't envy the tough choice Nathan was forced to make, but he made the call wisely. The Earther was decisive and objective in organising the crew: assigning the majority to protect and escort Jareth while leaving Russell, Harrt and the droid to search for Gordon.

It wasn't an easy choice, but in Koble's mind, it was the right one. Yes, Gordon was a member of the crew and a friend, but in the grand scheme of things, finding the Doctor wasn't going to solve the immediate issue. Objectively, Jareth was the key to resolving the situation in orbit and possibly preventing a war. Alastair Roth and his chums in the Society would know that, and they would no doubt attempt to stop Jareth from making his broadcast.

Once Nathan was done outlining the plan and they'd

geared up for what could be a perilous mission, he looked around the crew one last time:

"Let's just get through this in one piece".

▲

The group protecting Jareth was around the region of forty people strong. The sight of it reminded Koble of an old Sphinax legend about a prophet escorted through a great city by his followers. In the story, the Prophet stood at the centre of three-thousand devotees moments before a meteor strike. They surrounded the Prophet to protect him while he prayed to an Enkaye-god for their salvation. Despite his pleas for divine intervention, the meteor still struck: still destroyed the Prophet and the masses.

It was a pretty grim tale intended to teach its audience some meaningful lesson that Koble couldn't recall. Yet, at that moment, as he and thirty-nine others moved in a pack to defend Jareth, Koble drew comparisons. There he was, protecting the Prophet —aka Jareth— from certain death so he could deliver them salvation.

The 'wealther marines deployed several drones to cover the immediate airspace, while two gunships hovered above to provide cover. In Koble's mind, an aerial assault by the Paradisians was less likely because of the heavy storm: *pinpointing an exact target with limited visibility would be tricky, even for a seasoned pilot.*

That meant if Roth was going to target Jareth, it'd be on the ground: not from the air.

"Hey, boss," Rain said with a whisper.

Koble glanced at the pilot. Rain looked decidedly calm under the circumstances. Like the rest, Rain was soaked, so much so that his fur adopted a darker shade of blue than Koble was used to.

"Whassup?" Koble replied.

Rain raised both palms and gestured to the sky;

"Looks like I brought my namesake with us..."

It was a terrible pun but added some levity to the moment. Koble smiled and patted his friend's drenched shoulder:

"When this is done, we're taking a detour somewhere warm where the booze is strong".

"Don't forget a decent pipe of the vine," Rain added, making a smoking gesture with his fingers. "After weather like this I'll need something to warm my soul".

NATHAN

The first leg of the journey involved escorting Jareth through one of Valour's many business districts. Where Waife had imposed a planet-wide lockdown, there were no civilians wandering the normally busy streets, and no traffic in the skylanes above. The whole place felt like a different planet from the one Nathan had wandered just a few hours prior.

The second part of the journey began at a nondescript dome-shaped building on the edge of the civilian quarter. At first, Nathan was pretty sceptical about entering a closed space, but Dines assured him they'd be safe.

"This is what's known as the red loop," Dines said. "During the founding war, the Commonwealth built secret tunnels under the city to transport weapons and ammo between the key tactical locations".

"Is this place public knowledge?" Nathan asked.

"Not exactly..."

As Dines promised, they were led down a long, winding staircase that descended deep under the city. At the bottom was a tunnel, well illuminated, about seven metres across and seven metres tall. Retired tracks were still on the floor where the 'wealthers once used locomotives to carry supplies back-and-forth.

Despite Dines' assurances, Nathan didn't like the route. He was pretty sure that if something was going down, it'd be in a confined and secluded place just like it.

As the group walked along the tracks, James nudged Nathan;

"You remember trains?" he asked.

"A little," Nathan shrugged. "I think I remember my parents taking me on once".

James didn't say anything, he simply nodded a nostalgic nod, and they continued to walk in silence.

▲

It took fifteen minutes to reach the end of the tunnel, where a platoon of 'wealther soldiers were waiting for them. There was a moment of sheer alarm where everyone thought the worst, but thankfully, Dines was already prepared with a callsign to see if the unit was friendly.

They passed Dines' test, and he led the group past the soldiers up another staircase.

At the top, Nathan breathed a sigh of relief when he laid eyes on the Council Chambers just a few hundred feet away. Then he saw the stepped-up military presence and his face contorted. There must've been an entire Commonwealth battalion in the main square, with several tanks and gunnery towers covering the skies.

Nathan looked at Dines, "You people really put on a show, don't you?"

Dines frowned but didn't say anything.

David Jareth strode beside Nathan and peered out on the 'wealther troops guarding the Council Chambers. His eyes scanned everything —the soldiers, the tanks, the anti-aircraft emplacements.

Nathan knew the old man could see the same thing he did: *the consequences of poking the bear.*

"Good to know I'm popular," Jareth said.

HARRT

There was no sign of Gordon. The Phoenix's log recorded him making a coffee in the galley, then heading out the airlock and into the hangar. After that, there was no trace of his whereabouts.

Harrt, Russell and Kyp searched the hangar for the better part of twenty minutes to little avail. There was no sign of the portmaster, who'd been previously spotted at a desk that backed onto a restricted area. In her place was an armed officer guarding the doors and keeping a watchful eye.

Harrt made polite small talk before questioning him. The man had a sharp and regional accent, with a particularly odd way of pronouncing certain words. Harrt provided the guard with a brief description of Gordon, then asked if there had been any sightings.

The guard shook his head. "No, sir, can't say that I've seen anyone matching that description".

Harrt gestured to the metal door that led into the restricted area. "Mind if I take a look around?"

"I'm sorry, Commander. Given the security threat, I've been instructed to limit access to my people only".

Harrt wanted to pull rank: to tell the soldier that technically he was the senior officer. Of course, doing such a thing would result in drama and complaints, and Harrt wasn't willing to do that yet. He saluted the officer and returned to the Phoenix's cockpit, knowing that it was best to rule out the surrounding area that Russell was busy checking before ruffling any feathers.

Once Harrt was aboard the Phoenix, he sat in the pilot's seat, noticing the new cushioning added to the chairs since the last time he'd flown the ship. Sitting there reminded Harrt of better days: before his investigation, before the Artemis. Sure, the crew had been battling Seig and trying to find a long-lost Enkaye relic, but he'd felt a part of something tangible: something almost resembling a family.

That was the life he craved.

Harrt looked at the jumble of components that Gordon and Tariq had fashioned into the telegraph machine. The device was static: unable to confirm whether or not the message was received by the Sadalmelik.

Harrt imagined Vol, Hayward, Jaudi and his crew going toe-to-toe with Marx. As awful as it was to admit, there was no good outcome for that scenario. The thought stuck with Harrt right up until the moment Russell sprinted into the cockpit. The former barkeep presented Harrt with the remnants of a broken coffee cup.

"It belongs to the Doc," Russell panted. Then gesturing

to what had been the handle, "And look, blood..."

"Where did you find this?"

"Outside: one of the transport shelters".

That was when Harrt knew he had to take action and access the restricted area. The hangar's security logs were the next best way of finding Gordon. Harrt sprung to his feet. He grabbed his gun from the holotable and holstered it. Then he pushed past Russell and Kyp and barrelled toward the back of the Phoenix. By the time he'd dashed down the boarding ramp, Russell was following close behind.

"Whatcha gonna do?" he asked.

Harrt said, "We're gonna access the security logs for this place".

"Ain't that restricted?"

"It most certainly is".

They reached the officer, still guarding the doors to the restricted area. He was still clutching his gun and looking formidable and friendly at the same time.

"I'm sorry, Corporal, but I'm gonna need access to your security system," Harrt said, phrasing it as an order rather than a request. "One of our people is missing".

The guard's eyes hardened. "That is something I cannot do, Commander".

Harrt was ready to move forward and strike, but the guard pitched his rifle up.

"Sir," the guard warned. "Please—"

"I am ordering you to stand aside," Harrt said.

The guard moved in closer, pressing the barrel of his gun to Harrt's chest. That was a big mistake. Without hesitation, Harrt smacked the barrel to the left while he darted right. There was a spray of weapons fire where the guard clumsily pulled the trigger: clearly, he wasn't expecting the bold move. Rounds richoted against the ceiling, meeting nothing more than the steel of the hangar's roof. Something about the weapon sounded off to Harrt's well-trained ear: rather than the thump of a pulse weapon, this thing had a metallic clack.

Harrt's next move was to slam his closed fist into the soldier's head. With a hard right hook, the guard veered off to one side but still kept ahold of his gun. Before Harrt could move in, the guard raised his rifle and shot Harrt a bloody smile.

"I've been looking forward to—"

The guard didn't finish his sentence.

Over Harrt's shoulder, Russell fired a single, deadly round that veered into the *not-soldier's* skull. A cloud of blood flew into the air, and the man dropped back onto the ground. The sound of the gunshot echoed around the hangar for a moment.

Harrt turned to Russell.

Shock painted the young man's face.

"You alright?" Harrt asked.

Russell nodded; "That guy was no 'wealther". He moved up and grabbed the dead man's gun from the floor. Then after pulling the magazine from the weapon, Russell said, "Why would a 'wealther use bullets?"

A chill ran down Harrt's spine. The modified weapon was the kind of thing Paradisians would use. Not 'wealther standard. Not even close.

Harrt moved to the door that the imposter was previously guarding. Harrt pushed, but something heavy on the other side prevented him from opening the door. He applied more pressure, and slowly the door shifted but only marginally.

Harrt and Russell shared a look. Something wasn't right.

"That ain't right," Russell said.

Together they forced the door open and what they saw on the other side caused Harrt to freeze.

"Fuck..." Russell said, drawing the Earther curse words to two syllables.

The bodies of a dozen 'wealther officers, soldiers and mechanics carpeted the ground. They were fresh kills —less than an hour, by Harrt's estimate.

"The hell happened in here?" Russell shuddered.

Harrt didn't reply: he was too busy figuring out who could have murdered so many people without raising the alarm. He took a moment to examine one of the bodies: a forty-something human male who'd died from a single gunshot wound to the back of the head. The deceased didn't see his attacker coming. Harrt circled to the next body: the dockmaster. She too, had suffered a gunshot wound to the head. The more bodies Harrt examined, the more he began to form a picture of what happened. The kills were silent, clean, and meticulous. It was the work of professionals, not a lone nut with a gun.

"You think those marines did this?" Russell said. "The ones with Nate and the others".

Harrt said nothing.

He climbed to his feet, exhaled, and considered everything. There was substance to Russell's theory. Three-dozen 'wealther marines could quickly achieve the quick kills that Harrt was looking at, but there was one problem: *why would 'wealthers kill one another? Unless... they weren't 'wealthers. Unless they were like the man Russell shot seconds earlier.*

Harrt turned to Russell, about to ask if he'd seen anything fishy earlier that day, but something halted him. A red dot was on Russell's chest. For a hair of a second, Harrt saw it, didn't think anything of it, then realised what it was.

Without thinking, Harrt tackled Russell, forcing the young man to the ground. Gunfire erupted from the hangar. The shooting was relentless, tearing up the doors that they came through seconds earlier. The strange thing was that the weapons were quieter than Harrt expected. He'd heard Earther guns fired before, but this was different: muted, silenced.

Once Harrt and Russell were in cover, they looked at each other.

"You good?" Harrt yelled.

Russell took a second, patting his torso and legs, checking for any wounds. "Yeah, you?"

Harrt nodded and took up his gun. It was apparent that the weapons fire was coming from inside the hangar: not far from the Phoenix. By Harrt's estimate, there were at least five active shooters.

"What the hell is going on?" Russell yelled.

"The Artemis isn't Roth's only target," Harrt replied.

CHAPTER THIRTY
VOL

The smell of burning flesh permeated the air as Vol, the Sadalmelik's crew, and the five 'wealther marines made their way to the bridge. The rest of the Artemis was just as ravaged as the med-bay. The dark and empty corridors were now home to the dead. Bodies lined the halls, many shredded to pieces by Cadu's vicious elemental summons. He'd torn a path to the bridge, leaving a wave of destruction in his wake.

When the group reached the big metal doors to the bridge, Ralph Hayward looked around the group with steely resolve.

"We don't stop shooting until Cadu is dead," he whispered. "Understood?"

Nobody argued.

Like the others, Vol checked the ammo in her rifle, pressed the stock against her shoulder and prepared for what lay ahead.

Hayward was the first to enter the command deck, closely followed by Vol, Scruffy, the five marines and Riggs covering the rear. The bridge was utterly different from the one Vol left just twenty-five minutes earlier.

A shrill klaxon was sounding, thumping against Vol's eardrums without forgiveness. The emergency LEDs in the ceiling flicked on and off, casting short blasts of crimson light against the darkness. Then the cycle would repeat. The monitors and workstations were smashed, burning or flickering where they'd sustained damage in all the carnage. The walls were covered in entrails and scorch marks, and the floor was littered with the dismembered bodies of dead officers.

Vol peered at Hayward and the others, who didn't seem overly phased by what they saw. She figured they were accustomed to such violence, and she needed to be the same. There was no use in being frightened by the horrific nature of the slaughter. Otherwise, she'd end up joining the dead too.

Suddenly, Vol heard a guttural cough to her right. She turned her head to see Jaudi pressed against a command console, with a burning hole in her chest and blood covering her uniform. Vol and Hayward shared a quick look, and the Earther nodded to Vol to check on Jaudi whilst he and the others kept watch.

Vol rushed to Jaudi.

"He..." Jaudi's voice was weak. The wounds she'd sustained were beyond lethal: Vol didn't need medical training to know that.

"Save your energy," Vol said, squeezing her hand.

"The alarm..." Jaudi looked in the direction from where the klaxon was originating. "Self destruct is... active..."

Jaudi's voice trailed off, and her grip on Vol's hand loosened. As Lieutenant Jaudi Meera died in her arms, all Vol could hear was her dying thoughts: *If you want to be with him, be with him.*

Vol swallowed a lump in her throat. She gently let go of Jaudi's hand and respectfully closed her eyes. A million thoughts and emotions whirled there as Vol stepped away from the body, but one thing overwhelmed the majority: a burning desire to live.

A tapping sound from the far end of the bridge drew Vol's attention. Hayward and the others had heard it too, and they proceeded forward with their weapons raised at the mezzanine floor twenty feet up.

Cadu was there. He casually leaned against the railing: as though all the violence and destruction he'd caused was entirely normal. He was covered from head to toe in blood, and when he held up Gane's severed head, Cadu smiled with a mania in his eyes.

"Looks like you've been outplayed, Mr Hayward," Cadu taunted, hoisting his morbid trophy for all to see.

He tossed Gane's head over the railing as though it were nothing more than an unwanted burden. It landed with a moist thud.

Everyone stayed on point, refusing to cringe at the sickening noise, and instead keeping crosshairs trained on Cadu.

The klaxon sounded from a console two metres to Vol's right. If what Jaudi said was right, then that was the Commander's station, the quickest and most critical system to shut off the self-destruct protocols. The panels and screen flashed with a countdown timer that Vol couldn't see. The ship-wide announcement hadn't kicked-in yet, so Vol figured they had more than fifteen minutes. Before Vol could think of approaching the console, Cadu cast a pillar of elemental energy into the machine. The Commander's station exploded on impact, sending sparks and fire into the air.

A giddy arrogance appeared on Cadu's face.

"There is no stopping what is to come. *His* word is divine, and I am the instrument of his will. This vessel will create the most glorious explosion, and I am the one to light the kindling".

It was the ramblings of a madman.

The Artemis was a big ship carrying a great deal of lethal weaponry. Surely, if Roth wanted to level one of Valour's continents, it'd be wiser to use that weaponry rather than rely on the fallout from a self-destruct sequence.

Besides, the self-destruct would take out a significant proportion of the Paradisian blockade...

Then the realisation hit Vol:

Roth's intention was to destroy the blockade. It was nothing to do with Valour. *But why would he do such a thing?*

Vol considered the scale of the Artemis, the weapons that she was likely carrying, and the ship's position amongst the blockade. She calculated that the explosion would take out —at least— a third of the blockade.

She glared at Cadu. Feral joy burned his eyes as he chuckled at Hayward and the others. He clenched his blood-soaked fists, and for the first time, Vol heard his thoughts:

I will finally prove my worth to you, Elder Xanathur.

That didn't sound right at all. *Xanathur. What the hell did Elder Xanathur have to do with all this?*

Vol didn't have time to think about it. A slew of gunfire and elemental summons filled the command deck. She looked out of her eye at Hayward, tucked behind cover. The Earther was pulling the pin off of one of his grenades.

Hayward tossed the bomb at Cadu's feet. The grenade exploded beside the Evoker, and a thick green smog enveloped him. Scruffy, Riggs and the others did the same. More gas filled the mezzanine.

An eerie silence fell over the command deck.

Vol kept her rifle trained on the toxic cloud, watching for any movement. She could only hope that Hayward's grenades had done the trick and incapacitated Cadu.

The sound of slow clapping reverberated around the command deck. Then Cadu's voice emerged from within;

"You'll need something a little more potent than that".

A metal item flew down from within the gas, landing between Vol and Hayward. Vol glanced down at the thing, quickly realising it was an explosive.

There was a blast that sent flame and debris flying in all directions. Vol wasn't at the epicentre of it, but she still felt its effects as she scrambled away to safety. The sudden force of the detonation sent her rib-first into the floor, and she felt something crack in her ribs. It was painful but she was still alive. That was all that mattered.

Thick black smoke engulfed the command deck, making it difficult to see anything beyond a few metres. Vol knew it would be a good thirty seconds before the ship's environmental controls would filter the smog out of the room: assuming Cadu hadn't deactivated that functionality.

Once again, the sound of gunfire filled the Command Deck, but it only lasted seconds. The screams from within the smoke were proceeded only by the sound of something sharp cutting through flesh. A summon followed, and Vol saw Riggs cut down in a violent inferno. Though his screams lasted but a heartbeat, Vol would never forget the agony in his howls.

She became oddly aware that she should feel fear. Everything around her was unparalleled to anything she'd witnessed before, yet Vol felt something different.

She figured she would likely die aboard the Artemis, so why not take Cadu down with her: or at least make sure he died in the explosion with the rest of them: *at least the universe would have one less asshole to worry about.*

Vol took up her rifle and quietly crawled back toward her previous position. She shuffled past a decapitated body, then two of the 'wealther marines. Vol could feel her heart pounding in her chest as she crept deeper into the smoke.

Suddenly, there was the sound of a struggle, and Ralph Hayward flew directly over her and crashed into a nearby wall. Her first instinct was to check on the big man, but as Vol climbed to her feet, Cadu emerged from the smoke.

There was savagery in his eyes.

Cadu struck her in the face with his hand. The impact of the strike caused Vol to fall backward, tumbling over a wrecked workstation. As soon as she hit the floor, Vol took up her gun and began to fire, but Cadu's Evoker reactions were faster. He darted under the laser fire and whipped forward before booting her across the room.

Vol landed hard against the bulkhead, feeling her shoulder crunch as she collided with the unmoving steel mass. She willed herself to get up: to face her enemy. As the smoke began to clear, Vol spotted Cadu heading straight toward her.

On the right side of the room, Scruffy tried to stop him by firing round after round. The modified Sanctum ammo made some impact on Cadu, but it wasn't enough.

Without mercy or forgiveness, Cadu turned to Scruffy, raised his palm and fired a pillar of elemental energy straight through the man. The last thing Vol saw of the Sadalmelik's bearded pilot was an explosion of blood and viscera that painted the surrounding area red. There was no tormented shriek —only violence and death.

Vol retreated while Cadu was busy celebrating his kill. He laughed as what remained of Scruffy keeled over to one side with a gut-churning crunch.

"Childs-play," Cadu mocked.

NATHAN

Unlike Nathan's previous visit to the Council Chambers, he didn't undergo any security screening: none of the crew did. But the marine platoon was stopped and checked, raising new questions in Nathan's head.

Impulsively, he chose not to wait for the marines and pushed ahead with his crew and Jareth in tow. Tariq and Koble walked beside him as they strode through the giant building. The administrators and staff were present and doing their work, but they looked fearful.

"I don't like this," Tariq murmured.

"No shit," Koble replied. "The sooner we get this over and done with, the better".

▲

Inside the hexagonal-shaped council chamber, Inon Waife, the political representatives and about two dozen soldiers were waiting. As Nathan walked through the doors, he was met with intense looks of resentment from the council. As before, the delegates sat in tiered bench seating that went up in rows, while Inon Waife stood in his box against the front wall like a judge in a courtroom.

Nathan noticed a look of victory on Waife's face as he stared at Jareth. It was impossible to ignore. Waife no doubt saw Jareth's compliance as a sign of weakness, and Nathan realised then and there that he'd helped him to achieve that.

It didn't feel good, knowing he was aiding Waife in undermining Paradisium's democracy. Sure, the EWB was the product of the Society and other separatist groups, all with nefarious interests, but the vote was a democratic decision made by the people. It was their choice to make all the terrible decisions they wanted, not Nathan's, not Jareth's and certainly not Waife's.

"Mr Jareth," Waife said, his deep voice filling the vast chamber. "Welcome to our sacred house of democracy"

Nobody said a word: not even a peep from the delegation who had been full of entitled bluster hours earlier.

Waife continued, "I am so glad you chose to help quell the anger and rage brewing above our clouds. I'm sure you understand these... *terrorists* are disrupting the safe running of this world, this government and, by extension, the safeguarding of the galaxy from the ever-growing Revenant threat. These protestors cannot be allowed to continue a moment longer".

Jareth's sneer implied outrage. "You have no idea of the enemy you face. They have manufactured all of this because it serves their purpose: likely to distract you from their true intentions. The people up there are simply doing what they've been led to believe is the right action".

Nathan could tell from his eyes that the Master of the House didn't appreciate Jareth's words one bit.

"And what intentions might that be?" Waife said. "Are you going to spin this grand council lies and deceit like all the other capitalist pigs? This Commonwealth was founded upon—"

That was the moment that Nathan stepped in. He was sick of the political posturing, the games and the bullshit. People's lives were at risk, and his patience had snapped.

"You both need to put your fuckin' egos aside," Nathan placed himself between Jareth and Waife. Shocked gasps followed from the delegation, and Nathan imagined one or two of them fainting in shock at his use of coarse language. "You can continue your name-calling and political shit later. Right now, you've got a speech to make to put out the fire".

He raised his voice to cut through the bullshit. Nathan didn't realise it at first, but as he spoke the honest and harsh truth, he could hear Jack in himself, and *it was odd realising that the old man had passed something down.*

Nathan looked at Jareth, then Waife:

"There's more important things to worry about than

which of you has the moral high ground. So get off your high horses and make the speech".

He could practically hear Astrilla cringing and Leviticus Dines dying inside, but Nathan didn't care. Someone had to say what needed to be said: *even if it caused offence or outrage.*

He looked at his crew, noticing subtle nods of approval from Koble and Tariq. Rain appeared calm and collected, almost refusing to acknowledge the awkwardness. James stood at the back, looking like he simply didn't belong *—an ex-junkie in the presence of the galaxy's decision-makers.*

When Nathan turned to Jareth, he was surprised to see the old man's prideful expression. It made Nathan feel awkward and uncomfortable, but it was there nonetheless.

Inon Waife slowly descended the staircase from his box to the ground floor in silence, his heavy footsteps echoing around the room. He gestured to his assistant, and the young woman pushed on a combination of buttons on her datapad.

The marble floor beneath Nathan's feet shifted apart, creating a large opening in the ground. A stone plinth rose into the Council Chamber from below, containing two podiums and a backdrop intended for press events.

When Waife was on the floor with the Phoenix's crew and the others, he looked reluctant: *like a gambler deciding whether to play his cards or fold.*

Waife shuffled to Jareth, practically standing toe-to-toe with the man;

"I will not stand for a planet that weaponises media and lies to justify acts of bigotry like the blockade above". Waife spoke in a low voice, his eyes glued to Jareth. "Earth and its oppressive ways are long dead. If this broadcast fails to manoeuvre the people in orbit, then I cannot control what happens next".

Jareth didn't back down, and his penetrating gaze didn't waver.

"I am not your enemy, Inon," Jareth said. "Paradisium is not your enemy. Despite the Fall and EWB, I still believe we can embrace our differences and share an alliance that will one day see the end of the Revenant: I truly believe that".

The room was silent.

Waife lingered, stepped away, and finally breathed out. The Master of the House nodded in what looked like agreement. *Perhaps there was hope for the middle ground after all?*

Then something changed.

A gunshot filled the Council Chamber.

Inon Waife's head snapped back in a haze of blood as the round exploded through his skull. Nathan's adrenaline kicked in before Waife's body hit the ground. He reached for his gun as the cold rush of some innate primal instinct kicked in.

Guns were drawn. Laser sights met targets both among the Phoenix's crew and the delegation, but no shots were fired. Nathan shifted his gaze to get a look at the situation. He saw 'wealther marines with weapons pointed at each other. He saw big men in dark armour at all entrances to the chamber. There must have been somewhere in the region of forty hostiles: if not more.

Then he saw the man who'd executed Waife: James.

"Do not draw that weapon, little cousin," he warned. "My men will not hesitate to gun you down if you test me".

"You?" Nathan said, unable to hide his shock. "You?"

"Me," James sneered, then shifting his eyes to Tariq, who looked equally as stunned. "Sorry old pal, nothing personal. Just business," James smirked.

Tariq said something angry that came out as a garbled and emotional mess of at least three languages. The fact that he was taken by surprise meant that he wasn't a part of this; Nathan was sure of that much.

James shifted one hand from his still smoking pistol and tapped a comms device on his jacket. "Austin, if any of them move, kill 'em".

An American voice emerged from James' device:

"Understood".

Nathan felt the rage squeeze his chest. The sense of betrayal was overwhelming.

James circled the crew and stopped in front of Nathan.

He pointed his gun squarely at Nathan's chest, and a look of arrogant malice filled his eyes.

"Drop the gun, Nate," James warned. "Let's not make this any harder than it needs to be".

"James, what on Earth are you doing?" Tariq exclaimed.

"Shut your fuckin' mouth, Tariq," James hissed, turning his gun to the middle-eastern man.

A strange, uncomfortable silence followed.

Nathan could almost see the blood drain from Tariq's face as the realisation set in.

"I've been waiting nearly a decade to say that to you," James spat. "Do you know how fuckin' tiring it is to pretend I give a shit about your crusade?"

The malice behind James' voice was venomous. Nathan had heard that same tone before: *the night they'd parted ways —the night James destroyed the Loyalty in a drug induced rampage.*

"I've had you fooled for years, Tariq," James snarled. "Did you seriously think a powerhouse like Alastair Roth wouldn't notice some washed-up freedom fighters investigating him? He sees everything".

Tariq said nothing, but Nathan did.

"You're a bastard!"

James turned away from Tariq and peered at Nathan:

"You really think you have the right to talk to me like that, Nate?" James said. He pointed at Astrilla; "I can have my men gun down this bitch at the drop of a fuckin' hat. All I need to do is say the word. Sure, she's fast, but I don't like her odds: not with all this firepower".

Nathan's jaw clenched at the threat, refusing to give James the satisfaction of showing any weakness. Inside, he was screaming: panicking for Astrilla and all the others. Anxiety crept up his scalp, and he had to force himself to exhale.

Never let them see you bleed, Jack said in his mind.

Without warning, James turned and fired. For a heartbeat, Nathan wasn't sure who the target was, but then it became blindly apparent.

Tariq collapsed to one side and screamed in agony. The bullet had gone into his left hip just above the thigh.

Instinctively, Nathan moved, hoping to check on Tariq, but he was met with a strike to the head from James, who slammed the butt of his pistol into Nathan's head. The impact of the blow forced him to the floor. His eyesight became blurry and sluggish. Everything seemed to mute, and there was an overwhelming sense that the world was vibrating around him.

Nathan was aware that the others were protesting the attack, but they were quickly silenced when James spoke something into his communicator. Through the haze in his vision, Nathan made out a big man behind James, walking to the benches and into the delegation. Two shots followed, then the sound of frantic screaming.

Nathan attempted to sit up.

Koble was shouting obscenities at James, who'd now moved away and was talking into his datapad. "Objective one complete: we have the Doctor. Objective two: complete, the tango is down. Moving to reacquire the vital asset".

Nathan slowly climbed to his feet. He saw James swagger around the chamber, waving his gun at the terrified 'wealther delegates. Despite feeling dizzy and light-headed, Nathan locked eyes with Rain and Koble.

Rain was looking at his holster, while Koble was trying to subtly get Nathan's attention by looking to and from his pistol on the floor. He knew that the two Sphinax were planning on doing something ballsy. It was stupid, dangerous, and reckless, but something needed to be done.

James moved to Jareth and grabbed him by the collar. He snarled at the Paradisian elitist and licked his lips as though he were about to tuck into a three-course meal.

"Mr Roth was looking forward to having a good ol' catch-up with you," James smirked. "But I need all the space I can get on my ship, so I guess you died in all the carnage".

Jareth's expression was unreadable.

"Your father would be ashamed of you".

James bit his lip; narrowed his gaze, and nodded, but there was no guilt there: no regret whatsoever.

Out of nowhere he laid a punch into Jareth's head. The force wasn't quite enough to take the old man off his feet, but it looked painful enough.

When Jareth straightened up, James smiled sadistically. He kept his eyes on Jareth but called out to one of his men.

"Austin, you're with me," he barked. "Blake, take care of this mess and rendezvous at the rally point. Remember, no survivors".

James' moved toward the exit with four of his guys. The rest of his unit stayed behind to participate in whatever was to happen next.

As he reached the door, James looked at Nathan:

"Well, lil cousin, it was a lovely family reunion while it lasted, but as the old saying goes, all good things must end".

"Fuck you," Nathan spat. "Still the same hopped-up junkie prick you were all those years ago. I should've killed you back in that bar".

James' smile was entirely hostile.

He looked past Nathan to his men surrounding the room, with the guns trained on everyone.

"Have fun, boys," James said.

For a heartbeat, everything seemed to move in slow motion. The mercs turned their weapons on the councillors and the crew. From the corner of his eye, Nathan was aware of Koble diving to the ground for the pistol while Rain provided covering fire. Dines had a gun in each hand and was already lining up his target. Astrilla's hands were glowing white with elemental energy.

Then everything started to move.

CHAPTER THIRTY-ONE
VOL

Cadu cast a summon, pinning Vol against the bulkhead and rendering her unable to move. Despite knowing the power of Evoker abilities, she strained as hard as her body would allow, willing herself to break free from the hold, but the struggle was to no avail.

Cadu closed in with a look of lunacy painted across his pale features. He licked his lips as though craving his next kill like a junkie desperate for a high. Vol wasn't sure why but she could hear Cadu's deranged thoughts as he moved forward.

He wanted her to fear him: craved to see her beg for her life, all in service of someone he wanted to satisfy. It was a sick and twisted desire that overrode all other thoughts and emotions: a fracture in his mind so powerful that it chipped away all semblance of right and wrong. Vol refused to give him the satisfaction, refusing to let terror paint her features.

"Any last words?" Cadu taunted, drawing a white flame in his palm.

"Screw yourself," Vol replied through gritted teeth.

Cadu smirked: as though she'd given him a taste of what he craved. He raised a flaming palm, ready to deliver the killing blow. Vol didn't look away. If Cadu was going to kill her, she'd make sure that he looked her in the eye when he did it.

Cadu made a surprised noise: a single outward breath

with a tiny vocalisation that didn't fit the situation. A split second passed, and Vol realised she wasn't dead.

Ralph Hayward stood behind Cadu with his knife lodged in the Evoker's back.

Cadu lurched forward, releasing his hold on Vol. She slid against the wall, watching as Hayward twisted the knife in Cadu's spine. The Evoker turned to face Hayward, but the big man wasn't phased by him at all.

In a low voice, Hayward said, "That's for Claire".

Without mercy, Hayward grabbed Cadu by the throat, lifting him into the air and slamming him into a workstation. Sparks and glass flew upon impact.

"Little bastard!" Hayward barked, squeezing down on the young man's windpipe. "Did you kill her? Did you kill Claire?"

"No," Cadu choked. "If only I had".

Rage filled Hayward's eyes, and he began to beat Cadu atop the console. The sound of strikes meeting flesh was deafening. Hayward's fists rained down upon Cadu, but Vol knew it wouldn't be enough.

Before she could do or say anything, Cadu cast a summon directly into Ralph Hayward. From Vol's perspective, Vol saw a thin pillar of white light emerge through Hayward's back where Cadu's attack penetrated his chest.

Ralph Hayward dropped to the floor.

As Cadu sat up, Vol pulled her pistol from its holster. She fired wildly, but Cadu simply absorbed the attacks as he strode toward her. He stopped before Vol with the same hungry and desperate expression.

Knowing the gun would do little more for her, Vol tossed it aside.

"Why?" she asked. "Why kill all these people for Roth?"

"*Roth?*" Cadu laughed. "This act of beautiful violence is not for a lesser being like Alastair Roth: it is for someone far more deserving. For them. For Xanathur. For Baylum. For the Void".

His words took a moment to process. Then one thing stood out above all else. Elder Xanathur: the mole. The traitor that Harrt and Dines had been hunting all this time. He was the one the Revenant had under their control—a man with access not only to Commonwealth military movements but to Astrilla's whereabouts.

Cadu grabbed Vol by the throat just as Hayward had done to him seconds earlier and began to crush her airway. He forced her onto the shattered console, pinning her back against the shattered glass of the workspace. Vol struggled against the hold, attempting everything she could to break free.

Cadu's Evoker strength was simply too much.

"The void has shown Xanathur the way" Cadu screamed manically. "You will not stop our undertaking".

As Vol's sight began to fall to darkness, images of the ones she loved flashed before her; the crew of the Phoenix Titan, her parents, her late husband, Muhne, and, of course, Harrt Oxarri. If these were her final moments, she'd spend them thinking about everything she adored, not the grim reality of her situation.

As she faced death, Vol thought of all the things she'd achieved and all the things she regretted. There were good times and bad: more bad than good, but the Phoenix, the crew and, of course, Harrt were recent highlights in her long Uvan lifespan.

Then she thought more about Harrt and how she wished things could've been different. It could've been fantastic, but alas, the universe was a fickle bitch.

Still, it was nice to think that maybe —just maybe— if they'd had a chance, she and Harrt could've made a go of things. Perhaps there was a beauty to be found in that final thought: that love —for lack of a better word— could form in the least likely of places and times.

Something changed.

Maybe it was the lack of oxygen to the brain, but Vol could tell Cadu's grip had softened. She sensed thoughts of horror and alarm from him as he peeled his psychotic gaze away.

The next thing Vol's oxygen-starved brain processed was movement in the space around her. Cadu shifted his attention to a third party. An elemental summon flew across the room, cutting through Cadu's torso like a knife through butter. Blood exploded into the air, and Cadu keeled over.

Vol didn't quite comprehend it. Everything felt so distant and dream-like. She coughed and breathed, then realised she was covered in Cadu's entrails.

As Vol allowed oxygen to fill her lungs, she tried to move; to get a good look at what had happened. Cadu was on the floor, dying in a pool of his own blood, gasping for air where the summon had blown out his lung.

Elder Repla limped into Vol's line of sight. The Sillix was clutching a grizzly-looking wound on her leg, which seemed to be bleeding at an alarming rate. A nasty burn covered one half of her face, and something sharp had cut into her shoulder, leaving behind an open wound that looked grim but not as bad as the leg.

"Are you okay?" Repla asked as she limped past Vol.

Vol nodded, her mouth too dry to form the words.

Repla walked to one of the dead soldiers and took his sidearm. She shuffled to Cadu, who was still coughing and spluttering on the ground like a wounded animal.

"Where is Xanathur?" Repla demanded. "Where is that traitor?"

Cadu's frenzied smile was bloody and defiant. He refused to answer the question, but one of his thoughts bled into Vol's mind: *through death, I complete my service to you, oh great Void. And to you, Elder Xanathur.*

Repla shook her head, pointed the gun at Cadu's skull and pulled the trigger. It was a gruesome execution without honour or mercy: *it was the least Evoker-thing that Vol had ever seen.* Perhaps Cadu deserved it for what he'd done. The gunshot reverberated around the bridge, causing Vol to notice the new ringing in her ears.

Repla tossed the gun aside and turned her attention to Vol.

"The self-destruct sequence is active, isn't it?" she said.

Vol nodded and pointed at the station that Cadu destroyed minutes earlier.

"We can't disable it: not in the time we've got left".

Repla chewed the inside of her cheek. "We must abandon ship".

Vol wracked her brains for a way to stop Roth's plan from coming to fruition. They couldn't shut down the self-destruct, and a ship the size of the Artemis' wouldn't have autopilot. It was clear to Vol what she needed to do, but before she could say anything, a cough caught her attention.

Hayward was lying on his side, blood everywhere around him. He coughed again, and Vol rushed to his side. He looked like shit: pale and groggy with little colour left in his usually tanned complexion.

"Looks like I got pretty fucked up," he said with a long, drawn-out breath. "Is that lil' bastard dead?"

"Try not to move," Vol said, examining his injuries.

There was a lot of blood and what looked like a hole in his ribs the size of a fist: it was a miracle he was still clinging to life. Vol shared a grim look with Repla.

"Is the nav system still online?" Hayward asked, his voice weak, but filled with resolve.

Vol glanced over her shoulder at the workstation. It was covered in blood, and the screen was flickering, but the manual controls looked to be intact.

"Help me over there," Hayward said.

"Why?"

He groaned in pain; "Someone's gotta get this ship as far away from the blockade as possible".

Vol shook her head, "We leave no man behind".

Hayward smiled at her protest. "I ain't gonna survive a wound like this, and I ain't dying on my back in some corridor while I slow y'all down". He squeezed Vol's forearm, "Let me die flipping Alastair Roth the bird".

"There's no way that—"

"Let me die on *my* terms," Hayward insisted. "I'm gonna bleed out in a matter of minutes. Let me make a difference before that happens".

Vol nodded reluctantly.

▲

Repla and Vol moved Hayward to the helmsman's station, and a long trail of blood followed. As Hayward sat there, breathing laboured shallow breaths, he flipped switches and consoles and grabbed the manual flight controls. The ten minute warning klaxon began to sound, and Hayward looked at Vol;

"Take the Sadalmelik," he said, handing her a control key from his combat vest. "She might be fast enough to outrun the blast".

Vol welled up in sadness. She didn't want to leave him to die alone, but something he said resided with her in a way that couldn't be explained away. Hayward knew he was a dead man, and rather than waste his last few minutes on hope, he chose to stay. There was no fear in the man at all. Even then, staring death in the eye, Hayward's mind whirled with a single motivation: *to save as many people as possible.*

That was who he was: not the corporate man that Vol met a year prior.

"Do me a favour…" Hayward said in a low voice.

Vol nodded.

"Tell Mahmoot that I'd do it all over again. Tell him that this fight was always worth fighting for". Then turning his eyes to the displays around him with grit and determination, Ralph Hayward said, "Now get outta here".

Vol took ahold of Repla's arm, slinging it over her shoulder. Together they moved toward the crew elevators, and as the doors to the command centre closed, Vol took one final look at Hayward. The big man was activating the Artemis' impulse engines and talking to the ship;

"Okay, darlin', let's see what you got".

Inside the elevator, Vol tapped the control panel, then propped Repla against the wall. The Sillix was still bleeding profusely from the thigh but looked determined if a little pissed with everything going on.

"What is it?" Repla asked with no emotion in her voice.

"We always suspected a mole was working for Baylum," Vol said, shaking her head. "I never thought it'd be one of you guys".

Repla scowled as though what she was saying was irrelevant under the circumstances. *What else were they going to discuss on a sixty-second elevator ride?*

"Cadu had no idea what he was doing," Repla muttered. "His mind was twisted by Xanathur to do all of this". Her voice was free of the bitterness that any other creature would convey at the moment. "I just can't believe that a good friend that I trusted for so long is a part of the Revenant".

"Why would Xanathur do this?" Vol asked. "He always seemed so—"

"Baylum has his methods," Repla cut in. "The River Prynn, as they call it, is a powerful tool of manipulation".

"What the hell does that mean?"

Repla looked anxiously at the screen indicating the elevator journey. "It means that we need to survive this ordeal so that Xanathur doesn't get away with his crimes".

KOBLE

All hell broke loose inside the Council Chambers. On a different plane of consciousness, Koble was aware of Rain scooping up a gun and diving to the floor. His ears understood that James' men were opening fire; some slaughtering the politicians, others gunning for the Phoenix's crew. Koble swept up his own handgun out of nothing more than pure reflex. In that split second, he was sure he was a goner. There were too many of James' men to count amongst the mass of fleeing, terrified 'wealther councillors.

Then Astrilla's voice broke through the madness;

"Get down!" she yelled.

The next thing Koble processed was an elemental summon that came in the form of an energy barrier, spanning almost twelve feet in diameter. Bullets and laser fire ricocheted off Astrilla's summon, but it only accounted for the hostiles who had the high ground.

Koble turned his attention to Nathan, who was outside of the Evoker's shield. Much to Koble's surprise, Jareth had pulled Nathan into cover behind the media plinth that Inon Waife summoned seconds before death. The Earthers were tucked in against the stone base, but it was slowly being ripped to shreds by hostile gunfire. Koble's first instinct was to help Nathan, but he was quickly deterred from that inclination as a bolt of laser fire ricocheted past his ear.

"Move together," Astrilla yelled while nodding toward the entrance.

Koble turned his eyes to Nathan and Jareth, aware they were outside Astrilla's protective field.

"Koble!" Astrilla screamed. "Move!"

It was the only option that didn't result in a bullet to the brain. Koble figured Nathan would have to hold out a few more seconds. At least back in the corridor, Koble and the others would have the cover required to mount an offensive.

There was one other thing that itched in Koble's mind. He'd seen Astrilla use all kinds of crazy summons, and he knew she couldn't hold it for long. This particular defensive move looked powerful and all-consuming: likely enough to render her unconscious if she over exerted herself.

The group moved with Astrilla, retreating to cover, as James' militia slaughtered the politicians and genuine 'wealther marines. It was a bloodbath the likes of which Koble had never seen before. The Society mercs were brutal in their slaughter, opening fire on packs of people as they tried to flee.

Koble fired, clipping one of the hostiles in the process. Rain did the same. Leviticus Dines was dragging Tariq with one arm while firing a handgun with his free hand. The chaos and violence of it all were overwhelming.

In those few seconds, Koble's mind was fixed solely on surviving. Then the cacophony of gunfire and screaming filled his mind. Then one thought overrode all others: *Alastair Roth's mission was nothing to do with Jareth or the trade at Hawtrey House.* He'd staged Hawtrey House to get

James on the inside to do what he was doing now: to capture Gordon and to kill Inon Waife.

Fifteen seconds later, Koble and the others were back at the entrance, using the doorway for cover. Astrilla dropped the shield and leaned against the wall to catch her breath. Koble could tell that it had taken its toll on her, but she'd recover quickly under the circumstances.

"We gotta get back in there," Koble yelled over the chaos. "Nate is still in there".

He quickly surveyed the new area, ensuring nobody was waiting to spring a trap. It became painfully apparent that James and his other unit had made light work of the first responders: there were over a dozen dead soldiers further up the corridor and several more ahead.

Koble turned to the other side of the room, where Dines was lowering Tariq to sit behind cover. A trail of blood followed Tariq along the wall as he slumped down. He was barely conscious, still gripping the gunshot wound on his hip.

"Don't worry about me," Tariq murmured. "Do what needs to be done. Stop them!"

Dines nodded and moved to the doorway for cover with a pistol in each hand.

Koble darted to the opposite side of the hall and took up position beside Dines. Together they opened fire and picked off two of the hostiles. Koble couldn't see Nathan or Jareth in all the confusion.

With Astrilla trying to recover, Koble decided to take charge of the situation.

He looked at Dines; "We gotta get back in there! On my mark, we move in together. Dines, you cover the left flank."

The Agent acknowledged the command.

"Rain, you cover the right".

There was no reply.

"Rain?"

Koble turned to see his old friend laying against the wall, grasping his chest. Blood was gushing from between his blue, furry fingers. Koble dashed to Rain's side and saw the gaping bullet wound. He looked strangely defenceless: as though his very essence had diminished between the gunfight and that moment.

"Rain!" Koble took ahold of his friend's paw.

Rain turned his head to face Koble. His usually strong face twisted in agony, but his eyes were strong and steady.

Rain managed the words, "Pluvium... forever..."

His breathing quickened. Rain's eyes locked with Koble's, then lost all focus. His breath stopped, and his body settled. The strength and life went out of him.

Rain was gone.

"Pluvium forever". Koble whispered, still holding Rain. He brought his friend closer, hugging the lifeless and bloody body against his chest and wanting to mourn and cry.

But he couldn't.

The sound of gunfire pulled Koble back into the moment. This was not the time to grieve; that would have to wait. Nathan was still in danger, and James' men were still killing people.

Koble wiped away a tear and grabbed Rain's fedora from the ground. He placed the hat on his friends head as a kind of tribute to the man he'd been: suave and stylish no matter the situation. Koble decided his old pal would rock that look in death.

Koble climbed to his feet, with his gun to hand. He paced back toward the doorway: back to the fight.

Astrilla and Dines were waiting there. They didn't say anything.

"Let's kill these bastards," Koble growled.

NATHAN

Despite his groggy and undeniably concussed state, Nathan's aim did not falter. He lined up his sights on a man disguised as a 'wealther marine and squeezed the trigger. The imposter's head exploded in a shower of blood and brains. As Nathan lined up his next target, someone tackled him, and he felt the grip on his gun falter.

The impact was enough to take Nathan off his feet and force him behind the media plinth. A split second later, a burst of gunfire tore up the ground and surrounding area where Nathan had been.

Someone just saved his life, and that someone was David Jareth.

"Carter!" Jareth yelled, trying to snap him out of his dazed state.

Nathan blinked in confusion as gunfire rained down on the plinth.

"Carter!".

Something innate awoke inside Nathan. Maybe it was adrenaline kicking in or some deep-rooted human response to danger, but things suddenly became clear again. His eyes widened, and he came back to the here and now. Nathan noticed he was no longer holding his gun, and his holster was empty.

He grabbed Jareth by the collar and yelled, "Where's my fucking gun?"

Jareth swung his head out of cover, then back again, evidently, spotting Nathan's gun in the middle of the kill zone. He must've dropped it when Jareth tackled him.

"We may have a slight problem," Jareth mused.

As bullets ricocheted against the plinth, Nathan calmed his breathing and attempted to understand everything around him. He concentrated on his heartbeat: on the mild thumps of circulating blood around his veins. Then somehow, he was looking at everything around him from a different angle. His mind processed the active shooters, the situation and the best possible route to survival.

Jareth shook him by the shoulders, forcing Nathan out of his near-meditative state;

"We do not have time for that!" Jareth insisted.

From the other side of the room, Nathan heard an enraged Koble enter the hall, along with Dines and Astrilla. Koble was on the left flank, cursing and screaming as he proceeded forward while firing wildly into the mercenaries. Dines and Astrilla took the right and centre, picking off the hostiles as they moved together. Elemental summons began to fly, and Nathan saw the opportunity he needed.

He grabbed Jareth by the back of the shirt and practically dragged the old man from cover. Along the way, Nathan scooped his handgun from the floor and made toward a side door on the left. Then as Nathan got to within a hundred yards of the exit, a second group of Paradisian mercs burst through with their weapons raised. Nathan took aim, but before he could fire, an elemental summon struck one of the hostiles, sending her soaring over Nathan's head and crashing into the media plinth with a scream.

For a split second, Nathan wondered if perhaps he'd involuntarily cast an elemental summon, but he quickly realised that wasn't the case. The blast hadn't come from Astrilla: she was on the other side of the room fighting off the majority of the enemy force. So whoever had attacked was directly behind the hostiles.

Elder Yuta engaged the second group in combat. She made light work of the half dozen thugs, cutting them down with surprising ease.

Six against one was nothing to the seasoned Evoker.

Summons sliced and stabbed through torsos. Fire radiated around her. Within seconds Yuta stood in the middle of a circle of dead mercenaries —her chest heaving from the exertion.

She grabbed a rifle from the ground, and tossed it to Nathan.

"We must end this madness," Yuta said.

Nathan checked the weapon was loaded and shot the Elder a thumbs up.

She didn't respond in kind.

Now armed, Nathan moved back into the fight with Yuta at his side. He fired, shooting a bald man down in a haze of blood. He picked off a second. Then a third.

He lost count, and seconds later the fight was over.

An eerie silence fell over the Council Chambers as the last of James' militia fell, broken only by the sounds of wreckage falling from the walls and the cries of dying politicians.

The devastation was unreal: like something carved from a nightmare. Blood and bodies littered the once magnificent government building. Debris and spent bullets were everywhere. An acrid smell of death filled the space.

The silence wasn't welcome. Sure, the combat had ended, but the absence of sound allowed the mind to process the violence that just happened.

"Are you okay?" Nathan asked Astrilla, noting the wash of emotions on her delicate features.

Astrilla placed a hand against his temple, causing Nathan to feel a stinging sensation that he'd failed to notice. It hadn't even dawned on him that he'd suffered an injury, but he quickly recalled that James had struck him minutes earlier. *Perhaps that explained the woozy feeling that was slowly overpowering his senses.*

"You need a medic," Astrilla said.

Their quiet exchange was interrupted as Koble tossed a spent shotgun to the floor. The Sphinax moved slowly, his face flat and emotionless and his paws in tight fists, ready to break bones.

When Nathan's eyes met Koble's, he saw sadness and a desire to get even. Nathan looked around the chamber, accounting for everyone except Tariq and Rain: then Nathan felt sudden nausea as gravity pulled him back into reality.

Nathan asked, "Where's Rain?"

Koble shook his head and slid down against the wall with his face in his paws. A cold rage crept up Nathan's neck and into his skull. He refused to believe it. Rain, the self-proclaimed *finest pilot in the galaxy*, was gone.

James had done that: he'd robbed the universe of a wonderful, kind soul.

Violent thoughts filled Nathan's mind, but it felt wrong to talk of violence and revenge at that moment. Koble was suffering. Hundreds of others with families and friends were lying there, slaughtered by James' militia.

Grief came in all shapes and sizes, and Nathan wasn't sure how to process it. He chose anger, knowing he'd need that to fuel what was next.

Coughing came from one of the hundreds of bodies. Nathan moved toward the media podium only to find one of James' mercenaries struggling to reach for his gun. Both of his legs were broken, where he'd suffered a strike of elemental energy, and a gruesome gunshot wound was on his shoulder.

The man's eyes met Nathan, and he raised his hands in what looked like mock surrender.

"You got me…" He coughed, turned his head, and spat a mouthful of blood.

"Where the fuck is James heading?" Nathan demanded.

A calculating smirk formed on the merc's face.

"I ain't tellin' you shit".

Nathan thought about keeping him alive: about breaking the bones in his fingers and hands until he gave up James' location.

Then Nathan's mind turned to Rain, who was laying dead outside in the hall. He thought of the hundreds of unarmed politicians whose blood and bodies lined the stocks: of their families and loved ones

Then Nathan thought of the mercy James' men had shown him and his people.

His crew.

His friends.

His family.

His lover.

James and his unit had threatened all of that. It could've easily been another Mirotose Station incident.

Maybe that was exactly what James was going for? Maybe he wanted Nathan to lose another crew. Maybe James wanted history to repeat itself?

Never again.

Nathan pulled the trigger and a plume of scarlet blood flew up into the air as the mercs skull snapped violently to one side.

It was easier than he cared to admit.

▲

It took less than a minute for the Commonwealth's first emergency personnel to arrive on the scene. Medics attended to Tariq while others checked for survivors among the dead. Dines tried and failed to raise an alert with High Command. Instead, he contacted a buddy who was an ex-special agent. That was when everything about the situation became clear. The Council Chambers were one of several targets, all hit within five minutes of each other.

Two of Valour's four orbital cannons had been destroyed. The High Command building was a smoking wreck, and a broadcast station had been reduced to ash. There was also word of Paradisian terrorists gunning down innocent civilians as they fled the carnage. In summary, it was a shit show of the highest calibre.

One of the medics urged Nathan to allow her to examine him. The wound on his head hurt, but he'd live: that was better than a whole bunch of people. He politely declined the offer and insisted that he'd get checked out later.

After a minute of looking at the devastation in the Council Chamber, Nathan wanted to step outside. He moved to the outer corridor, where Tariq was sitting in a pool of blood. He'd been shot twice: once in the hip and another in his shoulder. He looked weak and pale, but there was clarity to his gaze. Tariq's eyes darted to Nathan as he knelt down beside him. The middle-eastern man gripped tightly on Nathan's sleeve, leaving a bloody handprint on the material.

"I'm sorry, Nathan. All of this was my fault..." Tariq exhaled. "I caused all of this... I brought you to James..."

"You didn't know," Nathan said, clinging to Tariq's hand for comfort. "This was the work of James and Roth".

James: just saying his name made Nathan seethe with anger.

"I played into Roth's hand," Tariq whimpered. "I was a pawn in his game. I—"

Nathan stopped him, "We'll make this right. I swear".

Nathan spotted Rain's body as he moved off. The Sphinax's face was covered by a jacket that had already soaked up the blood.

James had done that: he may not have been the one to pull the trigger, but he was undoubtedly responsible.

Knowing that his cousin was working for the enemy made Nathan feel sick, but it wasn't just for the violence there. He'd allowed James back into his life. Once again, he'd fallen for the lies and deception, only this time James wasn't looking for a chemical high.

Nathan swore that he would make James pay for what he'd done. All their history; their once brotherly bond was gone. Now, all that remained was Nathan's need for retribution.

Suddenly it dawned on him that James had nowhere to run —not with the blockade still in place. He wasn't finished on Valour. He had another objective: he'd said so right before the slaughter.

"Moving to reacquire the vital asset"

Nathan ventured back into the main chamber, trying his best to avoid looking at the dead. He spotted Astrilla, Koble, Dines and Yuta at the centre of the room. As Nathan approached, he could hear Dines relaying something he'd heard over the comms:

"They've hit another three sites in the last ten minutes," Dines said. "This was a highly organised and coordinated attack. Whoever did this—"

Nathan cut him off. "So where the fuck are they heading next? What other key targets haven't they hit yet?"

Dines' face darkened. "What do you mean?"

"Those fuckers have Gordon. They killed Rain and tried to kill the rest of us. I ain't letting them get away," Nathan said, gritting his teeth. "I'm going after them".

"Me too," Koble said, his voice low and angry.

Astrilla tilted her head at their remarks;

"You know it's not as simple as guessing where James is heading?"

"That is very correct," Jareth mused as he stepped into the conversation. "Fortunately, I think I know where they are going".

"Where?" Nathan demanded, darkness in his voice.

Jareth took up a rifle from one of the dead mercenaries,

checking the sights and grabbing a stash of ammo from the body.

"There is one thing that Roth cares about more than the Society," he said, pushing the magazine into the gun. "That, my friends, is his legacy. His son. His heir".

"The Containment Facility…" Nathan said. "They're gonna bust Christian Roth outta prison..."

Koble straightened as though he were in deep thought. Then he moved toward Jareth. For a moment, Nathan wondered if Koble would maul the elitist: it wouldn't be the first time emotion had gotten the best of him.

To Nathan's surprise, Jareth offered Koble the rifle, and the Sphinax accepted it.

"He's right," Koble nodded. "They'll go to the prison".

"Then we should take the Phoenix," Astrilla concluded. "It'll be faster than any inner-planet transport they're using".

Nathan glanced at Dines; "Can you contact the prison and give them a heads-up?"

"The blockade is still making comms difficult," Dines replied. "I'll set up a command centre here and try to coordinate emergency efforts, but you gotta assume you'll be on your own".

It wasn't an ideal situation, and Nathan knew it. Sure, using the Phoenix would speed things up, but James still had a ten minute headstart.

As Nathan turned to leave, Jareth handed him a stash of ammo.

"Be careful, Carter," he said.

CHAPTER THIRTY-TWO
NATHAN

Scenes of brutal bloodshed continued throughout the exterior halls of the Council Chambers. Bodies peppered with bullet wounds littered the floor like a slaughterhouse. The number of dead prompted Nathan to wonder how many people James had at his disposal. There'd been at least thirty inside the Council Chamber alone, which didn't include the eight or nine James left with —including the big man called *Austin*. At the same time, more strategic sites were attacked, including two of the orbital defence cannons: *both highly defended 'wealther assets.*

That meant James had more than a few dozen at his command. By Nathan's best guess, there was a minimum of a hundred thugs working alongside his traitorous cousin.

One question remained, *how many of those hundred-or-so guys would be at the Containment Facility?*

When Nathan, Koble and Astrilla made it outside, the devastation of James' attack became apparent. The battalion that had previously been stationed outside the Council Chamber was now replaced by a smoking crater and a scattering of bullet-riddled bodies. The tanks previously roaming the square were nothing more than charred debris: struck by something highly explosive.

To the naked eye, it looked as though someone in the blockade had fired a missile from orbit, taking out the bulk of the battalion in one fell swoop before a ground force had mopped up the survivors.

"We've gotta move," Nathan said to Koble and Astrilla.

RUSSELL

Bullets whipped around Russell and he'd never felt more outmatched in his life. The five-plus shooters in the hangar had the tactical advantage, with better gear and more room to manoeuvre. Russell and Harrt were effectively pinned down inside the restricted area, which consisted of a corridor full of dead 'wealthers and a closed office that led nowhere.

They had some cover in the form of a half-dozen tipped-over lockers, but Russell knew they wouldn't hold out for long. For three minutes, the hostiles outside fired into the corridor where Harrt and Russell took refuge. Then, as the lockers began to give way, they retreated into the office.

It was a closed space, with no windows and a single door. Three workstations to manage the inbound and outbound freight were at the centre. Another row of lockers was on the left side, and an old couch was on the right. Harrt hammered the door control, and a split second later, they were sealed in the office.

Minutes passed.

In Russell's head, this was to be a hold-out-as-long-as-possible scenario. He knew the odds were against them. After all, Russell wasn't armed for the situation, and his enemy certainly was. He and Harrt took cover behind the workstations, aiming their pistol at the door, anticipating someone to kick it open at any moment.

Nothing happened.

It was as though the hostiles were regrouping.

Then everything happened at once.

A charged explosion blew the door off its hinges and halfway across the office. Smoke grenades followed, and within seconds, Russell's visibility was dramatically reduced. He heard muted voices from the doorway: one American, the other something European: both sounding as though they belonged to people wearing breathing apparatus.

Russell couldn't see Harrt through the thick smoke.

Instead, he saw three different targeting lasers sweeping around the room. The hostiles were moving confidently, suggesting they were using thermal vision gear.

Suddenly Russell heard a yelp, then panic, then gunfire. Harrt was making a play: albeit a dangerous one.

Russell moved out, tracking the red targeting lasers and making an estimated guess as to where the hostiles were standing. He aimed his pistol into the smog and picked a target. He braced his wrist against the workstation and pulled the trigger three times.

The first round met flesh. Its recipient screamed, and the targeting laser dipped for a beat. The second met nothing but thin air while the third glanced against something metal: probably armour. Then another shooter must've spotted Russell and began firing in his direction.

One hostile was wounded, the other was fighting Harrt, and the third was on Russell. That meant there were two more, either outside the hangar or working to find an alternative route.

Russell dipped into cover and belly-crawled alongside the workstation, hoping to reposition and take his attacker by surprise. When he lifted up, the targeting laser was on him, and Russell immediately darted to the floor, barely avoiding a flurry of weapons fire.

HARRT

As Harrt tackled the first shooter, he became aware of clumsy gunfire from Russell's position. He'd hoped he could take down one guy, put a gun to his head and then use the man as a bargaining tool with the others.

Alas, that wasn't the case. Russell fired three shots, immediately giving away his position, which was precisely what Harrt was hoping to avoid. Russell was a good shot in a fair fight, but the men they were up against had a distinct advantage: better gear, guns, more training than Russell, and they could see him as clear as day using their visual headgear.

Russell's first gunshot hit one guy in the leg, causing the man to drop to one knee and yelp in agony. The second and third didn't register in Harrt's mind. All he knew was that he had to switch up his attack with the guy he was fighting. He landed hard on top of the hostile, pushing the man's gun to one side to avoid a burst of bullets that quickly followed. The stray gunfire whipped past the other goons and tore up the couch and wall.

Harrt's attacker was in full combat gear, including a metal helmet over his head, which made him slow and sluggish in a tight situation. Before the mercenary could offer a challenge, Harrt placed his pistol against the man's exposed neck and pulled the trigger.

He felt the man wretch as the laser round tore through flesh and airway. Blood hosed out of the wound, and Harrt felt the hostile go limp.

One down, two to go.

Harrt grabbed the first attacker's weapon, a heavily modified Earth rifle that felt like the kind of thing Hayward had aboard the Sadalmelik. More gunfire erupted from the back of the room, where Russell was fighting off one of the mercs.

Harrt's first thought was to go to him, but then he caught a glimpse of the third attacker that Russell shot seconds earlier.

The man spotted Harrt a second too late.

Harrt pulled the trigger.

The silenced burst of bullets smashed into the armoured thug, not enough to kill or break the protective layer of his chest plate but certainly enough to force the man to the floor. Harrt moved up, got to within a foot of the dazed mercenary and fired again. This time, the range of his weapon and the bullet spread combined was enough to cave in the thug's helmet.

Harrt could just about see human eyes beneath the metal.

Without ceremony or question, he forced the barrel of his gun into the crack of the helmet and fired. The hostile slumped over.

Harrt was about ready to go for the third merc, still attacking Russell when a blast of elemental energy flew past his shoulder and collided with the man, reducing him to a pile of ash.

When the smoke cleared seconds later, Astrilla was in the doorway, her hands still glowing from the attack.

"Are you okay?" she said.

"Damn good timing," Russell replied breathlessly.

NATHAN

When Nathan, Koble and Astrilla reached the hangar, they all heard the same unmistakable sound of silenced gunfire. Two men were positioned by the restricted area with their guns raised into a smog-filled corridor.

The first went down quickly. Nathan shot him in the leg and then hammered his skull into the wall, hoping to keep him alive for questioning. Koble was less kind to the second: his gunshot was precise and lethal and killed the armoured thug in a heartbeat.

Astrilla rushed ahead into the smoke-riddled passage. Seconds later, she emerged with Harrt and Russell, both fine but slightly shaken.

"What the hell happened here?" Nathan asked.

Russell blew out his lips and pointed over his shoulder.

"We found bodies, and the next thing we knew, these assholes were doing their best to kill us". Russell gestured to the unconscious mercenary that Nathan had taken down.

"Pretty sure these guys are Paradisian".

That part didn't come as a surprise.

"What happened to you guys?" Harrt asked.

"I'll tell you on the ship," Nathan replied. Then gesturing to the unconscious thug, "Koble, bring this piece of shit aboard. I've got questions for him".

As they headed to the Phoenix, Harrt walked alongside Nathan with a questioning look in his eye:

"Where exactly are we heading?" He asked.

"Containment Facility; on the double," Nathan replied.

VOL

Exhausted but driven by a will to survive, Vol dragged Repla toward the Sadalmelik. The Elder was just about conscious. She'd lost a lot of blood and could barely stand, but Vol wasn't going to leave her behind like Hayward.

Nobody else was going to die on her watch.

Klaxons and warning announcements of the imminent self-destruct assailed her ears. Red emergency lights flashed around the hangar. It would've been easier to access the escape pods, but with the thousands of Paradisian ships nearby, Vol was sure they'd shoot it down. Behind the stick of the Sadalmelik, she had access to weapons, shields and a semi-manoeuvrable ship. It might not get far, but it was the best option.

When Vol finally made it aboard the Sadalmelik, she breathed a sigh of relief. She hauled Repla through the gallery-like corridors of Tariq Mahmoot's ship, doing her best to ignore the trail of green blood that stained the white ceramic floor.

In the cockpit, she lowered Repla into the copilot's seat. The Evoker winced as Vol pulled two safety harnesses over her legs and torso.

"Have you ever flown a ship like this?" Repla mumbled.

Vol took the pilot's seat and buckled herself in. She took a cursory glance at Scruffy's workstation, figured out where the critical controls were, and then eyed Repla.

"Given the circumstances, we can't be picky".

Repla exhaled, tapping one of the copilot's screens and leaving a bloody fingerprint on the display.

"What can I do?" she asked.

Vol didn't reply and instead activated the engines.

She manually overrode the docking release, allowing the Sadalmelik to disengage the magnetic clamps holding it inside the Artemis. Vol skipped all pre-flight exercises, wary that the clock was ticking.

The ship lifted slightly. There was a loud mechanical whir, followed by a bang, as the clamp hit the hangar floor.

Then within seconds, the Sadalmelik left the confines of the Artemis. The moment should have served as a relief; however, once Vol laid eyes on the sheer magnitude of the blockade, she couldn't help but grimace.

There were thousands upon thousands of ships: all tightly sandwiched together. Most were civilian transports, but there was the odd corporate gunship in the mix. The scale of it was breathtaking in a horrifying way. All those people around the Artemis were at risk, and there was nothing anyone could do about it.

An alarm sounded beside Vol, and she craned her neck to look at one of the control panels. It showed that the Artemis was spinning up its gigantic impulse engines, and in return, the Paradisians were either targetting the warship or moving closer to keep it in place.

Vol swallowed a lump in her throat as she thought about Hayward. He was laying down his life to get that ship away from the blockade. It was an act of sheer bravery, and in return, the Paradisians would fire their weapons at him or get in his way.

The sheer ignorance of it was tragic.

Vol surveyed the area, trying to weigh up the best escape. She could head toward Valour and hope to outrun the imminent fallout, or she could try to make the jump to FTL.

Neither was great.

The FTL option required complex manoeuvring through the blockade and directly away from Valour. Unfortunately, Hayward was slowly heading in that direction with the Artemis, and Vol had no idea how much time the ship had left.

That meant the only viable solution was to gun it for Valour and hope the Sadalmelik could outrun the blast, the fallout and any Paradisian gunfire.

"Something tells me this isn't going to be pleasant," Repla frowned.

Vol could only nod in response.

HAYWARD

Aboard the Artemis, Ralph Hayward sat at the helm, blood pouring from his open chest wound. He'd grown lightheaded and was starting to pass in and out of consciousness. His initial plan was to send the ship into FTL and drop out in the middle of the sun or anywhere else, but it wasn't possible.

Cadu had damaged the Artemis beyond all repair. The main drive was out, leaving only impulse engines, which wouldn't get him far quickly.

So the plan had to change.

He put the Artemis into complete reverse, slowly backing the giant warship away from the blockade and toward an empty patch of space. He hoped that by doing so, he could minimise the fallout. People were going to die; that was a fact, but maybe —just maybe— he could save a few thousand by moving the Artemis back.

One minute to detonation, a ship-wide alarm announced.

Hayward stared at the protesting ships, wondering if the gullible idiots of Paradisium would ever know of his sacrifice. Maybe one day, when their cultural standards for leaders and role models had evolved, they'd appreciate what he'd given in his service.

"They better build a fuckin statue of me... I'll be pissed if there isn't a statue..."

Hayward took a cigar and lighter from his vest. He placed it in his mouth and pressed a flame to the tip. Then took a long drag and tossed his lighter across the room.

Twenty seconds until detonation.

Hayward couldn't help but shudder. He'd thought about death, worried about it and then accepted it all in minutes, but now the weight of the moment sunk in.

It was weird how the universe threw curveballs like this. He'd always hoped to live to some ripe old age after years of de-ageing therapy like the other pampered pricks on Paradisium.

Maybe one-hundred and thirty years old? Perhaps one-hundred fifty if his genes had been up to the challenge?

Alas, forty-something would have to do.

Weirdly, there was comfort in knowing his sacrifice would save lives. Maybe those people could go on and achieve great things? Maybe there was some future leader who'd usher in a new dawn for Paradisium out there in the mix.

Ten seconds to detonation.

Hayward puffed on the cigar. He pulled his datapad and gazed at his screensaver of Claire. Those days seemed so distant now, but he figured if there were life after death, she'd be first in line to greet him. *Maybe they could still make a go of it on the other side?*

Five. Four. Three.

Hayward leaned back. He pictured his childhood home in Texas and recalled how the sun used to set on the horizon. There was warmth in that memory: whimsy. Simpler times.

Two.

His final thoughts turned to the living: to Tariq, Nathan Carter, and the others. He hoped they were still out there: hoped that someone could take the fight to Roth and put a bullet between his pig-like eyes.

Maybe justice could one day be served.

One.

Hayward closed his eyes as the Artemis exploded.

NATHAN

Once the group was back aboard the Phoenix, Harrt threw himself into the pilot's seat as though he'd never left. It was good in a weird way to see him back at the helm, though Nathan wished it were under different circumstances.

The Phoenix lifted into the gloomy sky. Despite the torrential rainfall, long plumes of smoke from the Council Chambers could be seen on the horizon. From above, it looked like a scene of pure chaos, with medical ships and fire crews tending to the scene.

Nathan took the copilot's seat and told Harrt and Russell what had happened. He spared no detail, including James' betrayal, the deaths of Rain, Inon Waife, the Council and the severe injury Tariq had sustained.

Harrt was silent for a good minute, until finally he said;

"I thought your cousin was a little off, but I assumed it was his prior addiction. To think he was under our noses this entire time..."

"He played a lot of people," Nathan replied. "Including Tariq and Hayward for almost decade. Whatever he's doing, it's a part of something Roth's planned for a long time".

"You actually think they planned all of this?"

"Most of it," Nathan nodded. "But something this complex with so many moving parts isn't controllable. There has to be variables. Even if Roth is some great fuckin' mastermind, he can't account for every eventuality".

Russell grasped the back of Nathan's chair.

"What does that mean, Cap?"

"It means that Roth's plan has gone pretty well so far, but somewhere along the line, he fucked up," Nathan said. "Or rather his son, fucked up".

"You mean Christian?" Russell said.

Nathan nodded.

"Alastair Roth has targets, right? Waife, the Council, the Orbital cannons—"

"And Gordon..." Russell cut in. "Why the hell would Roth want Gordon?"

It was an excellent question that Nathan couldn't answer. *Why would one irrelevant man matter to the likes of Alastair Roth?* If it were Jareth, that'd be another story: he was an anticipated target that had pissed off Roth, but Gordon was a nobody.

Nathan peered at the back of the room, where Koble was still guarding the unconscious and bound mercenary they'd captured minutes earlier.

"That's a question for that guy," Nathan said. "But right now, we gotta intercept James and his unit and take 'em down before they can bust Christian Roth outta that jail".

"Then what?" Harrt replied. "With the Council and Inon Waife dead, the Commonwealth is without leadership. We can't take on Roth without—"

"One thing at a time," Nathan replied. "Objective one, we get Gordon back. Objective two is take down James and his unit. Anyone left alive can spill all of the Society's secrets, and hopefully, we can avoid any—"

A groan emerged from the back of the room and Koble called Nathan over. The unconscious hostile was awake. Without his armour, the prisoner was less physically impressive than he first appeared. For a mercenary, he wasn't what Nathan expected: average build, average height and not especially muscular.

He was around fifty, but the de-ageing treatments he'd undergone made him look thirty. He had dark buzz-cut hair and a perfectly trimmed beard interrupted by a newly formed cut where Nathan slammed his face into the wall earlier.

Nathan pulled his pistol from its holster and knelt to look the bound thug in the eye.

"Here's how this is gonna work: I ask, you answer," Nathan growled. "If you don't answer, I shoot you".

The man straightened up, smiled arrogantly and looked around at Nathan, Koble, and Astrilla. He eyed each of them thoughtfully as though making a mental note of their features so he could use them later. Nathan had already decided there wouldn't be a later: not for this guy or any of James' unit.

"So," he mused with a west coast American accent. "This is the Phoenix Titan..."

"Shut your mouth," Nathan snapped. He quickly composed himself, realising that he'd lost his cool and that interrogations tended to improve when he didn't rage. "How many of you are there? I want numbers, your targets, and your rendezvous location. Now".

"You got no clue, have you?" the thug laughed. "Y'all have lost. Game over. The Society has won. It'll always win".

Nathan pressed his gun into the man's head.

"Where is Taggart?"

"The guy with glasses?" The thug laughed again. There was no fear there at all. "Mr Roth wanted him for some *personal reasons*".

The thug wrenched his jaw and bit down; grinding his molars together. There was a loud click as something inside his mouth broke apart.

Nathan tried to act swiftly, grabbing the man before the poison he'd swallowed took effect, but it was too late. The thug's eyes glazed over, and he foamed at the mouth.

Nathan had seen the same drug back in the days aboard the Loyalty. Jack had cited it as something called cyanide, but in the Outer Worlds, it was colloquially referred to as *chow.* The drug had more or less the same end result as its Earth counterpart; immediate death upon ingestion, generally causing a massive stroke in its victim.

The fact that this seemingly low-level merc in the Society's operation was willing to kill himself rather than spill his guts told Nathan one thing: the Society's people were loyal.

He backed away from the body and asked Koble to throw it out of the airlock once they were over the ocean: *just in case the chow had any explosive element within.* It was unlikely, but Nathan wasn't willing to rule anything out at this stage. Alastair Roth had shown his wit and cunning in the field of deception.

Smoke and mirrors at its finest, as Tariq had said.

As Koble grabbed the corpse to haul it away, the partially deconstructed comms terminal beside Harrt began to alarm violently. It sounded like a distorted jumble of loud, high tones that evoked a primal feeling of danger in Nathan's mind. When he listened closer, he heard something that resembled screaming.

"What the?" Harrt said, punching the screen beside him.

Nathan and Astrilla gathered around the pilot's station as Harrt adjusted the settings on the terminal.

"Is that the long-range comms?" Astrilla asked. "How is that possible?"

"I'm not sure," Harrt replied, tapping the screen.

The display simplified the incoming transmissions, revealing that hundreds —if not thousands— of emergency broadcasts were coming from orbit. A flood of tangled communications began to play out from the speakers, and at that moment, Nathan felt a cold shudder pass down his spine.

"Please help!"

"The Commonwealth is killing us!"

"Mayday!"

"Help us!"

Nathan was grateful when Harrt muted the speakers. It was blindly apparent that something terrible had happened to the blockade.

"It's the Paradisians," Astrilla concluded grimly.

Nathan felt his chest tighten a little.

The entire time he and the others assumed that the blockade was a show of force or a distraction for the 'wealthers, but he'd been wrong.

The protestors were as much a target as Waife and the Council. Roth, through Markus Holland, had led the gullible, the righteous and the patriotic to Valour, like lambs to the slaughter.

INTERLUDE
ROTH

The blast was just as he imagined: *undeniably spectacular.*

Watching a Commonwealth Warship explode in a blinding ball of white fire from the comfort of his private quarters made Roth feel invincible: like a spectator from the heavens observing a tidal wave wipe away all life in its path.

At first, the bright light was contained, but it quickly spread into the blockade: consuming many Paradisian ships in its wake.

It was divine, but it wasn't perfect. Someone aboard the Artemis had moved the damn thing ever so slightly, but their sacrifice was nothing in the grand scheme of things.

Yes, the initial explosion killed less than Roth hoped, but the fallout was the grand finale: *at least to this part of the pièce de résistance.*

Roth keenly looked on as a Paradisian Cruiser collided with what he could only assume had been the bulkhead of the Artemis. The impact caused another explosion, then another, then another.

It was the most glorious ripple effect that was of Roth's creation.

The shockwave that followed the first explosion swept across the protest like a tsunami. While the larger ships could hold their position in orbit, the smaller ones felt the full effect of the impact.

The sheep will follow the shepherd.

Roth could only hope that he'd made Theodore Jareth proud. He raised his glass to the pandemonium outside and uttered the words that had defined the Society for generations.

"Novus ordo seclorum".

CHAPTER THIRTY-THREE
VOL

There was an initial burst of light that dwarfed everything. All at once, the Artemis exploded from within, shattering into a billion fragments. The fuel, oxygen, and chemicals that served as blood for the FTL engine burned in the endless void of space, only to be smothered in the vacuum seconds later. The warheads she was carrying ruptured a half-second later.

In the blink of an eye, the warship was gone: replaced by a blinding white radiance. The once-proud symbol of Commonwealth military strength was reduced to a cloud of vapour and debris.

Then as the burning light faded, all hell erupted.

Alarms and sensors screamed inside the Sadalmelik's cockpit. Vol made out over sixteen different proximity warnings on her monitor. The debris from the Artemis and surrounding ships was one thing, but the shockwave following the blast was terrifying.

Vol eyed the display, trying to make sense of the carnage around the Sadalmelik. The Paradisians were panicking. Some had been caught in the blast, while others collided in a frenzied stampede as they desperately tried to escape.

The tremendous force of the blast began rolling outward, spreading in all directions like an unstoppable sphere-shaped storm. Vol pictured it as a wall of unrelenting destruction as she pushed on the throttle. A heartbeat later, the shockwave met the bulk of the blockade. Paradisian ships began to collide as the burst forced them off course.

"Hold on to something; this is gonna get bumpy," Vol said to Repla.

There was no reply: not even an acknowledgement.

Vol didn't notice at first, but she peeked at Repla seconds later and noticed that the Sillix was unconscious, *or worse, dead.* Vol pushed her concerns aside in favour of the simple, primal desire to live.

She sent the Sadalmelik hurtling between two large corporate gunships, one of which belonged to Roth Industries. Vol could only hope the crew aboard was more concerned with the shockwave than a boat-shaped cruiser passing close by.

Sadly, that was not the case.

As the Sadalmelik cleared the blockade, with a clear path toward Valour, new alarms began to sound. Vol bit her lip in frustration, then shot a cursory glance at the red screen on her right.

WARNING - MISSILE LOCK.

Roth industries had fired: no doubt their orders were to ensure that nobody escaped.

"Give me a break!" Vol shouted.

As Valour drew closer, so too did the missiles fired by the Roth ships. Vol knew that a craft the size of the Sadalmelik would be unable to out-manoeuvre projectiles. The ship was a tub —not a fighter— so Vol didn't bother calculating the ideal aerial manoeuvre. Instead, she focused on rerouting every other system to the ship's engines in an attempt to outrun the projectiles and reach the surface.

"Shockwave approaching," the terminal said.

Vol eyed the screen. Six, maybe five seconds, until the seismic force of the explosion struck the Sadalmelik.

"C'mon!" she yelled at the rumbling ship.

As the Sadalmelik plunged toward Valour at a breakneck speed, Vol felt her organs crashing back against her seat: her neck aching from merely supporting the weight of her head. She glanced at the navigational display, watching the closing gap between the ship and the missiles.

That was when she knew the Sadalmelik wouldn't outrun the missiles.

"Shit".

The first missile collided with the Sadalmelik's rear, causing a small explosion off the stern. Klaxons began to sound that Vol could only assume meant that there was a breach in the hull.

She ignored it; glanced at the screen.

Missile's two and three were a second behind the first.

The Sadalmelik announced: "Brace for impact".

The rolling wall of destruction was on her back. A second passed. The shockwave passed over the missiles first, causing them to veer off course and explode amongst the debris.

Vol felt a strange moment of elation, knowing that she had survived that part at least. But of course, it lasted a heartbeat. The shockwave closed in: smashing into the rear of the Sadalmelik and forcing it into an uncontrollable downward spin.

Vol tried and failed to orient herself as the simulated gravity failed. She felt the blood rushing to her head as the spin accelerated tenfold, and her vision began to shake. She felt something in her chest that felt a like hammer blow: it was her heart.

Valour's gravity took over from the combined thrust of the shockwave and the Sadalmelik's velocity. When Vol opened her eyes, she saw the clouds. Vertigo washed over her, and she was sure that the planet's surface was rising toward her rather than the other way around. The new gravity took over, and all at once, Vol felt her body lurch against the safety harness on her torso. She tried to combat the sudden shift by switching the engines to complete reverse, but unfortunately, there was no reserve power: the missile must've taken care of that. When the tops of skyscrapers began to peek out from the dark clouds, Vol knew that this wouldn't be her finest landing.

She hammered on the shield control, willing the thing to spin up. A cheery-looking dialogue box appeared on the display, telling her the Sadalmelik had fifteen percent shield remaining. Vol pulled on the ship's manual air brakes, hoping it would slow the descent.

She rerouted the shields to the front of the Sadalmelik: right where the hull was —hopefully— at its thickest. Then Vol oriented the ship so that it would land shield first. With nothing else left to do but hope, she closed her eyes and braced for impact.

NATHAN

"The Artemis is gone..."

As Harrt uttered the words, Nathan saw his friend processing what it actually meant. It was the deaths of his crew and Vol in one single swoop. Confusion, denial, anger, and mourning were all present in the 'wealther's face.

Nathan wasn't sure how to process the idea that Vol was gone. The optimist in him wondered if perhaps she'd made it off the ship before the explosion, but the cynic within told him not to be stupid. There was no point in pretending otherwise.

As Nathan slid into the copilot's seat, he placed a hand on Harrt's shoulder. The 'wealther's gaze didn't wander. He kept his eyes focussed on the flight path ahead: quiet vengeance buried beneath the agony. Nathan recognised the hate buried beneath Harrt's hundred-mile stare: he felt it too.

Behind, Russell was questioning Astrilla and Koble;

"Is there any chance some of them made it off the ship in an escape pod?"

Nobody replied, and it stayed that way for thirty seconds: a mournful silence accompanied by a backdrop of the Phoenix's booming engine.

Nathan looked at what remained of his crew and immediately recognised the toll the situation had taken on them. In his heart, he wanted to say something to rally the team, but he instantly regretted saying the first thing that popped into his head.

"I will kill Alastair Roth for what he's done".

The bitterness in his voice wasn't surprising, but it was

deeper than he'd initially intended. He realised that he sounded just like Jack: bitter, vengeful and angry. That wasn't the man he wanted to be, but perhaps it was the man he needed to be now.

▲

In comparison to Dines' inner-planet shuttle, the Phoenix Titan was like a bullet out of a gun. Granted, there was little traffic in the skylanes, and Nathan was pretty sure that Harrt had violated a few dozen transport laws along the way, but it was undeniable how much quicker the journey had been using the Phoenix.

The Containment Facility was another scene of chaos.

A vast cloud of dark smoke loomed around the main entrance. The first security checkpoint was on fire, but rainfall slowed the spread. It was clear that James had already carved out a path of destruction.

"Wow," Harrt said with astonishment. "This is one of the most highly guarded facilities on the planet. How in the hell did they cause so much damage?"

Behind Nathan, Astrilla leaned between the pilot and copilot's stations to get a better look. She studied the view for a heartbeat, her dark eyes flicking between the raging fires and the debris.

"The element of surprise is one thing, but if I didn't know any better, I'd say that James' mercenaries are far more skilled than we initially thought".

"What do you mean?" Nathan turned to look at her.

Astrilla nodded at the fires:

"I'm confident this is the work of a highly experienced unit: not the handiwork of mere mercenaries". She stopped to consider something, peering at the proximity monitor beside Nathan. "Where is their ship?"

Nathan looked at the prison, then at the display. There were no vessels in the immediate vicinity, meaning James likely had a ship awaiting his instruction to scoop him up for a quick getaway.

It was a tactic that felt reminiscent: something straight

out of the Loyalty days. James was still using his father's old tricks: the same tricks Nathan knew, like the back of his hand.

Within seconds, the Phoenix touched down on the landing pad, metres away from the main entrance. Nathan wasted no time grabbing a rifle from Russell and heading to the landing pad.

He surveyed the area, noting over a dozen dead 'wealther guards, a blown portion of the prison's entrance and a raging fire burning where the security checkpoint had been.

The only thing moving was the vicious bursts of torrential rain falling from the sky. Thunder and lightning crashed from the dark clouds overhead while heavy gusts of wind pushed the downpour east.

The security checkpoint was a wreck: hit by an explosive device and riddled with bullets. The prison guards had been killed by precision gunfire, just like the bodies Harrt found back in the hangar.

"Damn," Russell said. "These Society guys work fast".

Nathan heard him, but something else pulled his attention away. He noticed something odd about one of the fires ahead. The flames flickered slowly and unnaturally: *as though time had slowed down*. Nathan blinked, and he felt his breathing synchronise with the crackle of the fire.

When he opened his eyes, everything changed.

He stood on the sandy dunes of the desert where he'd met his grandfather. There was a dry warmth to the air. A northerly breeze carried a hint of grit, but it wasn't unwelcome. Nathan could not see anything but the barren plains for miles in every direction. The park bench was there, looking out of place and antique but also friendly and inviting.

Bill Stephens was not there. Nobody was.

Instinctively, Nathan climbed one of the dunes to get his bearings on the place: *wherever this place was.* When he reached the top, nothing changed. The area was completely void of life, but Nathan knew he wasn't alone; he could feel it in his gut. A shadow lurked in the background: far away but somehow close at the same time.

"You must find me," a voice said.

Nathan had heard it before, from the video footage recovered on Levave. From the person that killed a squad of Society mercenaries at the Enkaye temple.

Subject C.

"You must find me".

Nathan tried to answer, but his voice didn't carry across the plains. He searched and searched, but there was nobody there. Just sand and the sky.

Something new flashed in his mind that he couldn't explain: *blood caught in a violent whirlpool that shifted into pure radiance.*

It was supposed to mean something profound, but not yet —not now.

His consciousness moved from one place to another, separated perhaps by time or distance or something else that slipped the bonds of the universe.

He returned to the Containment Facility. A gust of wind blew through his hair; a crash of thunder struck above, and a veil of rain caused Nathan to shudder.

When Astrilla tugged on his sleeve, gravity, reality and consciousness returned.

"Are you okay?" she asked.

Nathan's initial impulse was to tell her what he'd just experienced but quickly decided against it. There would be time to analyse any visions or hallucinations once James and his merry band of mercs were dead.

"Talk about it later," Nathan muttered.

Astrilla peered at him knowingly, evidently aware that something wasn't right.

As the group proceeded into the Containment Facility, Nathan tried to shake off the dazed feeling he'd developed. At first, he wondered if perhaps he was experiencing symptoms from where James struck him earlier. It would be easy to think that he'd suffered a concussion and was experiencing hallucinations, but Nathan knew better.

The desert —*elsewhere*— was calling to him.

JAMES

"Let's hurry this shit along," James yelled before taking another long drag from his cigarette.

He watched as Austin and three of his most trusted henchmen rigged charges against a cell door. Naturally, the team were being cautious: one poorly planted explosive could detonate at a bad angle or with the wrong payload and write the son's boss out of existence. Not the best outcome, but certainly not the worst: after all, the only reason James and his squad were at the 'wealther gulag and not aboard the Featon sipping champagne was because of Christian.

It was always because of Christian.

James' eyes flicked to his datapad to check timings, then yelled, "We ain't got long!"

Roth's plan was ballsy. Some —including James— called the pièce de résistance insane. Sure, the old bastard knew how to engineer feats of damn brilliance, but this was on a different scale with a cubic shit-ton of variables and a reliance on improvisation.

At first, James had doubted the project, citing it as bold and reckless, but there was no denying that Roth knew how to adapt when shit went sideways.

"It's called extemporisation," Roth had said. "Water will always roll downhill, regardless of rocks, fish or any other obstacle. The only thing that stops it is the building of a dam. We must all work together to reach our end goal even if that means punching a hole in that dam and drowning all the villagers".

Operation pièce de résistance had *mostly* stayed the course. James got aboard the Phoenix and convinced them that he was —almost— one of them. He even had Nathan fooled, which was an achievement in and of itself. All the sleeper cells on Valour had done their work well, blending among the 'wealthers: all biding their time before striking the relevant political and military assets in one fell swoop. Even Austin was able to sneak his unit onto Valour before the protest began.

The Doctor *—codename Humbug—* was captured and would soon be on his way to the Featon: just as Roth commanded. And, of course, the Commonwealth Council, including Inon Waife, was dead. Thus throwing the 'wealth into political pandemonium for the next part of the plan.

The Phoenix's crew, David Jareth and a bunch of dead marines would be found at the scene, prompting the 'wealth's military leaders to believe they were conspiring with Paradisium.

That was the hope, anyway.

Initially, Jareth was supposed to die at Hawtrey House, but that didn't go so well: primarily thanks to the infamous mercenary Chimera and his interference.

At first, James planned to kill Jareth while nobody was looking, but getting to him would compromise his cover. Fortunately, Jareth was just as stubborn as Roth predicted. Rather than ally with the Phoenix's crew, Jareth made an enemy of them and incited further division.

Big bad Jack's greatest crime was brought up, and emotions ran high. Jareth was hauled away and eventually brought back to Inon Waife, and in the end, James had exactly what he needed: *an opportunity to get to Waife.*

Thinking on one's feet.

The only unknown was the insurgency aboard the Artemis. It was hard to get updates from the ground, but the sudden burst of long-range distress signals from orbit suggested that Baylum's Evoker moles had completed his objective.

The only fuck-up belonged to Christian. The plan would've been flawless otherwise. That was where James had to think on his feet: he had to *extemporise,* as Roth would say. It pissed him off to know that the heir to the Society had been his usual reckless self. Had Christian followed his father's instructions, James would've been the only one acquired by the Phoenix's crew. Instead, Christian got himself captured by Koble because he was a naive asshole that believed he was untouchable.

So, once again, James adapted his plans on the fly. Sure he could leave Christian to rot in a containment chamber, but the boss wouldn't be too happy about that. Legacy meant everything in the Society, and James felt an immeasurable duty to Alastair Roth.

The sound of wailing brought James back into the moment. He gazed over his shoulder at the stockpile of dead 'wealther guards in the corridor. A Uvan woman in an officer's uniform was clawing her way up the hall, blood trailing from an exit wound on her back.

James snapped his fingers. "Austin, deal with this".

Bradley Austin's face lit up at the prospect of inflicting pain on another being: that was where he revelled —in pure savagery. The big American drew his trusted machete and followed the Uvan up the corridor. She'd barely moved six inches before Austin plunged the blade of his machete directly through her spine.

The Uvan's screams were unpleasant to hear, but fortunately, Austin didn't bask in the moment's violence for too long. Usually, he'd savour such things, but not today: not while they were on borrowed time. Austin pulled back his machete and stabbed her three more times in rapid succession. The sound of steel slicing into wet flesh filled the hallway.

When it was done, Austin sheathed his weapon and returned to James' side like a loyal protector. Together they waited as the others finished rigging the charges, and when the time came to detonate, Alexandria Martinez handed James the detonator.

If Austin was his right-hand man, then Martinez was undoubtedly his left: a skilled ex-corporate enforcer who knew her away around combat situations. Where Austin was like an untamed beast, Martinez was like a bird of prey: watchful, restricted and calculating.

"All on you, boss," she said.

When the cell door exploded, James shielded his eyes from the debris and smoke. The building's fire protection protocols kicked in, and water rained from the ceiling like the storm outside.

Inside the cell, Christian Roth sat on his standard issue 'wealther bed, looking decidedly calm. Despite the prison jumpsuit, he still looked like a future leader of Paradisium, which seemed somehow ironic to James, but he wasn't sure why.

"About fucking time, Stephens!" Christian snarled, climbing from his bunk and speaking with his overly-regal tone. "Do you have any idea how boring it is to stare at the same four walls for the better part of a day?"

James wanted nothing more than to strike the entitled little prick for jeopardising the mission. Still, as lovely as it'd be to put him on the ground, James knew it wasn't that simple. Christian was one of Paradisium's finest in the art of hand-to-hand combat: *trained by the best teachers money could buy.*

So James kept things civil.

"We don't have much time," James said. "The ship is coming to grab us, and I'm pretty sure we've got half the 'wealth on our ass".

Christian's lips turned upward. "Only half?"

"Do you wanna stick around to find out?" James said, this time inserting just the right amount of aggression in his voice to let Christian know how serious he was.

Christian smiled as he backed off and gestured to the restraints on his wrists. "Well, get these things off me before my skin starts to scar".

Something about Christian's sense of self-entitlement made James' flesh crawl. Christian had led a life of splendour, unlike James, who'd lived the direct opposite.

It made him jealous of all the stuff he'd missed out on in life. Had his father been less narcissistic, James could've enjoyed a privileged life on Paradisium: sipping champagne by the pool with a couple of pretty young things.

Alas, Jack Stephens had chosen a different path for him: the wrong path.

As Martinez cut the binds on Christian's wrists, the future president of Paradisium looked at James with excitement.

"Is it done?" Christian asked with the giddy excitement of a small child.

James nodded, pulling his spare sidearm from its holster and handing it to Christian. The grin on the younger man's face spanned from ear to ear: either delighted by the mission's success, the prospect of holding a gun, or both.

"For protection only," James warned.

Christian didn't acknowledge him.

Instead, he took ahold of the gun and tucked it into the back of his prison slacks.

"What about the Doctor?" Christian asked.

"Done," James said, ushering Christian toward the door.

While Christian punched the air in celebration, Austin entered the cell with a datapad. He urgently shoved the device into James' hands and gestured at the screen.

"Looks like your cousin and his pals survived," Austin said, pointing a meaty finger at the screen. "Security systems picked them up at the entrance about thirty seconds ago".

Once again, James found himself having to adapt his plan. The main entrance wasn't viable, so he needed an alternative. The roof was the next best option, and the ship could provide ample cover from the sky if worst came to the worst.

There was no denying it'd be a speedy getaway: *hop on the ship and high-tail back to the Featon.*

Before James could issue his command, Christian snatched the datapad from his hands.

"It's him!" Christian pointed to Koble in the footage. "That's the fucking Sphinax that attacked me!"

Christian started to walk in the opposite direction: readying himself to face the Phoenix's crew in combat like the arrogant fool he was.

James stopped him by grabbing him by the collar.

"If they are heading this way, then the 'wealthers won't be far behind," James barked. "We gotta be smart about this".

Christian tried to look thoughtful for a beat.

"Very well," he nodded reluctantly. "But I want that Sphinax's head on a spike at the first opportunity".

James didn't reply and instead turned to Austin, Martinez and the others;

"Comms the ship. Tell 'em to meet us on the roof".

CHIMERA

It took twenty-four hours for Chimera to arrive at Valour. With limited fuel and a busted FTL drive, the journey had been slow from Haydrium, but it provided him time to recover. He treated his recently relocated shoulder and took a few medical stimulants soothe his scrapes, bruises and burns. After a couple of hours, he was fighting fit.

When his shuttle dropped from the slipstream, Chimera was confronted by a scene of absolute destruction. Something gigantic had exploded near Valour, and the fallout left in the wake was apparent.

Thousands upon thousands of damaged ships floated in space, while thousands more were poised around Valour in what had been a blockade but had now descended into a chaotic panic. All the ships were Paradisian, with most being civilian vessels.

"What the hell happened here?"

Chimera tuned his ship's comms system to pick up any broadcasts in the sector. Both Commonwealth and Paradisian feeds were overwhelmed with chatter. He dialled back the newsfeed by twenty minutes, and only then could he establish an accurate picture of what happened.

"Roth…" he growled.

The blockade didn't matter. Chimera couldn't help the injured, and finding Alastair Roth amongst the sea of ships was like finding a needle in a haystack.

Now, the primary objective was to locate Nathan Carter.

Chimera tapped the navigation terminal and sent his shuttle hurtling toward Valour. Once the shuttle reached the appropriate velocity, Chimera deactivated the engines.

Given the amount of debris in the area, he hoped that by pulling off a drifting manoeuvre, the Paradisians would assume he was a piece of stray junk.

As he deactivated all systems inside his small ship, Chimera pulled up his datapad with the Commonwealth Citizen's Network.

"Locate David Jareth," he said into the device.

The computer failed to process his query.

"Locate Nathan Carter".

Same again.

He switched to the 'wealth's active ship registry.

"Locate the Phoenix Titan".

The device processed the query and, seconds later, returned the Phoenix's location.

CHAPTER THIRTY-FOUR
NATHAN

Eager to end his cousin's violent rampage, Nathan took the lead at the front of the pack, pointing his gun into the semi-darkness ahead. Together, the crew of the Phoenix pushed forward into the Containment Facility.

Much like the other places attacked by the Society's mercenaries, the 'wealther prison was a scene of homicidal destruction. Bodies, blood and guts filled the corridors, where James and his unit made light work of the unprepared guards. Even the guys wearing the premium 'wealther armour hadn't stood a chance.

All in all, Nathan counted over thirty bodies, and eventually, he stopped counting. Just as it had been on the streets, the Council Chambers, and all the other target sites, James and his team had acted with swift and brutal efficiency.

When all this began after Hawtrey House, Nathan assumed that James would be like before, an immature, unambitious pirate, simply living for each day.

Instead, he'd proven Nathan very wrong.

James was no longer the man Nathan had once known.

He'd evolved into something new: something callous and cold. He was now a part of something ruthlessly efficient.

He'd been the one calling the shots, suggesting that —at minimum— he had some sway in Roth's organisation.

The dead were riddled with gunshot wounds, just like the security team at the entrance. A handful had been finished with a sharp instrument —*likely an axe or sword*— which had been used barbarically to hack the limbs off of already-wounded victims.

That meant someone under James' command —if not James himself— had a sick taste for violence.

"Stay on your toes," Koble said. "This ain't gonna be straightforward".

▲

Christian's cell was deserted, and the corridor outside was drenched from the still-active fire system spewing water from silver pipes in the ceiling. The fact the sprinklers were still running meant that James wasn't far ahead. Where before there had been a big, heavy security door, there was now a hole in the wall where a controlled explosion had freed Christian. The blast was precise, blowing the door to smithereens while keeping the cell and its contents entirely untouched. It was the work of pros; of that, Nathan was sure.

"Nate," Koble called out, gesturing to a damp cigarette butt on the ground.

Nathan scowled at the sight of it.

"He's close," Astrilla said.

Nathan nodded, trying to figure out what James' escape plan would look like. There were no ships on the landing pad, meaning James and his goons were getting picked up by a vessel likely circling the area. They wouldn't risk landing there again for fear of running into reinforcements or the Phoenix Titan. With Christian now under their protection, James' unit needed a safe place to exfil.

"They'll use the roof," Nathan concluded. "What's the quickest way up there?"

Astrilla pulled the building's schematic on her datapad, quickly tracing her index finger from their current position to the nearest stairwell, then the elevator. She rotated the image a few times, and Nathan could see his paramour looking for the most effective route.

She pointed down the corridor, "This way".

Nathan nodded and once again took the lead. Rather than walking at a brisk speed, he found himself compelled to run. Then to sprint. Now, he was fuelled by one thing: getting even.

James had murdered dozens, including Rain and, by extension, Vol. Even if he wasn't the one to pull the trigger, he'd been a part of Roth's plan. That made James the enemy, and Nathan had to stop him.

Nathan dashed through long corridor after long corridor, boots splashing across the wet floor. Ahead he heard voices and the scrape of boots against metal.

Then he turned the corner.

A few hundred yards ahead was a small group of mercenaries, all clad in dark, unmarked gear. There were nine at most. All armed with heavy assault rifles with a prisoner in tow: still wearing his orange jumpsuit.

Then at the front of the pack, Nathan saw him: the man he'd once considered a brother. James.

Nathan aimed at the pack as he moved up the corridor. He opened fire, cutting down the guy covering the rear. His armour deflected the bulk of the impact, but it was still enough to take the thug by surprise and send him hurtling to the floor.

That was when all hell broke loose.

As gunfire began to fly down the narrow passageway, Nathan took up cover in a cell doorway while Astrilla and the others darted around the corner several metres behind.

Amidst the chaos, Nathan could hear Christian screaming at the top of his lungs;

"Kill them now!"

Nathan took aim, but before he could get off a shot, James and a tall guy began firing wide arcs toward him. The sudden onslaught of concentrated weaponsfire forced Nathan back into cover. Dust and debris kicked up around him, but he remained unharmed.

Nathan peered at the other end of the corridor where the others had taken refuge. He signalled, and Koble began firing down the hall at James while Nathan readied himself to reposition.

It looked as though a splinter group of James' men were holding a defensive position: likely buying time for their pals to escape. That meant that Nathan needed to find a way around them.

He peered at the doorway, spotting an access control on the wall. Without thinking, Nathan tapped the panel and unlocked the door. He moved inside, expecting to come across a very confused or very hostile prisoner, but instead, Nathan found an empty cell.

Logically, he knew he was at a dead end, but somehow in the deep recesses of his mind, Nathan saw a path. The human in him debated returning to the doorway and getting back in the fight, but the Enkaye in him suggested something new.

Nathan peered at the wall, separating him from the mercs and raised his left palm. His brain forged an image of the desert, the park bench, and the barren sandy dunes. He couldn't see Bill Stephens there, but through time, or space, or some different plain of existence, a voice spoke to him: just as it had aboard the Messorem:

"A great power lays within you, son of Earth".

Nathan slowed his breathing, allowing his body to relax, embracing the dormant elemental energy surrounding him. He imagined a blast emerging from his palm, strong enough to cut through anything.

Within seconds he could feel the energy course through his veins like fuel to an engine. Fire, electricity, and raw, untamed power whipped around him and coalesced into his palm. It felt like two rivers meeting and joining into a single channel: a confluence of elements unionising together to form a single blast.

In his mind, Nathan saw the shroud that was Subject C. The shadowy figure was standing on the dunes, watching like a strange spectator who simply didn't belong.

"You must find me," Subject C said.

A bolt of raw energy speared from Nathan's outstretched hand, and the wall opposite came down upon impact. Debris and dust kicked into the air as the unstoppable pulse cascaded through the walls, carving him a path that would create a new flanking position.

Without the need to celebrate his accomplishment, Nathan dashed forward. He found three startled mercenaries at the end of his newly forged path, two of which were still trying to fend off Harrt and the others. Nathan raised his gun, cutting down two of them in a haze of crimson. The third scrambled into the next room, slamming the door behind him.

This time Nathan waited for the others, and the group were together again within five to ten seconds.

Astrilla threw a summon into the door, blowing it off its hinges and straight into the next room.

The group rushed into the new chamber: a circular stairwell leading up several floors. There was no sign of the third guy, but Nathan could hear the sound of rushing footsteps above, accompanied by groans and panting. The mercenaries were retreating, no doubt, to reunite with James and make a getaway.

"We need to move!" Harrt said.

The group pressed ahead, rushing up several flights of stairs before reaching the top. There was a single unguarded door that led out to the roof. Nathan checked his gun, knowing that outside there'd be a fight to come.

"Do we take James alive?" Koble asked.

Nobody replied.

All eyes fell on Nathan.

"We save Gordon," he growled. "That's all that matters".

Without anything else to say, Nathan booted the door open.

The storm was still raging. Heavy rain pummelled the roof while a cold wind whipped through the air. Blue forks of lightning filled the skies while the intense rumble of thunder overpowered everything in the nearby space.

Nathan could see James about three hundred yards away, trying to guide a gunship down using a red flare. It was the kind of ship that would blend in but would also serve its purpose when it got down to the business: *the perfect getaway vehicle.*

In addition to James, there was a scattering of mercenaries and Christian Roth: all armed and desperate to flee. Without hesitation, Nathan took aim and fired at his cousin. A heartbeat later, he regretted the rash decision as the wind and rain caused his inaccurate shot to veer off by a good metre.

James turned to look at the source of the gunshot. His eyes met Nathan's.

For a moment, nothing happened. Then, as though flipping a switch, everything started moving very quickly.

JAMES

James took a dive, narrowly avoiding the sudden onslaught of weapons fire that Nathan sent toward him. Several bolts ricocheted overhead while another bounced off the gunship's hull. Austin, Martinez and a few others hugged a metal protrusion on the roof for cover. James crawled on his belly to join them as Christian decided to participate in the fight. As usual, Christian overestimated his ability, firing wildly at the Phoenix's crew and missing every shot.

"Whoever brings me that Sphinax's head will receive a lofty bonus," Christian yelled as he continued to shoot.

James wasted no time dragging Christian into cover. Koble had been a legendarily good shot back in the day, and James knew the Sphinax wouldn't hesitate in taking down Christian or anyone else if he deemed them a threat.

James snatched Christian's sidearm. "I ain't explaining why you ended up dead to your father, so stay in cover!"

Christian struggled but quickly settled down.

James released his grip on the boss's kid and gestured to Martinez to keep her eye on him. She nodded, and James pushed up the front of the pack as laser fire filled the space around him.

Austin was ahead of the pack, using a metal ventilation system for cover. James moved out and fired as he sprinted toward his trusted lieutenant.

An elemental summon blew by him, tearing up the floor and sending debris everywhere. When James got to Austin, the American looked at him with maniacal glee in his giant brown eyes.

"Any ideas, boss?" Austin said casually over the gunfire.

James pointed at the Phoenix's crew;

"Send our weakest men to meet them in combat on the frontlines. You an I will take the high ground to the east."

Austin began to issue commands through his ear-piece, sending six of the eleven mercs into the fold. They were nothing but cannon fodder in James' eyes, but he learned long ago that he had to be ruthless to survive.

As Roth would say, *sacrifices are necessary.*

James grabbed his comms device and opened a channel to Martinez;

"Once you get an opening, get Christian on that ship and hold the airspace for us".

"Roger," she replied.

James turned to Austin:

"We end this now; are you with me?"

Austin nodded with a gleeful bloodlust in his eyes.

Together they moved from cover and headed east, where a metal platform provided an elevated position. In the madness, James spotted Harrt Oxarri engaging in combat with the advancing forward team. The 'wealther was laying down suppressing fire to keep James' men on the back foot, likely to allow Koble to gain a good sniping position or so that the Evoker could work her magic.

James saw the tactic from a mile off. It was the kind of thing good ol' father Jack would've passed down in his many lessons, though James had written those off years ago.

He decided that Harrt would be his first target of the skirmish. James took aim and lined up the shot: imagining the burst of crimson that would follow as Harrt Oxarri met his bleak demise. He was just about to pull the trigger when —the kid— Russell spotted him and sent a burst of laser fire toward him.

James had to duck, but Austin had his back. The American began firing toward Russell's position, and the young man disappeared behind a ventilation shaft. James moved forward, hoping to gain a flanking position over the Phoenix's crew. Much to his surprise, the forward team —aka the cannon fodder— were holding their own quite nicely, though he was pretty sure that his side had suffered more casualties.

James eyeballed Martinez's unit. A couple of the guys were busy laying down covering fire, while another pair directed the ship to a suitable landing spot. Martinez had her hands full, trying to usher Christian to safety.

James was feeling pretty confident about the whole thing. He was sure that in less than thirty minutes, he'd be aboard Roth's ship sipping fine champagne and toasting a job well done.

Then Astrilla stepped into the battle: her hands glowing white and elemental energy rushing around her body like a storm. As James planned, the cannon fodder rushed to attack the Evoker, and she cut down two of them with minimal effort. A third merc fired her assault rifle at Astrilla, but the bullets failed to penetrate the elemental barrier that encircled the Evoker.

It was at that moment that James acted. He gestured to Austin, and together they opened fire on Astrilla from their elevated position. Austin's rifle spat incendiary rounds while James switched to a grenade launcher in the under-barrel of his gun. The grenade fired with a loud pop, and James watched as it soared toward its target.

Austin's gunfire was keeping her busy. Yes, she dodged the ferocious firey rounds with ease, but they served as the perfect distraction.

The grenade fell, and James readied himself to hear a perfect detonation.

Then the bitch surprised him.

As she eluded Austin's gunfire, Astrilla pivoted and threw herself upward in a graceful yet threatening way. She slapped the grenade in mid-air, causing it to veer off and explode a few metres away from his position.

James shielded his eyes from the blaze and switched back to standard rounds.

Wary that *team cannon fodder* didn't have much time, James yelled to Austin; "Get back to Martinez and hold those fuckers off! When the ship's ready, tell them to spin up the guns".

"What about you?" Austin yelled.

James gestured to Astrilla; "I've got an Evoker to kill".

Austin's delighted smile was born of his lust for violence. In another time or another place, someone like him would locked away, never to see the light of day, but the Society had its use for men like Bradley Austin. A vicious, violent murderer could be tamed into an instrument of blunt force and used effectively.

As Austin retreated, James moved from cover and took aim. He fired at Astrilla, but she was too fast: twisting, turning, and darting through the air quicker than his eyes could process. That was all well and good, but James knew that she would tire eventually. He emptied his entire mag, returned to cover, and reloaded.

James was about ready to take aim again, but suddenly something heavy slammed into him. Nathan was at the forefront of his vision, tackling him with sheer force. They tussled for a heartbeat, but Nathan had momentum on his side, and they both quickly fell over the edge of the eastern walkway.

James fell about twenty feet, hitting a metal conduit on the way down and landing hard on his spine. It hurt a lot, but he told himself the pain was temporary: that it was nothing compared to the crashes that followed an Ice rampage. James willed himself to climb to his feet, wary that Nathan was in the area and dangerous.

He looked around for his rifle, but there was no sign. He reached for his sidearm, but before James could fully draw the weapon, he felt something collide with his hand, and the pistol flipped away.

When James looked up, he saw Nathan.

"So," James spat. "It finally comes down to this: you and me mano-a-mano".

HARRT

Harrt saw Nathan disappear over the walkway's edge in a moment of sheer chaos. It was a foolish and overly emotional play, but he didn't expect less. The Earther was likely feeling vengeful and angry and responsible for everything that had happened, and Harrt could relate to all of those things.

Astrilla was at the leading edge of the engagement, casting summon after summon at the mercenary crew. Harrt was further back, using a ventilation shaft for cover. Russell and Koble were to his left, hugging the wall of a tall chimney while concentrating fire on the group further north.

The unmistakable sound of gunshots and yelling from both sides filled the roof. In all the carnage, Harrt found himself trying to focus on his kill count, of which there were none. He was sure he'd winged a guy earlier, but he couldn't confirm it.

James' men were well armed and held their defensive position exceptionally well. Astrilla had already killed two by Harrt's best guess, but there were at least another eight toward the north and another two or three between them.

There was no doubt in Harrt's mind that James' militia were the best of the best. From their tactical positioning and accuracy, it was clear that James had selected his people wisely. The question now was *how good were they compared to an Evoker, a former barkeep, and the two guys that had defeated Densius Olbori at the Battle of the Messorem.*

From the corner of his eye, Harrt saw a mercenary ten feet to his right, attempting a risky flanking manoeuvre. The man lifted his rifle but failed to realise that Harrt already had the drop on him. He pulled the trigger, and a laser round tore through the merc's chest, and his blood painted the wall behind.

"Oxarri," Koble yelled across the skirmish. "Get down!"

Harrt did as instructed before looking to see what had caused the Sphinax's alarm. From behind cover, Harrt peaked at the northernmost point of the roof, where James' unit was falling back. Then Harrt saw it; the gunship.

The small vessel spun up the two forward-facing cannons bolted to the front of its small frame. Then a trio of aerial drones emerged from its underbelly: all armed with explosive projectiles and cannons.

Harrt looked at Koble, and the big Sphinax looked at him as if to say, *yeah, things just got interesting.*

NATHAN

The impact with which Nathan tackled James was only felt when the pair crashed onto the hard metal floor twenty feet below the walkway. They fell and landed together, though Nathan was pretty sure James crashed into something on the way down. Nathan landed on his ribs and felt a moment of sheer daze afterwards. He was still groggy from the strike he'd received earlier, but adrenaline and rage were now in control and numbed most of the pain.

He shook off the daze, climbed to his feet, and booted James' pistol from his hand before he'd fully drawn his weapon. Nathan watched the gun tumble away: *far enough to guarantee that James couldn't simply reach for it.*

James laughed in a taunting manner.

"So, it finally comes down to this: you and me mano-a-mano".

Nathan didn't give him a chance to utter another word, striking James in the head with a closed fist. He hit him again. And again. Nathan allowed the impatient fury he'd held onto to fuel his assault.

On a primal level, he was back in that nightclub eleven years ago, beating the living shit out of the junkie cousin who'd destroyed the Loyalty. On an evolved level, he beat the man who'd killed Rain and Vol and many more.

Nathan threw himself at James, and the pair wrestled on the rain-soaked ground, beating each other nearly senseless.

Nathan shut out any thoughts of Jack, closing down the part of his mind that asked *what the old man would think of all this.*

"You bastard!" Nathan screamed.

He sent another closed fist into James' head before attempting to choke him. Nathan squeezed his throat, refusing to show mercy. The pain and suffering that James had inflicted in the last hour was unspeakable, he, and his troops, and Roth didn't deserve the mercy of an easy death.

But Jack wouldn't approve of this.

The family wouldn't.

The guys from the Loyalty wouldn't.

They'd expect better than this.

Nathan was suddenly taken off guard when James struck him in the head: the exact spot where he'd taken a heavy blow earlier that day. Nathan tumbled to one side.

His ears rang, and his vision expanded and narrowed and expanded again. His stomach rumbled as though the shock had vibrated through his entire body. Usually, such a strike wouldn't have impacted him so severely, but James had targeted that spot for a reason.

Always use their weakness against them; one of Jack's many lessons that he'd passed down to both of them.

Nathan scrambled to one side and took up his sidearm. He pointed the handgun at James, ready to open fire but discovered that his cousin had done the same: pulling a secondary sidearm from his jacket.

They stood there with guns pointed at one another in a horrible chilling moment that dragged on for an eternity.

Neither pulled the trigger, but neither backed down.

Cold rain continued to pound against Nathan's face as he looked down the sights of his pistol. He knew that if he pulled the trigger, it'd shred James' chest to pieces. Sure, he could shoot James in the foot or the arm, but anything less than a killing shot would put his own at risk. Above all else, it'd mean killing the last living member of his family.

But James had done terrible, unforgivable things.

What would Jack think of all this?

What would Grampa Bill think of it?

What would his mother think of it?

The silence of their standoff was broken when James opened his mouth:

"C'mon, Nate, put it down. We both know you don't have what it takes". James' smile was a taunt. "You and I are the last of us. You ain't gonna kill me. Just like you didn't kill me in that fuckin' nightclub".

Nathan felt his grip tighten on the gun.

"Why do this?" Nathan yelled. "After all the bullshit getting off Earth, why the fuck would you work for Roth?"

A crack of lightning struck overhead.

"You have no idea what happened during the Fall. You were too busy cowering to realise what really happened!" James licked his lips. "My father told me to shoot Roth's children if he didn't comply. Do you call that behaviour of a great man?"

Nathan said nothing.

"Roth got me off Ice. He gave me a home and purpose and reason to keep on going. But here's the thing, Nate, I don't work *for* Roth: I work *with* him. Partners. Brothers of the Society working together for the greater good".

The rumble of thunder followed.

"Look around, James," Nathan said. "How is all this bloodshed the greater good?"

James scoffed, "Project Erebus is gonna make things right. It's gonna give us the future that we —that I— deserve".

"Roth's lying to you," Nathan warned.

"Alastair Roth is more family to me than you or anyone else," James spat. "He will make this universe a better place".

Nathan could see the conviction in his cousin's eyes. He truly believed the words he was saying: that Roth's mission was moral and justified and righteous.

Nathan knew what he had to do, but some part of him resisted. He had to give James one final chance: for the cousin he'd once known. Before his Ice addiction. Before the Mirotose Station incident. Nathan saw the cousin he'd played with in his grandparent's garden. The cousin who'd given him a wooden train set one Christmas. He saw the cousin, who —despite being a decade older— had always treated him as a brother.

"Put the gun down, James," Nathan said, his voice low.

"Go ahead," James sneered. "Shoot".

Nathan hesitated.

James fired his gun.

Something instinctive inside Nathan awoke. It was as though his body could anticipate the incoming bullet, forcing him to turn slightly.

Metal seared through his shoulder, less than a few inches from his heart. The force of the gunshot was so severe that it sent him hurtling backwards, dropping his sidearm in the process.

Nathan tumbled over the edge of the roof and plummeted downward.

ASTRILLA

As the gunship spun up its cannons, Astrilla willed the elements cascading around her to create a protective barricade: an impulsive last-ditch attempt to shield herself and the others. Laser fire erupted from the enemy craft.

Astrilla's fingers weaved a web of electricity that rapidly built into a tapestry of light and heat, spanning several metres in diameter. The gunfire ricocheted off the shield, and a shower of sparks filled the space in front of her.

For a heartbeat, she wondered how long she could hold out. Koble was yelling something. Harrt was moving right while Russell was firing his assault rifle at the mercenaries. Astrilla's mind processed their movements, but only on a superficial level. All her focus was on her summon. It had to hold until the gunship's weapons array overheated.

For what felt like a lifetime, but was probably less than thirty seconds, Astrilla held the line. The gunship fired and fired, but no laser fire passed through.

Then the drones cycled around to gain a new vantage point while the gunship continued its onslaught. Out the corner of her eye, Astrilla saw the drones assume their new position, one to her right, the other to her left, and the gunship dead ahead.

It was right then that Astrilla knew she was out of options. She could only hold off one at a time. Maybe she could retreat and break off her defence, but that meant leaving the others exposed.

The drones span up their guns, but what was supposed to happen didn't.

A single round from far off in the distance penetrated the drone on Astrilla's left: causing it to lose power and crash to the floor in a large explosion. Whoever was operating the gunship's main cannons paused. Astrilla imagined the mercenary gawking at the sudden loss of the drone in confusion.

Astrilla didn't care what had happened; she simply saw an opportunity. She darted away, breaking off her barricade and hurling the residual power in her palms at the second drone.

The strike connected, winging the drone and causing smoke to pour from its metal frame. By the time the gunship reacquired her, Astrilla was in cover with the others.

"Where the hell did that shot come from?" Harrt yelled in a shrill panic.

CHAPTER THIRTY-FIVE
JAMES

With a victorious grin, James picked up Nathan's discarded pistol. He recognised it as the gun that once belonged to his father: a heavily modified Earth revolver complete with the same ridiculous carving of a wolf that spanned most of the barrel.

James didn't feel any hint of nostalgia or grief. It was but a remnant of the man who'd betrayed him. Still, it was a good gun, and James figured his father owed him a proper inheritance. He holstered the pistol and moved to the roof's edge, hoping to catch a glimpse of the moment Nathan plummetted to his death, but there was no sign of him.

From his vantage point, the visibility was maybe a hundred yards. Given the heavy rain, the steep incline of the drop, and the mist kicking up into the air, it was fair to assume that James missed the opportunity to witness his cousin's death.

"That's for abandoning me," James said bitterly.

Suddenly the sound of immense weapons fire came from the north. It sounded like a ship engaging with the drones and the shuttle, but James couldn't be entirely sure.

An explosion followed, which caused the ground beneath his feet to shake, suggesting that something had crashed nearby. James could only hope that it wasn't his escape ship: though he was pretty sure it was one of the drones.

He was about to look when suddenly laser fire echoed

passed him. James saw a small transport shuttle, flying circles around the Containment Facility and providing aerial support for the Phoenix's crew.

"Who the fuck are you?" James said.

Rather than find out, he retreated north. As he sprinted toward Austin, Martinez and the others, he fired over his shoulder at the pursuing shuttle. The ship returned fire, shooting up the ground around James as he moved to the best of his ability.

Austin appeared from behind a ventilation shaft with a rocket launcher and took aim at the ship. What followed was an explosion that sent the small shuttle off course. It spiralled and whipped to one side, crashing through the eastern walkway and smashing several yards from where the remainder of the Phoenix's crew were still holding out.

"C'mon, boss," Austin yelled, tossing the smoking launcher aside. "Let's get the hell outta here".

KOBLE

With the remaining drone effectively wounded, Koble saw an opportunity to put it down. He called to Russell, and pointed at the drone. The former barkeep peered up, seeing the same thing as Koble and nodded.

Koble was certain he pulled the trigger first, but it didn't matter who was the quicker shot. A flurry of laser fire rammed into the drone, causing it to explode in a ball of white fire.

The gunship was retreating, heading to the north to grab what remained of James' unit. Koble figured that by now, their only priority was to escape.

"C'mon," Koble yelled. "Let's finish these bastards".

"Right behind you!" Russell called out.

Koble didn't wait for Harrt or Astrilla to reply. Russell had his back, and Koble was confident that now was the one and only shot he'd have to avenge Rain. He was about ready to make his charge when suddenly a gunshot whizzed past him.

On some base level, Koble was aware that something wasn't right. He couldn't see the bullet, it wasn't like dealing with laser rounds, but he felt it flash by. Seconds later, his eyes processed his primitive suspicion, and Koble saw Russell fall.

A cloud of blood poofed into the air.

It was impossible to tell if Russell were alive or dead; all Koble knew was he'd been shot. At that moment, his mind processed the worst: it told him that James, Roth, and the Society, had stolen another close friend from him.

Koble roared in sheer anger as he spotted the shooter, forty feet north, clutching a smoking rifle and shifting his aim away. The man was human, hairless, maybe forty cycles old and retreating.

Unfortunately for the mercenary, he wasn't quick enough to escape. In brutal fashion, Koble took aim and fired, shooting the man in the back. It wasn't an honourable kill, but Koble didn't care. He'd shown the same mercy as they'd shown Rain and Vol and all the folks they'd murdered.

Koble pushed forward, knowing he had maybe a minute to stop the rest from escaping. He was only vaguely aware that Astrilla was covering the right flank.

Something from the northeast rumbled through the sky. When Koble turned to look, he saw James rushing away from a small shuttle that was in pursuit. The whole thing was about eighty feet from Koble's position: close enough for him to take a shot. The little craft was firing its laser cannons in an attempt to stop James from getting away.

For a moment, it looked like it would be successful, then a projectile was fired from the ground upward. The rocket collided with the new shuttle, causing it to spin off course. The small ship danced in the air in a firey haze and veered left; toward the east. It soared over Koble's head, and he subconsciously forced himself to take a dive.

The heat of the fire was so intense that Koble was certain his fur had been singed. The failing engines screeched, and the unwelcome smell of fuel filled his nostrils. As he sat up, Koble saw the shuttle collide with the eastern walkway: *Nathan's last position.* He turned to where

James had been, but the Earther was gone.

With every last ounce of strength and anger in his body, Koble forced himself to his feet and rushed north. He saw the gunship lift into the air with James Stephens looking out of the open airlock with a victorious expression all over his chiselled face.

His eyes met Koble's for all but a moment. The sense of achievement in James' eyes made everything else seem irrelevant: as though he were saying, *that's right, you lost, and I won.*

The airlock doors closed shut, and the gunship began its ascent. Refusing to quit, Koble lifted his rifle and fired until his gun ran dry. He then swapped to his sidearm and did the same.

It was pointless.

The gunship disappeared into the stormy clouds that oppressed the skies. Defeat rose from the ground like a mist as he watched James escape.

In frustration, Koble threw his gun on the ground, just in time for Astrilla to reach his side.

"Bastards got away," he said.

The Evoker didn't reply. Together they stared into the sky where James had escaped. For the first time since the Pluvium Civil War, Koble found himself vowing revenge against another.

Thirty seconds later, Harrt joined them with Russell in tow. The former barkeep's gunshot wound was limited to his upper bicep. Sure, Russell looked like he wanted to throw up, but at least he'd see another day. Koble found solace in that, but it didn't take away from the sting of defeat.

NATHAN

The gaping gunshot wound on Nathan's shoulder was agonising. The pain was increased ten-fold by the predicament he'd found himself in: clinging to dear life from a protruding panel on the side of the Containment Facility. It was hard enough to maintain his grip on the rain-soaked metal, but the bullet in his shoulder made things twenty times worse. Below him was a drop likely several miles down, but Nathan refused to look.

He clung on with both hands as the freezing rain hammered him. His mind shut out everything, refusing to allow him to think of James, the last few hours, or anything else. Human survival instinct was the only thing left.

At first, Nathan tried to pull himself up, but his shoulder was under excruciating pressure already. He tried to call out, but his voice was lost amongst the cacophony of gunfire and thunder. The human part of his mind fought the urge to let go and battled against his torment. He told himself that adrenaline would numb the pain and all he needed to do was hold out a little longer.

The gunfire ceased, and Nathan heard the sound of a ship's engine.

His grip wavered, and he called out, hoping the others would hear him.

"Help!"

There was nothing.

"Help!"

The next thing Nathan knew, he was standing in the middle of the desert. *Elsewhere*. The pain was gone, and a gentle breeze rolled across the dunes. The bench where Nathan once sat and spoke with Bill was sticking out like a sore thumb. As it had been before, there was no sign of Bill, but Subject C was there, lingering in the foreground.

"You must live. You must find me".

"How?" Nathan asked.

Subject C moved toward him, but Nathan couldn't see a face or a body or even a shadow. All he saw was an outreached hand: begging him to embrace it.

Nathan took hold, and it pulled him up.

"You will find me in the place you've seen in your dreams," Subject C said. "Helia is out there".

Lightning flashed in Nathan's vision. A star exploded in the distance, and he found himself back at the Containment Facility, but now he wasn't gripping to the wall for dear life.

Something *—no, someone—* was hoisting him to safety.

Nathan lay on the soaking wet ground for a few seconds, unable to process what was happening. He breathed, coughed, and acknowledged the awful sting radiating around his shoulder. Gravity was at his back, and Nathan had never been more relieved to feel it grounding him.

His saviour —whoever they were— was sitting on the ground beside him in silence, their chest heaving from the exertion.

"Thank you!" Nathan finally panted.

There wasn't an immediate response.

He turned with his eyes wide open and saw the masked visage of Chimera. For a moment of utter disbelief, Nathan stared at Jareth's accomplice, unable to fathom a sentence.

Silence whirled between them.

"You've been shot," Chimera remarked.

"No shit," Nathan replied, turning his head to cough.

If it were Jack, he hadn't changed. Sympathy and emotional reunions had never been his thing. If it wasn't Jack under the mask, the guy was pretty matter-of-fact.

As Nathan lay there, he embraced the defeat, knowing that James would go on to do much worse. He hated himself for not pulling the trigger, but he wouldn't make that mistake again.

"Don't worry, pal," Chimera muttered. "You'll live to fight another day,"

▲

The others found Nathan and Chimera at the roof's edge less than three minutes later. Koble had shouted, and Harrt had raised his gun, but to Nathan's surprise, Chimera surrendered without resistance. There was a moment where things got a little heated, but Nathan blacked out at some point, and the next thing he knew, he was woken by the sound of voices.

The Phoenix's living area had been his natural habitat for over a year, and his mind knew that he was there before his eyes processed it. An unfamiliar Uvan woman was on his left, with brown skin, green eyes and short hair that was a mix of cobalt blue and magenta.

She stopped and smiled at him; "Welcome back".

Then Nathan saw the medical tool buried deep in his open shoulder, and reality came crashing down on him like a wave from the ocean.

Truth and betrayal, and anger overcame him as he recalled everything. It was agony. It wasn't physical pain but rather a sense of bitter betrayal and disappointment — particularly in himself.

He'd opened himself to James. Perhaps on some level, Nathan optimistically hoped that they could reforge what had once been.

How wrong he was.

James had exploited that weakness: just like he would've done in the Loyalty days. The fact was that James was still dangerous and violent and determined, but now it wasn't because he lusted for chemical highs. Whatever his motivation, it didn't matter to Nathan: James' actions said all that needed to be said.

Nathan swore to himself that he wouldn't show that kind of mercy —that weakness— to anyone again.

Never let them see you bleed.

He vowed to find James and Roth and make them pay for all the lives they'd taken. He'd find Gordon, and most importantly of all, he'd end the Society.

Once Nathan processed his thoughts on the matter, he realised there was no real pain. The 'wealthers had dosed him with painkillers strong enough to put down a Sphinax, but there was clarity to his thinking. Sure, he was tired and bitter, but only one thing mattered, and that was his next action.

The sound of metal pinging into a medical tray drew Nathan's attention. He glanced down, seeing the blood-soaked bullet in the bowl.

The medic turned to him:

"All good," she said. "I'll scan for any shrapnel".

Nathan nodded, and as the medic continued her work, he glanced around the Phoenix's living area. Everyone looked rattled, exhausted and soaked from the rain. Gone was the casual candour that often filled the Phoenix's halls, and it didn't feel right.

Russell looked okay if a little shaken: *after all, the kid had never been shot before.* He was sat on one of the armchairs, being checked by a medic. Nathan figured the former barkeep would need a few days to recover from his injury but would be fighting fit soon enough.

Then his eyes settled on the masked man at the bar.

Chimera sat in silence, discreetly watching the room. It was almost as though he were analysing his surroundings for any threats, which Jack would often do under the same circumstances.

Who the hell are you?

It was the one question Nathan kept asking himself since they'd clashed at Hawtrey House. Chimera was efficient and ruthless in combat: clearly well trained. His combat style, tattoo, build, and weaponry was like Jack's. And he'd saved Nathan from certain death. *Surely that made him an ally?*

Yet the question remained; *who was he under the mask?*

Once the medic finished her scans and closed the wound on Nathan's shoulder, it took him a moment to realise that his answers were waiting for him at the bar. He moved to stand, but the medic halted him;

"I don't think there will be any permanent damage to the shoulder, but you probably shouldn't lift anything heavy for a few days".

Nathan was too distracted by Chimera's presence to reply. If it really was Jack sitting at the bar, he had questions to answer: eleven years worth by Nathan's estimate.

"Captain Carter?" The medic said, breaking his train of thought.

Nathan looked at her.

The medic regarded him with a kindly smile, then produced a small light that she began shining in his eyes. She continued checking his head, where James struck him earlier.

"I closed the laceration, but you've suffered a mild concussion. I suggest you take a few days to rest," the medic said.

She glanced at the bar, then at Koble, who was necking a bottle of whiskey.

"And no drinking". Her tone made it sound more like an order than advice. "Is that clear?"

Nathan was about to answer, but Astrilla cut him off;

"Crystal clear," she said.

The medic nodded, wished Nathan a speedy recovery, then walked to her colleague, still tending to Russell.

That was when Nathan looked at Chimera with purpose. The masked man didn't move an inch; he just sat at the bar, observing everyone's movements carefully.

Nathan wanted to stand, but he recognised that he needed a moment to catch his breath. He allowed himself to acknowledge the aches and pains that would present themselves once the painkillers wore off.

Astrilla knelt beside him, leaning on the arm of the chair to look him in the eye. She was frowning, no doubt feeling as defeated as everyone else, but she also looked thoughtful and concerned.

"What exactly happened back there?" she asked.

Nathan took a long, slow breath.

"James shot me," he said. "I wanted to end it, but *James...* I just couldn't shoot him. I hesitated, and he didn't". Nathan nodded in Chimera's general direction; "Then that guy saved me".

"And what are we going to do about him?" Astrilla said.

Nathan didn't say anything. Instead, he slowly climbed to his feet, embracing the woozy, lightheaded sensation that the painkillers provided and walked across the living area.

A tense silence fell over the room.

Koble was moving away from the wall, his paw poised over his holster. Russell was leaning forward in his chair, despite the instructions of the medics. Harrt appeared from the cockpit, looking especially wary.

Everyone was anticipating another brawl, but that wasn't the way Nathan wanted to handle the situation. There had been enough conflict for one day, and whoever Chimera was he clearly felt the same.

Nathan stopped within two metres of the masked man.

Chimera climbed from the barstool and stood to face him. It was the first time Nathan had truly taken a good look at the man dressed in all-black combat gear. Chimera's stance was rigid and military-like, juxtaposing his scratched, battle-worn armour and tattered military jacket.

The mask on his face was cloth and had little to no technological benefit: in fact, it more than likely hindered the man in combat. That fact alone told Nathan that the mask was not a practical choice but rather a shroud. A veil. A way to disguise what lay beneath.

Nathan was the one to break the silence.

"Who the hell are you?"

Chimera didn't move: didn't flinch. A vocal scrambler made his voice sound robotic and distorted, but human inflexion still existed in his tone.

"Back on Earth, it was customary to thank someone after they saved your ass," Chimera said.

Nathan didn't appreciate the masked man's attempt to dodge the question.

"Who are you?" He repeated.

Chimera said nothing.

Koble moved into the fray, placing himself beside Nathan;

"C'mon, Jack," Koble urged. "Whatever your reason is for this get-up, it doesn't matter.."

Chimera tilted his head to one side as if questioning the Sphinax but didn't say a word.

"Enough is enough," Nathan said, raising his voice. He pointed an accusatory finger at Chimera, "You have the same build as Jack Stephens. The same tattoo. The same kinda gear and guns. You even fight like an EDA agent".

Chimera said nothing, and Nathan stepped closer to him. He tried to soften his voice as best as possible as he started into the expressionless visage of the black mask.

"Jack, I know what happened on Earth with Baylum and Roth. I understand you were ashamed, but I get it now; you didn't have a choice," Nathan paused, hoping that he was appealing to the man who'd raised him. "The past is the past. All that matters now is stopping Roth".

Chimera turned his back and began pulling the mask

from his head. He detached his vocal scrambler from a battery unit on his neck.

As Nathan watched the mercenary pull the disguise away, he felt his heart pound against his chest. He didn't know what he wanted to see. More than a decade of emotion swelled around Nathan. It intensified as the mask lifted.

A heartbeat passed.

The first thing Nathan saw was hair. Not blonde like Jack, but black with hints of grey. A military buzz-cut: *all business, no style.*

Chimera turned.

It was a face that looked as though it hadn't seen the world in a lifetime. He was human with a tanned complexion: somewhere in his fifties, with a square jaw and piercing green eyes: laser-focussed. He was clean-shaven, with a scar running from his right eyebrow to his cheek.

Not the face of Jack Stephens.

All at the same time, Nathan felt a debilitating sadness and a welcome relief. He wasn't sure which to embrace.

Chimera tossed his mask on the bar.

"Sorry to disappoint you, kid".

His accent was American: gritty, saxophonic and sharp like a knife. He looked at Nathan with a degree of sympathy beneath his hardened expression.

"My name is Eric Garland. I'm the last living member of the Earth Defense Alliance".

JARETH

When the rain finally ceased, David Jareth stepped onto Inon Waife's platform of greeting: *otherwise known as a balcony*. For years, he'd watched the Master of the House on the newscasts waving to his subjects and delivering rousing speeches of tolerance and galactic unification from that very spot. As Jareth stood there, he realised that it must've been easy for Waife to feel powerful and god-like.

The Council Chamber was a building that could've been

designed by the ancient Greeks, with colossal stone columns and a gathering space below that could've easily trumped St. Peter's Square. The whole thing was built for greatness: to elevate the leader above the masses in a way that was completely and utterly anti-communist.

Man's desire for grandeur was potent.

As the sun rose on a new day, Jareth pondered the future. A hostile force had slaughtered an entire government in a violent and sadistic manner. There was no clear line of succession for the 'wealth, which meant there would be a gambit to seize control. If history was an indicator of things to come, then things were about to get complicated.

Maybe that was precisely what Roth wanted.

He noticed an easterly breeze passing by, carrying a scent he couldn't pinpoint. It was a damn sight better than the inside of the Council Chamber. Jareth took a deep breath of the fresh air, purging his lungs and nostrils of the pungent smell of death that seemed to cling to the walls inside. The government building and its exterior looked like a warzone: complete with bloodied bodies and bullet holes to add to the now ravaged decor.

For the first time in a very long while, Jareth felt the bitter sting of defeat. He'd arrogantly assumed that his plan would work: that he could finally put an end to the Society and Roth and Baylum and Project Erebus.

He had no doubt that Roth would be sipping his champagne in victory, but everything was still to play for.

He leant on the railing, knowing that his part in the coming war was just as Jack Stephens predicted all those years ago: *tied to the path of Nathan Carter.*

That was his destiny, and in some strange way, Jareth had accepted it long ago. He was exactly where the universe, god, or the Enkaye intended.

This was the righteous path: *the only path.*

"It's a long way down from this height".

Jareth craned his neck, spotting Elder Yuta standing in the doorway. The old woman pulled back the dark hood from her head and regarded him with a look of indifference.

"I have no intention of escaping," Jareth mused.

"Of course not," Yuta remarked as she shuffled to stand beside him. "You bear the look of a man who is exactly where he wants to be."

Jareth raised his brow, realising she was far more shrewd than he'd initially assumed.

"Tell me," she began. "What do you think the 'wealth will do to Paradisium for all of this?"

Jareth shook his head; "You and I know that the men who attacked Waife and the Council were part of a wider conspiracy. What they did does not represent the people of Paradisium".

Yuta exhaled as she produced a datapad from her cloak. She handed the device to Jareth, allowing him to look at a tactical view of the surrounding system. The remainder of the Paradisian ships were fleeing, and in their place were Commonwealth Warships meeting a small Revenant Armada in the field of battle.

Roth had done it again —smoke and mirrors and the act of manipulation. By bringing the Revenant —even if it was five or six ships— he'd only added to the already bleak picture of Paradisium and its citizens. The 'wealth already saw them as an enemy, but now they would see Paradisium as an ally to their greatest nemesis.

Jareth returned the datapad to Yuta:

"What do you think will happen next?"

The old woman shook her head and answered:

"Violence begets violence, Mr Jareth".

INTERLUDE
ROTH

The pièce de résistance, in ten simple steps. Note to self; know that victory comes with patience —you'll need it.

Step 1) Adopt a new stray. Get him sober; feed him; clothe him; train him. Now, wait. This lowly creature will — over time— evolve into a useful attack dog. Consider your dog a long-term investment that will pay dividends. In the meantime, drink brandy, and exercise patience.

Alastair Roth's personal assistant twisted a corkscrew into a thirty-three-year-old bottle of Château Latour. After it was placed on his desk, Roth dismissed the man. As he allowed the wine to breathe, Roth glanced out of his office window at the destruction that littered Valour's orbit.

Early reports indicated that the explosion and subsequent shockwave from the Artemis' wiped out over fifteen percent of the blockade. It wasn't quite the numbers Roth had hoped for, but fifteen percent was still high enough to incite a reaction.

Step 2) There comes the point where you need to validate if your investment is worthwhile. Give your dog a task to prove his value. Perhaps challenge him to infiltrate a particularly persistent thorn in your side, otherwise known as Tariq Mahmoot. If your investment has been wise, your dog will succeed in his mission. If he fails, cut your losses and return to Step 1.

By the time the remaining Paradisian ships started retreating, the wine was ready to drink. As Roth poured himself a glass, new reports came flooding in. James Stephens had been successful in his mission, right down to the last detail. He'd captured a most illusive man while assassinating the Commonwealth Council and rescuing Christian from a 'wealther gulag. *Good dog, indeed.*

Step 3) When the political conditions are finally right, create a movement that will grab the galaxy's attention. Something grand but modest; we don't need violence yet, but we certainly need a diversion.

For several minutes, Roth sipped his wine in quiet contemplation. The complicated part was over. That fact alone filled him with a sense of victory. Of course, he couldn't allow that feeling to cloud his judgement. Everything that was to happen next was critical. In completing this phase of the pièce de résistance, he'd built the foundation for his rise to power, but everything was still to play for.

Step 4) When the time is right, lure your enemies — including the aforementioned thorn in one's side— into the perfect trap. Like the Ancient Greeks, give your enemy a Trojan horse. Allow said 'horse' to gain the trust of the witless and be patient. The fall of Troy is coming. Allow the horse/dog to gather intel and confirm the identity of a man who's evaded you for decades.

Ten minutes later, the office doors opened, and Christian rushed inside, still wearing his prison jumpsuit. Roth frowned at his son in disappointment.

It had never been a part of the plan for Christian to be captured. He was supposed to be tucked away where the Commonwealth couldn't find him —perhaps shacked up with one of his many asinine conquests.

"How could you let that pudgy Sphinax capture you so easily?" Roth barked. "I spent a bloody fortune on your combat training to prevent things like that from happening".

Christian didn't immediately reply and instead snatched the open bottle of Château Latour from the desk. Christian pretended to examine the label as a way to cover his shame. Then like the smug, arrogant little shit he was, Christian drank directly from the bottle.

Silence loitered there.

Once he stopped drinking, Christian glared at Roth.

"Good to see you too, father".

A part of Roth wanted to scold his son for his failures: to tell him he'd jeopardised the pièce de résistance. He quickly changed his mind as James Stephens and Bradley Austin entered his office, dragging a battered and beaten prisoner with them.

Roth chose to savour the moment. He peered at Christian with indifference and, in a harsh tone, said, "See that you learn from this failure".

Christian scowled but didn't say anything.

Step 5) Using all of your influence and other investments, craft a new distraction, but this time something more aggressive: something that looks like war to the 'wealth. The enemy will no doubt take their eyes off your horse. Now your horse can behave like a dog.

The man James and Austin brought before him vaguely resembled the intel pictures from the first Project Erebus — twenty-six years prior. The man in the photographs had been in the prime of his life: *a more oblivious man, perhaps?* His eyes were the same, if maybe a little warier. His hair was marginally thinner, and undoubtedly greyer. The beard was the same but somehow looked different on a man approaching his sixties. Where before his facial hair looked like a statement piece, now it was something intended to lend to his surly, teacherly appearance.

"We found these," James said, producing a pair of thick dark-framed glasses.

Roth glanced at the spectacles and knew *they were the cherry on top of the cake.* Finally, after twenty-six years Roth had him: the final piece to unlock Project Erebus. The prisoner was the right-hand man of Bill Stephens *—the illusive Doctor Aubrey Gordon Beckett.*

Roth patted James on the back, "You've done well, my old friend,"

The prisoner scowled with his busted lip: hatred burning in his dark eyes.

"Doctor Beckett. We meet at long last!" Roth said. "I suppose congratulations are in order; you have been the single most slippery target the Society has ever known".

Beckett glared back.

James said, "He's been going by the name Gordon Taggart for quite some time"

For twenty-six years, Roth had searched for the man responsible for destroying the site buried deep beneath the Ural Mountains. To finally look upon Beckett felt slightly underwhelming. He expected better things, perhaps a dynamic mind or someone akin to Jack Stephens. Instead, Roth simply saw a man and nothing more.

Beckett tried to stand in protest, but James slammed his rifle into his back. The Doctor fell to the ground writhing in agony, and Roth laughed callously.

"I like this one," Roth mocked. He glanced at Austin, who watched Beckett's suffering as though it were light entertainment for the more depraved parts of his damaged psyche.

"Put him in a chair," Roth barked at Austin.

Step 6) Create tragedy. Note to self: this task is best delegated to your witless, gullible, Revenant ally. You don't want to be implicated in the matter if it all goes wrong. Make the King believe that he is the one in charge (it'll be critical later). Sit back and watch the fireworks as a 'wealther warship explodes, killing thousands.

Austin nodded, though there was a slight disappointment in his eyes. The big man dragged Beckett *—or Taggart—* into one of the vintage armchairs. Roth pulled up a seat opposite and waited as Austin, Christian, and the others left. James went to take his leave, but Roth called out to him;

"Not you, Stephens. I want you here for this".

James looked at him with scrutiny but didn't question the order. He returned to Roth's side, leaning against the wooden desk at the back of the room: hand poised over his pistol, looking more and more like his father —Jack— every day.

Roth turned his attention to Beckett and sipped his wine thoughtfully. He wanted the silence to feel eerie and uncomfortable, but alas, Beckett resisted:

"I'm not dead, so you clearly want something out of

me; so what the hell do you want?"

Roth noted the hatred on the Doctor's face. The simple answer to Beckett's question was that Roth desired power: the kind that would enable him to vanquish the Commonwealth and the Revenant in one fell swoop. Doing so would allow him to take his rightful place as the wise and wonderful ruler of the known galaxy. Of course, that was the simplified answer, and Roth had no intention of revealing his plans to the likes of Beckett.

Step 7) While step 6 takes place, take the other dogs off the leash. Assign each of the packs an objective and put them to work.

Roth held up his wine: "This is from a bottle of Château Latour. At one point, it was one of the most expensive bottles of wine you could purchase on Earth. I've waited thirty-three years to open this exquisite bottle. You could say I wanted to find the right moment to drink it".

There was another long silence.

"Do I look like I care about wine?" Beckett snarled.

Roth smiled. "You see, thirty-three years is a very long time, Doctor Beckett. It's almost as old as the Fall". Roth's voice turned slow and sibilant. "Decades ago, my organisation put Titus Rousseau and Sebastian Eli in charge of a critical operation in the Ural Mountains: I believe you know all too well what I am referring to".

Roth stared at Beckett, seeing something harrowing in the man's eyes: *memories of violence, perhaps?* Thanks to some *useful tools*, Roth had a good idea of what Beckett survived, but it wasn't a hundred percent. Fortunately, those same *useful tools* could finally be used as motivation for what came next.

Step 8) With all pieces in place, take your prize attack dog off his leash: he is no longer a horse. All dogs will execute their orders and, in doing so, kill your political rivals and cement the Paradisian movement as an act of war.

"You see, Rousseau and Sebastian failed me," Roth said. "They gave an order that was not theirs to give. Project Erebus was supposed to be mine. I was supposed to crack this bottle open the day they delivered what they promised".

"Then how about you take it up with Titus Rousseau?" Beckett spat a mouthful of blood onto the floor. "Your hit squad killed my friends and a whole bunch more for that... *thing"*.

There was ferocity in Beckett's voice: and Roth loved it. The man leaned forward, hands balling into fists.

"You have no idea what was inside Project Erebus, but I do. I saw it with my own eyes, and I tell you now, it was dangerous".

Roth quietly sipped his wine before slamming it violently into his desk. Glittering shards of handmade crystal flew up into the air like a dandelion exposed to a breeze.

"Listen to me, Beckett or Taggart or whatever fucking name you want to go by," Roth said, his voice rising into a bellow. "I want what Rousseau promised me all those years ago. I want Project Erebus opened, and I want that which lays inside. I want the power of the gods".

"Good thing Bill blew it to kingdom come," Beckett sneered defiantly. "He knew exactly what that thing was. We made damn sure to take it down so that mad bastards like you couldn't access it".

Step 9) Dog comes home to master. He brings you the catch of the day; the man who has evaded you for decades. Good dog.

Roth licked his lips, and a proud smile formed on his rotund face.

"It's such a shame that Doctor Stephens didn't account for more than one Project Erebus".

Roth could see the blood rush from Beckett's face. He moved from his chair and stood over the prisoner: *man and subject, the way it was always intended.*

"I've been waiting a lifetime to claim what is rightfully mine," Roth said. He gestured at James, "I have an Enkaye half-breed, willing to donate his blood to the mix. I have the galaxy's eyes locked on a conflict that will cause no end of controversy". Roth settled his eyes on Beckett, "And now, I have you: the man who opened the first Project Erebus".

"I won't do it," Beckett declared. "You may as well shoot me because I will not help you with this insanity".

Roth answered with a slight, unreadable smile.

"That's where you are so very wrong, Doctor Beckett. The Society has its methods. We saw to the desolation of Rome; the invention of nuclear weaponry; the fall of Earth, and the invention of the celebrity. We even forced Jack Stephens to do what we wanted". Roth paused for effect, leaning closer to Beckett. "When we reach Helia, you —like Jack Stephens— will do as I command. You will bend to my will".

"We'll see about that," Beckett spat.

"Indeed we shall".

Step 10) Drink brandy and celebrate as you head to Helia. For tomorrow you shall open Project Erebus unchallenged. Thus becoming the most powerful man in the universe.

▲

When Roth was done, James dragged Beckett away. It was only then that Roth noticed that the prisoner had dripped blood onto the armchair upholstery. Usually, such an imposition would drive him to the point of screaming, but today —on this most glorious of days— Alastair Roth allowed himself to let go of his indignation.

James returned seconds later, having ordered Martinez and Austin to escort Beckett to his cell. Roth gestured to his drinks cabinet, where many bottles of fine wine and port and whiskey were stored.

"Can I offer you a drink?" Roth asked.

James Stephens was covered in blood and sweat, looking like the vicious attack dog Roth had groomed him to become.

James shook his head with a distant expression.

"Rain check? I really feel the need to shower".

The dog knows when to wash. Good dog.

Roth nodded and began a slow walk toward the large window at the back of his office.

"You really proved yourself out there". Roth peered at James with a look of gratitude in his wrinkled eyes. "I'm proud of you, *son*".

James acknowledged the fatherly comment the way he always did, with an awkward and uneasy shrug.

A small part of Roth wished that Jack —the imbecile— Stephens could see what had become of his only son. It was revenge but in the most beautiful way.

Roth stopped at the long window and looked out at the destruction before him. A small battle between the Commonwealth's third fleet and a tiny scatter of Revenant Warships was taking place just beyond the Capital World of Gallantry. Though the fight wouldn't last long, it would be the perfect distraction for Roth and the remaining Paradisian ships to escape. It would also make it appear like the Revenant and Paradisium were now in cahoots, thus further fanning the flames of war.

Around Valour was a sea of debris from the detonation. It was picturesque in a way: a violent monument to Roth's success. As much as he wanted to take it all in like a piece of fine art, Roth knew that beauty was in the moment.

He tapped the comms device on his desk, and the Featon's pilot, Elwen Cameron, responded, awaiting his orders.

"Take us to Helia," Roth said.

A sobering thought ran through his mind as Valour disappeared behind the blue veil of the slipstream. So far, his mission had been a complete success, and Project Erebus was within reach, but Baylum was still a problem that needed fixing.

All in due time, Roth told himself.

CHAPTER THIRTY-SIX
NATHAN

Eric —Chimera— Garland was not Jack. He was a man who'd worked for the same agency back on Earth, with the same combat training and the same tattoo, but he wasn't Jack: that was for damn sure.

Garland seemed reserved and methodical in every which way. There was a slight abrasiveness to the way he spoke: like everyone around him was a threat.

He explained that after the encounter at Hawtrey House, he'd spied on a conversation between Roth and Baylum. Nathan was sceptical at first, but Garland produced a datapad with drone footage of the meeting, in which Roth had uttered to Baylum, *"The nephew of Jack Stephens will be yours"*.

Baylum's desire for revenge didn't surprise Nathan in the slightest. He figured it would only be a matter of time before the Revenant King would come looking for the people who killed his father and destroyed the Messorem. Still, it felt weird hearing it aloud: a gentle tug on the strings of reality.

Garland leaned on the bar, arms crossed uncomfortably as Nathan watched the footage.

"That was when I knew why you were calling me Jack," he said. "You are one of the guys from the Loyalty, right?"

"Yeah," Nathan straightened up on his barstool. "Why does that matter?"

Garland tensed his jaw and blinked uncomfortably.

"You gotta understand there was some bad blood with Jack and me. During the Fall, we had an encounter of sorts... one that resulted in me getting shot in the chest".

Nathan wondered if he needed to reach for his gun: wondered if perhaps Garland was a man out for revenge.

"But," Garland's voice lifted. "Jareth reintroduced me to Jack about eight years after the Fall, along with a few guys from the Loyalty".

Nathan peered at Koble, and the big Sphinax shrugged with his paws. "Two years before my time".

Garland continued, "Around that time Jack stumbled onto Enkaye tech, and it showed him some weird things".

"What things?"

Garland pointed around the room, "This ship for one; the Messorem; this crazy purpose that he had to fulfil. A load of shit that sounded farfetched and way out there".

Nathan said nothing.

"I didn't believe him," Garland said, rolling his jaw in angst. "But Jareth did, and that's something. So, over a decade, we pulled together the circumstances to ensure that Jack's visions and plans went smoothly".

There was a long pause.

"Then…" Garland counted on his fingers. "Eleven years ago, everything went to shit".

Nathan didn't need to count to know what he was referring to. It was the single moment wherein everything had gone very wrong. It was the day the Loyalty's crew were ambushed at Mirotose Station.

In a low voice, Garland said, "I was at Mirotose Station two days after it happened. By the time I got there, station security had cleared the whole thing up. They'd burned all the bodies, and there was no evidence. The principal investigator went missing, and his partner turned up with a bullet in his brain".

Garland paused for breath.

There was a hint of anger behind his eyes.

"After reports came in about the Loyalty crashing into the Xung-Sin hideout, everyone, including Jareth, concluded that Jack's crew —that you— were gone. Jareth told me y'all were dead and that all of our work was for nothing".

Some form of dark truth whirled there, and it caused Nathan to tremble slightly. He didn't know what to make of it all, but one thing was certain: Jareth knew more than he'd let on.

"Why are you telling me this?" Nathan asked.

Garland gave a look that suggested something deeply uncomfortable: *perhaps something extremely personal*. He coughed and quickly recovered his stoic gaze:

"When you a spend a decade of your life lining things up, so the supposed *saviour of the universe* has a fighting chance, you get a little invested," he said. "I went into containment storage for a few years after Mirotose; needed a bit of time for the galaxy to move on. I was woken up almost a year ago by Jareth with a new mission —to take down the Society once and for all. But he neglected to tell me you were still alive, which pisses me off more than you can imagine".

Nathan struggled to reconcile all the things Garland was saying. Jack had played a role in setting things up for him: ensuring that the Enkaye's destiny for him went according to plan. He'd never considered that others knew about it, but Garland's testimony proved different.

When Nathan lifted his head, he noticed Garland was glancing around the crew: analysing them individually.

He stopped at Nathan; "Is this the whole crew?"

"All but one," Harrt answered. "The Society captured Doctor Taggart earlier today".

"Who the fuck is Taggart?" Garland's face turned to concern, and his voice lifted. "Jack never mentioned anyone called Taggart".

All of a sudden, a klaxon sounded throughout the Phoenix, originating in the cockpit. Nathan wanted nothing more than to continue, but he couldn't shake the thought that Roth was making another play.

He glanced toward the cockpit, then back to Garland:

"I'll take you back to Jareth soon. Once that happens, the three of us will have a conversation".

Garland nodded. "Wouldn't have it any other way".

HARRT

The Phoenix's sensors buzzed with life. It wasn't a comms alert or a proximity alarm, which was a welcome change given the last few hours. Harrt felt a tiny piece of his adrenaline drop when he realised they weren't in imminent danger. He was the first one to the holotable, and by the time the others reached the cockpit, he'd already silenced the alarm.

A blue holographic message formed, and Harrt recognised it as a personalised notification he'd set up back at the hangar. His pulse thumped as he read the words aloud:

"Sadalmelik detected".

Harrt opened the notification, displaying the Sadalmelik's location on the other side of Valour, slightly southwest of the Phoenix's current position. Harrt glanced at Nathan, but the Earther was already heading for the pilot's station.

Harrt felt his throat constrict. With everything in the last few hours, he'd allowed anger and adrenaline to fuel his desire for revenge, simply assuming that Vol and Jaudi had died in the explosion. That was the right thing to do when facing an intense combat situation.

Denial, grief, hope and incomprehension overcame his every sense, and he wasn't sure which one to embrace. So, in the end, Harrt focused his mind on the flight ahead. He tapped the Phoenix's controls, and within seconds the ship punched its way across Valour's skyline.

▲

The journey took under four minutes. Sure, Harrt had violated every strict safety law in the book as he'd navigated Valour's barren skylanes, but he simply didn't care. If there was a chance in hell that someone —anyone— from the Sadalmelik, the Artemis, or both had made it, he had to get there.

He'd barely processed it over the last few hours, but now something inside him had awoken. *Optimism, perhaps?*

Maybe the calm had created headspace, or perhaps it was the slightest hint of hope that he felt, knowing someone had got out of there.

The Phoenix roared with an almost animal-like howl as Harrt pushed the ship to the safest maximum velocity. If he could've sent the ship into FTL without the consequence of certain death, he would've done so immediately.

The first thing of the Sadalmelik that Harrt saw was a plume of dark smoke looming against the sunrise. Then when the Phoenix got closer, Harrt felt a chill run up his spine.

Tariq Mahmoot's ship had crash-landed in a large municipal park. Where the trail of destruction began, there was a massive ripple of scorched ground where the ship's shield array had likely cushioned the initial impact. A long trail of mud, trees and charred debris followed to the entryway for one of Valour's many skyscrapers. And there was the Sadalmelik: a shell of its former self. The once magnificent vessel was embedded deep into the base of the building, with only its stern visible from the sky.

"Shit," Koble said, anxiously leaning between the pilot and copilot's seat to get a look. "That ship took one hell of a beating".

Harrt didn't say anything.

Instead, he focussed on landing the Phoenix as close as possible to the crash site. Emergency services were already at the scene, extinguishing what remained of the blaze while evacuating civilians from the area.

When the ship touched down, Harrt dashed out of the cockpit, through the living spaces and out of the airlock before the boarding ramp emerged from the Phoenix's underbelly. A law enforcer was waiting for him and tried to sanction him for a non-compliant landing.

Harrt ignored the man and sprinted as fast as his legs allowed, heading straight toward the Sadalmelik. He didn't have time for bureaucracy or stodgy 'wealther rules: he had to know if anyone survived.

Once he reached the Sadalmelik, Harrt rushed inside. The once pristine white corridors, full of art and sculptures, were ravaged. The walls were cracked and scorched and reeked of an extinguished fire. Broken glass covered the floor, and many of Tariq's paintings had fallen from the walls. A chunk of the roof was ripped to shreds: likely caused by a projectile, based on the violent way the hull had warped inward.

The bridge was the same as the corridors —a wreck. Most of the workstations had tipped over under the extreme impact. Everything was covered in thick shards of glass where the cockpit window smashed.

The early morning daylight spilt into the room just enough for Harrt to see two medics tending to a person in the copilot's chair.

When Harrt got closer, he recognised Elder Repla, sprawled out unconscious. Her scaley skin had turned pale, and her clothes were covered in green blood.

"Is she gonna make it?" Harrt asked.

One of the medics, a female Horrus, glanced at him with a severe expression.

"She's lost a lot of blood, but I'm pretty hopeful".

Harrt gestured to the pilot's station;

"Where's the pilot?"

"They took her out front," the medic answered gruffly, gesturing to the open void in the Sadalmelik's bow.

Harrt peered out of the broken cockpit window and into the reception area where the ship had crashed. There, sitting upon a metal bench, was Vol. A medic was checking her over, and she looked a little queasy but she was alive.

At that moment, Harrt felt his anxiety melt away. Everything that wasn't Vol became a blur. He climbed through the window frame and slid down the Sadalmelik's hull. Once his feet hit the floor, he dashed toward her.

Vol's pink skin was slightly ashen. Her typically kind eyes were bloodshot and weary and exhausted. She was covered in cuts and bruises, and her clothes were stained with dried blood. Despite all those things, she was the most beautiful thing he'd seen in a very long time. Seeing her there, knowing she was alive and well, was like returning home after a long voyage.

When Vol saw him, she smiled, though it was an expression of relief, sadness, and something else that Harrt couldn't quite pinpoint. When he reached her, Harrt pulled her into a hug and, for a long moment, refused to let go.

Nathan, Astrilla and Koble were about twenty seconds behind. Once the initial shock and relief and emotion had calmed, Koble gestured to the Sadalmelik;

"Hell of a landing," he said, lightly nudging Vol.

She laughed, but Harrt could tell it was slightly forced.

"You don't know the half of it," she said.

▲

Harrt had to sit down as Vol recounted everything that happened aboard the Artemis. To think that Cadu, the innocent-seeming kid Harrt had saved on the Equus, was a Revenant mole was beyond words. Vol's account of the massacre was harrowing. She spared no detail, and to her credit, emotion didn't get the best of her.

Harrt failed to push aside a part of his brain that blamed himself: after all, he'd brought Cadu aboard and trusted him. In return for that kindness, Cadu murdered not only the Sadalmelik's crew but also everyone that had staffed the Artemis, including Jaudi.

That one stung more than Harrt cared to say.

He'd known the woman for nearly thirty years. She'd been at his wedding. He'd fought beside her at Maru Seven. Jaudi's death was on him. Harrt figured he was the one to save Cadu and bring him aboard the Artemis. Like a gullible moron, he'd enabled Cadu to complete his mission.

"You gotta stop thinking that way," Vol whispered as she walked beside him toward the Phoenix. "Cadu had Marx and Repla fooled. He was a clever little bastard. We could've never known what he was".

Harrt shook his head, clearing the violent images his mind imagined.

"It just doesn't make sense," he said. "I spent a year investigating politicians and officials because they were the people with access to intel and Waife. I never thought a lone

Evoker would have such privileges".

Vol looked at him with narrowed eyes. "Cadu wasn't working alone".

"What do you mean?"

"Xanathur," Vol said in a low voice. "The whole time Cadu was killing the crew, he..." she paused as though pulling back something painful. "He kept saying he was doing this for Xanathur".

"Elder Xanathur?" Harrt said, his voice lifting in surprise. "That's impossible; Yuta received reports confirming that his ship was destroyed en route to Valour..."

Vol looked at him with hard eyes, "Cadu said he wasn't doing this for Roth. He said it was for Xanathur, Baylum and the Great Void".

The Great Void: the Revenant's sacred waters. It was the machine that turned the dead into mindless husks and whispered into the ears of Revenant Purebloods.

Harrt wondered for a moment if Xanathur, an Evoker with almost a century of dedicated service, could've betrayed his creed in such a way.

At first, it sounded absurd, but an Elder would have all the same accesses as a politician or an admiral. He'd be privy to crucial operational intel, especially during the tumultuous period where Astrilla was on the run from the Revenant. Maybe Xanathur was the mole he'd been looking for this entire time, but if he was, that made things much more complicated.

ASTRILLA

What Vol said made little sense. Hearing that Xanathur, a man Astrilla had known since her formative years, was working for the Revenant made her sick to her stomach. She'd barely processed the prospect that he'd —supposedly — died a few hours ago; that would've been easier to accept.

To think of him now as a turncoat was beyond words.

Granted, there was only mild substance to Vol's argument, with no actual proof, but it didn't replace the fact that Repla had known something aboard the Vertex. *Maybe Cadu's insane ramblings had given away some detail of Xanathur's true intentions?*

"Could you say it one more time?" Astrilla said, craning her eyes to look at Vol. "What exactly did Cadu say?"

Vol folded her arms, still traumatised and shocked by everything that'd happened. The Uvan sighed, pressing her fingers against her eyelids as if she were in deep thought.

"Cadu said that it was an act of beautiful violence," Vol shuddered at the words. "It was for Xanathur. For Baylum and for the Void".

Astrilla said nothing.

"Could it be true?" Nathan asked.

"In theory, it's possible," she said, finally forcing herself to speak. "I just don't understand why he'd do such a thing".

"The Void," Nathan mused. "Maybe the Revenant fed him to their holy water, and it fried his brain?"

Harrt nodded; "It's certainly done worse".

"It doesn't work like that," Astrilla shook her head. "The mutation process can only affect the dead. If Xanathur did this, then he did it knowingly: consciously".

"He did it," Vol said with finality. "Xanathur is a part of this now, and Repla was sure of it too. In his dying thoughts Cadu was consumed by this idea that he was completing a divine act for Xanathur and Baylum".

Astrilla was quiet for a long moment: unsure of what to say. Vol was rarely wrong when it concerned her sporadic mind-reading abilities, and of course, why would she lie about such a thing? *Perhaps Cadu had been lying that entire time, but why would he continue his deception in his dying thoughts?*

That left only one option—the horrible truth.

NATHAN

Finding Vol alive and well provided the crew with a much-needed dose of relief, but Nathan couldn't help but grimace at what happened aboard the Artemis.

Cadu, the weird-looking kid with a shitty haircut, had committed mass murder: all in the name of Elder Xanathur. Not Roth.

Nathan couldn't quite get his head around the prospect of Xanathur as the traitor who'd screwed them over several times. Unlike the other Elders, he'd always been cordial and polite with Nathan: always treating him with respect and dignity.

Better than the other Elders.

If anything, he was the least likely to be the mole, and yet, Nathan found himself questioning all of that.

As Nathan stepped aboard the Phoenix, he considered his next play. The angry, vengeful, and very human part of him acknowledged that James and Roth had caused this, and they deserved to pay. Then there was Gordon, captured by Roth for unknown reasons. He didn't know why, but something in his gut told him that Gordon was critical to Roth. If he'd wanted the Doctor dead, he would be like Waife and the Council —slaughtered.

No, Roth needed him alive, and that was important.

Then there was the final piece of the puzzle; Subject C. Whoever they were, they could access the desert: the elsewhere —*whatever the hell that place was*. They could communicate to Nathan on a different plane of existence, just like Bill had done on the Messorem.

There was one thing that Nathan hadn't acknowledged yet, and that was the fallout for Paradisium. In many ways, he felt no allegiance toward the sunny little rock and its idiotic and shallow inhabitants. They were the ones who had been foolish enough to follow Markus Holland into protest. They were the ones who'd never questioned the nature of the celebrities they heralded as gods.

Despite all that, the Paradisians were all that remained of Earth. Some would go so far as to say that they were Nathan's people: that he should feel some semblance of allegiance, but it wasn't that simple.

He wasn't one of them.

He'd never been one of them.

Upon entering the living area, Nathan spotted Garland

and Russell sitting at the bar. Despite his injuries, Russell watched Garland like a hawk while clutching Gordon's trusted shotgun. Russell's supervision of the man known as Chimera ceased when he saw Vol. He rushed to his feet to hug her, and once he released the Uvan from his hold, she stared at Garland with a degree of caution.

"Who the hell is this?" Vol asked.

Garland didn't say a word.

"That is another long story," Astrilla answered, stepping beside Vol.

Before Nathan could say anything else on the matter, Harrt entered with his datapad on loudspeaker, and the voice of Leviticus Dines filled the living area.

"It's bad, Oxarri," Dines was saying anxiously.

Harrt placed his datapad on the bar, and a hologram, no larger than six inches, formed above. Dines looked like he usually did: grumpy and slightly on edge. It was amazing how the man seemed both in his element and completely bewildered at the same time.

"What now?" Harrt asked.

Dines brushed a stray piece of silver hair back and sighed into the holo-recorder.

"Nothing like this has ever happened. Most of the council is dead or in critical condition". Dines looked worried about that. "Commissioner Kamen is the highest member of government that seems to be alive, but she isn't a councillor; she's technically part of the legal system".

Harrt leaned on the bar and put his head in his hands.

"What does that mean?" Nathan asked.

Dines tensed his jaw.

"As a caretaker to the Commonwealth leadership, she would be perfect, but because Kamen is the legal link between the politicians and high command, the Admiralty technically out-ranks her".

"What does that mean?" Nathan repeated.

Dines was awkwardly silent.

Harrt jumped in; "It means that the military is going to make a play for power".

The thought of an already corrupt government at the

hands of someone controlling the military and the political system sent a chill down Nathan's spine. Anyone with the faintest grasp of history knew that was a dangerous combination: the perfect way to create a tyrant.

Dines cleared his throat;

"Admirals Wexell, Embala and Deffu are holding an emergency summit to decide what happens next".

"Well, it's simple, isn't it?" Harrt replied. "We go after Roth and stop him".

"You know the Admiralty will only work with facts," Dines sighed. "We know this is the work of Alastair Roth, but Markus Holland was the one who made all the public addresses. He was the one all over the Paradisian social feeds. He was the one making all the speeches. As far as anyone is concerned, Holland is the public face of this".

Nathan felt his stomach twist at what Dines was saying. He was completely and utterly correct.

"The Commonwealth will react," Dines surmised. "If I were Paradisium, I'd be worried".

"That's exactly what Roth wants," Nathan argued.

"Then we must make our case," Harrt said. "Give the Admiralty our account of the situation".

"You really think they'll believe us?" Nathan snapped.

Harrt shrugged, his dark eyes narrow.

"We've got to try at least," he said. "The Paradisians may be foolish, but they do not deserve violence for being victims of deception".

The room was silent for a moment.

"Oxarri's right," Russell nodded. "Paradisium was my home for a long time. Sure, a bunch of those people are fuckin' morons, but there are good people there too".

In Nathan's head, he saw a million red flags but felt the overwhelming need to bring a metric ton of 'wealther justice upon Alastair Roth. He couldn't do that if the 'wealth had its guns pointed at Paradisium.

"Fine," Nathan sighed. Then looking at the hologram of Dines, "Bring Jareth with you: it's about fuckin' time he started pulling his weight".

Dines nodded.

CHAPTER THIRTY-SEVEN
ASTRILLA

The Verulanum was to be the venue for the emergency summit: where the fate of Paradisium and the future of the 'wealth would be decided. It was an old building, pre-dating the 'wealth by a century, and was considered by many to be one of the most significant historical landmarks on Valour. It was where the Founders first signed the accords, thus forming the Commonwealth. It was a wonder how the 'wealth hadn't bulldozed it and built a few high-rise towers, but Astrilla presumed it was because of that historic moment:

The birth of a new order.

She suspected there was a rationale behind choosing the Verulanum that went beyond the damage at the Council Chambers.

Perhaps the birth of another new order?

Astrilla's gut told her that the gathering to come was not going to be pleasant. There was no doubt in her mind that the Admiralty would seek revenge for what had happened: it was the only logical outcome.

The interior of the Verulanum was set up in the model of an ancient Commonwealth amphitheatre. At the centre of the room was a long table that could seat over thirty.

Massive stone pillars went from floor to ceiling at regular intervals spanning over two hundred feet in height. It was a building from a different era, opulent and grandiose: designed by a long-dead emperor whose name had been purged from history.

When the Phoenix's crew arrived, most of the 'wealth's new delegation had already assembled around the long table. The vast majority were military, but there were a few civic members among the forty or so attendees, including Public Commissioner Nephthys Kamen, Illuminator high-priest Jimea Hummel and of course Agent Leviticus Dines.

"This ain't gonna be fun," Nathan grimaced.

"Hey, at least we didn't bring the whole gang," Koble shrugged. "That could've made things a lot more interesting".

The Sphinax was right.

The group had opted to leave Russell, Garland and Vol back at the Phoenix, which in Astrilla's view, was the right call. Vol had been through hell and back, and the last thing she needed was an interrogation from a group of angry, militant 'wealthers. Eric Garland was an unknown quantity, and Russell was still light on his feet and a little emotional about Paradisium.

"Well, well," Koble said, nudging Harrt, then Astrilla. "Look who it is".

He pointed out David Jareth at the back of the room, who was under the scrutinous supervision of Elder Yuta. As always, Jareth looked calm and collected, like a man in his element.

Astrilla followed Nathan as he moved through the attendees toward Jareth. Koble and Harrt were close behind. When Nathan stopped at Jareth's side, the old man regarded him with an unsurprised expression.

"Looks like you took a bit of a tumble?" Jareth gestured to Nathan's shoulder.

Nathan leaned in, keeping his voice low and threatening:

"We got your man, Garland, back on the Phoenix".

Jareth's lips curled upward into a thin smile.

"Not who you were hoping for, I presume?"

Astrilla sensed that Nathan was readying to take a swing at the elitist, so she stepped in, forcefully placing her hand over Nathan's forearm.

She took a step closer to Jareth:

"Why didn't you tell us the truth about Chimera?" Astrilla scowled. "You could've—"

Jareth cut her off: "When you've been in this game as long as I have, you learn that leverage is as valuable as the oxygen you breathe or the water you drink".

It was a cold and callous thing to say: the typical mindset of a privileged corporate man.

"You reap what you sow, Mr Jareth," Astrilla said, scowling at the old man. "Remember that when nobody comes to your aid".

NATHAN

Dines gave an opening statement that described the events of the last twelve hours. It was factual and fair, and in Nathan's view, everything the Agent said was correct. He didn't paint the Paradisians as terrorists, like many would prefer to believe, and he made mention of Roth and the Society, which raised a few sceptical eyebrows. The —*mostly*— military delegation seemed phased by Dines' opening statement, especially the part that described the death of Waife and the Council.

When Dines moved on to the part about the Artemis, he stammered:

"It is my solemn duty to inform you that the Warship Artemis and her entire crew were killed as part of this attack," Dines said, pausing as though he were expecting questions. "Only two survived, and they claim that it was a traitor that committed these heinous crimes".

Dines tapped a console on the table before him, and a holographic image of Cadu formed at the centre of the room. The murderous little bastard was smiling in the picture.

Dines said, "Cadu Menos was an Evoker who gained access to the Artemis by posing as an injured kidnap victim. Survivors report that he was killed in combat".

Dines went on a little longer about the estimated number of casualties and the other strikes around Valour before finally opening up the floor to questions.

Silence fell over the room.

A red-haired human-Uvan woman stood from her

chair: one of the civilian representatives, based on her lack of military garb. The holographic placard in front of her read *Commissioner Nephthys Kamen.*

"Thank you for the update," she said, nodding to Dines. "Regarding this secret group on Paradisium —*the Society I believe it was?* Do we have any hard evidence beyond mere witness accounts that this cabal exists?"

Dines cleared his throat.

"Not at this moment," he shook his head. "The theory is that they are working with King Baylum as part of a—"

Kamen raised her hand in a dismissive nature.

"As you know, we cannot base our decisions on theory. Unfortunately, that is the job of facts".

"Commissioner," Dines argued. "If I may—"

"That'll be all, Agent Dines".

Like the good 'wealther he was, Dines took his seat.

Kamen looked around the delegation, and her eyes settled on the Admiralty. There were three of them —two Uvan's and one human: all sour-looking, stereotypical 'wealthers, with stiff upper lips and prideful nationalism radiating from them.

"Constitutionally, we are in a bind," Kamen said warily. "I firmly believe that we must uphold political representation just as the Founders said all those years ago".

One of the Admirals, a white-haired Uvan male that Nathan recognised as Harrt's CO, Dolian Wexell, slowly climbed to his feet and faced Kamen.

"My apologies, Commissioner, but now is not the time for an electoral decision," Wexell said, his voice low and considered. "We've been attacked by a group of hateful bigots who oppose our way of life. This is the consequence of separatism. My colleagues in the Admiralty agree that the time for action is upon us. An attack on one of us is an attack on all of us. We must act swiftly and strike back for this crime against our precious Commonwealth".

The rest of the military types climbed to their feet in support. Voices rose, most in agreement, none in protest.

The delegates eventually reseated themselves, and as the hall quietened, another Admiral addressed the room. She was Uvan, with lime-coloured skin and juniper hair pulled into a tight bun. Nathan read the name Admiral Deffu from her place setting.

Deffu stood beside Wexell in support. "My esteemed comrade is right. A show of force is the only way to keep these decadent hogs under control. We must ensure unification to stamp out this threat".

The room was silent. Nathan was sure that he was witnessing the start of the end for Paradisium.

Then Jareth moved to the table, and Nathan had to look twice. Every eye in the room was locked on him, but Jareth was completely unphased.

"Let's not dress up the word invasion," Jareth said, his voice echoing from the corners of the room. "A grand unification, as you say, is exactly what Alastair Roth and Baylum want. While you sit here and debate the future of Paradisium, Alastair Roth is en route to activate an Enkaye weapon that makes the Messorem look like a supply cruiser. Now, I know we are not friends. Hell, I've probably been a massive thorn in the side of this Commonwealth for two decades..." Jareth shifted his gaze to Nathan and smiled for a beat. "But I, like you, am a citizen of this universe. If you take your eyes off of Roth, we all lose".

It was not what Nathan expected.

The Admiralty looked positively offended by Jareth's presence.

Wexell tensed his jaw; "Alastair Roth is a businessman, not a terrorist. All intel confirms that he was on Paradisium, skiing at his mountain lodge". The Admiral tossed his datapad onto the table, and an image of Markus Holland appeared where Cadu had been. "The attack was led by this man".

Jareth chuckled at the remark; "The day that a rotund fool like Roth skis down a mountain is the day that hell freezes over. Markus Holland was a puppet".

Admiral Wexell frowned at Jareth.

"And why should we trust a single word that comes out of your mouth, Mr Jareth? Lest we forget, *you* were our prisoner less than six hours ago: under charges of conspiracy to trade with the Revenant".

Jareth smiled to himself, leaving Nathan to assume the old man was revelling at the opportunity to prove the 'wealthers wrong.

"My good man, I may be a decadent capitalist, as you may say, but I am also a man who has sought revenge against the Revenant for many years," Jareth paused for effect. "There was a saying we once had back on Earth: *the enemy of my enemy is my friend*".

Wexell looked at him with contempt and judgement. The Uvan waved aside Jareth's comment like a cloud of smoke.

"The time for debate is over," Wexell shook his head at Jareth. The Admiral turned to his fellow military personnel. "Our forces will place those ungrateful dogs on Paradisium under strict martial law. We will revoke the EWB and enforce a grand unification, thus welcoming them back to the 'wealth and ensuring they receive ample re-education". Wexell turned to Jareth with steely eyes; "If the Paradisians are foolish enough to resist, then we will eradicate them: just as the Revenant should've done twenty-six years ago".

Nathan felt the hairs on his arms stand to attention as he listened to the angry yells of agreement. Everything being said made him wonder if Jack had always been right. The lessons and warnings of years gone by came crashing into the forefront of Nathan's mind. Every single one boiled down to the same message; *under no circumstances should you trust the 'wealth.*

Nathan looked at Dines, and the Agent shook his head as if saying; *please don't involve yourself.*

Nathan ignored it.

He stomped to Jareth's side, but none of the 'wealthers acknowledged him, which served to outrage him a little more. He was, after all, the man who'd saved all their asses by killing Seig and destroying the Messorem.

Without ceremony or invitation, Nathan climbed onto the table, drew his gun and fired a single round into the ceiling. The bolt made a small dent on the stone surface. A tiny trail of chalky, white dust followed, distorting the image of Markus Holland. Everyone, from military to civilian, froze; many out of fear; others out of confusion.

Nathan glared at Wexell as he holstered his pistol. *A part of him wondered if he shot the man, would history thank him?*

"I am a survivor of the Fall," Nathan declared, his voice breaking as he spoke. "I'm not a Paradisian, and I'm no 'wealther, but I saw what the Revenant did on that day, and you have no fuckin' right to wish that on anyone".

Wexell scoffed at his statement. The ignorance of the Uvan made Nathan's blood boil, but he had to say his piece: he had to try and convince them that war was not the answer.

"What is the point of this rant, Captain Carter?" Wexell said.

"My *point* is that everything Jareth and Dines have said is true," Nathan said. "Take your eyes off of Roth, and he will return to destroy you. Let's see how far your precious 'wealth lasts when that happens".

Nobody said a word.

Nathan allowed the delegates to assimilate what he'd said and climbed from the table. Initially, his plan was to scold Wexell and his little entourage, but he'd somehow been able to push the impulse aside and focus on the big problem. He'd just about reached Astrilla and the others when Wexell called out across the vast room;

"And what is it that Alastair Roth is supposedly doing in the shadows, Captain Carter? Opera? Skiing?"

A short burst of chuckles crackled among the delegation.

Nathan didn't acknowledge it.

When Wexell didn't get a reaction, he bellowed across the room, "Don't waste our time, you filthy Earther".

More laughing and scoffing followed.

Nathan stopped, and naturally, his hand sank to his holster.

Shoot this prick, the imaginary version of Jack said inside his head. *C'mon, you don't have to kill him. Just wipe that smug smile off his fuckin' face.*

The voice of Elder Yuta pulled Nathan away from his violent fantasy.

"You are not in charge yet, Admiral," she yelled. "This

is still a democracy".

Nathan turned, peering at Wexell and the other Admirals, who, at first, were slightly taken aback by the Evoker's warning. The collective surprise of the Admiralty only lasted a second.

Wexell proudly gestured to his military comrades:

"We control the military, while you, Elder Yuta, control nothing. Lest we remind you that it was one of your own that destroyed the Artemis: that slaughtered hundreds".

"That is enough!" Yuta barked, banging her fist on the table. "You need to stop and think about what you're proposing. This Commonwealth was built on the ideals of the founders: men and women who opposed tyranny. What would they say about this course of action?".

Nathan had never seen Yuta so enraged. He could almost feel the indignation in her every word.

Wexell turned his gaze to Nathan, and his crewmates and a group of armed guards moved toward them. Every fibre of Nathan's being suggested that things were about to go very wrong. His hand lingered over his pistol, but when he looked at Astrilla, she shook her head.

"The Phoenix Titan is grounded, effective immediately," Wexell declared. "Captain Carter, you and your crew will surrender your weapons. You'll be placed under house arrest until this situation is resolved."

The guards closed in, many with apologetic looks. Nathan and Koble were stripped of their guns, and Astrilla showed open palms in a non-aggressive manner. Inhibiting binds were placed around her wrists, preventing the casting of any summons.

The angry voice of Jack was at the back of Nathan's mind again:

See what you've gone and done now? If you'd have just done as I said and stayed away from these commie bastards, you wouldn't be headin' to some fuckin' gulag to eat porridge and slop.

Wexell stopped the guards from arresting Harrt.

"Not Oxarri. He is still a member of this grand military, and this council has many questions regarding the Artemis".

"You're making a huge mistake," Jareth said, raising his voice in protest. "This will not end well for you".

Wexell snapped his fingers at the guards, and one of them grabbed Jareth by the arm.

"Take this capitalist scum with them," Wexell sneered. Then turning on his toes to the crew of the Phoenix. "I recognise that you're heroes to the Commonwealth. You have my word you will be treated with the utmost respect. When our policing action is complete on Paradisium you will be released: I swear it".

C'mon, Jack said, nudging at the insides of Nathan's skull. *You ain't gonna stand for this shit, right?*

HARRT

Harrt could almost feel the anger radiating from Nathan as he was dragged away with the others. He sensed something wasn't above board with Wexell. The Admiral was always an honourable man, at least in the public eye, but what Harrt was witnessing were the behaviours of a warmonger. For most of his career, Harrt had respected Wexell, but to see the man so pleased by the prospect of war threw everything into question.

He wondered if perhaps Wexell's loyalty to the 'wealth was so uncompromising that he was blinded by every argument. Once the crew, plus Jareth, were hauled away, Wexell addressed the remaining personnel.

"See to it that any others aboard the Phoenix are taken into custody as well".

Harrt had never felt his allegiance as challenged as it was at that moment. Sure, he'd been running an investigation with Dines for over a year, but this felt different: *as though the 'wealth he'd been fighting for was a thing of the past.*

"Oxarri," Wexell said with a raised voice. "You will take command of the Redemption and join me and the fleet at Paradisium. You will command the ground operation and impose martial law".

Harrt fixed his gaze on the doors where Nathan and the

others were dragged away.

Everything Wexell was doing went against the values of the Founders. He'd overridden the democratic decision-making process. He'd treated allies as enemies. There had been no vote and no trial. War was being declared out of emotion, not logic.

Harrt asked himself, *is this the 'wealth I've been fighting to save?*

No.

Harrt said the word aloud, and Wexell narrowed his eyes. The big Uvan stomped across the room toward Harrt, hands balling into fists, a vein on his forehead practically bursting.

"What was that, Commander?" Wexell bellowed. "You dare question my authority?"

Harrt remained still.

Wexell had gone too far.

Harrt Oxarri tore the metal commander's pin from his uniform and tossed it at Wexell's feet.

"This is not the Commonwealth I've dedicated my life to. I will not follow you into war," Harrt pointed at his discarded pin, "Consider that my declaration of retirement".

Wexell looked positively stunned. As though Harrt was the first person to ever challenge his command. Harrt allowed his eyes to wander to Leviticus Dines. The Agent shot him an approving smirk, but his default stoic expression returned in heartbeat.

Harrt shifted his gaze to Wexell: "This Commonwealth was built upon values of friendship, unity, bravery and truth. Running into a war with Paradisium goes against those most sacred values"..

The Admiral shook his head in mock disappointment.

"Having you, the Hero of Maru Seven, on the ground with us would've been tremendous". Then, turning to his security personnel, Wexell yelled, "Take this coward with the rest of the Phoenix's crew".

Two burly-looking guards closed in, but Wexell halted them when they reached his side. He edged closer to Harrt, rage in his sharp Uvan eyes:

"When we've shown Paradisium the true force of our Commonwealth, I will launch an investigation into the destruction of the Artemis". Wexell spoke with untamed malice to his voice. "It seems convenient that you abandoned your crew *before* the attack. One has to wonder if perhaps you and Densius Olbori share a similar secret allegiance".

Something snapped inside Harrt, and it took control.

He swung a hard right into Wexell's head, and the Admiral crumbled to the side. Harrt debated going in for another strike, but before he had the chance, the two guards were already on him. Harrt held up both palms, and the guards seemed to calm, leaving him wondering if perhaps they covertly agreed with him.

A man in a Commander's uniform helped Wexell to his feet. The Admiral dusted off his uniform, refusing to show any sign of weakness.

"Take him away," Wexell yelled at the guards.

NATHAN

Guards escorted Nathan, Koble, Astrilla and Jareth through the twisted maze of Valour's streets. They were being taken to a place called Deference House: a high-rise tower a half kilometre from the Verulanum. It was fair to assume that once they arrived at their *safe house,* the crew would be separated—or even isolated.

That meant time was of the essence.

There was no way Nathan would stand by and let Roth and James get away with what they'd done. With Wexell in charge of the 'wealth, there would be a war. That was inevitable, and Nathan figured there was very little he could do to stop that from happening.

Stopping Roth had to become the priority, which meant returning to the Phoenix and getting the hell off Valour.

Nathan glanced at the armed marines surrounding them. By his best guess, there were seventeen —all well armed and ready for a scrap. Astrilla had been forced into inhibiting binds, which meant that getting those off her had to be step one.

The ordinarily busy district they were taken through was empty, leading Nathan to believe that Wexell had already imposed a lockdown on the city.

It felt like a ghost town.

As they turned a corner, Koble started to walk beside Nathan and subtly nudged him in the ribs. Nathan couldn't help but notice the exhaustion on the chunky Sphinax's face.

"I'm sorry about Rain," Nathan said in a low voice. "For what it's worth, he was a good guy and a damn fine pilot".

"The best," Koble replied thoughtfully.

Nathan looked Koble in the eyes, "We will make this right. Rain's death will not be in vain".

Koble nodded; "Just gotta get outta this little situation," he said in a low voice.

There was a sudden disturbance to the rear of the pack. Harrt was shoved into the middle of the group by one of the guards, almost tripping over in the process. Nathan steadied the 'wealther, and they continued to walk.

"I take it Wexell didn't like what you had to say," Nathan said with mild sarcasm.

"You could say that," Harrt replied with just a hint of humour in his voice. "Still, I was never the reasoning type".

"You ready for what comes next?" Nathan asked.

Harrt's eyes darted around the seventeen marines, then at the binds on Astrilla's wrists.

"Pretty terrible odds, I'd say".

"Is that a no, Oxarri?" Nathan mused.

Harrt shrugged with a wry smile; "We've seen worse".

"So," Nathan said, drawing the word out. "On my go?"

▲

Two minutes later, the marines led the crew into a courtyard with a stone fountain in the middle. By Nathan's best guess, they had three —maybe four— minutes before they reached their destination.

He was about ready to give the signal to Harrt and Koble when suddenly, a laser pulse sailed by Nathan's head and struck one of the marines. The shooting was coming from an unknown location to the south, but Nathan didn't have the time to look. Laser fire filled the courtyard. The lone shooter was highly effective and had already taken out three of the seventeen by the time Nathan was in cover.

The others did the same, taking up defensive positions with Nathan. Astrilla held out her inhibitor binds expectantly, and Nathan wasted no time snapping the wires between her wrists. The Evoker pulled what remained of the shackles apart, her palms already lighting up.

"Go," Nathan yelled.

The Evoker was over the fountain in the blink of an eye with white-hot elemental energy burning at her fingertips. Nathan looked to Koble, then Harrt, who was busy dragging Jareth into cover.

"Hell of a signal, Nate," Koble yelled sarcastically. "You ready?"

"Let's go!".

As he moved from cover, Nathan tackled one of the marines from behind, slamming the man to the ground and grabbing his rifle. Nathan considered shooting him, but instead, he smashed the butt of the gun against the 'wealther's military-grade helmet: enough to knock him out cold. Without wasting time, Nathan grabbed the marine's sidearm and tossed it to Harrt.

"Incapacitate only," Harrt yelled.

By the time Nathan returned to cover, only a handful of the marines were left standing. Between Astrilla, the unknown shooter and the rest, they were a formidable team, and the 'wealthers didn't stand a chance.

When the dust settled, Nathan peered out from cover and dragged Jareth to his feet. The old man nodded in thanks, then, after pulling a stray thread from the cuff of his jacket, he surveyed the courtyard.

"It would seem that we have an ally," Jareth remarked.

Nathan didn't acknowledge the comment and watched as Dines moved into the courtyard, holstering his smoking pistol. The Agent regarded him with a nod as he rushed over.

"Quite the show, Dines," Koble drawled. "You're one hell of a shot".

"We don't have much time," the Agent said hurriedly. "You all need to get out of here and stop Roth".

"What about you?" Harrt asked.

"Wexell wants me aboard one of his warships to oversee the operation at Paradisium," Dines said. "I'm going to try my best to put the brakes on it".

"Hate to say it, pal," Koble interrupted, "You just took out a whole bunch of your buddies. How you gonna explain that one away".

Dines sighed with dread.

"Hit me," he said, flinching slightly. "I've already hacked the security feeds in the area. I figure you guys have a five-minute head start, but I need it to look like you took me out".

Koble raised his big fist, ready to strike, but Dines stopped him. The Agent looked at Nathan.

"Tariq Mahmoot... is he trustworthy?"

Nathan nodded. "Yeah, I think so".

"Good," Dines remarked. "I think I'm gonna need him".

With nothing else left to say Leviticus Dines turned to Koble. He welcomed the strike as though it were an old friend.

CHAPTER THIRTY-EIGHT
JAMES

A warm shower and a glass of expensive whiskey were just what the doctor ordered. It'd never replace the electric high from a fresh hit of Ice, but it allowed James to centre himself, to accept his actions —both past and present— and decide how to learn from it: how to become strong from it.

James reclined in a padded armchair in one of the Featon's guest quarters. It was nice to feel himself again. Pretending to be a reworked version of himself to fool Nathan and his crew had been an exhausting affair. The fact was that he'd never forgiven Nathan for leaving him at the bar eleven years ago.

How could he ever forgive such betrayal?

He pulled a cigar from a selection box that Roth's staff left in his quarters. As he watched the blue ribbons of FTL pass by, James wondered what his father, Merri, or any of the Loyalty's crew would think of the whole thing.

Nothing good: of that, James could be sure.

Merri would call him irresponsible, and they'd argue until someone threw a hard enough punch —likely James. She'd never understood him back in the day: *how could she?* James was a trauma victim, and Merri was too consumed by her desire to be his saviour.

Working for Roth would hold a different meaning for his father. Jack's reaction to it all would be similar, but he'd be far more pissed than Merri.

"How could you work for a monster like that?" The imaginary version of his father was enraged. Just as James recalled him: a bitter, twisted old man who'd denied him a life of splendour on Paradisium. His own father had pushed him into a life of crime, forcing him to live with a crew of degenerates aboard the Loyalty. If anything, Jack made him an addict by denying him the same counselling and treatments that the Paradisians received.

Fuck you, James thought. *You might as well have shoved that fucking vial into my arm yourself.*

It felt good to be rid of his father, and James had discovered that it felt even better to be on the winning side.

After a decade on Roth's payroll, James had grown to see Alastair Roth as a mentor and father figure. He'd been there when James was at his lowest.

Not Nathan.

Not Jack.

Not the supposed love of his life, Merri.

None of them.

Roth had. He was the one who'd found James when he was at rock bottom: sprawled out in a gutter on some godforsaken rock, starving, penniless. Abandoned.

As James placed the cigar in a cutter, he thought of Tariq Mahmoot. Despite his mission to infiltrate the Sadalmelik's crew and act as a double agent, James couldn't deny that he'd grown to respect Tariq and Hayward and the others: not as people or even as foes but as radical, idealists. He'd miss the absurd notion that a group of disgruntled freedom fighters believed they stood a chance against the Society.

Nobody won against the Society: that was a fact of life. James was a part of it now, and it felt fucking amazing: like he was a part of something bigger than himself. Like he was a part of history. Like being on the winning team.

James was halfway through the cigar when a knock came at his door. He slowly climbed from the armchair, and when he opened the door, he came face to face with Alastair Roth.

His mentor and friend was still in his grey suit, carrying a large glass of port in his right hand and looking regal, noble, and proud.

James invited him into the cabin, and Roth accepted.

"I wanted to come down here and congratulate you," Roth said, walking into the room. "I owe you a debt of gratitude for saving Christian".

"It's nothing," James replied awkwardly. "I couldn't leave him there with the 'wealthers. The plan had to change, so I adapted: just as you taught me".

Roth patted him on the shoulder and settled down into a chair. He folded one large leg over the other and sipped at his port as he eyed James thoughtfully.

"I spoke with Baylum earlier," he said methodically. "The King wants us to rendezvous with his asset en route to Helia".

James raised his brow. "I thought his asset died aboard the Artemis".

Roth made a humming noise and nodded.

"It would appear that the Evoker responsible for the incursion on the Artemis was not operating alone. There was another, a man named Xanathur".

A shiver ran down James' spine.

"You think Baylum suspects something? Do I need my men to keep an eye on this Xanathur guy when we bring him aboard?"

"Not necessary," Roth raised his palm, and cooly added, "Baylum is far too busy worrying about his lack of numbers to suspect a thing. He needs us more than we need him".

"For the record, I don't like it," James argued. "You don't wanna fuck with an Evoker".

"James, my boy, we will handle it if we must," Roth replied with a friendly tone. "Our main priority is to open Project Erebus and claim the prize inside. Once we have it under our control, Baylum will be history".

"I'd sleep better if we kept Xanathur confined to the docks," James said. "If he tries anything, we can jettison his ass into the void".

Roth sighed through his nostrils. "Very well".

James returned to his armchair and took a long drag on his cigar.

"So what about the 'wealthers?" He asked. "Do you think they'll take the bait?"

Roth smiled. "The Commonwealth will react, and when they do, Paradisium will be the only thing in their sights".

James accepted his answer: *after all, why would he challenge it?* Still, there was one thing that could throw a spanner in the works, and Roth hadn't acknowledged it since James returned. He didn't want to say it, but the situation required him to speak his mind:

"What about Subject C?"

There it was: the elephant in the room. Just uttering the name of Roth's lab rat made James nervous.

Roth was silent.

"That little fucker is on the warpath," James went on. "I saw Rhoades' body-cam footage on the Phoenix. Subject C diced him and his unit into pieces. He'll be heading for Helia next".

Roth sipped his brandy and kept his eyes forward: directly at the slipstream.

"Let him come," Roth snarled. "Subject C will have an army to get through before he reaches the dig site".

Roth's answer was oversimplifying it, but he was — mostly— right. Sure, Subject C could summon elemental energy, but Roth had over a thousand mercenaries on Helia: all highly trained, lethal killers. There was no way the lab rat could carve through all of them without taking a bullet.

For a while, Roth and James sat in companionable silence, the feint hum of the FTL serving as white noise for the break in their conversation.

"I want you to know how very proud I am," Roth leaned forward, looking James in the eyes. "You've come so far from that boy I met the day of the Fall: simply following your father's orders, clutching that ridiculous hunting rifle and threatening my family".

"You know I didn't want to do it," James replied. "My father… he—"

"Your father was a cruel man," Roth interrupted. "You

are not your father. You are a man of action who understands that terrible things must be done for the greater good. History will remember that sort of thing".

James felt uncomfortable with the praise, but he wasn't sure why. *Maybe some repressed childhood trauma prevented him from accepting that kind of thing.*

He climbed to his feet and moved to the cabinet, grabbing a bottle of whiskey and a fresh glass for Roth. James topped up his drink, and the pair raised their glasses in toast, saying the ancient words of the Society:

"Novus ordo seclorum".

GORDON

When Gordon awoke, he found himself in an almost pitch-black cell. There was a faint slither of light coming down from a thin grate in the ceiling, but it didn't help him to study his new surroundings. He felt around on the ground and in his jacket for his glasses to no avail.

"Perfect, just bloody perfect," he huffed.

The cat was finally out of the bag. His cover was blown. Aubrey Gordon Beckett had —on paper— died during the Fall, along with the rest of Bill's research team. He'd never liked the name Aubrey anyway. Even as a child, he preferred to be called Gordon. So unofficially, that was what he went by.

He'd lived as Gordon for over fifty-five years, and he'd lived as Gordon Taggart since the Fall. His Commonwealth identity documents all had the name Gordon Taggart, not Aubrey Beckett. No one —not even the Phoenix's crew— knew his real name, and that was how it was supposed to stay.

His instructions had been clear from day one: *Aubrey Beckett is dead.*

The Society was not supposed to find him, but they had. Which meant something had gone very wrong. Maybe he'd slipped up? Or perhaps someone in Roth's organisation had put two and two together. Either way, there was no point in debating now.

Gordon sat up, and the ache in his jaw became apparent. In an attempt to take his mind off the pain, he decided that understanding the layout of his enclosure could help formulate an escape plan. Gordon felt his way around the edges of the dark cell, using his shoe as a marker to signal where he'd started. Unfortunately, it only took seconds to feel around the four walls before returning to the beginning. By Gordon's best estimate, he was in a compartment no larger than six feet by six feet: *barely enough room to lay down for sleep.*

"Bastards locked me in a bloody broom closet".

Regardless of his dire situation, Gordon continued to feel around the floor and walls, hoping he could find an electrical conduit or an air vent to aid in his breakout. Sadly, there was nothing, and he concluded that the only way out was through the opening in the ceiling.

He took a deep breath and sighed, wondering how he would pass the time inside his cramped cell.

Gordon slumped against the wall and asked the universe: "How am I gonna get out of this one?"

Nobody answered.

NATHAN

After Dines sprung them from capture, the crew —along with Jareth— dashed back to the Phoenix harboured outside the Verulanum. The streets were free of citizens, making the return sprint much quicker.

As the Phoenix came into view, Nathan saw that a group of soldiers had beaten them there. Two had taken up defensive positions outside the ship, while the sound of commotion from inside was more than apparent.

Astrilla made light work of the pair, and Nathan was the first up the boarding ramp.

Once he reached the interior, a big marine moved out of cover and pointed his weapon at Nathan. To his surprise, the unsuspecting 'wealther was tackled into the opposite bulkhead by Eric —Chimera— Garland. As a brawl ensued between Garland and the 'wealther, Nathan pushed ahead and into the living area. Russell and Vol were behind the bar, throwing liquor bottles at a pair of soldiers who'd taken refuge behind the faux fireplace.

"Y'all better back the fuck up," Russell threatened with a bottle in his hand.

"Put the bottles down," a marine warned.

Nathan didn't waste time and pulled the stolen sidearm from his holster. He shot the first man in the knee and the second in the shoulder, incapacitating both in seconds. He looked at Russell, still clutching a bottle.

"Run out of ammo, did we?" Nathan said.

"Mine wasn't loaded," Russell admitted. "And Vol was asleep when they stormed in".

Nathan pointed at the bottle in Russell's hand: a fine Yariam rum from the Outer Worlds that fetched a modest price tag but tasted terrific on the rocks.

"New rule," Nathan said, grabbing the bottle from Russell. "Don't start by throwing the good stuff. Start with the Sphinax Fish Wine".

▲

Harrt and Vol took their places in the cockpit while Koble and Garland dumped the unconscious marines on the landing pad. Nathan waited for the pair at the top of the docking ramp, keeping his gun pointed toward the Verulanum. It was only a matter of time until Wexell would have reinforcements heading their way, so he didn't want any nasty surprises.

Fortunately, it didn't take Garland and Koble much time, and they were back on the ship in less than sixty seconds. With everyone aboard, Nathan sealed the airlock and passed through the Phoenix's living quarters on his way to the cockpit.

"Time to go!" Nathan yelled.

Before he'd walked through the cockpit doors, the Phoenix's engines roared to life. Nathan steadied himself in the doorway, watching Vol and Harrt at the ship's controls.

The sight of the pair at the helm filled Nathan with a sense of nostalgia: something he rarely felt. It was about damn time that the gang was back together again.

"Everyone strap in," Harrt said. "This is gonna be one bumpy flight".

As Nathan sat down, his eyes met Jareth's. The old man regarded him with a nod, and as Nathan strapped himself into the chair, he wondered if this was a turning point for Jareth. He was all out of allies. His organisation was under Roth's control: his family prisoners to the Society. The only people Jareth had were those aboard the Phoenix.

The ship lifted off at breakneck speed. Harrt made a bee-line toward the skies, sending the Phoenix upward at an eighty-five-degree angle. The manoeuvre was so extreme that the ship's artificial gravity system began to fail: *no doubt baffled by the sudden change in velocity.*

Valour's orbital cannons must've detected the Phoenix, as suddenly a warning klaxon sounded. Harrt yanked the ship hard to port, and something explosive caused the Phoenix to rumble and jolt.

"We could have a lot of trouble heading our way once we're clear of the atmosphere," Vol said as she checked one of her terminals. "We'll need someone in the gunnery chambers".

"No," Harrt said. "I can plot an FTL jump once we're clear of the debris fields".

White clouds fell toward the Phoenix as the ship rose toward space. The natural blue of Valour's skies faded away, and the featureless black of space replaced it. The artificial gravity kicked in once it detected that the Phoenix was in zero-g. Then what had been the Paradisian blockade came into view. Nathan unbuckled himself from his chair and moved toward the front to get a better look.

The destruction left in the wake of Alastair Roth's plot became apparent as he stared at the field of wreckage now orbiting Valour. Chunks of burnt-up debris littered the vast openness of space, along with the asphyxiated, frozen bodies of Roth's victims.

Nathan knew that the damage Roth had inflicted was staggering, but seeing it up close was harrowing. It gave weight to James' actions and made Nathan realise that he should've taken the shot and put an end to his cousin when he had the chance. He'd hesitated, and one of the men responsible for everything he was seeing had escaped.

Harrt swallowed a lump in his throat as he gazed out the window. Nathan placed a hand on his friend's shoulder, struggling to imagine how difficult it must be to see what had once been the Artemis. His ship: his crew.

It was unthinkable.

VOL

The leap to FTL couldn't come sooner. Once the Phoenix cleared the debris field, Vol plotted a jump to take them out of 'wealther space. It was a direct route, likely to last around five hours, so the crew had some time to discuss their next move.

Nathan had scheduled a crew meeting in ten minutes, so Vol figured she could grab a quiet moment before everything got busy. She remained in the co-pilot's seat, watching the blue and white ribbons of the slipstream pass by. She'd always hated FTL, it gave her headaches and generally left her with a queasy feeling in her gut, but for the first time, Vol appreciated the calm.

After everything, she'd found a moment of pure, unadulterated peace. Knowing she was finally out of danger was meditative and soothing, but Vol knew it wouldn't last, and she wouldn't have it any other way.

Hayward, Scruffy, Riggs, Jaudi and all the countless others that died fighting Cadu deserved justice. Rain too. And Claire. Thousands of people deserved that, and Vol was just fine with being on the frontlines if it meant putting an end to Alastair Roth, Xanathur and all the other pricks who'd caused so much pain.

Five minutes before Nathan's crew meeting, Harrt took the seat beside her. He handed her a glass of Kor, and they toasted to all those who'd perished. It was a sombre moment that hit harder than Vol expected.

Harrt leaned back, sipped his drink and gazed at her.

"I'm glad you made it," he said. "I don't know what I would've done if I'd lost you like the rest".

Vol placed a hand on his, debating what to say next. She could tell him that Jaudi died a hero and that his crew had fought valiantly. But Vol knew that words couldn't take the sting out of the pain.

Vengeance had to come first.

"They won't get away with what they did,' Vol said.

"I know".

"Good," she nodded. Then with a wry smile, Vol said, "Glad you made it as well... 'wealther".

XANATHUR

Fifty years before the Battle of the Messorem, Elendrion Xanathur faced Baylum in combat at the battle of Iom three. It'd been a bloody and violent conflict that lasted days on the ash-soaked plains of the Illuminator terraforming project. Prince Baylum, as was his title then, had proven himself to be a cunning and vicious tactician, and Xanathur was forced to make several tough decisions when working with the Commonwealth to push back the Revenant forces.

The fighting culminated at Iom Three's northernmost mountainscape, where the Commonwealth and Evokers made their final stand.

As the people evacuated, Xanathur heroically went ahead to hold off the hostile Revenant force. That was when he faced Baylum in combat. The young Prince was an exceptional warrior in every mode of warfare, and he overpowered Xanathur before the 'wealth or Evokers could evacuate.

Baylum killed them all, but he spared Xanathur and took him aboard a flagship. At the time, Xanathur expected the worst, but what followed surprised him. He wasn't subjected to torture or mutation, or violence. Instead, the

Revenant Purebloods treated him with respect and dignity. He was fed, clothed, and provided a warm bed to rest.

It was like that for eight days and seven nights.

Then on the eighth night, he was summoned for a meeting with Baylum. He met the young Prince aboard a different ship, known to the Revenant as the Chalice: *a holy place where the River Prynn originated.* The vessel was undoubtedly Enkaye, a planet-sized sphere filled to the brim with trillions of gallons of the strange grey sludge.

That night, Baylum showed him the Revenant's true origins. They were children of the Enkaye, provided with a holy mission to cleanse chaos from the universe.

Naturally, Xanathur challenged Baylum's supposed truth, but the Great Void was there in the room with them, and it showed Xanathur all he needed to know. There was only fact in the River Prynn: no trickery, no mutation, just the cold hard truth.

The truth about the Enkaye's demise...

The truth about their destroyer...

The true injustice of the universe they fostered...

And the truth about the Enkaye's final plan.

That was the day Elendrion Xanathur became Baylum's, right-hand man. He turned away from the Evokers, from the 'wealth and all of it. His purpose was to ensure that the Enkaye's final plan failed and that meant becoming a traitor to those he'd once called friend.

And so, Xanathur went to work and returned to the 'wealth and Evokers with a new purpose: biding his time until Baylum finally called upon him.

Twelve hours after the attack on Valour and Cadu's brave sacrifice, Xanathur stared out at a red sun flaring against the blackness of space. He was somewhere beyond 'wealther territory, teetering on the edge of an asteroid field where no one could find him.

The shuttle he'd travelled aboard was not as roomy as his old Evoker transport, but it was undoubtedly far more subtle. It wasn't easy to abandon his personal ship, but destroying it was vital to the mission. He needed to cover his tracks and make it look like he'd perished in the explosion; that way, his final message to Yuta would make Marx appear the guilty party. The 'wealth would blame the conceited Florus for the attack while Cadu went down with the Artemis.

Xanathur's new craft comprised of two small chambers: a cockpit and a bathroom. Nothing else. It was a ship for a two-man crew, designed for short-haul FTL only. It wouldn't do for the pilgrimage before him: to Helia. To the great singularity: the place where the path shown to him by the mighty river would finally begin.

As Xanathur sat alone watching the nearby sun, he meditated on his recent actions. He'd turned away from his Evoker roots in favour of the River Prynn's noble path, thus betraying his fellow elders: *dear friends on the surface but virtuous fools beneath.* He felt no sorrow for that. Like all the other Elders, they walked a fine line to keep the Commonwealth appeased, and the 'wealth returned their friendship by viewing Evokers as war assets.

He wouldn't miss that.

Cadu's death was a necessary evil. The boy had been impressionable and easy to control and believed he was doing something righteous. Cadu had only seen a slither of the noble path, and it'd been enough for him to commit mass murder. There was no questioning Cadu's bravery and dedication, but in Xanathur's eyes, he was but a tool to achieve a goal; which he'd undoubtedly achieved.

Now, Alastair Roth believed he was in control, just as Baylum and the River Prynn intended. The rotund fool now had everything he needed to open what he called Project Erebus, and by doing so, the noble path would finally begin. Baylum would achieve his god-like status, and Xanathur would be at his side to witness order overcome chaos.

Xanathur was awoken from his meditation by an incoming transmission. He tapped the console before him, and a blue hologram of King Baylum illuminated his otherwise darkened cockpit.

They exchanged quick greetings, then, without wasting time, Baylum moved to the task at hand. He informed Xanathur, that Alastair Roth would rendezvous with him in the next twelve hours, and take him on to Helia. That was all well and good, but Xanathur could tell from the King's expression that something else was troubling him.

"I have a new undertaking for you, my old friend," Baylum said, his voice thoughtful. "Roth has deceived us in more ways than one".

Xanathur and the King were anticipating it; after all, Roth's hubris knew no bounds. He'd eventually get greedy and try to kill Baylum to make a play for control. That was always inevitable. The plan for Roth was simple; *ensure he opens Project Erebus, then kill him and his people. So why was Baylum bringing it up now?*

The King pulled a datapad from under his cloak and tapped the screen a few times, sending a flurry of data to Xanathur's workstation. A cargo manifest appeared on-screen, mostly detailing Roth's collection of art, wine and furniture. Xanathur scrolled through the seemingly mundane list for several seconds as Baylum waited patiently.

Then Xanathur saw it, and his jaw fell.

"How did Roth—"

Baylum cut him off, "I do not know".

Xanathur considered it. Indeed, Roth had betrayed them, but not in a way that was expected. This was something different: *personal maybe?*

"Shall I kill Roth when I get aboard the Featon?"

"No," Baylum shook his head. "Your primary objective has changed. When you reach Helia, find it, extract it and get it to the fleet".

"What about Roth?" Xanathur frowned.

Baylum's black eyes narrowed, and his jaw clenched with anger, "I will deal with Roth myself".

The hologram of Baylum dissolved into the air, plunging Xanathur into darkness once again; the distant red star his only source of light. Amidst the shadows, Xanathur readied himself for whatever fate awaited him. Then as he looked out on the vast expanse of the starfield, glittering from aeons ago, he wondered which of them was Helia: *the last battleground of the Enkaye.*

NATHAN

The crew were defeated and tired, but they were also angry and ready to take the fight to Roth. Nathan gathered them around the holotable, including David Jareth and Garland. Having those two standing right there seemed odd, but they were a part of this now: they'd always been a part of it. Nathan wasn't sure if he could trust Jareth entirely, but the part about trying to end Baylum and Roth back at Hawtrey was genuine: he knew that now.

"So," Harrt said, drawing the word out. "I think I speak for all of us when I say that the next move is to save Gordon, right?"

Nobody offered a challenge.

"Good," Nathan nodded.

He opened a star map above the holotable and began collapsing the image until only the charted regions of the universe were visible. He pointed to an area that lay beyond Nebar Point just on the outskirts of Revenant space.

No man's land.

The Breach.

Where civilisation ended, and the unknown began.

Roth was heading there: Nathan didn't know how he knew, but he did, and when he looked at Astrilla, she nodded in agreement. Something Enkaye was there: Nathan could feel it. Both of them could.

"The planet is called Helia," Jareth said with a grimace.

Nathan narrowed his eyes; "You knew about this place?"

Jareth shook his head. "Only the name. One of the Society's men gave it up to myself and Mr Garland a few days ago. You could say we loosened his tongue..."

Vol leaned on the table, reviewing the distant location with scrutiny.

"That is quite a way away," she said, raising a brow. "You sure about this?"

Nathan nodded with certainty. Astrilla too.

"This is gonna sound crazy," Nathan began. "Something is there. I couldn't feel it before, but now it's like a magnet".

Astrilla nodded in confirmation. "Whatever it is, it's powerful".

"Ah, great," Koble exhaled. "I take it this is this one of those, *Enkaye-save-the-universe-type* feelings?"

Silence answered for a beat.

"I think so," Nathan nodded.

Harrt began analysing potential routes on the star map with a worried expression. Eventually, he settled on a flight path that wasn't ideal, but given the circumstances, it was the only option. First, the Phoenix would have to pass the Outer Worlds, avoiding attention from the Criminal Syndicate and the Corporations. Then they'd need to travel through Nebar Point, *the last outpost before known space became somewhat unknown.* Once that *small challenge* was complete, there would be a long journey into the Breach: into the sector where the Revenant were supposedly born.

▲

With the Phoenix safely in the slipstream, the crew finally had a chance to breathe. Now, all that remained was a long wait, so Nathan suggested to the others that they rest up. He knew that what lay ahead was a battle with an enemy who'd already proven himself to be as cunning as he was ruthless. Alastair Roth was far more shrewd than anyone could've predicted: including Nathan, Tariq and even David Jareth.

But now, things were different.

Where before, Roth had been the puppet master in shadows using gutless fools to do his dirty work, now he had no other cards to play.

Smoke and mirrors were his way of operating. He'd shown his hand early, and Nathan knew he could use that somehow.

Finding a spare moment to reflect, Nathan headed to the bar and grabbed his bottle of rescued Yarian Rum. He poured himself a shot and knocked it back, allowing the mild alcoholic hit to wash over him.

It didn't help at all.

What James had done seemed far worse than what he'd done after the Loyalty. Back then, the Ice had made him do terrible things. He hurt the people who loved him most: Jack, Nathan, and his on-again-off-again lover, Merri. *Or perhaps Ice was just an excuse. Maybe he'd always been a dreadful person. Maybe he'd simply swapped Ice for the Society.*

Nathan leant on the bar with his face in his hands and sighed, wondering if he had the strength to face James again.

"You do," someone said.

Nathan lifted his head and was confronted by a man he'd not seen since the Battle of the Messorem. He hadn't been on the desert plains of that strange place that wasn't quite reality.

He stood behind the bar as though he'd always been there. The spectre stood at five-foot-eleven with his grey hair combed back over his ears, and regarded Nathan with a severe expression.

"I think you and I need to have a little chat," Bill Stephens said.

Nathan froze at the sight of his long-dead Grandfather, but before he could even wonder if he was dreaming or hallucinating, the sound of raised voices erupted from behind. Nathan turned to look, but when he glanced back to the bar, Bill was gone.

"Fuck," Nathan cursed.

He knocked back another shot as Koble shoved David Jareth into an armchair. Jareth still had a million secrets, and now if he was going to ally himself with the Phoenix's crew, it was time to talk. Nathan slammed his glass down on the bar and ambled slowly toward the man with all the answers.

Koble stepped aside, and Eric Garland offered no challenge as Nathan leaned down to look Jareth in the eyes.

"So, Mr Jareth..." Nathan said, his voice low and impatient. "I think it's about fuckin' time you told us everything".

EPILOGUE
SUBJECT C

For what he'd assumed was a century, the humans of Earth referred to him by a designation; Subject C. He wasn't sure when that started, but he'd been in a vegetative state for the first decade of his incarceration. Still, he'd woken and told them his birth name, but the humans refused to call him by it. He was Subject C to them.

Melponyn, or Nyn for short, was the name he recalled, though he wasn't entirely certain it was his own. Details from his highly evolved Enkaye brain seemed cloudier than they were supposed to, but he still remembered his origin, so he assumed Nyn was his name.

He still remembered the Enkaye Dynasty in all its beauty and order. He still remembered how it felt to be part of a connected network of creatures, all seeking to foster the galaxy one race at a time. It had been glorious and beautiful.

But then it happened: the purge.

Nyn couldn't recall how it happened, only that it did. An enemy of great power rose and began a systemic slaughter of his people. Battles were fought and lives were lost, but in Nyn's memory he couldn't recall how or why.

He'd fought in that war, but it was a hazy picture in a broken mind. After, he and the handful that remained tried to lay the foundation for what was next. Then Nyn's memories ceased to exist, and for a long time there was darkness that lasted multiple millennia.

The only thing he knew after was torture and agony;

inflicted by humans who called themselves the Society. They wanted something from him: information regarding a location and a machine at that location.

The Desmoterion, or as the humans called it, Project Erebus: the forbidden place where slivers of evil were to remain until the end of time. They had no idea what it was, only that one of them existed somewhere on their planet.

A mistake of Prynn's, perhaps?

Before she and Sebek went their separate ways...

Maybe the Desmoterion on Earth wasn't as sealed as she'd hoped?

All Nyn knew was that he couldn't allow the humans to access it. So, he refused to tell them, and for years, all Nyn knew was suffering: so much so that it severed parts of his psyche to keep them from knowing where it was.

Maybe that's why his mind was so damaged?

Then one day, a new human came to him, one they called Roth, and he brought with him a creature that was a bastardised mongrel monster known as Baylum: *a child of Prynn, but not as she intended.*

They subjected Nyn to torture far worse than anything he'd ever known: a cruel mix of chemical-induced agony and elemental torment that tore through the very essence of his being. Nyn tried to be strong, but he wasn't built for such cruelty. Nobody was.

What followed was a cloudy period that seemed to go on forever. At some point, the humans sedated him and moved him, and it was hard to tell how long that age lasted. Where there should've been consciousness or at least a vague measure of time, there was nothing; just a barren gap.

When Nyn became aware, he felt the loss of the Earth in his veins. He didn't need it confirmed. He knew in his mind that it was gone: destroyed by the same men that had tortured him for answers.

Time passed: a decade perhaps.

Then, he became aware again. Someone was out there, doing the work of the Enkaye Dynasty: *the final plan.* A human —no, that wasn't right. A human with glitters of Enkaye buried in his genetic code.

A man called Jack Stephens. A man who was willing to die to ensure that the final plan became a reality. He'd seen it somehow. The seed of hope had been planted, but it'd take time to grow. So Nyn waited. And waited. He felt the presence of Jack Stephens fade, but it wasn't over. Others were out there, sewing their destiny upon the great universal tapestry.

Time continued, and Nyn embraced the progress.

Then seven days ago, a human who wasn't just human appeared before him, but he wasn't there. He was a projection: a ghost from the elsewhere, somehow still living in the old networks.

The spectre called himself Bill and miraculously helped Nyn escape the prison that had held him for so very long.

Once he was safely aboard a primitive shuttle, too large for his kind, Nyn looked at the ghost and asked;

"What happens now?"

The one called Bill smiled: a very human gesture. "I died closing one of the machines that your kind called the Desmoterion. I'd like to tell you that was the last one, but as you know..."

"There is more than one," Nyn concluded with a sigh. "So, the Society seeks to open another?"

Bill nodded quietly. "They do".

"Then I must stop them".

"Not yet," Bill replied. "You'll need allies in the battle to come".

A primitive sensor on the shuttle made an unpleasant shrill. Nyn stretched on his toes to look at the workstation, and then he saw that Roth's people were in pursuit.

He looked at the ghost.

"They fitted you with a tracker, my friend," Bill Stephens warned, "There is a planet nearby called Levave. I think it's about time you got them off your back and got yourself a new —faster— ship".

▲

Combat was not something the Enkaye took lightly. There had been two wars during the Dynasty's long reign, and Nyn had only lived to see one of them: the final war. Killing was not pleasant, but if one's destiny was tied to *the final plan,* one had to ensure one's survival.

He landed the small craft on the poorly terraformed planet of Levave, close to what had once been an Enkaye research station. The dormant technology detected his presence, and a massive burst of air blew the brown sand upward, creating a reverse blister in the ground.

Nyn entered the facility knowing he needed to set a trap for Roth's people. Yes, they were primitive beings, but he was out of practice by a few thousand years.

He spent thirty minutes clawing the archaic tracking device from his shoulder, using a sharp instrument he'd found in the temple. The pain should've been terrible, but after decades of torture, it felt like nothing more than a splinter. Once removed, Nyn tossed the still-active tracking device onto the floor.

Two hours later, Roth's people landed in the desert above. Nyn sensed there were several: all armed and very dangerous people by human standards. They entered the temple with primaeval projectile weapons pointed into the darkness: hunting him.

They were arrogant to assume they could kill or capture an Enkaye.

One shone his light on Nyn's bloodsoaked tracking device.

"Are you seriously telling me he pulled that thing out? How the fuck did he—"

"Shut your mouth, Hiller," another said in sheer panic. "Fan out; he's here".

That was when Nyn struck. Centuries of pent-up anger and hostility fueled his attack. The elements swelled around him as they had the day he fought Ganmaru.

That was *his* name: *Ganmaru.*

The one responsible for the Enkaye's downfall.

Nyn fought brutally, using the darkness as his ally until only one remained. One of Nyn's many torturers: the one who'd broken his fingers using a pincer utensil. Rhoades — the others called him Rhoades.

The torturer called out, "They'll never stop looking for you, Subject C".

"You should walk away while you still can," Nyn warned, but he had no intention of letting him live. He'd given in to a base instinct to toy with his prey before the kill.

"You know I can't do that," Rhoades yelled. "You know what Mr Roth is looking for. It means too much to him".

He was referring to the Desmoterion: the thing they called Project Erebus.

"Turn around and go back to Paradisium. This is your final warning".

Rhoades ignored the opportunity to live.

Nyn tore the man limb from limb. The torturer's bones cracked and snapped and went in entirely unnatural directions. His skin boiled as if exposed to the raw energy of a star, and his fragile human eyes exploded into a million fragments.

When the violence was done, Nyn tossed the smoking body aside, and a horrible crack followed. A lesser being would try to call it justice, but Nyn knew it was barbaric and cruel. He accepted the flaw in his character and knew he'd need to atone for such savagery, but not until Project Erebus was buried once and for all.

Nyn glanced at a shiny item that had fallen from the torturer's combat vest. It was a small imaging device, recording and perhaps transmitting everything.

Nyn held up the cracked device, hoping that Alastair Roth was listening. He spoke into it as though the man were there in front of him: as though they'd be the last words Roth would hear before dying like his platoon;

"Alastair Roth... as long as I draw breath, I will not allow you to open the singularity. Mark my words; I will stop you. I will find you, and I will end you for everything you and the Society did to me".

Nyn tossed the device aside, and the ghost —Bill— was standing there looking at him with a strange human expression that was supposed to convey patience.

"What now?" Nyn asked.

The ghost looked around at the bloodshed, then with a long, drawn-out breath, "To Helia".

"But you said I can't do this alone".

Bill smiled a knowing smile, "You won't have to. Others will join you, but they have a different path to walk".

"A part of the final plan?"

Bill nodded, "Let's call it a mild detour".

ACKNOWLEDGEMENTS

I never included acknowledgements in Heritage, as page count was a huge concern in making the work printable. Now that I'm pulling together my first acknowledgements section, I find myself with a list covering both books.

This book --and this series thus far-- wouldn't exist without the hard proofreading and editing process undertaken by my fantastic mother-in-law, Kim. Thank you!

Big thanks to Dad and Paul Lawlor for the upfront proofreading efforts on both books.

Thanks to my wife, Tamsin, for all the proofreading, patience, and support you have given throughout my writing journey since day one.

Cheers to Zak Jordan of BrightestDay Audiobook Productions for turning my work into its audio form and being a great collaborator in this space.

To my fellow independent author, Adrian Cousins, it's always great exchanging ways to navigate the world of self-publishing. For any time travel fans, I recommend you go and check out his body of work.

And last but certainly not least, thank you to everyone who has made the gamble to purchase my work. Your support has been instrumental in the success of these books, and I couldn't have done it without you.

ABOUT THE AUTHOR

S.M. Warlow is a best-selling Sci-fi author from the United Kingdom. He was born in Welwyn Garden City, Hertfordshire --a town once dubbed the home of the breakfast cereal.

From a young age, S.M. Warlow had a keen love for all things science fiction, and in 2022 he published his debut novel Heritage.

The original concept for the Phoenix Titan books came to S.M. Warlow in 2003. However, thanks to years of study and a busy career in Retail strategy and operations, it would be another fifteen years before he'd eventually put pen to paper.

After four years of writing, rewriting, and editing, he published Heritage in January 2022. In its first week on sale, Heritage held a strong position at #8 on the Amazon science fiction charts, and in May 2022, Heritage surged up the sci-fi charts to #1.

S.M. Warlow now resides in Bedfordshire with his wife and son.

SMWARLOW_AUTHOR

THE CREW WILL RETURN IN...

TALES OF THE PHOENIX TITAN
VOLUME III

PRISONER

COMING 2024